W.i.t.c.h.

Will Irma Taranee Cornelia Hay Lin

Part I. The Twelve Portals
Volume 2

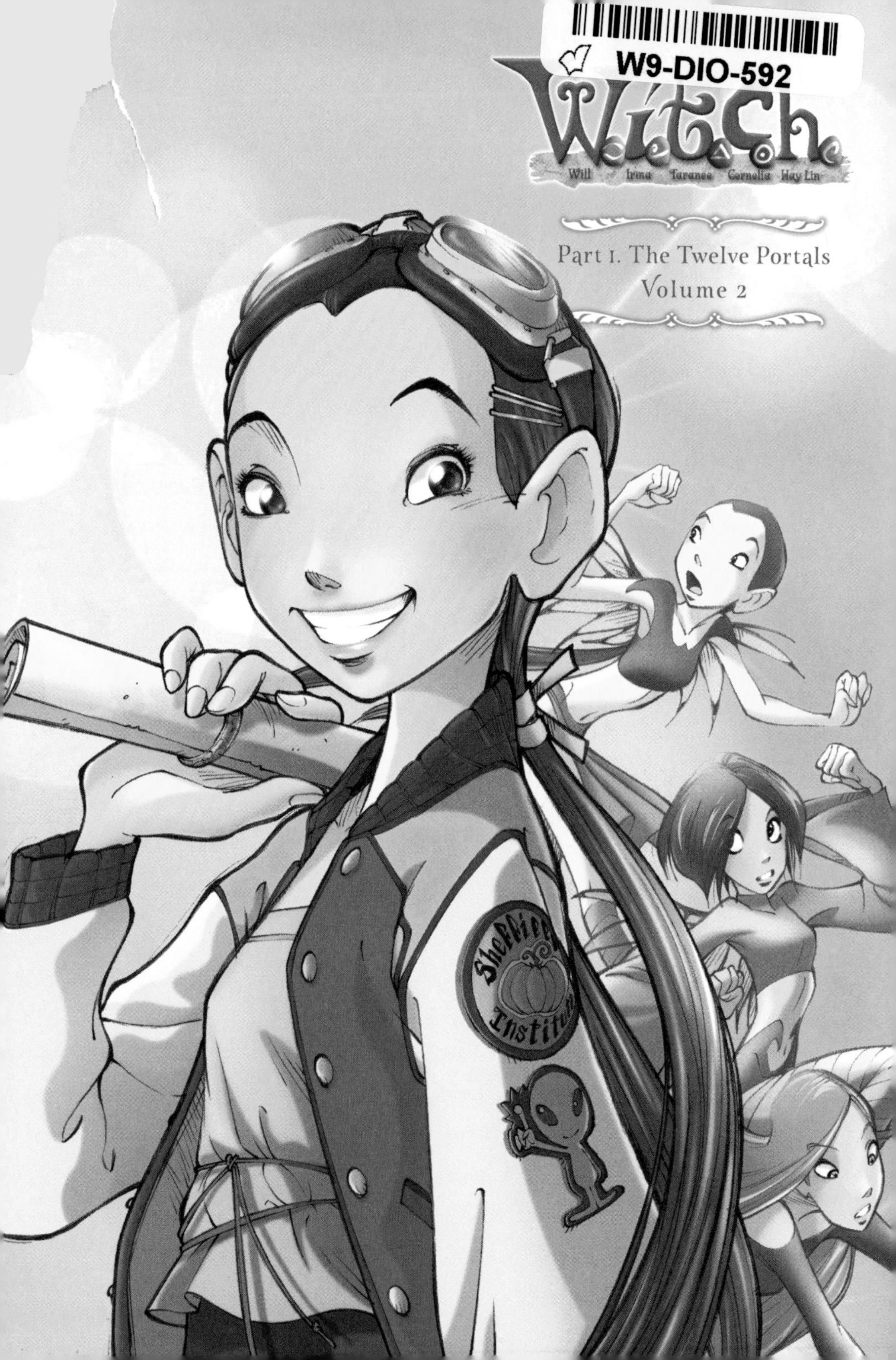
Sheffield Institute

W.i.t.c.h.

Will Irma Taranee Cornelia Hay Lin

Part 1. The Twelve Portals
Volume 2

CONTENTS

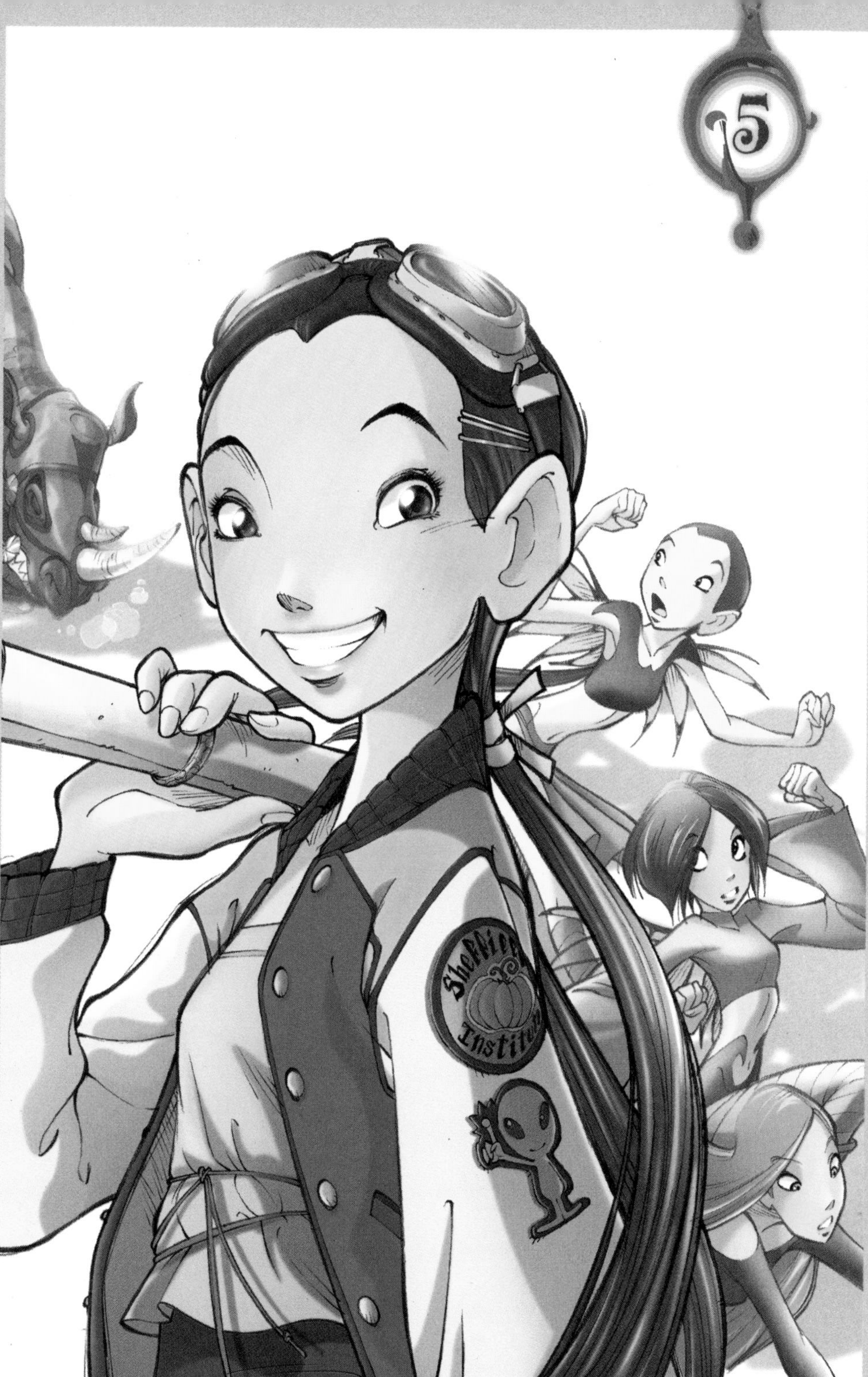
5

THE LAST TEAR

"A world unable to change is a world without hope."

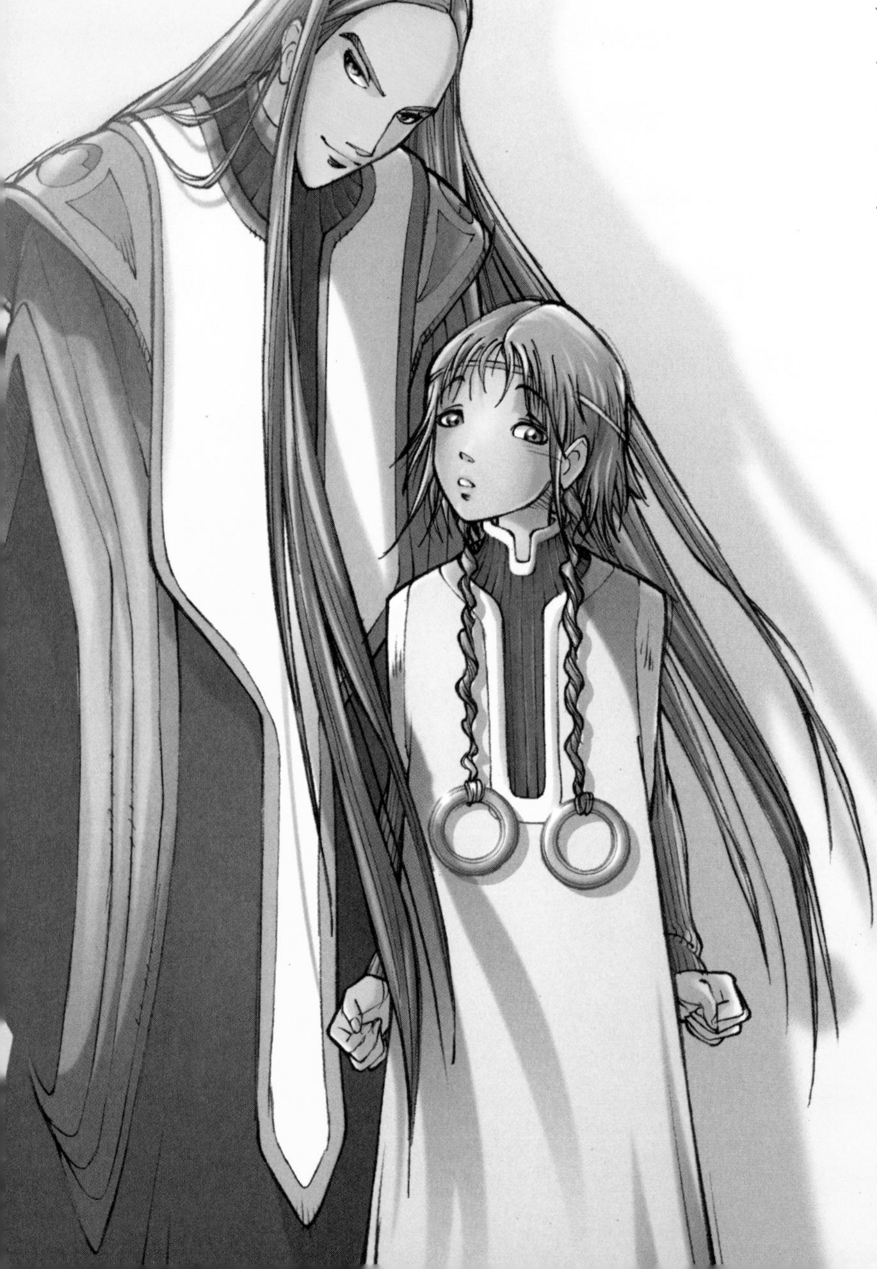

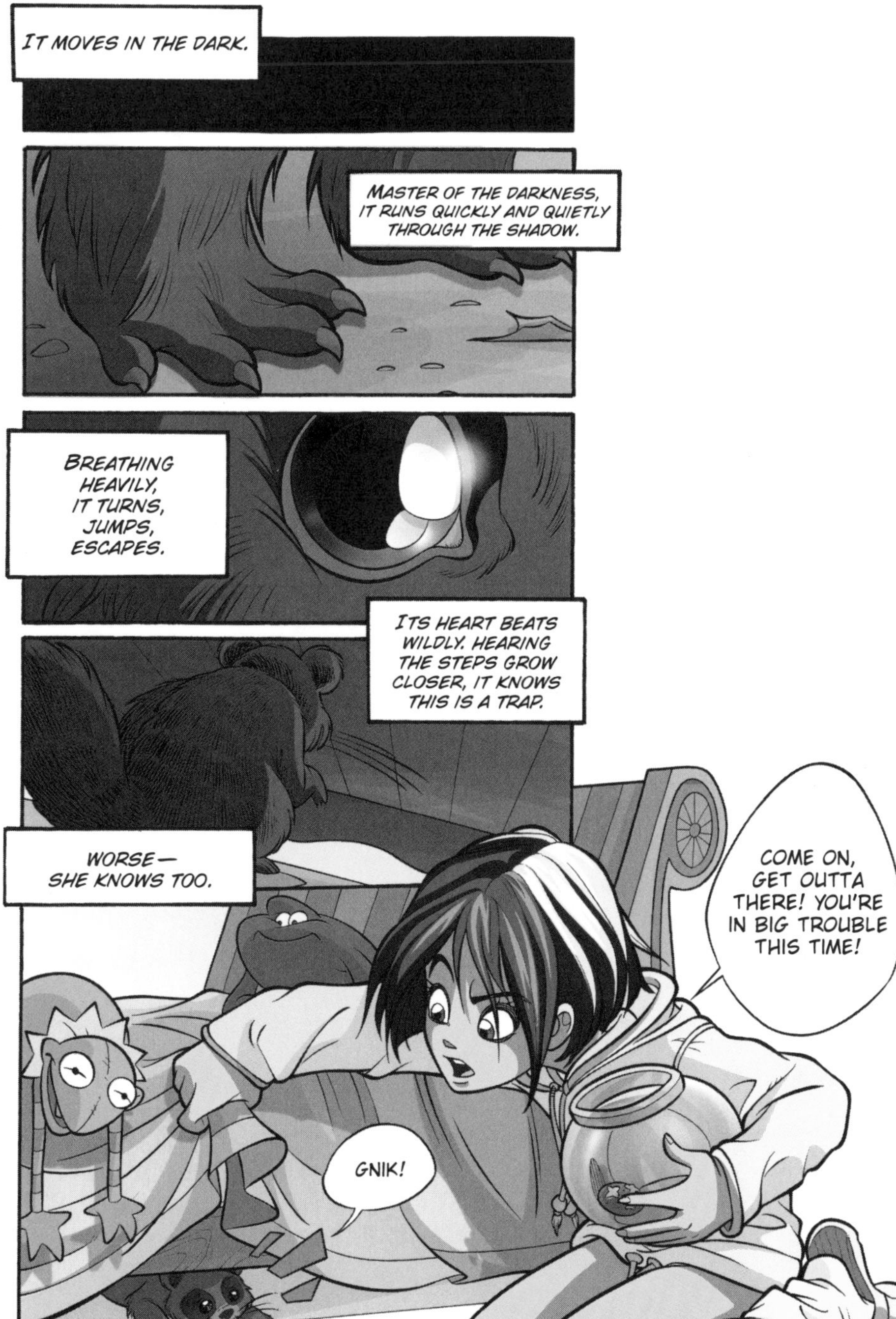
IT MOVES IN THE DARK.
MASTER OF THE DARKNESS, IT RUNS QUICKLY AND QUIETLY THROUGH THE SHADOW.
BREATHING HEAVILY, IT TURNS, JUMPS, ESCAPES.
ITS HEART BEATS WILDLY. HEARING THE STEPS GROW CLOSER, IT KNOWS THIS IS A TRAP.
WORSE— SHE KNOWS TOO.
COME ON, GET OUTTA THERE! YOU'RE IN BIG TROUBLE THIS TIME!
GNIK!

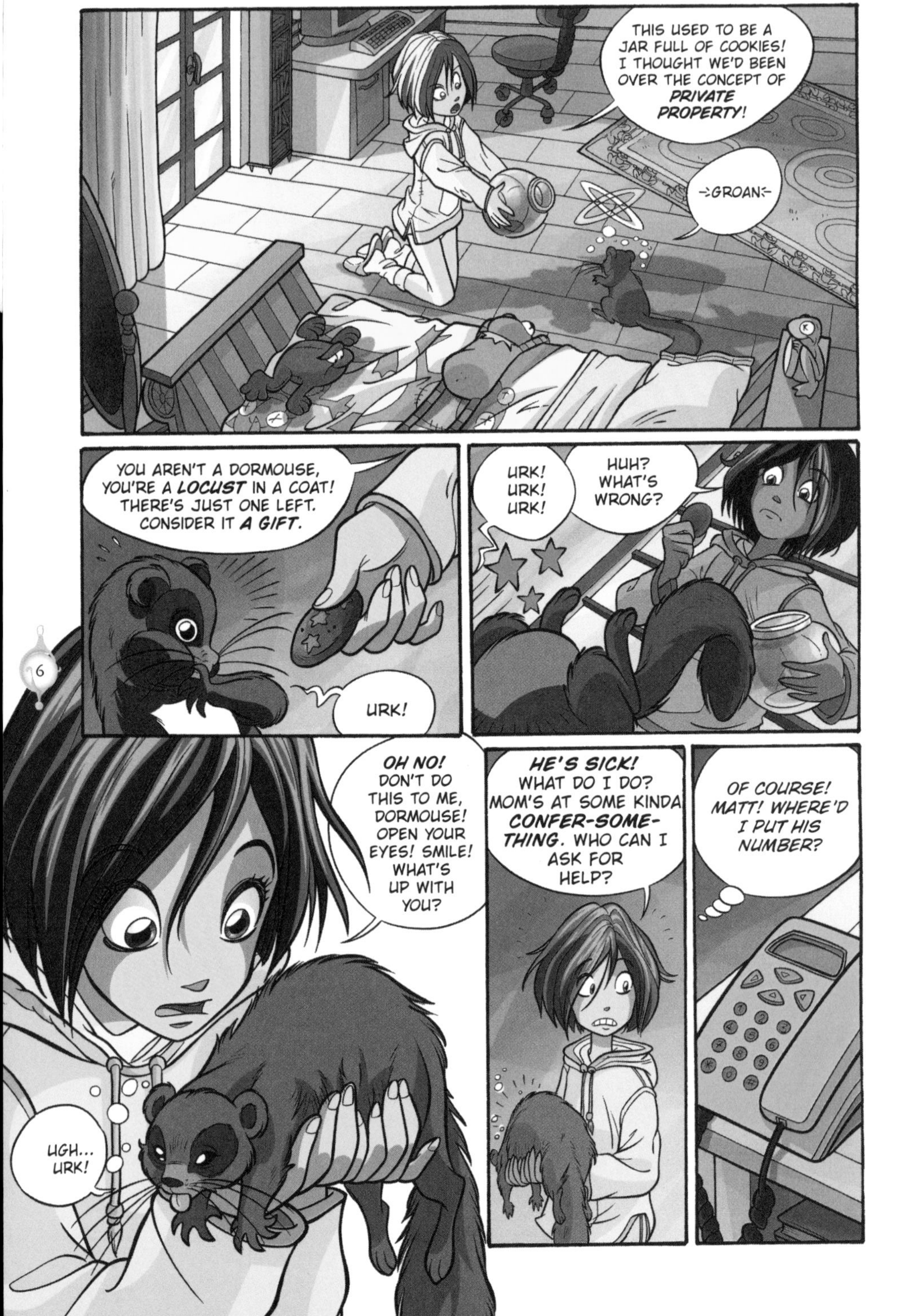
THIS USED TO BE A JAR FULL OF COOKIES! I THOUGHT WE'D BEEN OVER THE CONCEPT OF PRIVATE PROPERTY!
-GROAN-
YOU AREN'T A DORMOUSE, YOU'RE A LOCUST IN A COAT! THERE'S JUST ONE LEFT. CONSIDER IT A GIFT.
URK!
URK! URK! URK!
HUH? WHAT'S WRONG?
OH NO! DON'T DO THIS TO ME, DORMOUSE! OPEN YOUR EYES! SMILE! WHAT'S UP WITH YOU?
UGH... URK!
HE'S SICK! WHAT DO I DO? MOM'S AT SOME KINDA CONFER-SOME-THING. WHO CAN I ASK FOR HELP?
OF COURSE! MATT! WHERE'D I PUT HIS NUMBER?

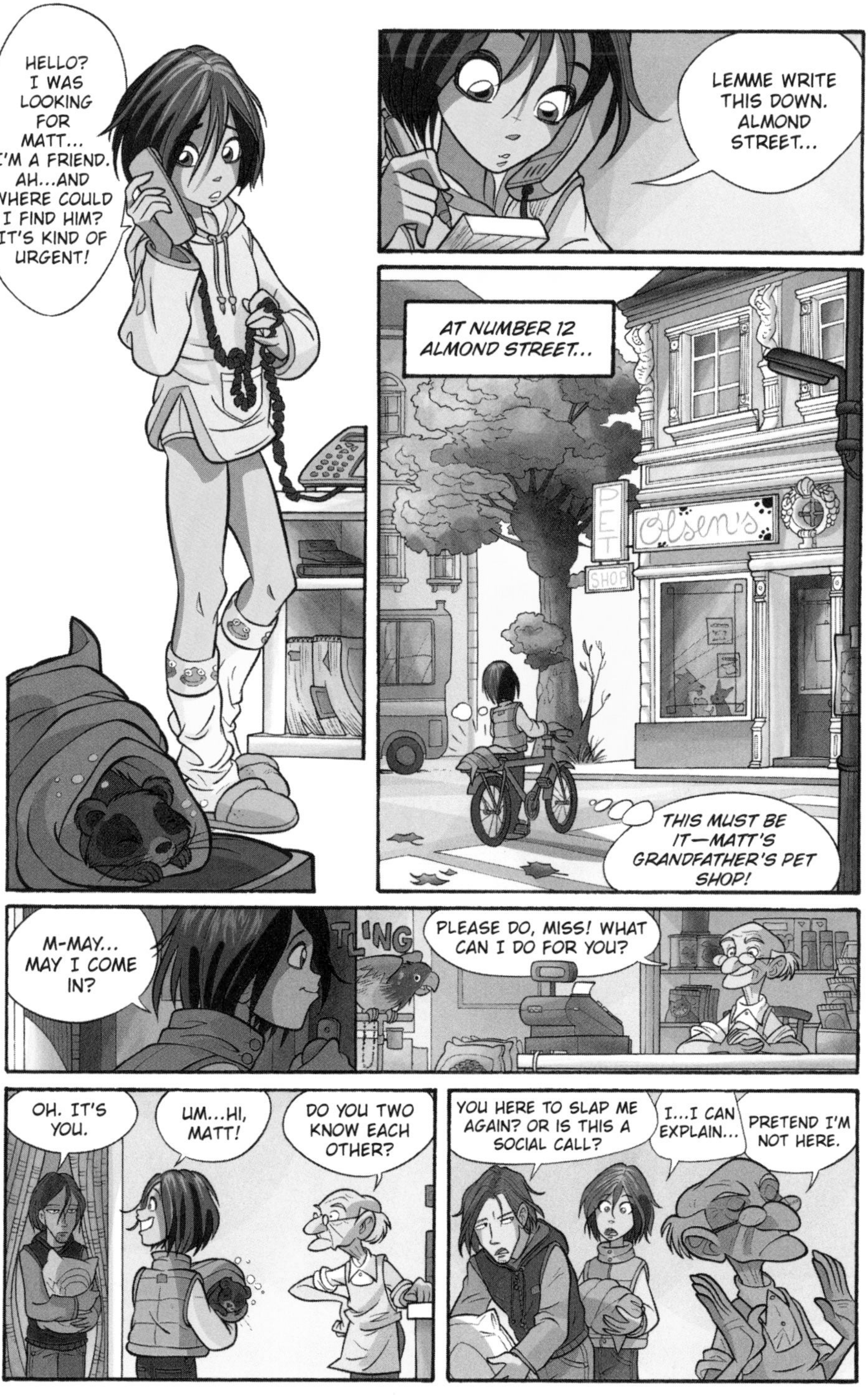
HELLO? I WAS LOOKING FOR MATT... I'M A FRIEND. AH...AND WHERE COULD I FIND HIM? IT'S KIND OF URGENT!
LEMME WRITE THIS DOWN. ALMOND STREET...
AT NUMBER 12 ALMOND STREET...
PET SHOP
Olsen's
THIS MUST BE IT—MATT'S GRANDFATHER'S PET SHOP!
M-MAY... MAY I COME IN?
TLING
PLEASE DO, MISS! WHAT CAN I DO FOR YOU?
OH. IT'S YOU.
UM...HI, MATT!
DO YOU TWO KNOW EACH OTHER?
YOU HERE TO SLAP ME AGAIN? OR IS THIS A SOCIAL CALL?
I...I CAN EXPLAIN...
PRETEND I'M NOT HERE.

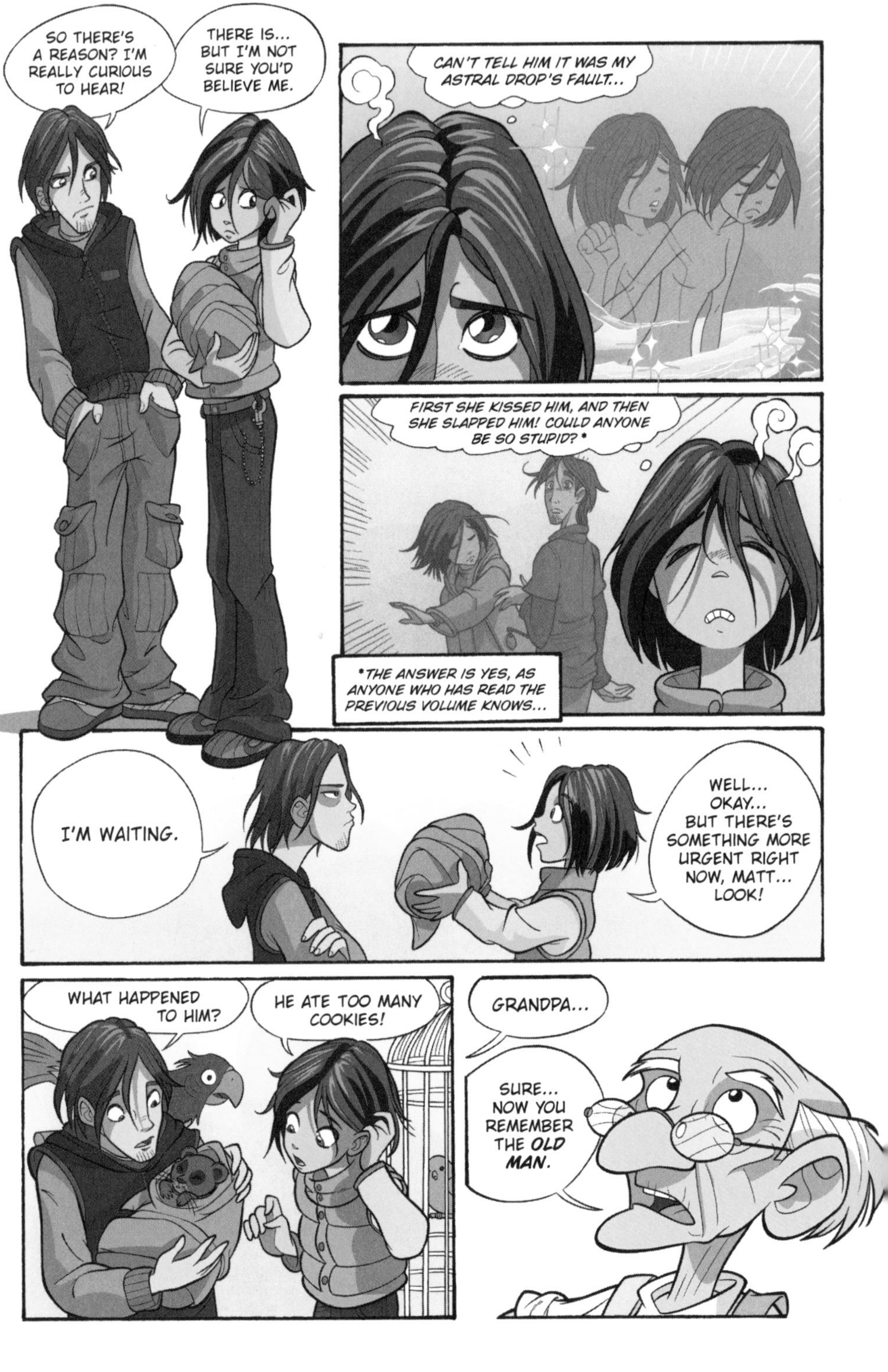
SO THERE'S A REASON? I'M REALLY CURIOUS TO HEAR!
THERE IS... BUT I'M NOT SURE YOU'D BELIEVE ME.
CAN'T TELL HIM IT WAS MY ASTRAL DROP'S FAULT...
FIRST SHE KISSED HIM, AND THEN SHE SLAPPED HIM! COULD ANYONE BE SO STUPID? *
*THE ANSWER IS YES, AS ANYONE WHO HAS READ THE PREVIOUS VOLUME KNOWS...
I'M WAITING.
WELL... OKAY... BUT THERE'S SOMETHING MORE URGENT RIGHT NOW, MATT... LOOK!
WHAT HAPPENED TO HIM?
HE ATE TOO MANY COOKIES!
GRANDPA...
SURE... NOW YOU REMEMBER THE OLD MAN.

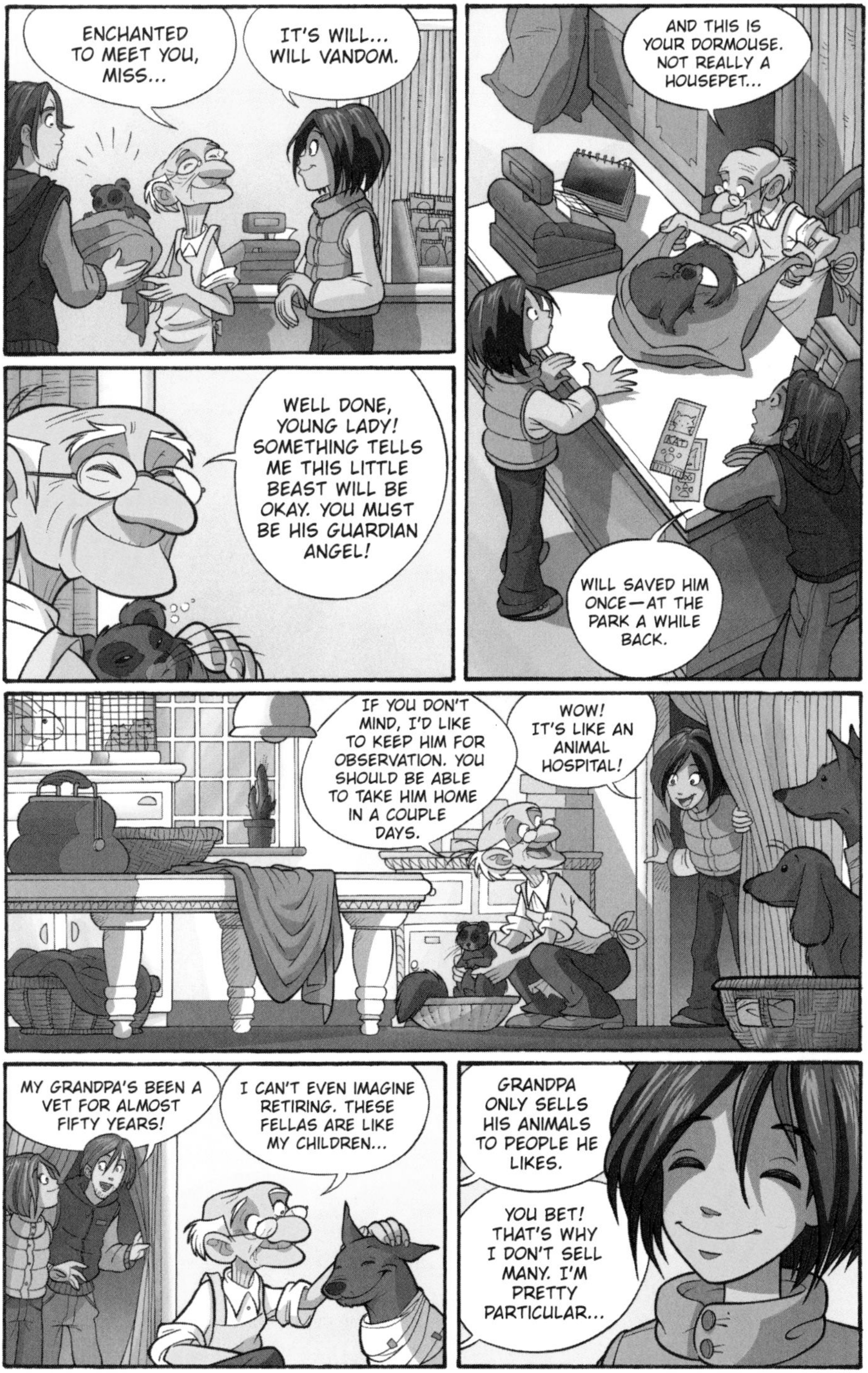
ENCHANTED TO MEET YOU, MISS...
IT'S WILL... WILL VANDOM.
AND THIS IS YOUR DORMOUSE. NOT REALLY A HOUSEPET...
WILL SAVED HIM ONCE—AT THE PARK A WHILE BACK.
WELL DONE, YOUNG LADY! SOMETHING TELLS ME THIS LITTLE BEAST WILL BE OKAY. YOU MUST BE HIS GUARDIAN ANGEL!
IF YOU DON'T MIND, I'D LIKE TO KEEP HIM FOR OBSERVATION. YOU SHOULD BE ABLE TO TAKE HIM HOME IN A COUPLE DAYS.
WOW! IT'S LIKE AN ANIMAL HOSPITAL!
MY GRANDPA'S BEEN A VET FOR ALMOST FIFTY YEARS!
I CAN'T EVEN IMAGINE RETIRING. THESE FELLAS ARE LIKE MY CHILDREN...
GRANDPA ONLY SELLS HIS ANIMALS TO PEOPLE HE LIKES.
YOU BET! THAT'S WHY I DON'T SELL MANY. I'M PRETTY PARTICULAR...

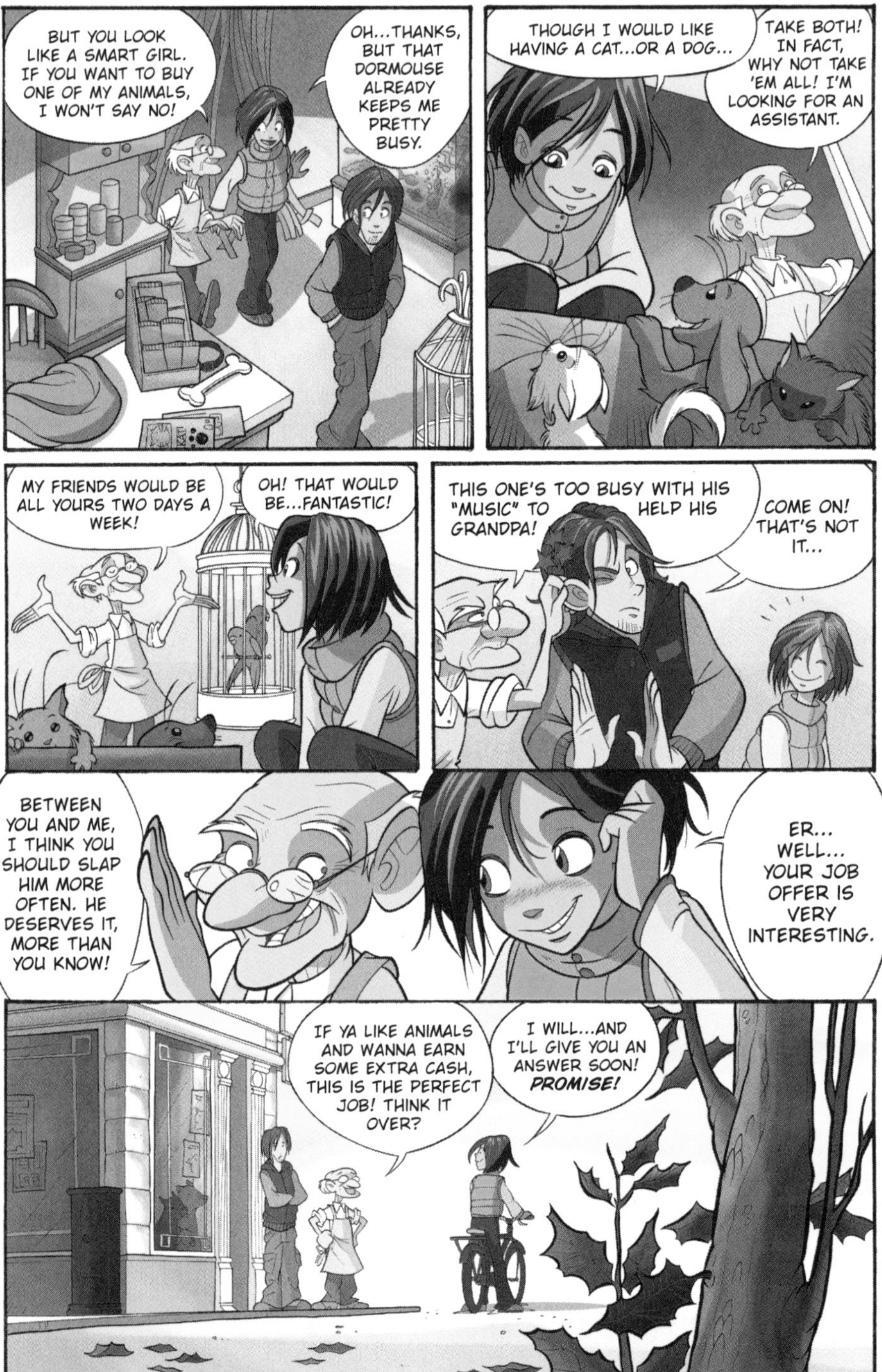

BUT YOU LOOK LIKE A SMART GIRL. IF YOU WANT TO BUY ONE OF MY ANIMALS, I WON'T SAY NO!
OH...THANKS, BUT THAT DORMOUSE ALREADY KEEPS ME PRETTY BUSY.
THOUGH I WOULD LIKE HAVING A CAT...OR A DOG...
TAKE BOTH! IN FACT, WHY NOT TAKE 'EM ALL! I'M LOOKING FOR AN ASSISTANT.
MY FRIENDS WOULD BE ALL YOURS TWO DAYS A WEEK!
OH! THAT WOULD BE...FANTASTIC!
THIS ONE'S TOO BUSY WITH HIS "MUSIC" TO HELP HIS GRANDPA!
COME ON! THAT'S NOT IT...
BETWEEN YOU AND ME, I THINK YOU SHOULD SLAP HIM MORE OFTEN. HE DESERVES IT, MORE THAN YOU KNOW!
ER... WELL... YOUR JOB OFFER IS VERY INTERESTING.
IF YA LIKE ANIMALS AND WANNA EARN SOME EXTRA CASH, THIS IS THE PERFECT JOB! THINK IT OVER?
I WILL...AND I'LL GIVE YOU AN ANSWER SOON! ***PROMISE!***

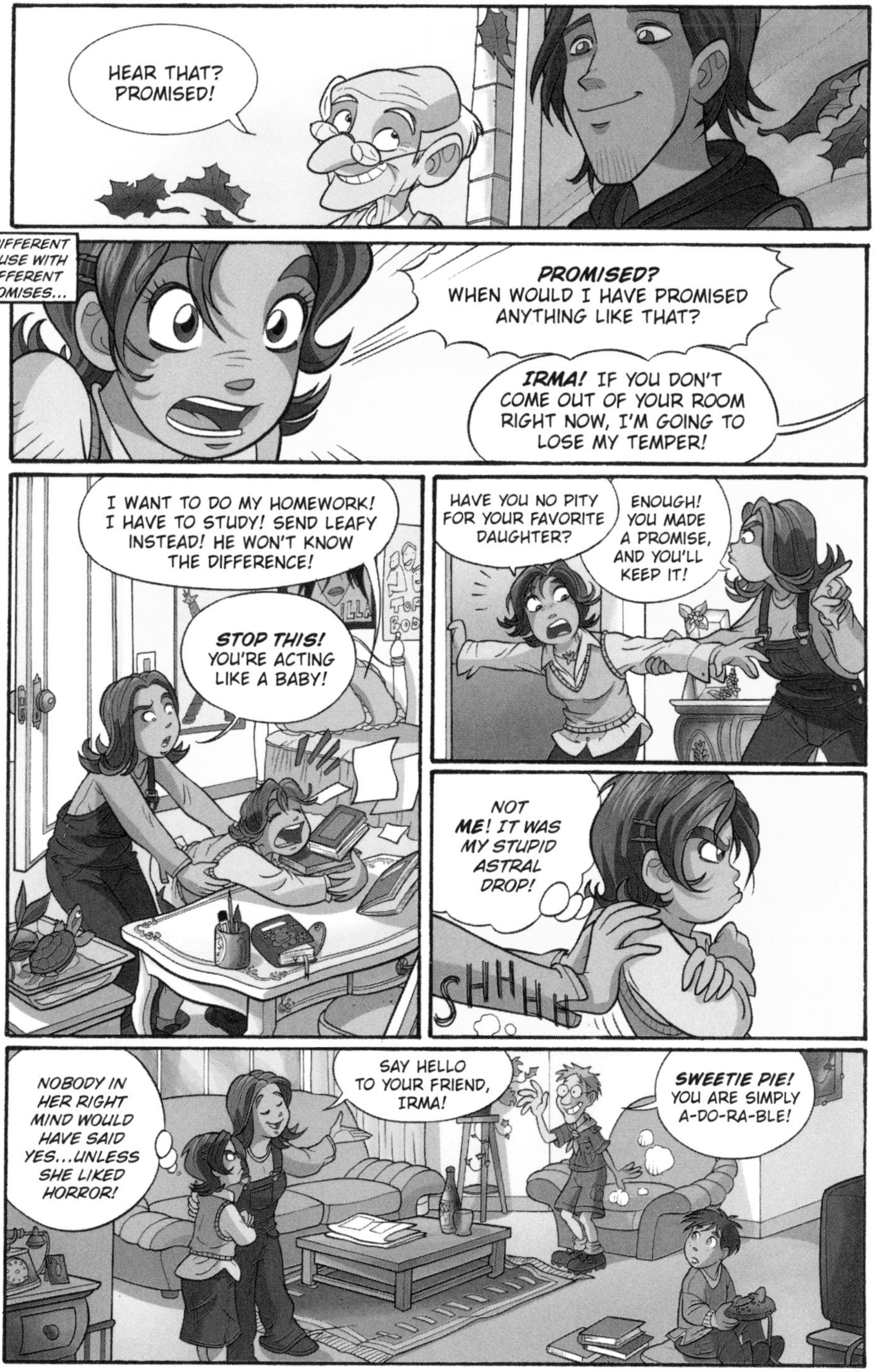
HEAR THAT? PROMISED!
A DIFFERENT HOUSE WITH DIFFERENT PROMISES...
PROMISED? WHEN WOULD I HAVE PROMISED ANYTHING LIKE THAT?
IRMA! IF YOU DON'T COME OUT OF YOUR ROOM RIGHT NOW, I'M GOING TO LOSE MY TEMPER!
I WANT TO DO MY HOMEWORK! I HAVE TO STUDY! SEND LEAFY INSTEAD! HE WON'T KNOW THE DIFFERENCE!
STOP THIS! YOU'RE ACTING LIKE A BABY!
HAVE YOU NO PITY FOR YOUR FAVORITE DAUGHTER?
ENOUGH! YOU MADE A PROMISE, AND YOU'LL KEEP IT!
NOT ME! IT WAS MY STUPID ASTRAL DROP!
SHHHH
NOBODY IN HER RIGHT MIND WOULD HAVE SAID YES...UNLESS SHE LIKED HORROR!
SAY HELLO TO YOUR FRIEND, IRMA!
SWEETIE PIE! YOU ARE SIMPLY A-DO-RA-BLE!

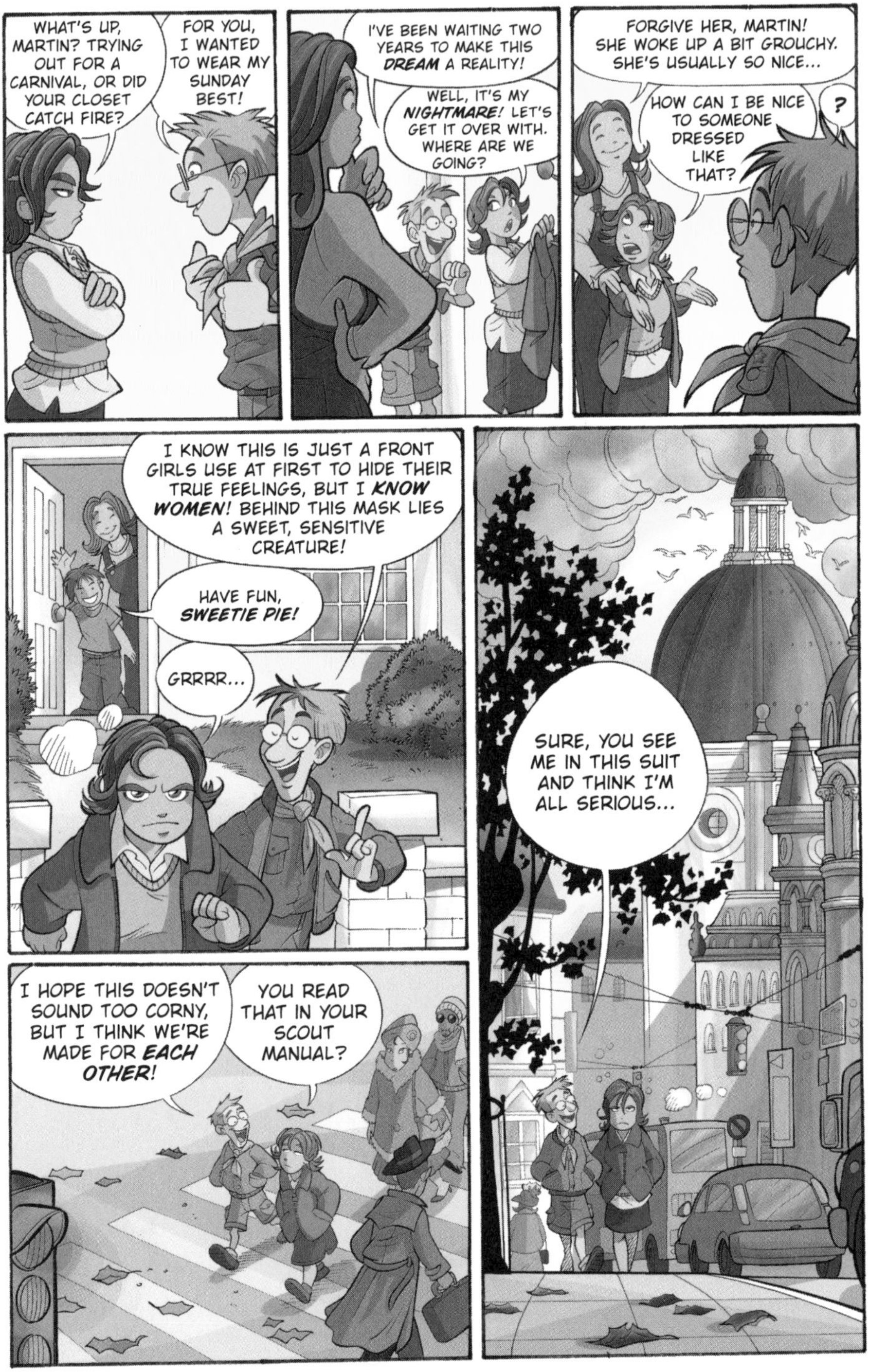
WHAT'S UP, MARTIN? TRYING OUT FOR A CARNIVAL, OR DID YOUR CLOSET CATCH FIRE?
FOR YOU, I WANTED TO WEAR MY SUNDAY BEST!
I'VE BEEN WAITING TWO YEARS TO MAKE THIS DREAM A REALITY!
WELL, IT'S MY NIGHTMARE! LET'S GET IT OVER WITH. WHERE ARE WE GOING?
FORGIVE HER, MARTIN! SHE WOKE UP A BIT GROUCHY. SHE'S USUALLY SO NICE...
HOW CAN I BE NICE TO SOMEONE DRESSED LIKE THAT?
?
I KNOW THIS IS JUST A FRONT GIRLS USE AT FIRST TO HIDE THEIR TRUE FEELINGS, BUT I KNOW WOMEN! BEHIND THIS MASK LIES A SWEET, SENSITIVE CREATURE!
HAVE FUN, SWEETIE PIE!
GRRRR...
SURE, YOU SEE ME IN THIS SUIT AND THINK I'M ALL SERIOUS...
I HOPE THIS DOESN'T SOUND TOO CORNY, BUT I THINK WE'RE MADE FOR EACH OTHER!
YOU READ THAT IN YOUR SCOUT MANUAL?

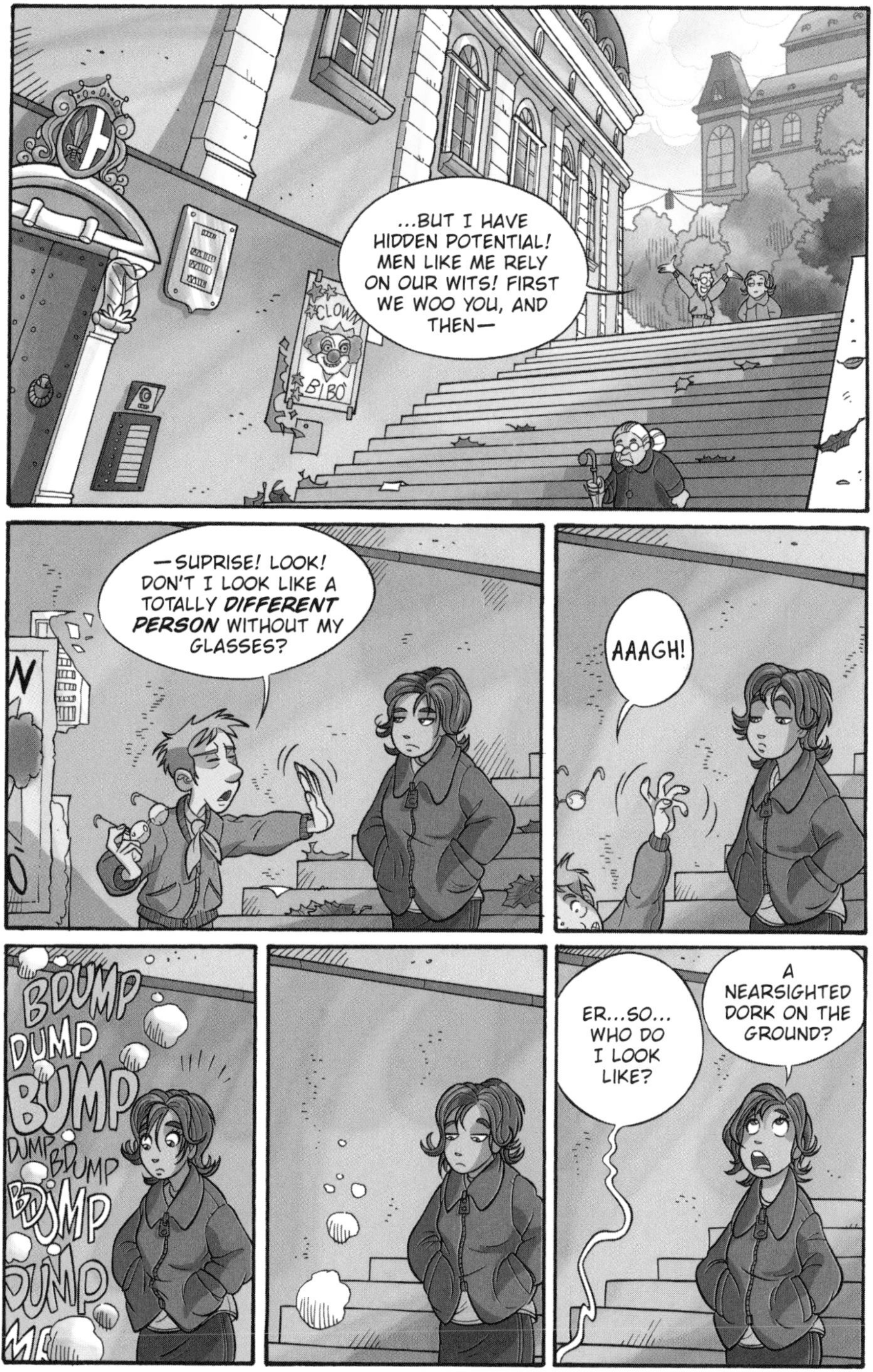
...BUT I HAVE HIDDEN POTENTIAL! MEN LIKE ME RELY ON OUR WITS! FIRST WE WOO YOU, AND THEN—
CLOWN BIBO
—SUPRISE! LOOK! DON'T I LOOK LIKE A TOTALLY *DIFFERENT PERSON* WITHOUT MY GLASSES?
AAAGH!
BDUMP DUMP BUMP DUMP BDUMP BDUMP DUMP
ER...SO... WHO DO I LOOK LIKE?
A NEARSIGHTED DORK ON THE GROUND?

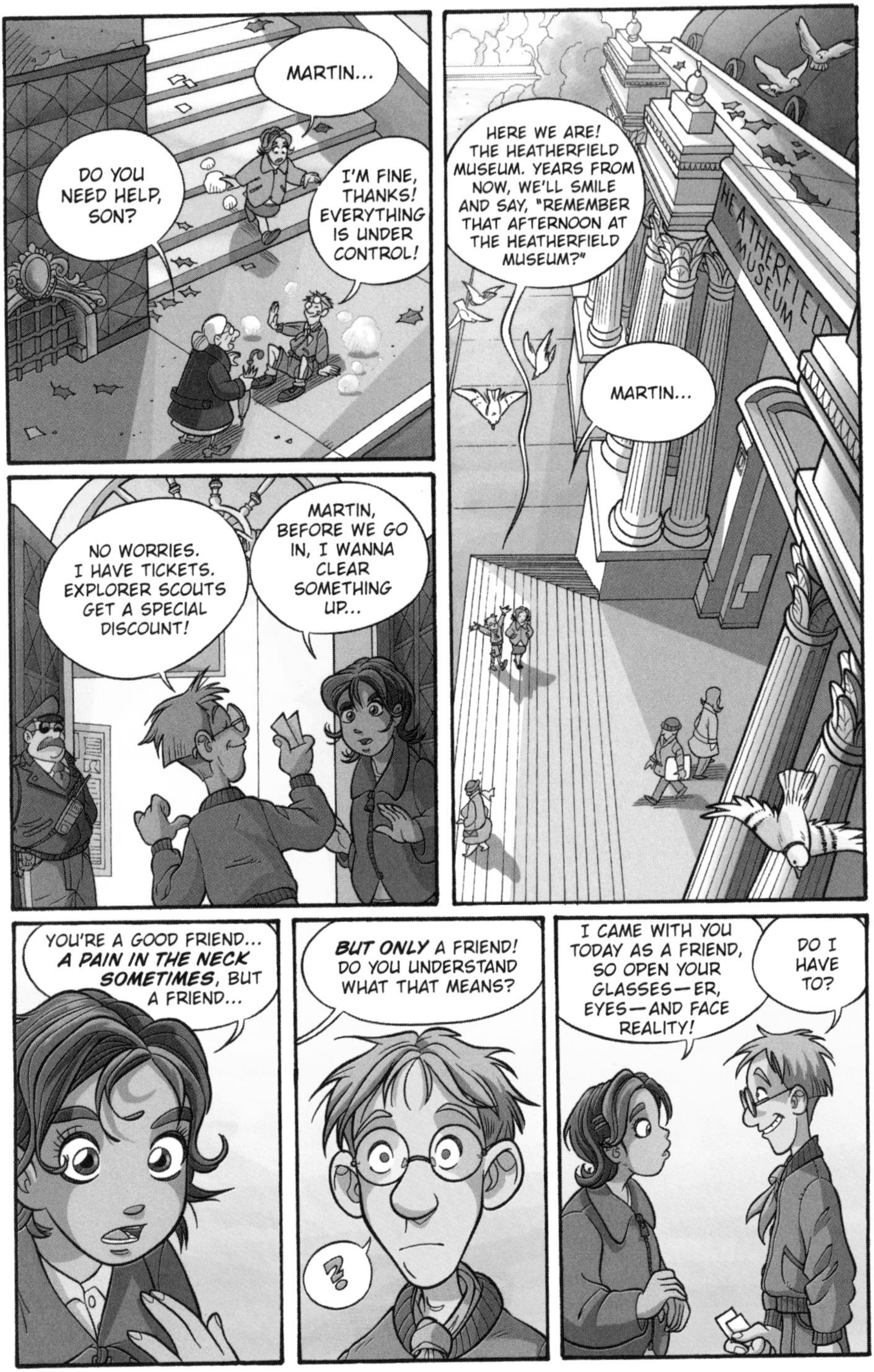
MARTIN...
DO YOU NEED HELP, SON?
I'M FINE, THANKS! EVERYTHING IS UNDER CONTROL!
HERE WE ARE! THE HEATHERFIELD MUSEUM. YEARS FROM NOW, WE'LL SMILE AND SAY, "REMEMBER THAT AFTERNOON AT THE HEATHERFIELD MUSEUM?"
HEATHERFIELD MUSEUM
MARTIN...
NO WORRIES. I HAVE TICKETS. EXPLORER SCOUTS GET A SPECIAL DISCOUNT!
MARTIN, BEFORE WE GO IN, I WANNA CLEAR SOMETHING UP...
YOU'RE A GOOD FRIEND... ***A PAIN IN THE NECK SOMETIMES***, BUT A FRIEND...
BUT ONLY A FRIEND! DO YOU UNDERSTAND WHAT THAT MEANS?
?
I CAME WITH YOU TODAY AS A FRIEND, SO OPEN YOUR GLASSES—ER, EYES—AND FACE REALITY!
DO I HAVE TO?

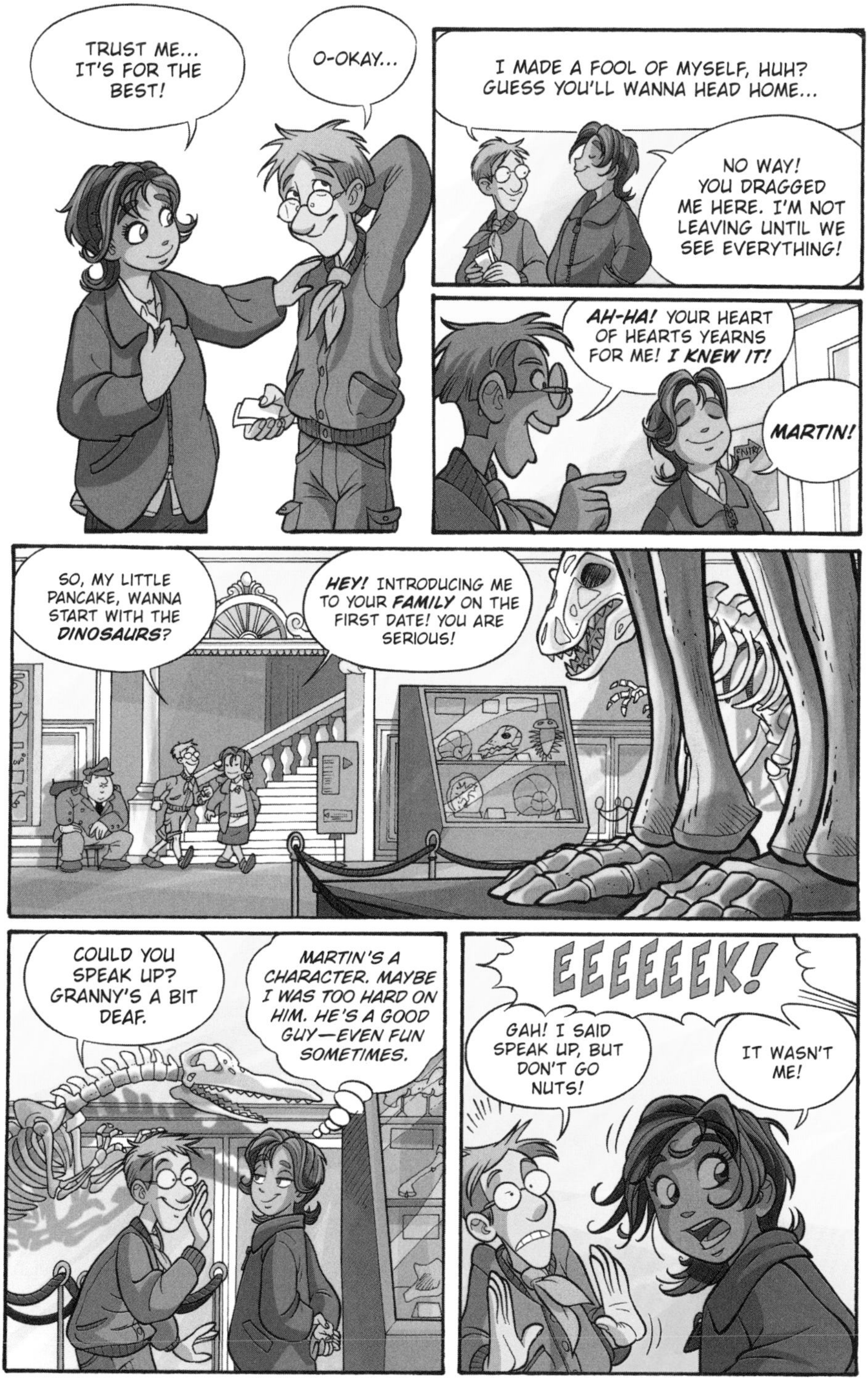
TRUST ME... IT'S FOR THE BEST!
O-OKAY...
I MADE A FOOL OF MYSELF, HUH? GUESS YOU'LL WANNA HEAD HOME...
NO WAY! YOU DRAGGED ME HERE. I'M NOT LEAVING UNTIL WE SEE EVERYTHING!
AH-HA! YOUR HEART OF HEARTS YEARNS FOR ME! I KNEW IT!
MARTIN!
SO, MY LITTLE PANCAKE, WANNA START WITH THE DINOSAURS?
HEY! INTRODUCING ME TO YOUR FAMILY ON THE FIRST DATE! YOU ARE SERIOUS!
COULD YOU SPEAK UP? GRANNY'S A BIT DEAF.
MARTIN'S A CHARACTER. MAYBE I WAS TOO HARD ON HIM. HE'S A GOOD GUY—EVEN FUN SOMETIMES.
EEEEEEK!
GAH! I SAID SPEAK UP, BUT DON'T GO NUTS!
IT WASN'T ME!

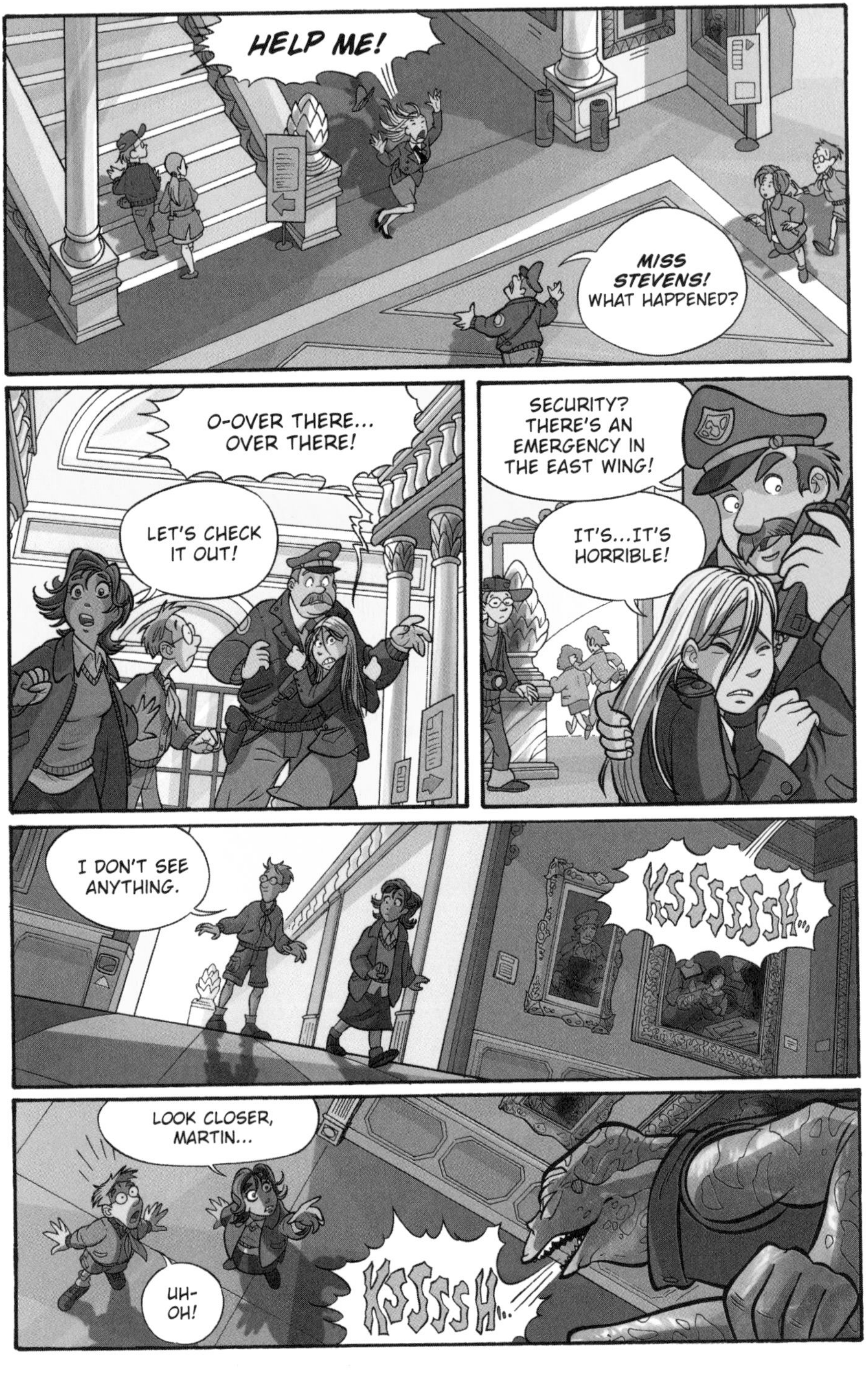
HELP ME!
MISS STEVENS! WHAT HAPPENED?
O-OVER THERE... OVER THERE!
LET'S CHECK IT OUT!
SECURITY? THERE'S AN EMERGENCY IN THE EAST WING!
IT'S...IT'S HORRIBLE!
I DON'T SEE ANYTHING.
KSSSSSSH...
LOOK CLOSER, MARTIN...
UH-OH!
KSSSSH...

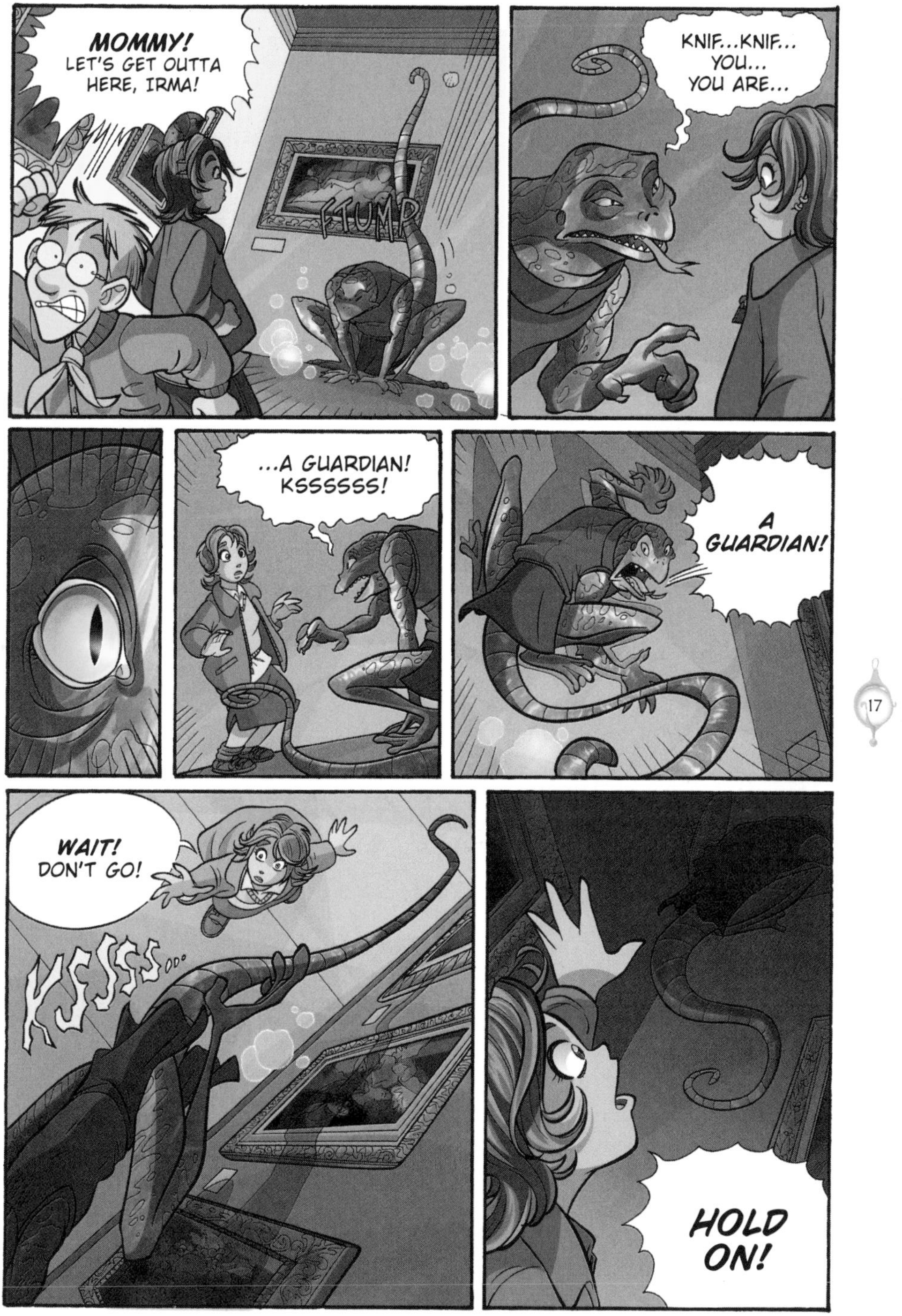
MOMMY! LET'S GET OUTTA HERE, IRMA!
FTUMP
KNIF...KNIF... YOU... YOU ARE...
...A GUARDIAN! KSSSSSS!
A GUARDIAN!
WAIT! DON'T GO!
KSSSS
HOLD ON!

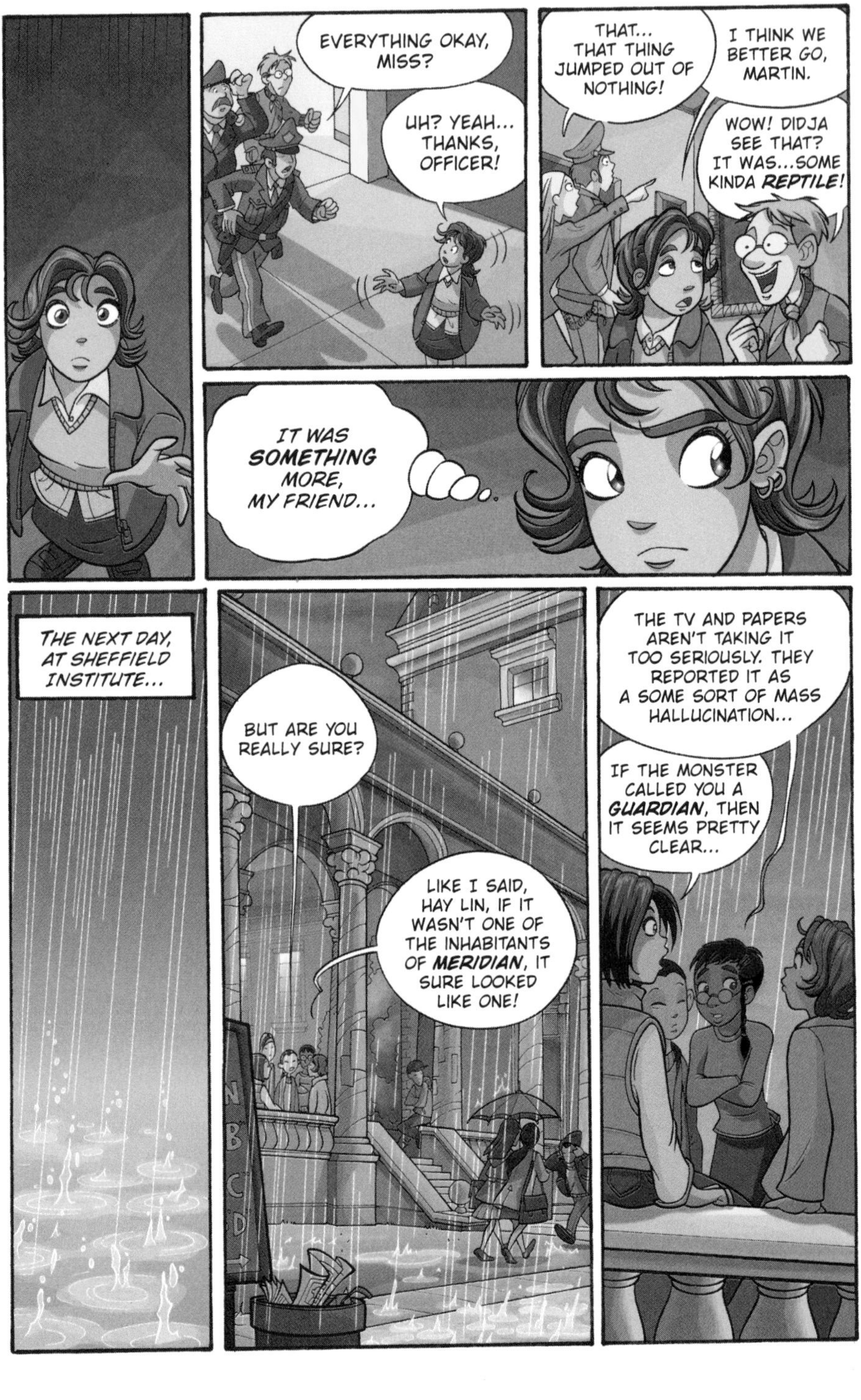
EVERYTHING OKAY, MISS?
UH? YEAH... THANKS, OFFICER!
THAT... THAT THING JUMPED OUT OF NOTHING!
I THINK WE BETTER GO, MARTIN.
WOW! DIDJA SEE THAT? IT WAS...SOME KINDA REPTILE!
IT WAS SOMETHING MORE, MY FRIEND...
THE NEXT DAY, AT SHEFFIELD INSTITUTE...
BUT ARE YOU REALLY SURE?
LIKE I SAID, HAY LIN, IF IT WASN'T ONE OF THE INHABITANTS OF MERIDIAN, IT SURE LOOKED LIKE ONE!
THE TV AND PAPERS AREN'T TAKING IT TOO SERIOUSLY. THEY REPORTED IT AS A SOME SORT OF MASS HALLUCINATION...
IF THE MONSTER CALLED YOU A GUARDIAN, THEN IT SEEMS PRETTY CLEAR...

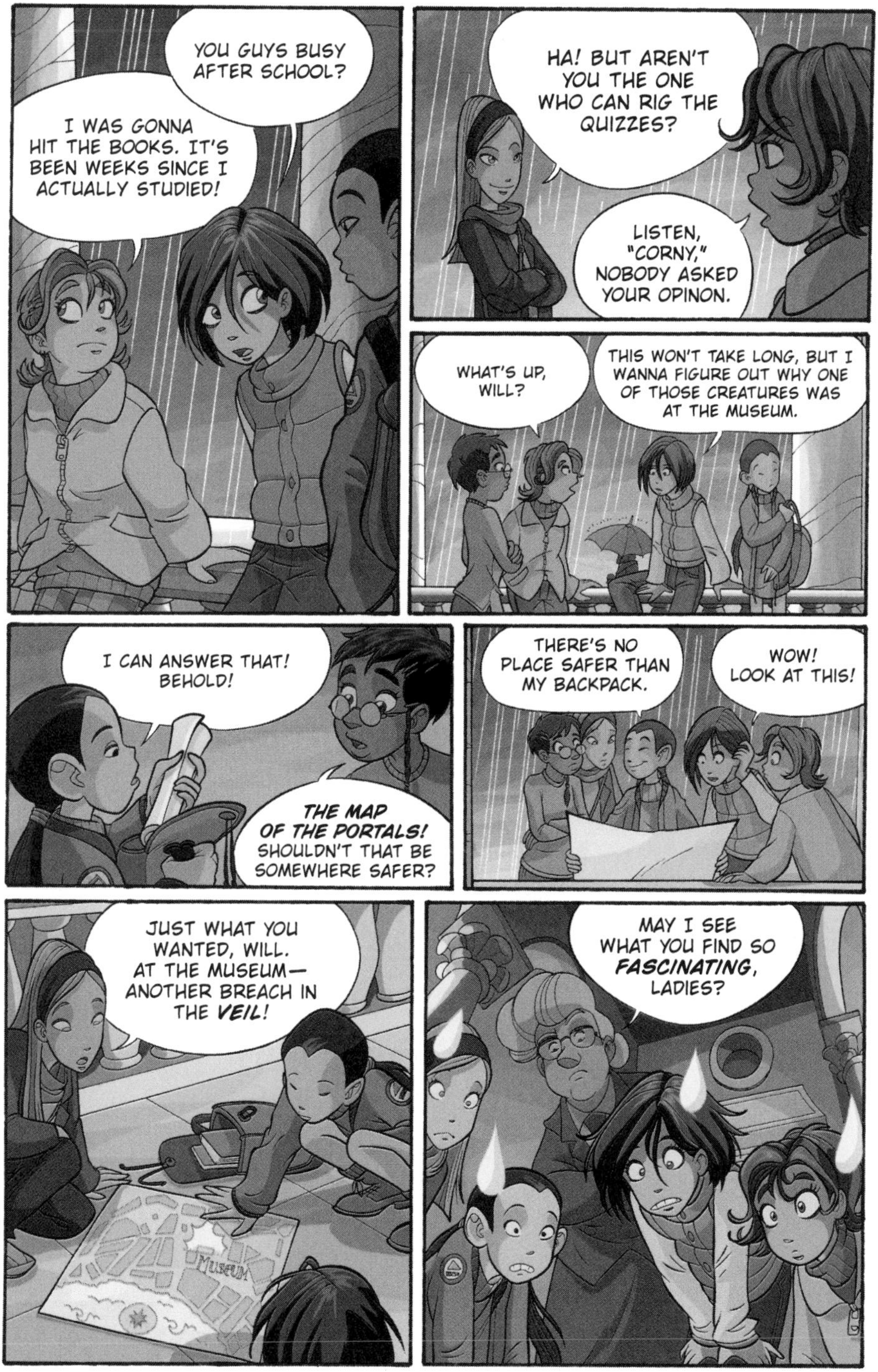
YOU GUYS BUSY AFTER SCHOOL?
I WAS GONNA HIT THE BOOKS. IT'S BEEN WEEKS SINCE I ACTUALLY STUDIED!
HA! BUT AREN'T YOU THE ONE WHO CAN RIG THE QUIZZES?
LISTEN, "CORNY," NOBODY ASKED YOUR OPINON.
WHAT'S UP, WILL?
THIS WON'T TAKE LONG, BUT I WANNA FIGURE OUT WHY ONE OF THOSE CREATURES WAS AT THE MUSEUM.
I CAN ANSWER THAT! BEHOLD!
THE MAP OF THE PORTALS! SHOULDN'T THAT BE SOMEWHERE SAFER?
THERE'S NO PLACE SAFER THAN MY BACKPACK.
WOW! LOOK AT THIS!
JUST WHAT YOU WANTED, WILL. AT THE MUSEUM— ANOTHER BREACH IN THE VEIL!
MUSEUM
MAY I SEE WHAT YOU FIND SO FASCINATING, LADIES?

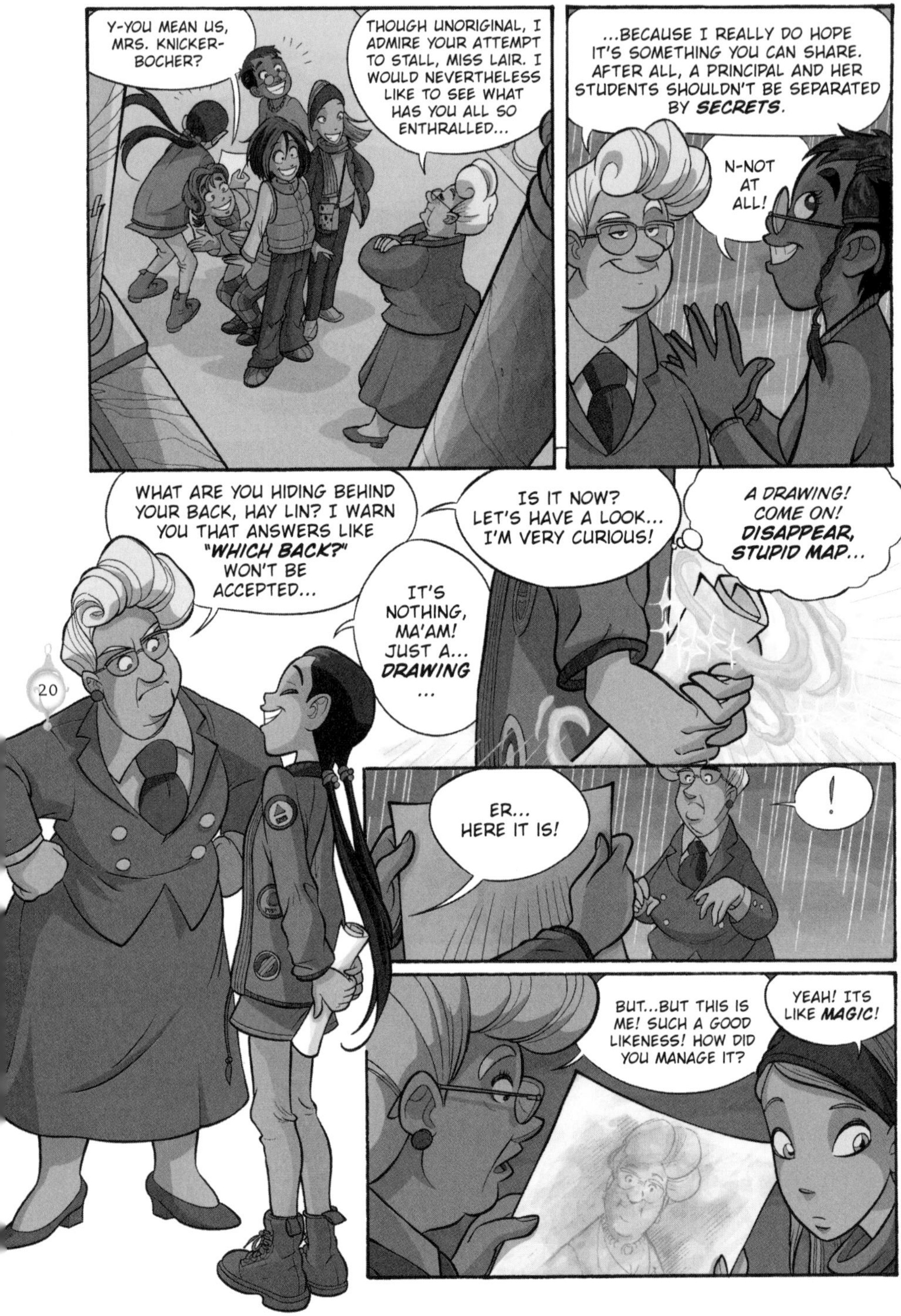

Y-YOU MEAN US, MRS. KNICKER-BOCHER?
THOUGH UNORIGINAL, I ADMIRE YOUR ATTEMPT TO STALL, MISS LAIR. I WOULD NEVERTHELESS LIKE TO SEE WHAT HAS YOU ALL SO ENTHRALLED...
...BECAUSE I REALLY DO HOPE IT'S SOMETHING YOU CAN SHARE. AFTER ALL, A PRINCIPAL AND HER STUDENTS SHOULDN'T BE SEPARATED BY SECRETS.
N-NOT AT ALL!
WHAT ARE YOU HIDING BEHIND YOUR BACK, HAY LIN? I WARN YOU THAT ANSWERS LIKE "WHICH BACK?" WON'T BE ACCEPTED...
IT'S NOTHING, MA'AM! JUST A... DRAWING...
IS IT NOW? LET'S HAVE A LOOK... I'M VERY CURIOUS!
A DRAWING! COME ON! DISAPPEAR, STUPID MAP...
ER... HERE IT IS!
!
BUT...BUT THIS IS ME! SUCH A GOOD LIKENESS! HOW DID YOU MANAGE IT?
YEAH! ITS LIKE MAGIC!

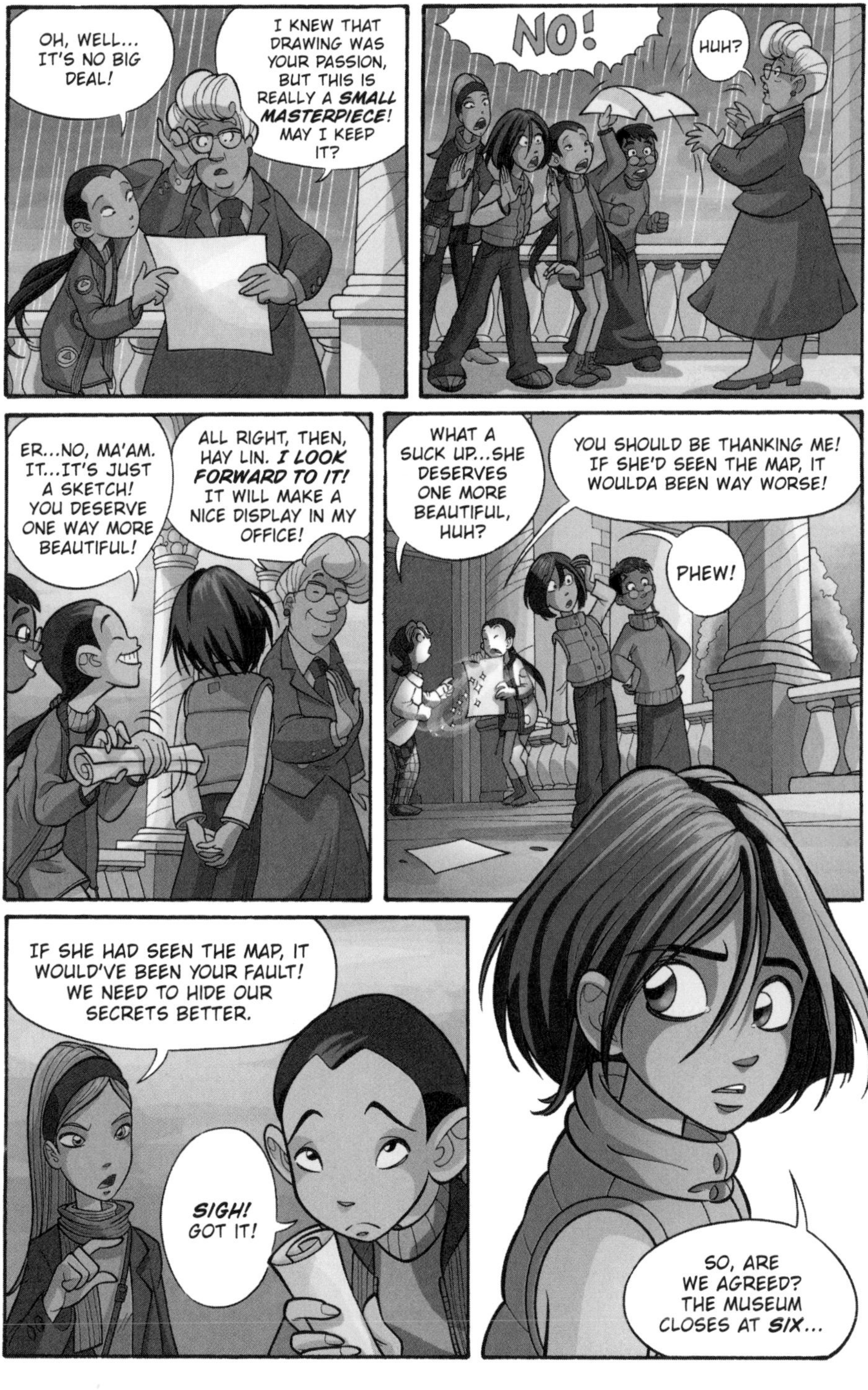
OH, WELL... IT'S NO BIG DEAL!
I KNEW THAT DRAWING WAS YOUR PASSION, BUT THIS IS REALLY A SMALL MASTERPIECE! MAY I KEEP IT?
NO!
HUH?
ER...NO, MA'AM. IT...IT'S JUST A SKETCH! YOU DESERVE ONE WAY MORE BEAUTIFUL!
ALL RIGHT, THEN, HAY LIN. I LOOK FORWARD TO IT! IT WILL MAKE A NICE DISPLAY IN MY OFFICE!
WHAT A SUCK UP...SHE DESERVES ONE MORE BEAUTIFUL, HUH?
YOU SHOULD BE THANKING ME! IF SHE'D SEEN THE MAP, IT WOULDA BEEN WAY WORSE!
PHEW!
IF SHE HAD SEEN THE MAP, IT WOULD'VE BEEN YOUR FAULT! WE NEED TO HIDE OUR SECRETS BETTER.
SIGH! GOT IT!
SO, ARE WE AGREED? THE MUSEUM CLOSES AT SIX...

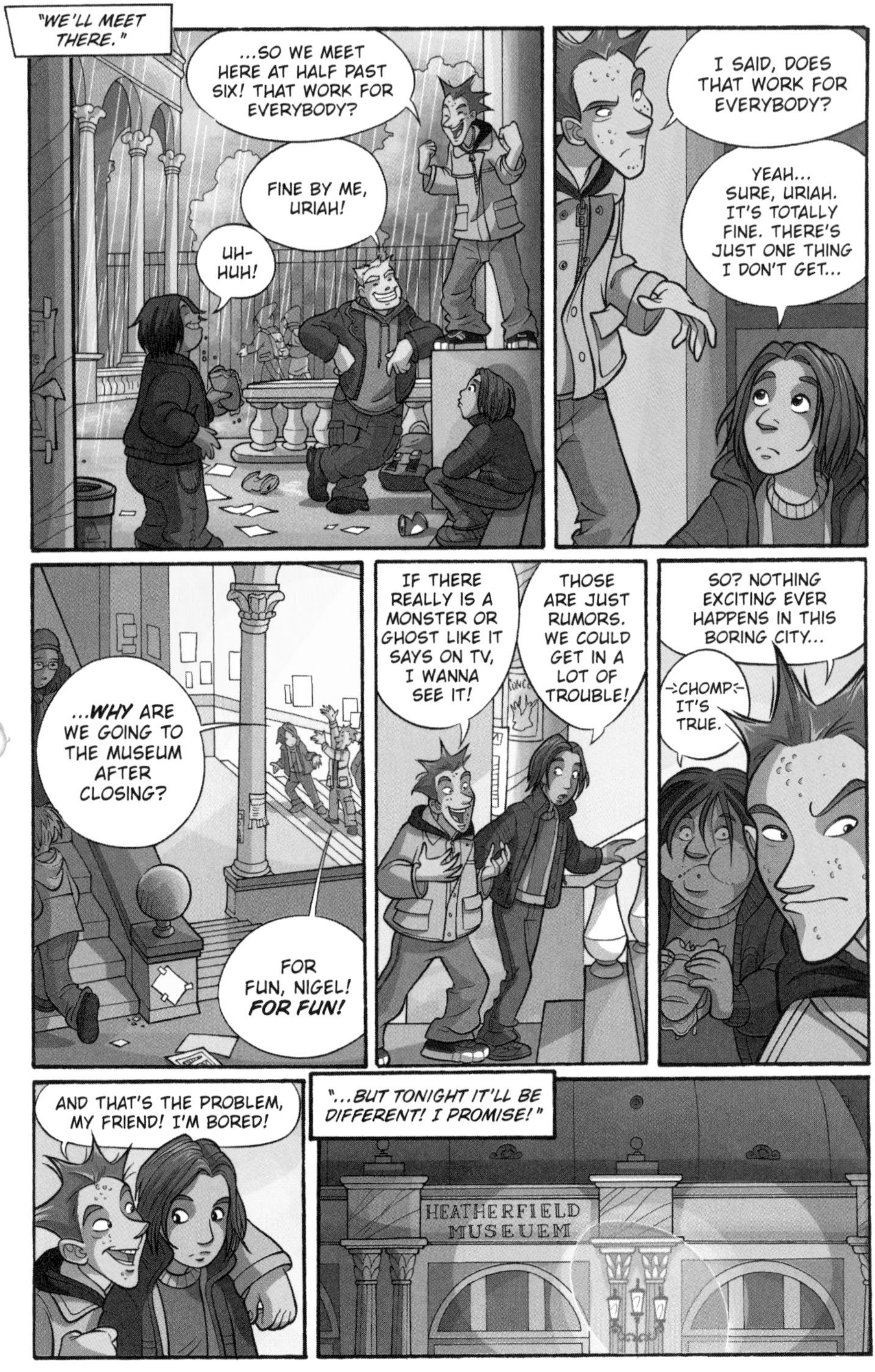
"WE'LL MEET THERE."
...SO WE MEET HERE AT HALF PAST SIX! THAT WORK FOR EVERYBODY?
FINE BY ME, URIAH!
UH-HUH!
I SAID, DOES THAT WORK FOR EVERYBODY?
YEAH... SURE, URIAH. IT'S TOTALLY FINE. THERE'S JUST ONE THING I DON'T GET...
...WHY ARE WE GOING TO THE MUSEUM AFTER CLOSING?
FOR FUN, NIGEL! FOR FUN!
IF THERE REALLY IS A MONSTER OR GHOST LIKE IT SAYS ON TV, I WANNA SEE IT!
THOSE ARE JUST RUMORS. WE COULD GET IN A LOT OF TROUBLE!
SO? NOTHING EXCITING EVER HAPPENS IN THIS BORING CITY...
CHOMP
IT'S TRUE.
AND THAT'S THE PROBLEM, MY FRIEND! I'M BORED!
"...BUT TONIGHT IT'LL BE DIFFERENT! I PROMISE!"
HEATHERFIELD MUSEUEM

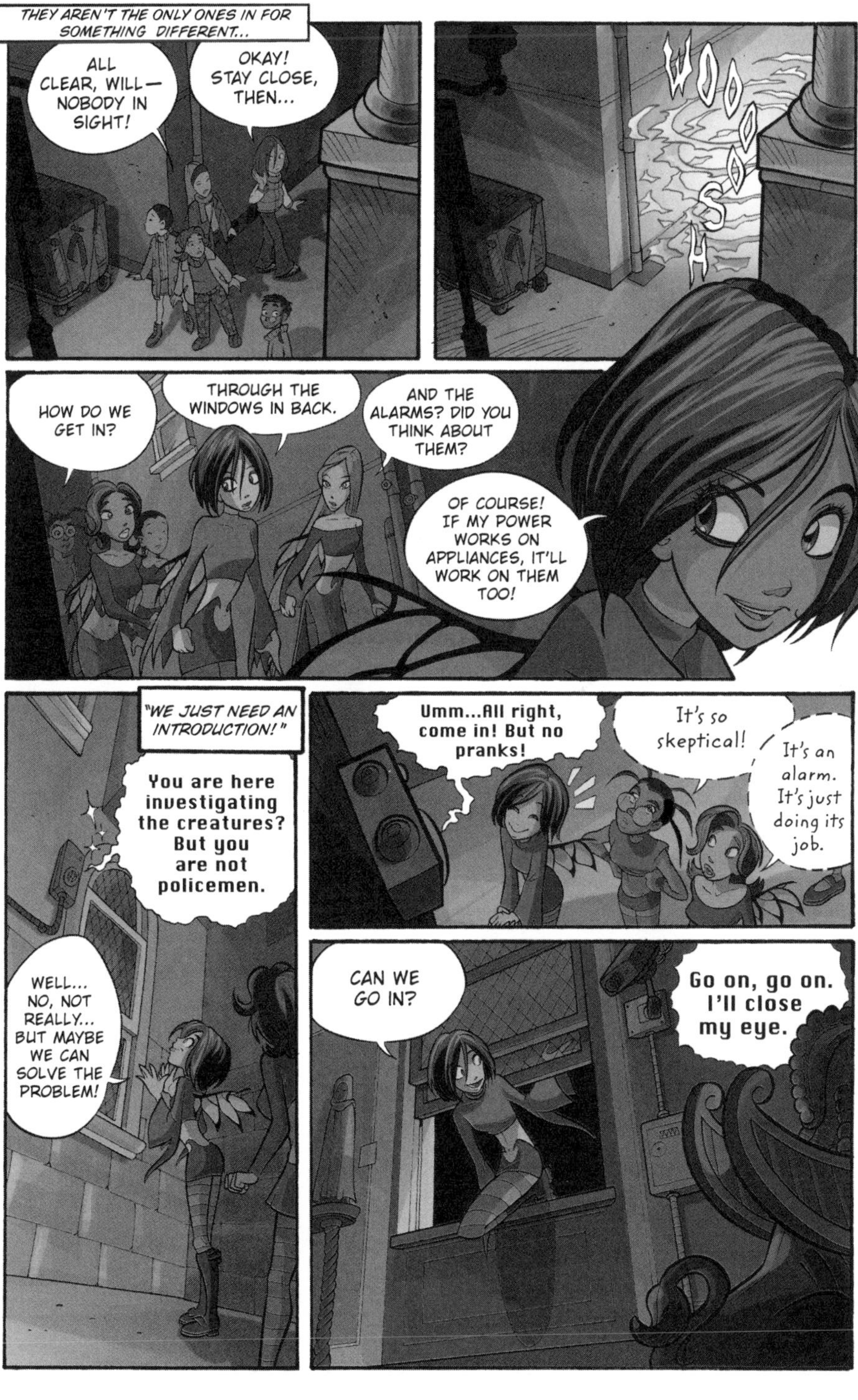
THEY AREN'T THE ONLY ONES IN FOR SOMETHING DIFFERENT...
ALL CLEAR, WILL—NOBODY IN SIGHT!
OKAY! STAY CLOSE, THEN...
WOOOOOSH
HOW DO WE GET IN?
THROUGH THE WINDOWS IN BACK.
AND THE ALARMS? DID YOU THINK ABOUT THEM?
OF COURSE! IF MY POWER WORKS ON APPLIANCES, IT'LL WORK ON THEM TOO!
"WE JUST NEED AN INTRODUCTION!"
You are here investigating the creatures? But you are not policemen.
WELL... NO, NOT REALLY... BUT MAYBE WE CAN SOLVE THE PROBLEM!
Umm...All right, come in! But no pranks!
It's so skeptical!
It's an alarm. It's just doing its job.
CAN WE GO IN?
Go on, go on. I'll close my eye.

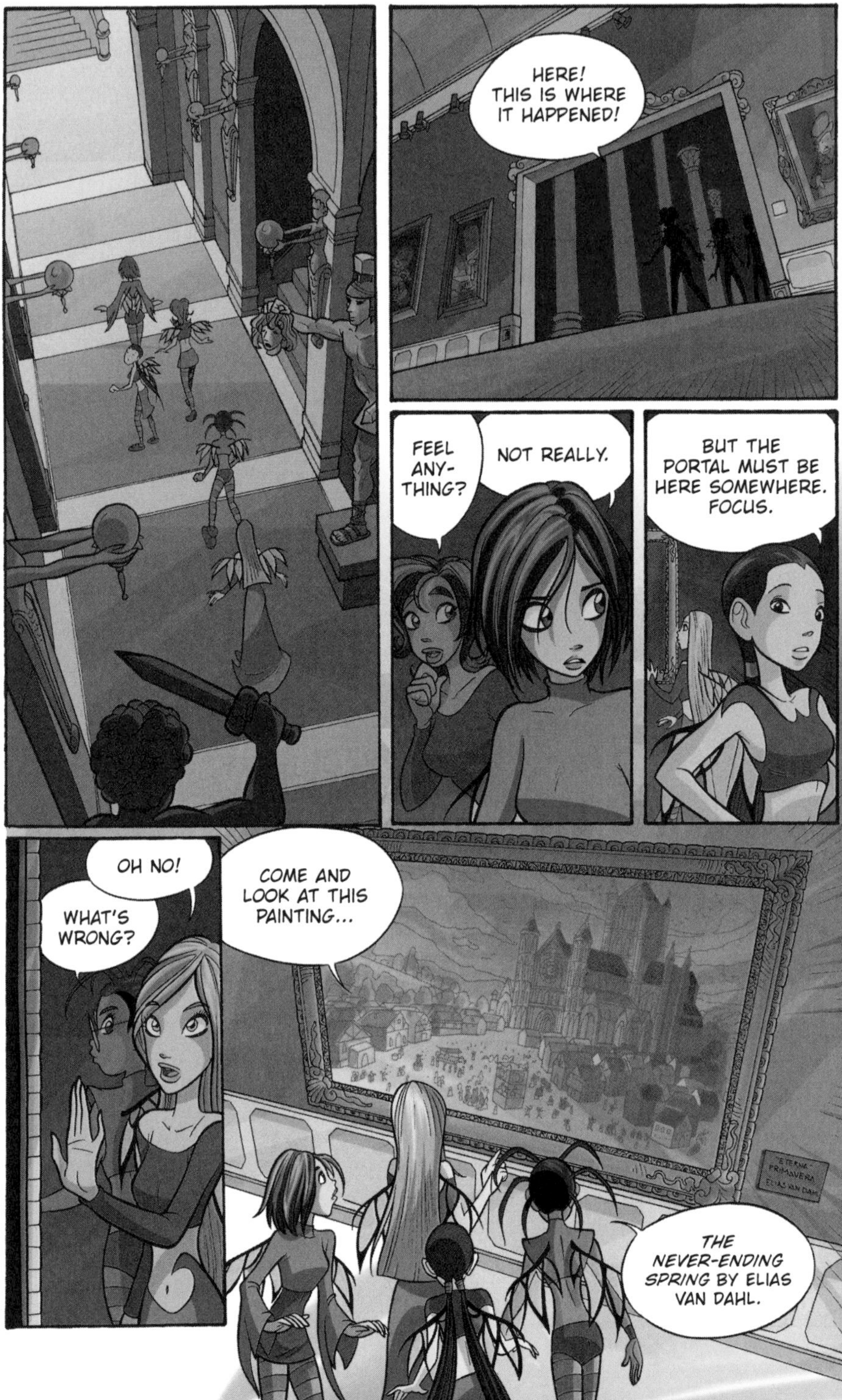
HERE! THIS IS WHERE IT HAPPENED!
FEEL ANY-THING?
NOT REALLY.
BUT THE PORTAL MUST BE HERE SOMEWHERE. FOCUS.
OH NO!
WHAT'S WRONG?
COME AND LOOK AT THIS PAINTING...
THE NEVER-ENDING SPRING BY ELIAS VAN DAHL.

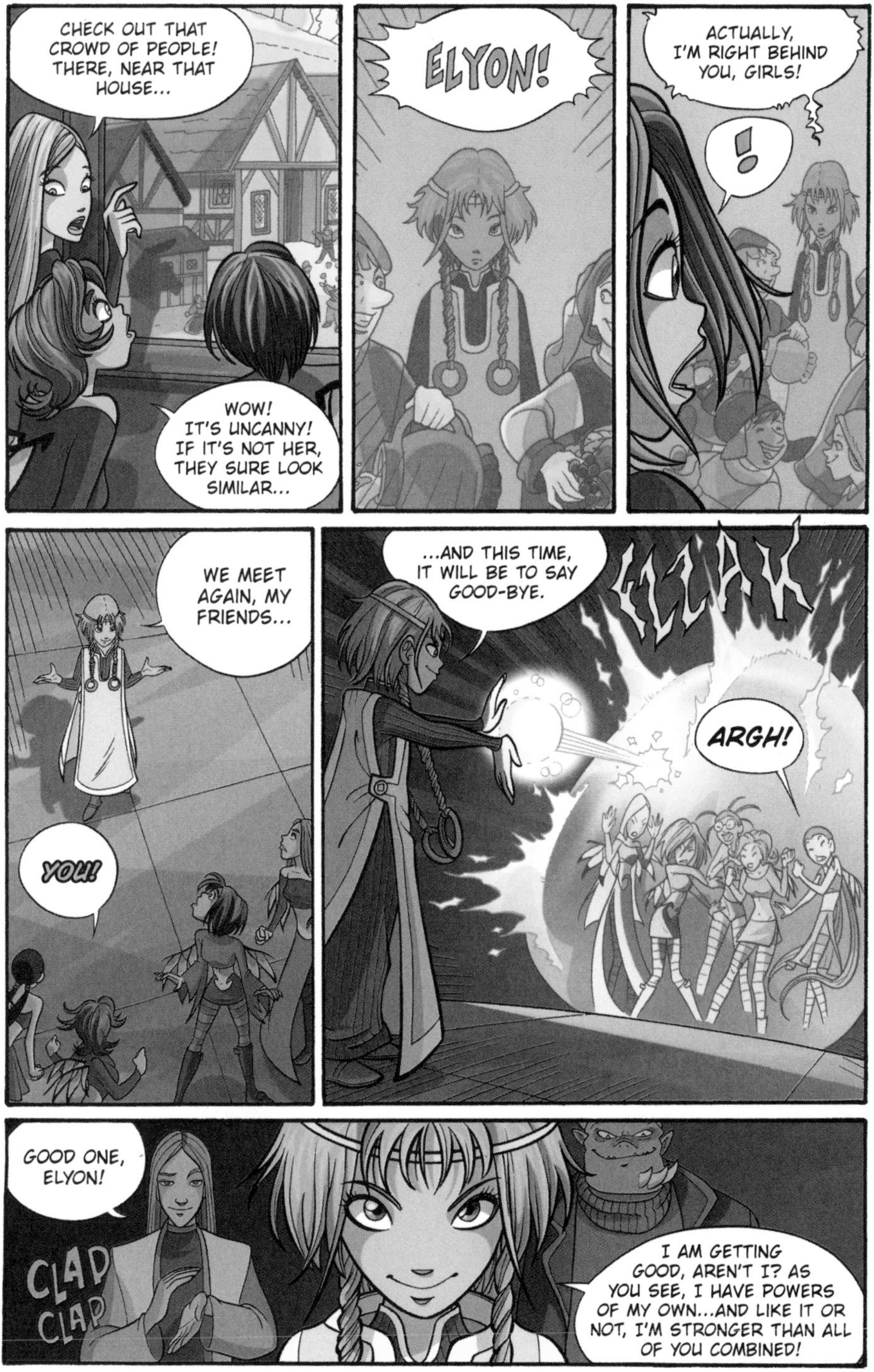
CHECK OUT THAT CROWD OF PEOPLE! THERE, NEAR THAT HOUSE...
WOW! IT'S UNCANNY! IF IT'S NOT HER, THEY SURE LOOK SIMILAR...
ELYON!
ACTUALLY, I'M RIGHT BEHIND YOU, GIRLS!
!
WE MEET AGAIN, MY FRIENDS...
YOU!
...AND THIS TIME, IT WILL BE TO SAY GOOD-BYE.
ARGH!
GOOD ONE, ELYON!
CLAP CLAP
I AM GETTING GOOD, AREN'T I? AS YOU SEE, I HAVE POWERS OF MY OWN...AND LIKE IT OR NOT, I'M STRONGER THAN ALL OF YOU COMBINED!

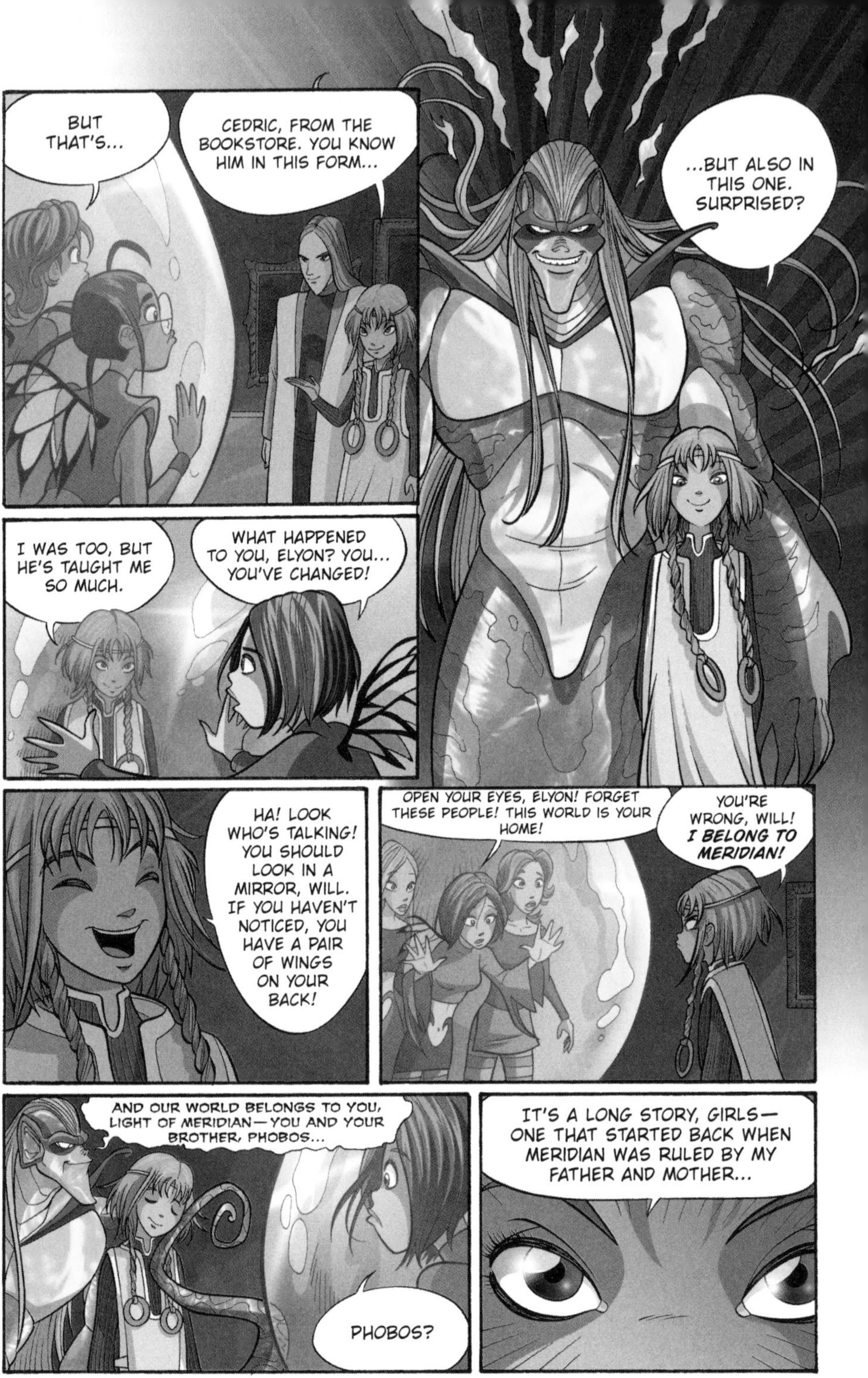
BUT THAT'S...
CEDRIC, FROM THE BOOKSTORE. YOU KNOW HIM IN THIS FORM...
...BUT ALSO IN THIS ONE. SURPRISED?
I WAS TOO, BUT HE'S TAUGHT ME SO MUCH.
WHAT HAPPENED TO YOU, ELYON? YOU... YOU'VE CHANGED!
HA! LOOK WHO'S TALKING! YOU SHOULD LOOK IN A MIRROR, WILL. IF YOU HAVEN'T NOTICED, YOU HAVE A PAIR OF WINGS ON YOUR BACK!
OPEN YOUR EYES, ELYON! FORGET THESE PEOPLE! THIS WORLD IS YOUR HOME!
YOU'RE WRONG, WILL! *I BELONG TO MERIDIAN!*
AND OUR WORLD BELONGS TO YOU, LIGHT OF MERIDIAN—YOU AND YOUR BROTHER, PHOBOS...
PHOBOS?
IT'S A LONG STORY, GIRLS—ONE THAT STARTED BACK WHEN MERIDIAN WAS RULED BY MY FATHER AND MOTHER...

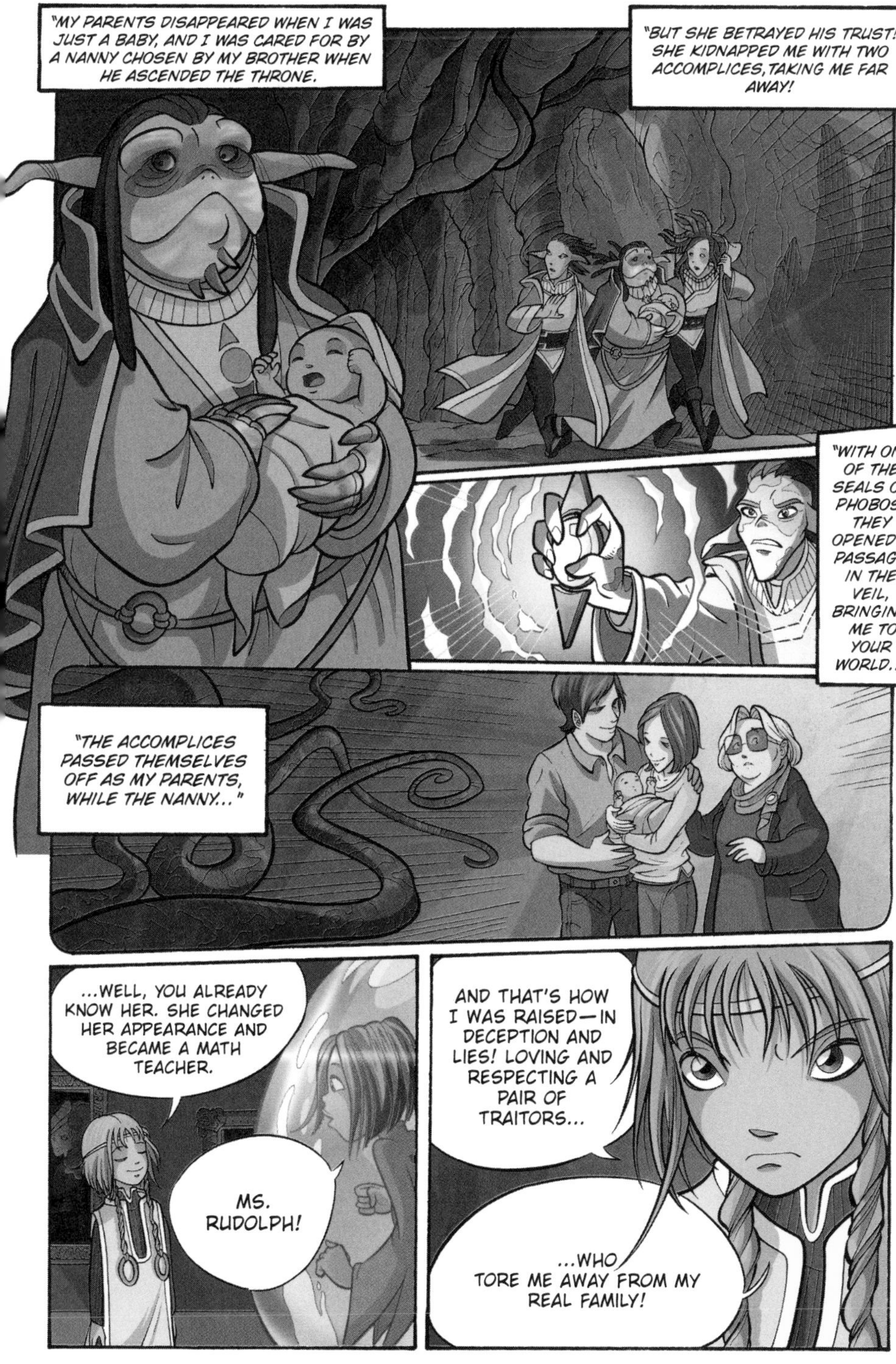
"MY PARENTS DISAPPEARED WHEN I WAS JUST A BABY, AND I WAS CARED FOR BY A NANNY CHOSEN BY MY BROTHER WHEN HE ASCENDED THE THRONE.
"BUT SHE BETRAYED HIS TRUST! SHE KIDNAPPED ME WITH TWO ACCOMPLICES, TAKING ME FAR AWAY!
"WITH ONE OF THE SEALS OF PHOBOS, THEY OPENED A PASSAGE IN THE VEIL, BRINGING ME TO YOUR WORLD...
"THE ACCOMPLICES PASSED THEMSELVES OFF AS MY PARENTS, WHILE THE NANNY..."
...WELL, YOU ALREADY KNOW HER. SHE CHANGED HER APPEARANCE AND BECAME A MATH TEACHER.
MS. RUDOLPH!
AND THAT'S HOW I WAS RAISED—IN DECEPTION AND LIES! LOVING AND RESPECTING A PAIR OF TRAITORS...
...WHO TORE ME AWAY FROM MY REAL FAMILY!

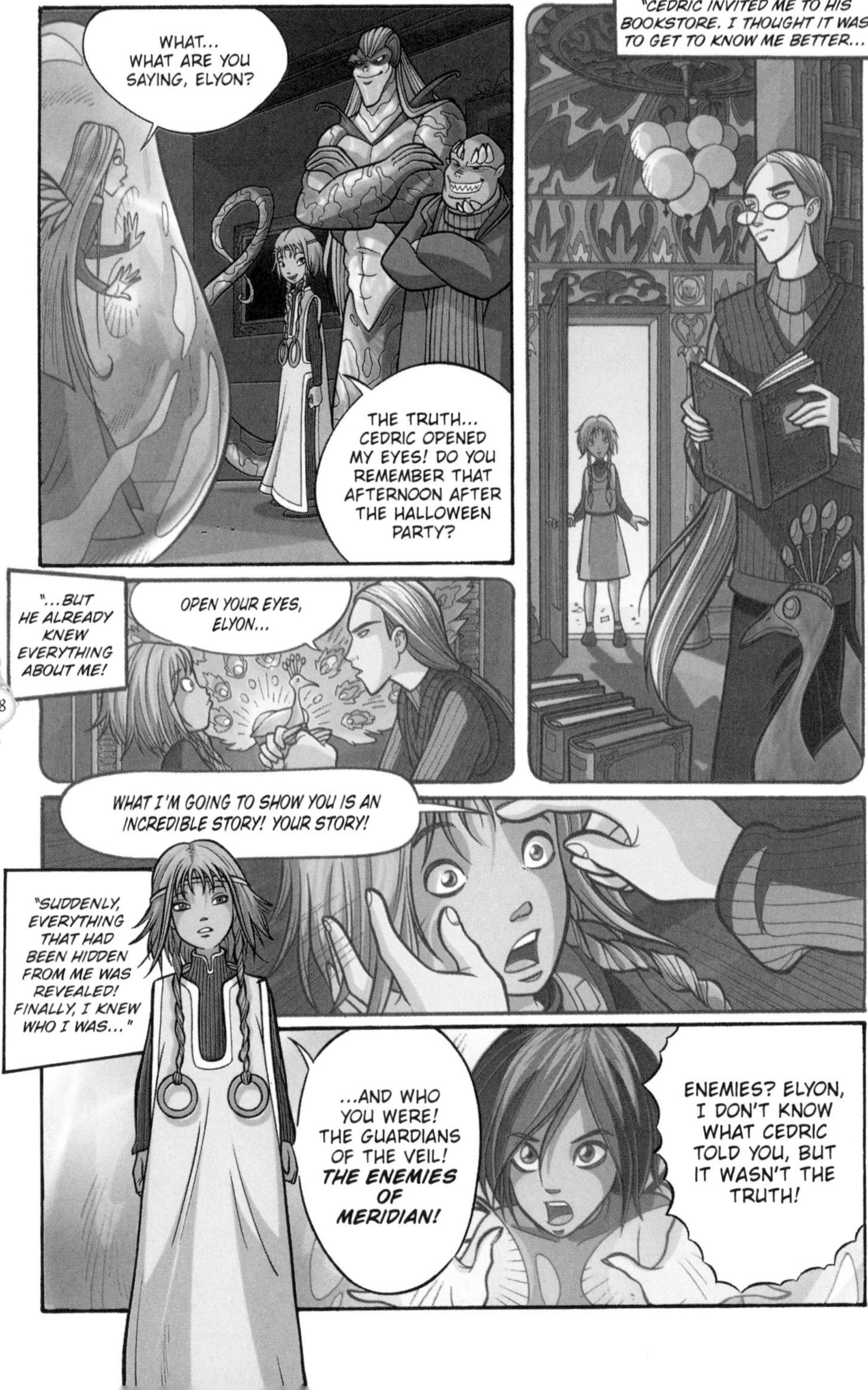
WHAT... WHAT ARE YOU SAYING, ELYON?
THE TRUTH... CEDRIC OPENED MY EYES! DO YOU REMEMBER THAT AFTERNOON AFTER THE HALLOWEEN PARTY?
"CEDRIC INVITED ME TO HIS BOOKSTORE. I THOUGHT IT WAS TO GET TO KNOW ME BETTER...
"...BUT HE ALREADY KNEW EVERYTHING ABOUT ME!
OPEN YOUR EYES, ELYON...
WHAT I'M GOING TO SHOW YOU IS AN INCREDIBLE STORY! YOUR STORY!
"SUDDENLY, EVERYTHING THAT HAD BEEN HIDDEN FROM ME WAS REVEALED! FINALLY, I KNEW WHO I WAS..."
...AND WHO YOU WERE! THE GUARDIANS OF THE VEIL! THE ENEMIES OF MERIDIAN!
ENEMIES? ELYON, I DON'T KNOW WHAT CEDRIC TOLD YOU, BUT IT WASN'T THE TRUTH!

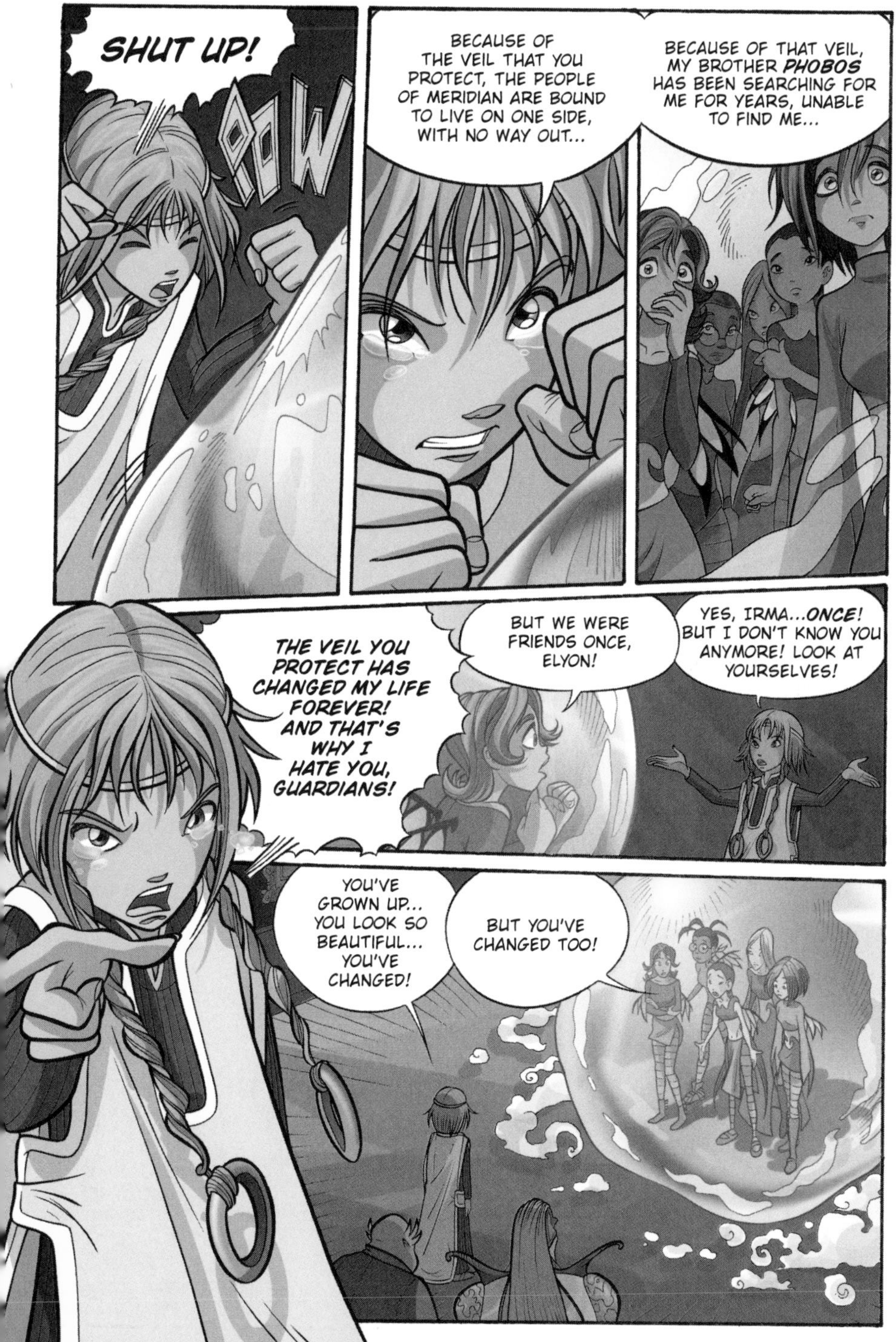
SHUT UP!
POW
BECAUSE OF THE VEIL THAT YOU PROTECT, THE PEOPLE OF MERIDIAN ARE BOUND TO LIVE ON ONE SIDE, WITH NO WAY OUT...
BECAUSE OF THAT VEIL, MY BROTHER PHOBOS HAS BEEN SEARCHING FOR ME FOR YEARS, UNABLE TO FIND ME...
THE VEIL YOU PROTECT HAS CHANGED MY LIFE FOREVER! AND THAT'S WHY I HATE YOU, GUARDIANS!
BUT WE WERE FRIENDS ONCE, ELYON!
YES, IRMA...ONCE! BUT I DON'T KNOW YOU ANYMORE! LOOK AT YOURSELVES!
YOU'VE GROWN UP... YOU LOOK SO BEAUTIFUL... YOU'VE CHANGED!
BUT YOU'VE CHANGED TOO!

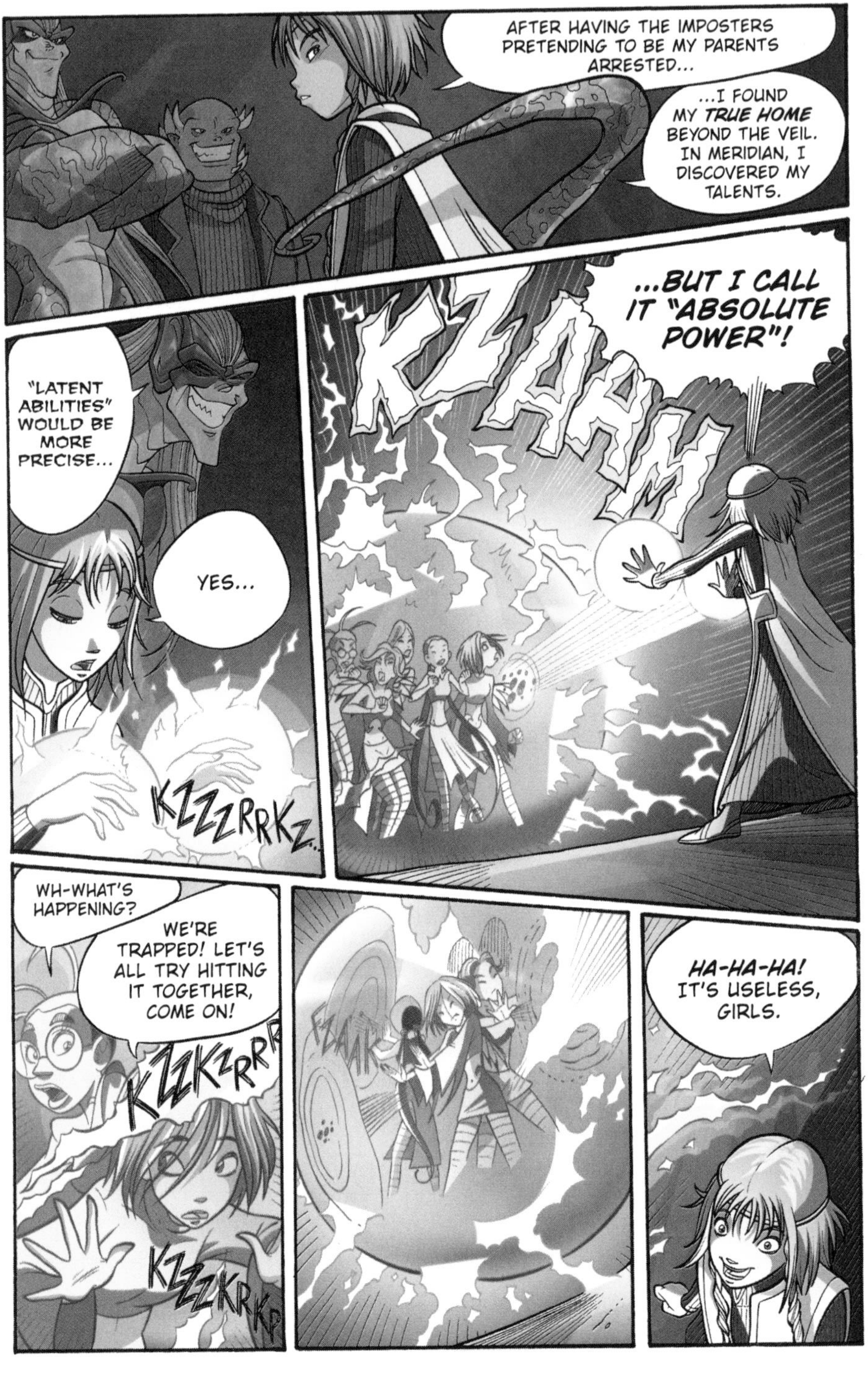
AFTER HAVING THE IMPOSTERS PRETENDING TO BE MY PARENTS ARRESTED...
...I FOUND MY TRUE HOME BEYOND THE VEIL. IN MERIDIAN, I DISCOVERED MY TALENTS.
"LATENT ABILITIES" WOULD BE MORE PRECISE...
YES...
KZZZRRKZ...
...BUT I CALL IT "ABSOLUTE POWER"!
KZAAM
WH-WHAT'S HAPPENING?
WE'RE TRAPPED! LET'S ALL TRY HITTING IT TOGETHER, COME ON!
KZZKZRRR
KZZZKRKP
FZAAK
HA-HA-HA! IT'S USELESS, GIRLS.

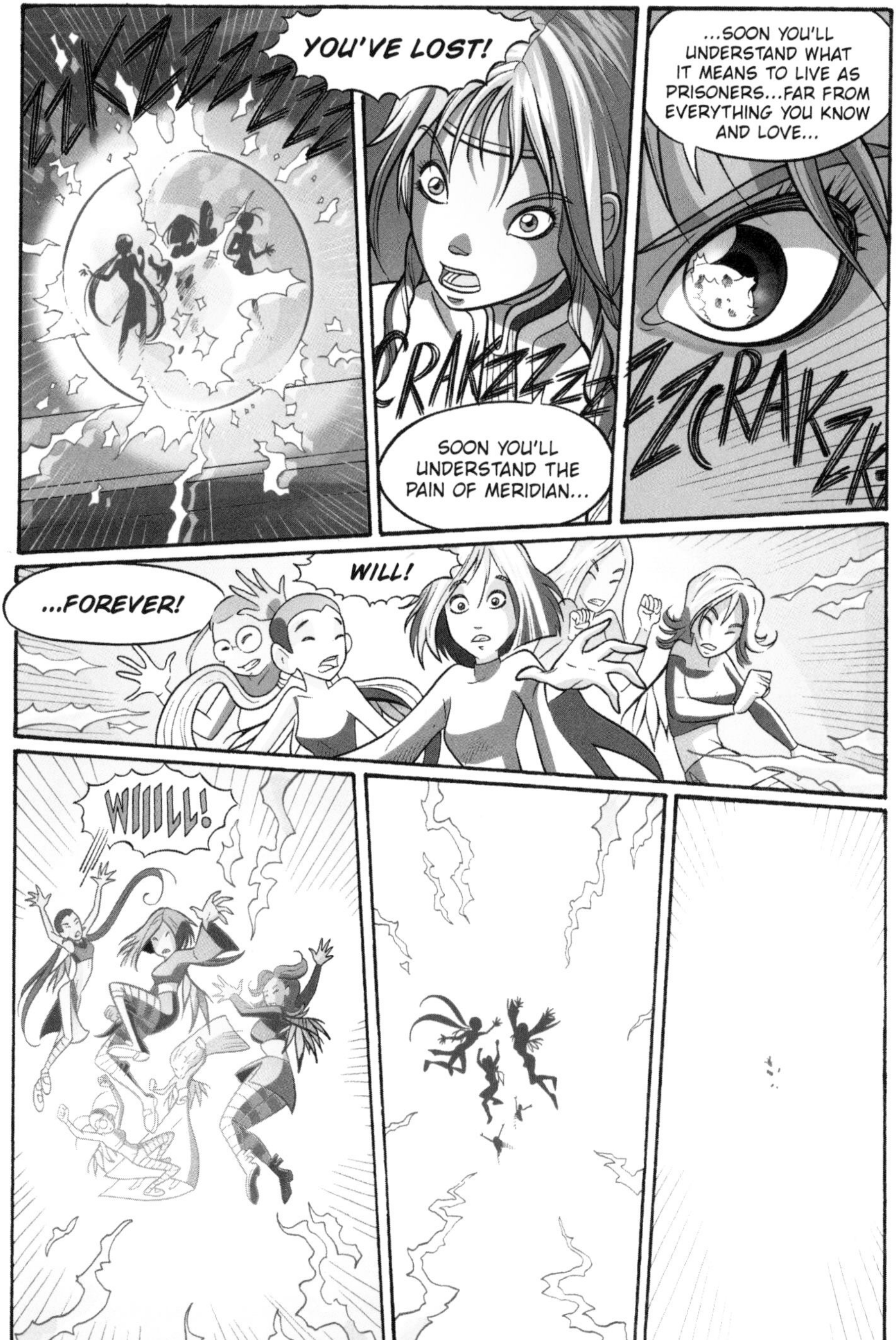
ZZKZZZZZZZ
YOU'VE LOST!
...SOON YOU'LL UNDERSTAND WHAT IT MEANS TO LIVE AS PRISONERS...FAR FROM EVERYTHING YOU KNOW AND LOVE...
CRAKZZZZZ
ZZCRAKZK
SOON YOU'LL UNDERSTAND THE PAIN OF MERIDIAN...
...FOREVER!
WILL!
WIIILL!

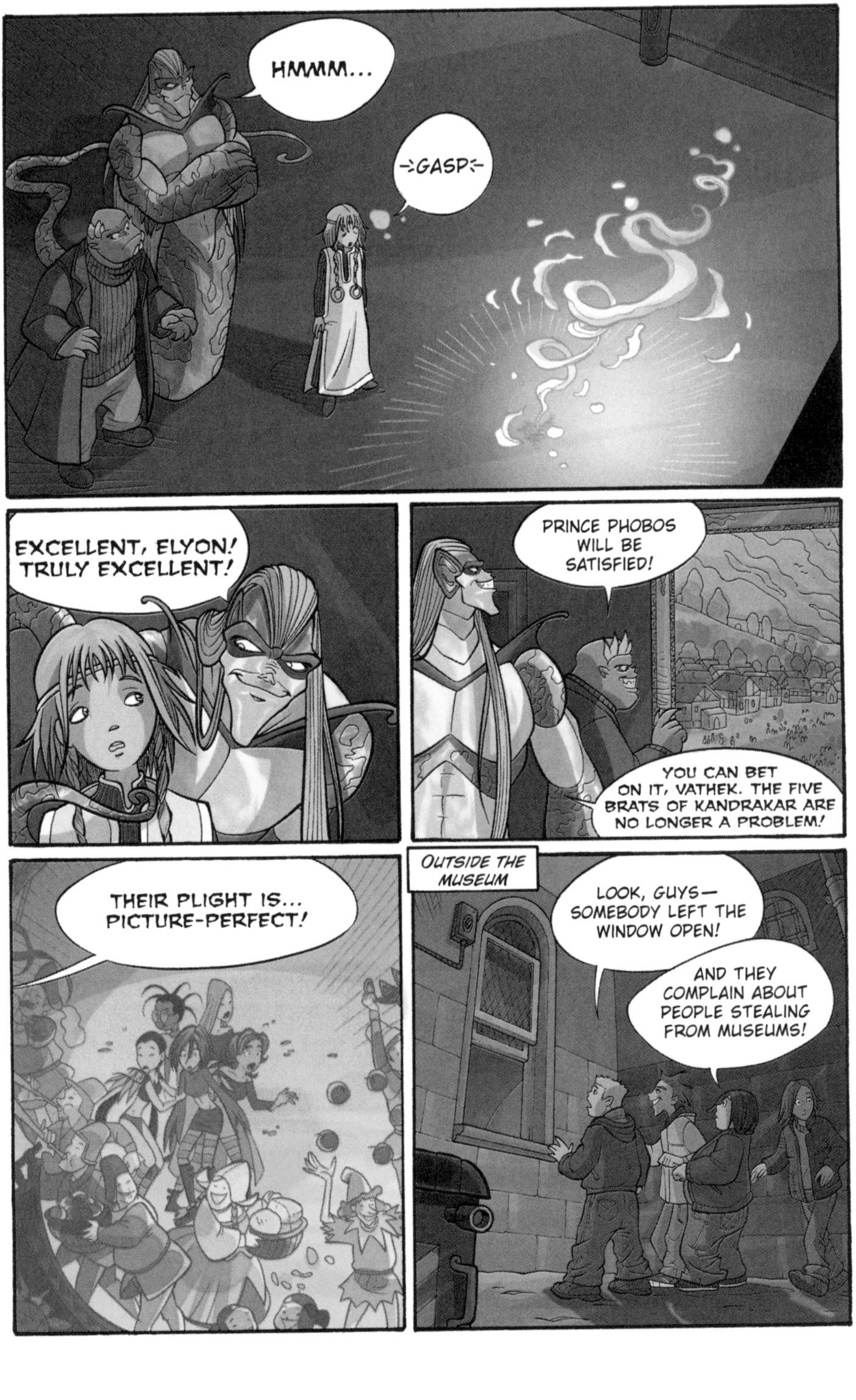
HMMM...
-GASP-
EXCELLENT, ELYON! TRULY EXCELLENT!
PRINCE PHOBOS WILL BE SATISFIED!
YOU CAN BET ON IT, VATHEK. THE FIVE BRATS OF KANDRAKAR ARE NO LONGER A PROBLEM!
THEIR PLIGHT IS... PICTURE-PERFECT!
OUTSIDE THE MUSEUM
LOOK, GUYS— SOMEBODY LEFT THE WINDOW OPEN!
AND THEY COMPLAIN ABOUT PEOPLE STEALING FROM MUSEUMS!

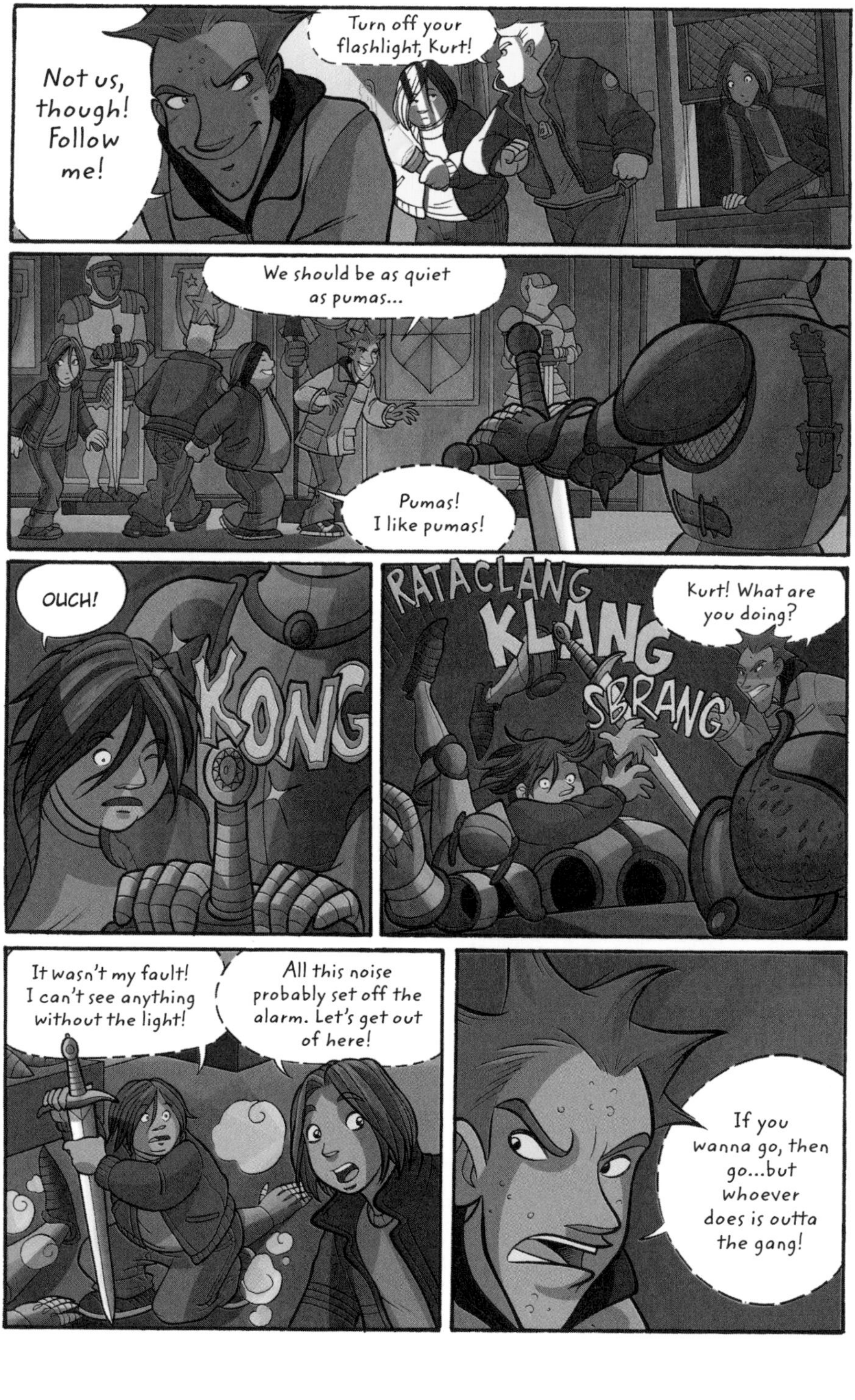
Turn off your flashlight, Kurt!
Not us, though! Follow me!
We should be as quiet as pumas...
Pumas! I like pumas!
OUCH!
KONG
RATACLANG
KLANG
SBRANG
Kurt! What are you doing?
It wasn't my fault! I can't see anything without the light!
All this noise probably set off the alarm. Let's get out of here!
If you wanna go, then go...but whoever does is outta the gang!

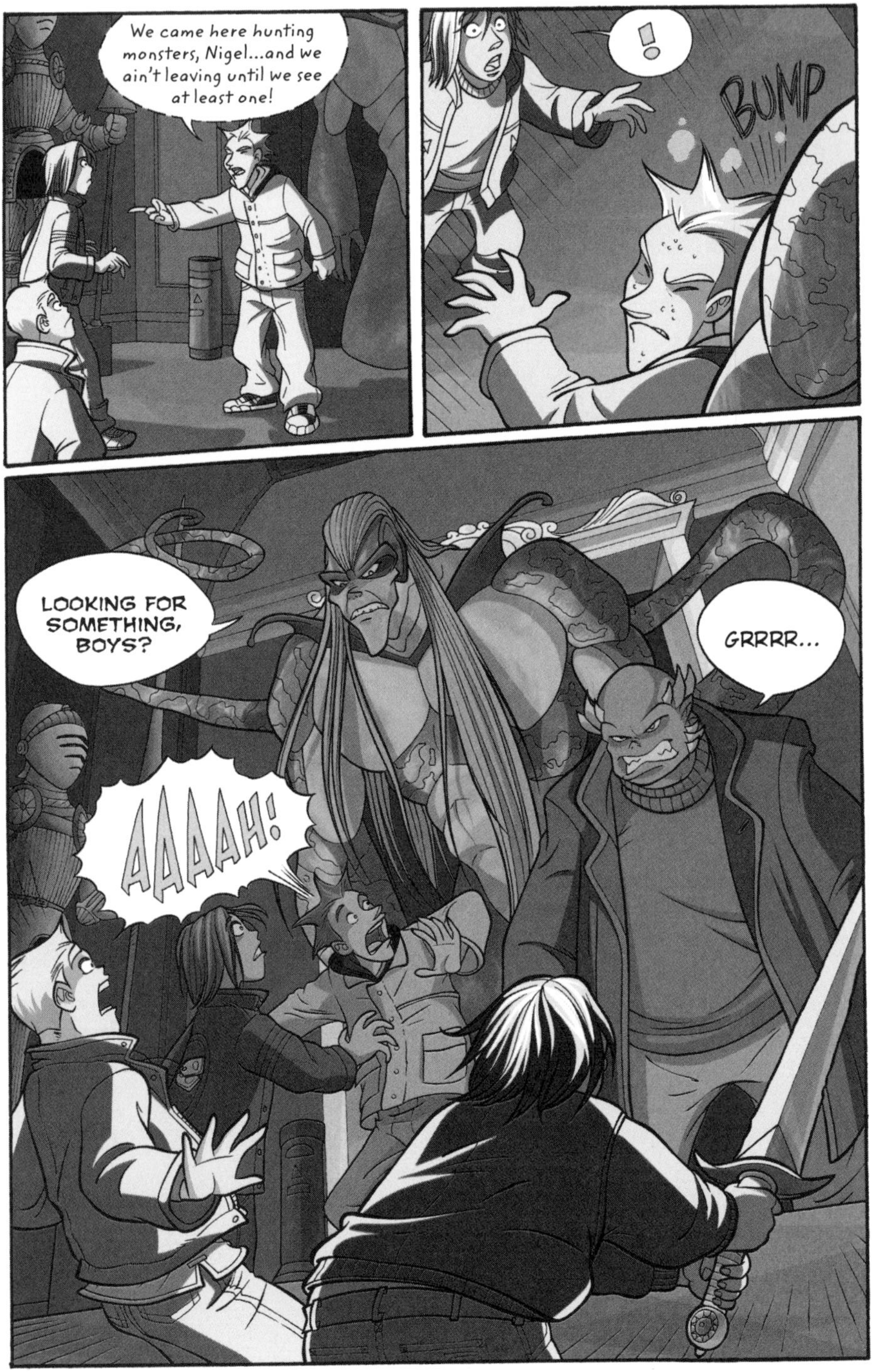
We came here hunting monsters, Nigel...and we ain't leaving until we see at least one!
!
BUMP
LOOKING FOR SOMETHING, BOYS?
GRRRR...
AAAAH!

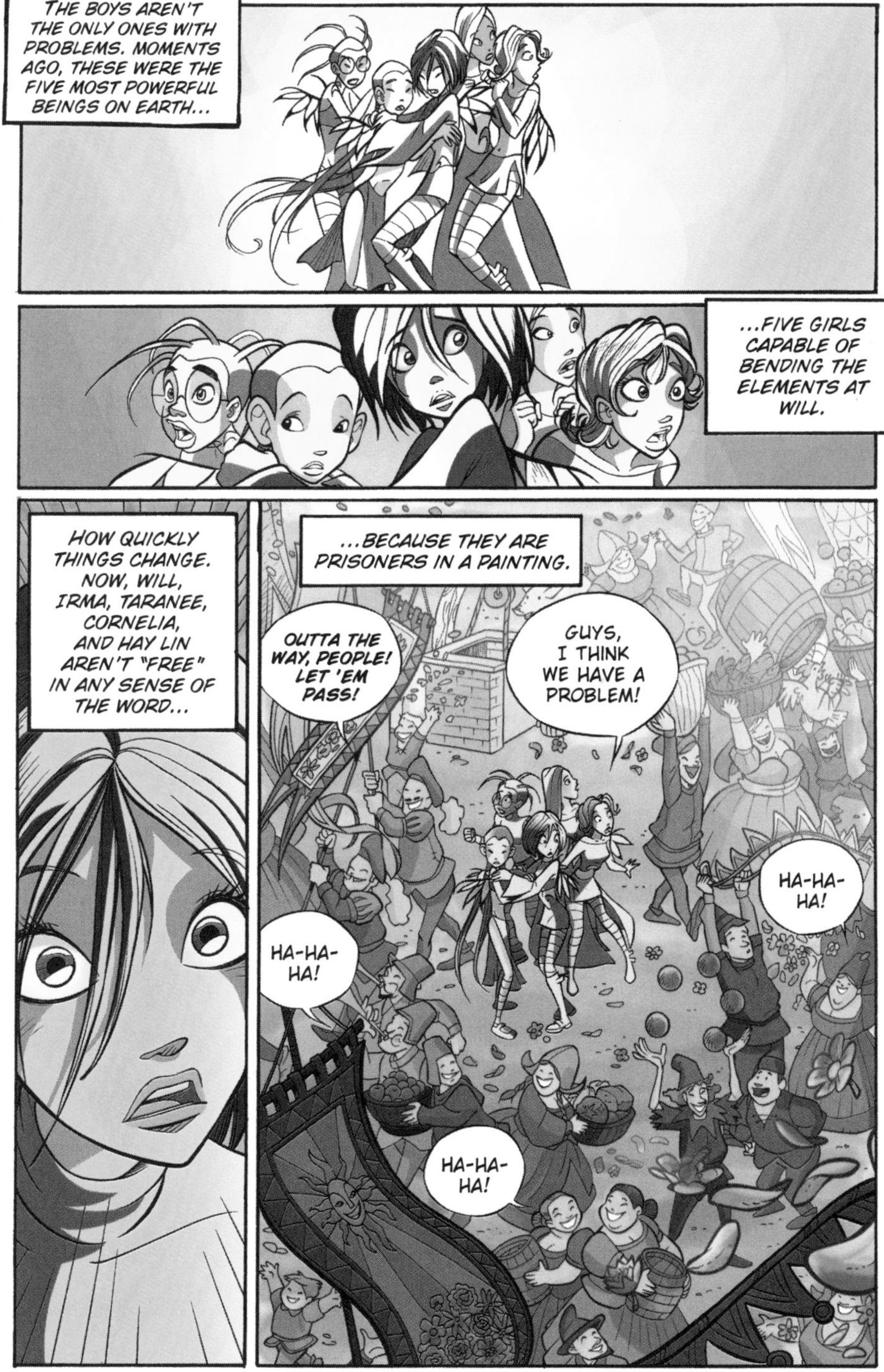
THE BOYS AREN'T THE ONLY ONES WITH PROBLEMS. MOMENTS AGO, THESE WERE THE FIVE MOST POWERFUL BEINGS ON EARTH...
...FIVE GIRLS CAPABLE OF BENDING THE ELEMENTS AT WILL.
HOW QUICKLY THINGS CHANGE. NOW, WILL, IRMA, TARANEE, CORNELIA, AND HAY LIN AREN'T "FREE" IN ANY SENSE OF THE WORD...
...BECAUSE THEY ARE PRISONERS IN A PAINTING.
OUTTA THE WAY, PEOPLE! LET 'EM PASS!
GUYS, I THINK WE HAVE A PROBLEM!
HA-HA-HA!
HA-HA-HA!
HA-HA-HA!

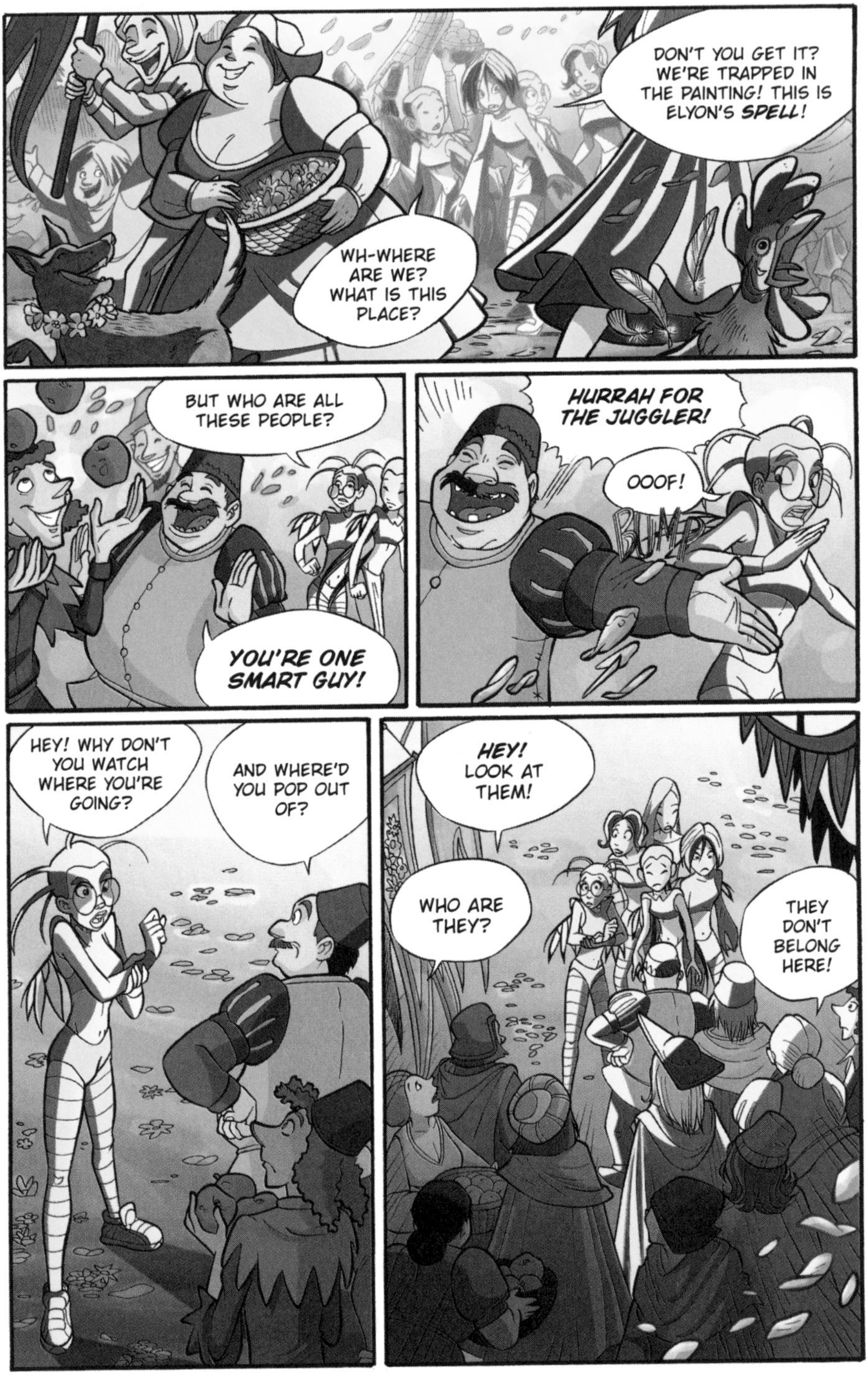
DON'T YOU GET IT? WE'RE TRAPPED IN THE PAINTING! THIS IS ELYON'S SPELL!
WH-WHERE ARE WE? WHAT IS THIS PLACE?
BUT WHO ARE ALL THESE PEOPLE?
YOU'RE ONE SMART GUY!
HURRAH FOR THE JUGGLER!
OOOF!
BUMP
HEY! WHY DON'T YOU WATCH WHERE YOU'RE GOING?
AND WHERE'D YOU POP OUT OF?
HEY! LOOK AT THEM!
WHO ARE THEY?
THEY DON'T BELONG HERE!

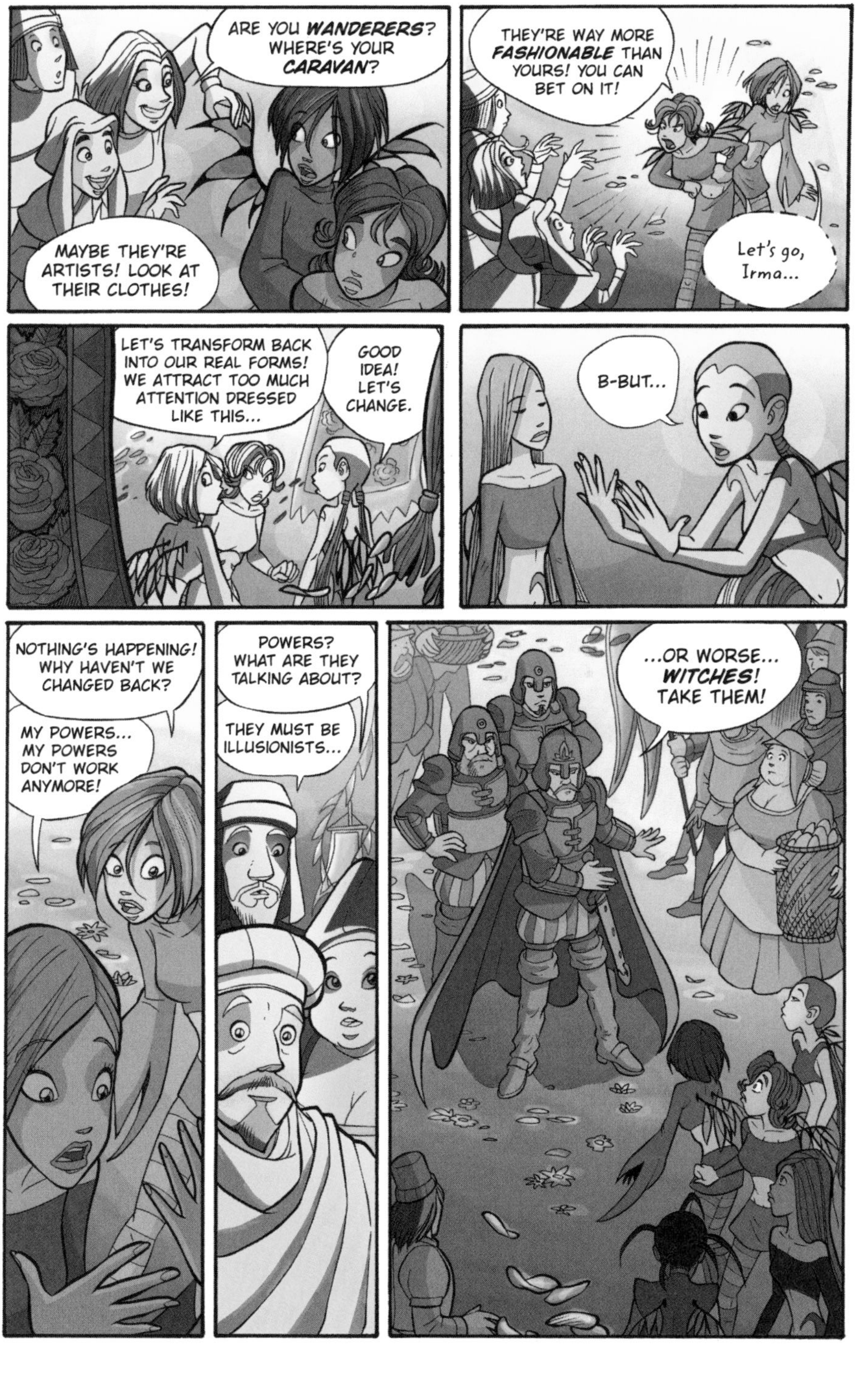
ARE YOU WANDERERS? WHERE'S YOUR CARAVAN?
MAYBE THEY'RE ARTISTS! LOOK AT THEIR CLOTHES!
THEY'RE WAY MORE FASHIONABLE THAN YOURS! YOU CAN BET ON IT!
Let's go, Irma...
LET'S TRANSFORM BACK INTO OUR REAL FORMS! WE ATTRACT TOO MUCH ATTENTION DRESSED LIKE THIS...
GOOD IDEA! LET'S CHANGE.
B-BUT...
NOTHING'S HAPPENING! WHY HAVEN'T WE CHANGED BACK?
MY POWERS... MY POWERS DON'T WORK ANYMORE!
POWERS? WHAT ARE THEY TALKING ABOUT?
THEY MUST BE ILLUSIONISTS...
...OR WORSE... WITCHES! TAKE THEM!

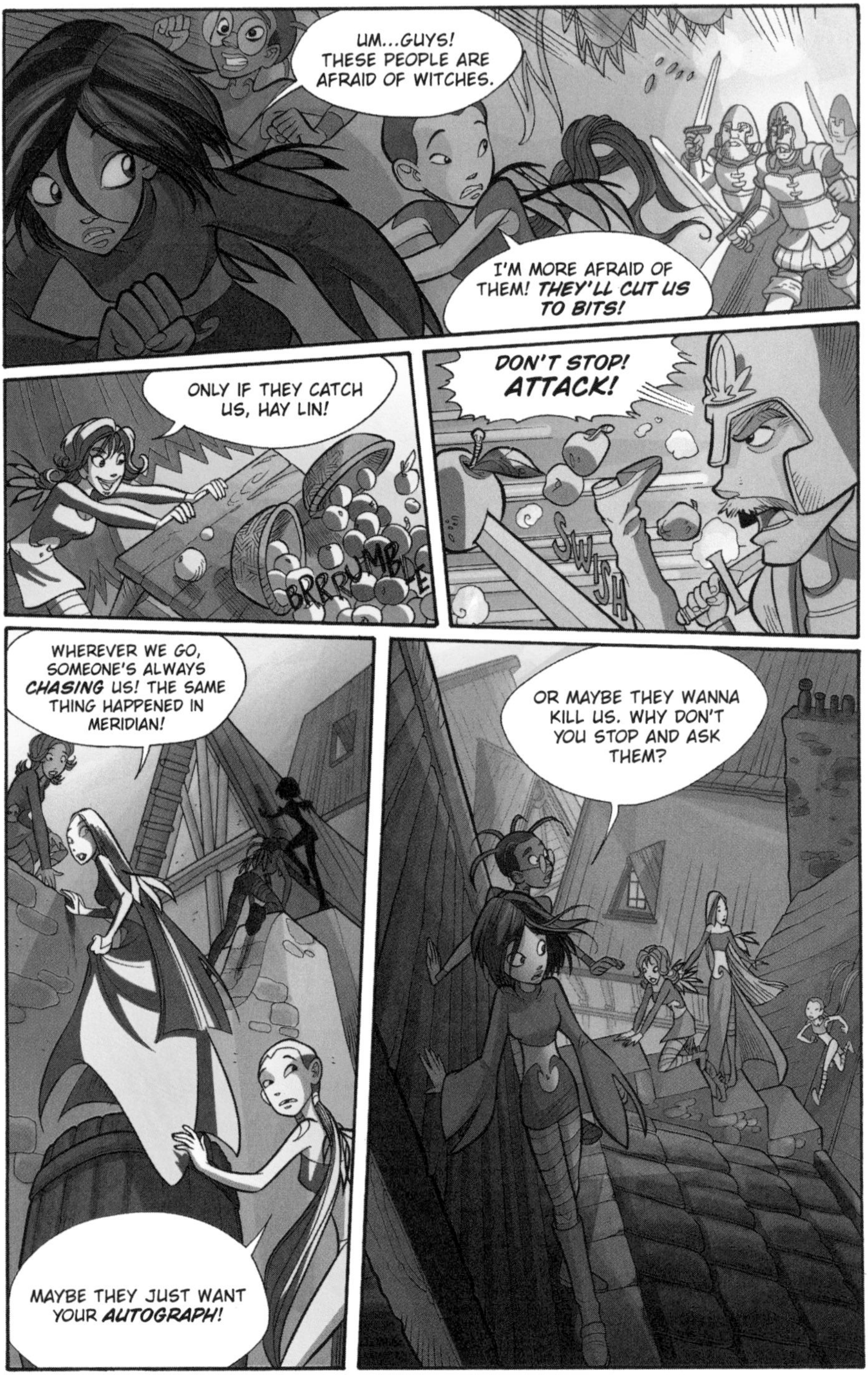
UM...GUYS! THESE PEOPLE ARE AFRAID OF WITCHES.
I'M MORE AFRAID OF THEM! THEY'LL CUT US TO BITS!
ONLY IF THEY CATCH US, HAY LIN!
BRRRUMBLE
DON'T STOP! ATTACK!
SWISH
WHEREVER WE GO, SOMEONE'S ALWAYS CHASING US! THE SAME THING HAPPENED IN MERIDIAN!
MAYBE THEY JUST WANT YOUR AUTOGRAPH!
OR MAYBE THEY WANNA KILL US. WHY DON'T YOU STOP AND ASK THEM?

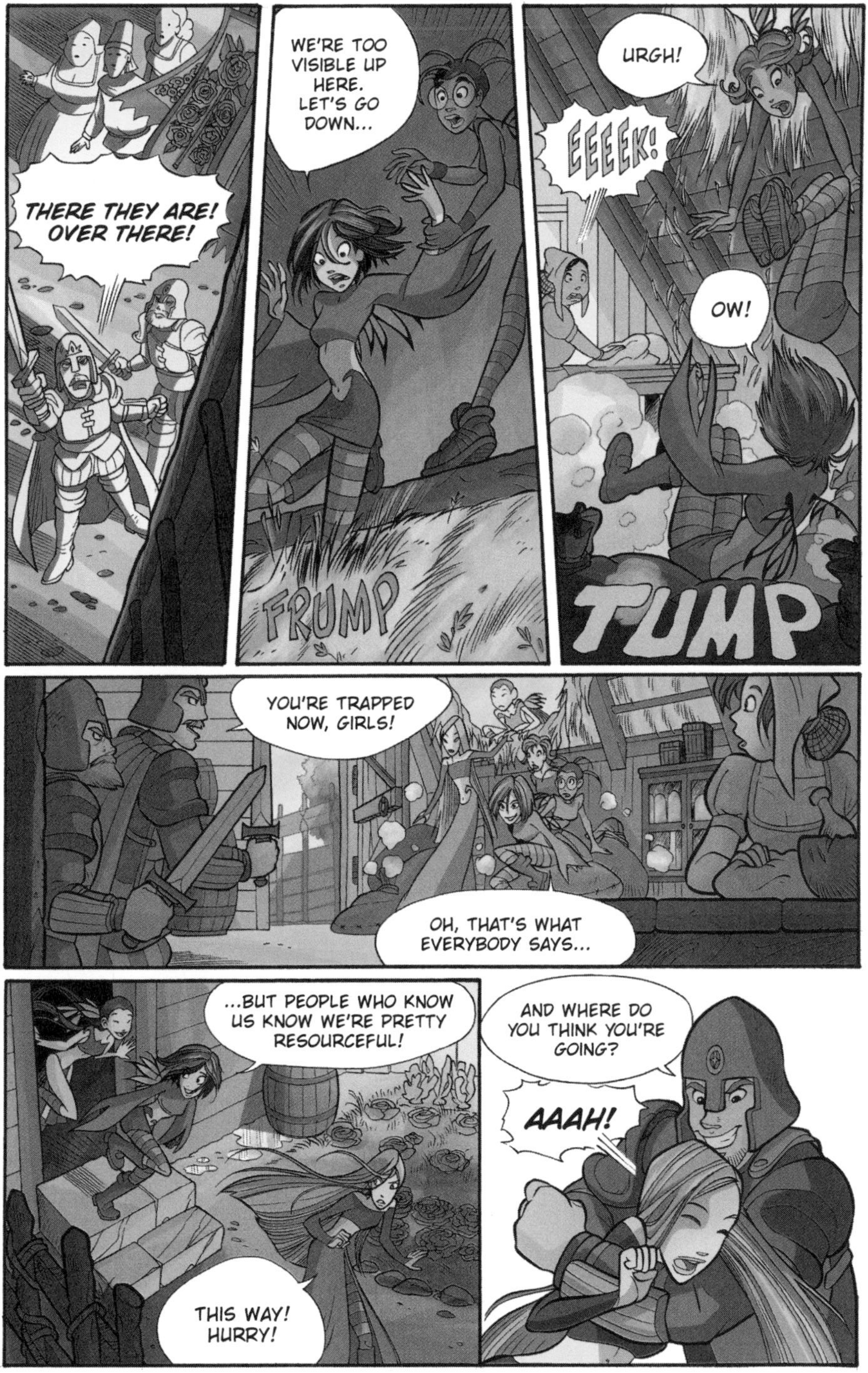
THERE THEY ARE! OVER THERE!
WE'RE TOO VISIBLE UP HERE. LET'S GO DOWN...
FRUMP
URGH!
EEEEK!
OW!
TUMP
YOU'RE TRAPPED NOW, GIRLS!
OH, THAT'S WHAT EVERYBODY SAYS...
...BUT PEOPLE WHO KNOW US KNOW WE'RE PRETTY RESOURCEFUL!
THIS WAY! HURRY!
AND WHERE DO YOU THINK YOU'RE GOING?
AAAH!

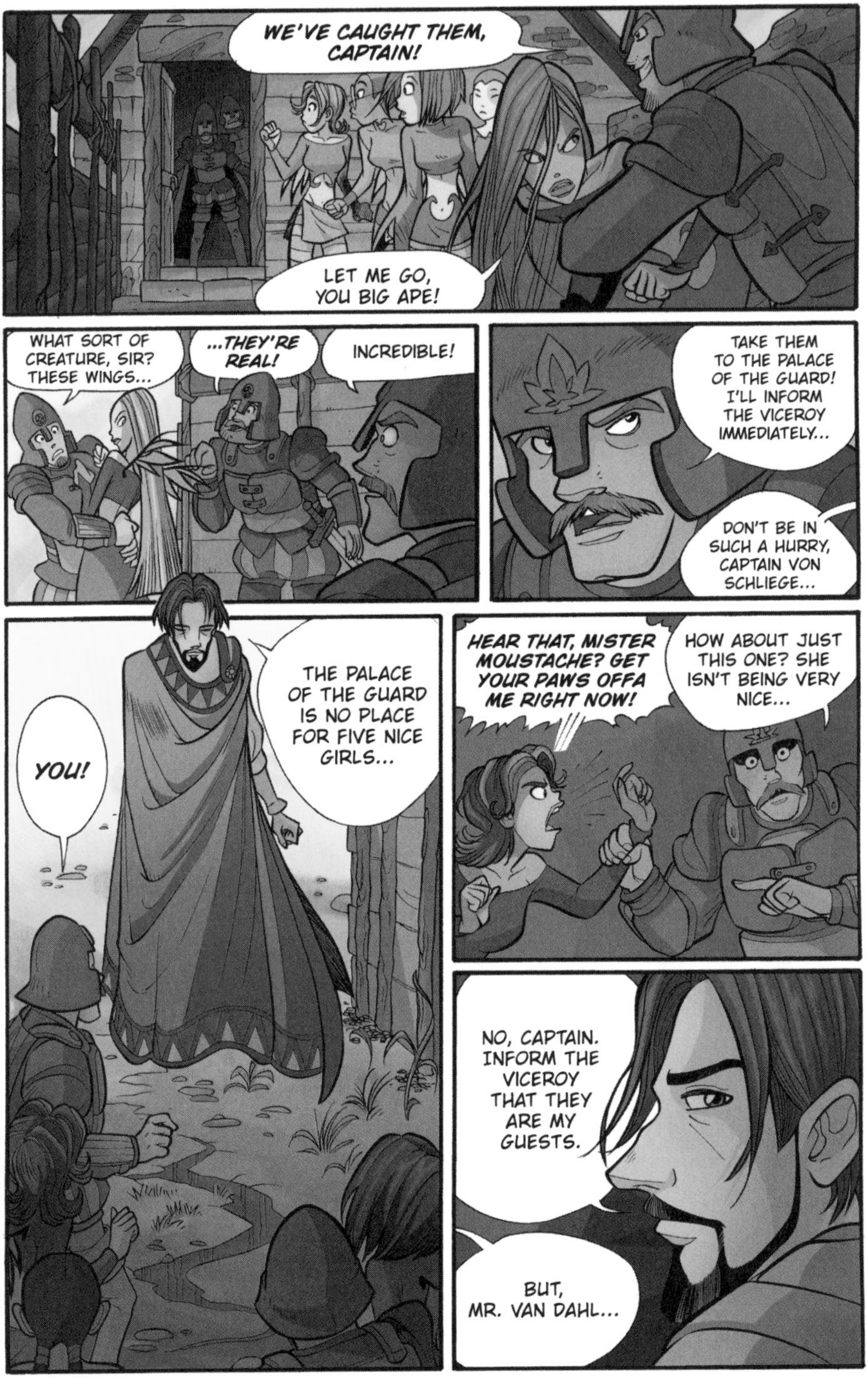
WE'VE CAUGHT THEM, CAPTAIN!
LET ME GO, YOU BIG APE!
WHAT SORT OF CREATURE, SIR? THESE WINGS...
...THEY'RE REAL!
INCREDIBLE!
TAKE THEM TO THE PALACE OF THE GUARD! I'LL INFORM THE VICEROY IMMEDIATELY...
DON'T BE IN SUCH A HURRY, CAPTAIN VON SCHLIEGE...
THE PALACE OF THE GUARD IS NO PLACE FOR FIVE NICE GIRLS...
YOU!
HEAR THAT, MISTER MOUSTACHE? GET YOUR PAWS OFFA ME RIGHT NOW!
HOW ABOUT JUST THIS ONE? SHE ISN'T BEING VERY NICE...
NO, CAPTAIN. INFORM THE VICEROY THAT THEY ARE MY GUESTS.
BUT, MR. VAN DAHL...

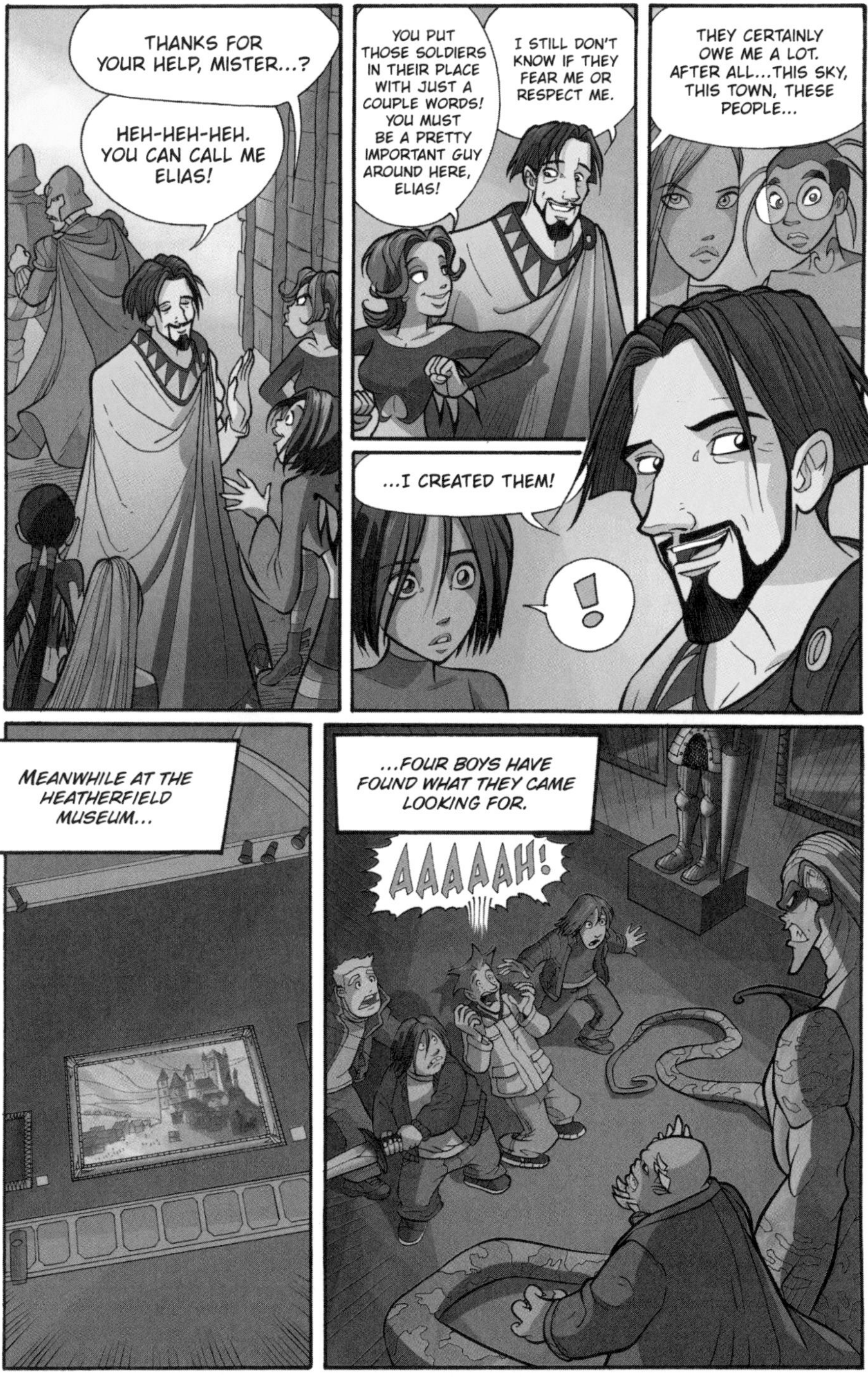
THANKS FOR YOUR HELP, MISTER...?
HEH-HEH-HEH. YOU CAN CALL ME ELIAS!
YOU PUT THOSE SOLDIERS IN THEIR PLACE WITH JUST A COUPLE WORDS! YOU MUST BE A PRETTY IMPORTANT GUY AROUND HERE, ELIAS!
I STILL DON'T KNOW IF THEY FEAR ME OR RESPECT ME.
THEY CERTAINLY OWE ME A LOT. AFTER ALL...THIS SKY, THIS TOWN, THESE PEOPLE...
...I CREATED THEM!
!
MEANWHILE AT THE HEATHERFIELD MUSEUM...
...FOUR BOYS HAVE FOUND WHAT THEY CAME LOOKING FOR.
AAAAAH!

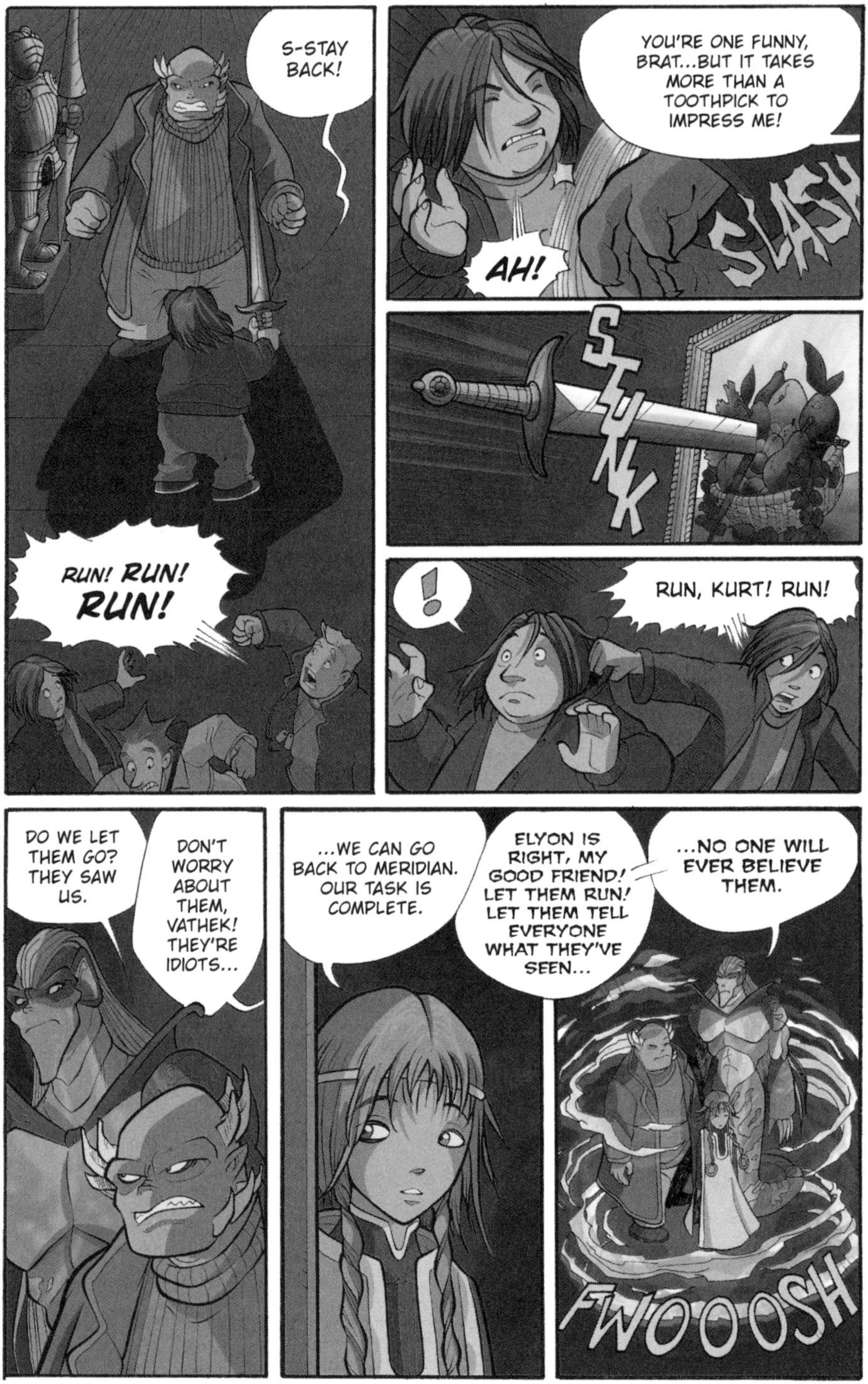
S-STAY BACK!
YOU'RE ONE FUNNY, BRAT...BUT IT TAKES MORE THAN A TOOTHPICK TO IMPRESS ME!
AH!
SLASH
STUNK
RUN! RUN! RUN!
!
RUN, KURT! RUN!
DO WE LET THEM GO? THEY SAW US.
DON'T WORRY ABOUT THEM, VATHEK! THEY'RE IDIOTS...
...WE CAN GO BACK TO MERIDIAN. OUR TASK IS COMPLETE.
ELYON IS RIGHT, MY GOOD FRIEND! LET THEM RUN! LET THEM TELL EVERYONE WHAT THEY'VE SEEN...
...NO ONE WILL EVER BELIEVE THEM.
FWOOOSH

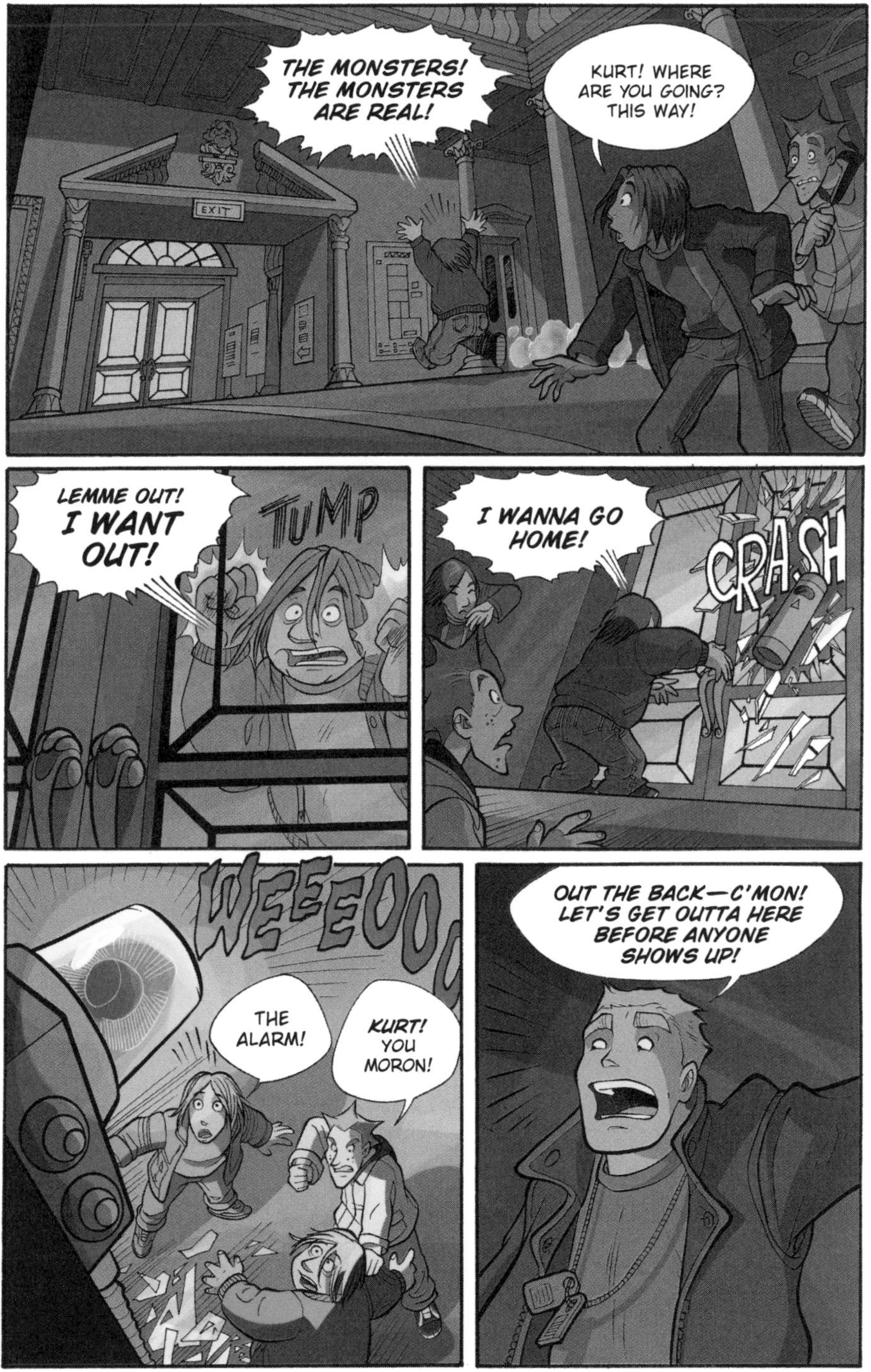
THE MONSTERS! THE MONSTERS ARE REAL!
KURT! WHERE ARE YOU GOING? THIS WAY!
EXIT
LEMME OUT! I WANT OUT!
TUMP
I WANNA GO HOME!
CRASH
WEEEOOO
THE ALARM!
KURT! YOU MORON!
OUT THE BACK—C'MON! LET'S GET OUTTA HERE BEFORE ANYONE SHOWS UP!

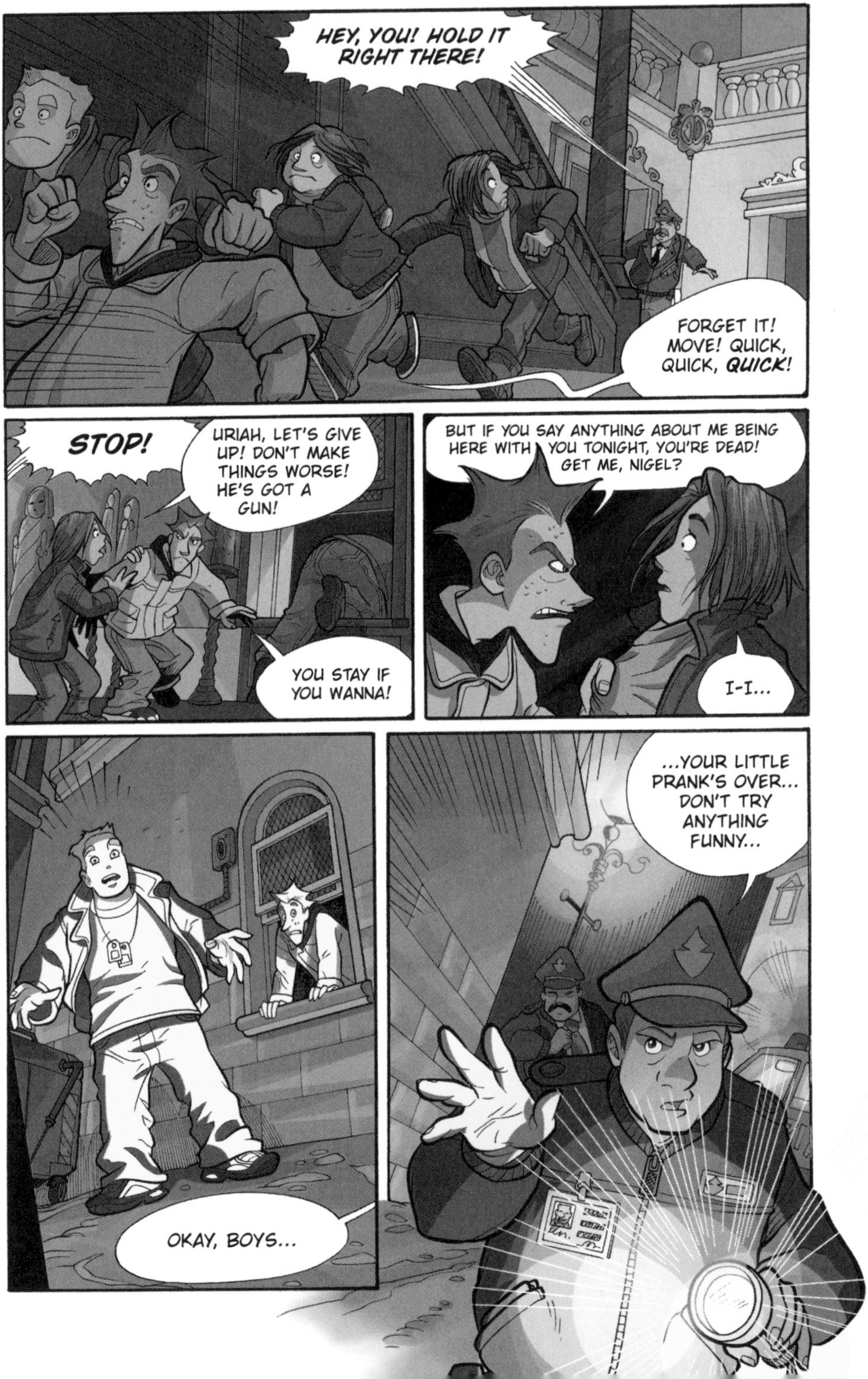
HEY, YOU! HOLD IT RIGHT THERE!
FORGET IT! MOVE! QUICK, QUICK, **QUICK**!
STOP!
URIAH, LET'S GIVE UP! DON'T MAKE THINGS WORSE! HE'S GOT A GUN!
YOU STAY IF YOU WANNA!
BUT IF YOU SAY ANYTHING ABOUT ME BEING HERE WITH YOU TONIGHT, YOU'RE DEAD! GET ME, NIGEL?
I-I...
OKAY, BOYS...
...YOUR LITTLE PRANK'S OVER... DON'T TRY ANYTHING FUNNY...

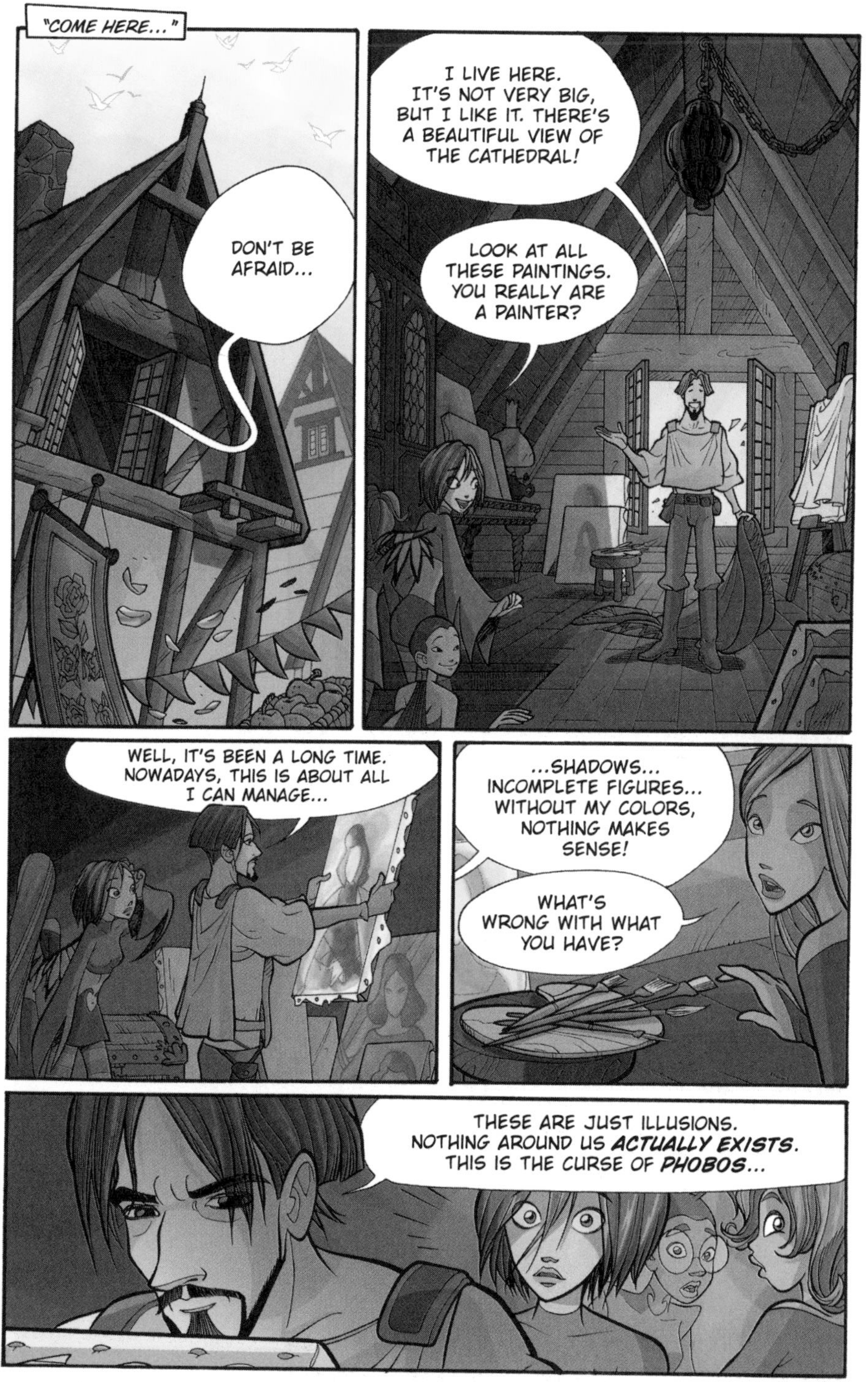
"COME HERE..."
DON'T BE AFRAID...
I LIVE HERE. IT'S NOT VERY BIG, BUT I LIKE IT. THERE'S A BEAUTIFUL VIEW OF THE CATHEDRAL!
LOOK AT ALL THESE PAINTINGS. YOU REALLY ARE A PAINTER?
WELL, IT'S BEEN A LONG TIME. NOWADAYS, THIS IS ABOUT ALL I CAN MANAGE...
...SHADOWS... INCOMPLETE FIGURES... WITHOUT MY COLORS, NOTHING MAKES SENSE!
WHAT'S WRONG WITH WHAT YOU HAVE?
THESE ARE JUST ILLUSIONS. NOTHING AROUND US **ACTUALLY EXISTS**. THIS IS THE CURSE OF **PHOBOS**...

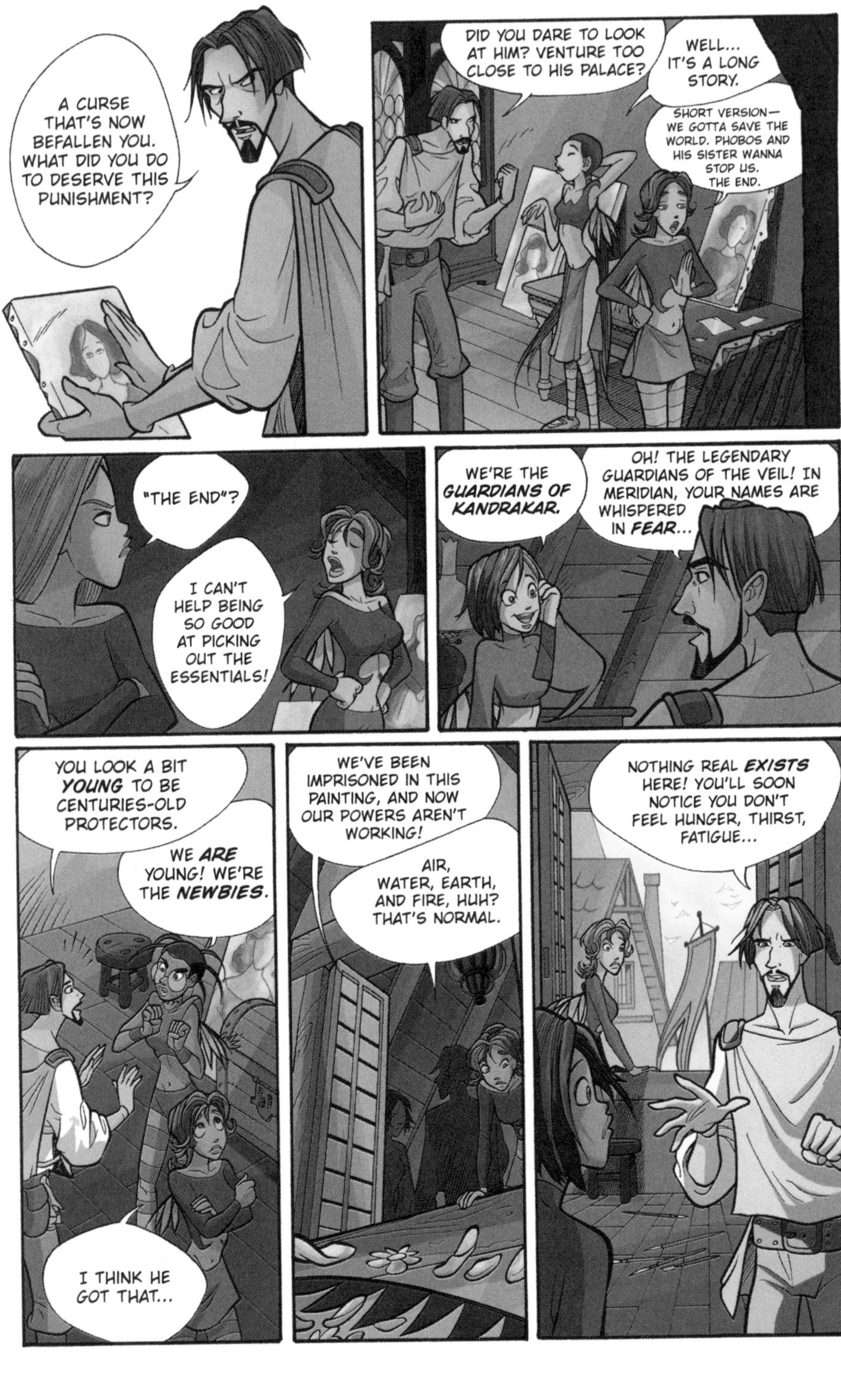
A CURSE THAT'S NOW BEFALLEN YOU. WHAT DID YOU DO TO DESERVE THIS PUNISHMENT?
DID YOU DARE TO LOOK AT HIM? VENTURE TOO CLOSE TO HIS PALACE?
WELL... IT'S A LONG STORY.
SHORT VERSION— WE GOTTA SAVE THE WORLD. PHOBOS AND HIS SISTER WANNA STOP US. THE END.
"THE END"?
I CAN'T HELP BEING SO GOOD AT PICKING OUT THE ESSENTIALS!
WE'RE THE **GUARDIANS OF KANDRAKAR.**
OH! THE LEGENDARY GUARDIANS OF THE VEIL! IN MERIDIAN, YOUR NAMES ARE WHISPERED IN **FEAR**...
YOU LOOK A BIT **YOUNG** TO BE CENTURIES-OLD PROTECTORS.
WE **ARE** YOUNG! WE'RE THE **NEWBIES**.
I THINK HE GOT THAT...
WE'VE BEEN IMPRISONED IN THIS PAINTING, AND NOW OUR POWERS AREN'T WORKING!
AIR, WATER, EARTH, AND FIRE, HUH? THAT'S NORMAL.
NOTHING REAL **EXISTS** HERE! YOU'LL SOON NOTICE YOU DON'T FEEL HUNGER, THIRST, FATIGUE...

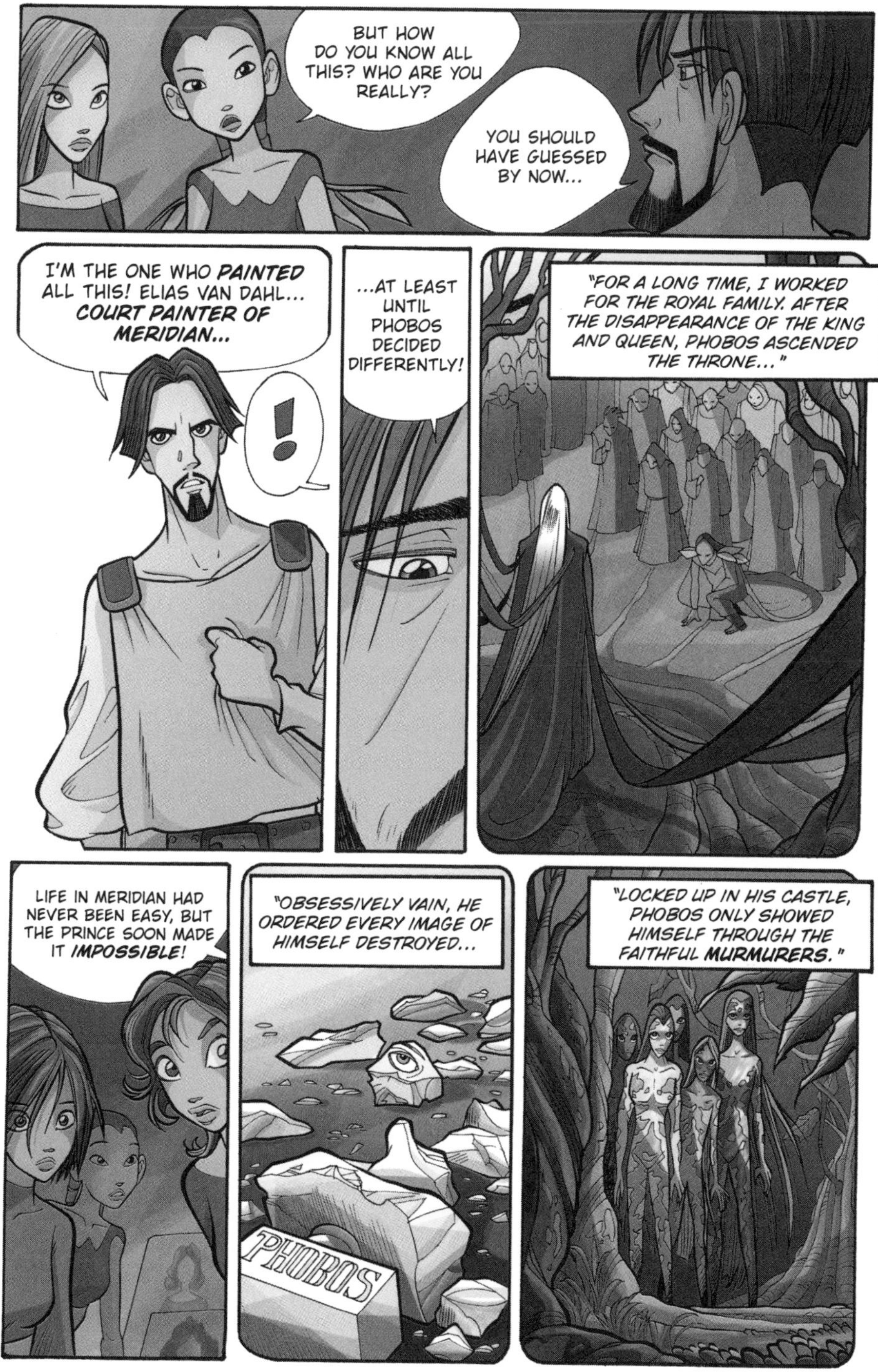
BUT HOW DO YOU KNOW ALL THIS? WHO ARE YOU REALLY?
YOU SHOULD HAVE GUESSED BY NOW...
I'M THE ONE WHO PAINTED ALL THIS! ELIAS VAN DAHL... COURT PAINTER OF MERIDIAN...
!
...AT LEAST UNTIL PHOBOS DECIDED DIFFERENTLY!
"FOR A LONG TIME, I WORKED FOR THE ROYAL FAMILY. AFTER THE DISAPPEARANCE OF THE KING AND QUEEN, PHOBOS ASCENDED THE THRONE..."
LIFE IN MERIDIAN HAD NEVER BEEN EASY, BUT THE PRINCE SOON MADE IT IMPOSSIBLE!
"OBSESSIVELY VAIN, HE ORDERED EVERY IMAGE OF HIMSELF DESTROYED...
PHOBOS
"LOCKED UP IN HIS CASTLE, PHOBOS ONLY SHOWED HIMSELF THROUGH THE FAITHFUL MURMURERS."

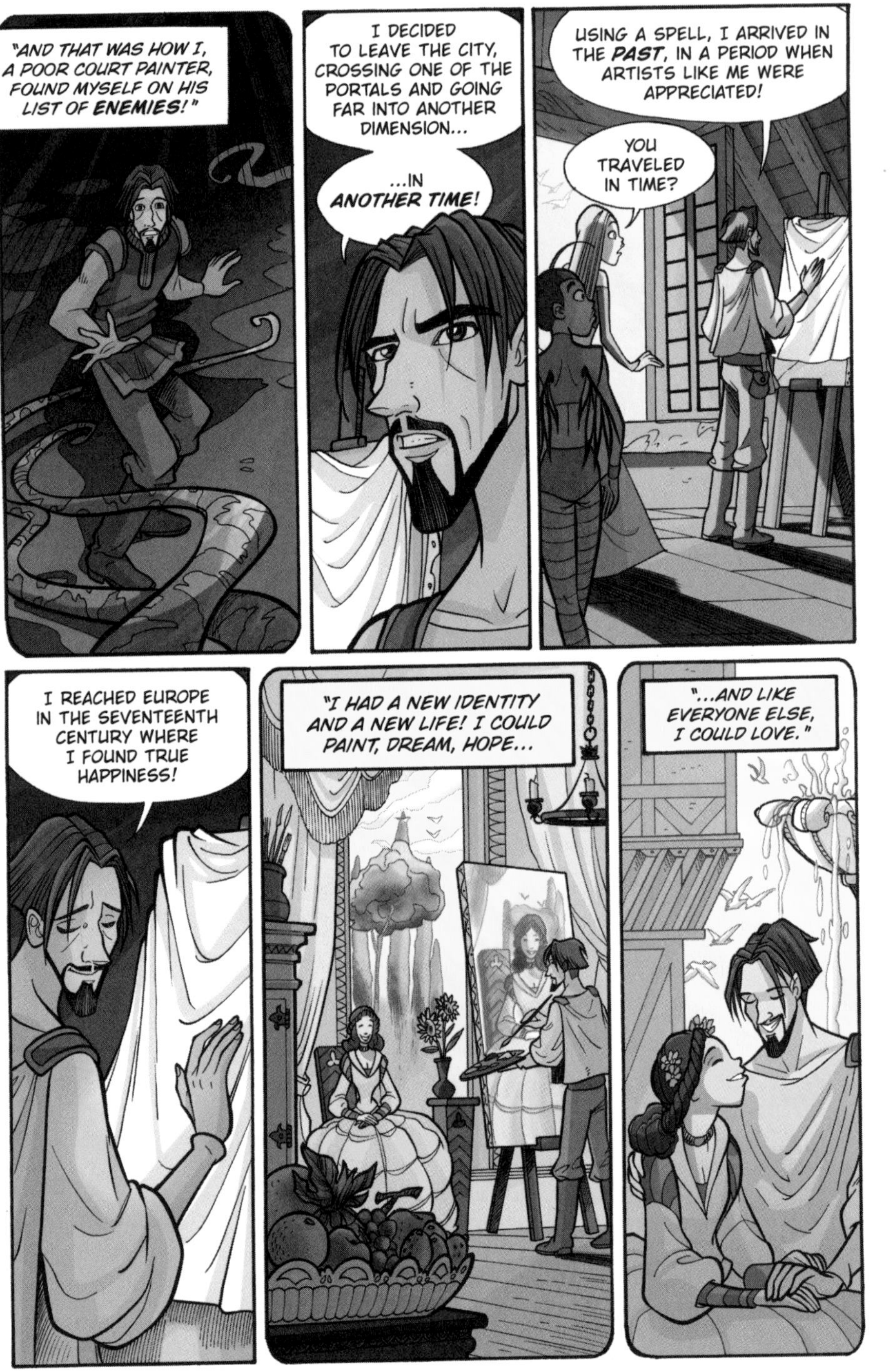
"AND THAT WAS HOW I, A POOR COURT PAINTER, FOUND MYSELF ON HIS LIST OF ENEMIES!"
I DECIDED TO LEAVE THE CITY, CROSSING ONE OF THE PORTALS AND GOING FAR INTO ANOTHER DIMENSION...
...IN ANOTHER TIME!
USING A SPELL, I ARRIVED IN THE PAST, IN A PERIOD WHEN ARTISTS LIKE ME WERE APPRECIATED!
YOU TRAVELED IN TIME?
I REACHED EUROPE IN THE SEVENTEENTH CENTURY WHERE I FOUND TRUE HAPPINESS!
"I HAD A NEW IDENTITY AND A NEW LIFE! I COULD PAINT, DREAM, HOPE...
"...AND LIKE EVERYONE ELSE, I COULD LOVE."

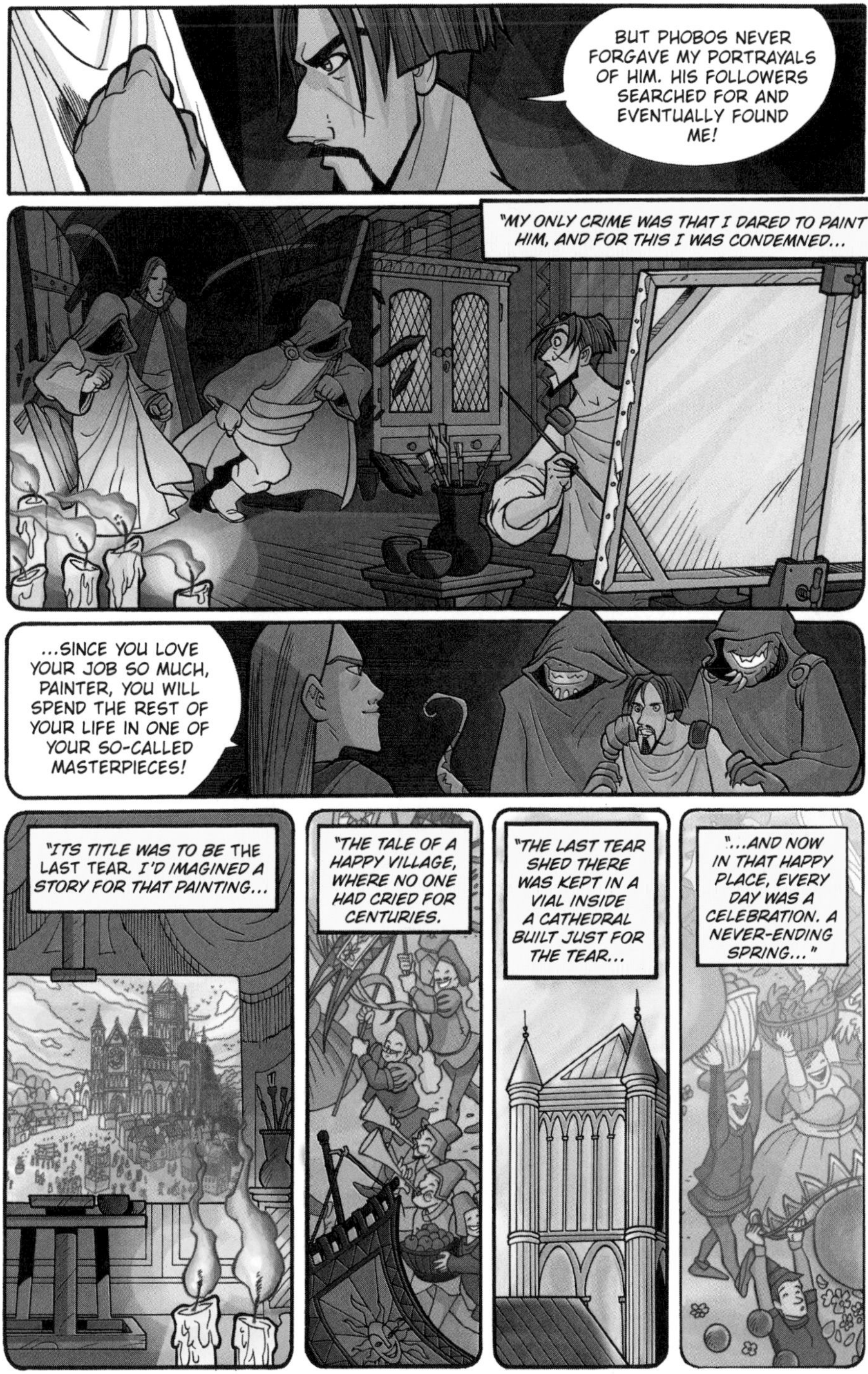
BUT PHOBOS NEVER FORGAVE MY PORTRAYALS OF HIM. HIS FOLLOWERS SEARCHED FOR AND EVENTUALLY FOUND ME!
"MY ONLY CRIME WAS THAT I DARED TO PAINT HIM, AND FOR THIS I WAS CONDEMNED...
...SINCE YOU LOVE YOUR JOB SO MUCH, PAINTER, YOU WILL SPEND THE REST OF YOUR LIFE IN ONE OF YOUR SO-CALLED MASTERPIECES!
"ITS TITLE WAS TO BE THE LAST TEAR. I'D IMAGINED A STORY FOR THAT PAINTING...
"THE TALE OF A HAPPY VILLAGE, WHERE NO ONE HAD CRIED FOR CENTURIES.
"THE LAST TEAR SHED THERE WAS KEPT IN A VIAL INSIDE A CATHEDRAL BUILT JUST FOR THE TEAR...
"...AND NOW IN THAT HAPPY PLACE, EVERY DAY WAS A CELEBRATION. A NEVER-ENDING SPRING..."

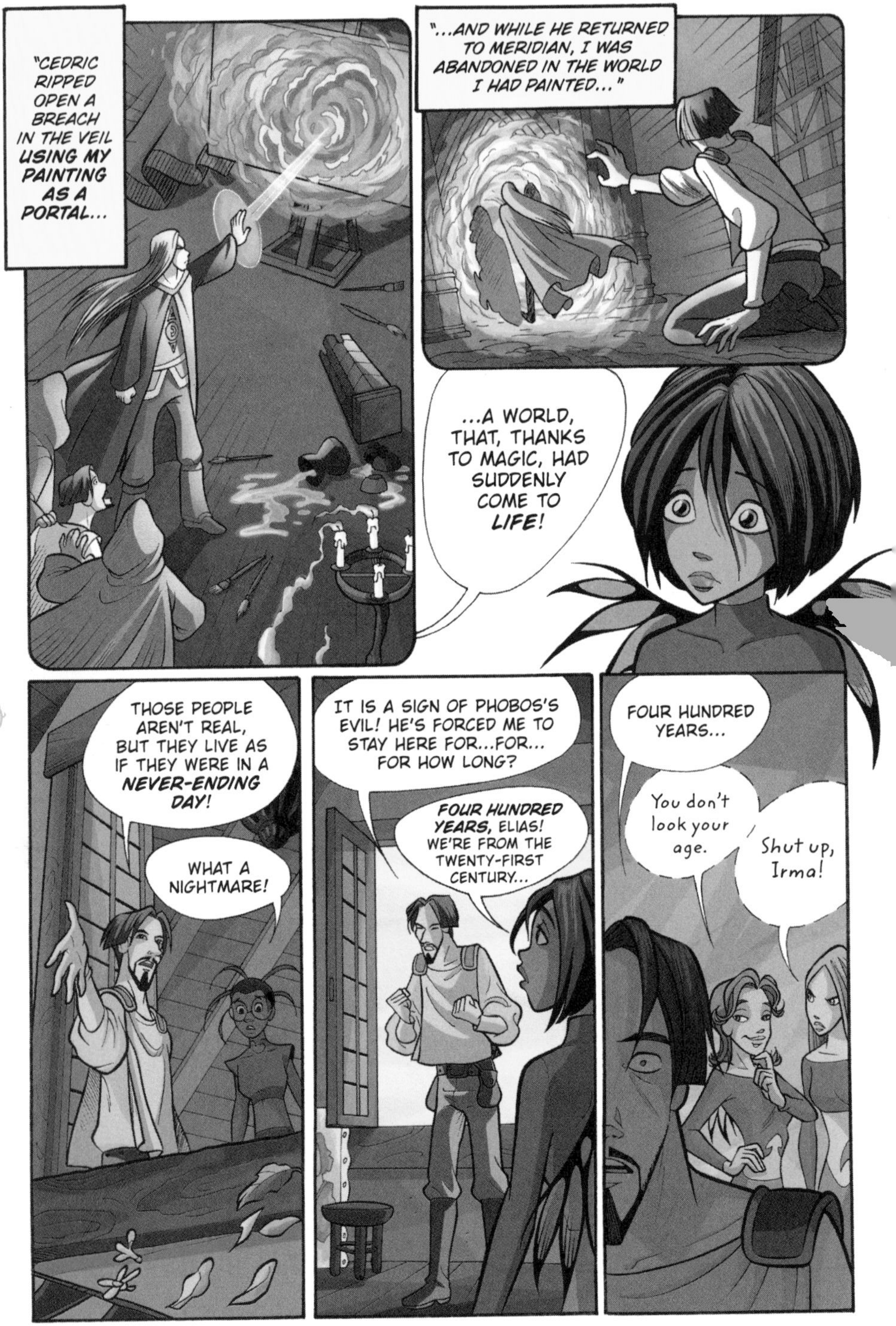
"CEDRIC RIPPED OPEN A BREACH IN THE VEIL **USING MY PAINTING AS A PORTAL...**
"...AND WHILE HE RETURNED TO MERIDIAN, I WAS ABANDONED IN THE WORLD I HAD PAINTED..."
...A WORLD, THAT, THANKS TO MAGIC, HAD SUDDENLY COME TO ***LIFE!***
THOSE PEOPLE AREN'T REAL, BUT THEY LIVE AS IF THEY WERE IN A ***NEVER-ENDING DAY!***
WHAT A NIGHTMARE!
IT IS A SIGN OF PHOBOS'S EVIL! HE'S FORCED ME TO STAY HERE FOR...FOR... FOR HOW LONG?
FOUR HUNDRED YEARS, ELIAS! WE'RE FROM THE TWENTY-FIRST CENTURY...
FOUR HUNDRED YEARS...
You don't look your age.
Shut up, Irma!

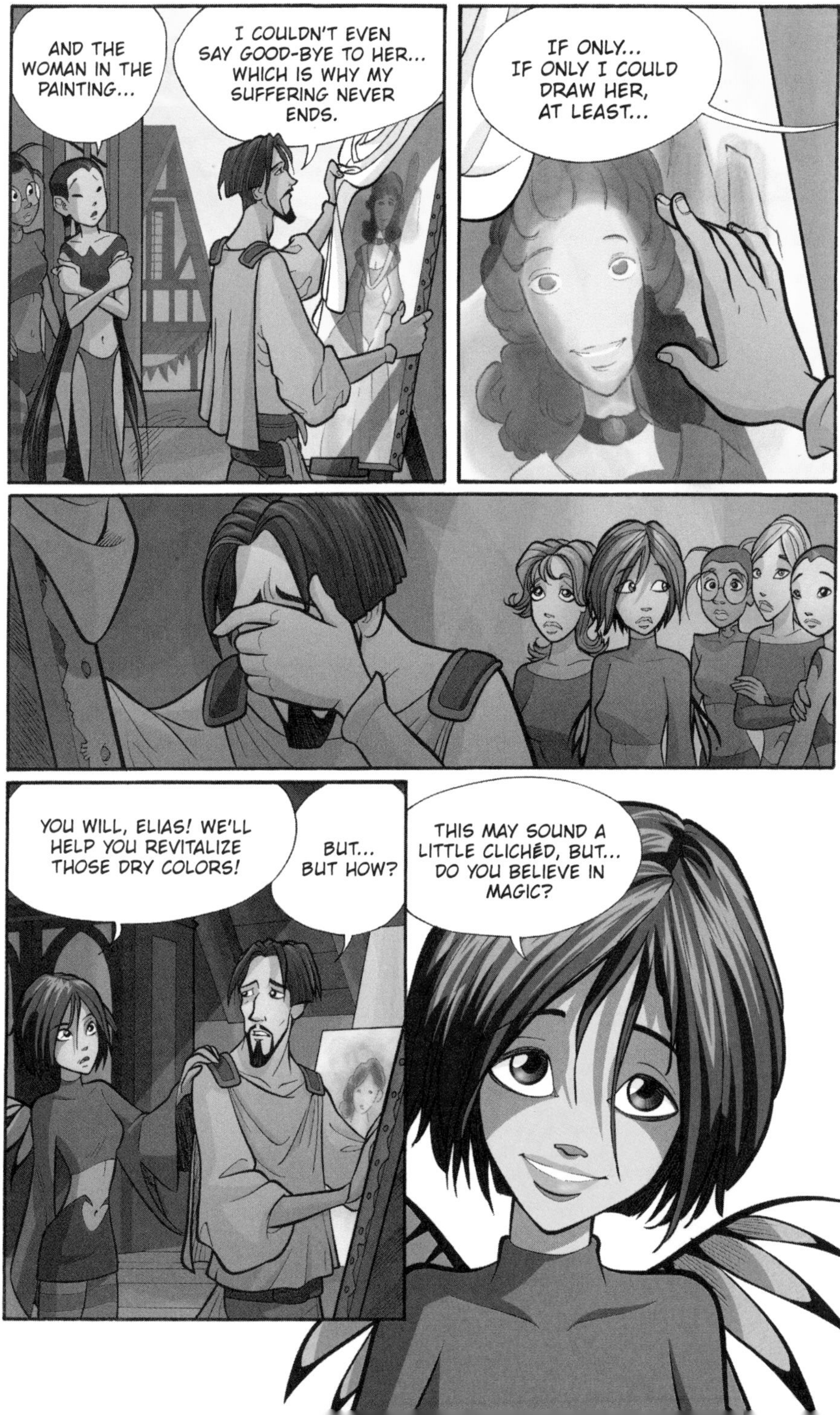

AND THE WOMAN IN THE PAINTING...
I COULDN'T EVEN SAY GOOD-BYE TO HER... WHICH IS WHY MY SUFFERING NEVER ENDS.
IF ONLY... IF ONLY I COULD DRAW HER, AT LEAST...
YOU WILL, ELIAS! WE'LL HELP YOU REVITALIZE THOSE DRY COLORS!
BUT... BUT HOW?
THIS MAY SOUND A LITTLE CLICHÉD, BUT... DO YOU BELIEVE IN MAGIC?

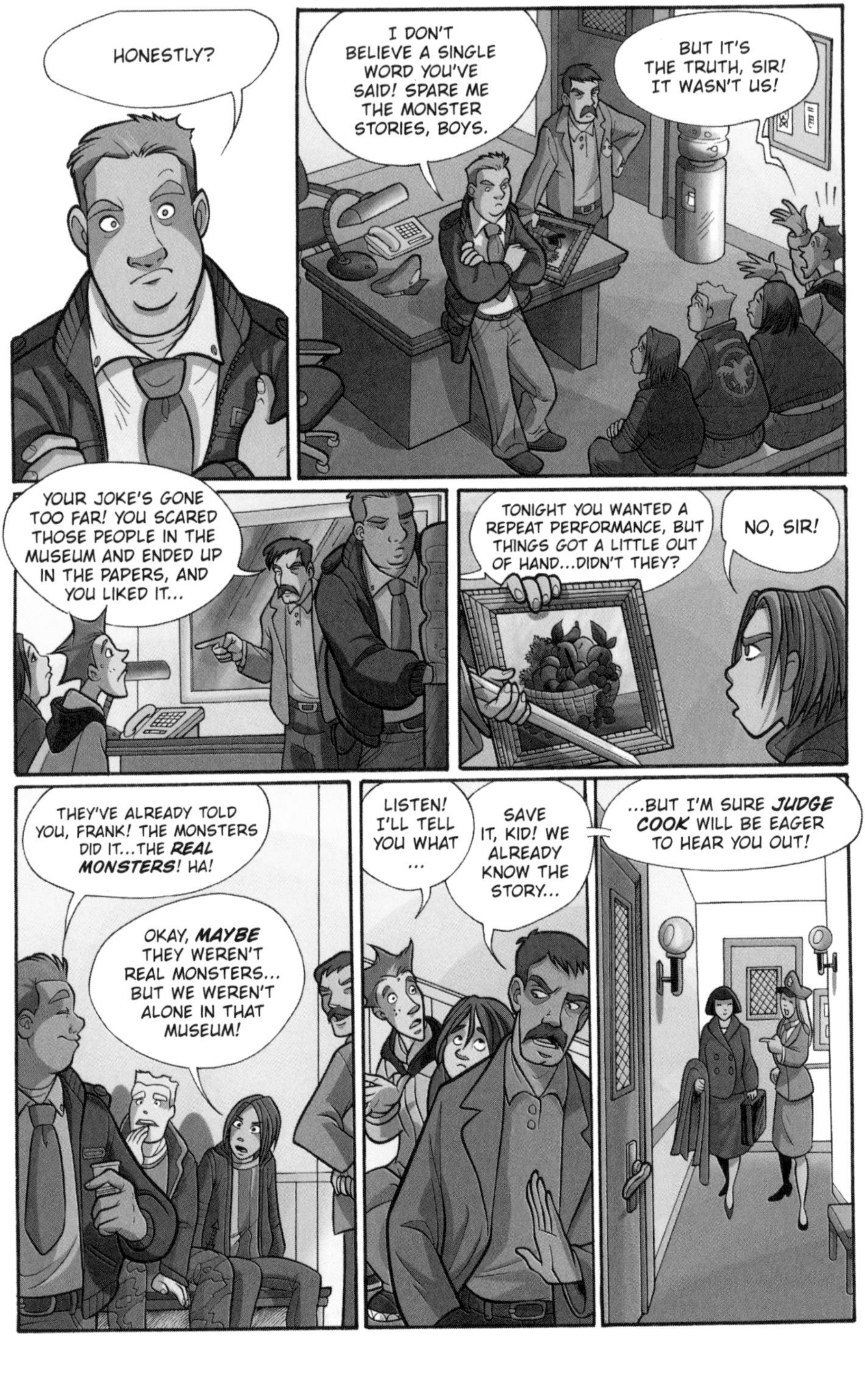
HONESTLY?
I DON'T BELIEVE A SINGLE WORD YOU'VE SAID! SPARE ME THE MONSTER STORIES, BOYS.
BUT IT'S THE TRUTH, SIR! IT WASN'T US!
YOUR JOKE'S GONE TOO FAR! YOU SCARED THOSE PEOPLE IN THE MUSEUM AND ENDED UP IN THE PAPERS, AND YOU LIKED IT...
TONIGHT YOU WANTED A REPEAT PERFORMANCE, BUT THINGS GOT A LITTLE OUT OF HAND...DIDN'T THEY?
NO, SIR!
THEY'VE ALREADY TOLD YOU, FRANK! THE MONSTERS DID IT...THE **REAL MONSTERS**! HA!
OKAY, **MAYBE** THEY WEREN'T REAL MONSTERS... BUT WE WEREN'T ALONE IN THAT MUSEUM!
LISTEN! I'LL TELL YOU WHAT ...
SAVE IT, KID! WE ALREADY KNOW THE STORY...
...BUT I'M SURE **JUDGE COOK** WILL BE EAGER TO HEAR YOU OUT!

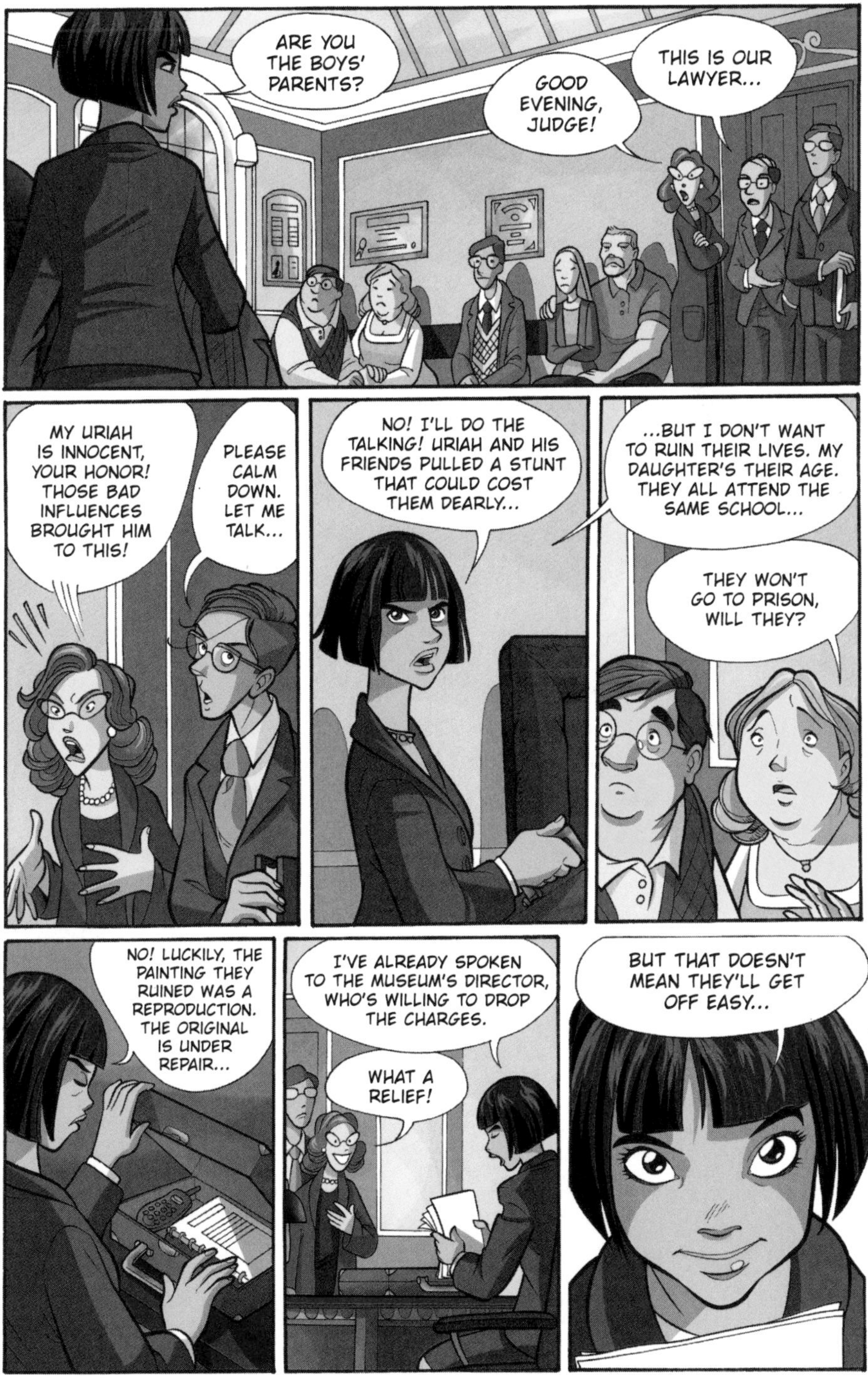
ARE YOU THE BOYS' PARENTS?
GOOD EVENING, JUDGE!
THIS IS OUR LAWYER...
MY URIAH IS INNOCENT, YOUR HONOR! THOSE BAD INFLUENCES BROUGHT HIM TO THIS!
PLEASE CALM DOWN. LET ME TALK...
NO! I'LL DO THE TALKING! URIAH AND HIS FRIENDS PULLED A STUNT THAT COULD COST THEM DEARLY...
...BUT I DON'T WANT TO RUIN THEIR LIVES. MY DAUGHTER'S THEIR AGE. THEY ALL ATTEND THE SAME SCHOOL...
THEY WON'T GO TO PRISON, WILL THEY?
NO! LUCKILY, THE PAINTING THEY RUINED WAS A REPRODUCTION. THE ORIGINAL IS UNDER REPAIR...
I'VE ALREADY SPOKEN TO THE MUSEUM'S DIRECTOR, WHO'S WILLING TO DROP THE CHARGES.
WHAT A RELIEF!
BUT THAT DOESN'T MEAN THEY'LL GET OFF EASY...

OHHH...

THERE THEY ARE!

WHAT IMPUDENCE!

CHEER UP, PEOPLE! THESE GIRLS ARE OUR FRIENDS! THEY CAME TO HELP US...

...At least, that's what you told me!

It was just an idea, Elias...

...but it's crazy enough to work!

THE MAIN CHARACTERISTIC OF THIS WORLD IS ITS STILLNESS. WE'RE LIVING IN A MOMENT THAT NEVER CHANGES...

...SO LET'S TRY TO CHANGE THE RULES! FACE PHOBOS'S SPELL AND SEE WHAT HAPPENS!

HOW? YOU DON'T HAVE YOUR POWERS.

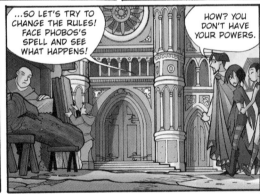

WE DON'T NEED OUR POWERS! SOMETIMES A DROP IS ALL IT TAKES.

UP TO NOW, YOU'VE ONLY MIXED YOUR COLORS WITH THE WATER FROM THE WELL...

RIGHT...

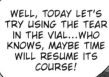

WELL, TODAY LET'S TRY USING THE TEAR IN THE VIAL...WHO KNOWS, MAYBE TIME WILL RESUME ITS COURSE!

THE DOOR'S JAMMED!

HEY, YOU! COME HELP US PUSH!

!

A WORLD UNABLE TO CHANGE IS A WORLD WITHOUT HOPE, HUH?

EXACTLY! MAYBE NOTHING WILL HAPPEN, BUT HECK...

55

...WHY NOT AT LEAST TRY?

TUMP

I CAN'T BELIEVE IT...

TUMP

THOSE GIRLS ARE TRYING MY PATIENCE!

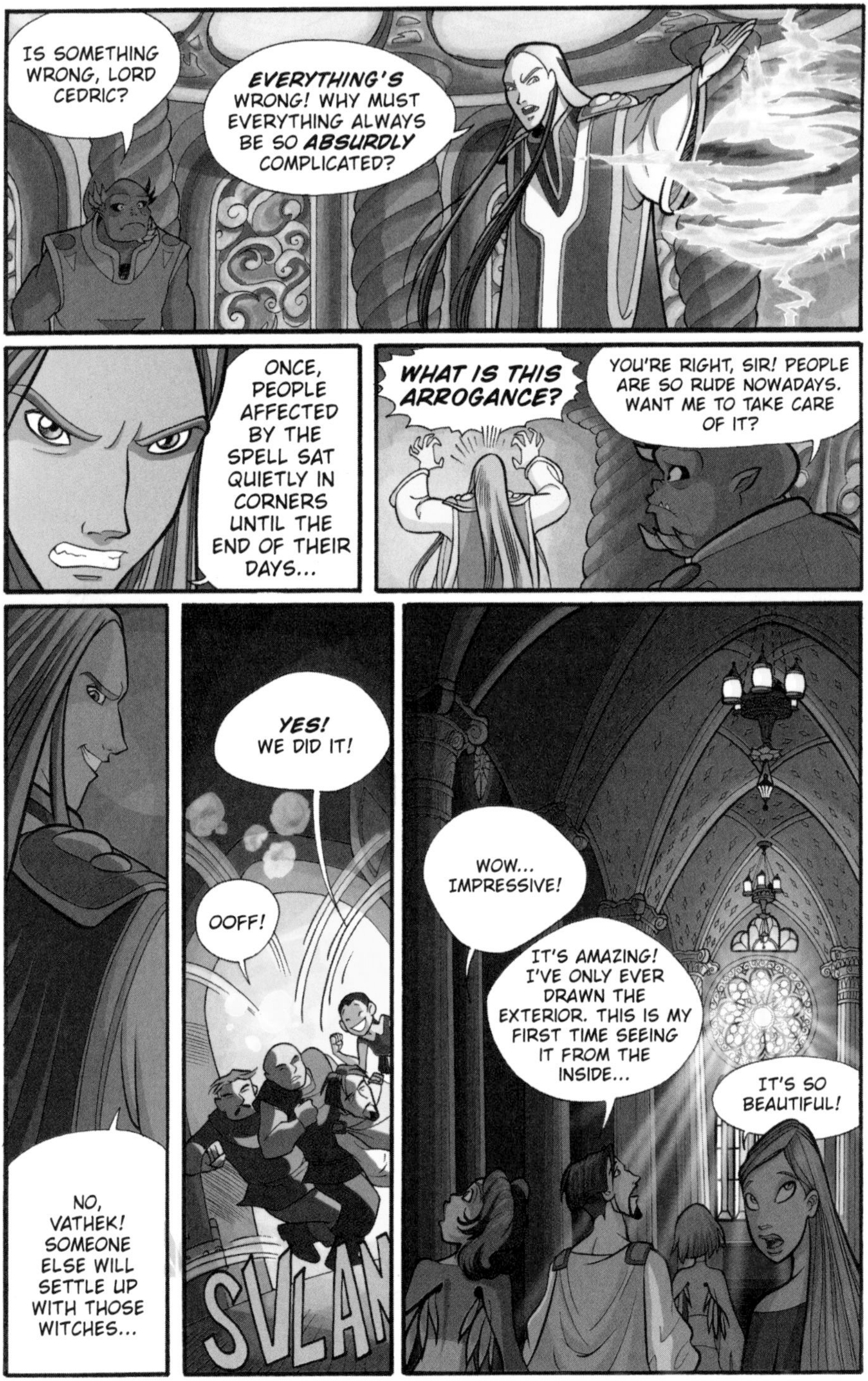

IS SOMETHING WRONG, LORD CEDRIC?
EVERYTHING'S WRONG! WHY MUST EVERYTHING ALWAYS BE SO ABSURDLY COMPLICATED?
ONCE, PEOPLE AFFECTED BY THE SPELL SAT QUIETLY IN CORNERS UNTIL THE END OF THEIR DAYS...
WHAT IS THIS ARROGANCE?
YOU'RE RIGHT, SIR! PEOPLE ARE SO RUDE NOWADAYS. WANT ME TO TAKE CARE OF IT?
NO, VATHEK! SOMEONE ELSE WILL SETTLE UP WITH THOSE WITCHES...
YES! WE DID IT!
OOFF!
SLAM
WOW... IMPRESSIVE!
IT'S AMAZING! I'VE ONLY EVER DRAWN THE EXTERIOR. THIS IS MY FIRST TIME SEEING IT FROM THE INSIDE...
IT'S SO BEAUTIFUL!

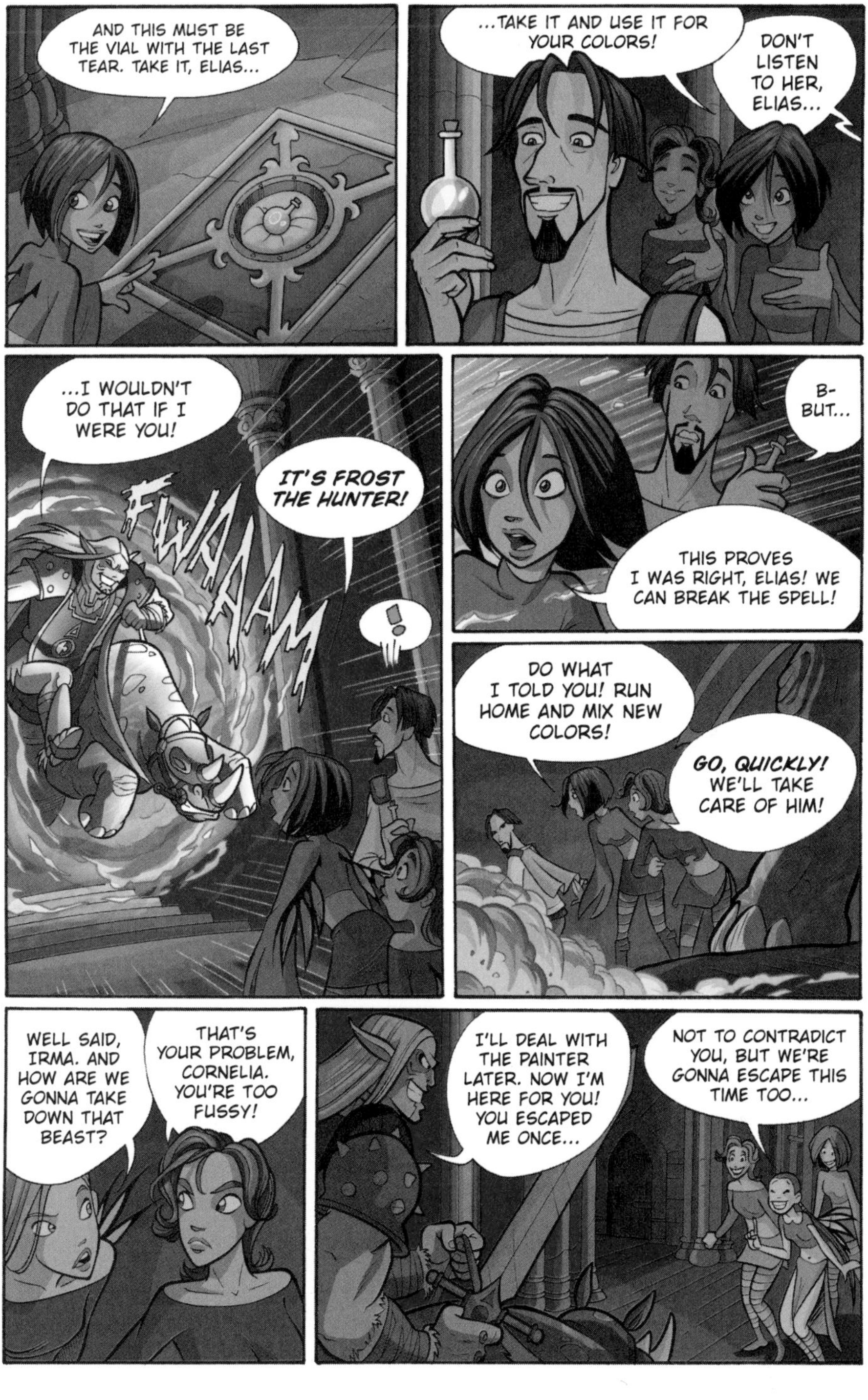
AND THIS MUST BE THE VIAL WITH THE LAST TEAR. TAKE IT, ELIAS...
...TAKE IT AND USE IT FOR YOUR COLORS!
DON'T LISTEN TO HER, ELIAS...
...I WOULDN'T DO THAT IF I WERE YOU!
FWAAAM
IT'S FROST THE HUNTER!
!
B-BUT...
THIS PROVES I WAS RIGHT, ELIAS! WE CAN BREAK THE SPELL!
DO WHAT I TOLD YOU! RUN HOME AND MIX NEW COLORS!
GO, QUICKLY! WE'LL TAKE CARE OF HIM!
WELL SAID, IRMA. AND HOW ARE WE GONNA TAKE DOWN THAT BEAST?
THAT'S YOUR PROBLEM, CORNELIA. YOU'RE TOO FUSSY!
I'LL DEAL WITH THE PAINTER LATER. NOW I'M HERE FOR YOU! YOU ESCAPED ME ONCE...
NOT TO CONTRADICT YOU, BUT WE'RE GONNA ESCAPE THIS TIME TOO...

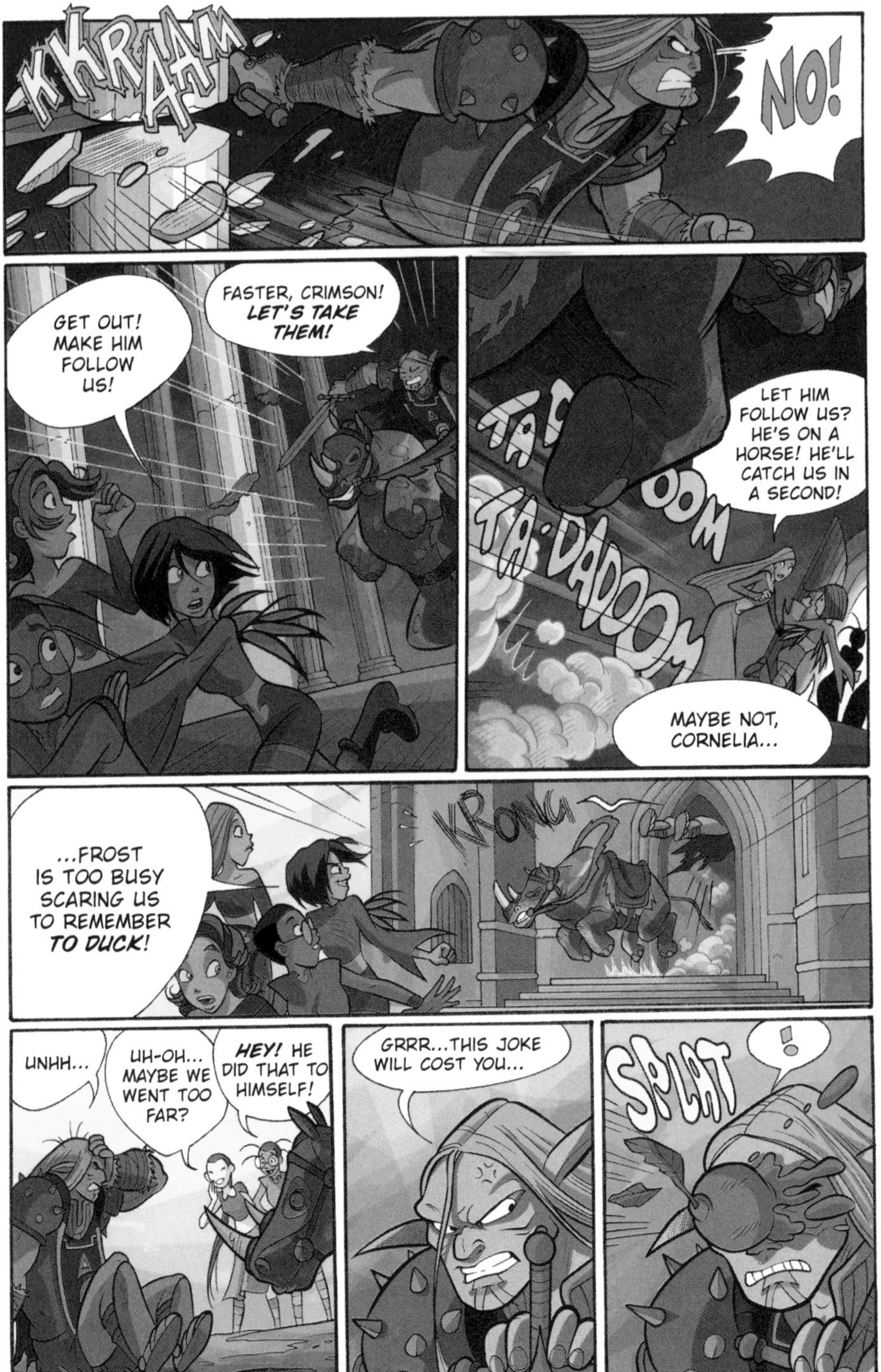

KKRAAM
NO!
GET OUT! MAKE HIM FOLLOW US!
FASTER, CRIMSON! LET'S TAKE THEM!
LET HIM FOLLOW US? HE'S ON A HORSE! HE'LL CATCH US IN A SECOND!
TA-DADOOM
MAYBE NOT, CORNELIA...
...FROST IS TOO BUSY SCARING US TO REMEMBER TO DUCK!
KRONCH
UNHH...
UH-OH... MAYBE WE WENT TOO FAR?
HEY! HE DID THAT TO HIMSELF!
GRRR...THIS JOKE WILL COST YOU...
SPLAT
!

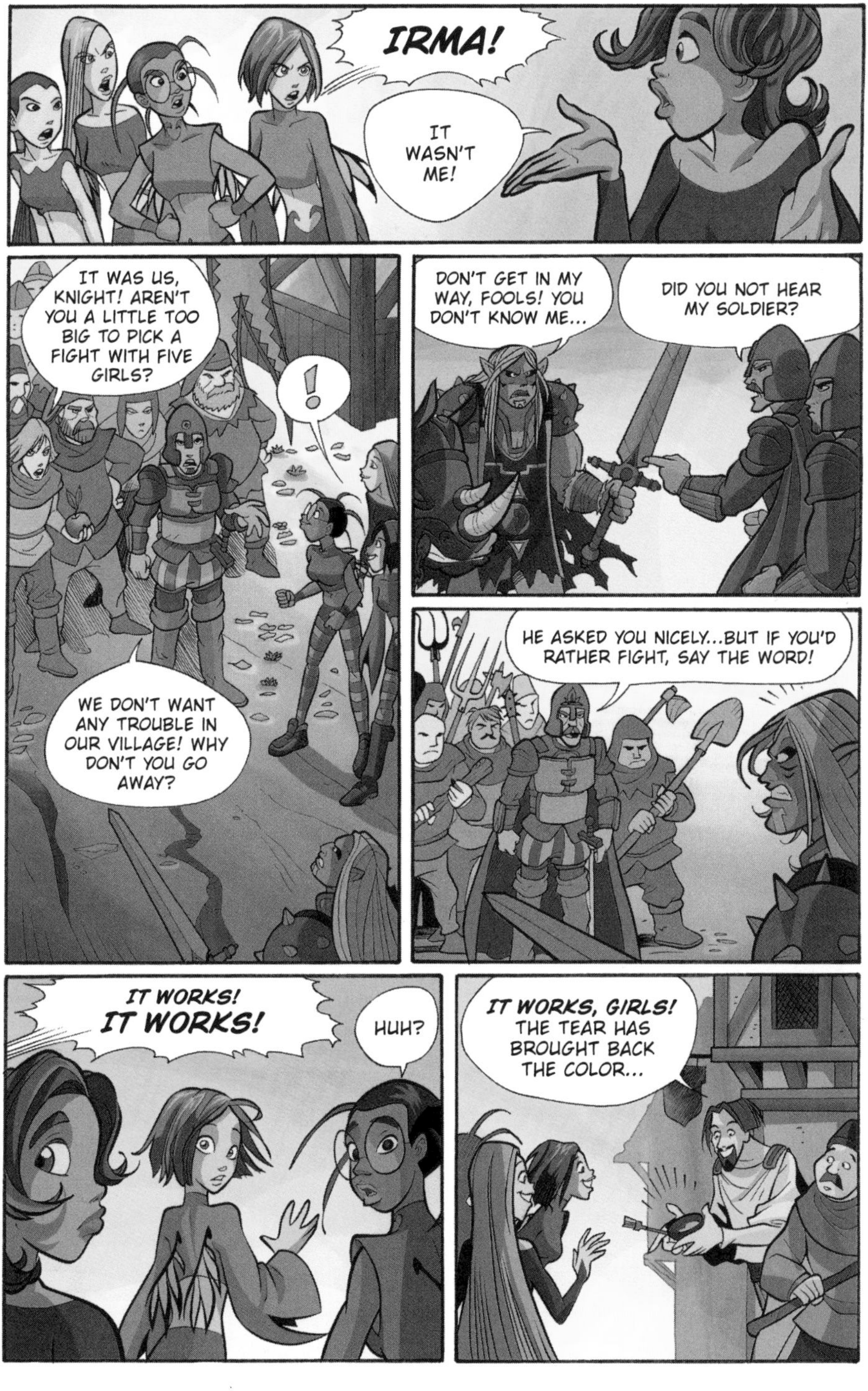

IRMA!
IT WASN'T ME!
IT WAS US, KNIGHT! AREN'T YOU A LITTLE TOO BIG TO PICK A FIGHT WITH FIVE GIRLS?
!
WE DON'T WANT ANY TROUBLE IN OUR VILLAGE! WHY DON'T YOU GO AWAY?
DON'T GET IN MY WAY, FOOLS! YOU DON'T KNOW ME...
DID YOU NOT HEAR MY SOLDIER?
HE ASKED YOU NICELY...BUT IF YOU'D RATHER FIGHT, SAY THE WORD!
IT WORKS! IT WORKS!
HUH?
IT WORKS, GIRLS! THE TEAR HAS BROUGHT BACK THE COLOR...

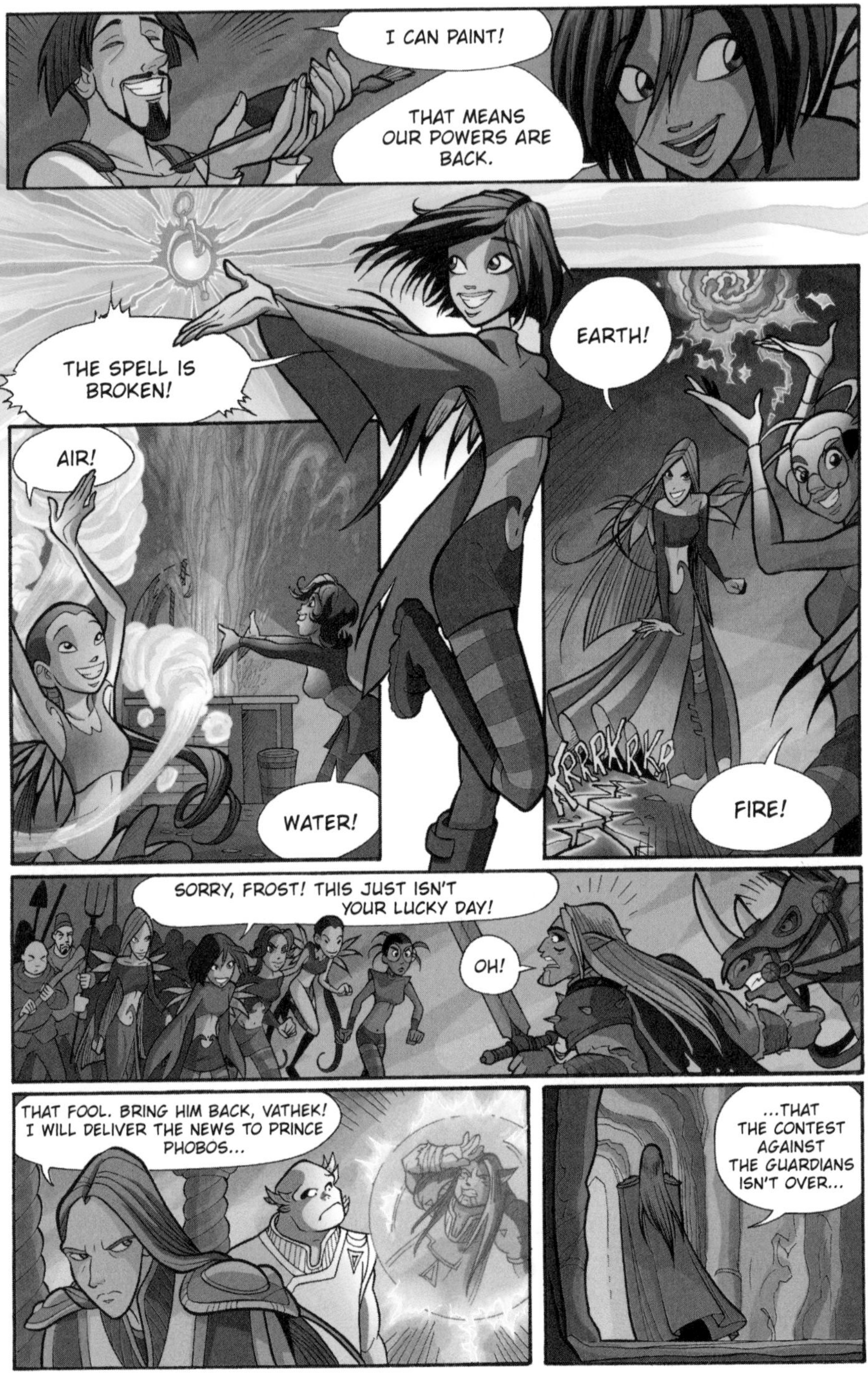
I CAN PAINT!
THAT MEANS OUR POWERS ARE BACK.
THE SPELL IS BROKEN!
EARTH!
AIR!
WATER!
KRRRKRKR
FIRE!
SORRY, FROST! THIS JUST ISN'T YOUR LUCKY DAY!
OH!
THAT FOOL. BRING HIM BACK, VATHEK! I WILL DELIVER THE NEWS TO PRINCE PHOBOS...
...THAT THE CONTEST AGAINST THE GUARDIANS ISN'T OVER...

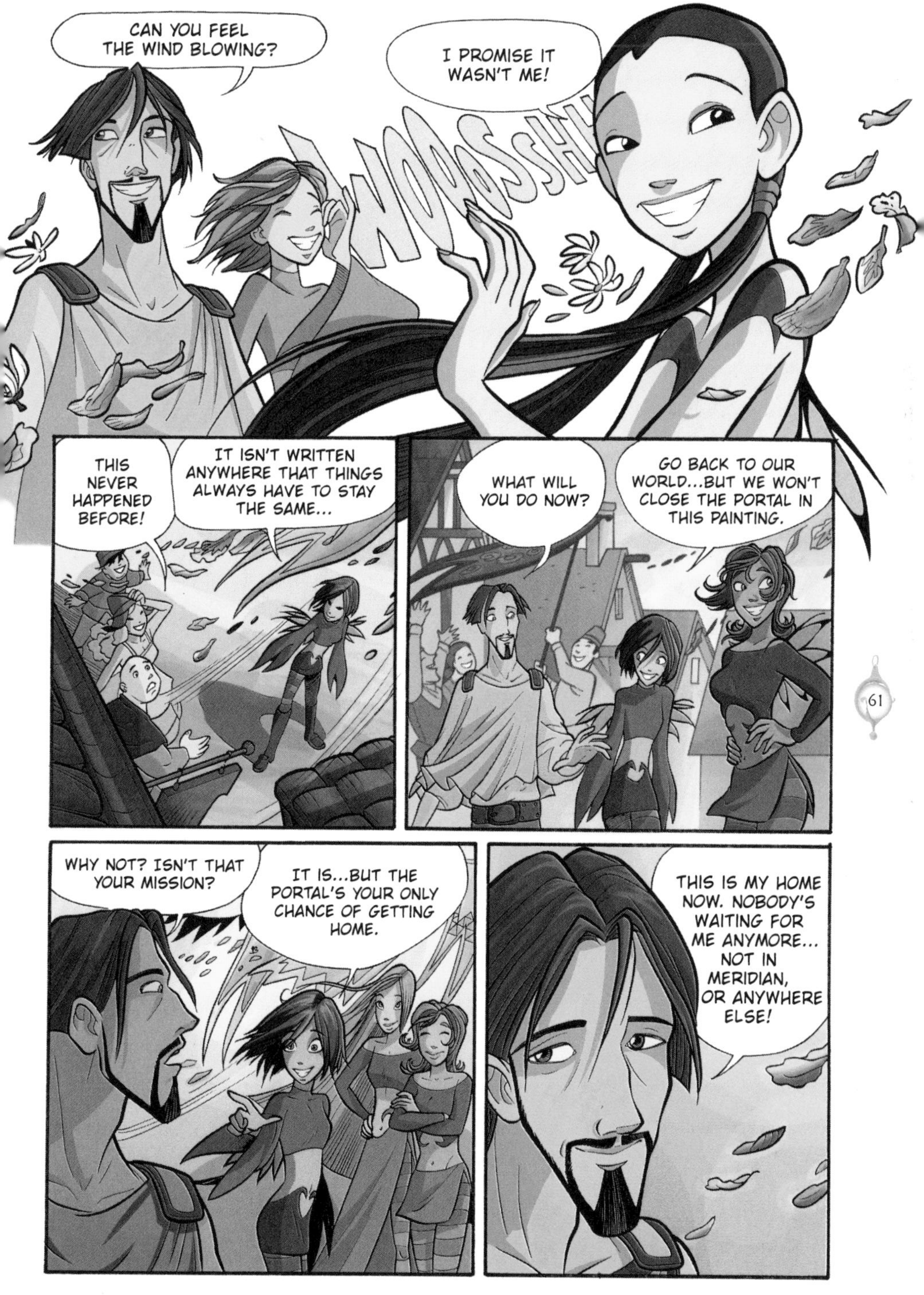
CAN YOU FEEL THE WIND BLOWING?
I PROMISE IT WASN'T ME!
WHOOSSHH
THIS NEVER HAPPENED BEFORE!
IT ISN'T WRITTEN ANYWHERE THAT THINGS ALWAYS HAVE TO STAY THE SAME...
WHAT WILL YOU DO NOW?
GO BACK TO OUR WORLD...BUT WE WON'T CLOSE THE PORTAL IN THIS PAINTING.
WHY NOT? ISN'T THAT YOUR MISSION?
IT IS...BUT THE PORTAL'S YOUR ONLY CHANCE OF GETTING HOME.
THIS IS MY HOME NOW. NOBODY'S WAITING FOR ME ANYMORE... NOT IN MERIDIAN, OR ANYWHERE ELSE!

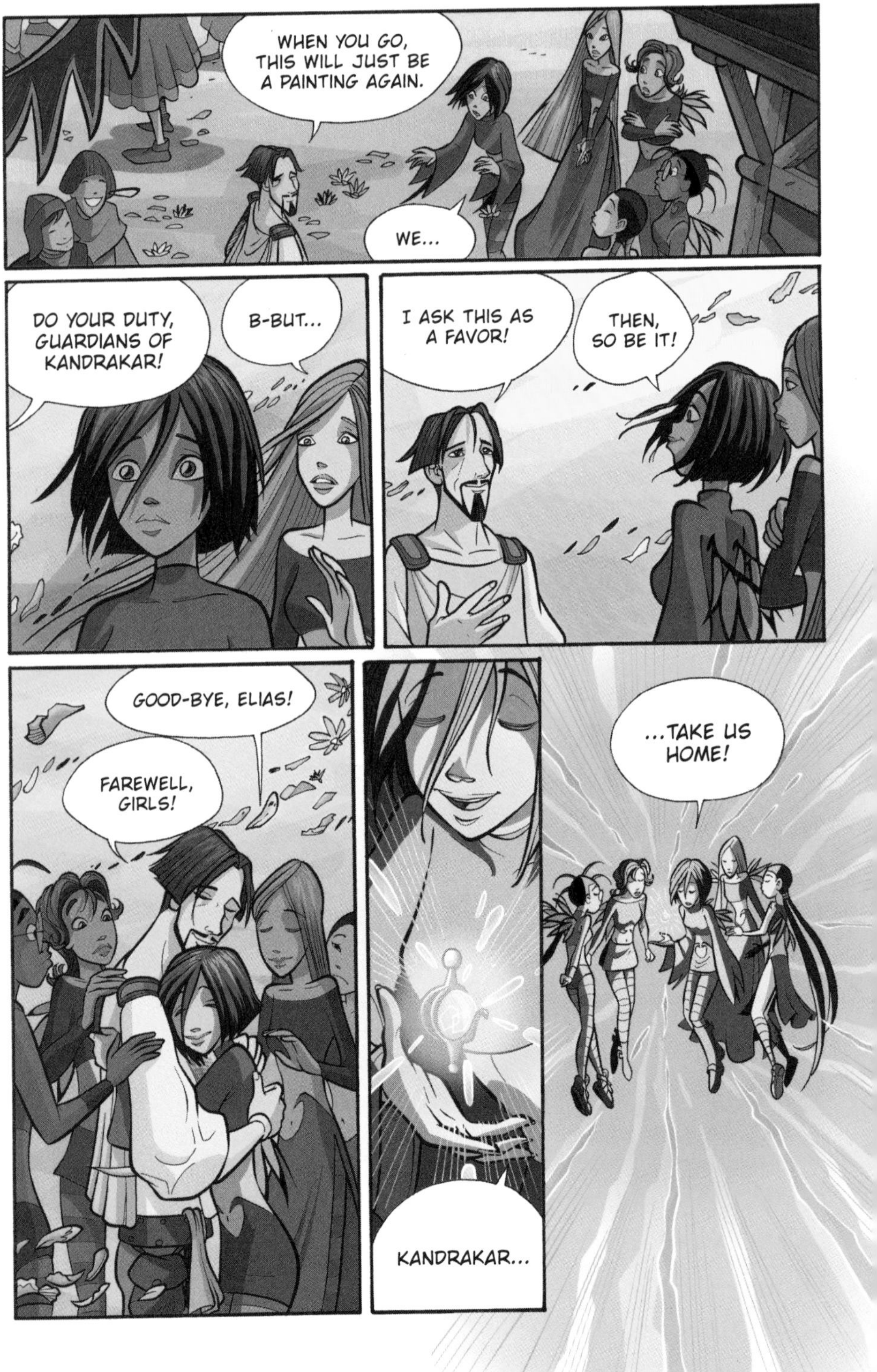

WHEN YOU GO, THIS WILL JUST BE A PAINTING AGAIN.
WE...
DO YOUR DUTY, GUARDIANS OF KANDRAKAR!
B-BUT...
I ASK THIS AS A FAVOR!
THEN, SO BE IT!
GOOD-BYE, ELIAS!
FAREWELL, GIRLS!
KANDRAKAR...
...TAKE US HOME!

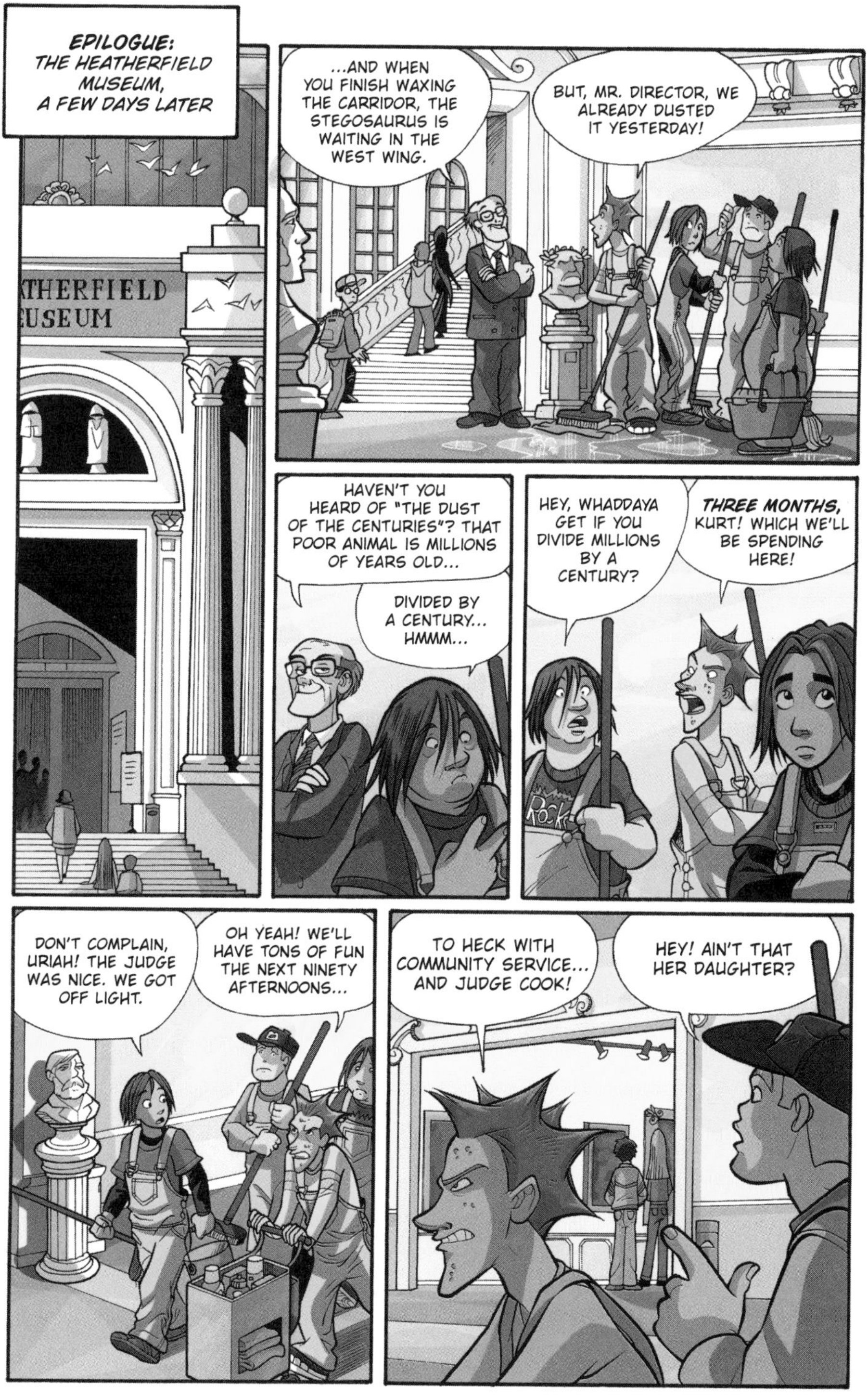
EPILOGUE:
THE HEATHERFIELD MUSEUM, A FEW DAYS LATER
...THERFIELD
...USEUM
...AND WHEN YOU FINISH WAXING THE CARRIDOR, THE STEGOSAURUS IS WAITING IN THE WEST WING.
BUT, MR. DIRECTOR, WE ALREADY DUSTED IT YESTERDAY!
HAVEN'T YOU HEARD OF "THE DUST OF THE CENTURIES"? THAT POOR ANIMAL IS MILLIONS OF YEARS OLD...
DIVIDED BY A CENTURY... HMMM...
HEY, WHADDAYA GET IF YOU DIVIDE MILLIONS BY A CENTURY?
THREE MONTHS, KURT! WHICH WE'LL BE SPENDING HERE!
DON'T COMPLAIN, URIAH! THE JUDGE WAS NICE. WE GOT OFF LIGHT.
OH YEAH! WE'LL HAVE TONS OF FUN THE NEXT NINETY AFTERNOONS...
TO HECK WITH COMMUNITY SERVICE... AND JUDGE COOK!
HEY! AIN'T THAT HER DAUGHTER?

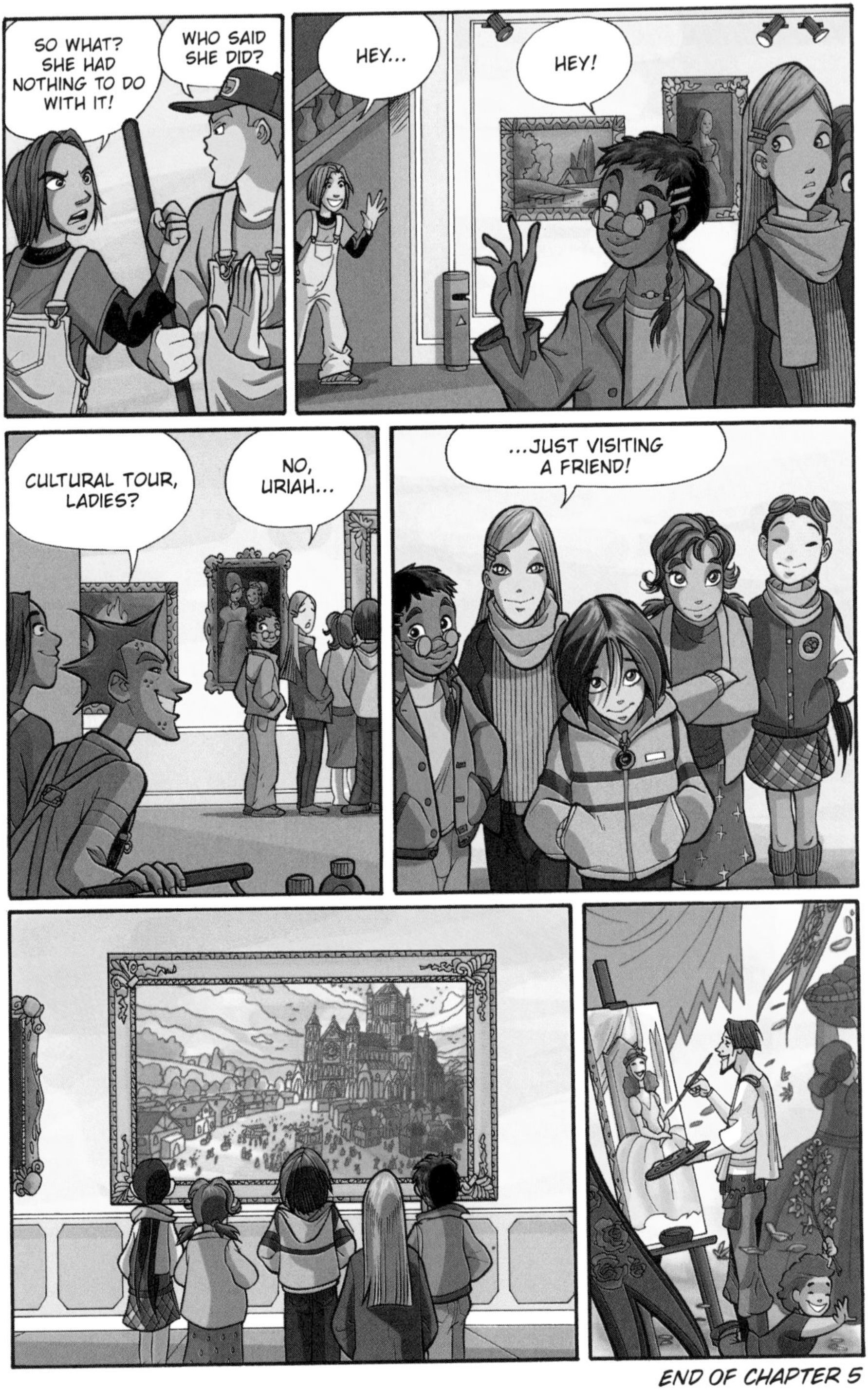
SO WHAT? SHE HAD NOTHING TO DO WITH IT!
WHO SAID SHE DID?
HEY...
HEY!
CULTURAL TOUR, LADIES?
NO, URIAH...
...JUST VISITING A FRIEND!

END OF CHAPTER 5

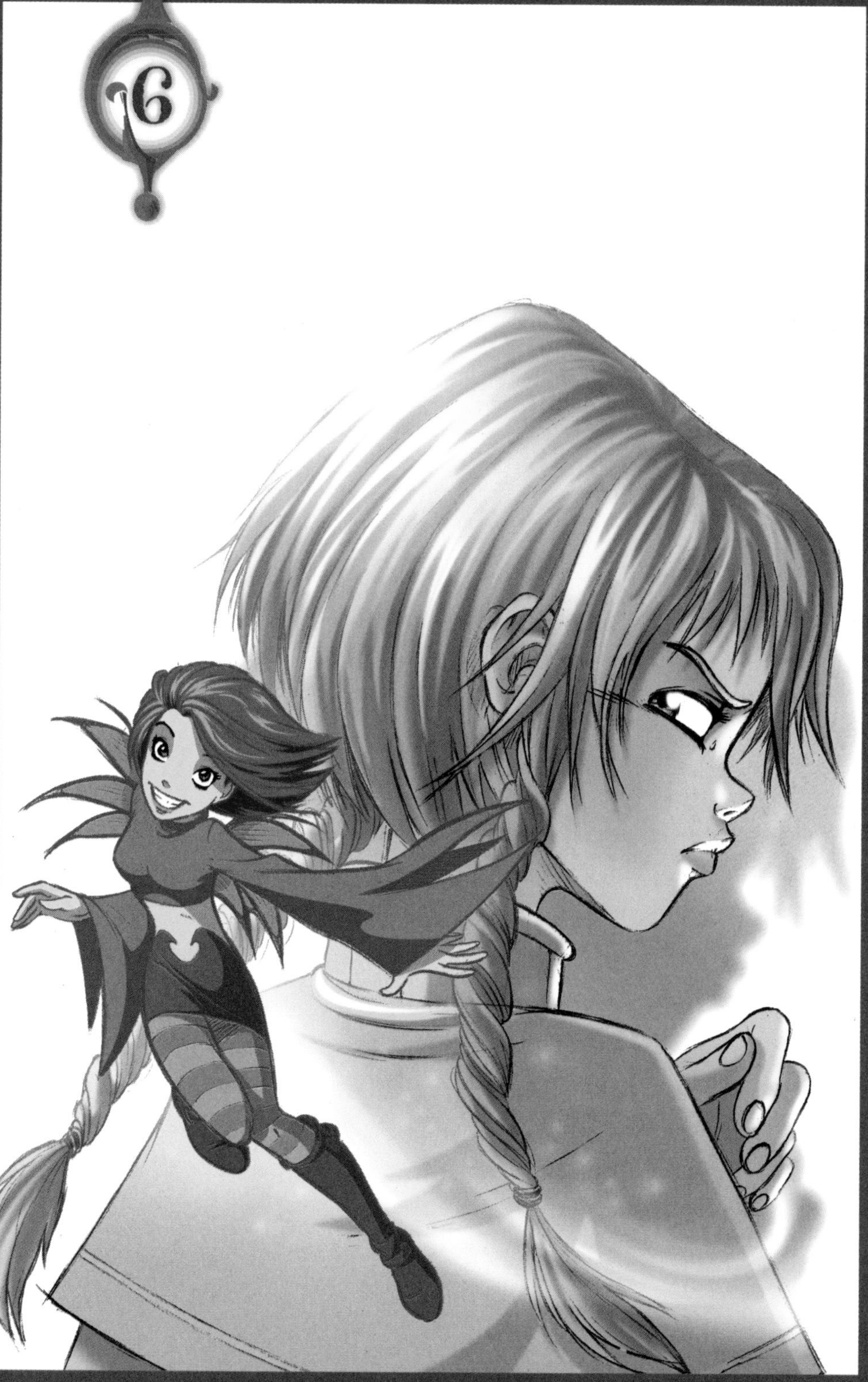

ILLUSIONS AND LIES

"Sometimes words
are not enough
for feelings..."

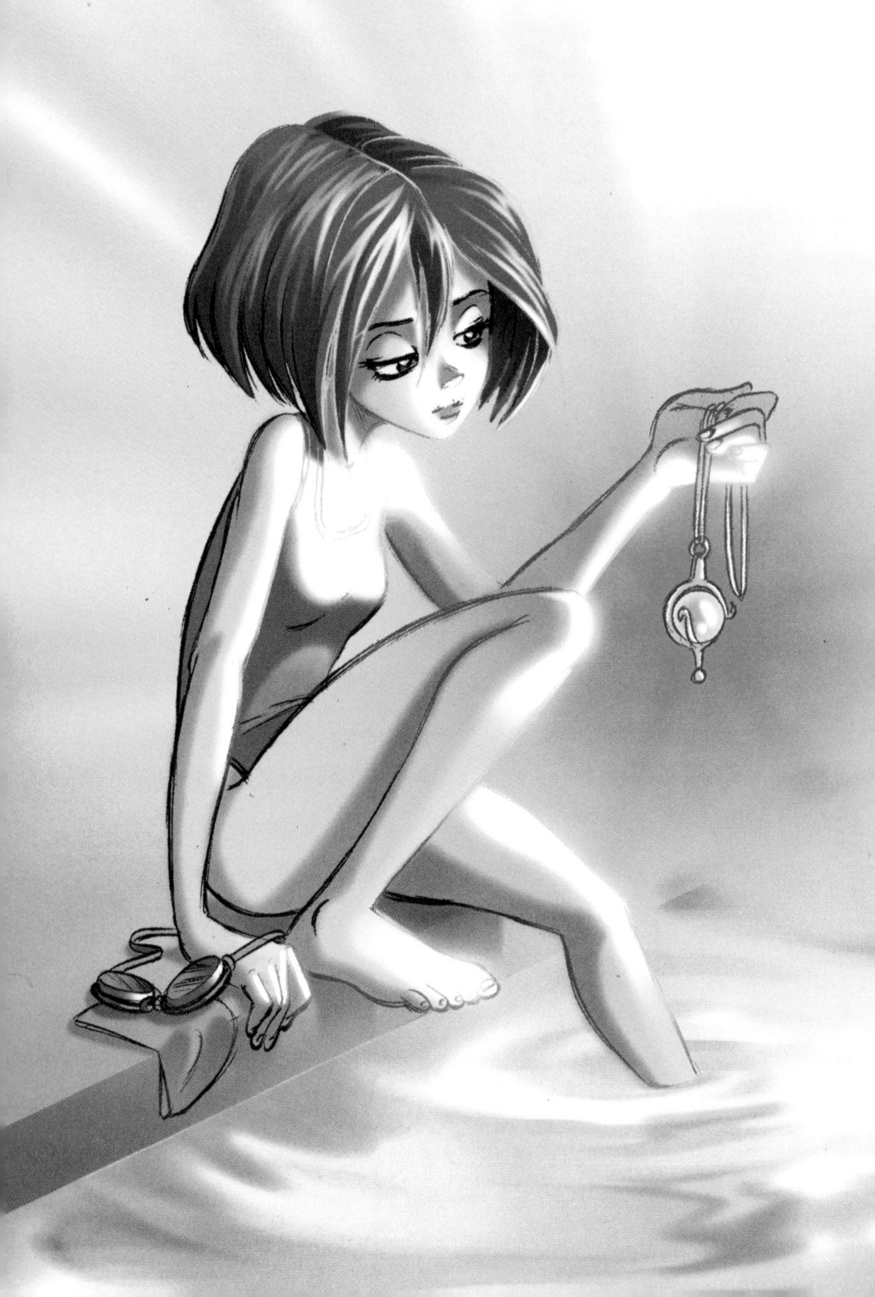

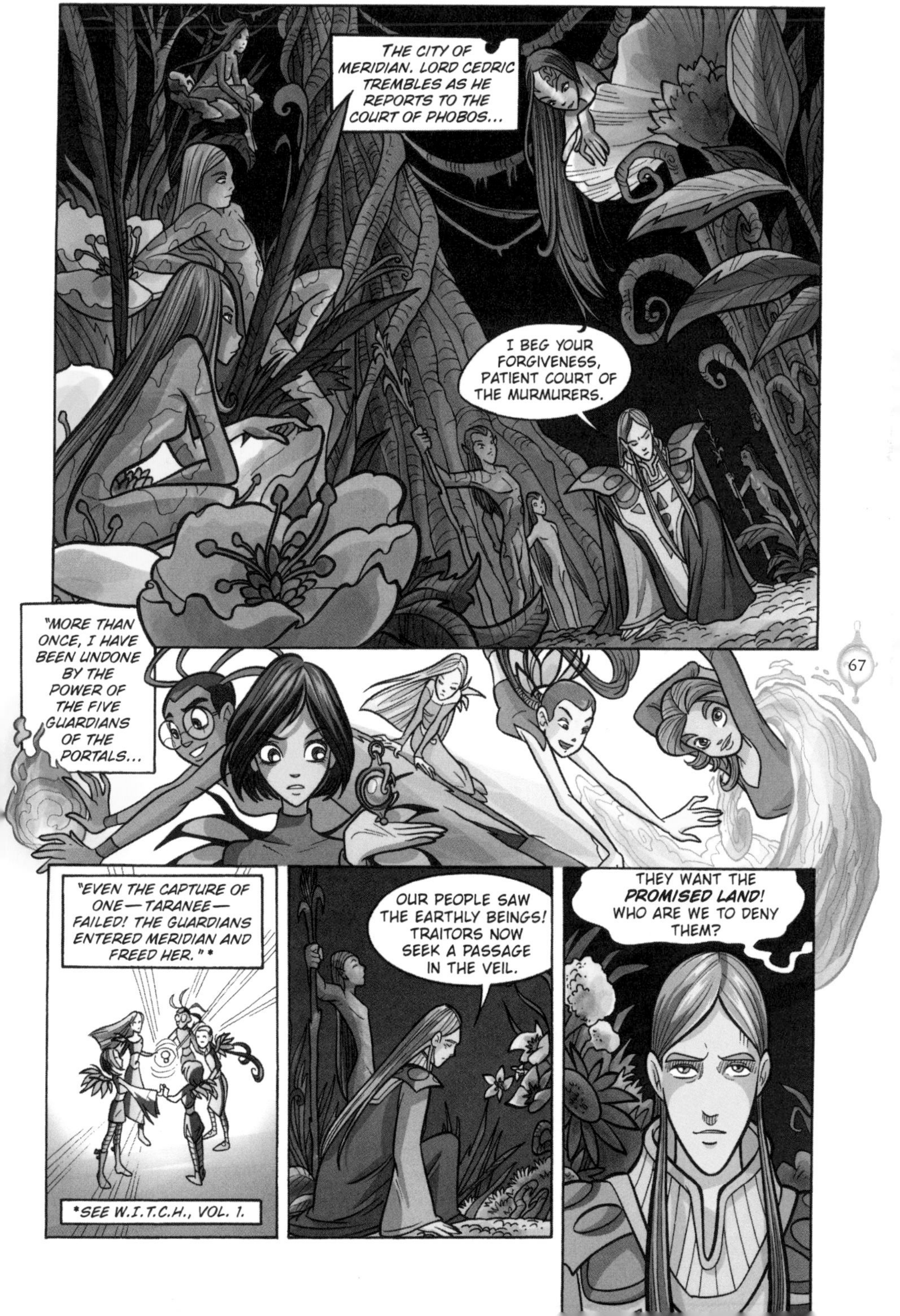
THE CITY OF MERIDIAN. LORD CEDRIC TREMBLES AS HE REPORTS TO THE COURT OF PHOBOS...
I BEG YOUR FORGIVENESS, PATIENT COURT OF THE MURMURERS.
"MORE THAN ONCE, I HAVE BEEN UNDONE BY THE POWER OF THE FIVE GUARDIANS OF THE PORTALS...
"EVEN THE CAPTURE OF ONE—TARANEE—FAILED! THE GUARDIANS ENTERED MERIDIAN AND FREED HER." *
*SEE W.I.T.C.H., VOL. 1.
OUR PEOPLE SAW THE EARTHLY BEINGS! TRAITORS NOW SEEK A PASSAGE IN THE VEIL.
THEY WANT THE **PROMISED LAND**! WHO ARE WE TO DENY THEM?

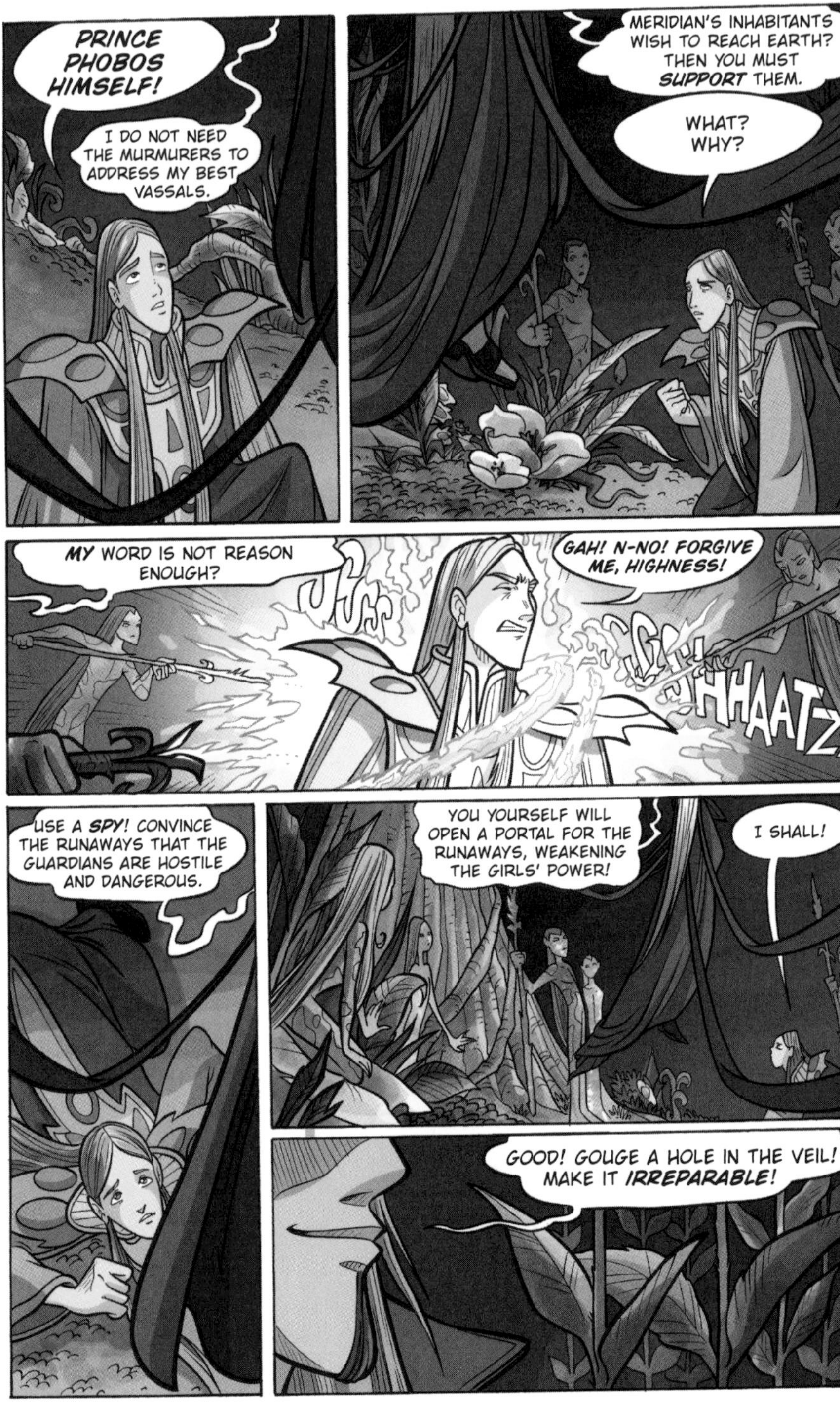
PRINCE PHOBOS HIMSELF!
I DO NOT NEED THE MURMURERS TO ADDRESS MY BEST VASSALS.
MERIDIAN'S INHABITANTS WISH TO REACH EARTH? THEN YOU MUST SUPPORT THEM.
WHAT? WHY?
MY WORD IS NOT REASON ENOUGH?
GAH! N-NO! FORGIVE ME, HIGHNESS!
HHAATZZ
USE A SPY! CONVINCE THE RUNAWAYS THAT THE GUARDIANS ARE HOSTILE AND DANGEROUS.
YOU YOURSELF WILL OPEN A PORTAL FOR THE RUNAWAYS, WEAKENING THE GIRLS' POWER!
I SHALL!
GOOD! GOUGE A HOLE IN THE VEIL! MAKE IT IRREPARABLE!

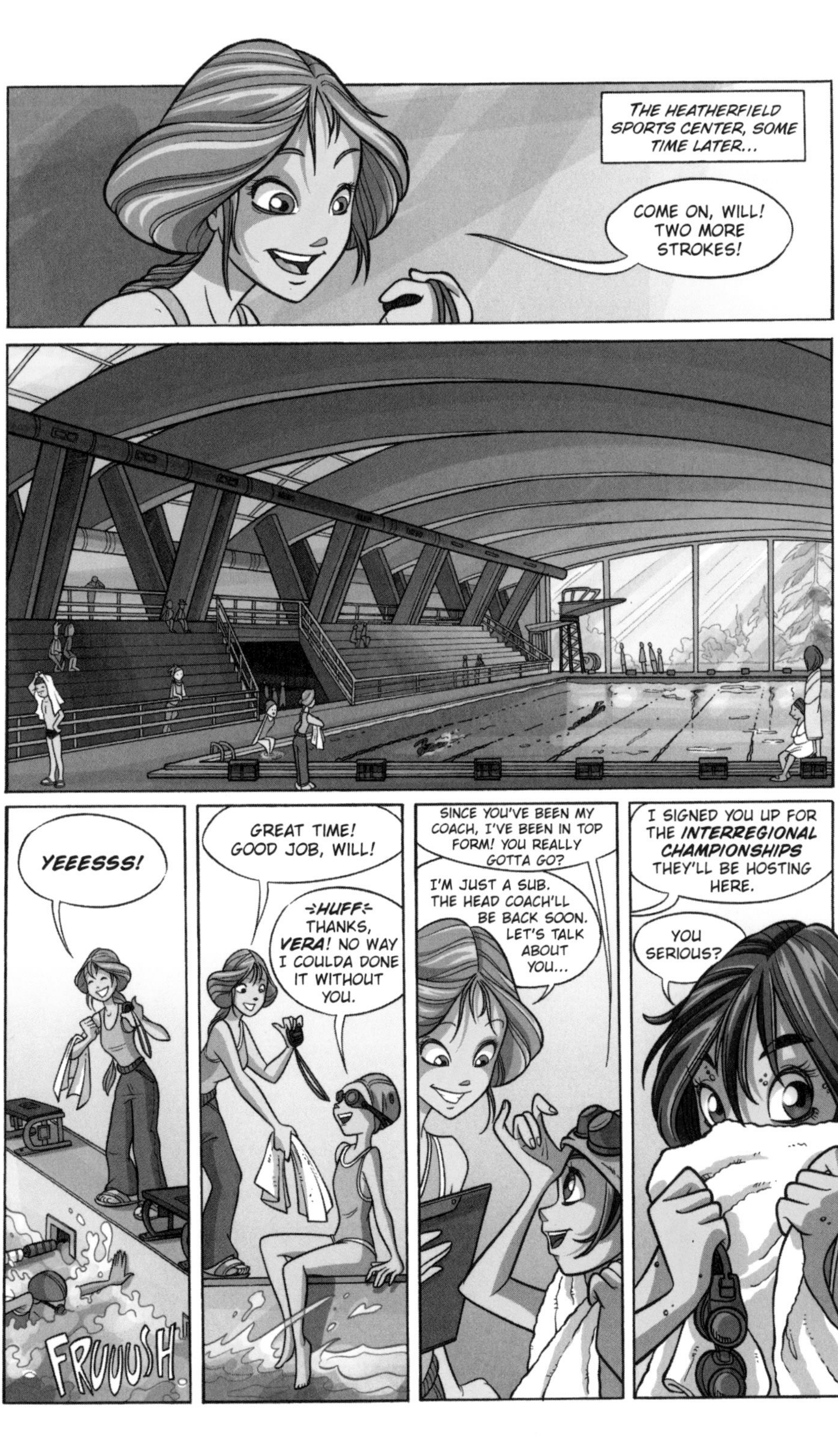

THE HEATHERFIELD SPORTS CENTER, SOME TIME LATER...
COME ON, WILL! TWO MORE STROKES!
YEEESSS!
FRUUUSH
GREAT TIME! GOOD JOB, WILL!
HUFF THANKS, VERA! NO WAY I COULDA DONE IT WITHOUT YOU.
SINCE YOU'VE BEEN MY COACH, I'VE BEEN IN TOP FORM! YOU REALLY GOTTA GO?
I'M JUST A SUB. THE HEAD COACH'LL BE BACK SOON. LET'S TALK ABOUT YOU...
I SIGNED YOU UP FOR THE INTERREGIONAL CHAMPIONSHIPS THEY'LL BE HOSTING HERE.
YOU SERIOUS?

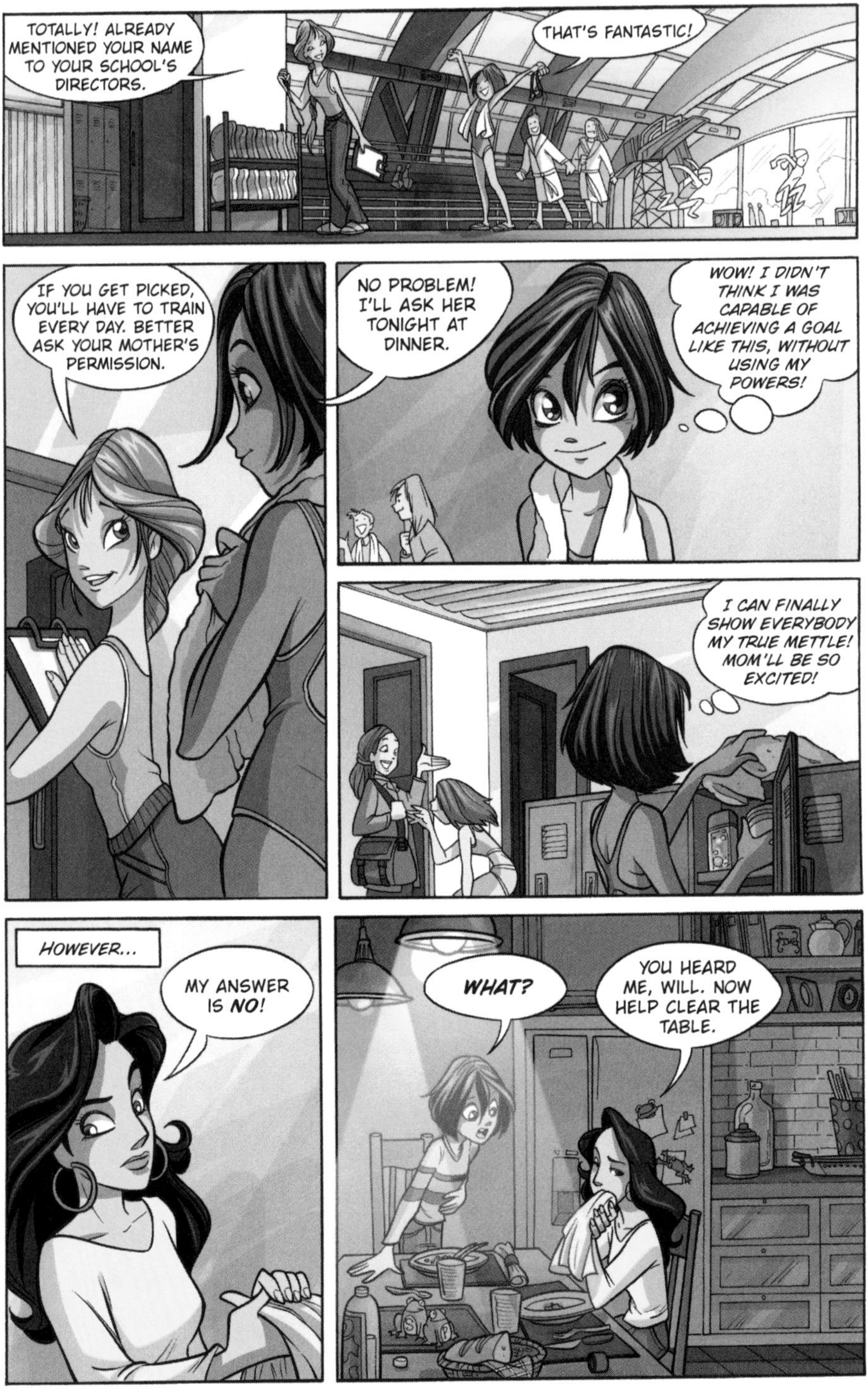
TOTALLY! ALREADY MENTIONED YOUR NAME TO YOUR SCHOOL'S DIRECTORS.
THAT'S FANTASTIC!
IF YOU GET PICKED, YOU'LL HAVE TO TRAIN EVERY DAY. BETTER ASK YOUR MOTHER'S PERMISSION.
NO PROBLEM! I'LL ASK HER TONIGHT AT DINNER.
WOW! I DIDN'T THINK I WAS CAPABLE OF ACHIEVING A GOAL LIKE THIS, WITHOUT USING MY POWERS!
I CAN FINALLY SHOW EVERYBODY MY TRUE METTLE! MOM'LL BE SO EXCITED!
HOWEVER...
MY ANSWER IS NO!
WHAT?
YOU HEARD ME, WILL. NOW HELP CLEAR THE TABLE.

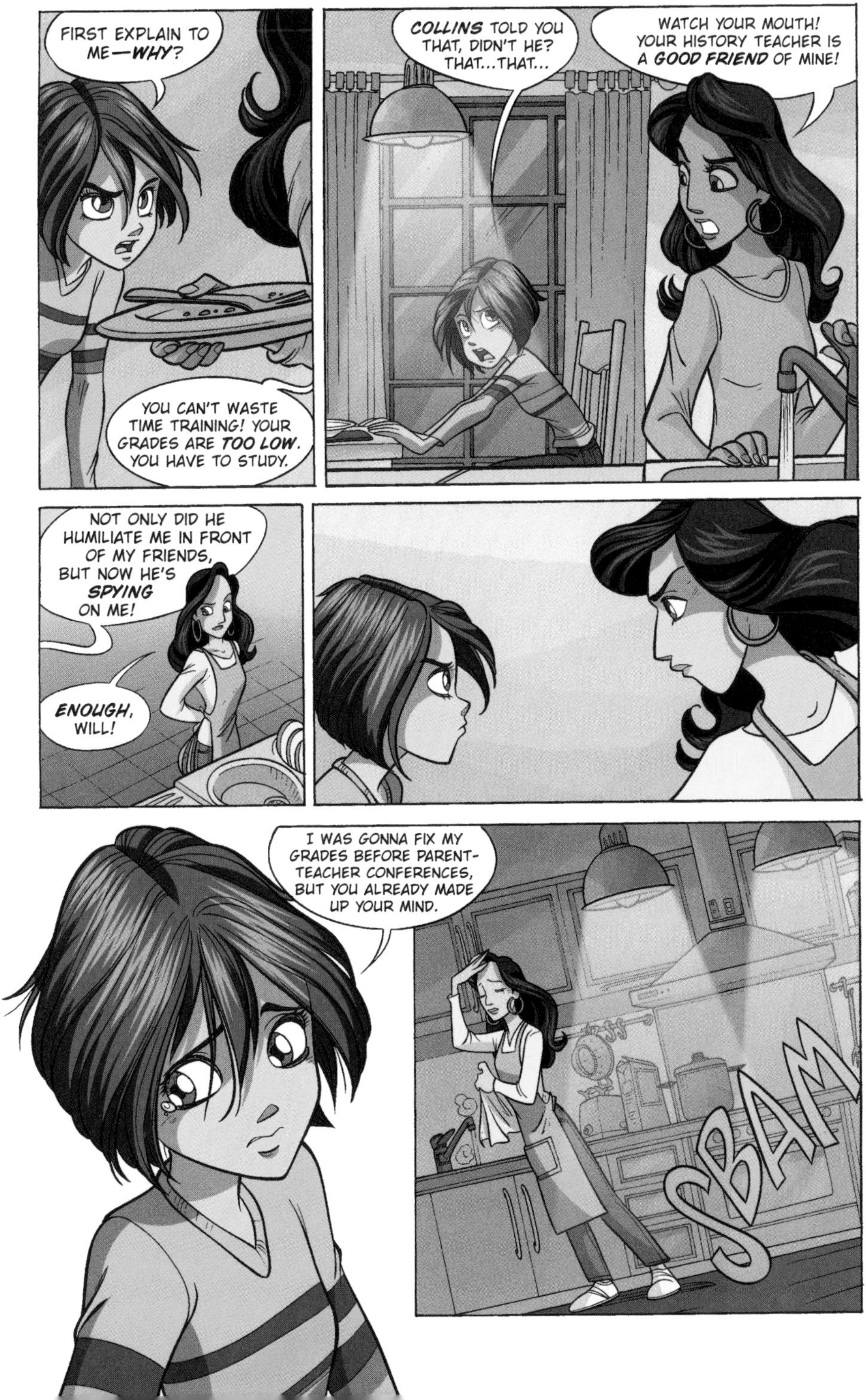
FIRST EXPLAIN TO ME—WHY?
YOU CAN'T WASTE TIME TRAINING! YOUR GRADES ARE TOO LOW. YOU HAVE TO STUDY.
COLLINS TOLD YOU THAT, DIDN'T HE? THAT...THAT...
WATCH YOUR MOUTH! YOUR HISTORY TEACHER IS A GOOD FRIEND OF MINE!
NOT ONLY DID HE HUMILIATE ME IN FRONT OF MY FRIENDS, BUT NOW HE'S SPYING ON ME!
ENOUGH, WILL!
I WAS GONNA FIX MY GRADES BEFORE PARENT-TEACHER CONFERENCES, BUT YOU ALREADY MADE UP YOUR MIND.
SBAM

THE NEXT MORNING, IN FRONT OF THE SHEFFIELD INSTITUTE...

WHY? WHY?

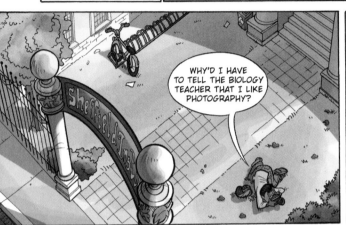

WHY'D I HAVE TO TELL THE BIOLOGY TEACHER THAT I LIKE PHOTOGRAPHY?

"THAT'S WONDERFUL, TARANEE! TAKE A PHOTO OF THREE BUGS AND WRITE A REPORT ABOUT IT!"

EXCEPT THEY *TOTALLY DISGUST ME!*

AND WITH THE ZOOM, THEY LOOK EVEN BIGGER!

A BUTTERFLY! MY SAVIOR!

STOP A MINUTE, BEAUTIFUL BUTTERFLY. HOLD STILL NOW...DON'T MOVE YOUR LITTLE WINGS...

FRUSH

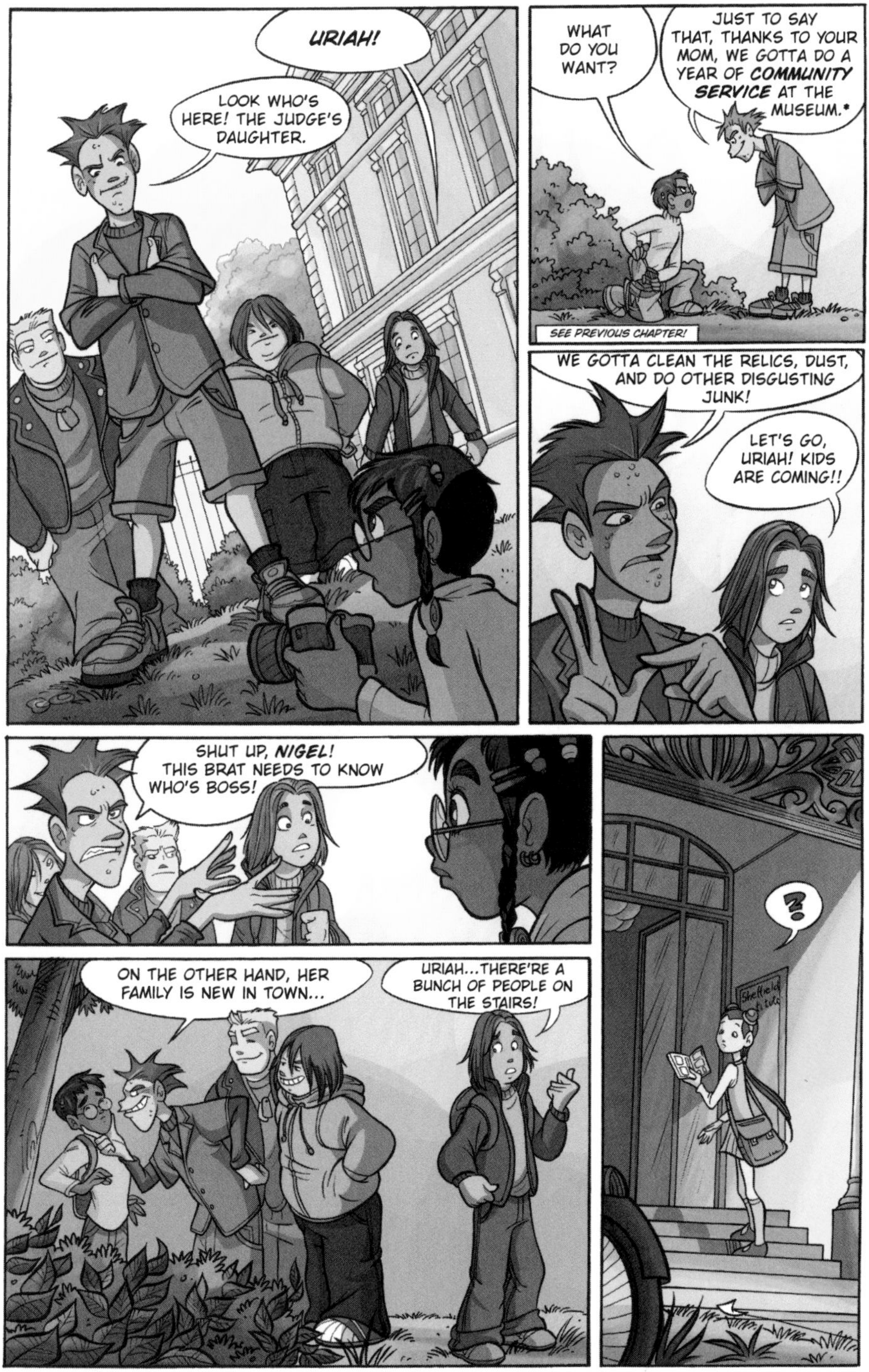
URIAH!
LOOK WHO'S HERE! THE JUDGE'S DAUGHTER.
WHAT DO YOU WANT?
JUST TO SAY THAT, THANKS TO YOUR MOM, WE GOTTA DO A YEAR OF **COMMUNITY SERVICE** AT THE MUSEUM.*
SEE PREVIOUS CHAPTER!
WE GOTTA CLEAN THE RELICS, DUST, AND DO OTHER DISGUSTING JUNK!
LET'S GO, URIAH! KIDS ARE COMING!!
SHUT UP, **NIGEL**! THIS BRAT NEEDS TO KNOW WHO'S BOSS!
?
ON THE OTHER HAND, HER FAMILY IS NEW IN TOWN...
URIAH...THERE'RE A BUNCH OF PEOPLE ON THE STAIRS!

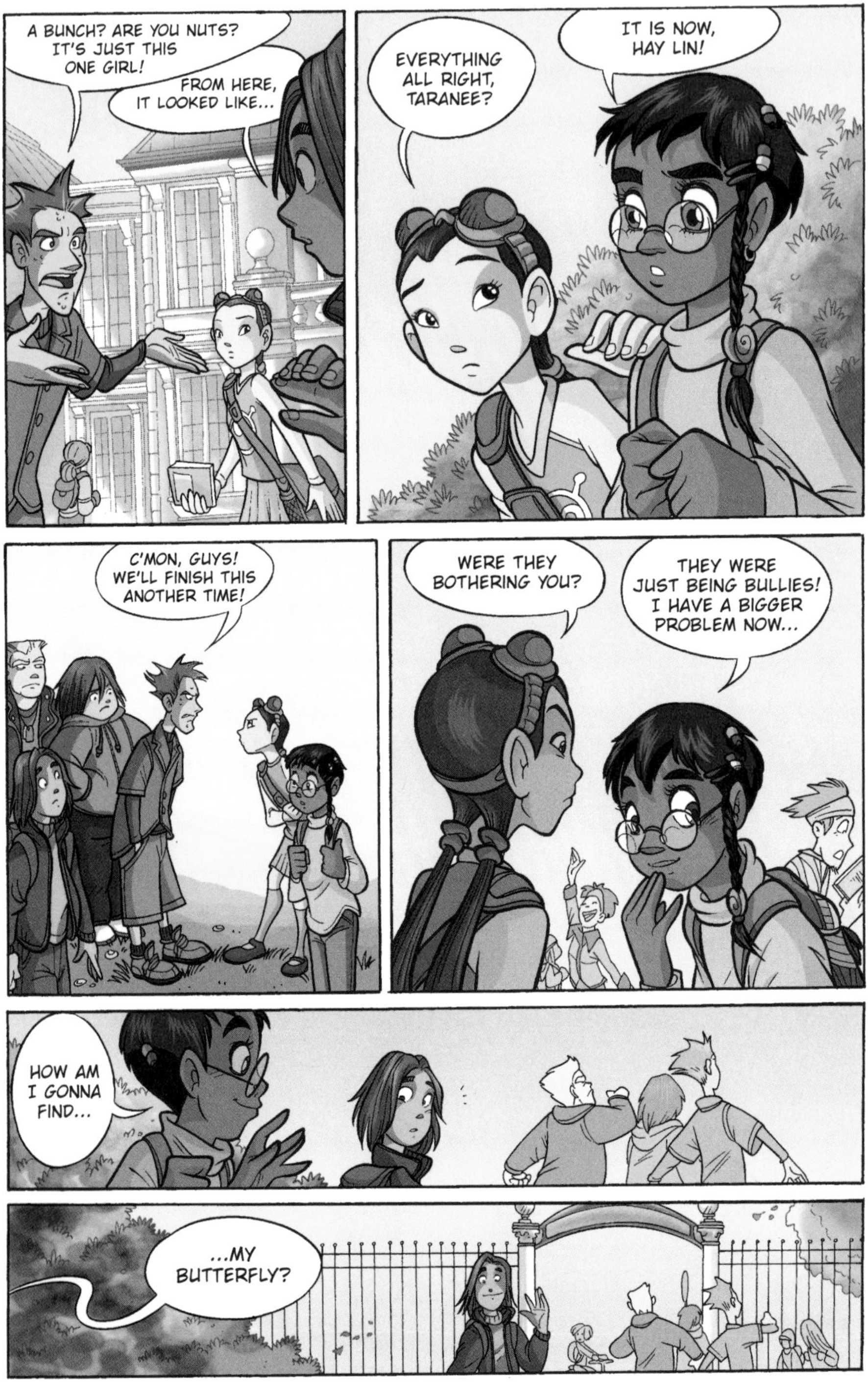
A BUNCH? ARE YOU NUTS? IT'S JUST THIS ONE GIRL!
FROM HERE, IT LOOKED LIKE...
EVERYTHING ALL RIGHT, TARANEE?
IT IS NOW, HAY LIN!
C'MON, GUYS! WE'LL FINISH THIS ANOTHER TIME!
WERE THEY BOTHERING YOU?
THEY WERE JUST BEING BULLIES! I HAVE A BIGGER PROBLEM NOW...
HOW AM I GONNA FIND...
...MY BUTTERFLY?

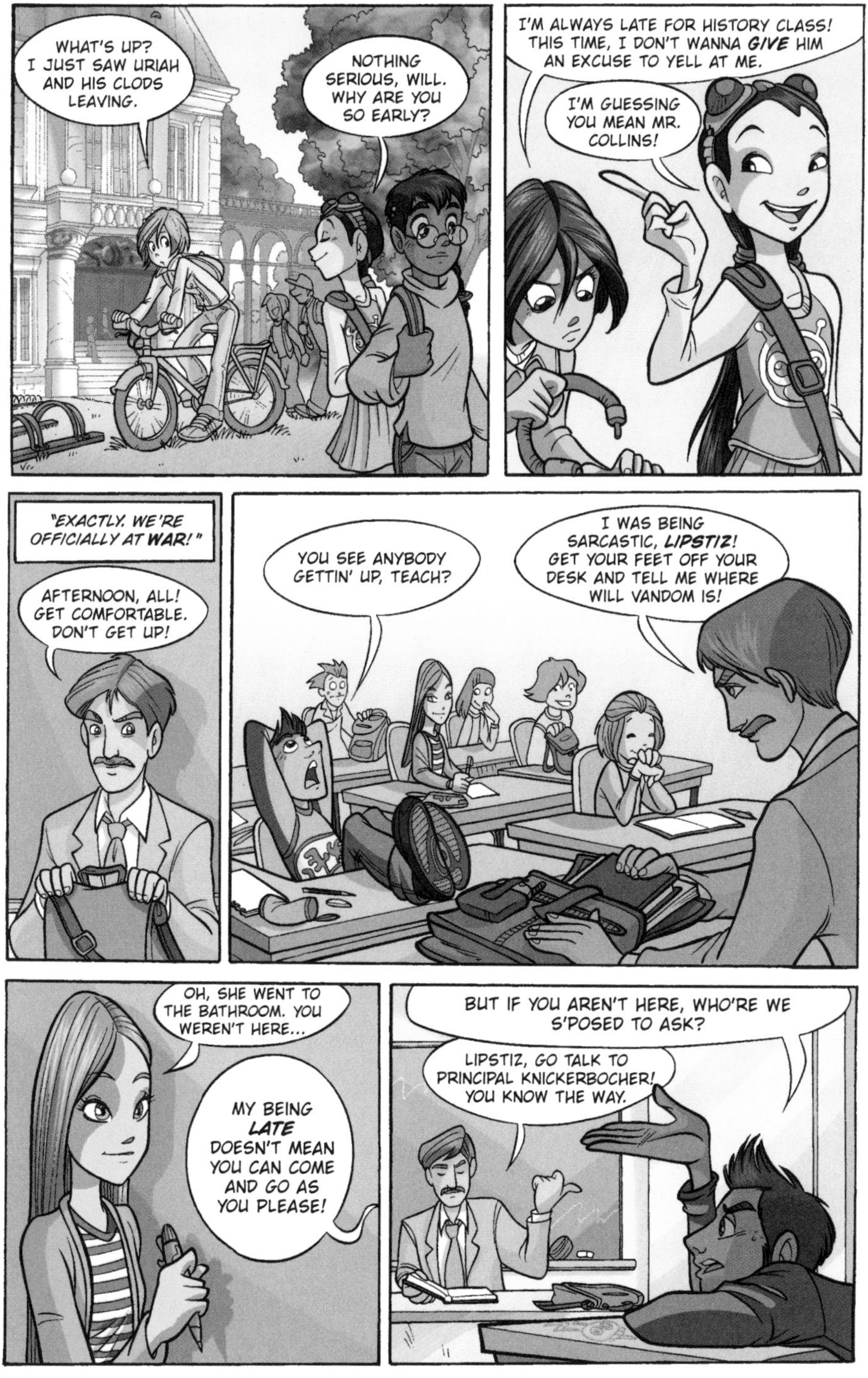
WHAT'S UP? I JUST SAW URIAH AND HIS CLODS LEAVING.
NOTHING SERIOUS, WILL. WHY ARE YOU SO EARLY?
I'M ALWAYS LATE FOR HISTORY CLASS! THIS TIME, I DON'T WANNA GIVE HIM AN EXCUSE TO YELL AT ME.
I'M GUESSING YOU MEAN MR. COLLINS!
"EXACTLY. WE'RE OFFICIALLY AT WAR!"
AFTERNOON, ALL! GET COMFORTABLE. DON'T GET UP!
YOU SEE ANYBODY GETTIN' UP, TEACH?
I WAS BEING SARCASTIC, LIPSTIZ! GET YOUR FEET OFF YOUR DESK AND TELL ME WHERE WILL VANDOM IS!
OH, SHE WENT TO THE BATHROOM. YOU WEREN'T HERE...
MY BEING LATE DOESN'T MEAN YOU CAN COME AND GO AS YOU PLEASE!
BUT IF YOU AREN'T HERE, WHO'RE WE S'POSED TO ASK?
LIPSTIZ, GO TALK TO PRINCIPAL KNICKERBOCHER! YOU KNOW THE WAY.

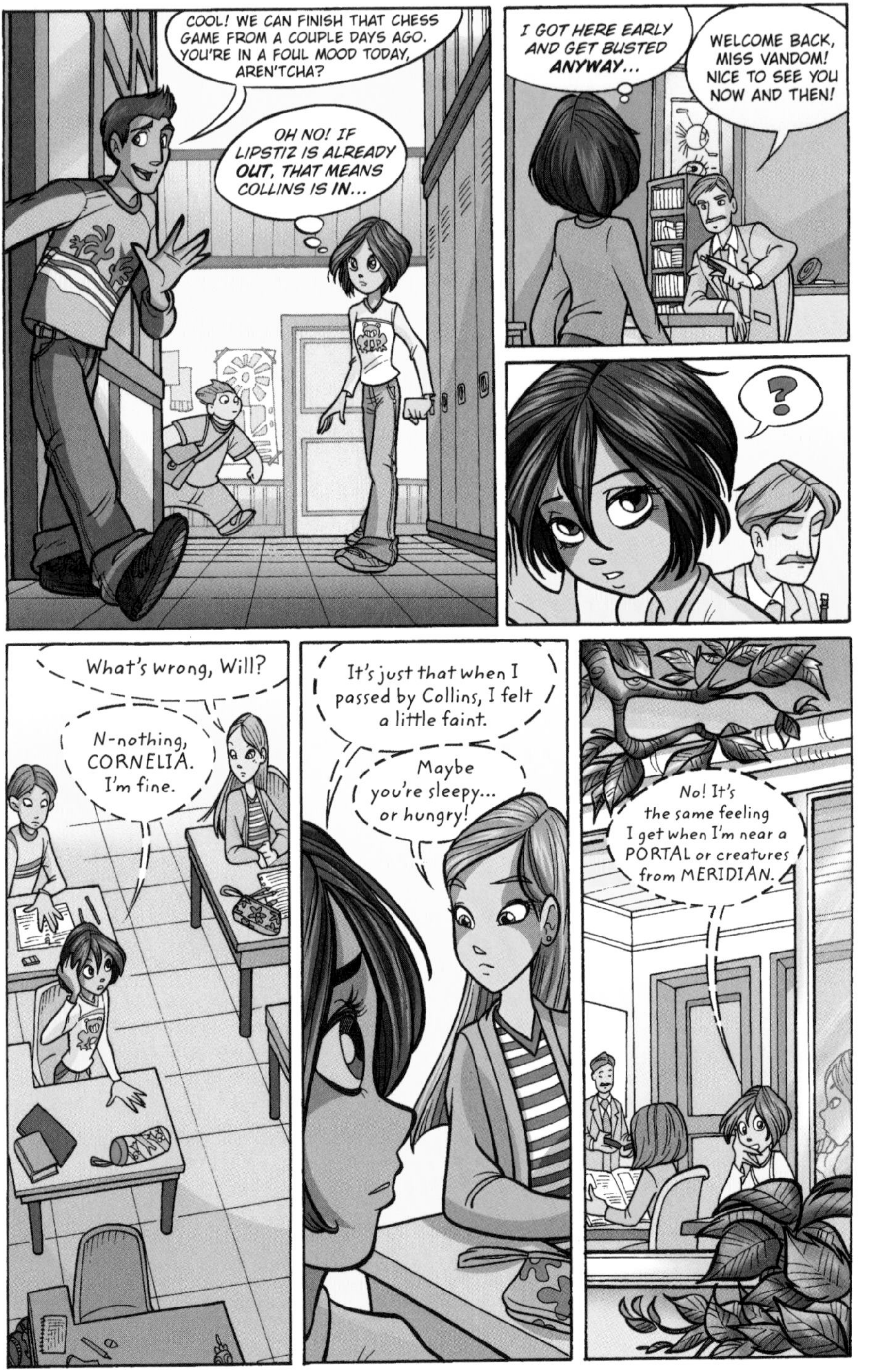
COOL! WE CAN FINISH THAT CHESS GAME FROM A COUPLE DAYS AGO. YOU'RE IN A FOUL MOOD TODAY, AREN'TCHA?
OH NO! IF LIPSTIZ IS ALREADY **OUT**, THAT MEANS COLLINS IS **IN**...
I GOT HERE EARLY AND GET BUSTED **ANYWAY**...
WELCOME BACK, MISS VANDOM! NICE TO SEE YOU NOW AND THEN!
?
What's wrong, Will?
N-nothing, CORNELIA. I'm fine.
It's just that when I passed by Collins, I felt a little faint.
Maybe you're sleepy... or hungry!
No! It's the same feeling I get when I'm near a PORTAL or creatures from MERIDIAN.

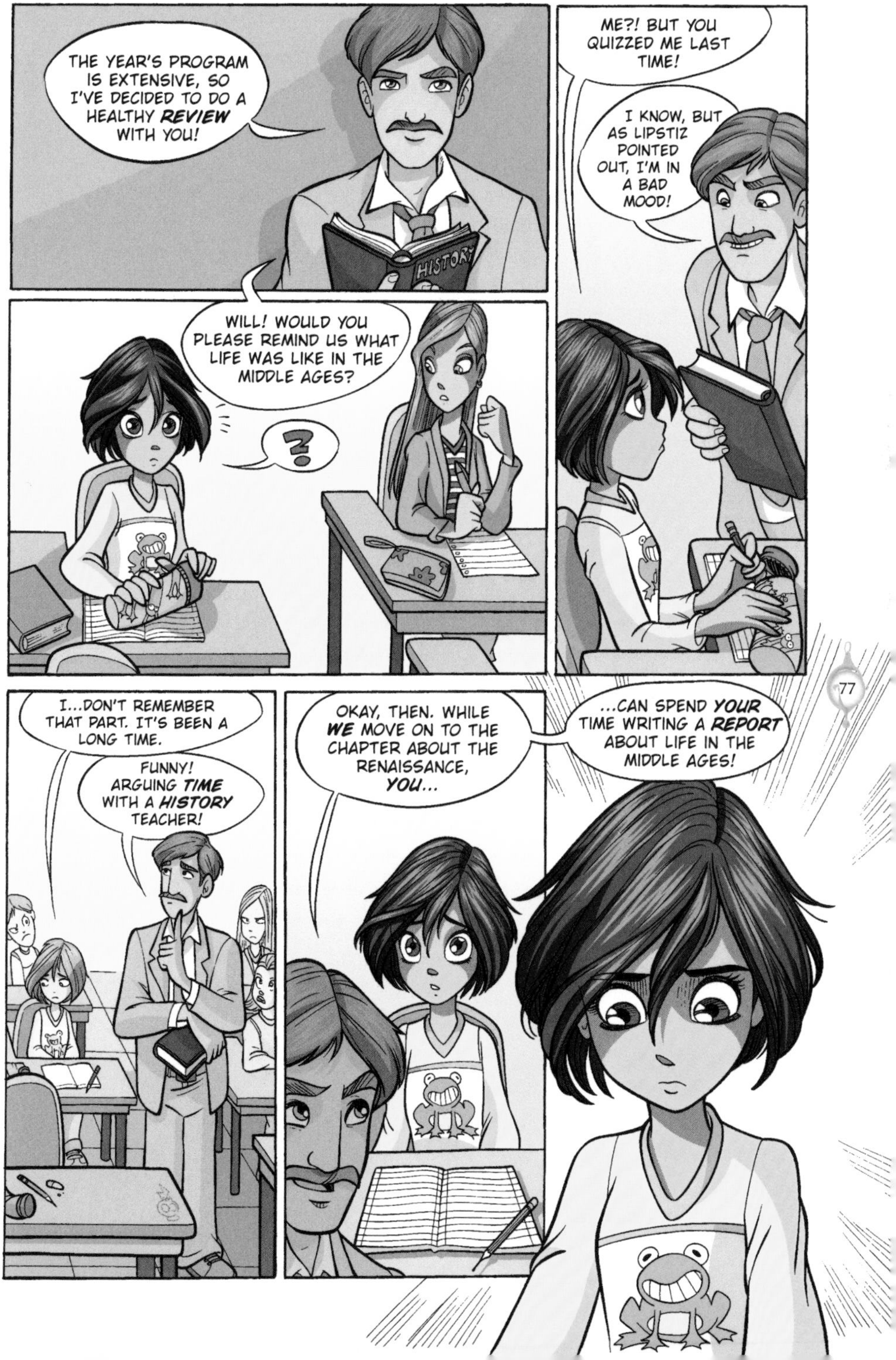
THE YEAR'S PROGRAM IS EXTENSIVE, SO I'VE DECIDED TO DO A HEALTHY *REVIEW* WITH YOU!
HISTORY
WILL! WOULD YOU PLEASE REMIND US WHAT LIFE WAS LIKE IN THE MIDDLE AGES?
?
ME?! BUT YOU QUIZZED ME LAST TIME!
I KNOW, BUT AS LIPSTIZ POINTED OUT, I'M IN A BAD MOOD!
I...DON'T REMEMBER THAT PART. IT'S BEEN A LONG TIME.
FUNNY! ARGUING *TIME* WITH A *HISTORY* TEACHER!
OKAY, THEN. WHILE *WE* MOVE ON TO THE CHAPTER ABOUT THE RENAISSANCE, *YOU*...
...CAN SPEND *YOUR* TIME WRITING A *REPORT* ABOUT LIFE IN THE MIDDLE AGES!

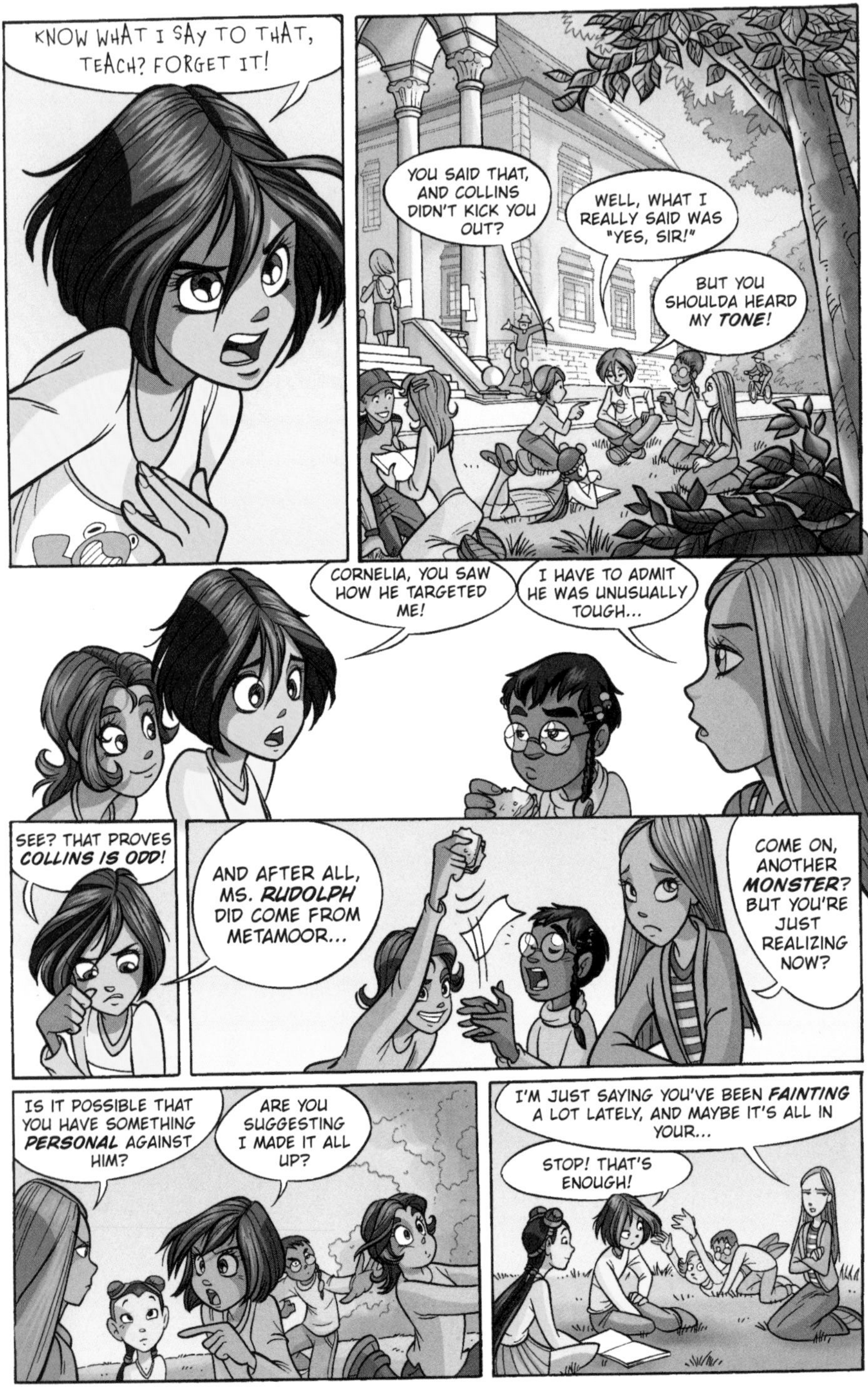
KNOW WHAT I SAY TO THAT, TEACH? FORGET IT!
YOU SAID THAT, AND COLLINS DIDN'T KICK YOU OUT?
WELL, WHAT I REALLY SAID WAS "YES, SIR!"
BUT YOU SHOULDA HEARD MY TONE!
CORNELIA, YOU SAW HOW HE TARGETED ME!
I HAVE TO ADMIT HE WAS UNUSUALLY TOUGH...
SEE? THAT PROVES COLLINS IS ODD!
AND AFTER ALL, MS. RUDOLPH DID COME FROM METAMOOR...
COME ON, ANOTHER MONSTER? BUT YOU'RE JUST REALIZING NOW?
IS IT POSSIBLE THAT YOU HAVE SOMETHING PERSONAL AGAINST HIM?
ARE YOU SUGGESTING I MADE IT ALL UP?
I'M JUST SAYING YOU'VE BEEN FAINTING A LOT LATELY, AND MAYBE IT'S ALL IN YOUR...
STOP! THAT'S ENOUGH!

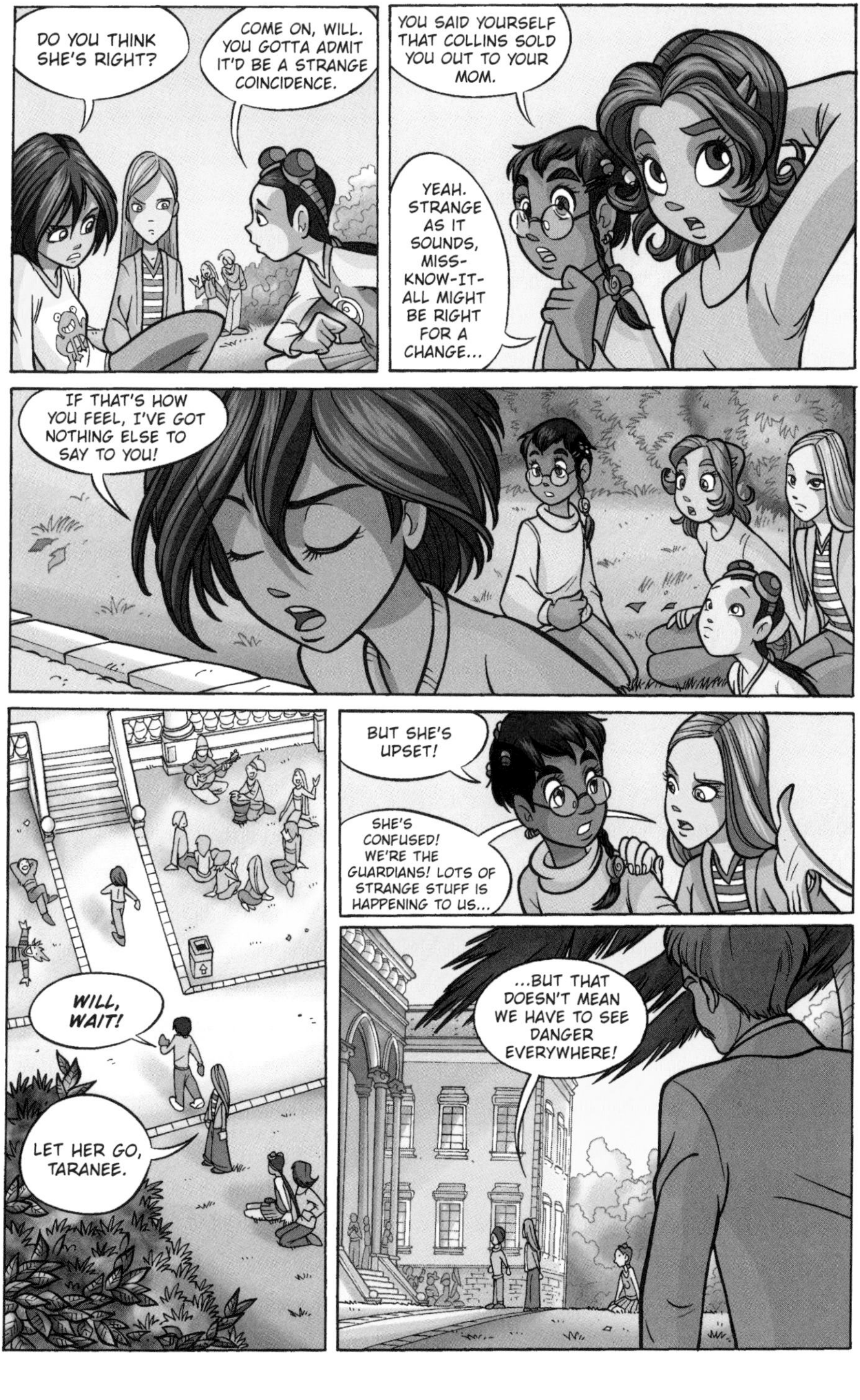
DO YOU THINK SHE'S RIGHT?
COME ON, WILL. YOU GOTTA ADMIT IT'D BE A STRANGE COINCIDENCE.
YOU SAID YOURSELF THAT COLLINS SOLD YOU OUT TO YOUR MOM.
YEAH. STRANGE AS IT SOUNDS, MISS-KNOW-IT-ALL MIGHT BE RIGHT FOR A CHANGE...
IF THAT'S HOW YOU FEEL, I'VE GOT NOTHING ELSE TO SAY TO YOU!
WILL, WAIT!
LET HER GO, TARANEE.
BUT SHE'S UPSET!
SHE'S CONFUSED! WE'RE THE GUARDIANS! LOTS OF STRANGE STUFF IS HAPPENING TO US...
...BUT THAT DOESN'T MEAN WE HAVE TO SEE DANGER EVERYWHERE!

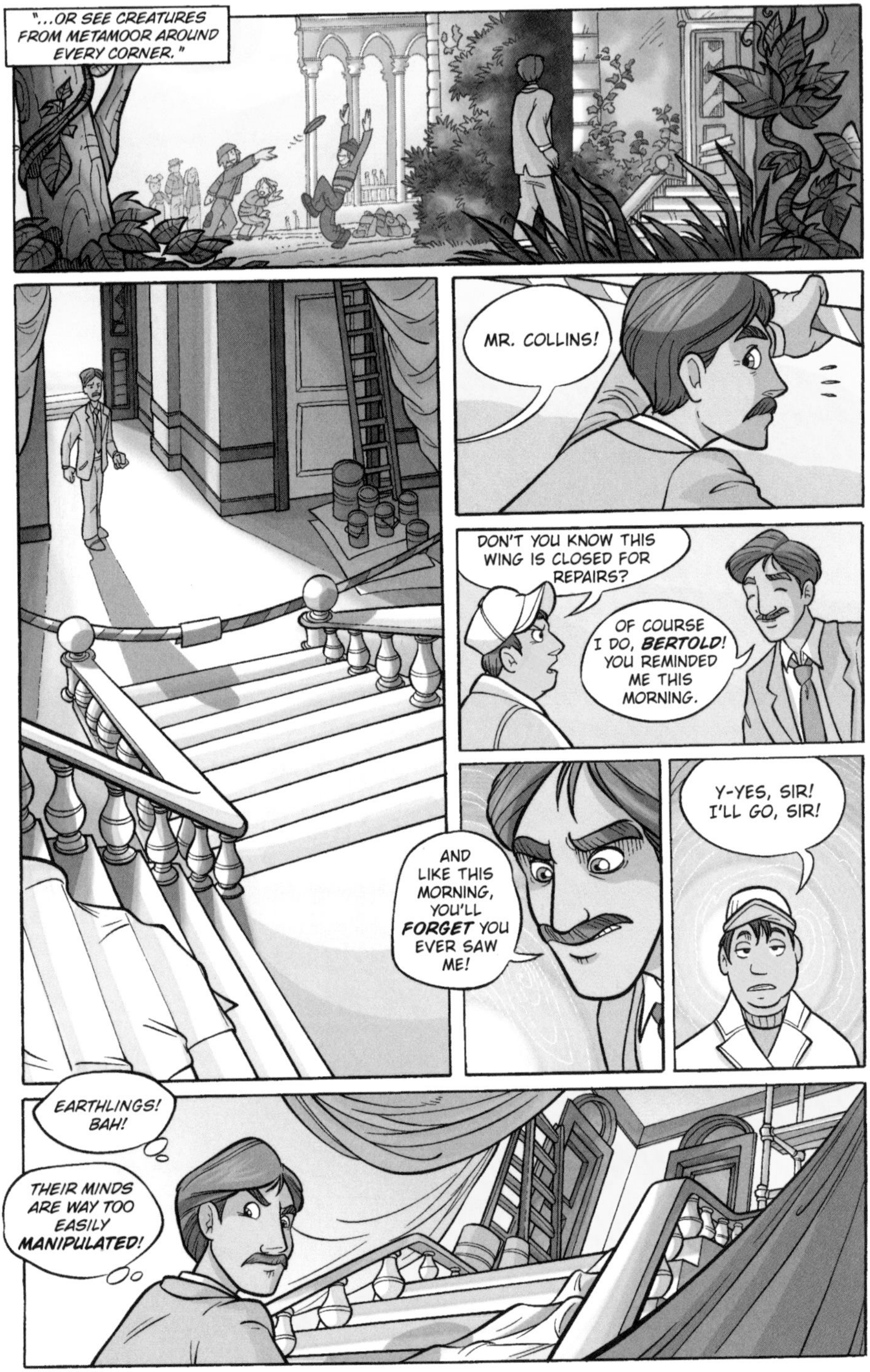
"...OR SEE CREATURES FROM METAMOOR AROUND EVERY CORNER."
MR. COLLINS!
DON'T YOU KNOW THIS WING IS CLOSED FOR REPAIRS?
OF COURSE I DO, **BERTOLD**! YOU REMINDED ME THIS MORNING.
AND LIKE THIS MORNING, YOU'LL **FORGET** YOU EVER SAW ME!
Y-YES, SIR! I'LL GO, SIR!
EARTHLINGS! BAH!
THEIR MINDS ARE WAY TOO EASILY **MANIPULATED**!

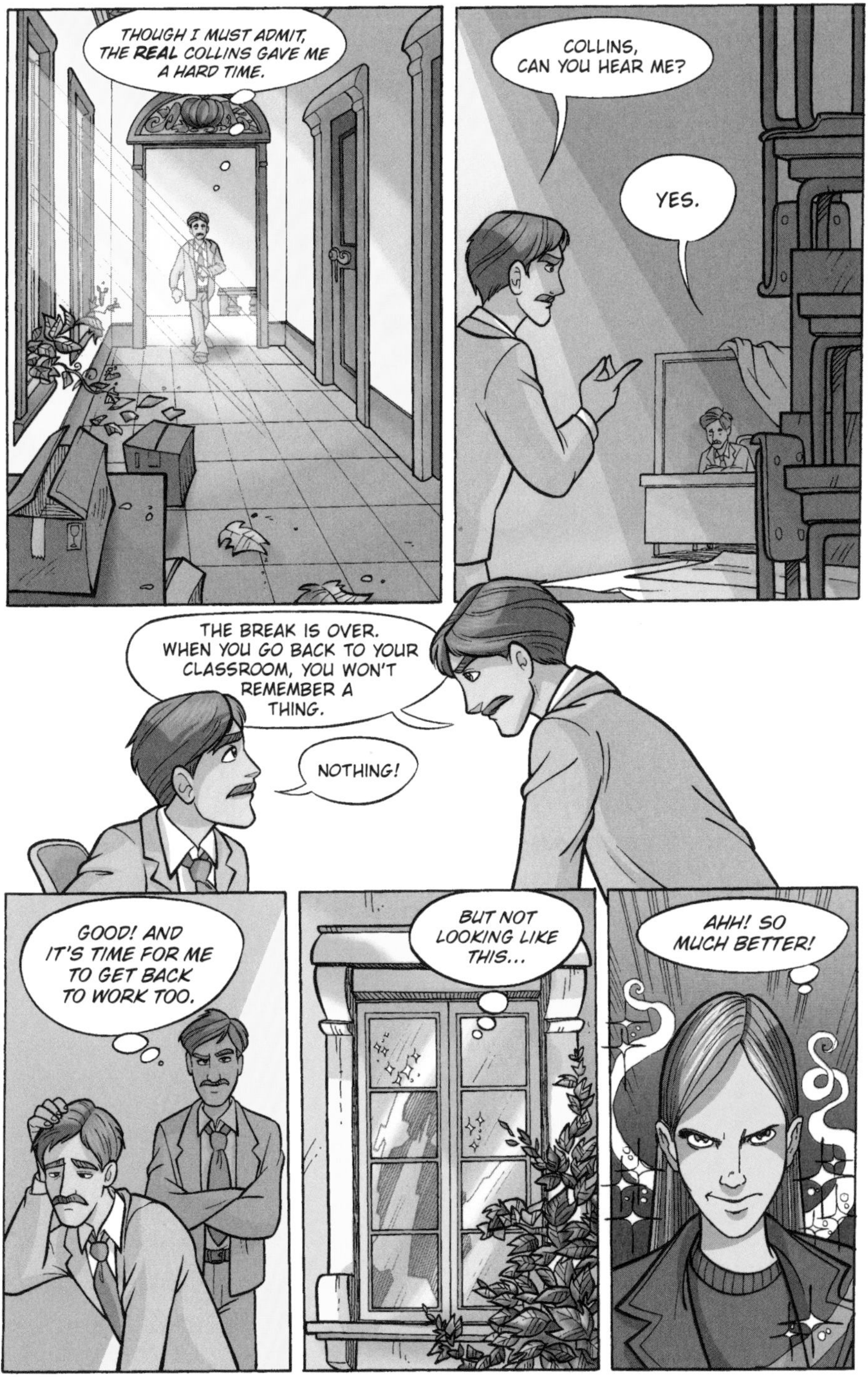
THOUGH I MUST ADMIT, THE REAL COLLINS GAVE ME A HARD TIME.
COLLINS, CAN YOU HEAR ME?
YES.
THE BREAK IS OVER. WHEN YOU GO BACK TO YOUR CLASSROOM, YOU WON'T REMEMBER A THING.
NOTHING!
GOOD! AND IT'S TIME FOR ME TO GET BACK TO WORK TOO.
BUT NOT LOOKING LIKE THIS...
AHH! SO MUCH BETTER!

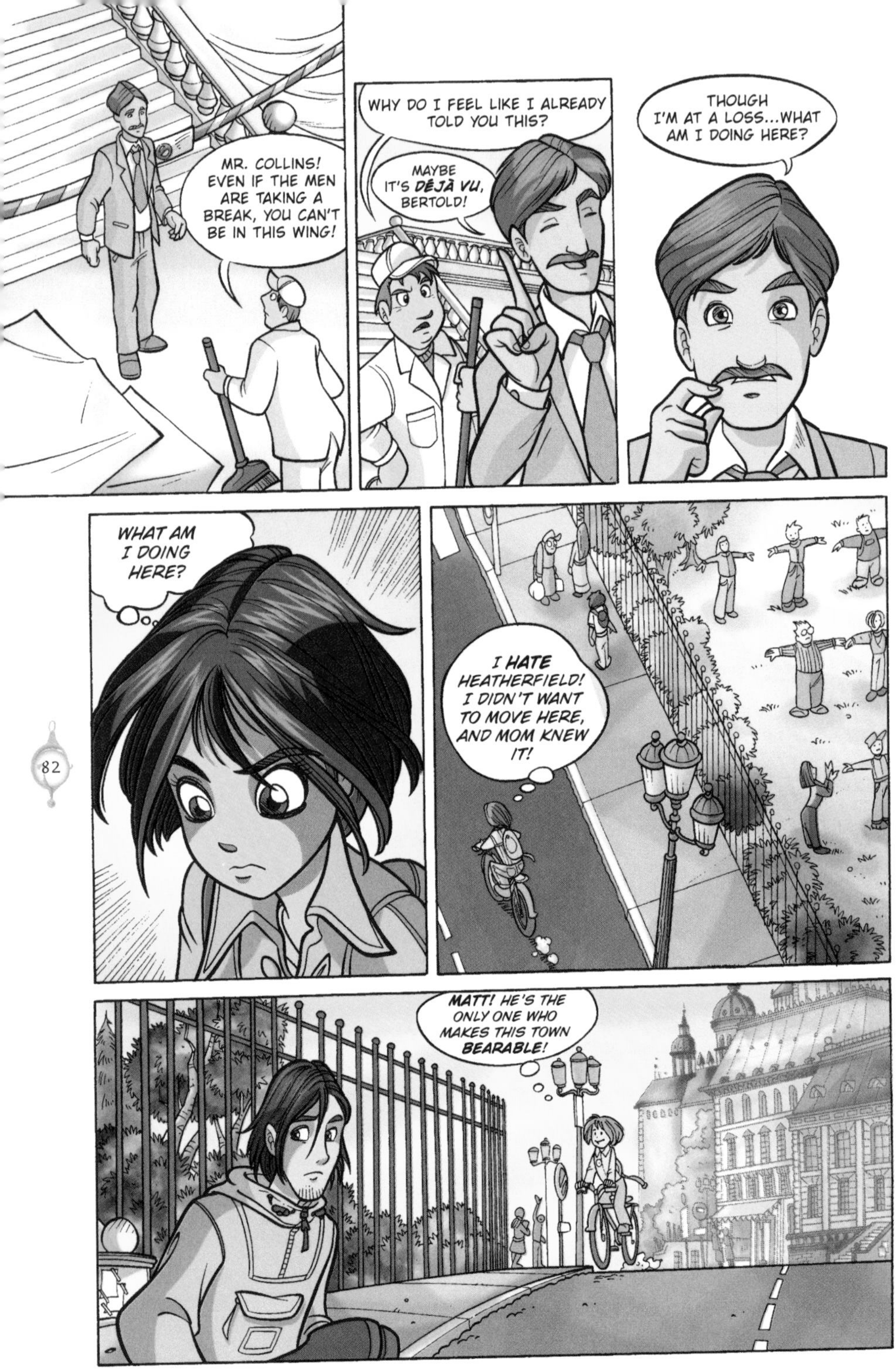
MR. COLLINS! EVEN IF THE MEN ARE TAKING A BREAK, YOU CAN'T BE IN THIS WING!
WHY DO I FEEL LIKE I ALREADY TOLD YOU THIS?
MAYBE IT'S DÉJÀ VU, BERTOLD!
THOUGH I'M AT A LOSS...WHAT AM I DOING HERE?
WHAT AM I DOING HERE?
I HATE HEATHERFIELD! I DIDN'T WANT TO MOVE HERE, AND MOM KNEW IT!
MATT! HE'S THE ONLY ONE WHO MAKES THIS TOWN BEARABLE!

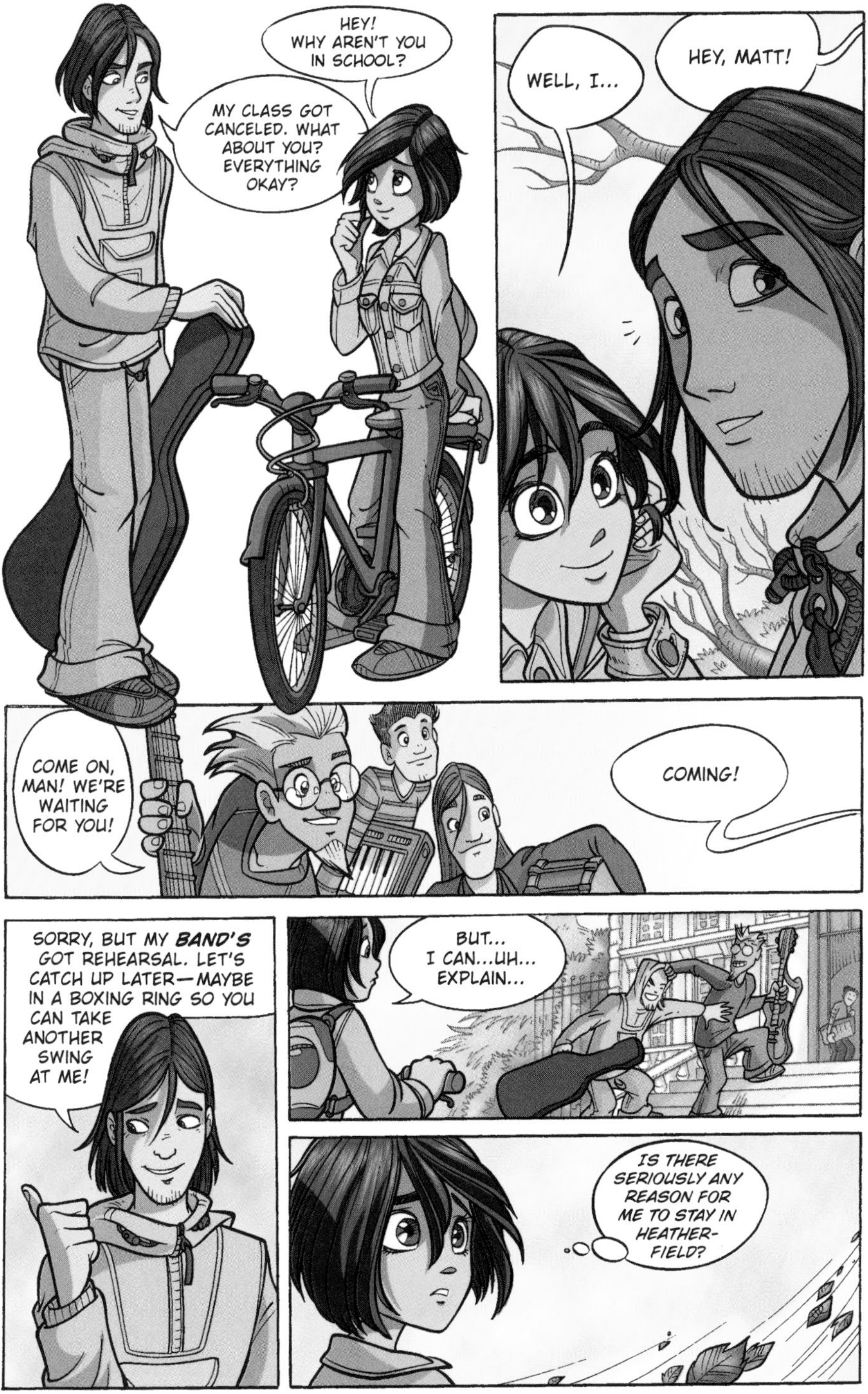
HEY!
WHY AREN'T YOU
IN SCHOOL?
MY CLASS GOT CANCELED. WHAT ABOUT YOU? EVERYTHING OKAY?
HEY, MATT!
WELL, I...
COME ON, MAN! WE'RE WAITING FOR YOU!
COMING!
SORRY, BUT MY ***BAND'S*** GOT REHEARSAL. LET'S CATCH UP LATER—MAYBE IN A BOXING RING SO YOU CAN TAKE ANOTHER SWING AT ME!
BUT... I CAN...UH... EXPLAIN...
IS THERE SERIOUSLY ANY REASON FOR ME TO STAY IN HEATHER-FIELD?

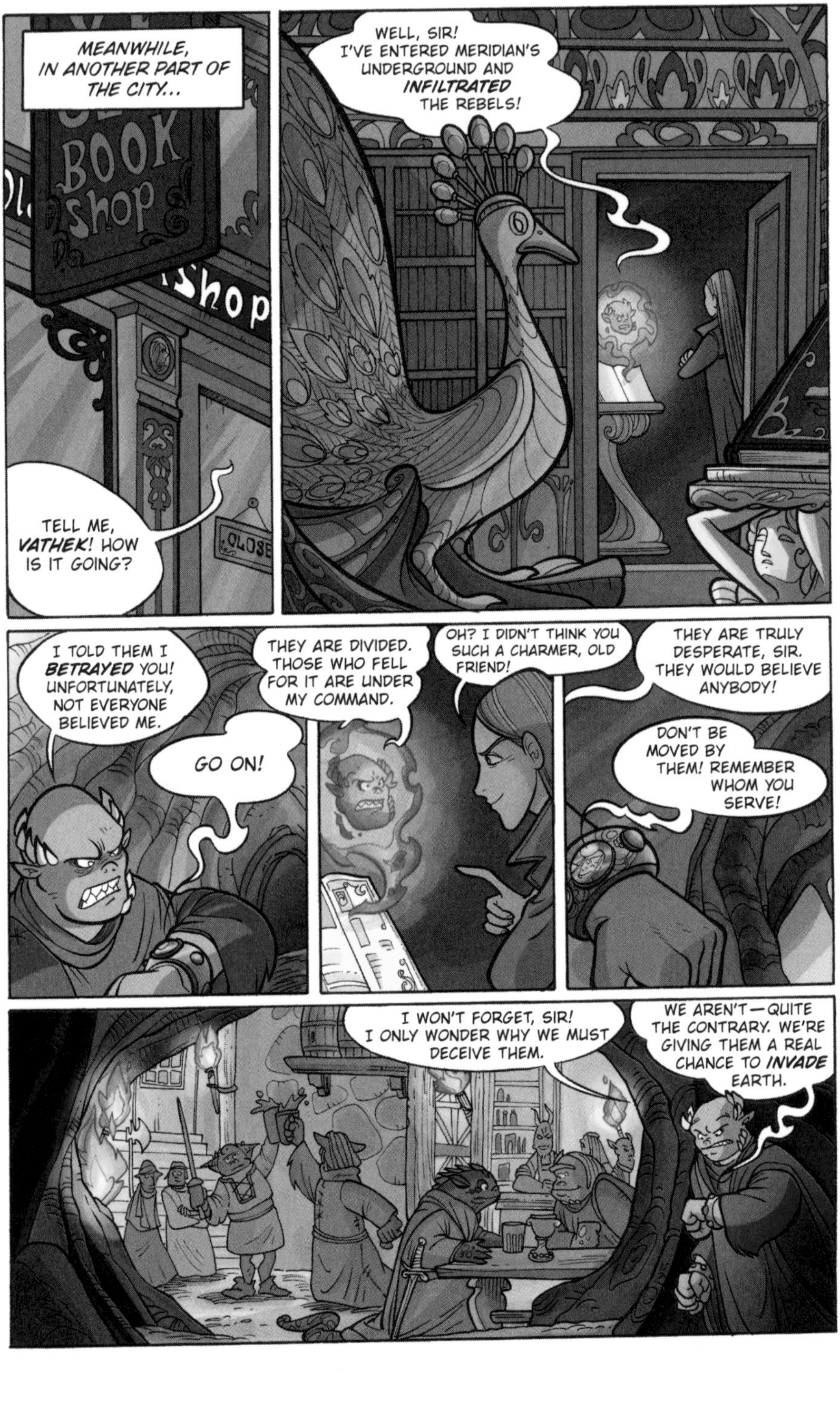
MEANWHILE, IN ANOTHER PART OF THE CITY...
BOOK shop
Shop
TELL ME, VATHEK! HOW IS IT GOING?
WELL, SIR! I'VE ENTERED MERIDIAN'S UNDERGROUND AND INFILTRATED THE REBELS!
I TOLD THEM I BETRAYED YOU! UNFORTUNATELY, NOT EVERYONE BELIEVED ME.
GO ON!
THEY ARE DIVIDED. THOSE WHO FELL FOR IT ARE UNDER MY COMMAND.
OH? I DIDN'T THINK YOU SUCH A CHARMER, OLD FRIEND!
THEY ARE TRULY DESPERATE, SIR. THEY WOULD BELIEVE ANYBODY!
DON'T BE MOVED BY THEM! REMEMBER WHOM YOU SERVE!
I WON'T FORGET, SIR! I ONLY WONDER WHY WE MUST DECEIVE THEM.
WE AREN'T—QUITE THE CONTRARY. WE'RE GIVING THEM A REAL CHANCE TO INVADE EARTH.

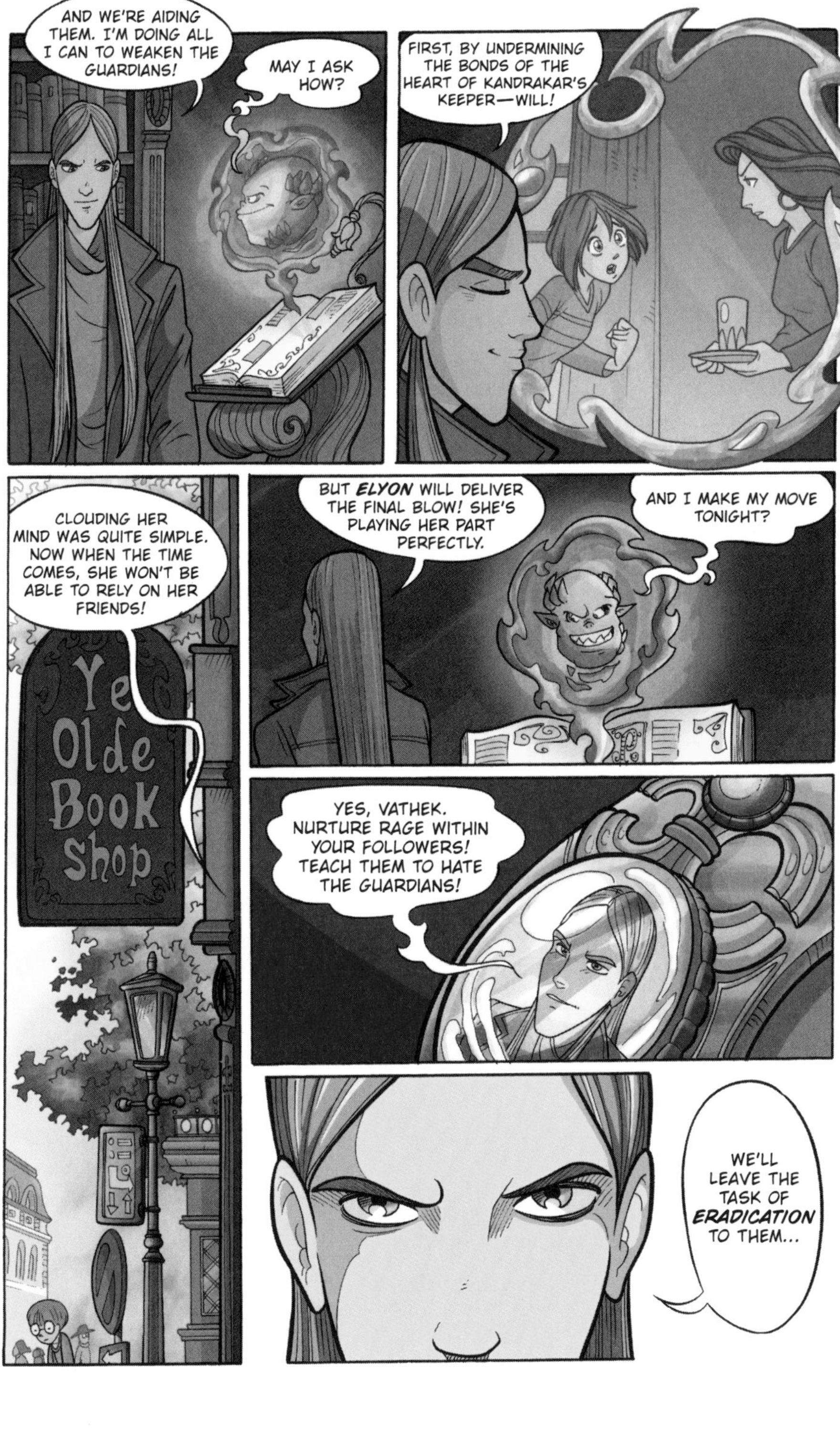
AND WE'RE AIDING THEM. I'M DOING ALL I CAN TO WEAKEN THE GUARDIANS!
MAY I ASK HOW?
FIRST, BY UNDERMINING THE BONDS OF THE HEART OF KANDRAKAR'S KEEPER—WILL!
CLOUDING HER MIND WAS QUITE SIMPLE. NOW WHEN THE TIME COMES, SHE WON'T BE ABLE TO RELY ON HER FRIENDS!
Ye Olde Book Shop
BUT ELYON WILL DELIVER THE FINAL BLOW! SHE'S PLAYING HER PART PERFECTLY.
AND I MAKE MY MOVE TONIGHT?
YES, VATHEK. NURTURE RAGE WITHIN YOUR FOLLOWERS! TEACH THEM TO HATE THE GUARDIANS!
WE'LL LEAVE THE TASK OF ERADICATION TO THEM...

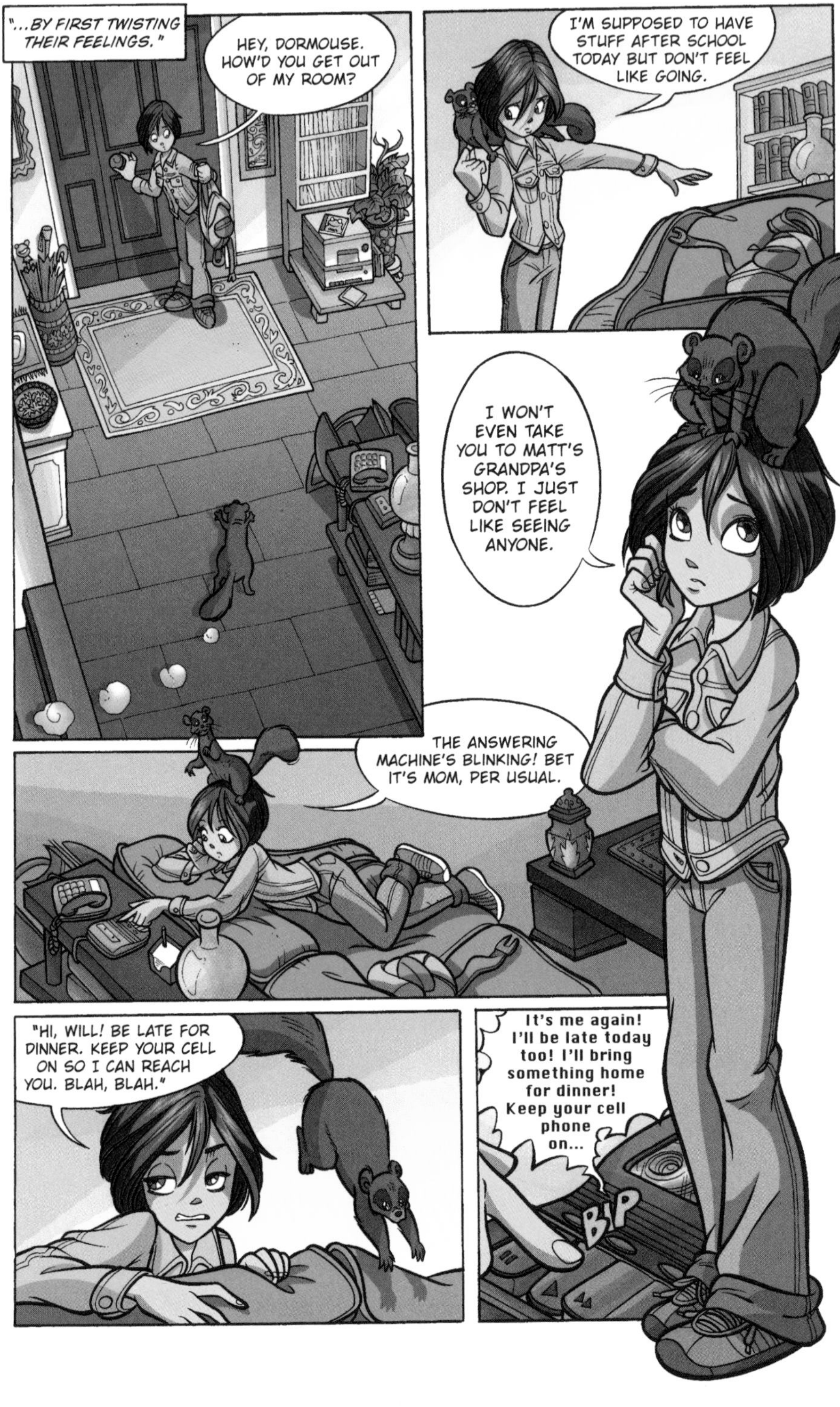
"...BY FIRST TWISTING THEIR FEELINGS."
HEY, DORMOUSE. HOW'D YOU GET OUT OF MY ROOM?
I'M SUPPOSED TO HAVE STUFF AFTER SCHOOL TODAY BUT DON'T FEEL LIKE GOING.
I WON'T EVEN TAKE YOU TO MATT'S GRANDPA'S SHOP. I JUST DON'T FEEL LIKE SEEING ANYONE.
THE ANSWERING MACHINE'S BLINKING! BET IT'S MOM, PER USUAL.
"HI, WILL! BE LATE FOR DINNER. KEEP YOUR CELL ON SO I CAN REACH YOU. BLAH, BLAH."
It's me again! I'll be late today too! I'll bring something home for dinner! Keep your cell phone on...
BLIP

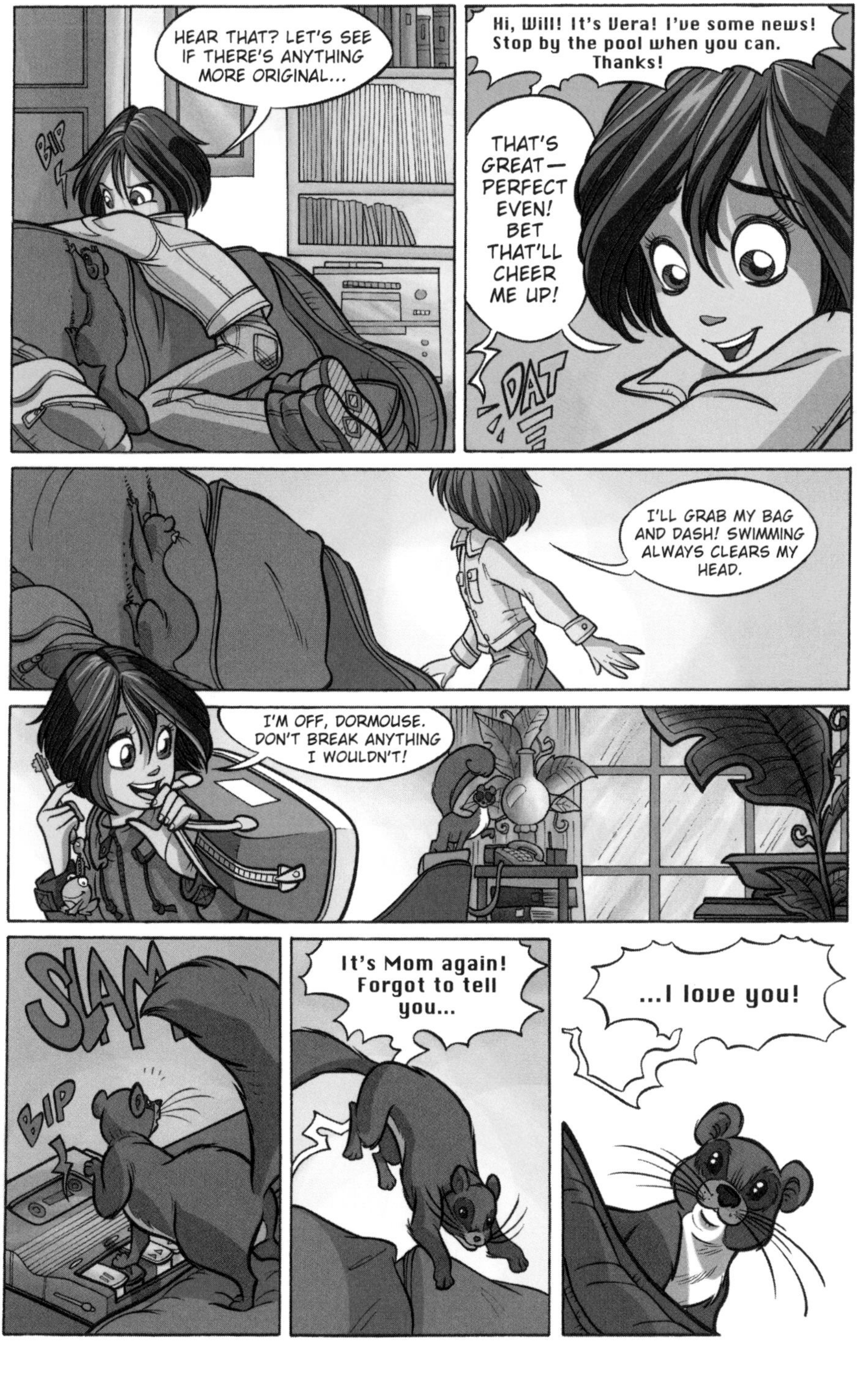
HEAR THAT? LET'S SEE IF THERE'S ANYTHING MORE ORIGINAL...
BIP
Hi, Will! It's Vera! I've some news! Stop by the pool when you can. Thanks!
THAT'S GREAT—PERFECT EVEN! BET THAT'LL CHEER ME UP!
DAT
I'LL GRAB MY BAG AND DASH! SWIMMING ALWAYS CLEARS MY HEAD.
I'M OFF, DORMOUSE. DON'T BREAK ANYTHING I WOULDN'T!
SLAM
BIP
It's Mom again! Forgot to tell you...
...I love you!

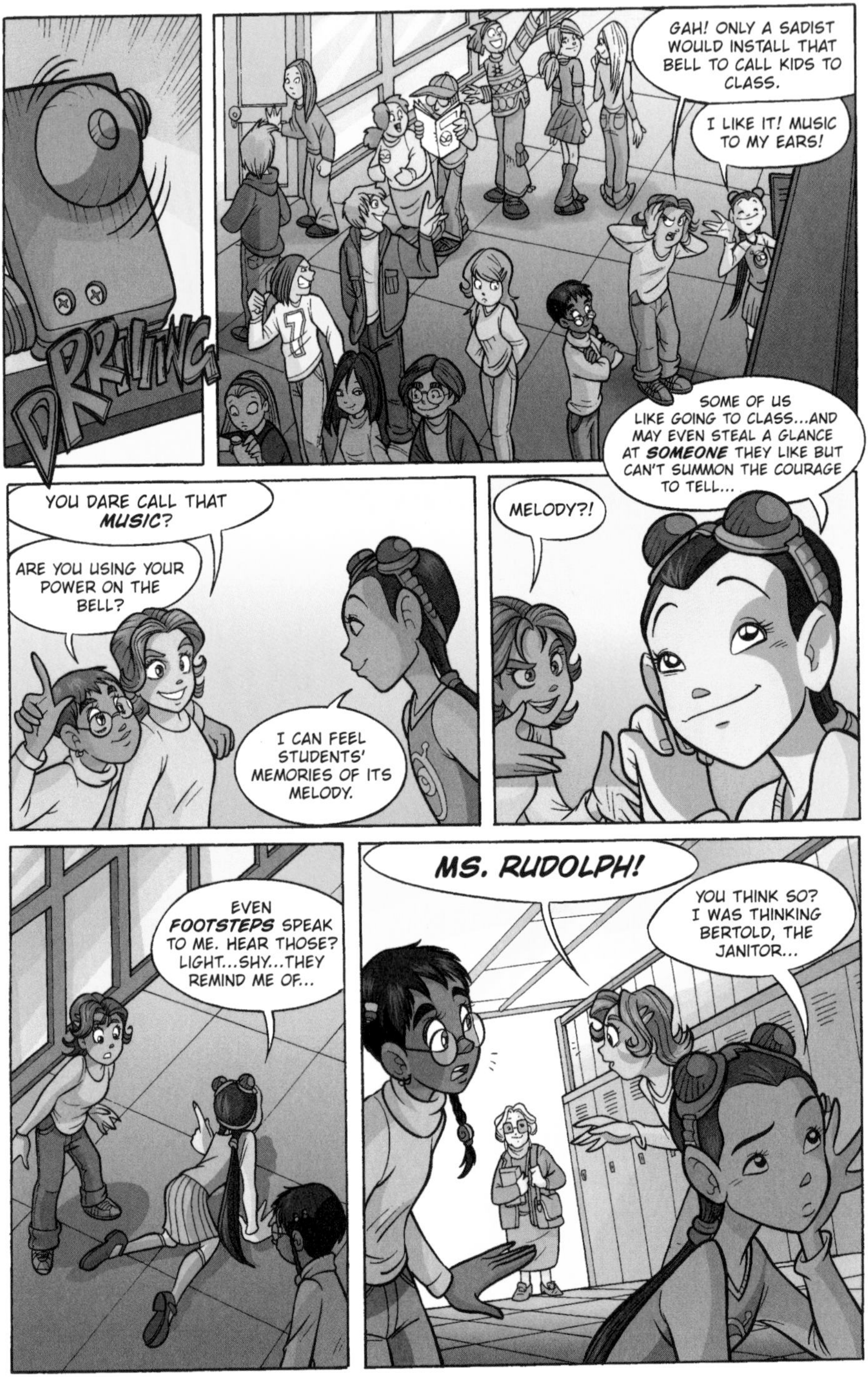
DRRIIIING
GAH! ONLY A SADIST WOULD INSTALL THAT BELL TO CALL KIDS TO CLASS.
I LIKE IT! MUSIC TO MY EARS!
SOME OF US LIKE GOING TO CLASS...AND MAY EVEN STEAL A GLANCE AT SOMEONE THEY LIKE BUT CAN'T SUMMON THE COURAGE TO TELL...
YOU DARE CALL THAT MUSIC?
ARE YOU USING YOUR POWER ON THE BELL?
I CAN FEEL STUDENTS' MEMORIES OF ITS MELODY.
MELODY?!
EVEN FOOTSTEPS SPEAK TO ME. HEAR THOSE? LIGHT...SHY...THEY REMIND ME OF...
MS. RUDOLPH!
YOU THINK SO? I WAS THINKING BERTOLD, THE JANITOR...

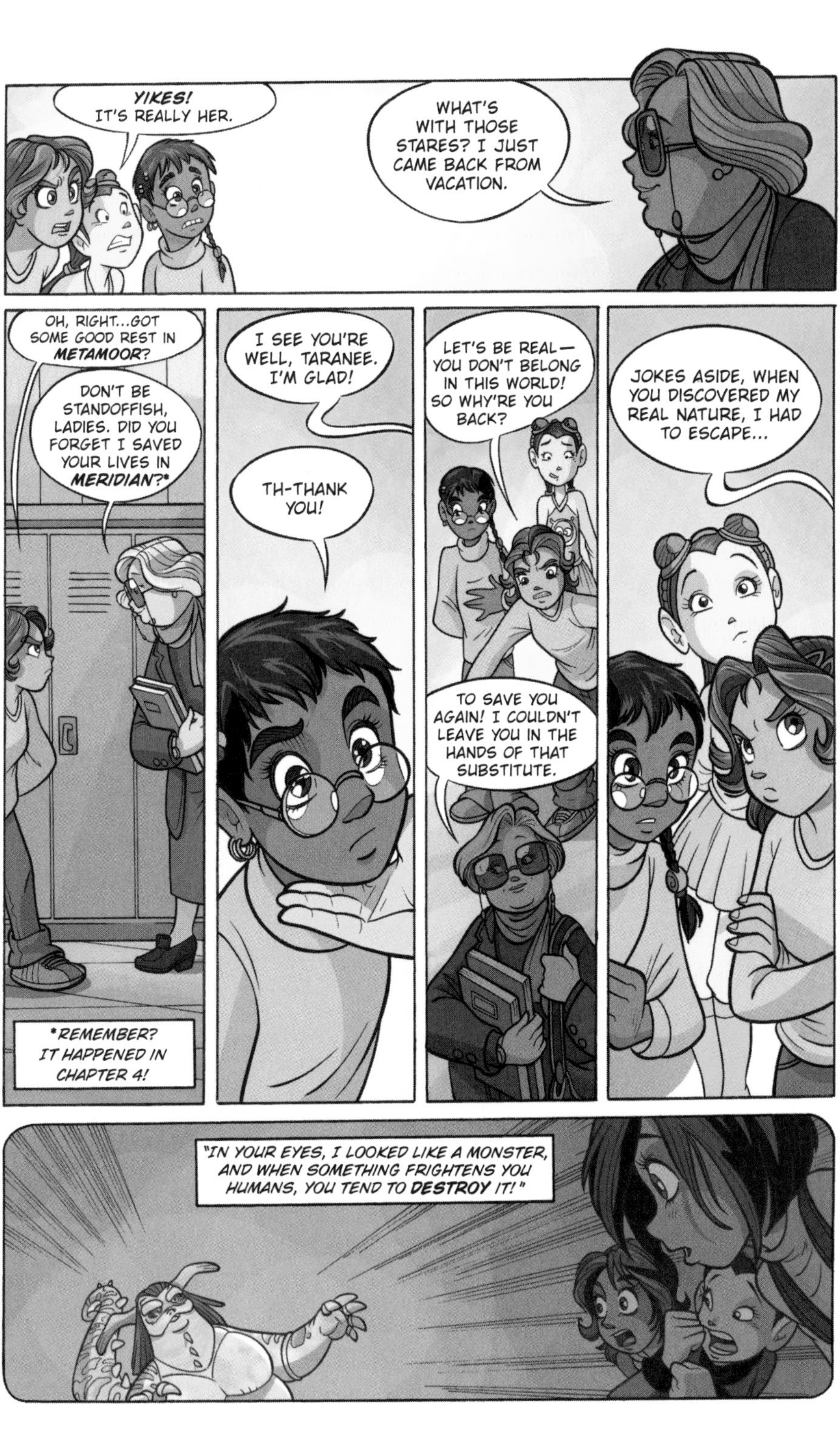
YIKES! IT'S REALLY HER.
WHAT'S WITH THOSE STARES? I JUST CAME BACK FROM VACATION.
OH, RIGHT...GOT SOME GOOD REST IN METAMOOR?
DON'T BE STANDOFFISH, LADIES. DID YOU FORGET I SAVED YOUR LIVES IN MERIDIAN?*
*REMEMBER? IT HAPPENED IN CHAPTER 4!
I SEE YOU'RE WELL, TARANEE. I'M GLAD!
TH-THANK YOU!
LET'S BE REAL—YOU DON'T BELONG IN THIS WORLD! SO WHY'RE YOU BACK?
TO SAVE YOU AGAIN! I COULDN'T LEAVE YOU IN THE HANDS OF THAT SUBSTITUTE.
JOKES ASIDE, WHEN YOU DISCOVERED MY REAL NATURE, I HAD TO ESCAPE...
"IN YOUR EYES, I LOOKED LIKE A MONSTER, AND WHEN SOMETHING FRIGHTENS YOU HUMANS, YOU TEND TO DESTROY IT!"

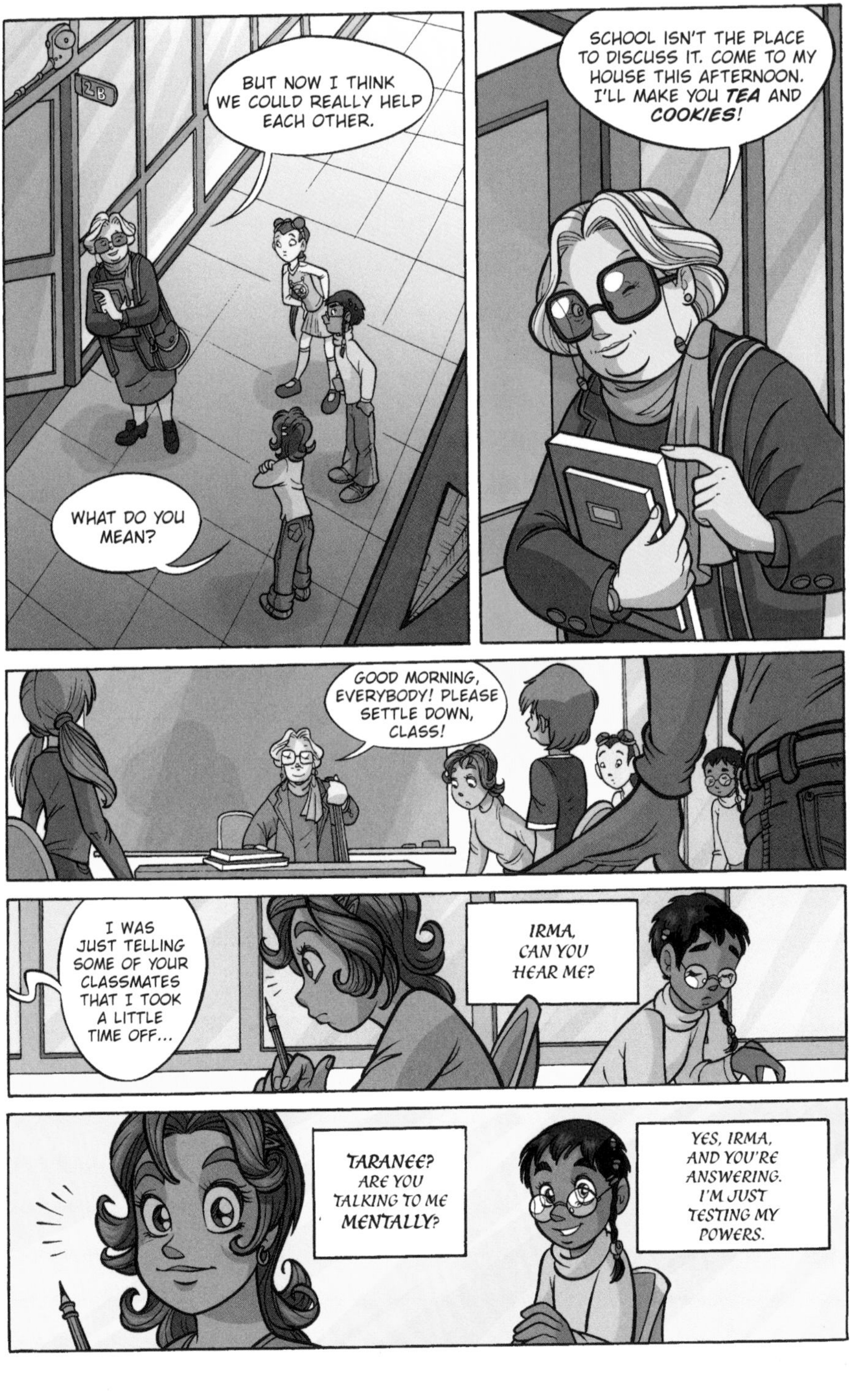
BUT NOW I THINK WE COULD REALLY HELP EACH OTHER.
WHAT DO YOU MEAN?
SCHOOL ISN'T THE PLACE TO DISCUSS IT. COME TO MY HOUSE THIS AFTERNOON. I'LL MAKE YOU TEA AND COOKIES!
GOOD MORNING, EVERYBODY! PLEASE SETTLE DOWN, CLASS!
I WAS JUST TELLING SOME OF YOUR CLASSMATES THAT I TOOK A LITTLE TIME OFF...
IRMA, CAN YOU HEAR ME?
TARANEE? ARE YOU TALKING TO ME MENTALLY?
YES, IRMA, AND YOU'RE ANSWERING. I'M JUST TESTING MY POWERS.

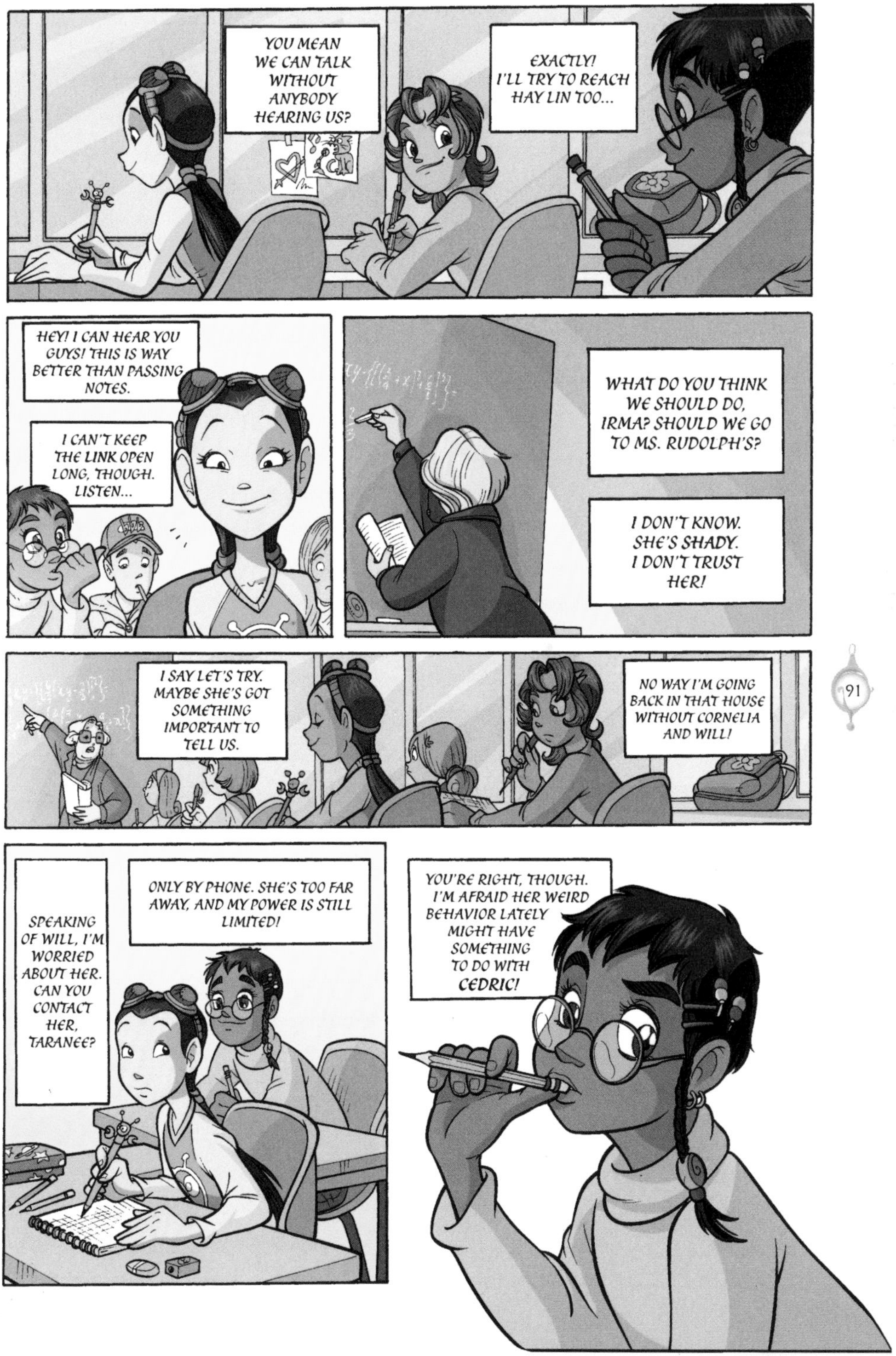
YOU MEAN WE CAN TALK WITHOUT ANYBODY HEARING US?
EXACTLY! I'LL TRY TO REACH HAY LIN TOO...
HEY! I CAN HEAR YOU GUYS! THIS IS WAY BETTER THAN PASSING NOTES.
I CAN'T KEEP THE LINK OPEN LONG, THOUGH. LISTEN...
WHAT DO YOU THINK WE SHOULD DO, IRMA? SHOULD WE GO TO MS. RUDOLPH'S?
I DON'T KNOW. SHE'S SHADY. I DON'T TRUST HER!
I SAY LET'S TRY. MAYBE SHE'S GOT SOMETHING IMPORTANT TO TELL US.
NO WAY I'M GOING BACK IN THAT HOUSE WITHOUT CORNELIA AND WILL!
SPEAKING OF WILL, I'M WORRIED ABOUT HER. CAN YOU CONTACT HER, TARANEE?
ONLY BY PHONE. SHE'S TOO FAR AWAY, AND MY POWER IS STILL LIMITED!
YOU'RE RIGHT, THOUGH. I'M AFRAID HER WEIRD BEHAVIOR LATELY MIGHT HAVE SOMETHING TO DO WITH CEDRIC!

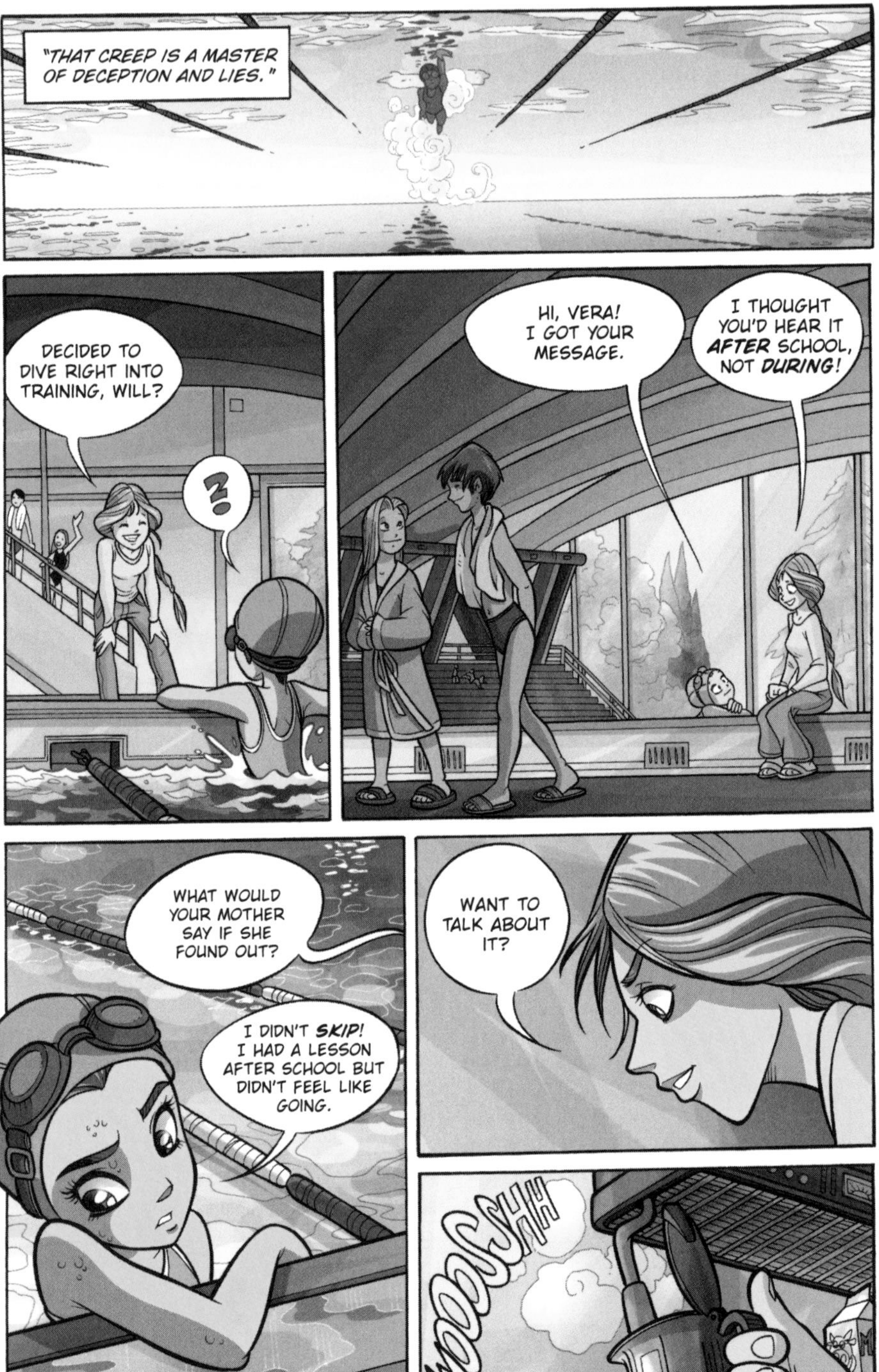
"THAT CREEP IS A MASTER OF DECEPTION AND LIES."
DECIDED TO DIVE RIGHT INTO TRAINING, WILL?
?
HI, VERA! I GOT YOUR MESSAGE.
I THOUGHT YOU'D HEAR IT AFTER SCHOOL, NOT DURING!
WHAT WOULD YOUR MOTHER SAY IF SHE FOUND OUT?
I DIDN'T SKIP! I HAD A LESSON AFTER SCHOOL BUT DIDN'T FEEL LIKE GOING.
WANT TO TALK ABOUT IT?
WOOOSSHH

92

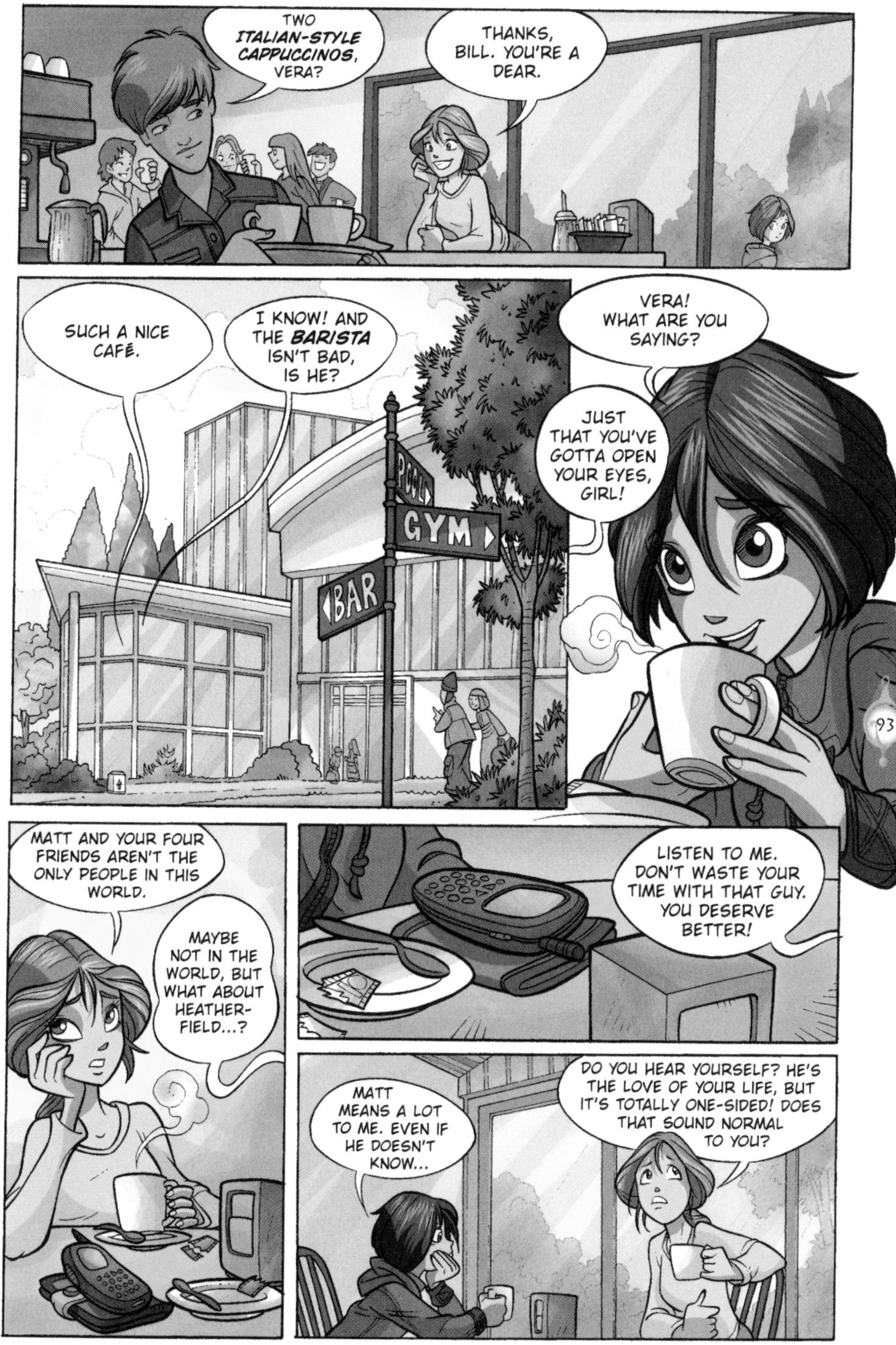
TWO *ITALIAN-STYLE CAPPUCCINOS*, VERA?
THANKS, BILL. YOU'RE A DEAR.
SUCH A NICE CAFÉ.
I KNOW! AND THE *BARISTA* ISN'T BAD, IS HE?
POOL
GYM
BAR
VERA! WHAT ARE YOU SAYING?
JUST THAT YOU'VE GOTTA OPEN YOUR EYES, GIRL!
MATT AND YOUR FOUR FRIENDS AREN'T THE ONLY PEOPLE IN THIS WORLD.
MAYBE NOT IN THE WORLD, BUT WHAT ABOUT HEATHER-FIELD...?
LISTEN TO ME. DON'T WASTE YOUR TIME WITH THAT GUY. YOU DESERVE BETTER!
MATT MEANS A LOT TO ME. EVEN IF HE DOESN'T KNOW...
DO YOU HEAR YOURSELF? HE'S THE LOVE OF YOUR LIFE, BUT IT'S TOTALLY ONE-SIDED! DOES THAT SOUND NORMAL TO YOU?

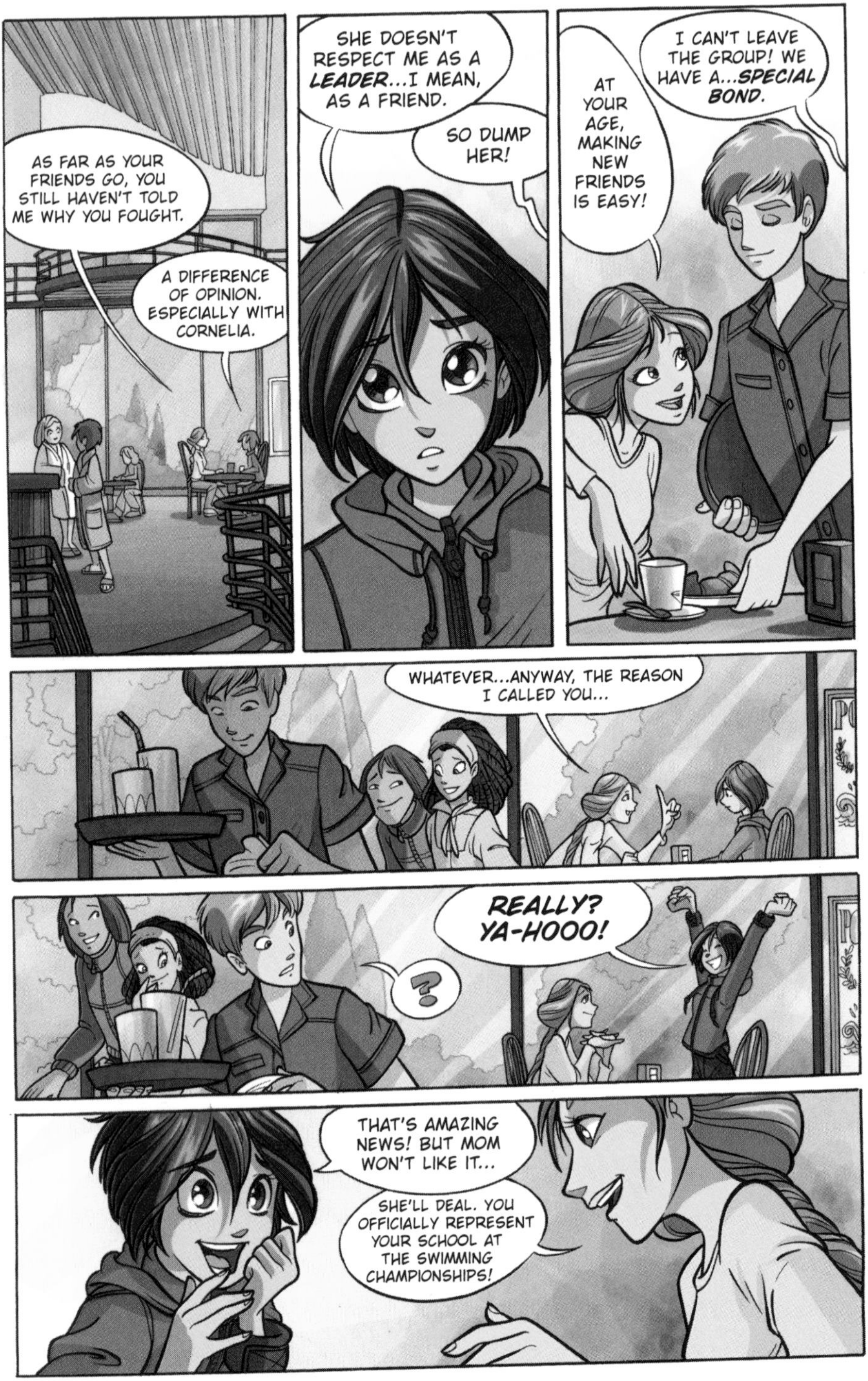
AS FAR AS YOUR FRIENDS GO, YOU STILL HAVEN'T TOLD ME WHY YOU FOUGHT.
A DIFFERENCE OF OPINION. ESPECIALLY WITH CORNELIA.
SHE DOESN'T RESPECT ME AS A LEADER...I MEAN, AS A FRIEND.
SO DUMP HER!
AT YOUR AGE, MAKING NEW FRIENDS IS EASY!
I CAN'T LEAVE THE GROUP! WE HAVE A...SPECIAL BOND.
WHATEVER...ANYWAY, THE REASON I CALLED YOU...
REALLY? YA-HOOO!
?
THAT'S AMAZING NEWS! BUT MOM WON'T LIKE IT...
SHE'LL DEAL. YOU OFFICIALLY REPRESENT YOUR SCHOOL AT THE SWIMMING CHAMPIONSHIPS!

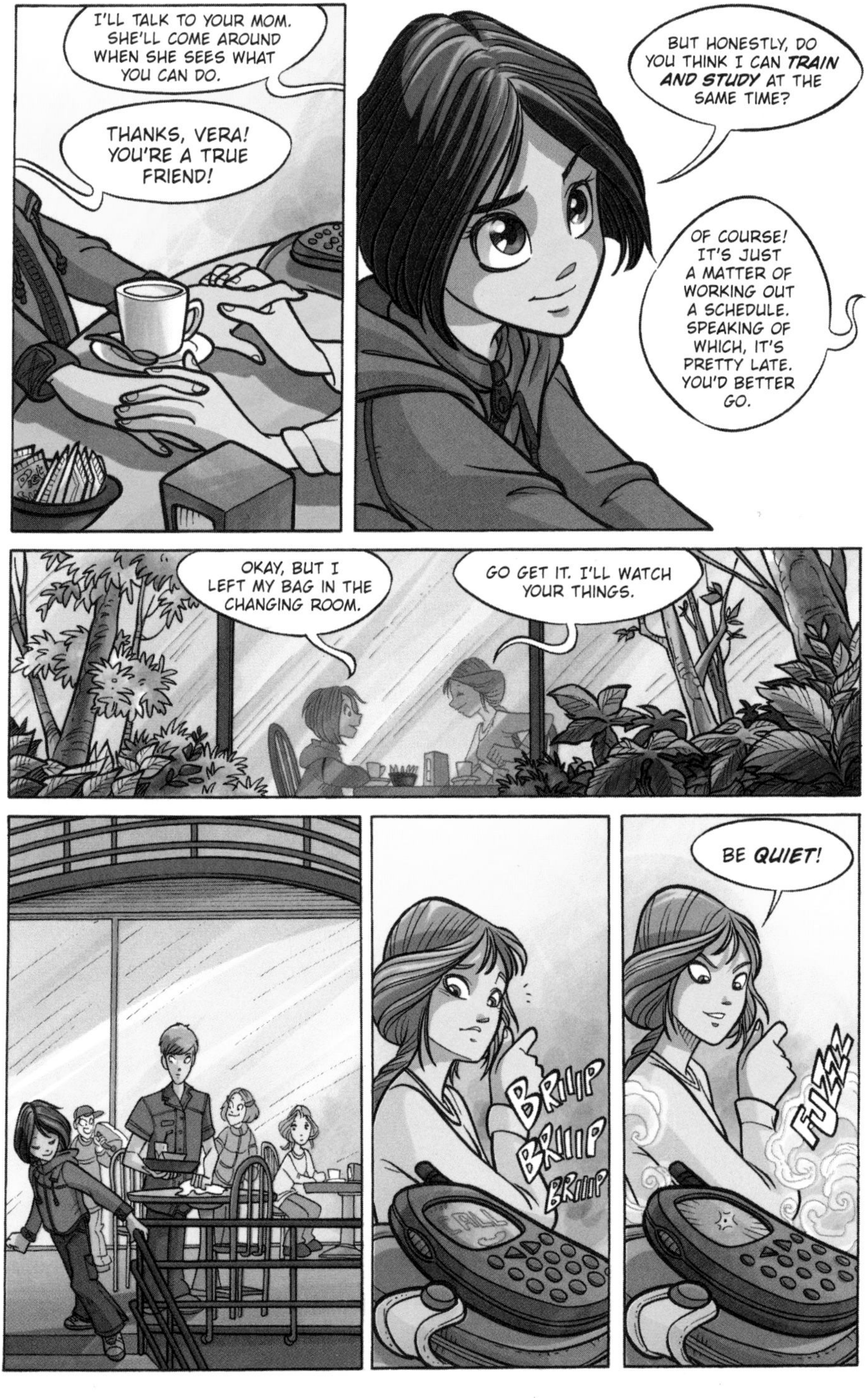
I'LL TALK TO YOUR MOM. SHE'LL COME AROUND WHEN SHE SEES WHAT YOU CAN DO.
THANKS, VERA! YOU'RE A TRUE FRIEND!
BUT HONESTLY, DO YOU THINK I CAN TRAIN AND STUDY AT THE SAME TIME?
OF COURSE! IT'S JUST A MATTER OF WORKING OUT A SCHEDULE. SPEAKING OF WHICH, IT'S PRETTY LATE. YOU'D BETTER GO.
OKAY, BUT I LEFT MY BAG IN THE CHANGING ROOM.
GO GET IT. I'LL WATCH YOUR THINGS.
BRIIIP
BRIIIP
BRIIIP
BE QUIET!
FUZZZ

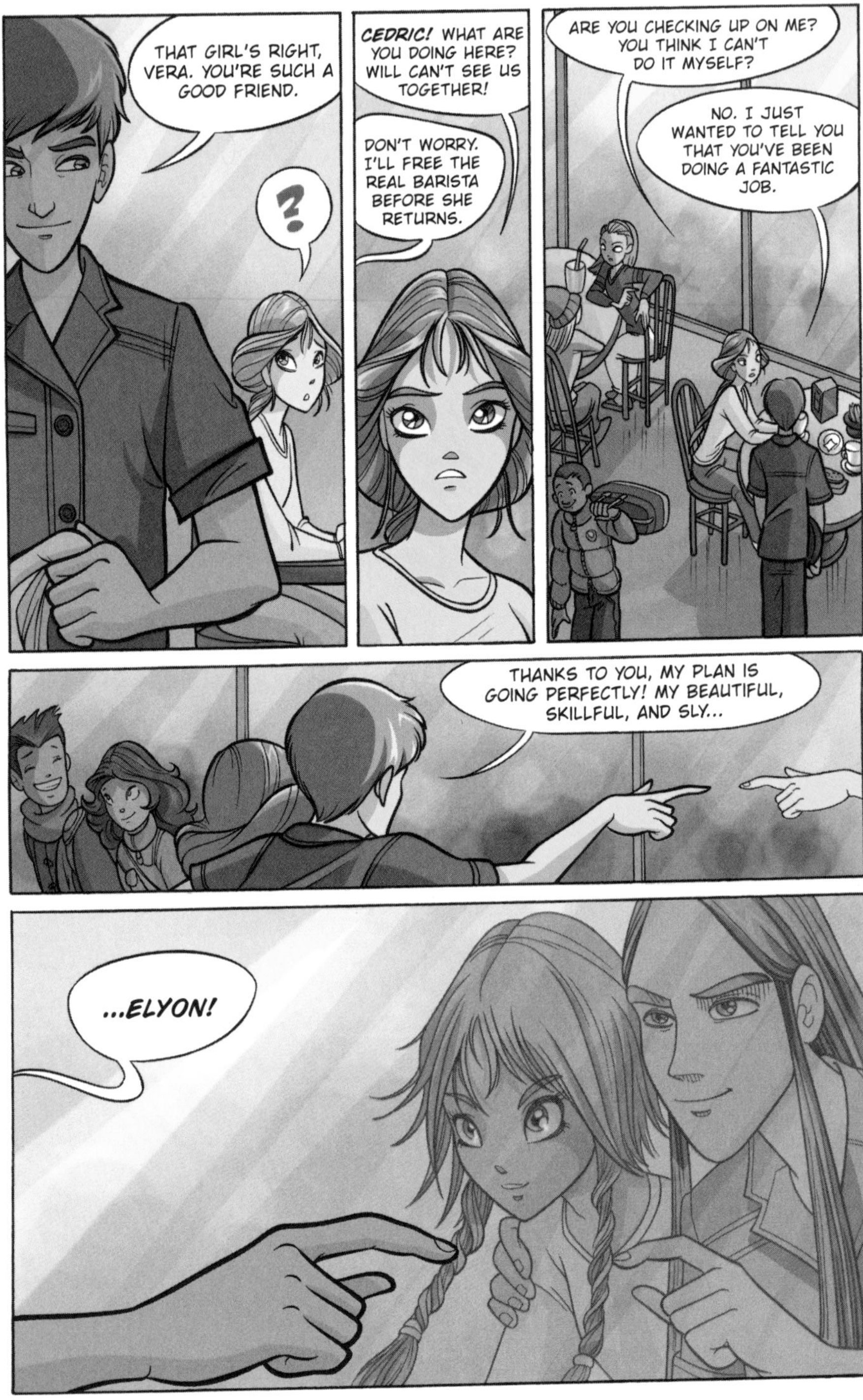
THAT GIRL'S RIGHT, VERA. YOU'RE SUCH A GOOD FRIEND.
?
CEDRIC! WHAT ARE YOU DOING HERE? WILL CAN'T SEE US TOGETHER!
DON'T WORRY. I'LL FREE THE REAL BARISTA BEFORE SHE RETURNS.
ARE YOU CHECKING UP ON ME? YOU THINK I CAN'T DO IT MYSELF?
NO. I JUST WANTED TO TELL YOU THAT YOU'VE BEEN DOING A FANTASTIC JOB.
THANKS TO YOU, MY PLAN IS GOING PERFECTLY! MY BEAUTIFUL, SKILLFUL, AND SLY...
...ELYON!

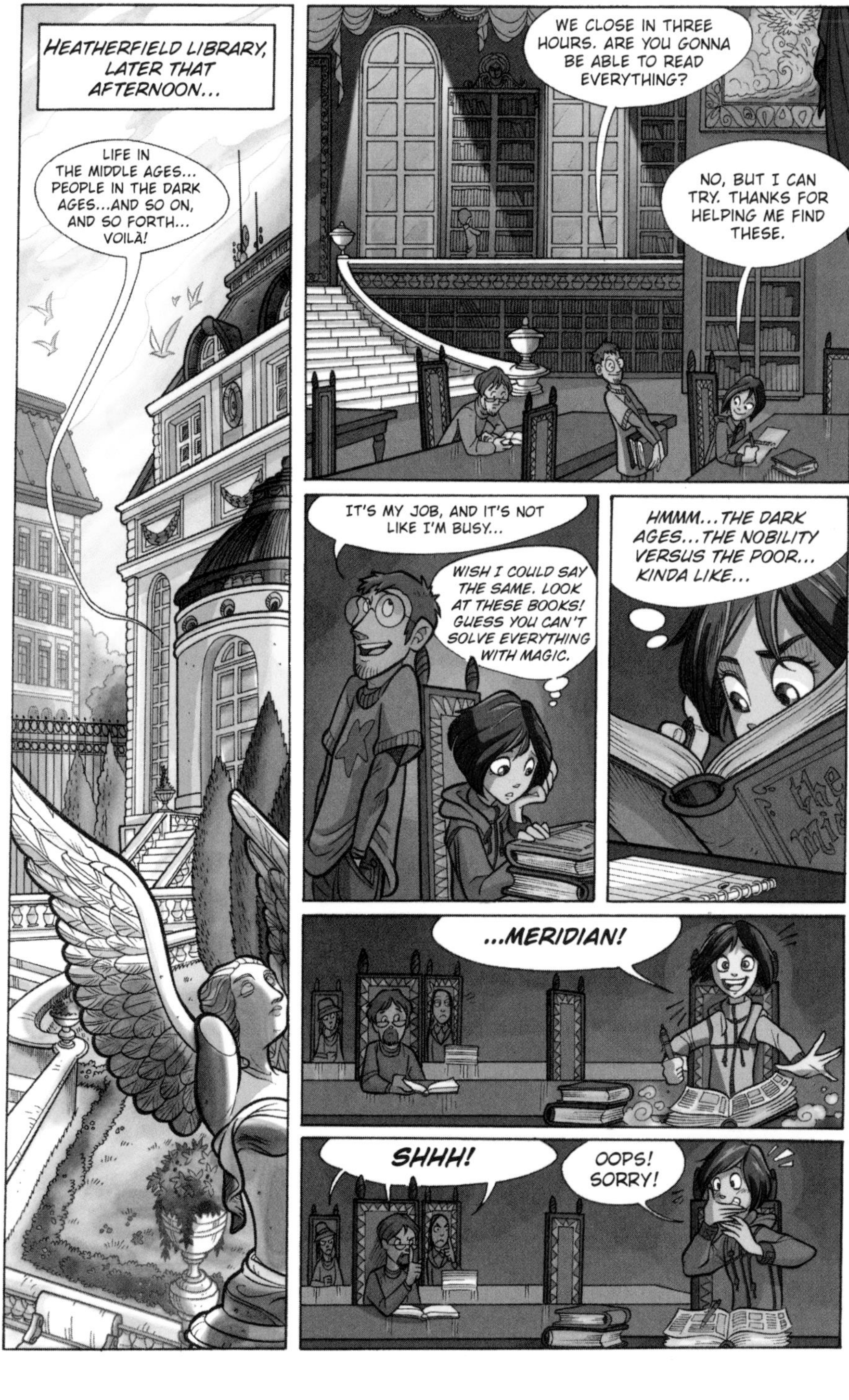
HEATHERFIELD LIBRARY, LATER THAT AFTERNOON...
LIFE IN THE MIDDLE AGES... PEOPLE IN THE DARK AGES...AND SO ON, AND SO FORTH... VOILÀ!
WE CLOSE IN THREE HOURS. ARE YOU GONNA BE ABLE TO READ EVERYTHING?
NO, BUT I CAN TRY. THANKS FOR HELPING ME FIND THESE.
IT'S MY JOB, AND IT'S NOT LIKE I'M BUSY...
WISH I COULD SAY THE SAME. LOOK AT THESE BOOKS! GUESS YOU CAN'T SOLVE EVERYTHING WITH MAGIC.
HMMM...THE DARK AGES...THE NOBILITY VERSUS THE POOR... KINDA LIKE...
...MERIDIAN!
SHHH!
OOPS! SORRY!

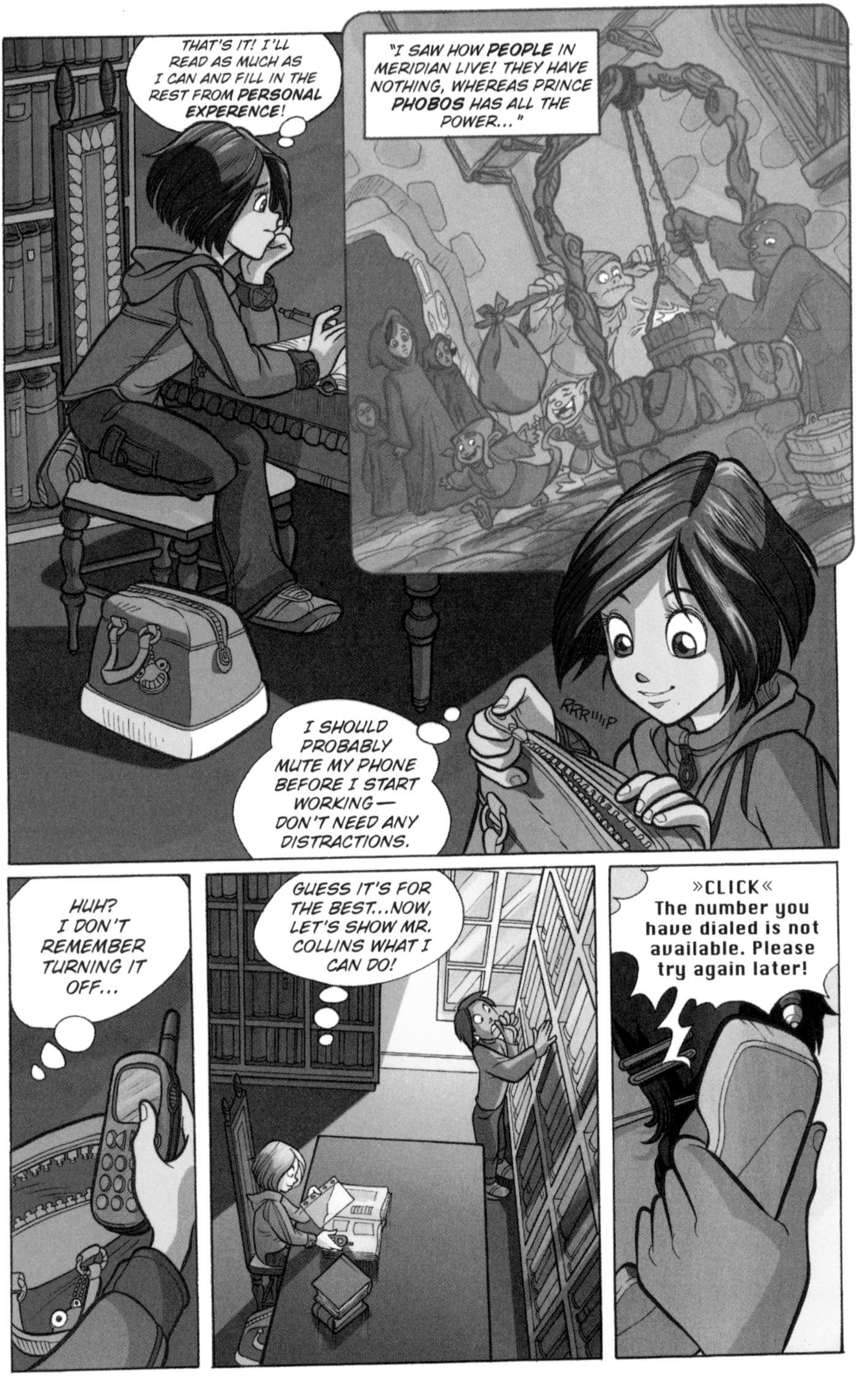
THAT'S IT! I'LL READ AS MUCH AS I CAN AND FILL IN THE REST FROM PERSONAL EXPERENCE!
"I SAW HOW PEOPLE IN MERIDIAN LIVE! THEY HAVE NOTHING, WHEREAS PRINCE PHOBOS HAS ALL THE POWER..."
RRRIIIIP
I SHOULD PROBABLY MUTE MY PHONE BEFORE I START WORKING—DON'T NEED ANY DISTRACTIONS.
HUH? I DON'T REMEMBER TURNING IT OFF...
GUESS IT'S FOR THE BEST...NOW, LET'S SHOW MR. COLLINS WHAT I CAN DO!
»CLICK«
The number you have dialed is not available. Please try again later!

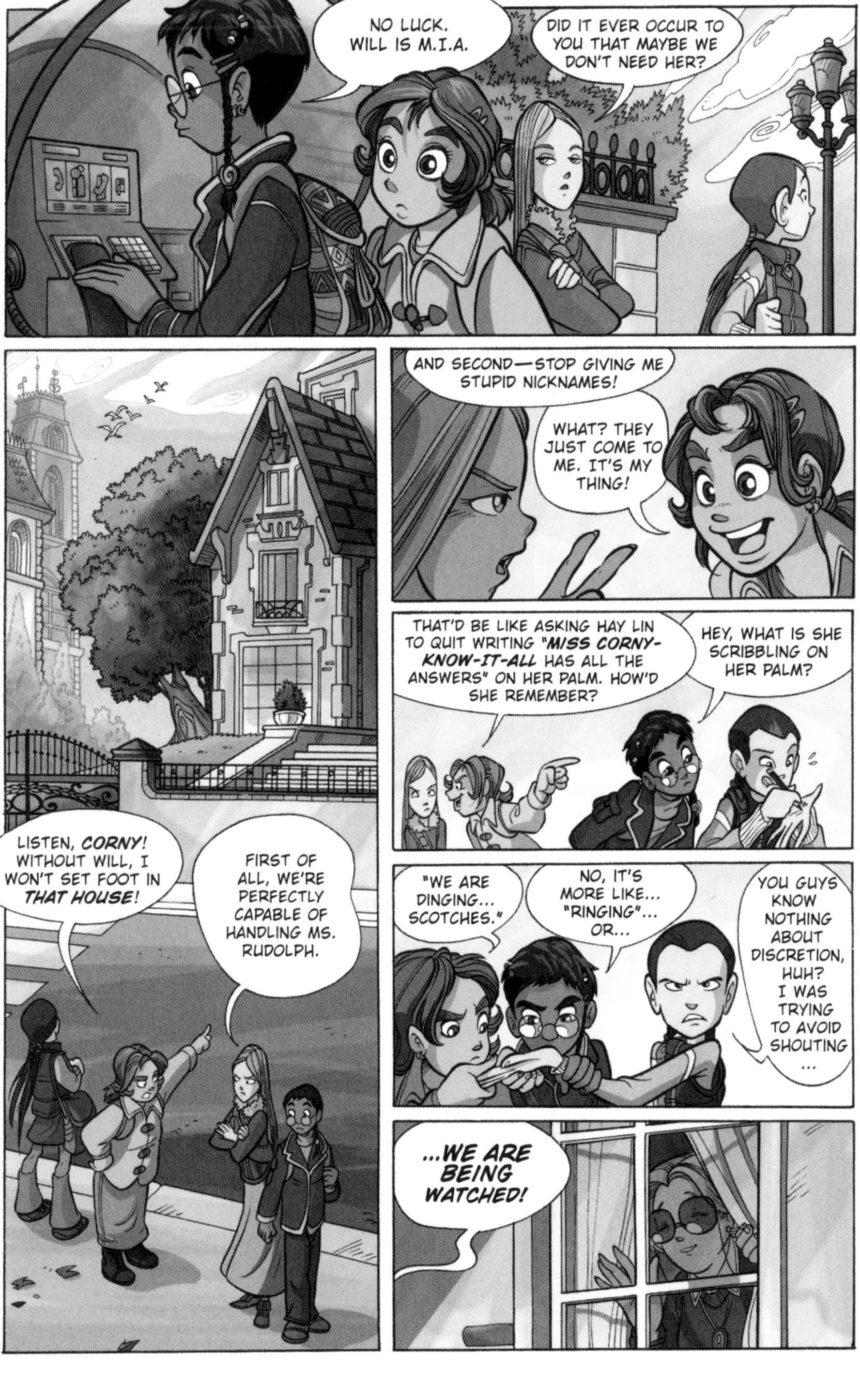
NO LUCK. WILL IS M.I.A.
DID IT EVER OCCUR TO YOU THAT MAYBE WE DON'T NEED HER?
LISTEN, CORNY! WITHOUT WILL, I WON'T SET FOOT IN THAT HOUSE!
FIRST OF ALL, WE'RE PERFECTLY CAPABLE OF HANDLING MS. RUDOLPH.
AND SECOND—STOP GIVING ME STUPID NICKNAMES!
WHAT? THEY JUST COME TO ME. IT'S MY THING!
THAT'D BE LIKE ASKING HAY LIN TO QUIT WRITING "MISS CORNY-KNOW-IT-ALL HAS ALL THE ANSWERS" ON HER PALM. HOW'D SHE REMEMBER?
HEY, WHAT IS SHE SCRIBBLING ON HER PALM?
"WE ARE DINGING... SCOTCHES."
NO, IT'S MORE LIKE... "RINGING"... OR...
YOU GUYS KNOW NOTHING ABOUT DISCRETION, HUH? I WAS TRYING TO AVOID SHOUTING ...
...WE ARE BEING WATCHED!

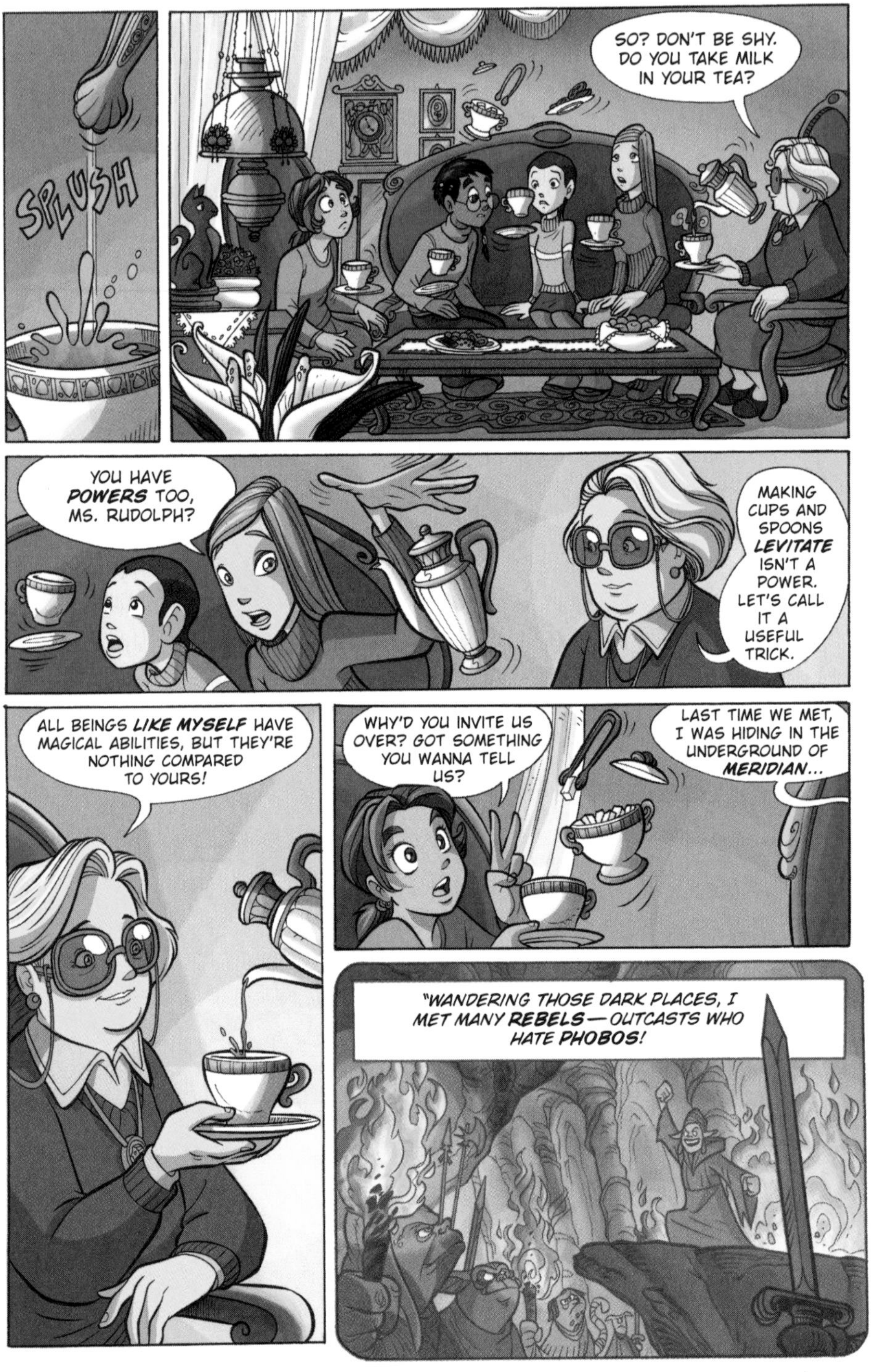
SPLUSH
SO? DON'T BE SHY. DO YOU TAKE MILK IN YOUR TEA?
YOU HAVE POWERS TOO, MS. RUDOLPH?
MAKING CUPS AND SPOONS LEVITATE ISN'T A POWER. LET'S CALL IT A USEFUL TRICK.
ALL BEINGS LIKE MYSELF HAVE MAGICAL ABILITIES, BUT THEY'RE NOTHING COMPARED TO YOURS!
WHY'D YOU INVITE US OVER? GOT SOMETHING YOU WANNA TELL US?
LAST TIME WE MET, I WAS HIDING IN THE UNDERGROUND OF MERIDIAN...
"WANDERING THOSE DARK PLACES, I MET MANY REBELS—OUTCASTS WHO HATE PHOBOS!

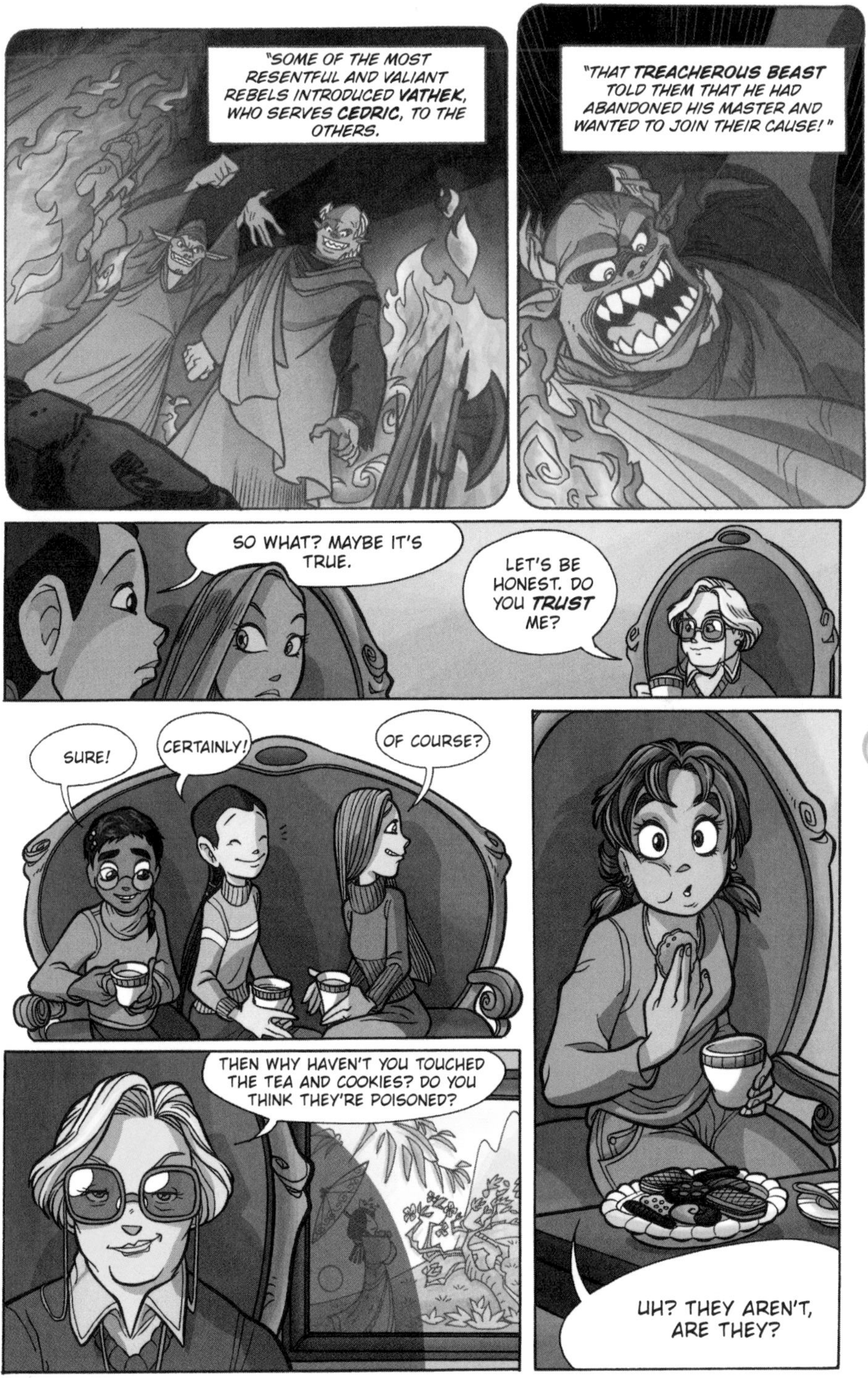
"SOME OF THE MOST RESENTFUL AND VALIANT REBELS INTRODUCED VATHEK, WHO SERVES CEDRIC, TO THE OTHERS.
"THAT TREACHEROUS BEAST TOLD THEM THAT HE HAD ABANDONED HIS MASTER AND WANTED TO JOIN THEIR CAUSE!"
SO WHAT? MAYBE IT'S TRUE.
LET'S BE HONEST. DO YOU TRUST ME?
SURE!
CERTAINLY!
OF COURSE?
THEN WHY HAVEN'T YOU TOUCHED THE TEA AND COOKIES? DO YOU THINK THEY'RE POISONED?
UH? THEY AREN'T, ARE THEY?

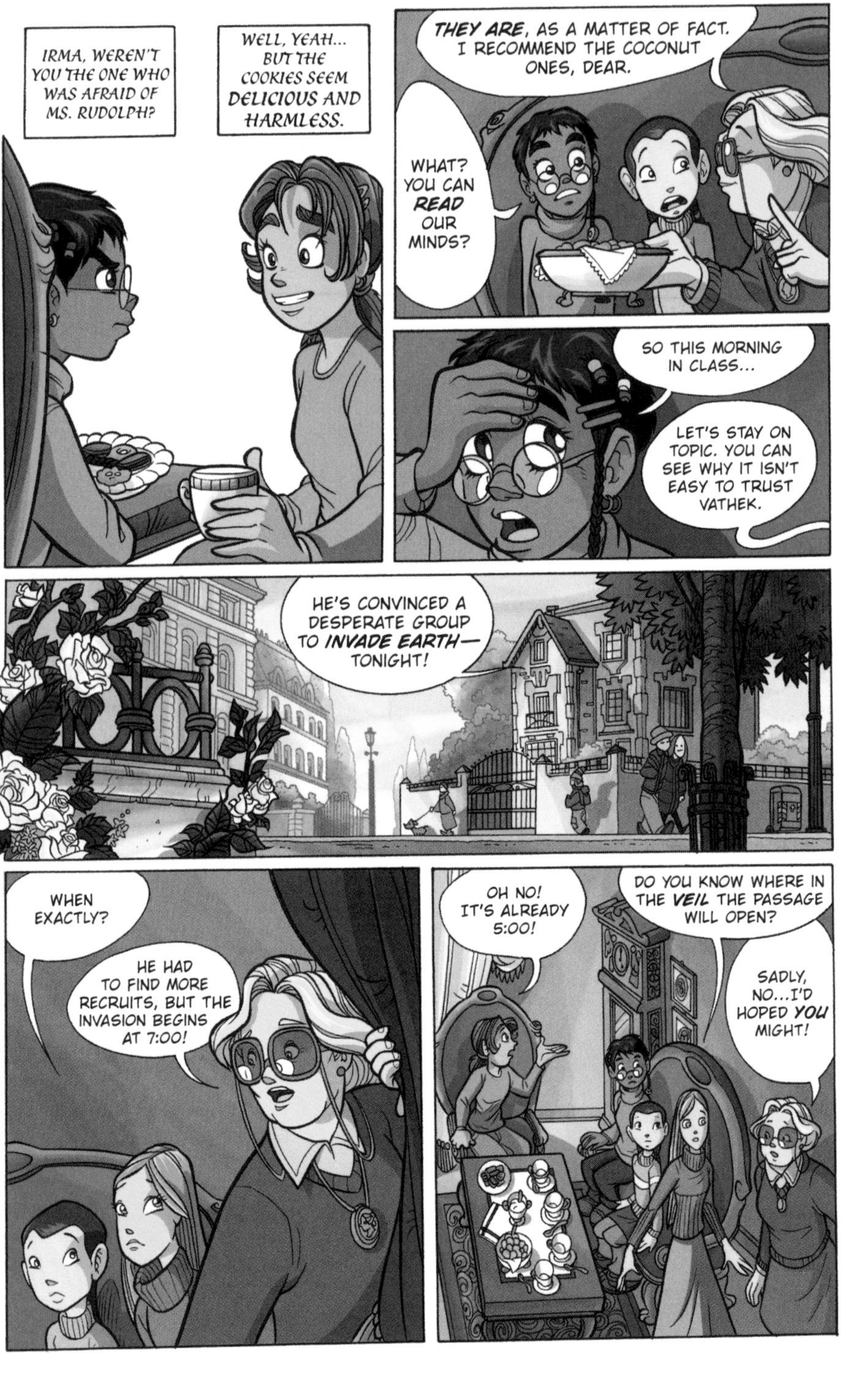
IRMA, WEREN'T YOU THE ONE WHO WAS AFRAID OF MS. RUDOLPH?
WELL, YEAH... BUT THE COOKIES SEEM DELICIOUS AND HARMLESS.
THEY ARE, AS A MATTER OF FACT. I RECOMMEND THE COCONUT ONES, DEAR.
WHAT? YOU CAN READ OUR MINDS?
SO THIS MORNING IN CLASS...
LET'S STAY ON TOPIC. YOU CAN SEE WHY IT ISN'T EASY TO TRUST VATHEK.
HE'S CONVINCED A DESPERATE GROUP TO INVADE EARTH—TONIGHT!
WHEN EXACTLY?
HE HAD TO FIND MORE RECRUITS, BUT THE INVASION BEGINS AT 7:00!
OH NO! IT'S ALREADY 5:00!
DO YOU KNOW WHERE IN THE VEIL THE PASSAGE WILL OPEN?
SADLY, NO...I'D HOPED YOU MIGHT!

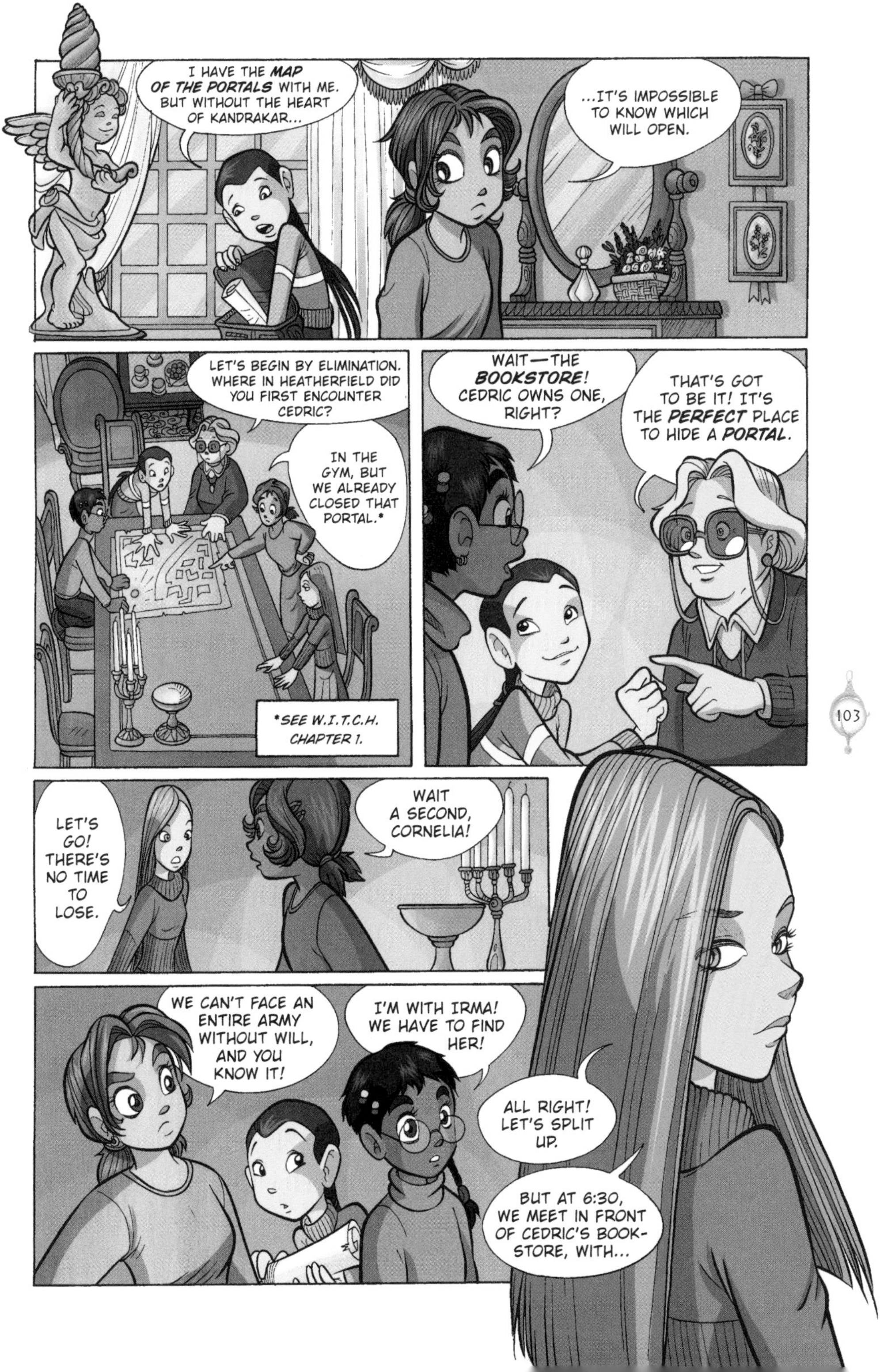
I HAVE THE MAP OF THE PORTALS WITH ME. BUT WITHOUT THE HEART OF KANDRAKAR...
...IT'S IMPOSSIBLE TO KNOW WHICH WILL OPEN.
LET'S BEGIN BY ELIMINATION. WHERE IN HEATHERFIELD DID YOU FIRST ENCOUNTER CEDRIC?
IN THE GYM, BUT WE ALREADY CLOSED THAT PORTAL.*
*SEE W.I.T.C.H. CHAPTER 1.
WAIT—THE BOOKSTORE! CEDRIC OWNS ONE, RIGHT?
THAT'S GOT TO BE IT! IT'S THE PERFECT PLACE TO HIDE A PORTAL.
LET'S GO! THERE'S NO TIME TO LOSE.
WAIT A SECOND, CORNELIA!
WE CAN'T FACE AN ENTIRE ARMY WITHOUT WILL, AND YOU KNOW IT!
I'M WITH IRMA! WE HAVE TO FIND HER!
ALL RIGHT! LET'S SPLIT UP.
BUT AT 6:30, WE MEET IN FRONT OF CEDRIC'S BOOKSTORE, WITH...

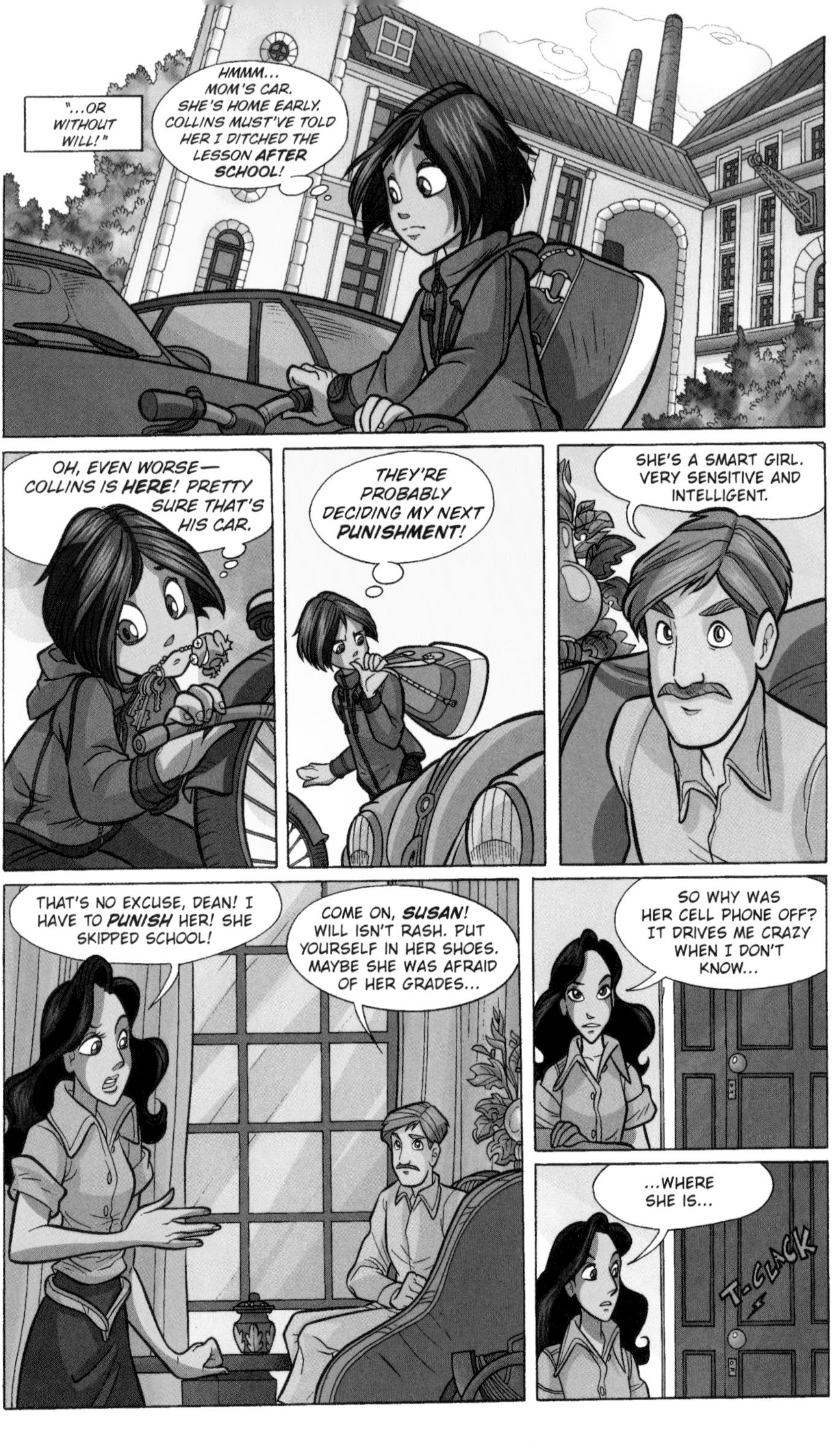
"...OR WITHOUT WILL!"
HMMM... MOM'S CAR. SHE'S HOME EARLY. COLLINS MUST'VE TOLD HER I DITCHED THE LESSON AFTER SCHOOL!
OH, EVEN WORSE— COLLINS IS HERE! PRETTY SURE THAT'S HIS CAR.
THEY'RE PROBABLY DECIDING MY NEXT PUNISHMENT!
SHE'S A SMART GIRL. VERY SENSITIVE AND INTELLIGENT.
THAT'S NO EXCUSE, DEAN! I HAVE TO PUNISH HER! SHE SKIPPED SCHOOL!
COME ON, SUSAN! WILL ISN'T RASH. PUT YOURSELF IN HER SHOES. MAYBE SHE WAS AFRAID OF HER GRADES...
SO WHY WAS HER CELL PHONE OFF? IT DRIVES ME CRAZY WHEN I DON'T KNOW...
...WHERE SHE IS...
T-CLACK

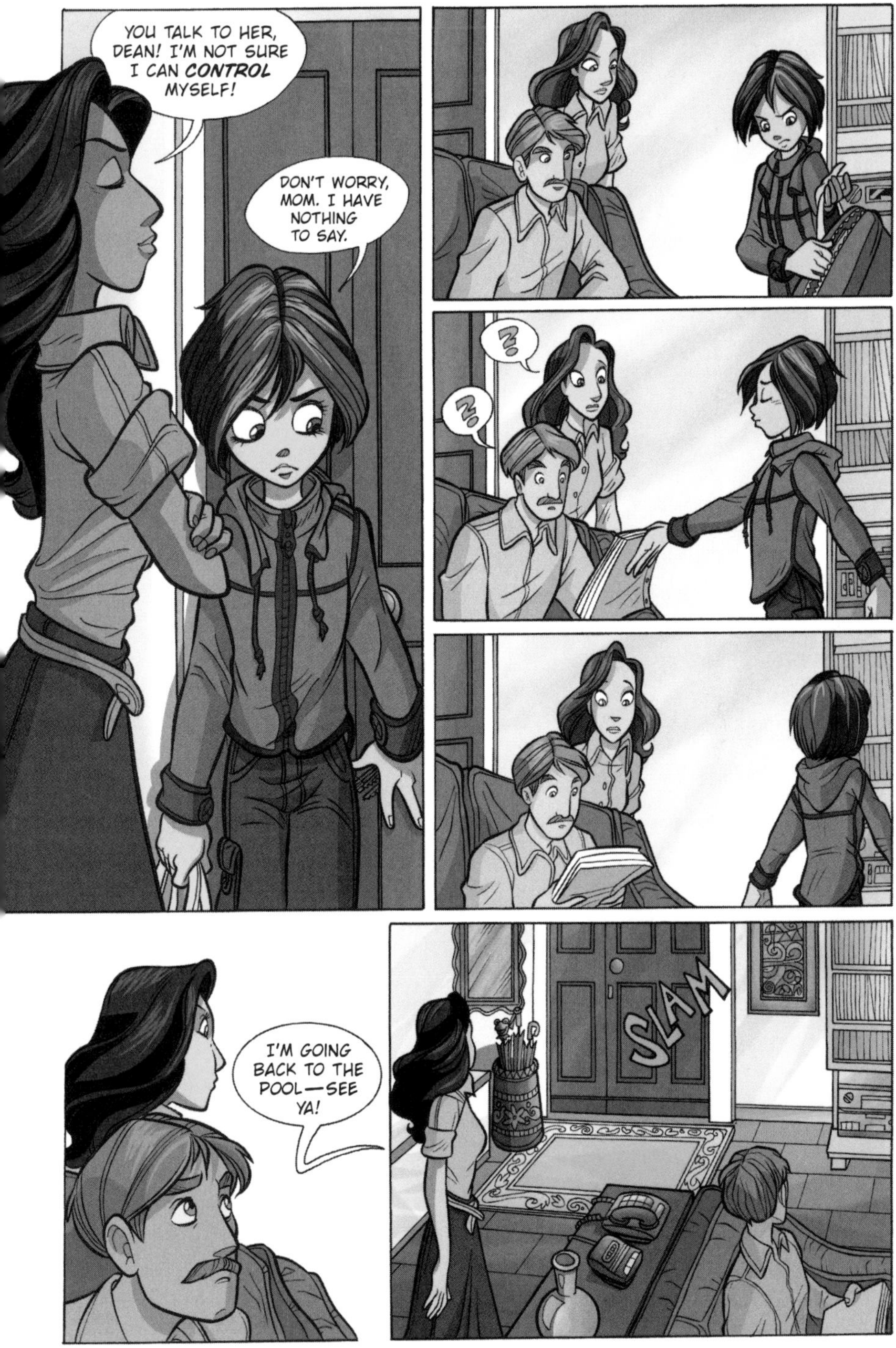
YOU TALK TO HER, DEAN! I'M NOT SURE I CAN **CONTROL** MYSELF!
DON'T WORRY, MOM. I HAVE NOTHING TO SAY.
?
?
I'M GOING BACK TO THE POOL—SEE YA!
SLAM

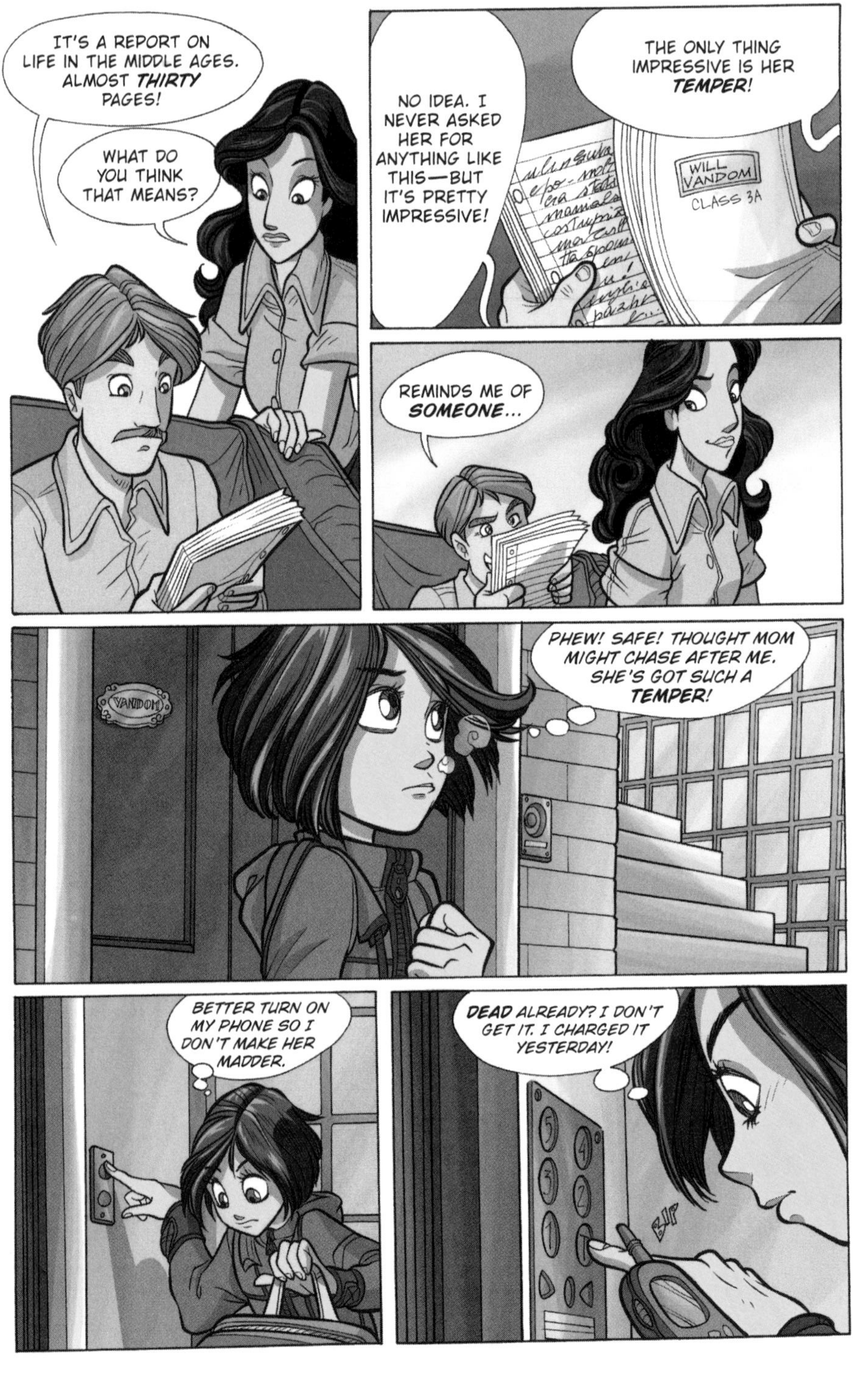
IT'S A REPORT ON LIFE IN THE MIDDLE AGES. ALMOST *THIRTY* PAGES!
WHAT DO YOU THINK THAT MEANS?
NO IDEA. I NEVER ASKED HER FOR ANYTHING LIKE THIS—BUT IT'S PRETTY IMPRESSIVE!
THE ONLY THING IMPRESSIVE IS HER *TEMPER*!
WILL VANDOM
CLASS 3A
REMINDS ME OF *SOMEONE*...
VANDOM
PHEW! SAFE! THOUGHT MOM MIGHT CHASE AFTER ME. SHE'S GOT SUCH A *TEMPER*!
BETTER TURN ON MY PHONE SO I DON'T MAKE HER MADDER.
DEAD ALREADY? I DON'T GET IT. I CHARGED IT YESTERDAY!
BIP

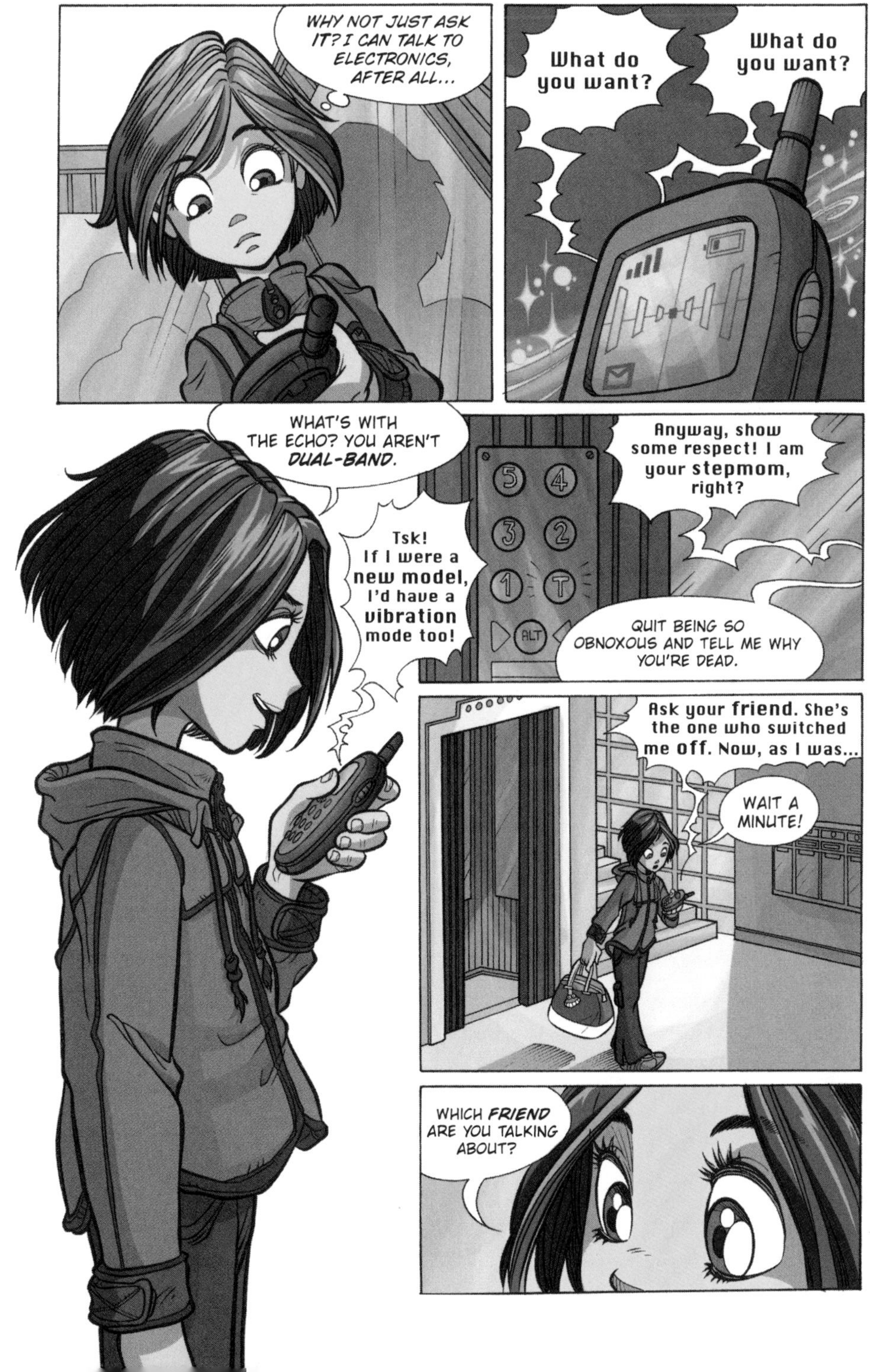
WHY NOT JUST ASK IT? I CAN TALK TO ELECTRONICS, AFTER ALL...
What do you want?
What do you want?
WHAT'S WITH THE ECHO? YOU AREN'T DUAL-BAND.
Tsk! If I were a new model, I'd have a vibration mode too!
Anyway, show some respect! I am your stepmom, right?
QUIT BEING SO OBNOXIOUS AND TELL ME WHY YOU'RE DEAD.
Ask your friend. She's the one who switched me off. Now, as I was...
WAIT A MINUTE!
WHICH FRIEND ARE YOU TALKING ABOUT?

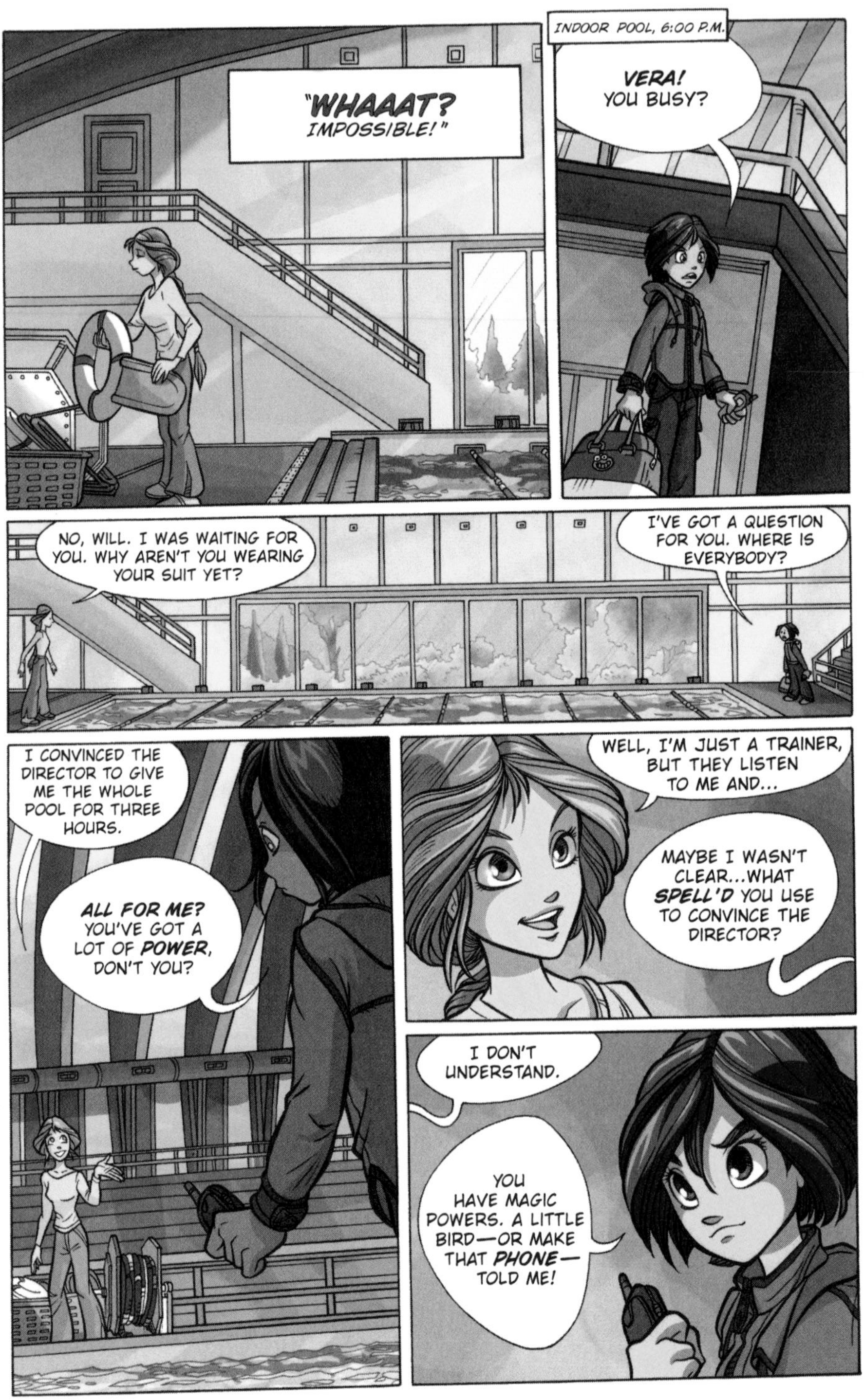

"WHAAAT? IMPOSSIBLE!"
INDOOR POOL, 6:00 P.M.
VERA! YOU BUSY?
NO, WILL. I WAS WAITING FOR YOU. WHY AREN'T YOU WEARING YOUR SUIT YET?
I'VE GOT A QUESTION FOR YOU. WHERE IS EVERYBODY?
I CONVINCED THE DIRECTOR TO GIVE ME THE WHOLE POOL FOR THREE HOURS.
ALL FOR ME? YOU'VE GOT A LOT OF POWER, DON'T YOU?
WELL, I'M JUST A TRAINER, BUT THEY LISTEN TO ME AND...
MAYBE I WASN'T CLEAR...WHAT SPELL'D YOU USE TO CONVINCE THE DIRECTOR?
I DON'T UNDERSTAND.
YOU HAVE MAGIC POWERS. A LITTLE BIRD—OR MAKE THAT PHONE—TOLD ME!

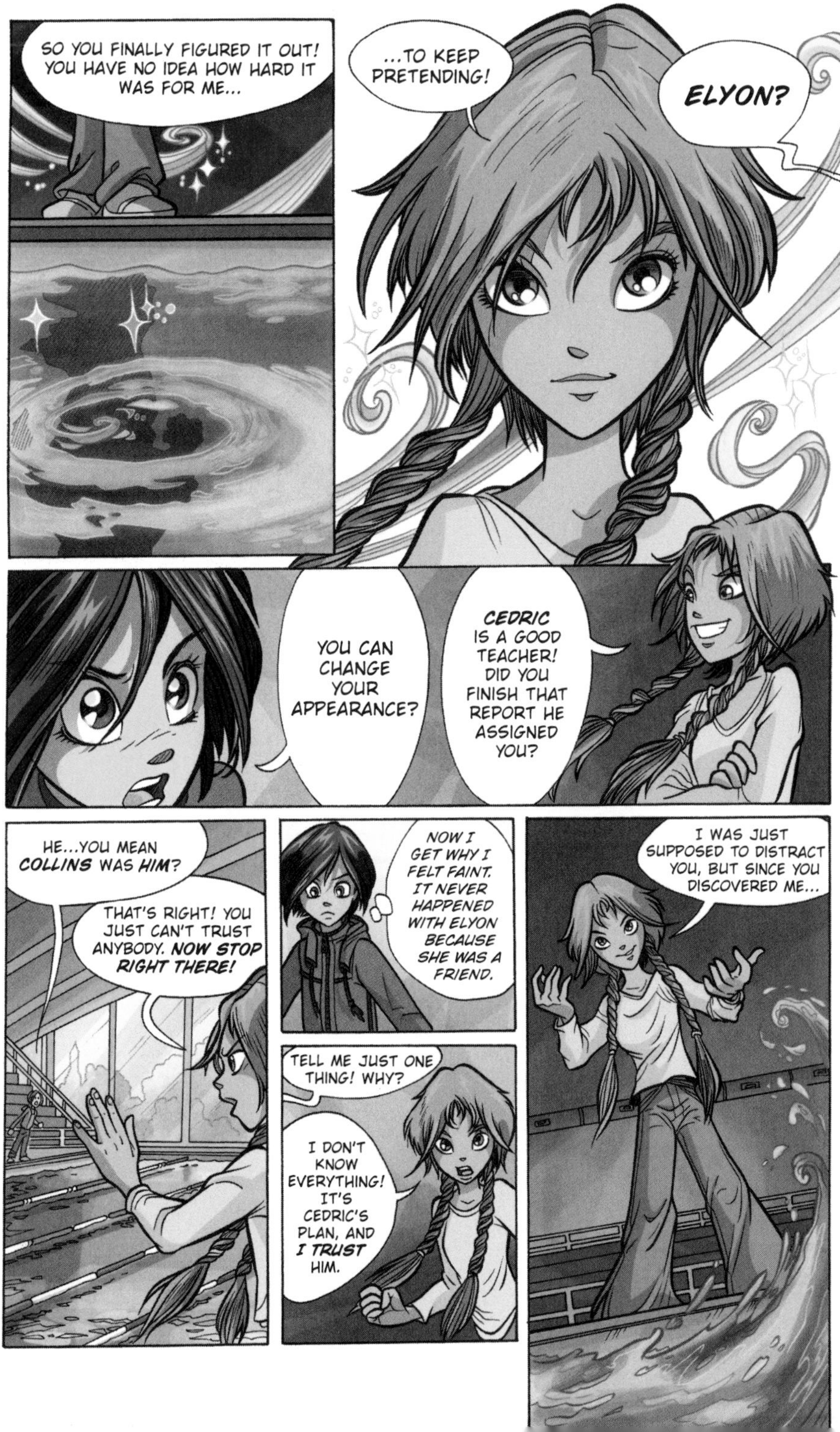
SO YOU FINALLY FIGURED IT OUT! YOU HAVE NO IDEA HOW HARD IT WAS FOR ME...
...TO KEEP PRETENDING!
ELYON?
YOU CAN CHANGE YOUR APPEARANCE?
CEDRIC IS A GOOD TEACHER! DID YOU FINISH THAT REPORT HE ASSIGNED YOU?
HE...YOU MEAN COLLINS WAS HIM?
THAT'S RIGHT! YOU JUST CAN'T TRUST ANYBODY. NOW STOP RIGHT THERE!
NOW I GET WHY I FELT FAINT. IT NEVER HAPPENED WITH ELYON BECAUSE SHE WAS A FRIEND.
TELL ME JUST ONE THING! WHY?
I DON'T KNOW EVERYTHING! IT'S CEDRIC'S PLAN, AND I TRUST HIM.
I WAS JUST SUPPOSED TO DISTRACT YOU, BUT SINCE YOU DISCOVERED ME...

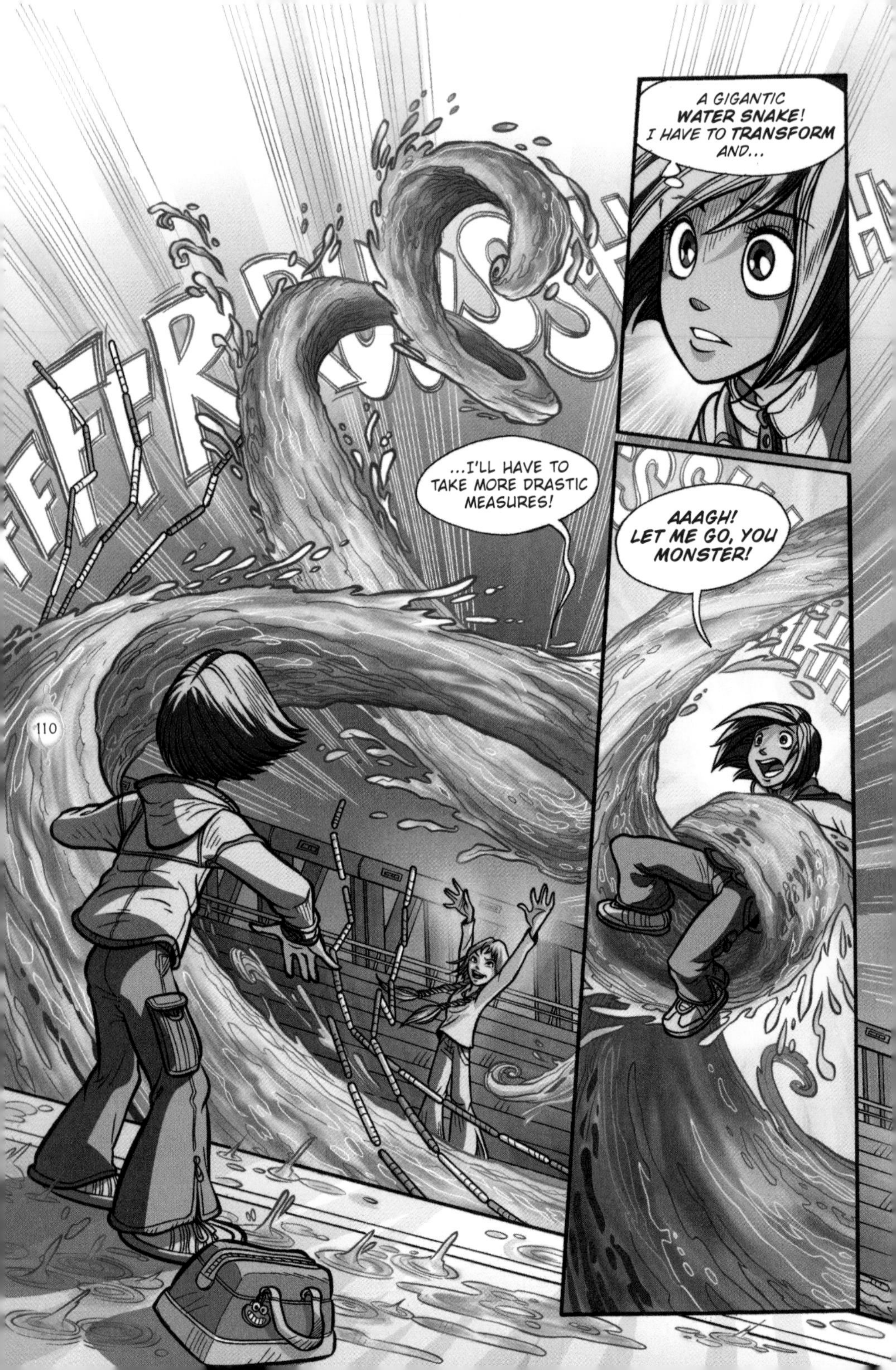
A GIGANTIC WATER SNAKE! I HAVE TO TRANSFORM AND...
...I'LL HAVE TO TAKE MORE DRASTIC MEASURES!
AAAGH! LET ME GO, YOU MONSTER!

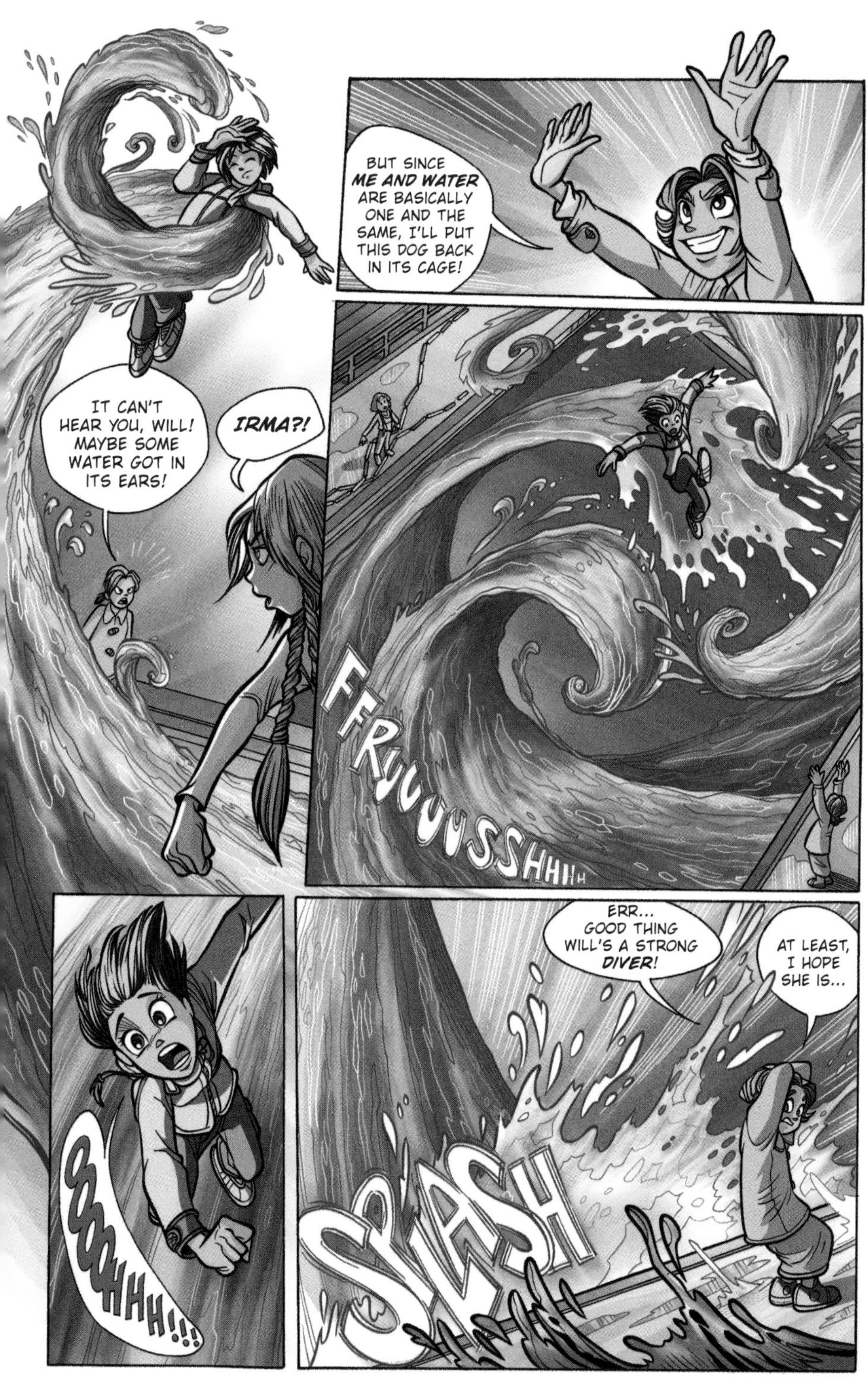
BUT SINCE ME AND WATER ARE BASICALLY ONE AND THE SAME, I'LL PUT THIS DOG BACK IN ITS CAGE!
IT CAN'T HEAR YOU, WILL! MAYBE SOME WATER GOT IN ITS EARS!
IRMA?!
FFRUUUUSSHHHH
OOOOHHH!!!
ERR... GOOD THING WILL'S A STRONG DIVER!
AT LEAST, I HOPE SHE IS...
SPLASH

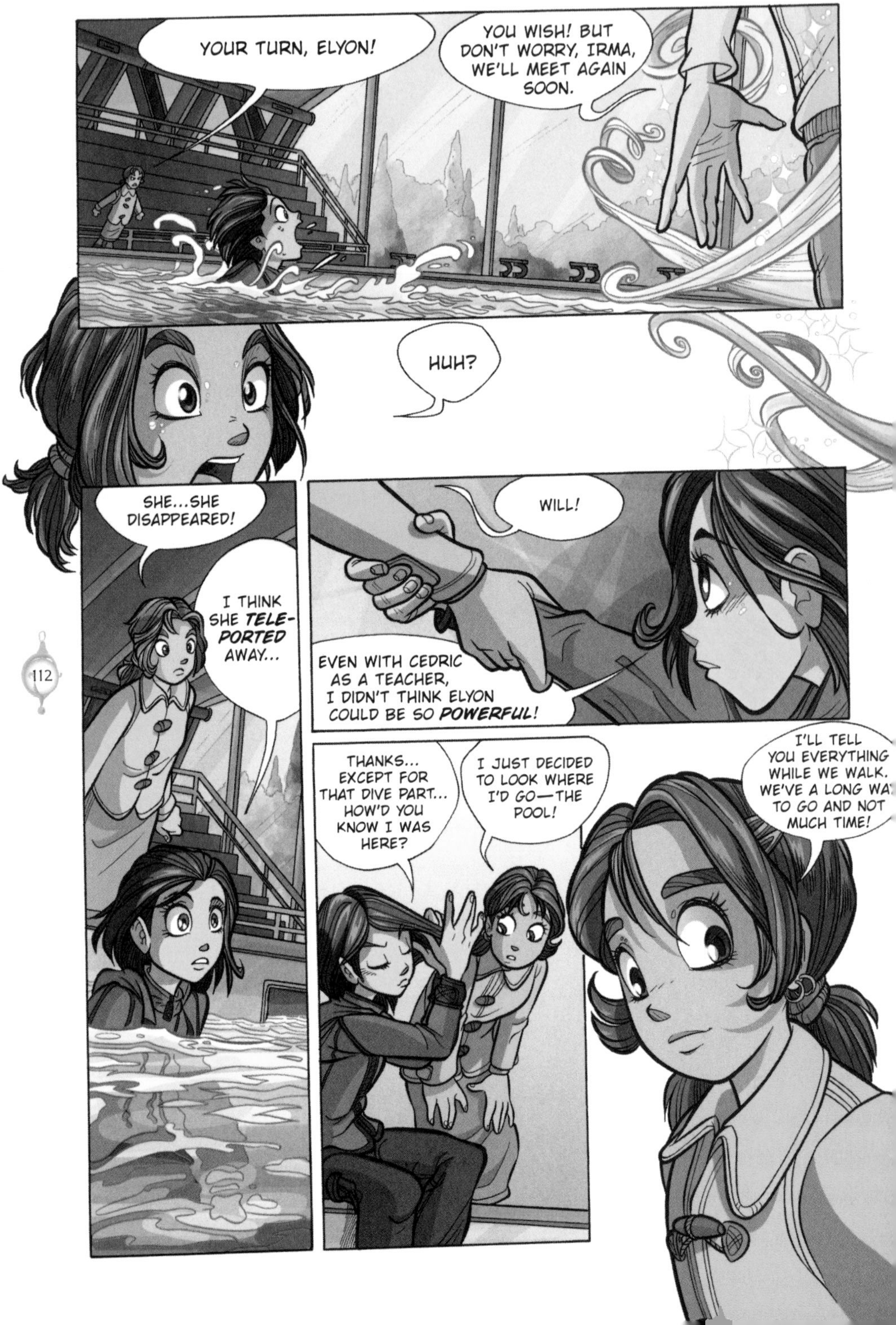
YOUR TURN, ELYON!
YOU WISH! BUT DON'T WORRY, IRMA, WE'LL MEET AGAIN SOON.
HUH?
SHE...SHE DISAPPEARED!
I THINK SHE TELE-PORTED AWAY...
WILL!
EVEN WITH CEDRIC AS A TEACHER, I DIDN'T THINK ELYON COULD BE SO POWERFUL!
THANKS... EXCEPT FOR THAT DIVE PART... HOW'D YOU KNOW I WAS HERE?
I JUST DECIDED TO LOOK WHERE I'D GO—THE POOL!
I'LL TELL YOU EVERYTHING WHILE WE WALK. WE'VE A LONG WA TO GO AND NOT MUCH TIME!

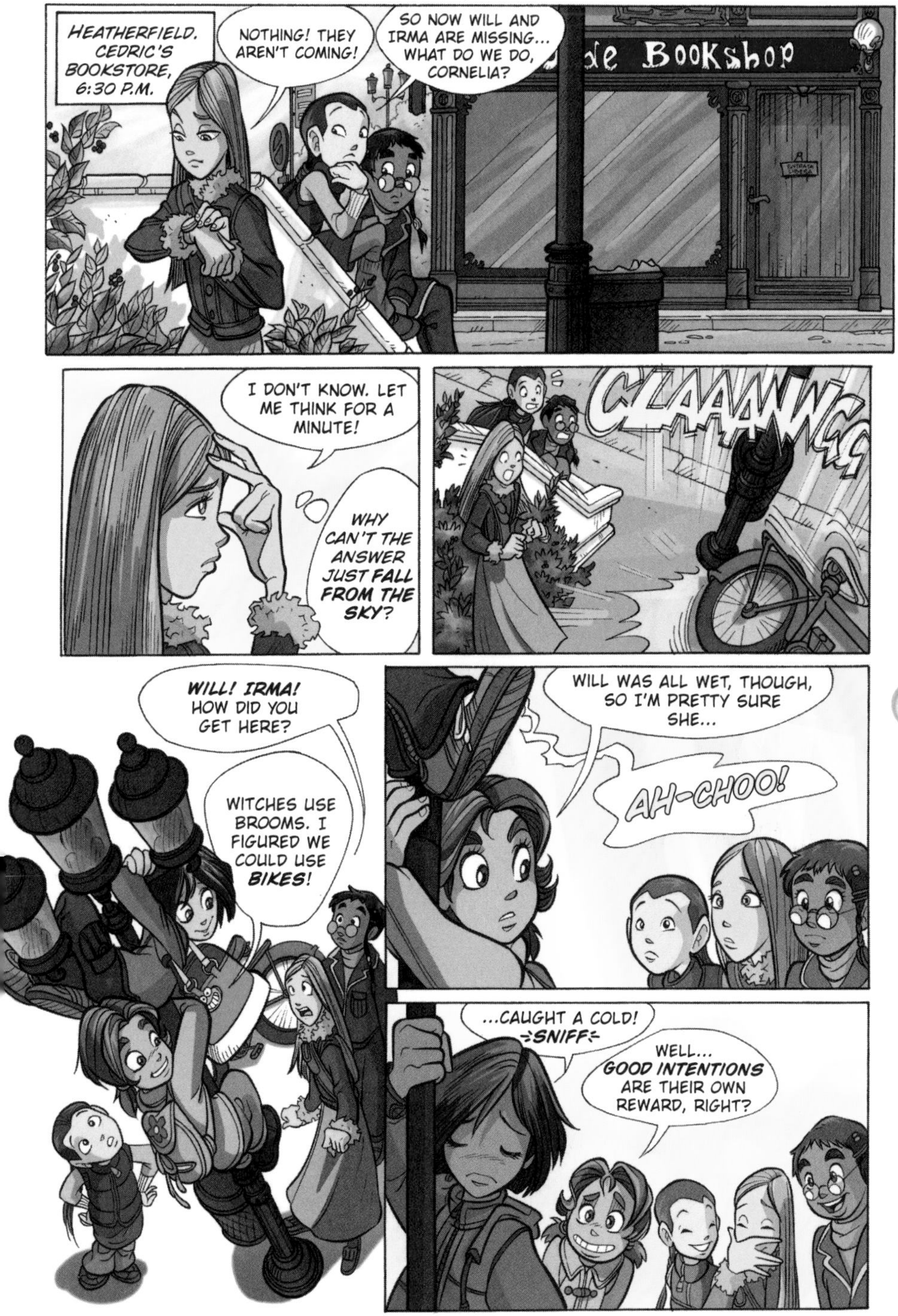
HEATHERFIELD. CEDRIC'S BOOKSTORE, 6:30 P.M.
NOTHING! THEY AREN'T COMING!
SO NOW WILL AND IRMA ARE MISSING... WHAT DO WE DO, CORNELIA?
Bookshop
I DON'T KNOW. LET ME THINK FOR A MINUTE!
WHY CAN'T THE ANSWER JUST FALL FROM THE SKY?
CLAAANNGG
WILL! IRMA! HOW DID YOU GET HERE?
WITCHES USE BROOMS. I FIGURED WE COULD USE BIKES!
WILL WAS ALL WET, THOUGH, SO I'M PRETTY SURE SHE...
AH-CHOO!
...CAUGHT A COLD! SNIFF
WELL... GOOD INTENTIONS ARE THEIR OWN REWARD, RIGHT?

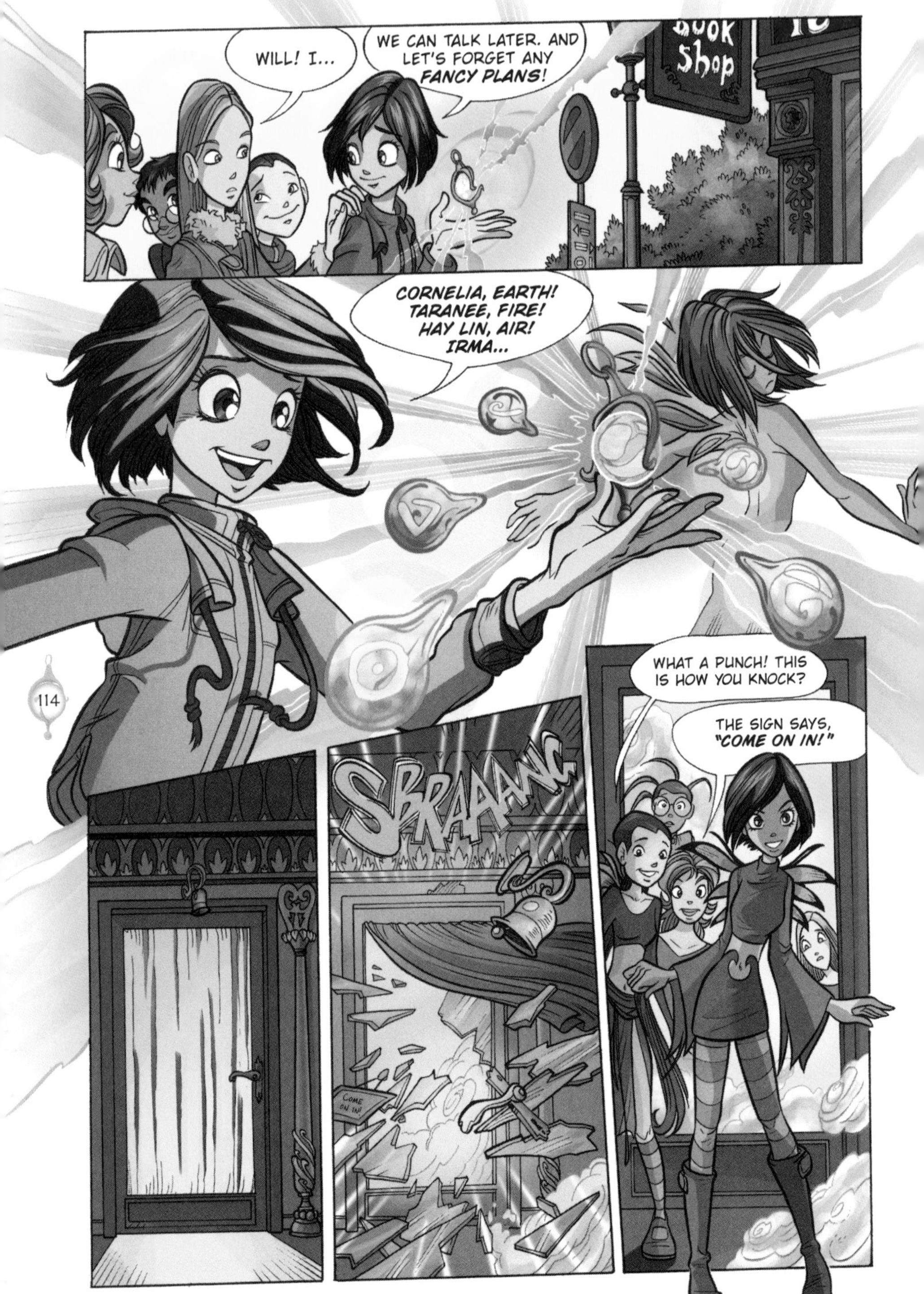
WILL! I...
WE CAN TALK LATER. AND LET'S FORGET ANY FANCY PLANS!
Book Shop
CORNELIA, EARTH! TARANEE, FIRE! HAY LIN, AIR! IRMA...
SBRAAANG
WHAT A PUNCH! THIS IS HOW YOU KNOCK?
THE SIGN SAYS, "COME ON IN!"

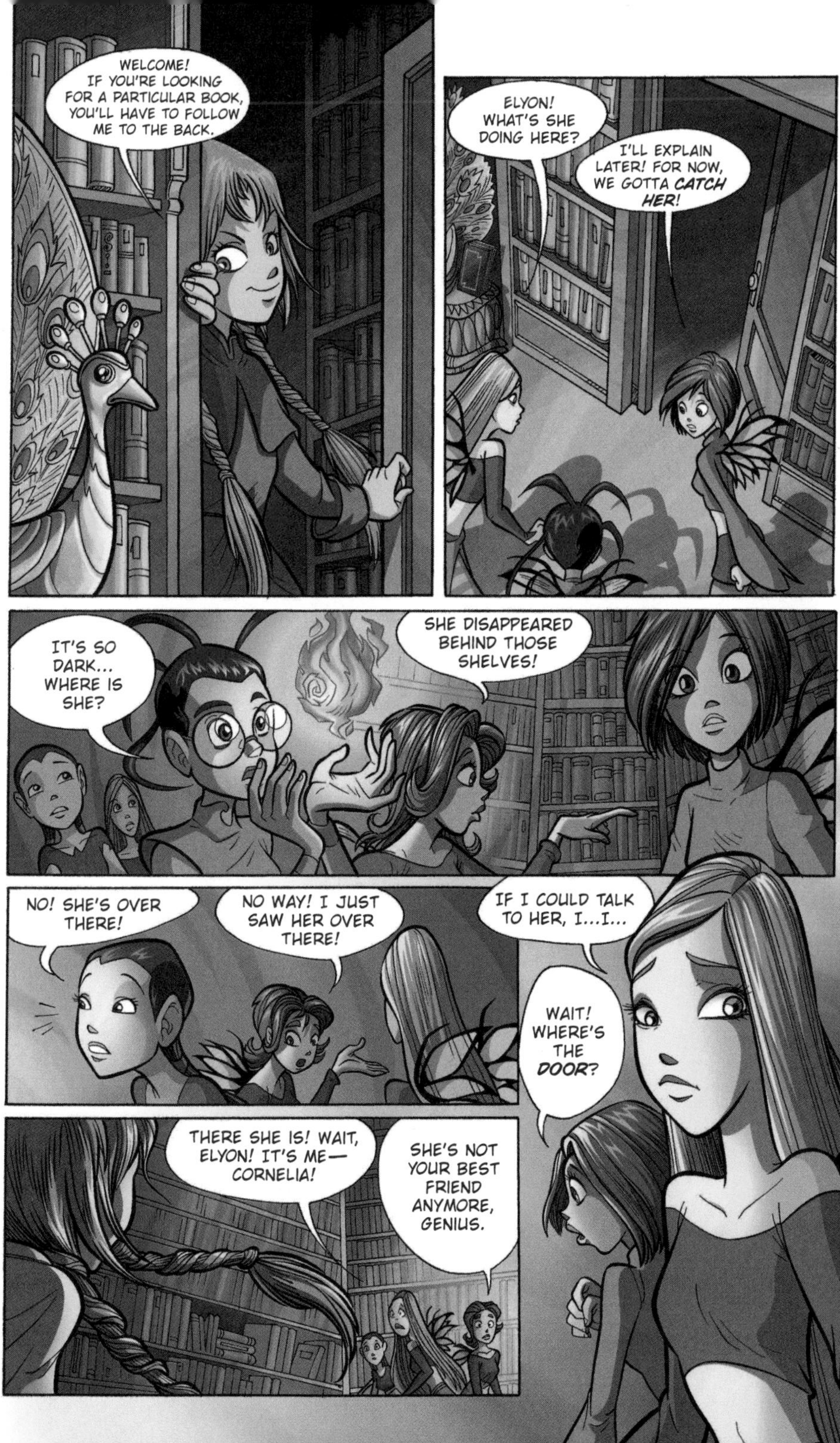
WELCOME! IF YOU'RE LOOKING FOR A PARTICULAR BOOK, YOU'LL HAVE TO FOLLOW ME TO THE BACK.
ELYON! WHAT'S SHE DOING HERE?
I'LL EXPLAIN LATER! FOR NOW, WE GOTTA **CATCH HER**!
IT'S SO DARK... WHERE IS SHE?
SHE DISAPPEARED BEHIND THOSE SHELVES!
NO! SHE'S OVER THERE!
NO WAY! I JUST SAW HER OVER THERE!
IF I COULD TALK TO HER, I...I...
WAIT! WHERE'S THE **DOOR**?
THERE SHE IS! WAIT, ELYON! IT'S ME—CORNELIA!
SHE'S NOT YOUR BEST FRIEND ANYMORE, GENIUS.

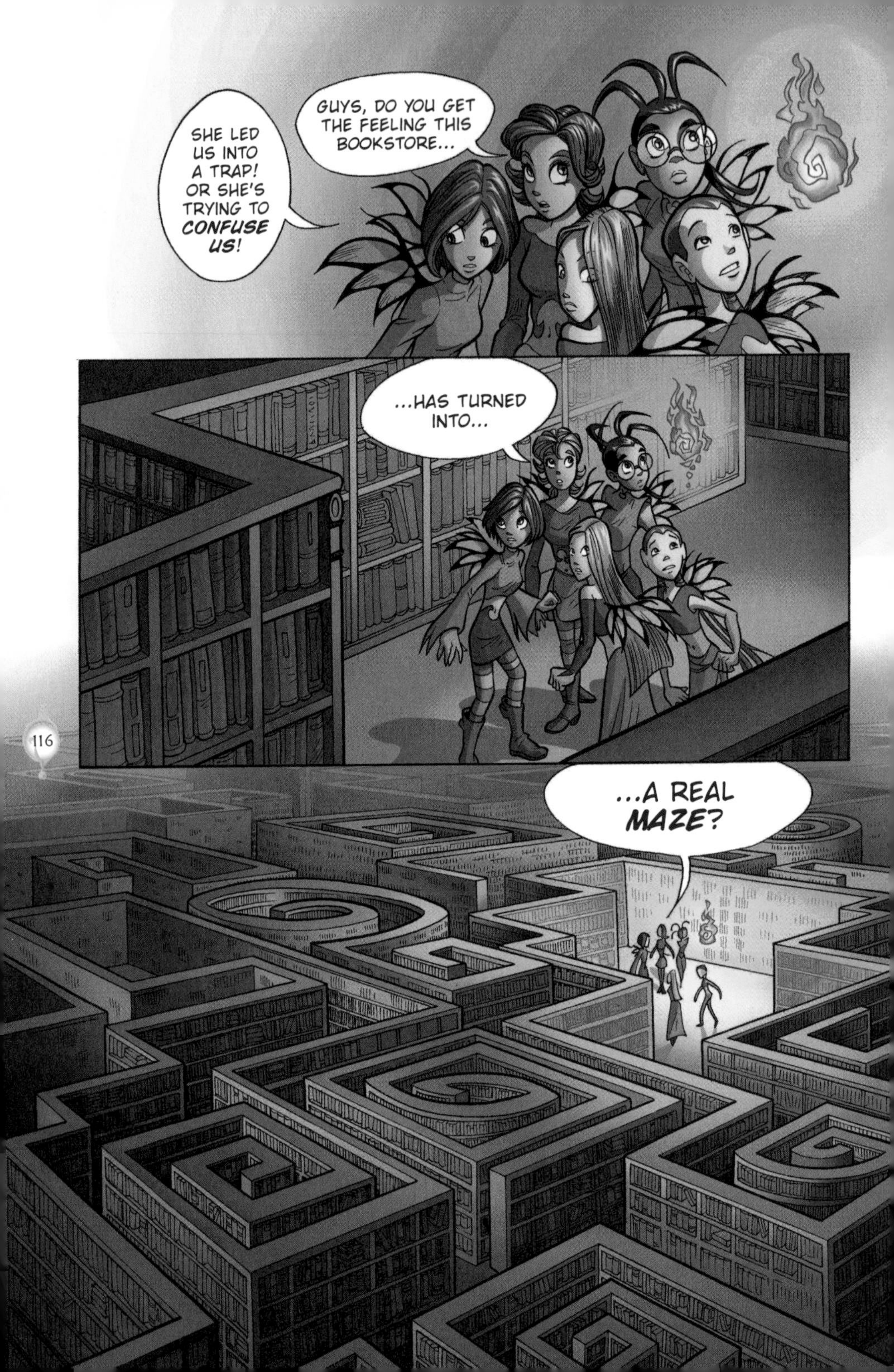
SHE LED US INTO A TRAP! OR SHE'S TRYING TO **CONFUSE US**!
GUYS, DO YOU GET THE FEELING THIS BOOKSTORE...
...HAS TURNED INTO...
...A REAL **MAZE**?

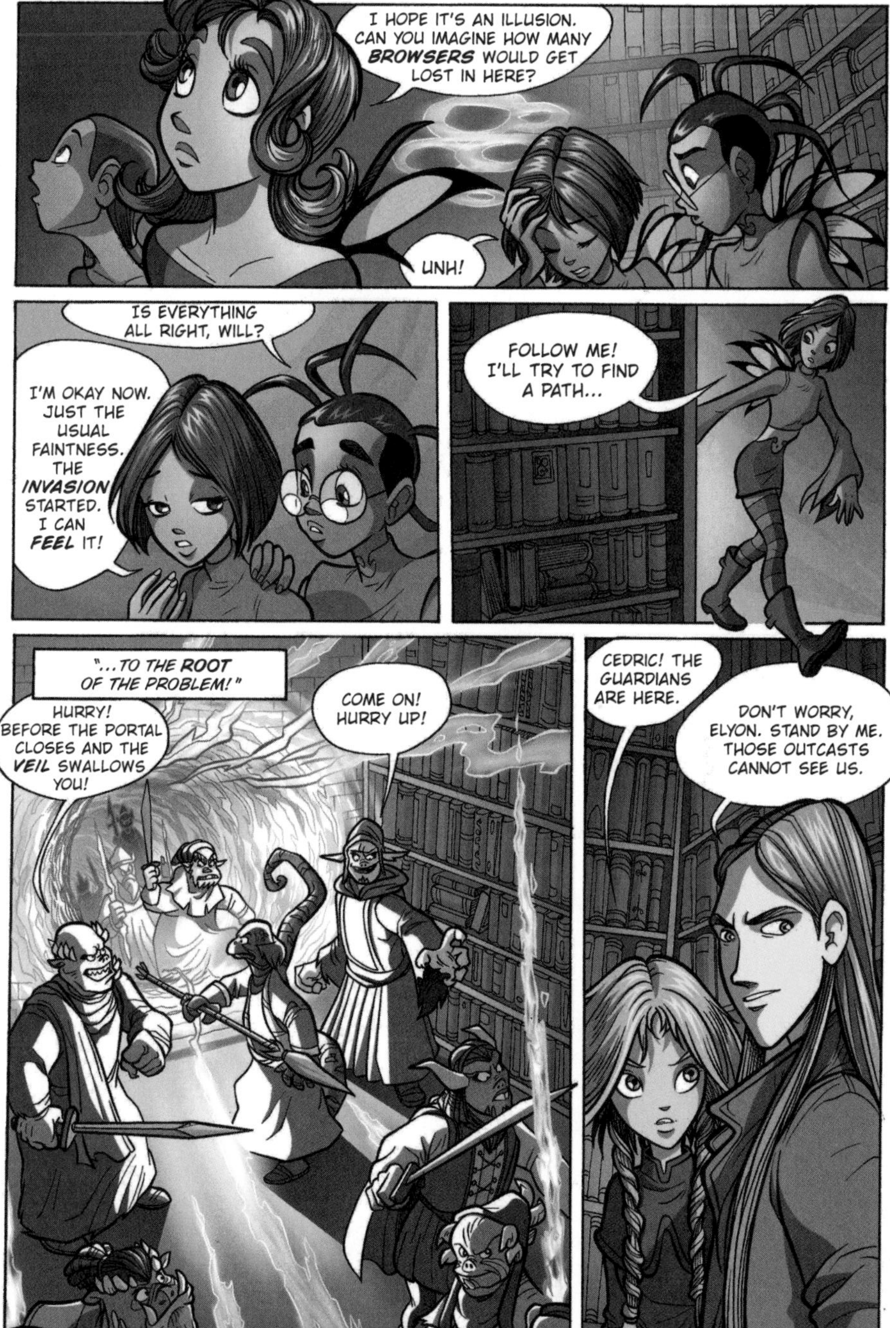

I HOPE IT'S AN ILLUSION. CAN YOU IMAGINE HOW MANY BROWSERS WOULD GET LOST IN HERE?
UNH!
IS EVERYTHING ALL RIGHT, WILL?
I'M OKAY NOW. JUST THE USUAL FAINTNESS. THE INVASION STARTED. I CAN FEEL IT!
FOLLOW ME! I'LL TRY TO FIND A PATH...
"...TO THE ROOT OF THE PROBLEM!"
HURRY! BEFORE THE PORTAL CLOSES AND THE VEIL SWALLOWS YOU!
COME ON! HURRY UP!
CEDRIC! THE GUARDIANS ARE HERE.
DON'T WORRY, ELYON. STAND BY ME. THOSE OUTCASTS CANNOT SEE US.

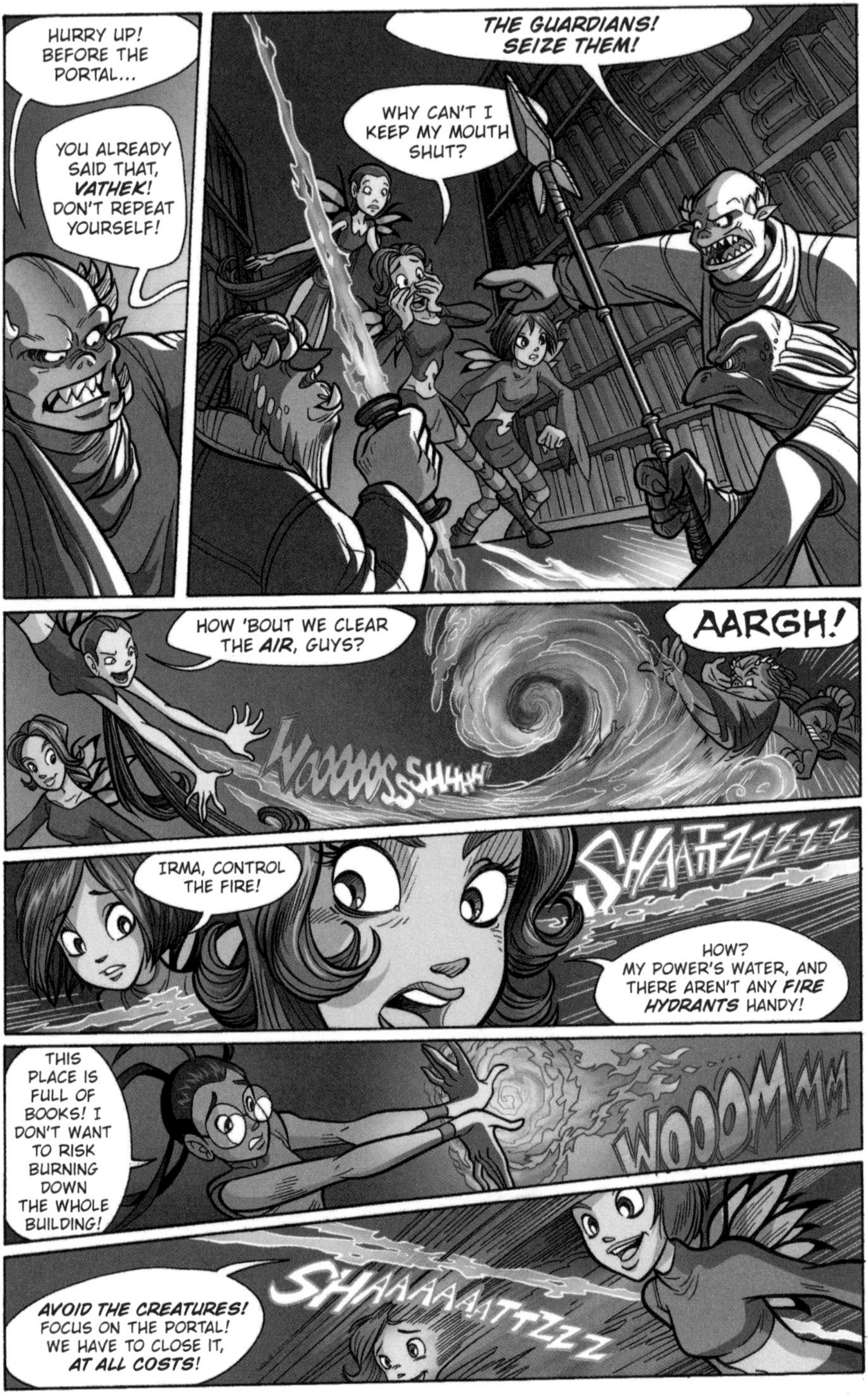
HURRY UP! BEFORE THE PORTAL...
YOU ALREADY SAID THAT, VATHEK! DON'T REPEAT YOURSELF!
THE GUARDIANS! SEIZE THEM!
WHY CAN'T I KEEP MY MOUTH SHUT?
HOW 'BOUT WE CLEAR THE AIR, GUYS?
AARGH!
WOOOOOSSSHHHH
IRMA, CONTROL THE FIRE!
SHAATTZZZZZ
HOW? MY POWER'S WATER, AND THERE AREN'T ANY FIRE HYDRANTS HANDY!
THIS PLACE IS FULL OF BOOKS! I DON'T WANT TO RISK BURNING DOWN THE WHOLE BUILDING!
WOOOMMMM
SHAAAAAATTZZZZ
AVOID THE CREATURES! FOCUS ON THE PORTAL! WE HAVE TO CLOSE IT, AT ALL COSTS!

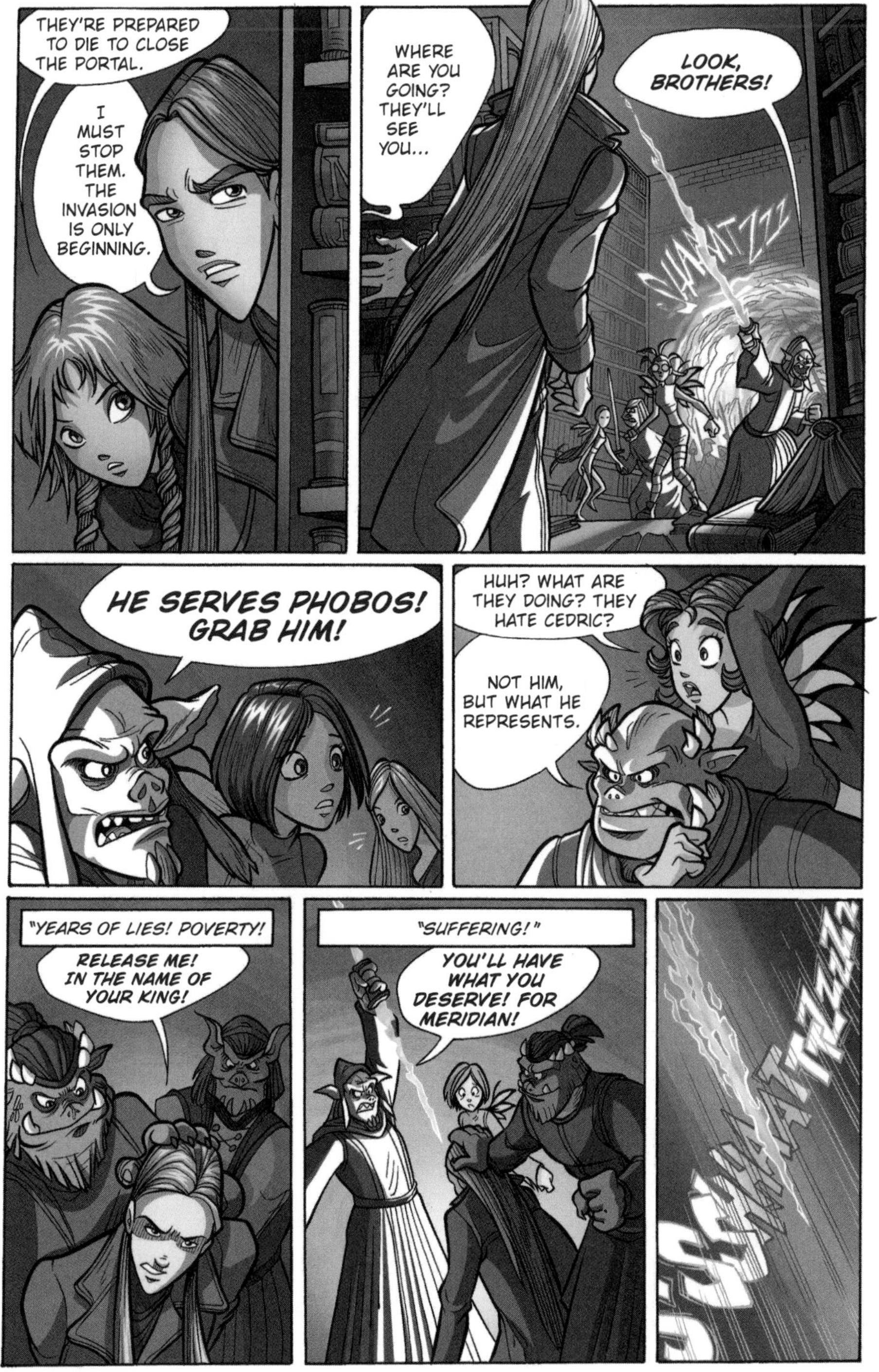
THEY'RE PREPARED TO DIE TO CLOSE THE PORTAL.
I MUST STOP THEM. THE INVASION IS ONLY BEGINNING.
WHERE ARE YOU GOING? THEY'LL SEE YOU...
LOOK, BROTHERS!
HE SERVES PHOBOS! GRAB HIM!
HUH? WHAT ARE THEY DOING? THEY HATE CEDRIC?
NOT HIM, BUT WHAT HE REPRESENTS.
"YEARS OF LIES! POVERTY!
RELEASE ME! IN THE NAME OF YOUR KING!
"SUFFERING!"
YOU'LL HAVE WHAT YOU DESERVE! FOR MERIDIAN!

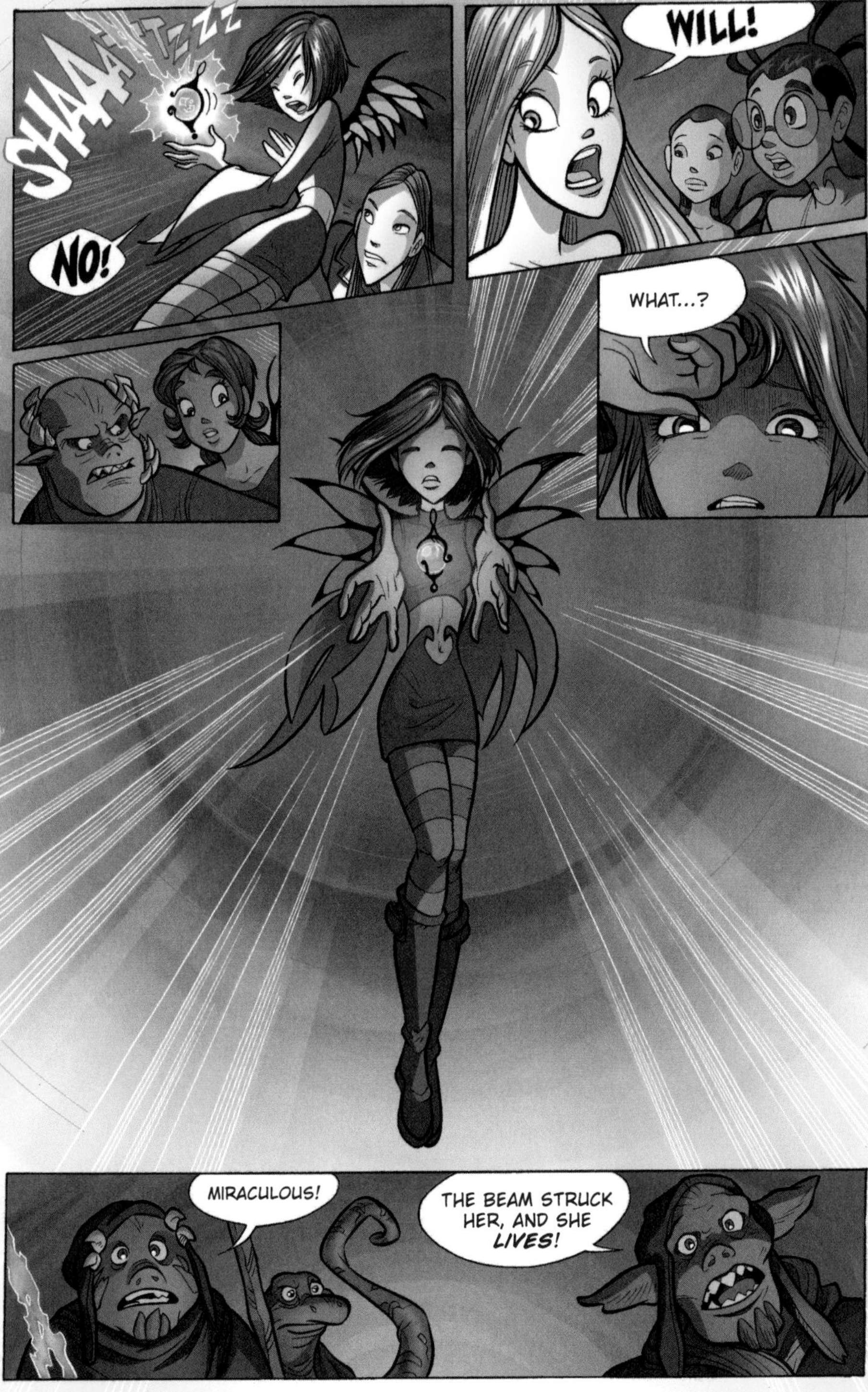
SHAAA TZZZ
NO!
WILL!
WHAT...?
MIRACULOUS!
THE BEAM STRUCK HER, AND SHE LIVES!

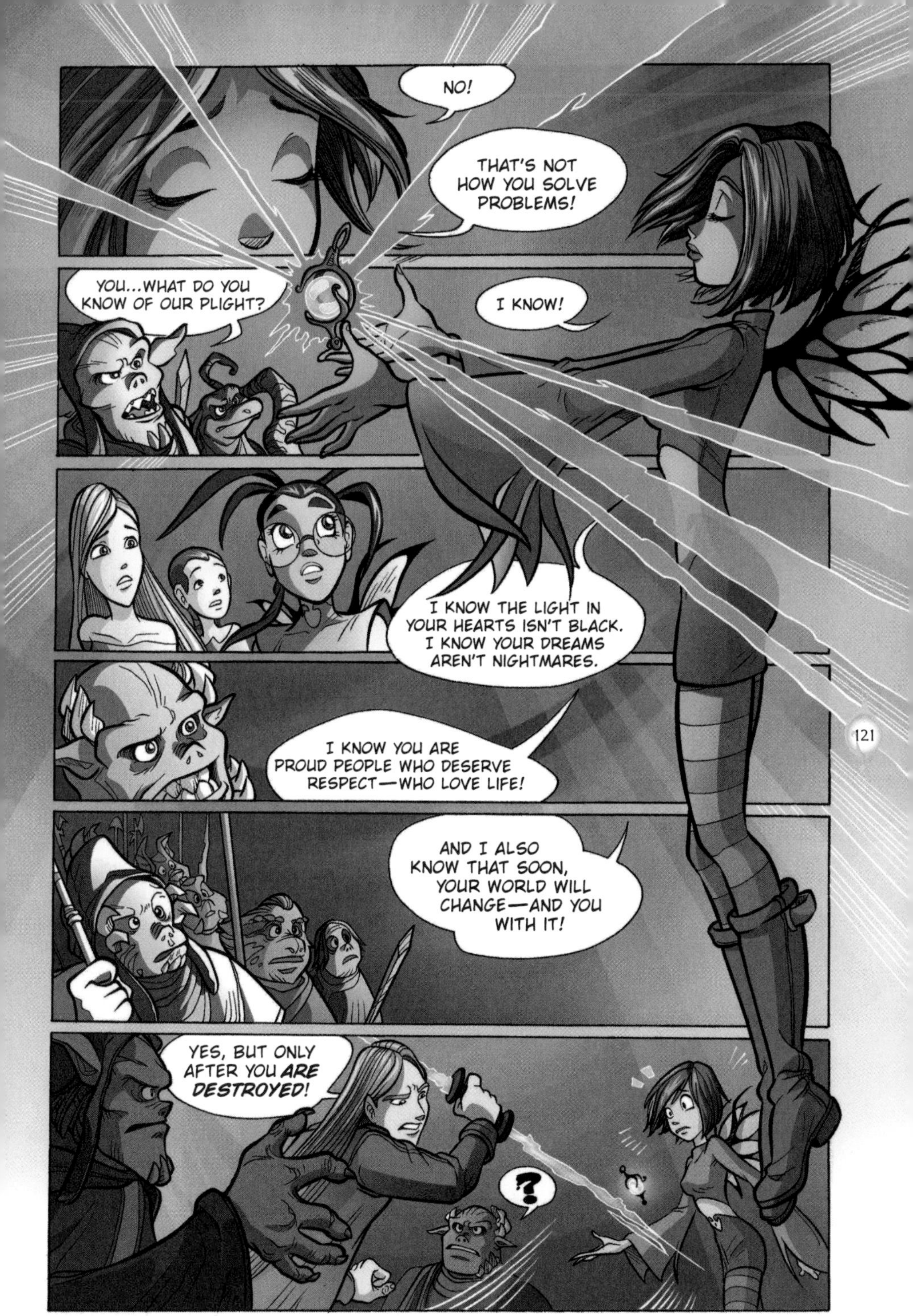
NO!
THAT'S NOT HOW YOU SOLVE PROBLEMS!
YOU...WHAT DO YOU KNOW OF OUR PLIGHT?
I KNOW!
I KNOW THE LIGHT IN YOUR HEARTS ISN'T BLACK. I KNOW YOUR DREAMS AREN'T NIGHTMARES.
I KNOW YOU ARE PROUD PEOPLE WHO DESERVE RESPECT—WHO LOVE LIFE!
AND I ALSO KNOW THAT SOON, YOUR WORLD WILL CHANGE—AND YOU WITH IT!
YES, BUT ONLY AFTER YOU ***ARE DESTROYED***!
?

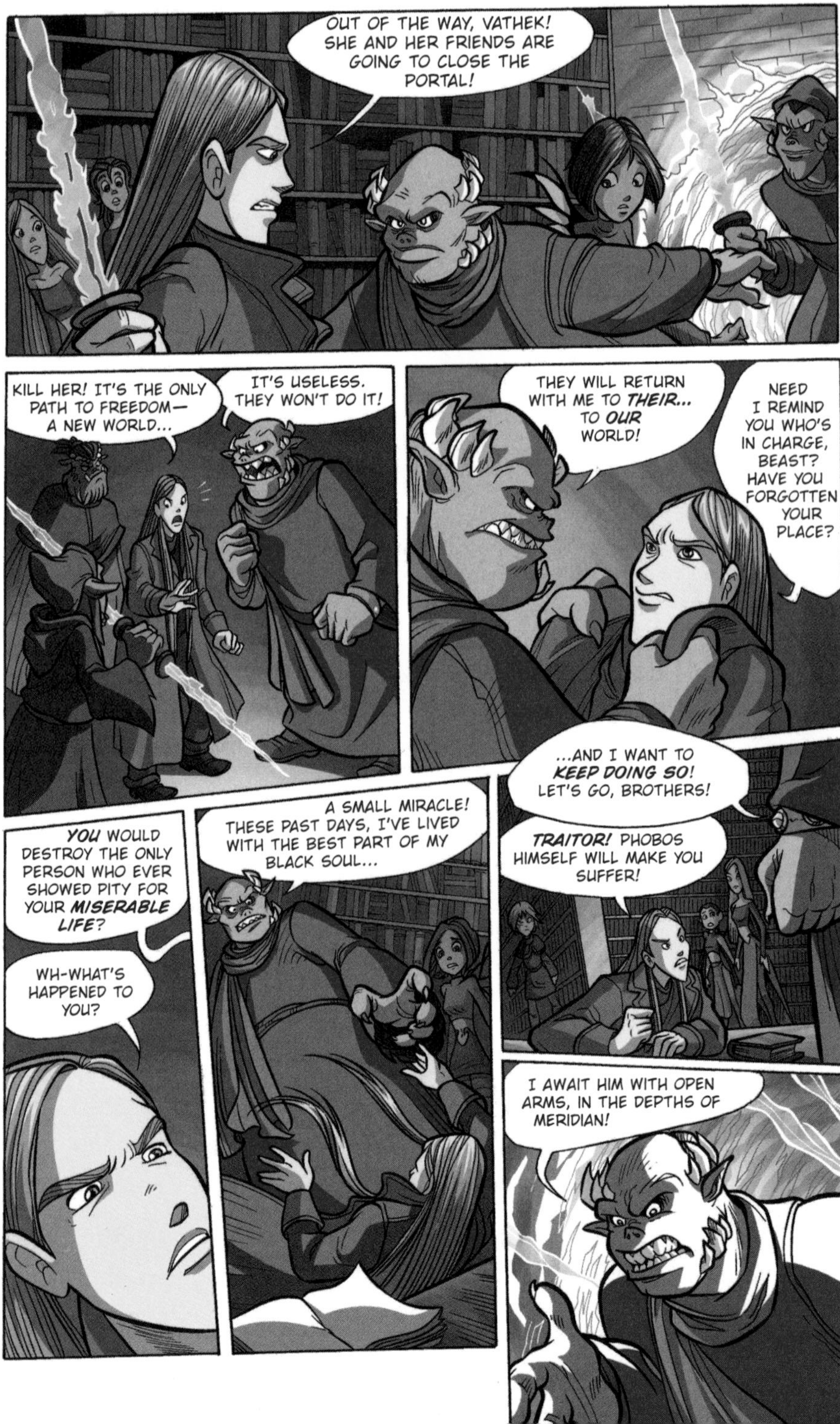
OUT OF THE WAY, VATHEK! SHE AND HER FRIENDS ARE GOING TO CLOSE THE PORTAL!
KILL HER! IT'S THE ONLY PATH TO FREEDOM— A NEW WORLD...
IT'S USELESS. THEY WON'T DO IT!
THEY WILL RETURN WITH ME TO THEIR... TO OUR WORLD!
NEED I REMIND YOU WHO'S IN CHARGE, BEAST? HAVE YOU FORGOTTEN YOUR PLACE?
YOU WOULD DESTROY THE ONLY PERSON WHO EVER SHOWED PITY FOR YOUR MISERABLE LIFE?
WH-WHAT'S HAPPENED TO YOU?
A SMALL MIRACLE! THESE PAST DAYS, I'VE LIVED WITH THE BEST PART OF MY BLACK SOUL...
...AND I WANT TO KEEP DOING SO! LET'S GO, BROTHERS!
TRAITOR! PHOBOS HIMSELF WILL MAKE YOU SUFFER!
I AWAIT HIM WITH OPEN ARMS, IN THE DEPTHS OF MERIDIAN!

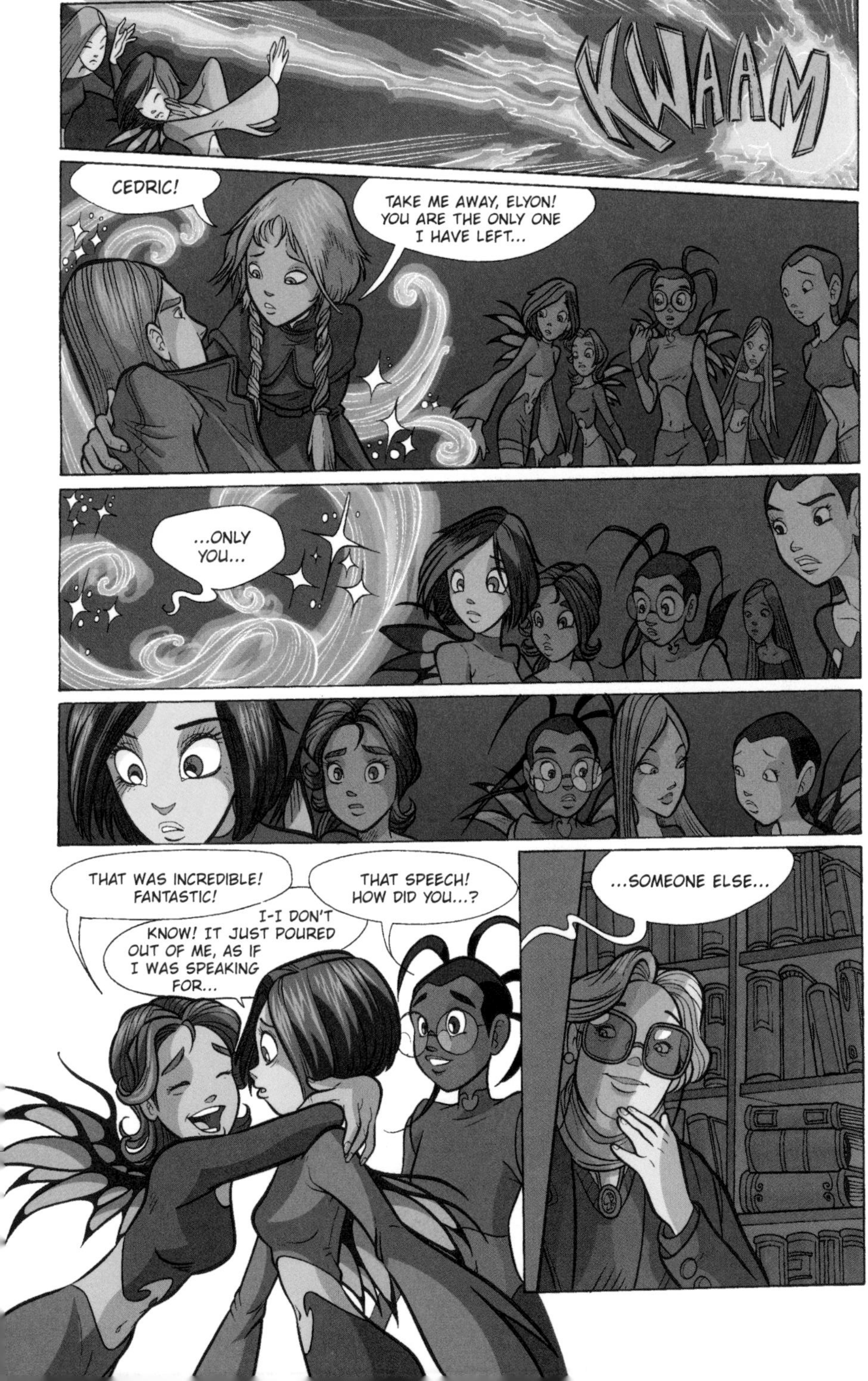
KWAAM
CEDRIC!
TAKE ME AWAY, ELYON! YOU ARE THE ONLY ONE I HAVE LEFT...
...ONLY YOU...
THAT WAS INCREDIBLE! FANTASTIC!
THAT SPEECH! HOW DID YOU...?
I-I DON'T KNOW! IT JUST POURED OUT OF ME, AS IF I WAS SPEAKING FOR...
...SOMEONE ELSE...

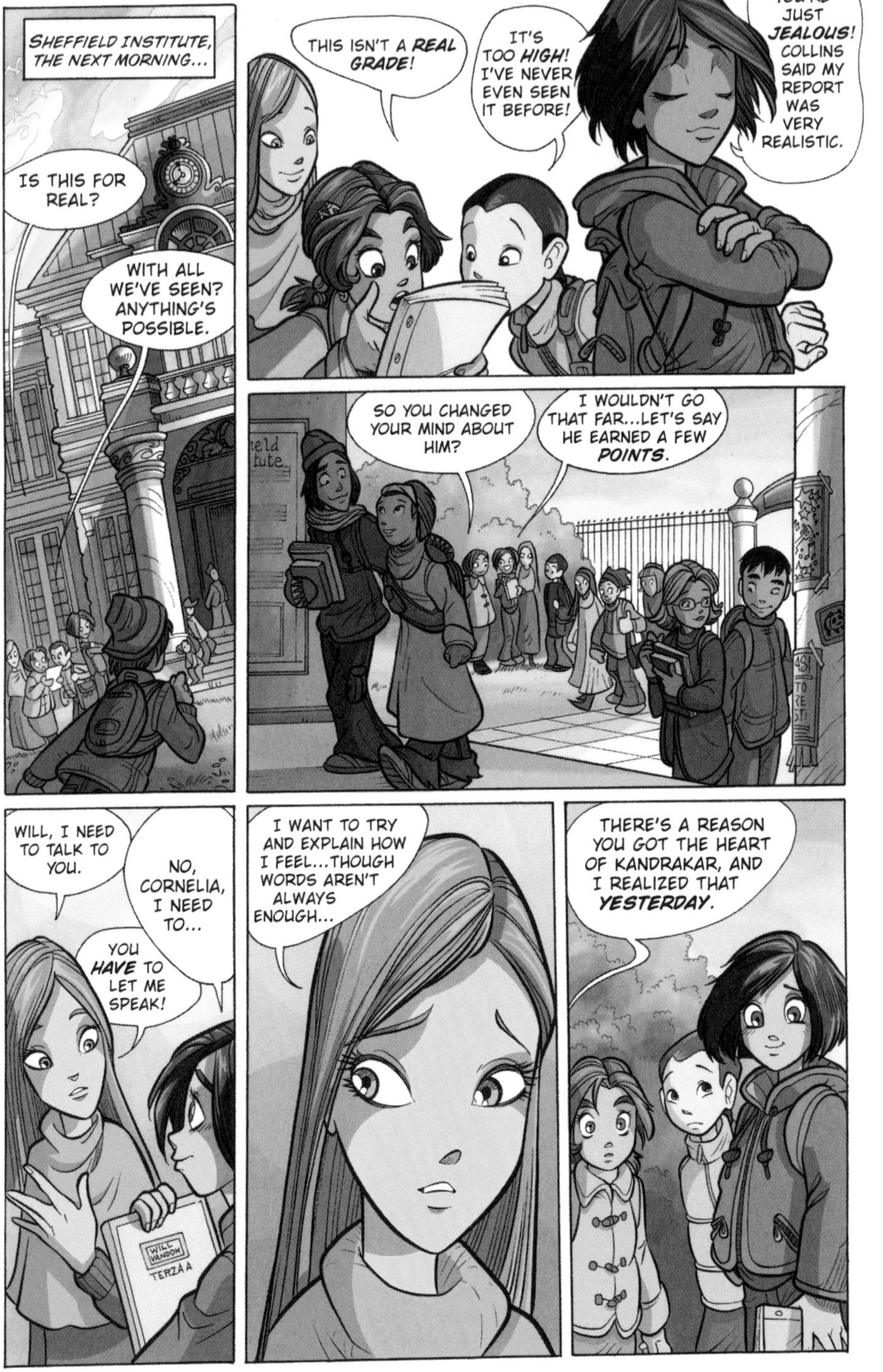
SHEFFIELD INSTITUTE, THE NEXT MORNING...
IS THIS FOR REAL?
WITH ALL WE'VE SEEN? ANYTHING'S POSSIBLE.
THIS ISN'T A *REAL GRADE*!
IT'S TOO *HIGH*! I'VE NEVER EVEN SEEN IT BEFORE!
YOU'RE JUST *JEALOUS*! COLLINS SAID MY REPORT WAS VERY REALISTIC.
SO YOU CHANGED YOUR MIND ABOUT HIM?
I WOULDN'T GO THAT FAR...LET'S SAY HE EARNED A FEW *POINTS*.
WILL, I NEED TO TALK TO YOU.
NO, CORNELIA, I NEED TO...
YOU *HAVE* TO LET ME SPEAK!
WILL VANDOM
TERZA A
I WANT TO TRY AND EXPLAIN HOW I FEEL...THOUGH WORDS AREN'T ALWAYS ENOUGH...
THERE'S A REASON YOU GOT THE HEART OF KANDRAKAR, AND I REALIZED THAT *YESTERDAY*.

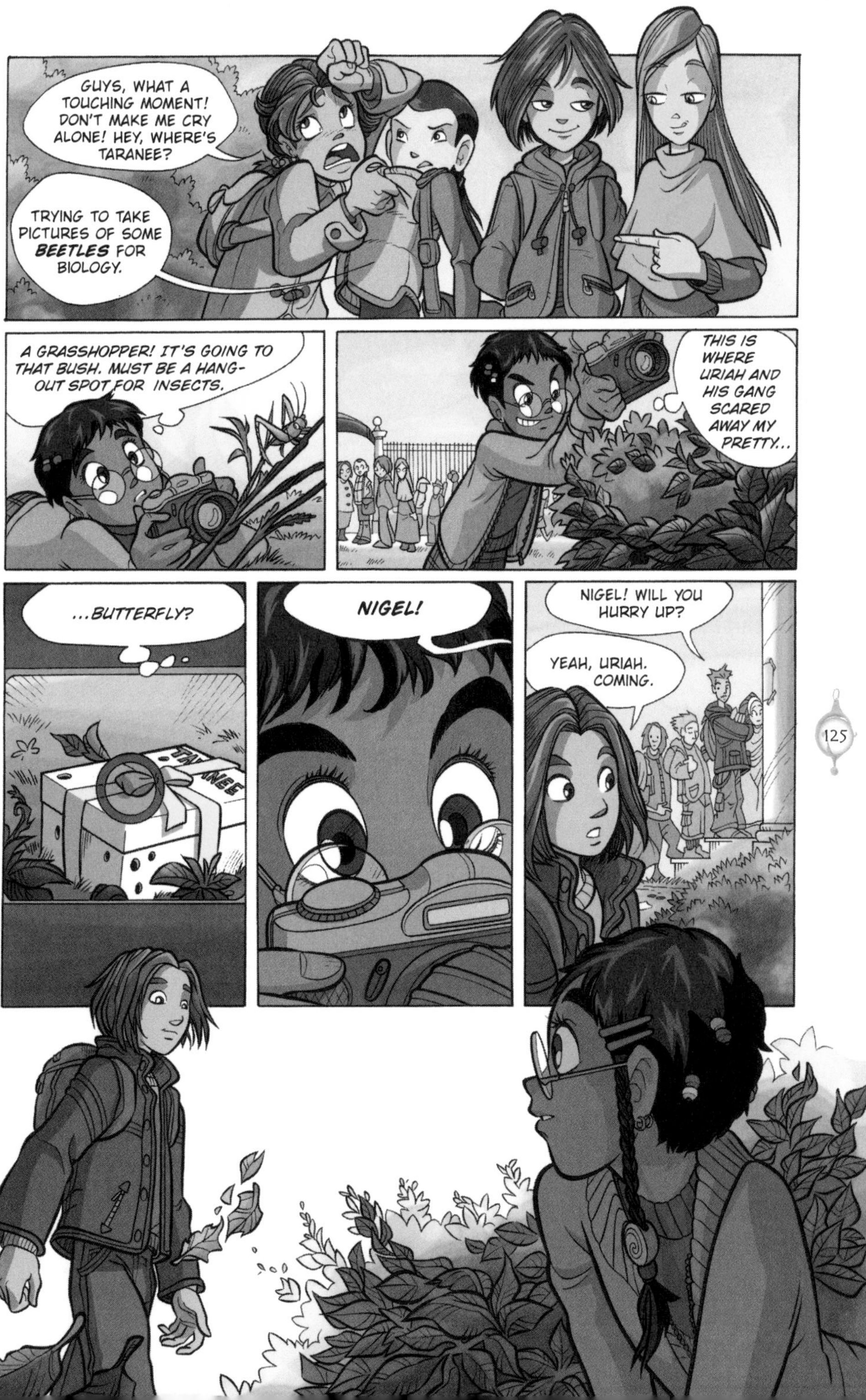
GUYS, WHAT A TOUCHING MOMENT! DON'T MAKE ME CRY ALONE! HEY, WHERE'S TARANEE?
TRYING TO TAKE PICTURES OF SOME ***BEETLES*** FOR BIOLOGY.
A GRASSHOPPER! IT'S GOING TO THAT BUSH. MUST BE A HANG-OUT SPOT FOR INSECTS.
THIS IS WHERE URIAH AND HIS GANG SCARED AWAY MY PRETTY...
...BUTTERFLY?
NIGEL!
NIGEL! WILL YOU HURRY UP?
YEAH, URIAH. COMING.

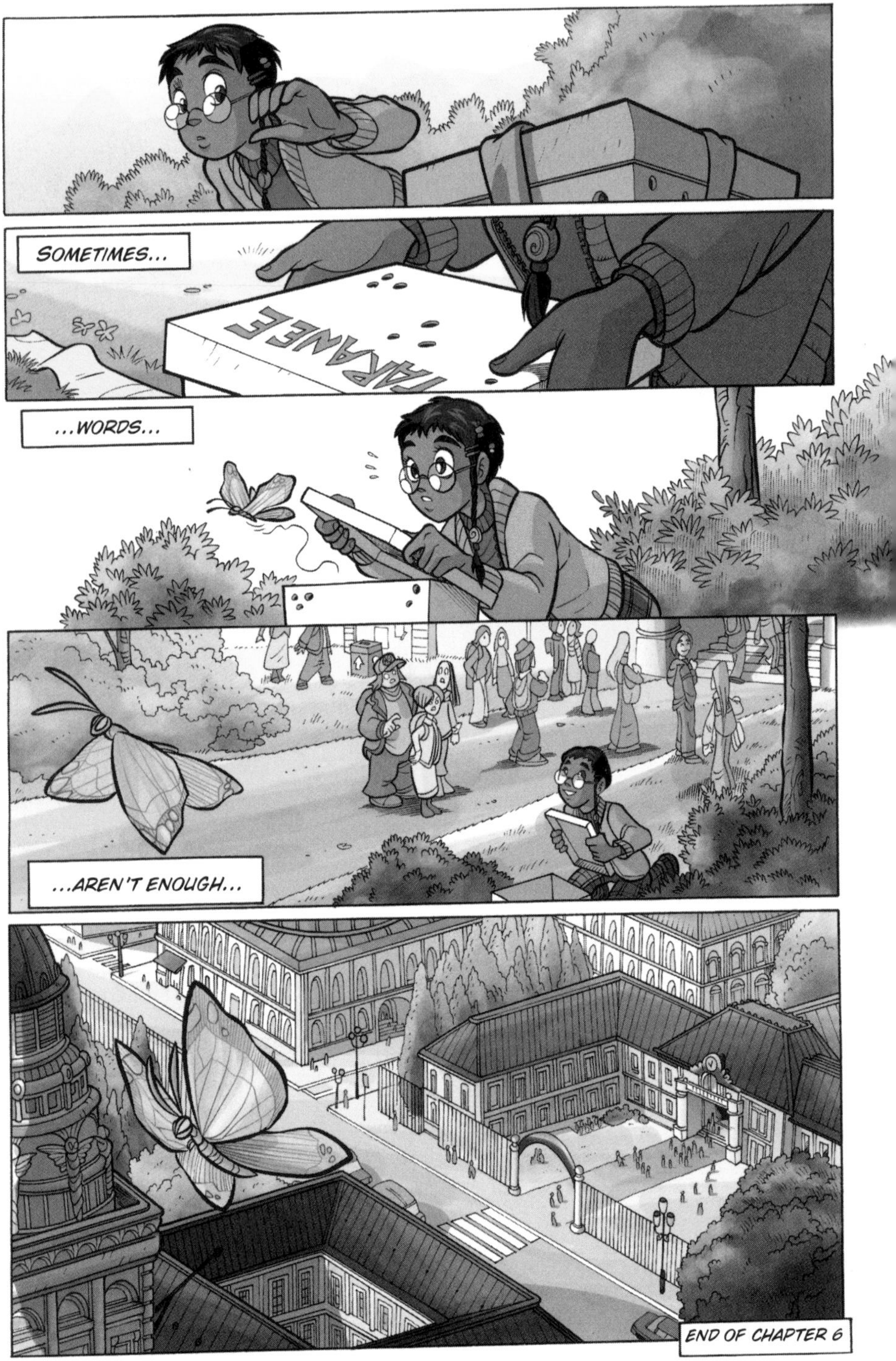
SOMETIMES...
...WORDS...
...AREN'T ENOUGH...
END OF CHAPTER 6

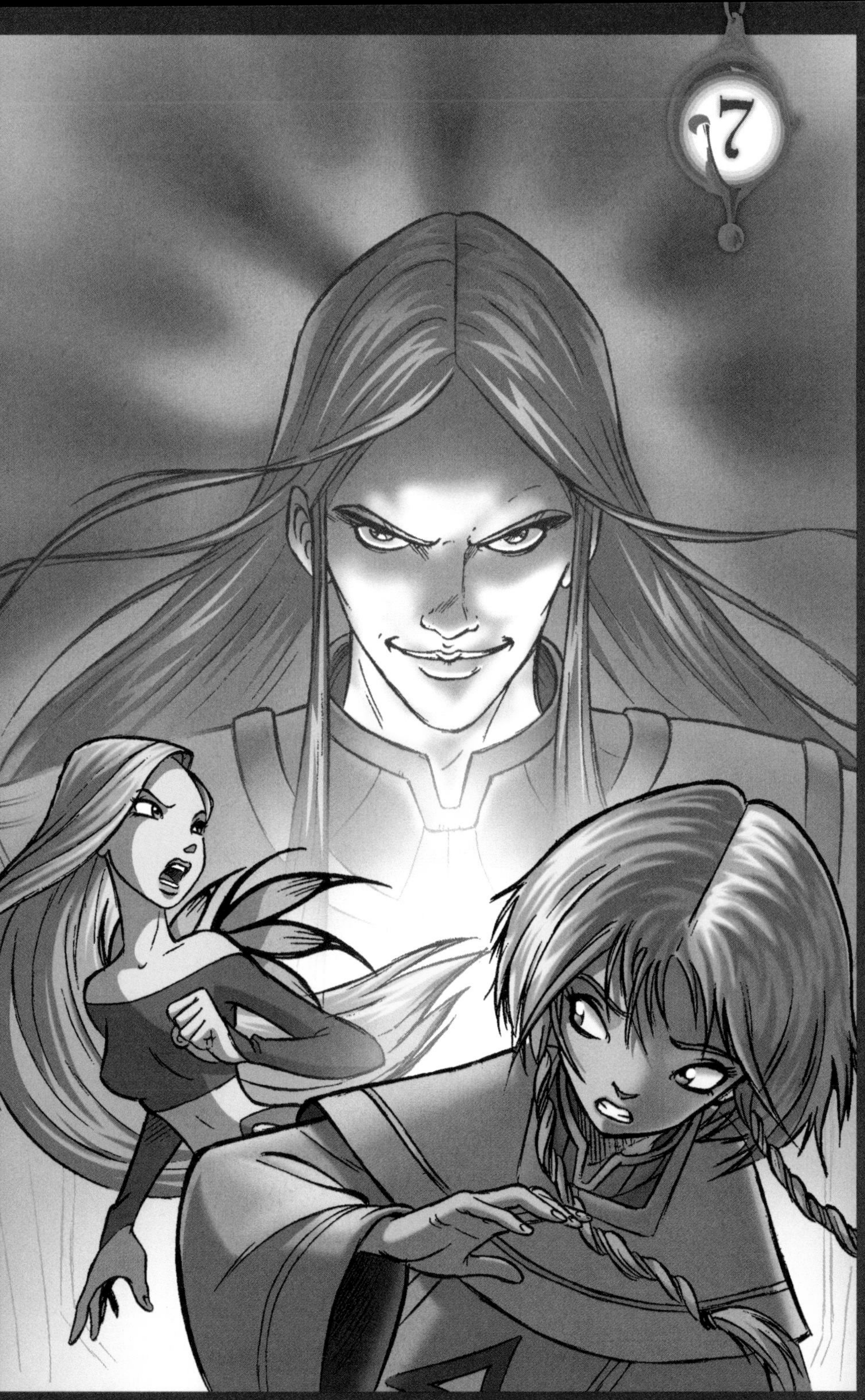
7

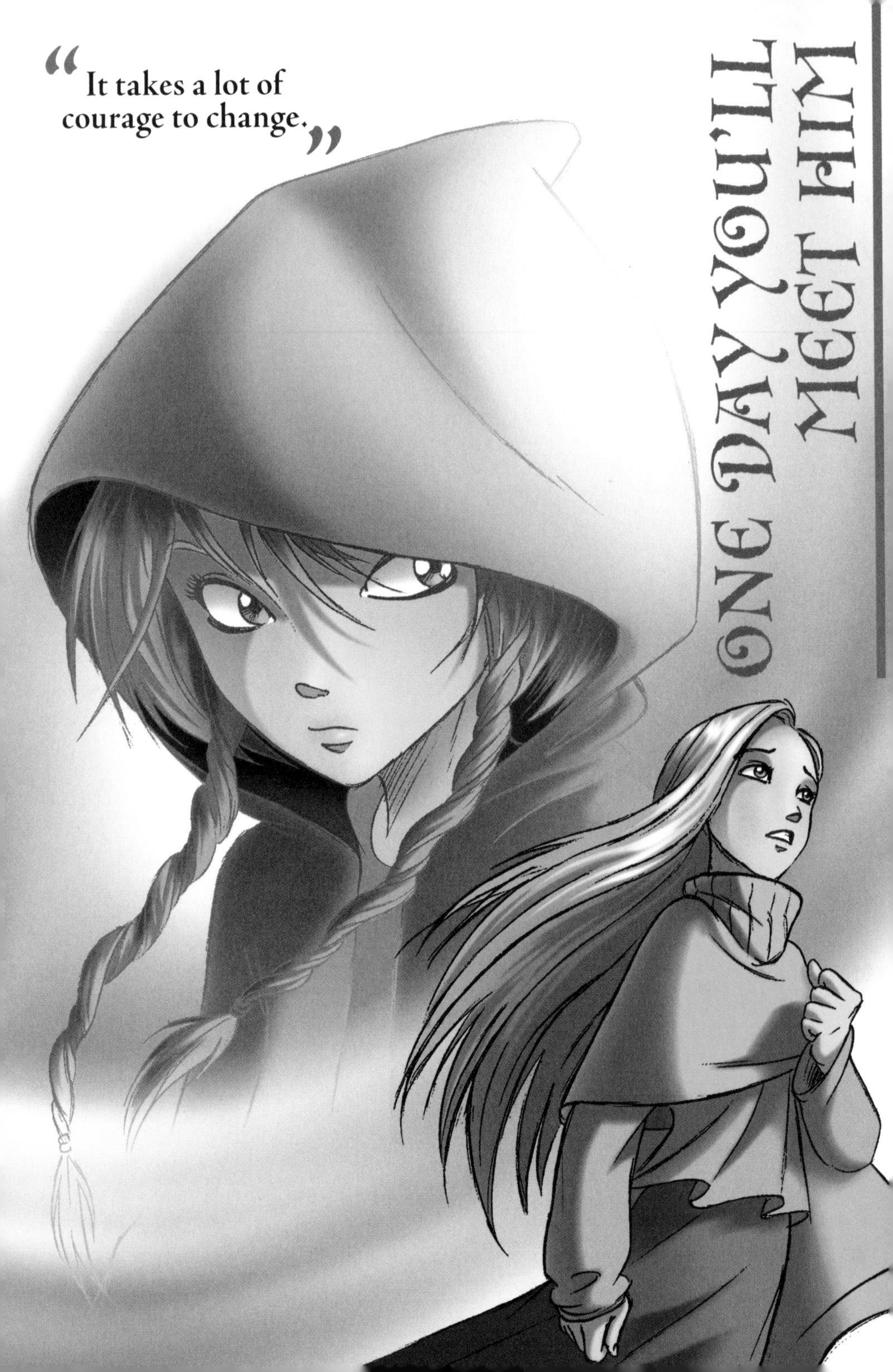
"It takes a lot of courage to change."
ONE DAY YOU'LL MEET HIM

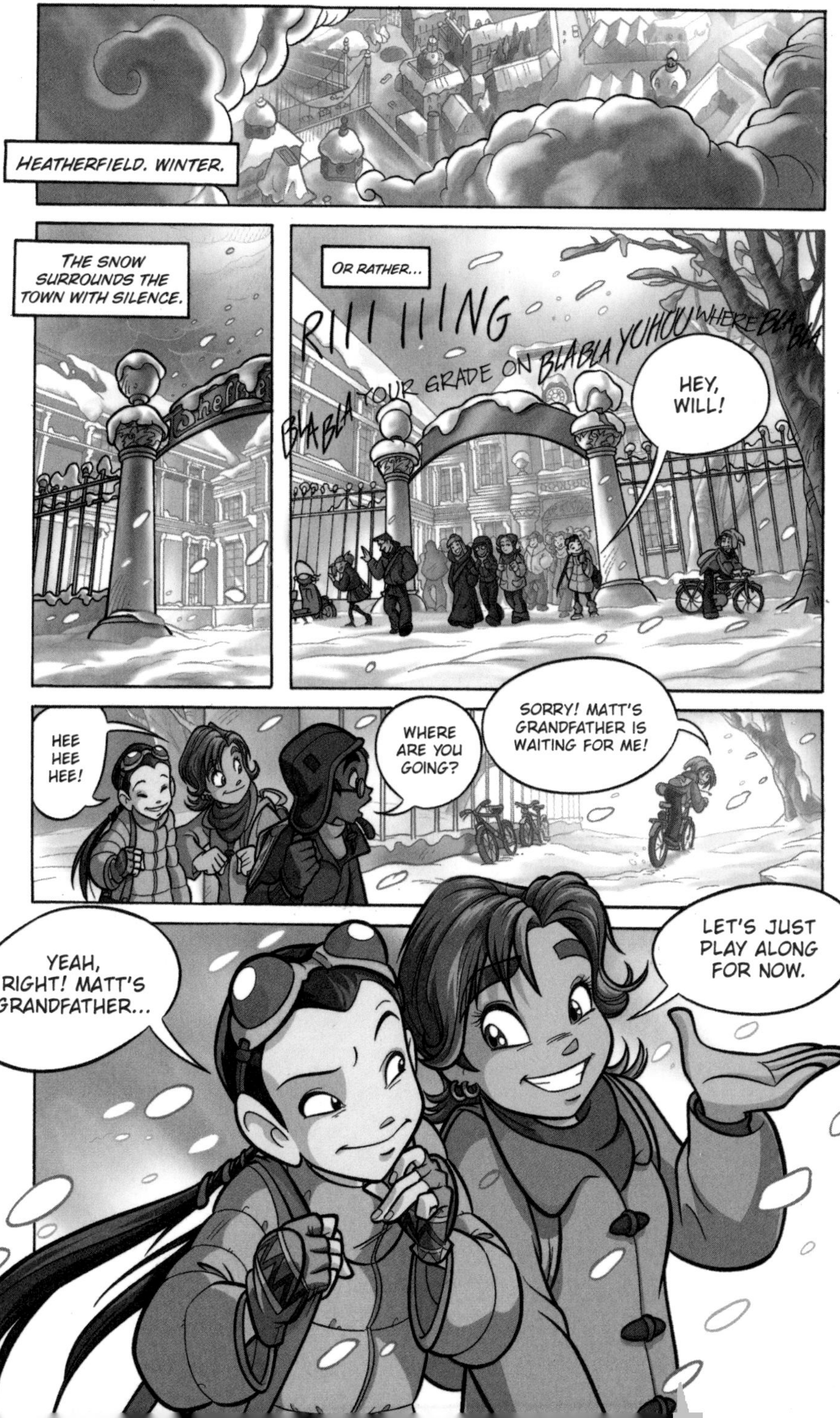
HEATHERFIELD. WINTER.
THE SNOW SURROUNDS THE TOWN WITH SILENCE.
OR RATHER...
RIII IIING
BLA BLA YOUR GRADE ON BLABLA YUHOU WHERE BLA BLA
HEY, WILL!
HEE HEE HEE!
WHERE ARE YOU GOING?
SORRY! MATT'S GRANDFATHER IS WAITING FOR ME!
YEAH, RIGHT! MATT'S GRANDFATHER...
LET'S JUST PLAY ALONG FOR NOW.

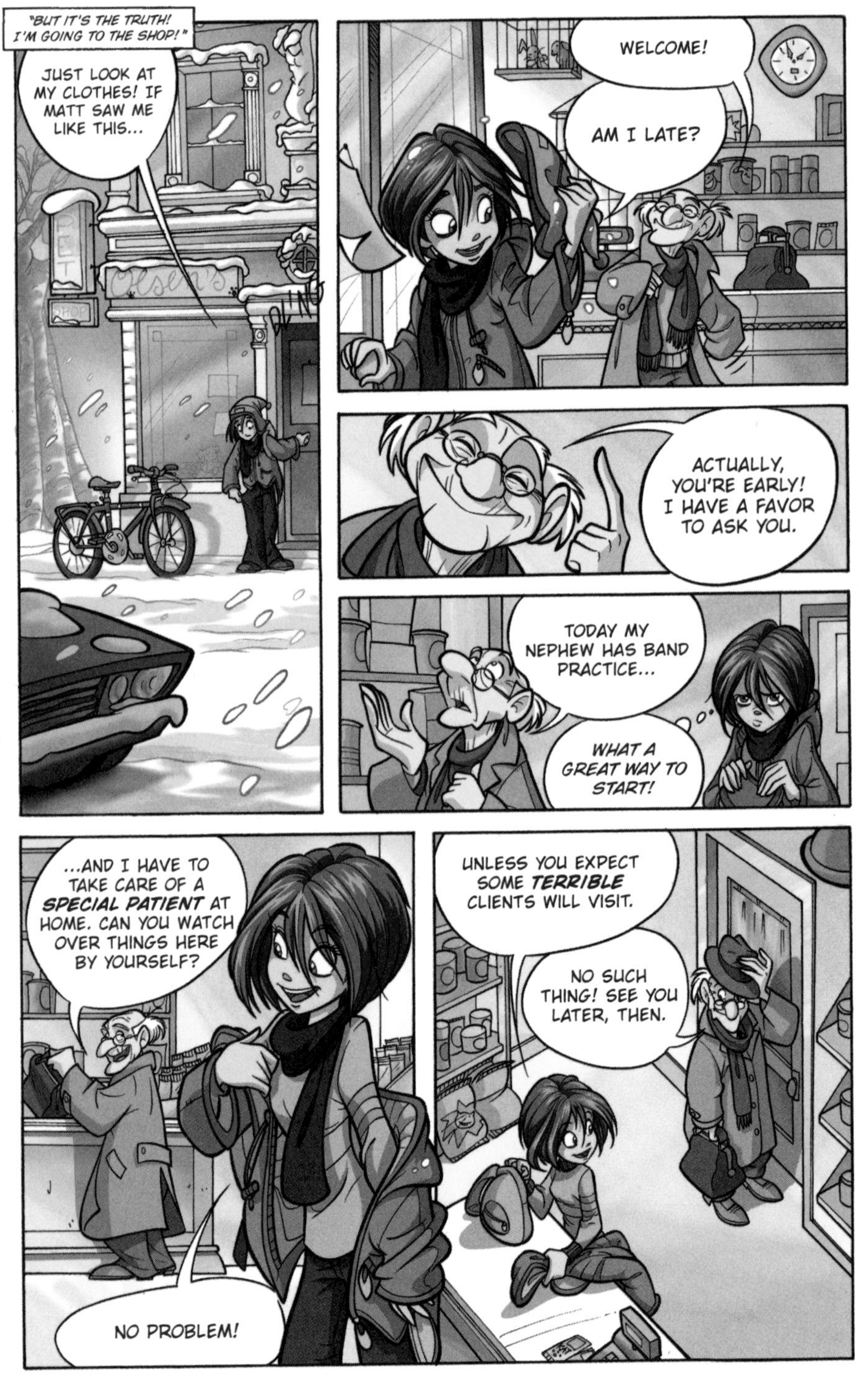
"BUT IT'S THE TRUTH! I'M GOING TO THE SHOP!"
JUST LOOK AT MY CLOTHES! IF MATT SAW ME LIKE THIS...
PET
SHOP
Olsen's
DING
WELCOME!
AM I LATE?
ACTUALLY, YOU'RE EARLY! I HAVE A FAVOR TO ASK YOU.
TODAY MY NEPHEW HAS BAND PRACTICE...
WHAT A GREAT WAY TO START!
...AND I HAVE TO TAKE CARE OF A SPECIAL PATIENT AT HOME. CAN YOU WATCH OVER THINGS HERE BY YOURSELF?
NO PROBLEM!
UNLESS YOU EXPECT SOME TERRIBLE CLIENTS WILL VISIT.
NO SUCH THING! SEE YOU LATER, THEN.

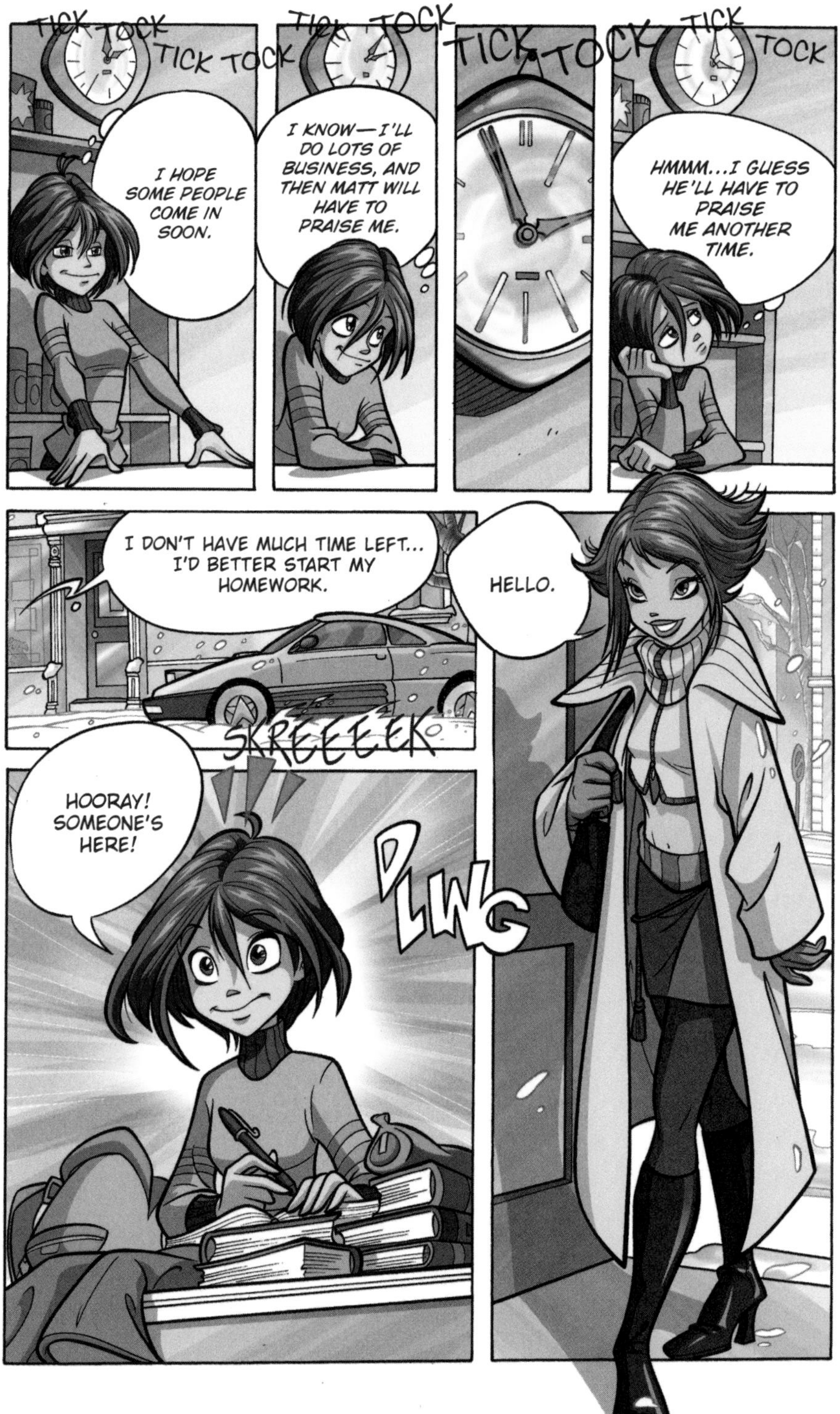
TICK TOCK
TICK TOCK
I HOPE SOME PEOPLE COME IN SOON.
TICK TOCK
I KNOW—I'LL DO LOTS OF BUSINESS, AND THEN MATT WILL HAVE TO PRAISE ME.
TICK TOCK
TICK TOCK
HMMM...I GUESS HE'LL HAVE TO PRAISE ME ANOTHER TIME.
I DON'T HAVE MUCH TIME LEFT... I'D BETTER START MY HOMEWORK.
SKREEEEEK
HELLO.
HOORAY! SOMEONE'S HERE!
DLING

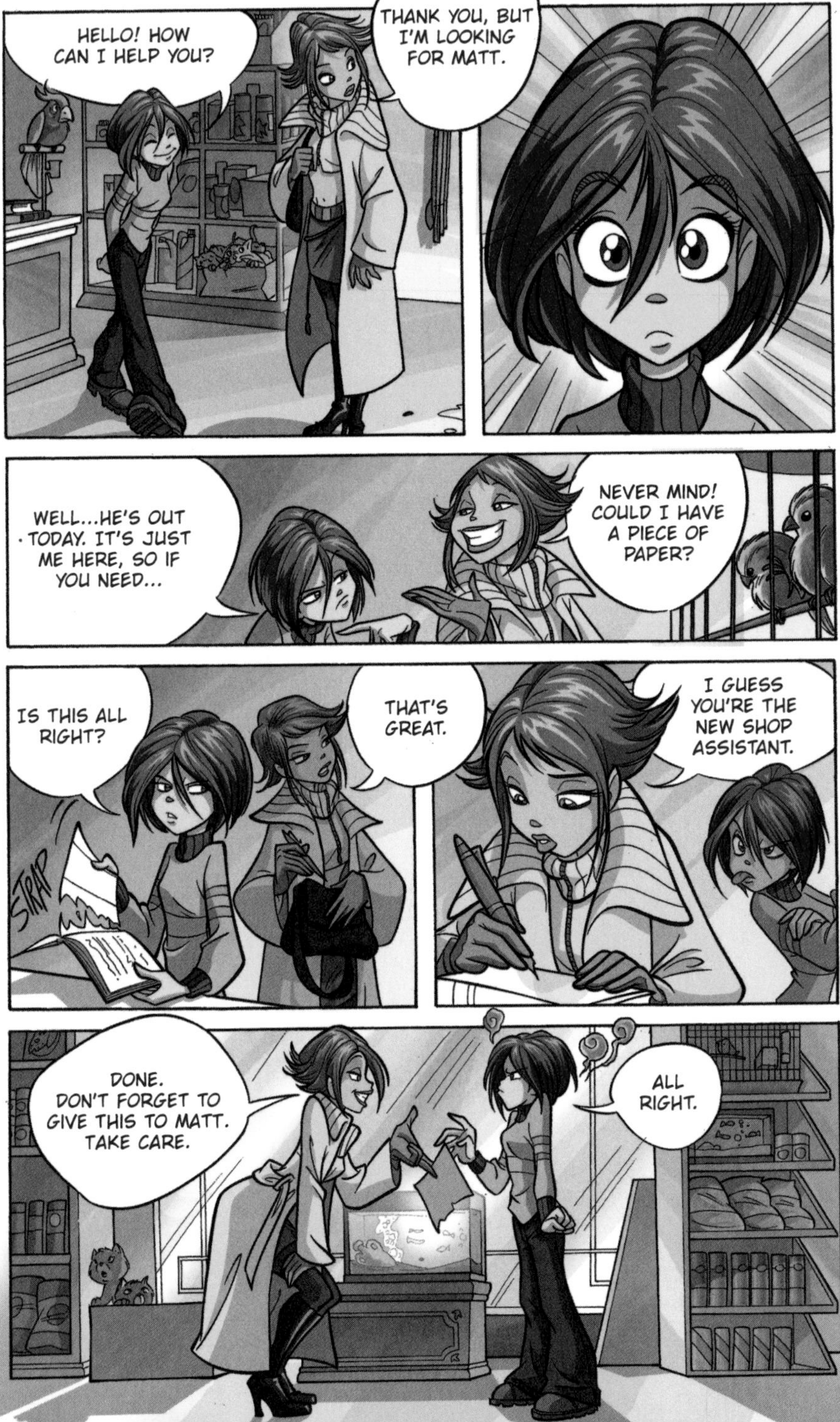
HELLO! HOW CAN I HELP YOU?
THANK YOU, BUT I'M LOOKING FOR MATT.
WELL...HE'S OUT TODAY. IT'S JUST ME HERE, SO IF YOU NEED...
NEVER MIND! COULD I HAVE A PIECE OF PAPER?
IS THIS ALL RIGHT?
STRAP
THAT'S GREAT.
I GUESS YOU'RE THE NEW SHOP ASSISTANT.
DONE. DON'T FORGET TO GIVE THIS TO MATT. TAKE CARE.
ALL RIGHT.

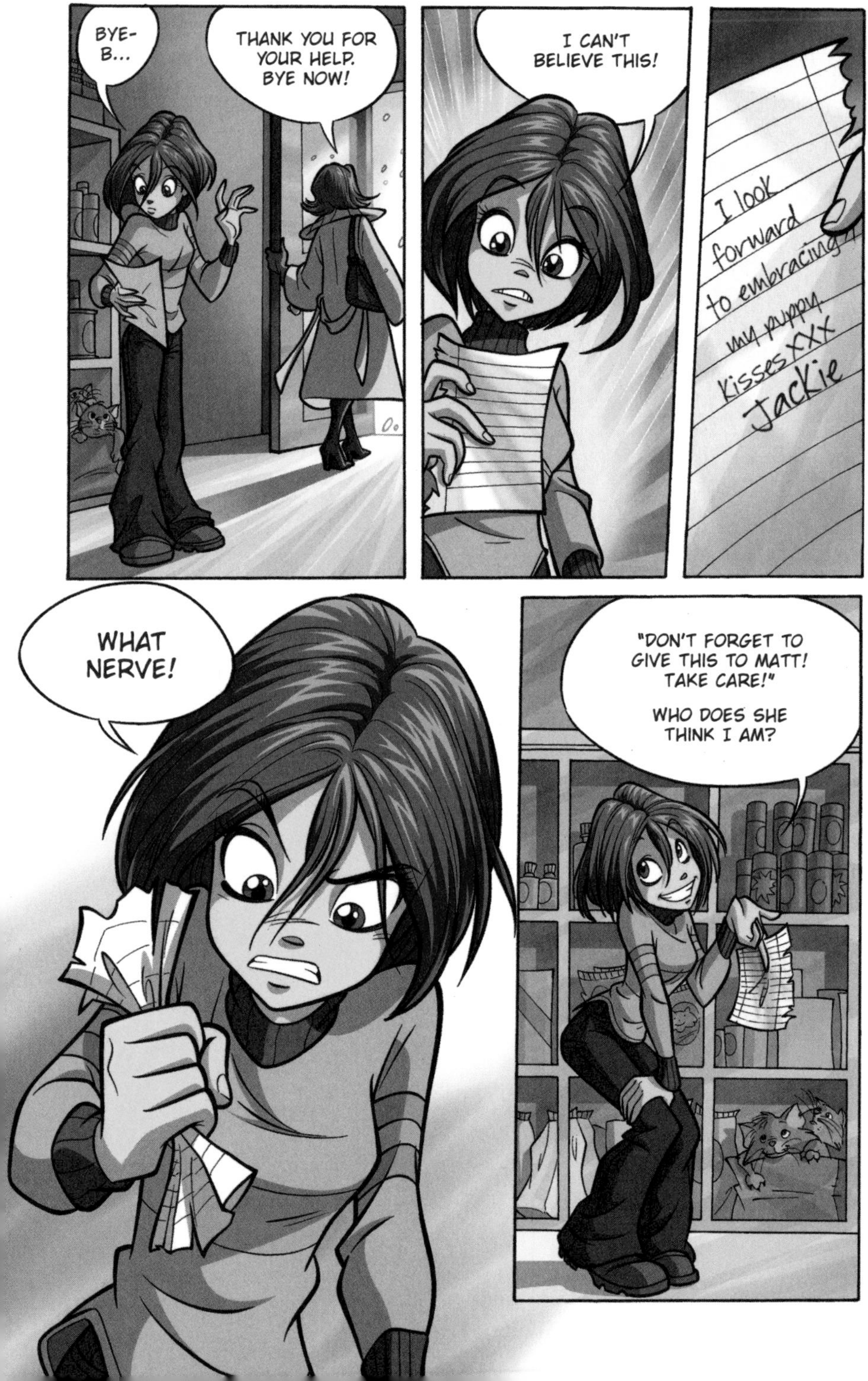
BYE-
B...
THANK YOU FOR YOUR HELP. BYE NOW!
I CAN'T BELIEVE THIS!
I look forward to embracing my puppy. kisses XXX Jackie
WHAT NERVE!
"DON'T FORGET TO GIVE THIS TO MATT! TAKE CARE!"
WHO DOES SHE THINK I AM?

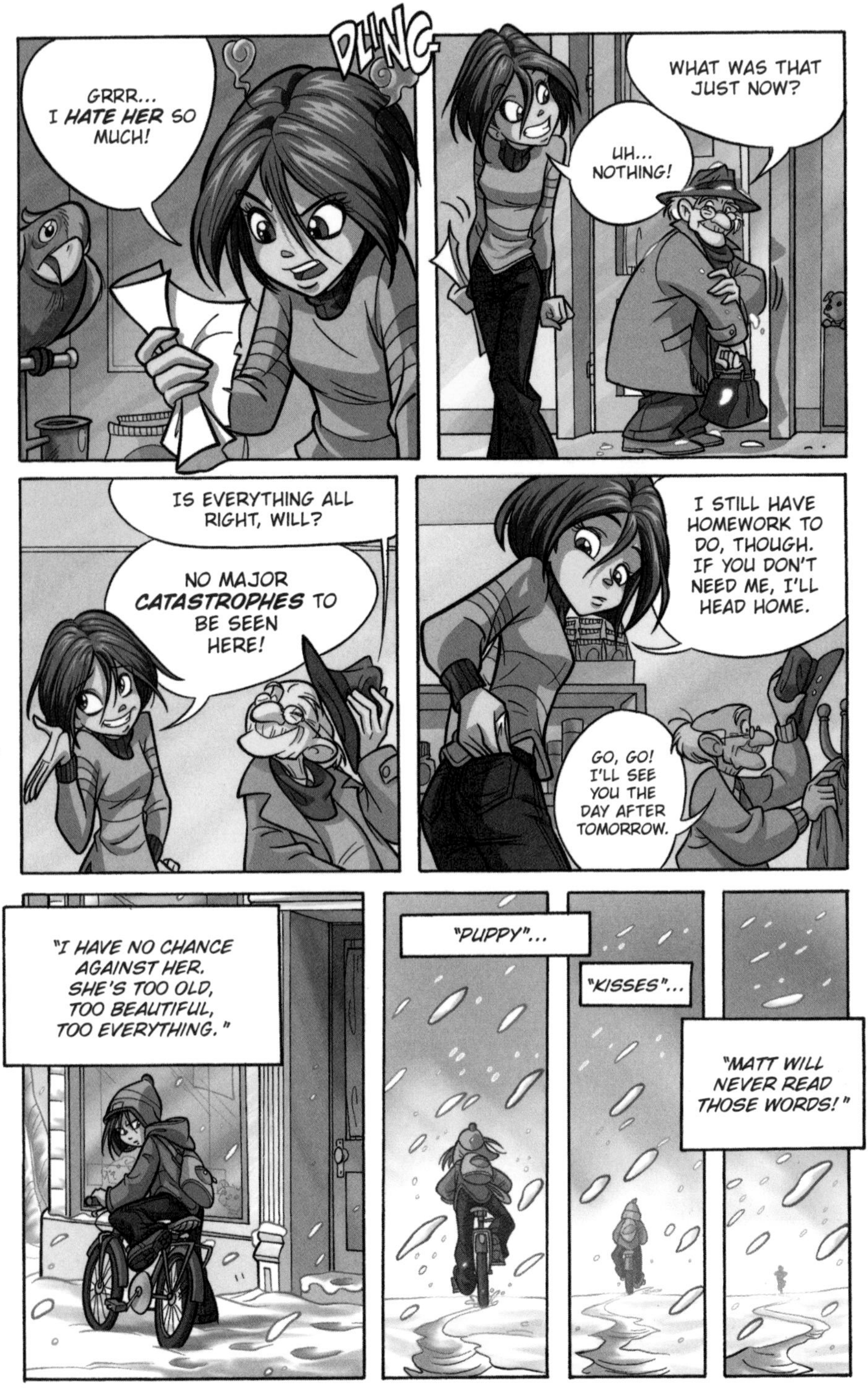
GRRR...
I HATE HER SO MUCH!
DLING
WHAT WAS THAT JUST NOW?
UH... NOTHING!
IS EVERYTHING ALL RIGHT, WILL?
NO MAJOR CATASTROPHES TO BE SEEN HERE!
I STILL HAVE HOMEWORK TO DO, THOUGH. IF YOU DON'T NEED ME, I'LL HEAD HOME.
GO, GO! I'LL SEE YOU THE DAY AFTER TOMORROW.
"I HAVE NO CHANCE AGAINST HER. SHE'S TOO OLD, TOO BEAUTIFUL, TOO EVERYTHING."
"PUPPY"...
"KISSES"...
"MATT WILL NEVER READ THOSE WORDS!"

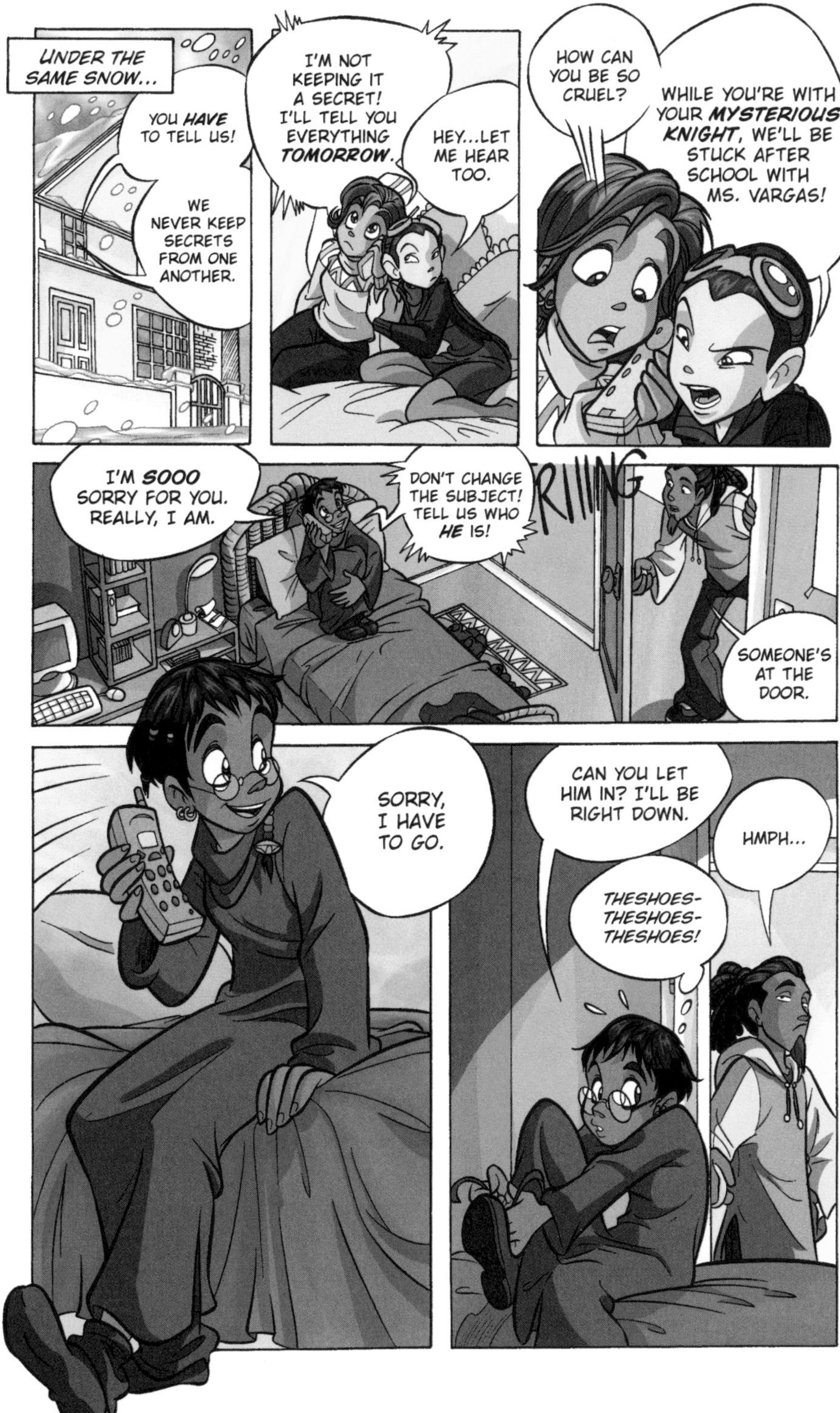
UNDER THE SAME SNOW...
YOU HAVE TO TELL US!
WE NEVER KEEP SECRETS FROM ONE ANOTHER.
I'M NOT KEEPING IT A SECRET! I'LL TELL YOU EVERYTHING TOMORROW.
HEY...LET ME HEAR TOO.
HOW CAN YOU BE SO CRUEL?
WHILE YOU'RE WITH YOUR MYSTERIOUS KNIGHT, WE'LL BE STUCK AFTER SCHOOL WITH MS. VARGAS!
I'M SOOO SORRY FOR YOU. REALLY, I AM.
DON'T CHANGE THE SUBJECT! TELL US WHO HE IS!
RIIING
SOMEONE'S AT THE DOOR.
SORRY, I HAVE TO GO.
CAN YOU LET HIM IN? I'LL BE RIGHT DOWN.
HMPH...
THESHOES-THESHOES-THESHOES!

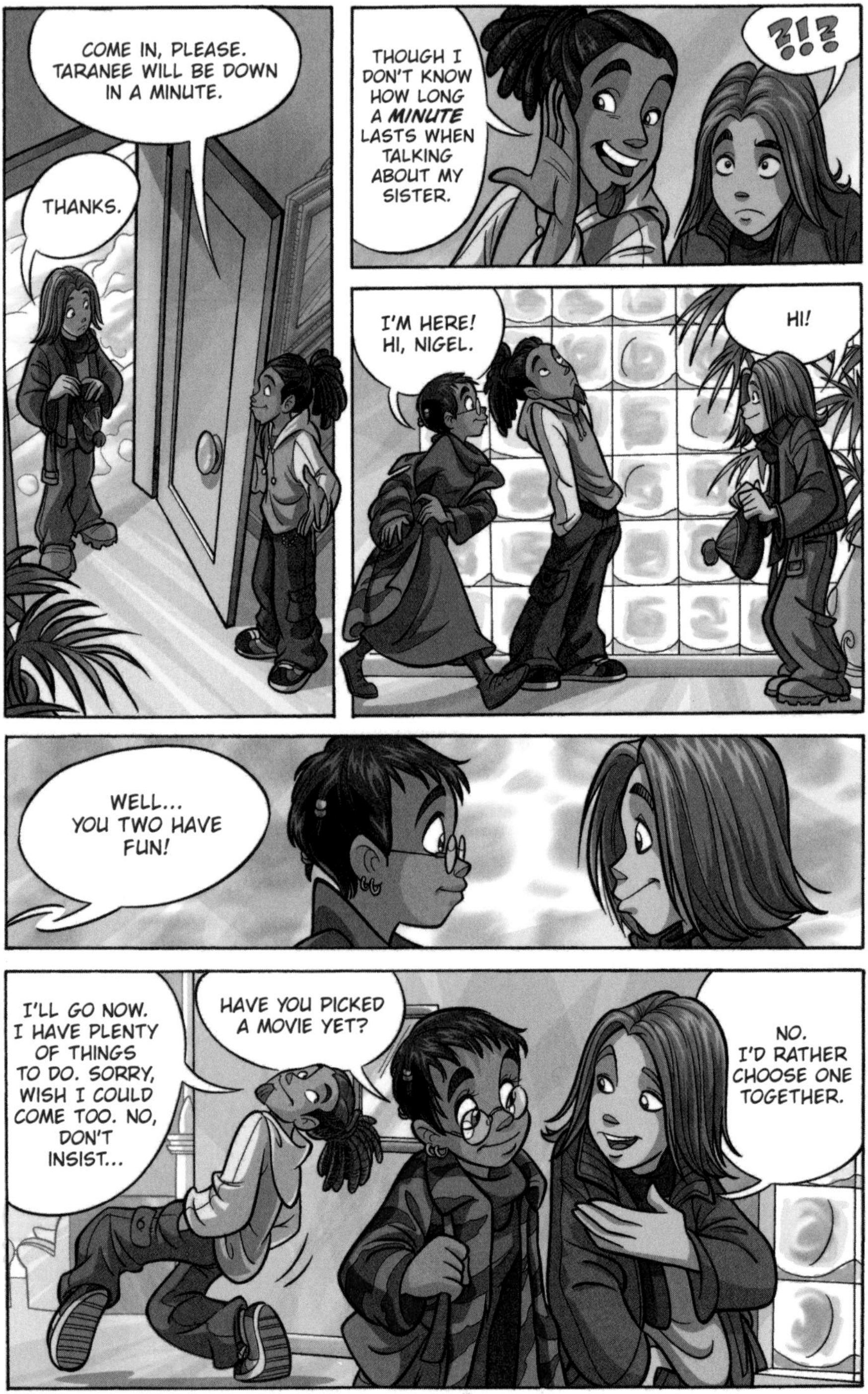
COME IN, PLEASE. TARANEE WILL BE DOWN IN A MINUTE.
THANKS.
THOUGH I DON'T KNOW HOW LONG A MINUTE LASTS WHEN TALKING ABOUT MY SISTER.
?!?
I'M HERE! HI, NIGEL.
HI!
WELL... YOU TWO HAVE FUN!
I'LL GO NOW. I HAVE PLENTY OF THINGS TO DO. SORRY, WISH I COULD COME TOO. NO, DON'T INSIST...
HAVE YOU PICKED A MOVIE YET?
NO. I'D RATHER CHOOSE ONE TOGETHER.

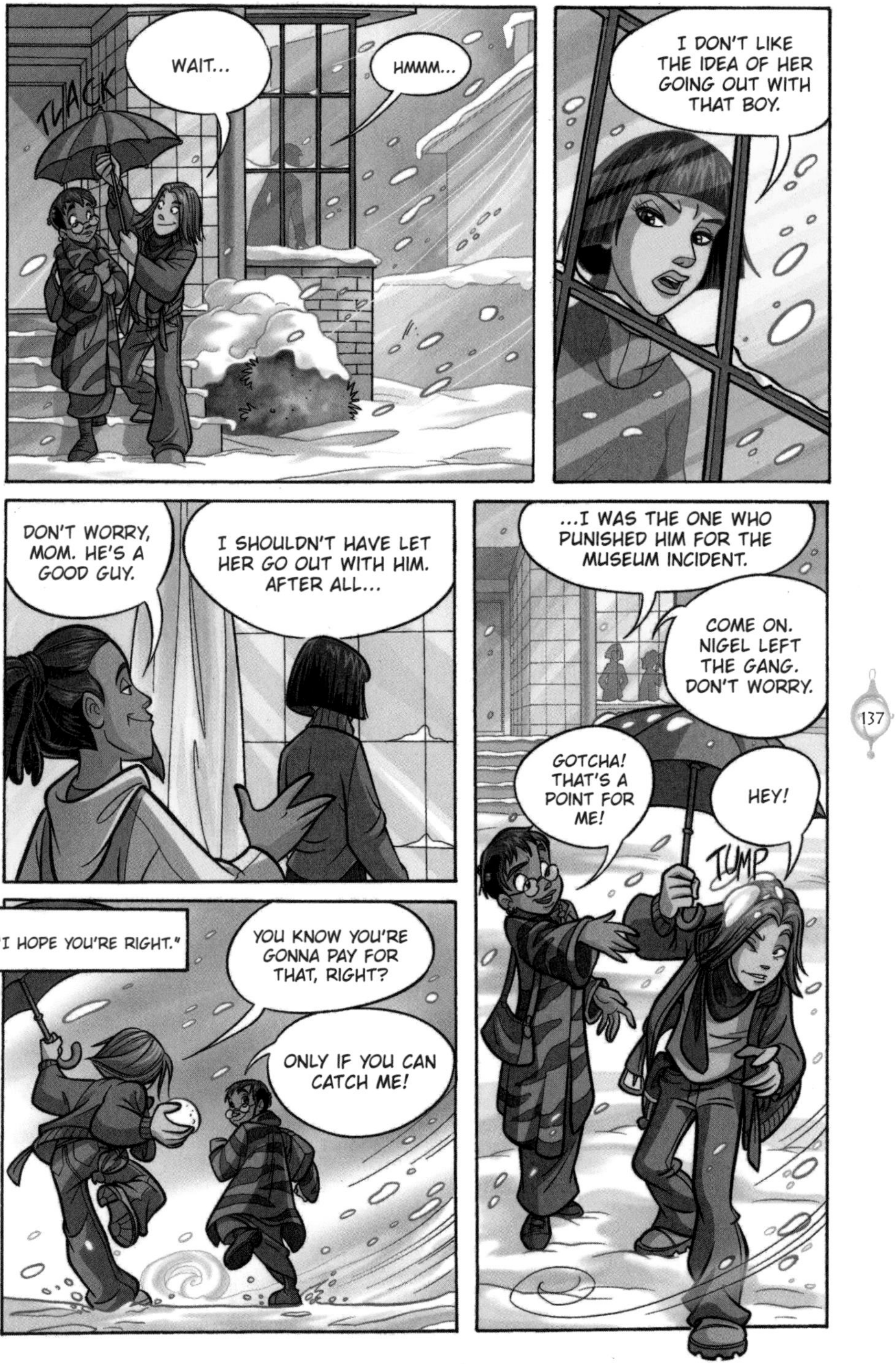
TLACK
WAIT...
HMMM...
I DON'T LIKE THE IDEA OF HER GOING OUT WITH THAT BOY.
DON'T WORRY, MOM. HE'S A GOOD GUY.
I SHOULDN'T HAVE LET HER GO OUT WITH HIM. AFTER ALL...
...I WAS THE ONE WHO PUNISHED HIM FOR THE MUSEUM INCIDENT.
COME ON. NIGEL LEFT THE GANG. DON'T WORRY.
GOTCHA! THAT'S A POINT FOR ME!
HEY!
TUMP
"I HOPE YOU'RE RIGHT."
YOU KNOW YOU'RE GONNA PAY FOR THAT, RIGHT?
ONLY IF YOU CAN CATCH ME!

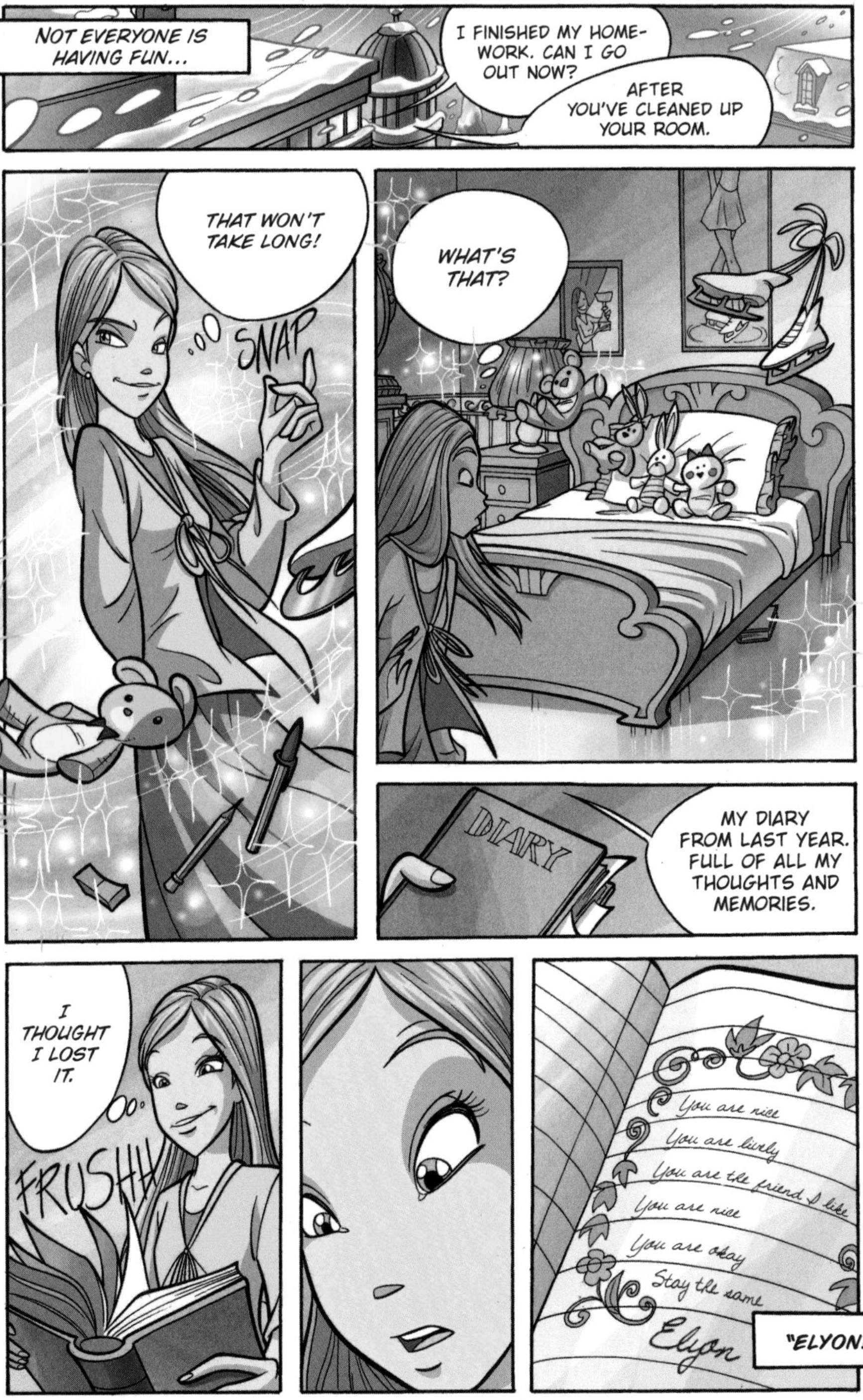
NOT EVERYONE IS HAVING FUN...
I FINISHED MY HOME-WORK. CAN I GO OUT NOW?
AFTER YOU'VE CLEANED UP YOUR ROOM.
THAT WON'T TAKE LONG!
SNAP
WHAT'S THAT?
DIARY
MY DIARY FROM LAST YEAR. FULL OF ALL MY THOUGHTS AND MEMORIES.
I THOUGHT I LOST IT.
FRUSHH
You are nice
You are lively
You are the friend I like
You are nice
You are okay
Stay the same
Elyon
"ELYON!

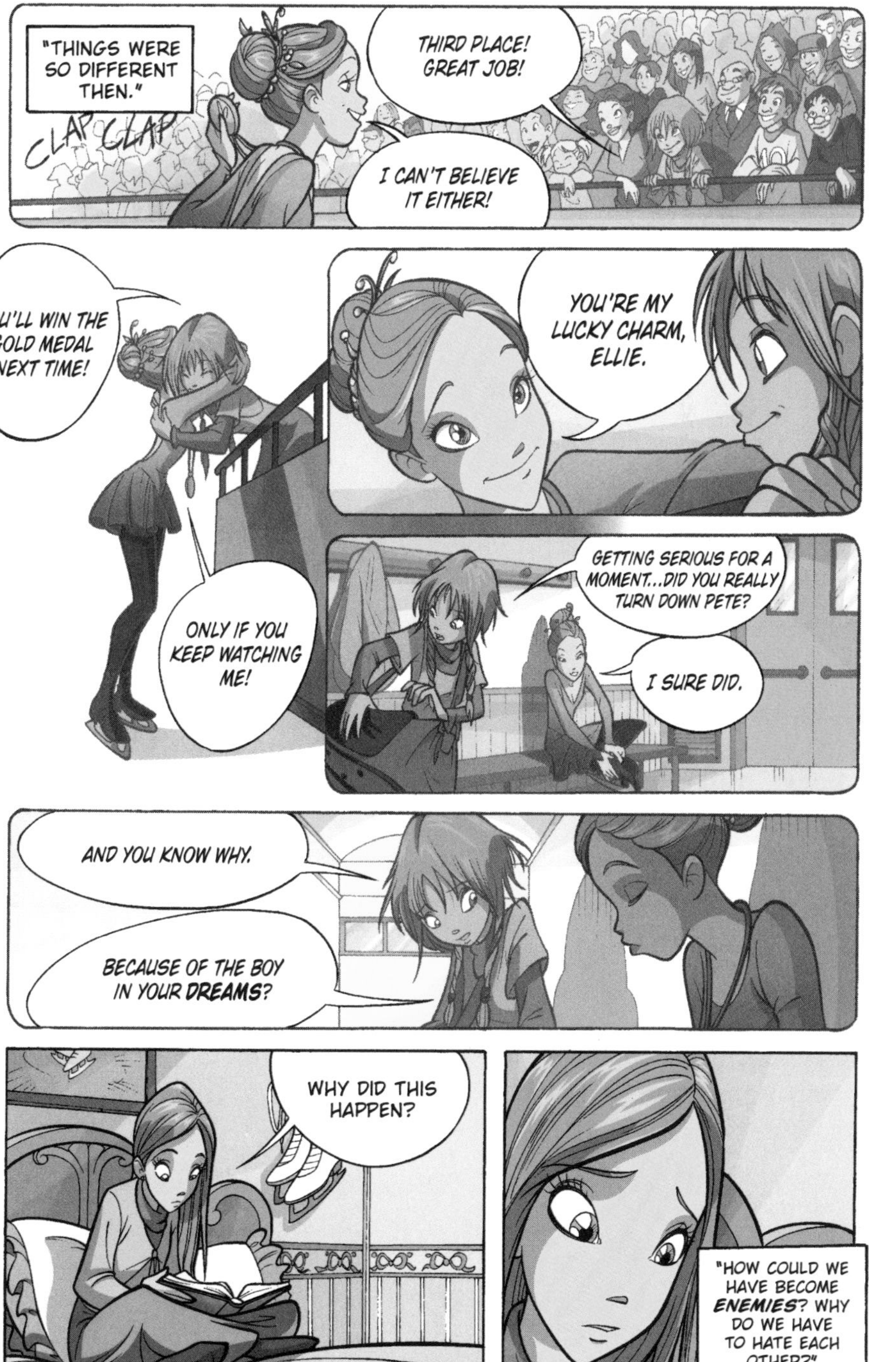
"THINGS WERE SO DIFFERENT THEN."
CLAP CLAP
THIRD PLACE! GREAT JOB!
I CAN'T BELIEVE IT EITHER!
YOU'LL WIN THE GOLD MEDAL NEXT TIME!
YOU'RE MY LUCKY CHARM, ELLIE.
ONLY IF YOU KEEP WATCHING ME!
GETTING SERIOUS FOR A MOMENT...DID YOU REALLY TURN DOWN PETE?
I SURE DID.
AND YOU KNOW WHY.
BECAUSE OF THE BOY IN YOUR DREAMS?
WHY DID THIS HAPPEN?
"HOW COULD WE HAVE BECOME ENEMIES? WHY DO WE HAVE TO HATE EACH OTHER?"

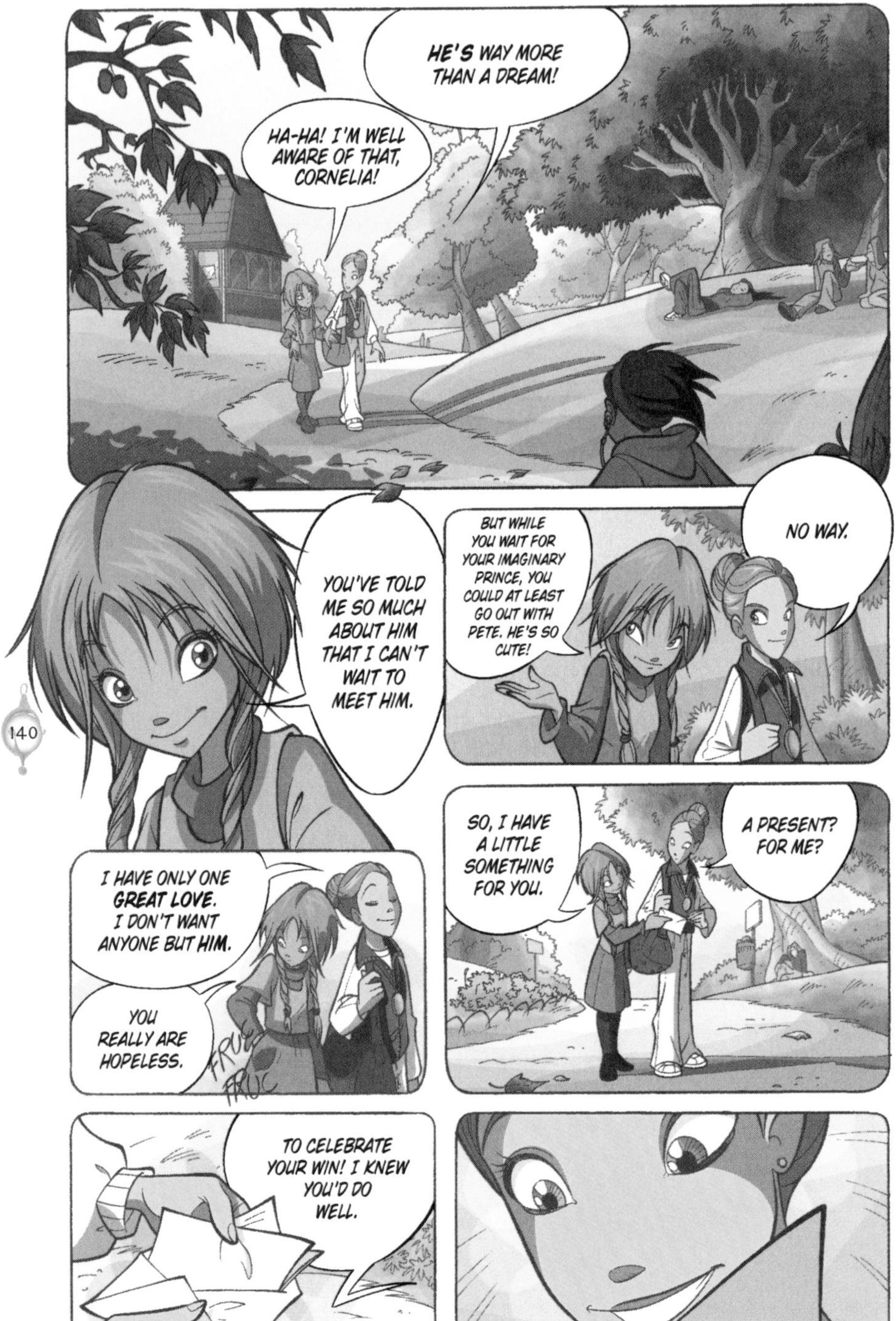
HE'S WAY MORE THAN A DREAM!
HA-HA! I'M WELL AWARE OF THAT, CORNELIA!
YOU'VE TOLD ME SO MUCH ABOUT HIM THAT I CAN'T WAIT TO MEET HIM.
BUT WHILE YOU WAIT FOR YOUR IMAGINARY PRINCE, YOU COULD AT LEAST GO OUT WITH PETE. HE'S SO CUTE!
NO WAY.
I HAVE ONLY ONE GREAT LOVE. I DON'T WANT ANYONE BUT HIM.
YOU REALLY ARE HOPELESS.
FRUC FRUC
SO, I HAVE A LITTLE SOMETHING FOR YOU.
A PRESENT? FOR ME?
TO CELEBRATE YOUR WIN! I KNEW YOU'D DO WELL.

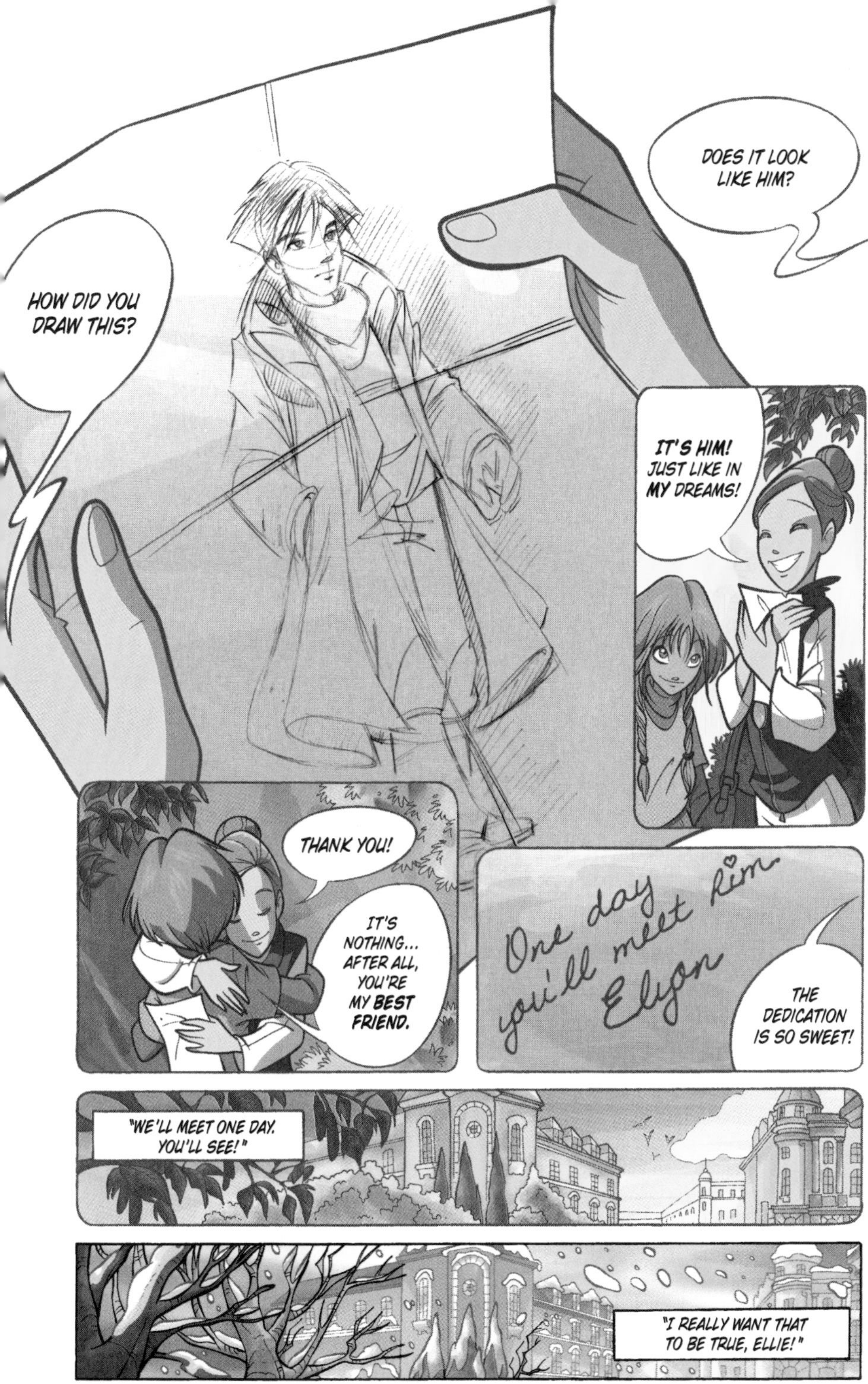
DOES IT LOOK LIKE HIM?
HOW DID YOU DRAW THIS?
IT'S HIM! JUST LIKE IN MY DREAMS!
THANK YOU!
IT'S NOTHING... AFTER ALL, YOU'RE MY BEST FRIEND.
One day you'll meet him. Elyon
THE DEDICATION IS SO SWEET!
"WE'LL MEET ONE DAY. YOU'LL SEE!"
"I REALLY WANT THAT TO BE TRUE, ELLIE!"

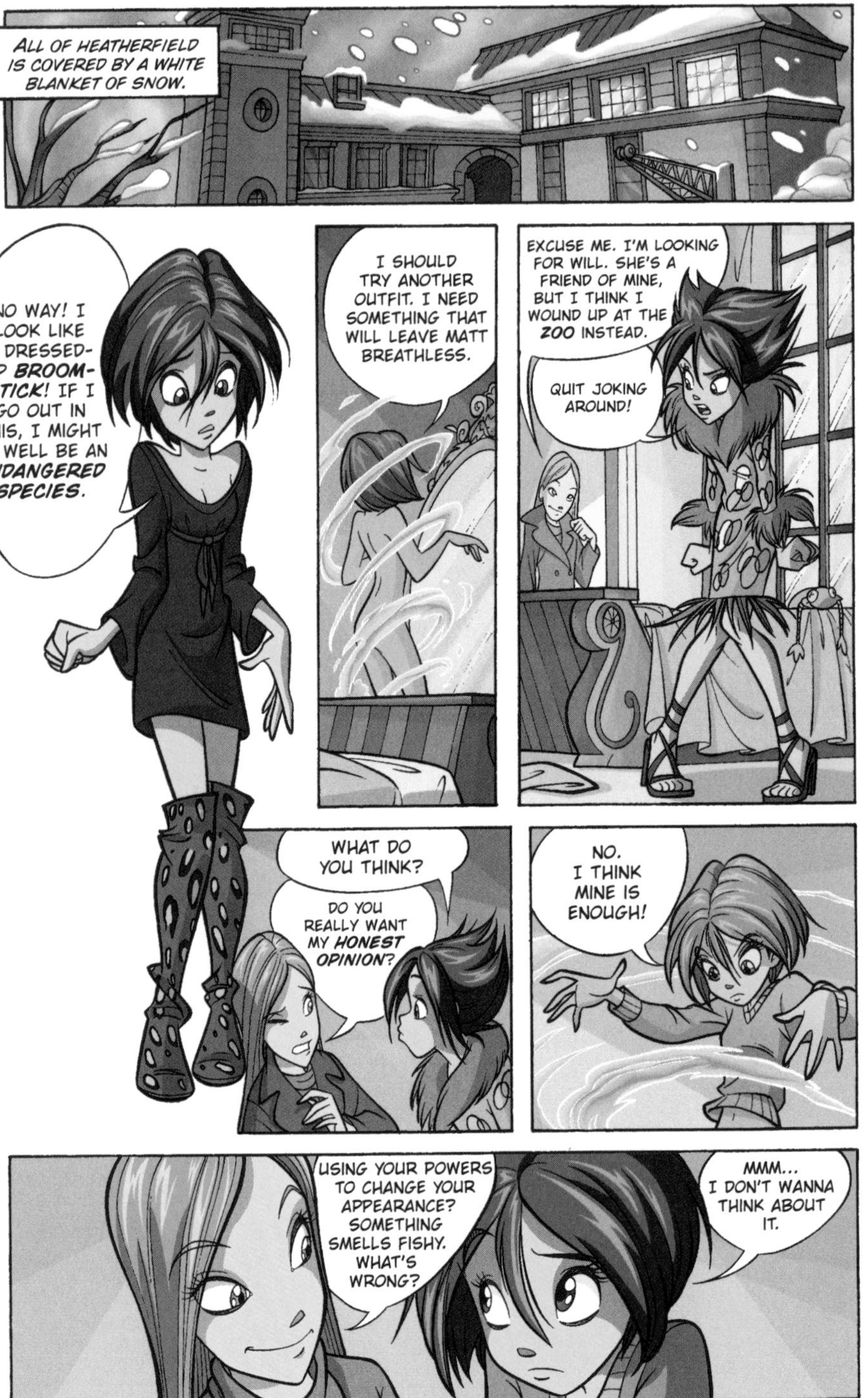
ALL OF HEATHERFIELD IS COVERED BY A WHITE BLANKET OF SNOW.
NO WAY! I LOOK LIKE A DRESSED-UP **BROOMSTICK**! IF I GO OUT IN THIS, I MIGHT AS WELL BE AN **ENDANGERED SPECIES**.
I SHOULD TRY ANOTHER OUTFIT. I NEED SOMETHING THAT WILL LEAVE MATT BREATHLESS.
EXCUSE ME. I'M LOOKING FOR WILL. SHE'S A FRIEND OF MINE, BUT I THINK I WOUND UP AT THE **ZOO** INSTEAD.
QUIT JOKING AROUND!
WHAT DO YOU THINK?
DO YOU REALLY WANT MY **HONEST OPINION**?
NO. I THINK MINE IS ENOUGH!
USING YOUR POWERS TO CHANGE YOUR APPEARANCE? SOMETHING SMELLS FISHY. WHAT'S WRONG?
MMM... I DON'T WANNA THINK ABOUT IT.

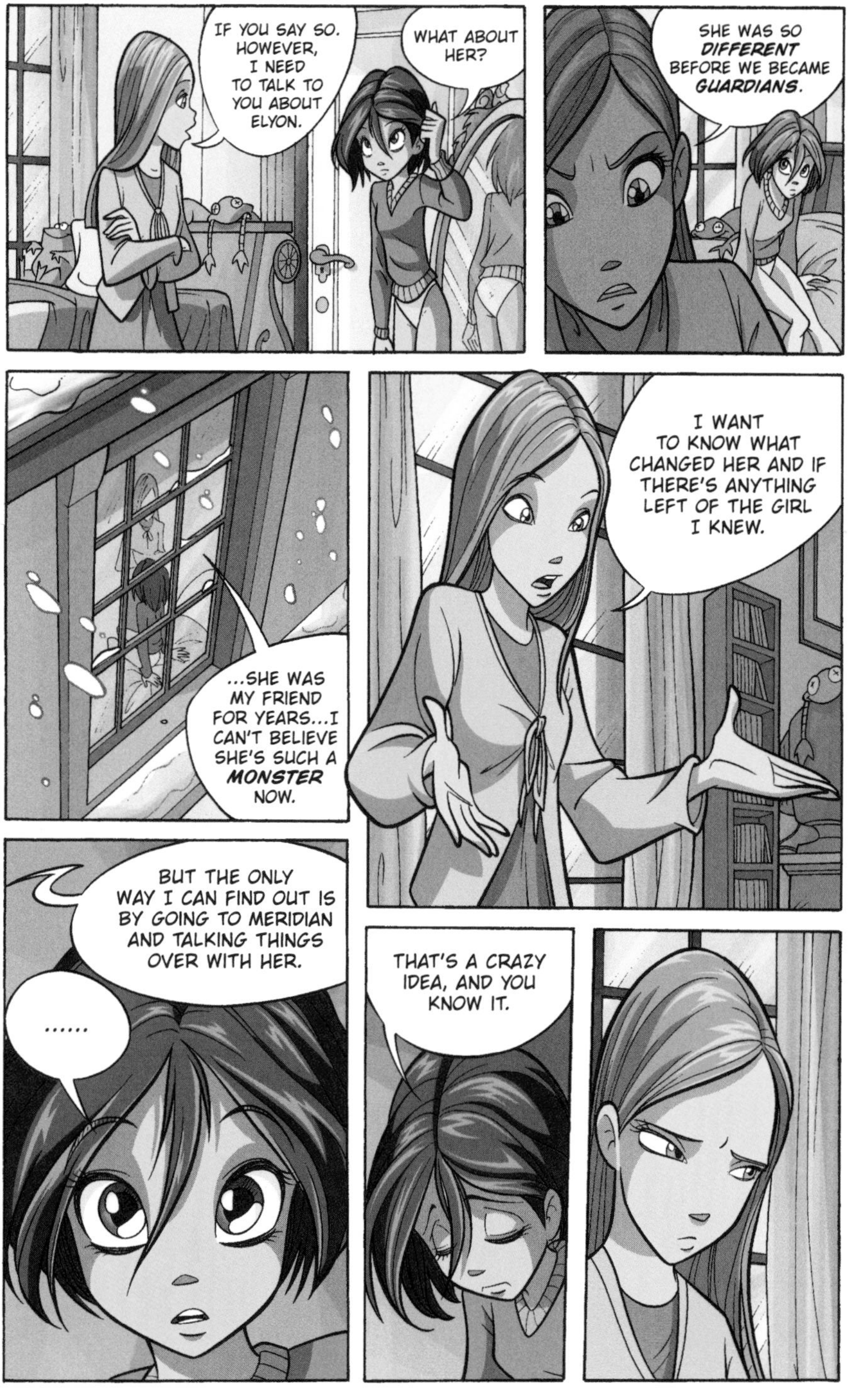
IF YOU SAY SO. HOWEVER, I NEED TO TALK TO YOU ABOUT ELYON.
WHAT ABOUT HER?
SHE WAS SO *DIFFERENT* BEFORE WE BECAME *GUARDIANS*.
...SHE WAS MY FRIEND FOR YEARS...I CAN'T BELIEVE SHE'S SUCH A *MONSTER* NOW.
I WANT TO KNOW WHAT CHANGED HER AND IF THERE'S ANYTHING LEFT OF THE GIRL I KNEW.
BUT THE ONLY WAY I CAN FIND OUT IS BY GOING TO MERIDIAN AND TALKING THINGS OVER WITH HER.
......
THAT'S A CRAZY IDEA, AND YOU KNOW IT.

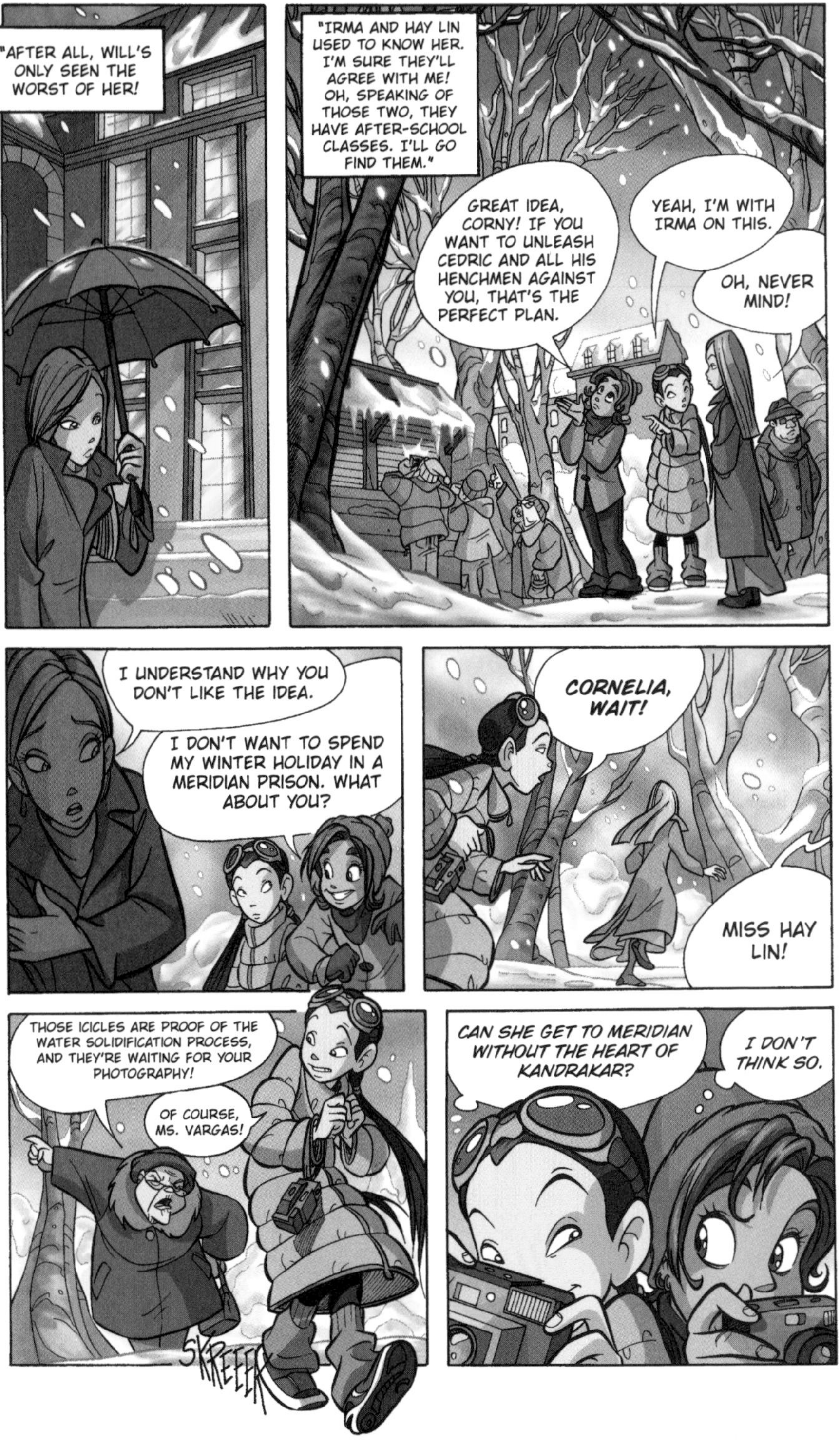

"AFTER ALL, WILL'S ONLY SEEN THE WORST OF HER!
"IRMA AND HAY LIN USED TO KNOW HER. I'M SURE THEY'LL AGREE WITH ME! OH, SPEAKING OF THOSE TWO, THEY HAVE AFTER-SCHOOL CLASSES. I'LL GO FIND THEM."
GREAT IDEA, CORNY! IF YOU WANT TO UNLEASH CEDRIC AND ALL HIS HENCHMEN AGAINST YOU, THAT'S THE PERFECT PLAN.
YEAH, I'M WITH IRMA ON THIS.
OH, NEVER MIND!
I UNDERSTAND WHY YOU DON'T LIKE THE IDEA.
I DON'T WANT TO SPEND MY WINTER HOLIDAY IN A MERIDIAN PRISON. WHAT ABOUT YOU?
CORNELIA, WAIT!
MISS HAY LIN!
THOSE ICICLES ARE PROOF OF THE WATER SOLIDIFICATION PROCESS, AND THEY'RE WAITING FOR YOUR PHOTOGRAPHY!
OF COURSE, MS. VARGAS!
SKREEEK
CAN SHE GET TO MERIDIAN WITHOUT THE HEART OF KANDRAKAR?
I DON'T THINK SO.

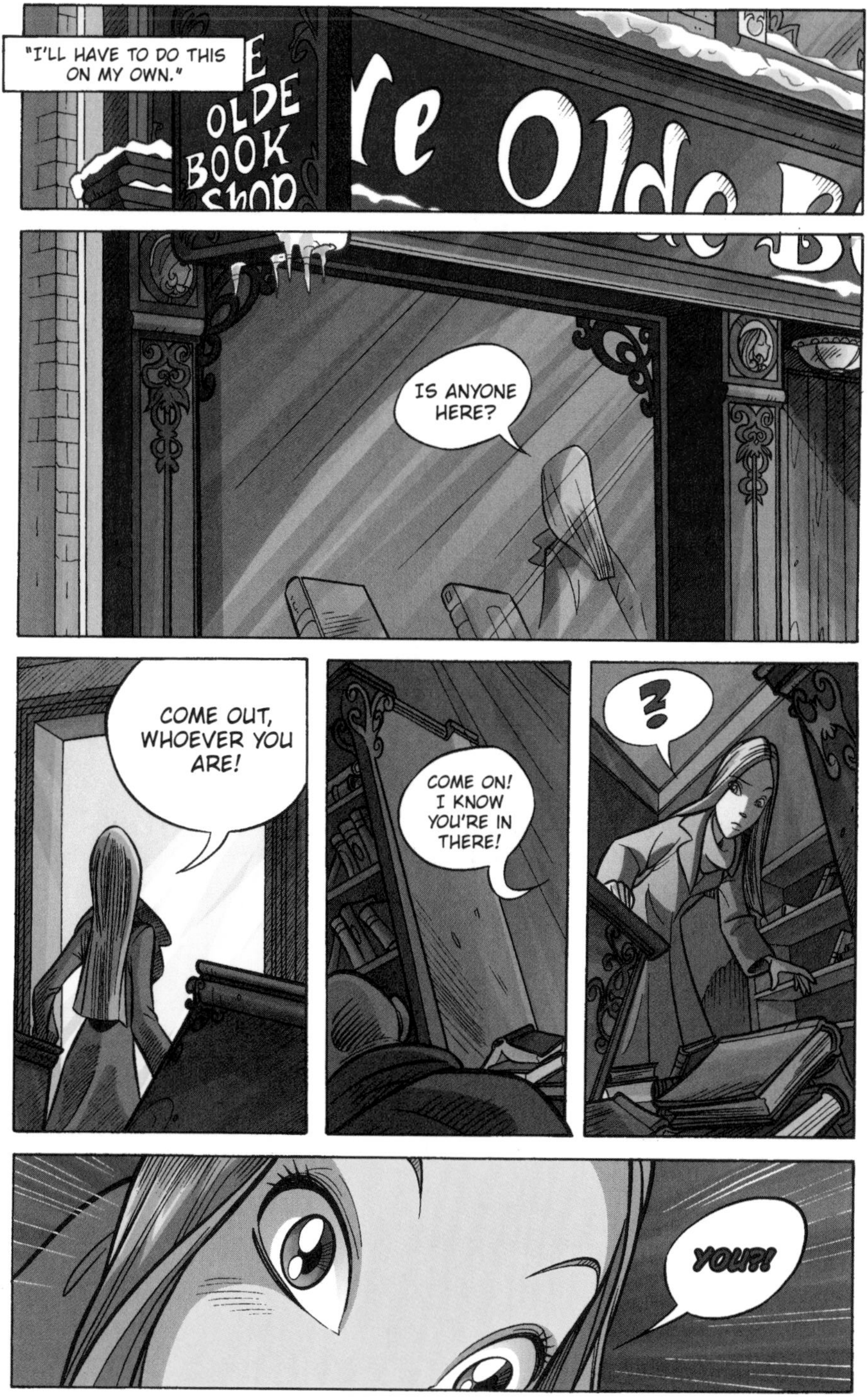
"I'LL HAVE TO DO THIS ON MY OWN."
OLDE BOOK SHOP
OLDE
IS ANYONE HERE?
COME OUT, WHOEVER YOU ARE!
COME ON! I KNOW YOU'RE IN THERE!
?
YOU?!

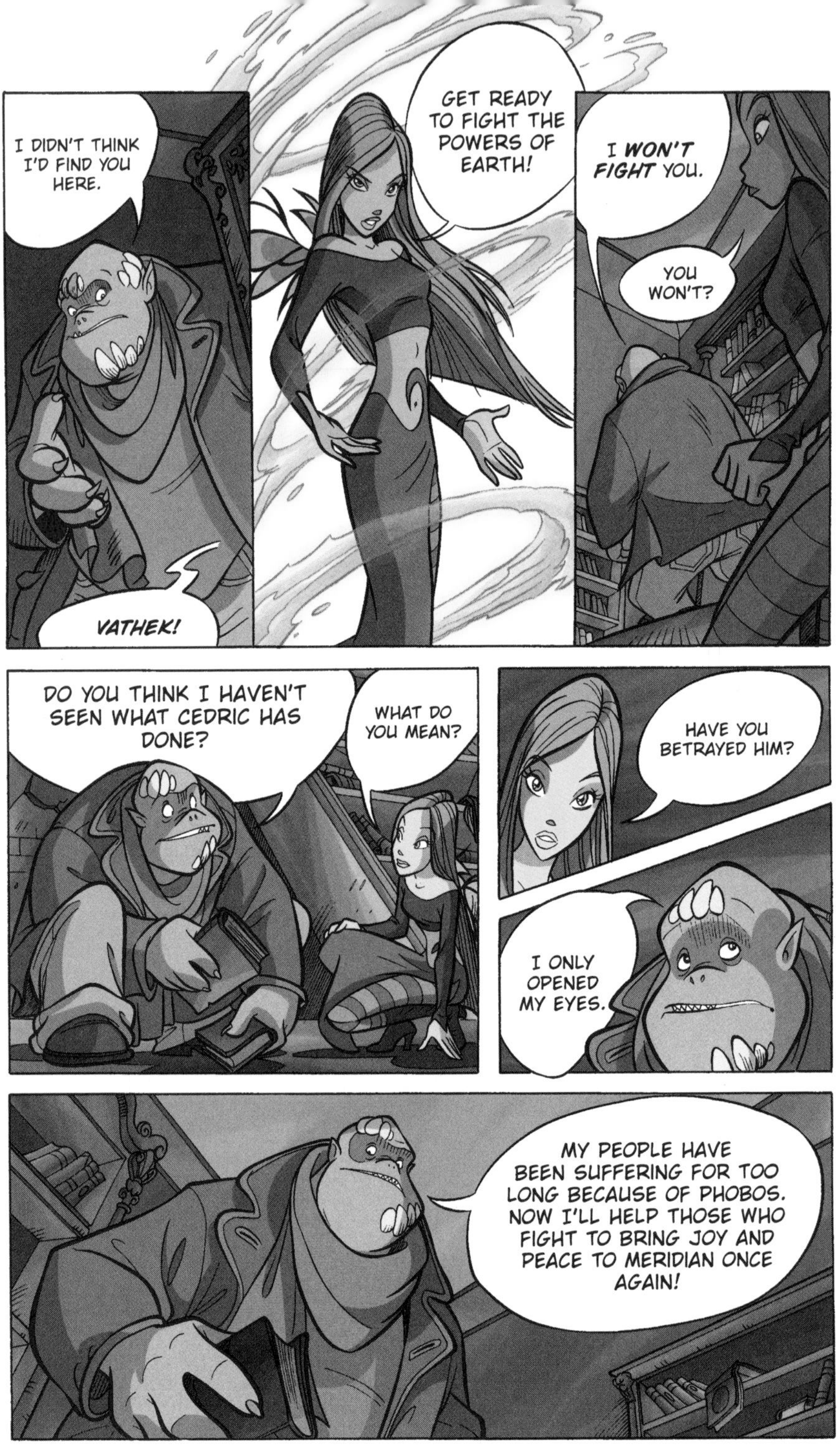

I DIDN'T THINK I'D FIND YOU HERE.
VATHEK!
GET READY TO FIGHT THE POWERS OF EARTH!
I **WON'T FIGHT** YOU.
YOU WON'T?
DO YOU THINK I HAVEN'T SEEN WHAT CEDRIC HAS DONE?
WHAT DO YOU MEAN?
HAVE YOU BETRAYED HIM?
I ONLY OPENED MY EYES.
MY PEOPLE HAVE BEEN SUFFERING FOR TOO LONG BECAUSE OF PHOBOS. NOW I'LL HELP THOSE WHO FIGHT TO BRING JOY AND PEACE TO MERIDIAN ONCE AGAIN!

ENOUGH TALKING! I HAVE EVERYTHING **CALEB** ASKED FOR.

CALEB...

CALEB.

CALEB.

CALEB.

WHAT'S HAPPENING TO ME? THAT NAME...

NO WAY!

CLANG

GOOD-BYE, GUARDIAN.

WAIT! TAKE ME WITH YOU!

IF YOU'VE CHANGED, MAYBE ELYON HAS TOO...

MMM... DON'T COUNT ON IT. SHE FOLLOWS CEDRIC'S EVERY WORD.

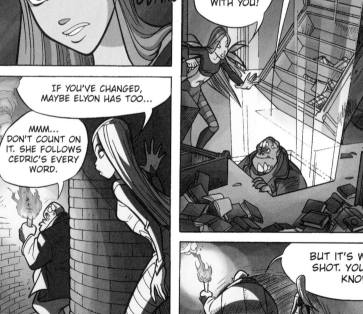

BUT IT'S WORTH A SHOT. YOU NEVER KNOW.

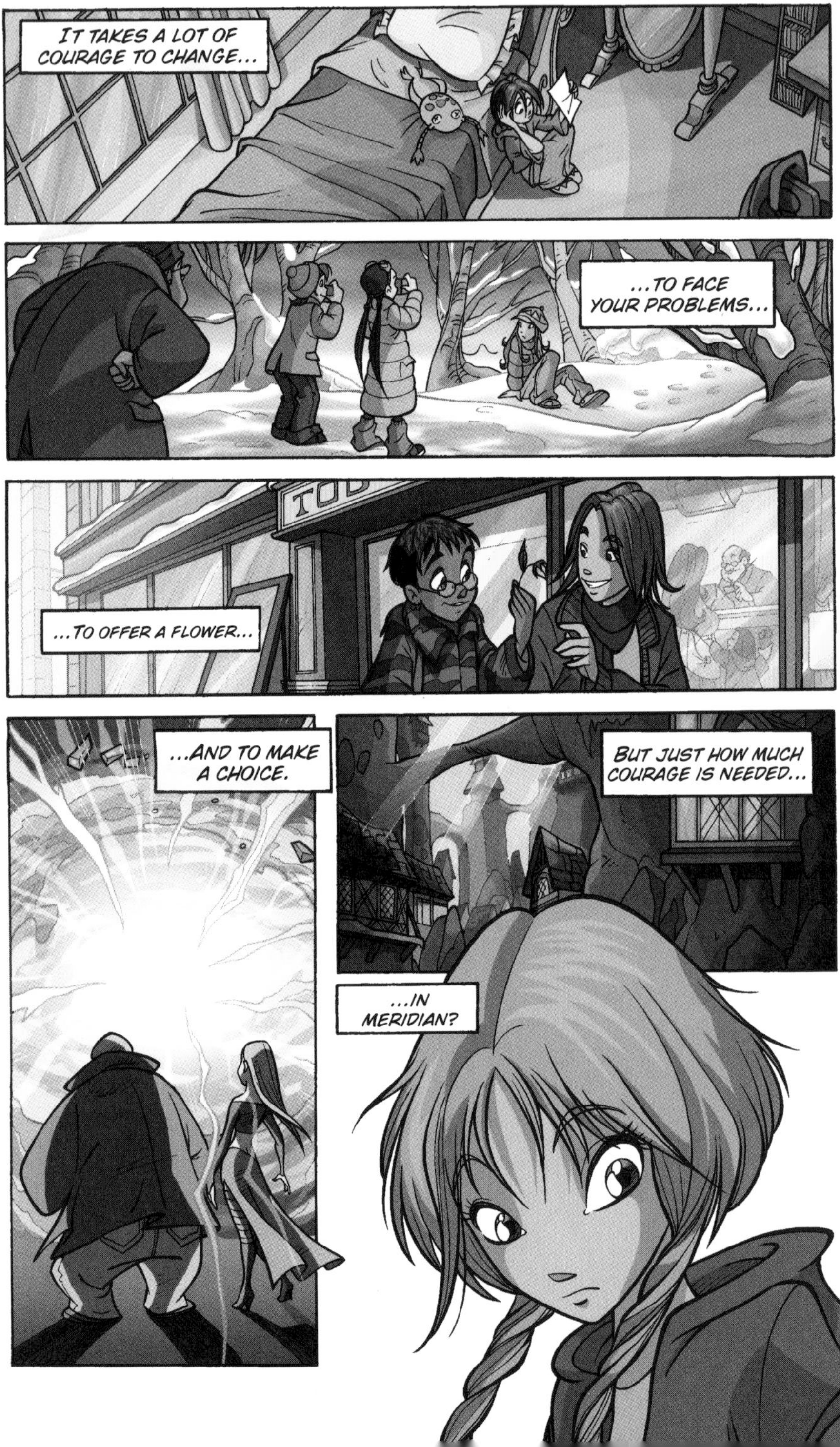
IT TAKES A LOT OF COURAGE TO CHANGE...
...TO FACE YOUR PROBLEMS...
TOD
...TO OFFER A FLOWER...
...AND TO MAKE A CHOICE.
BUT JUST HOW MUCH COURAGE IS NEEDED...
...IN MERIDIAN?

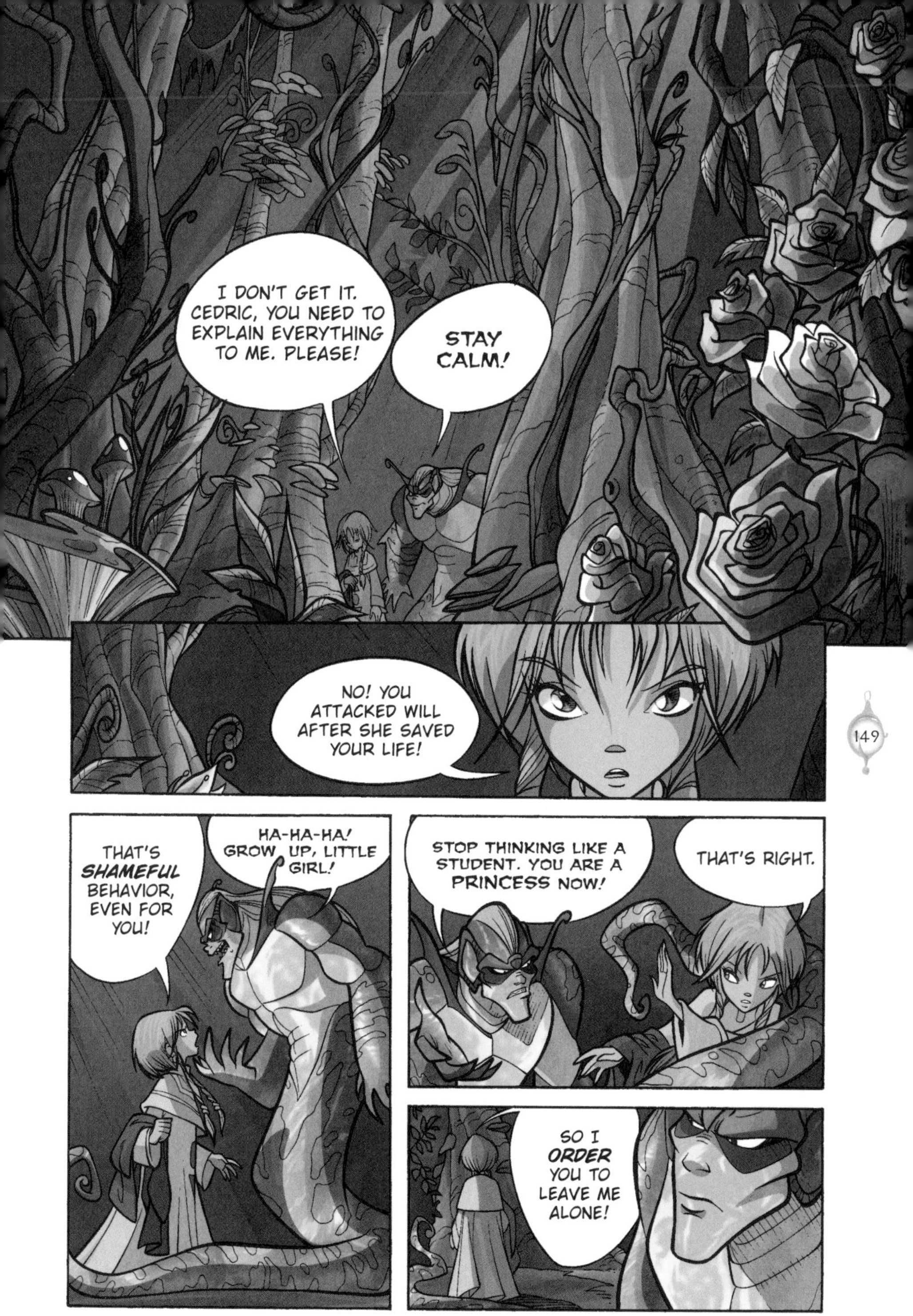
I DON'T GET IT. CEDRIC, YOU NEED TO EXPLAIN EVERYTHING TO ME. PLEASE!
STAY CALM!
NO! YOU ATTACKED WILL AFTER SHE SAVED YOUR LIFE!
THAT'S SHAMEFUL BEHAVIOR, EVEN FOR YOU!
HA-HA-HA! GROW UP, LITTLE GIRL!
STOP THINKING LIKE A STUDENT. YOU ARE A PRINCESS NOW!
THAT'S RIGHT.
SO I ORDER YOU TO LEAVE ME ALONE!

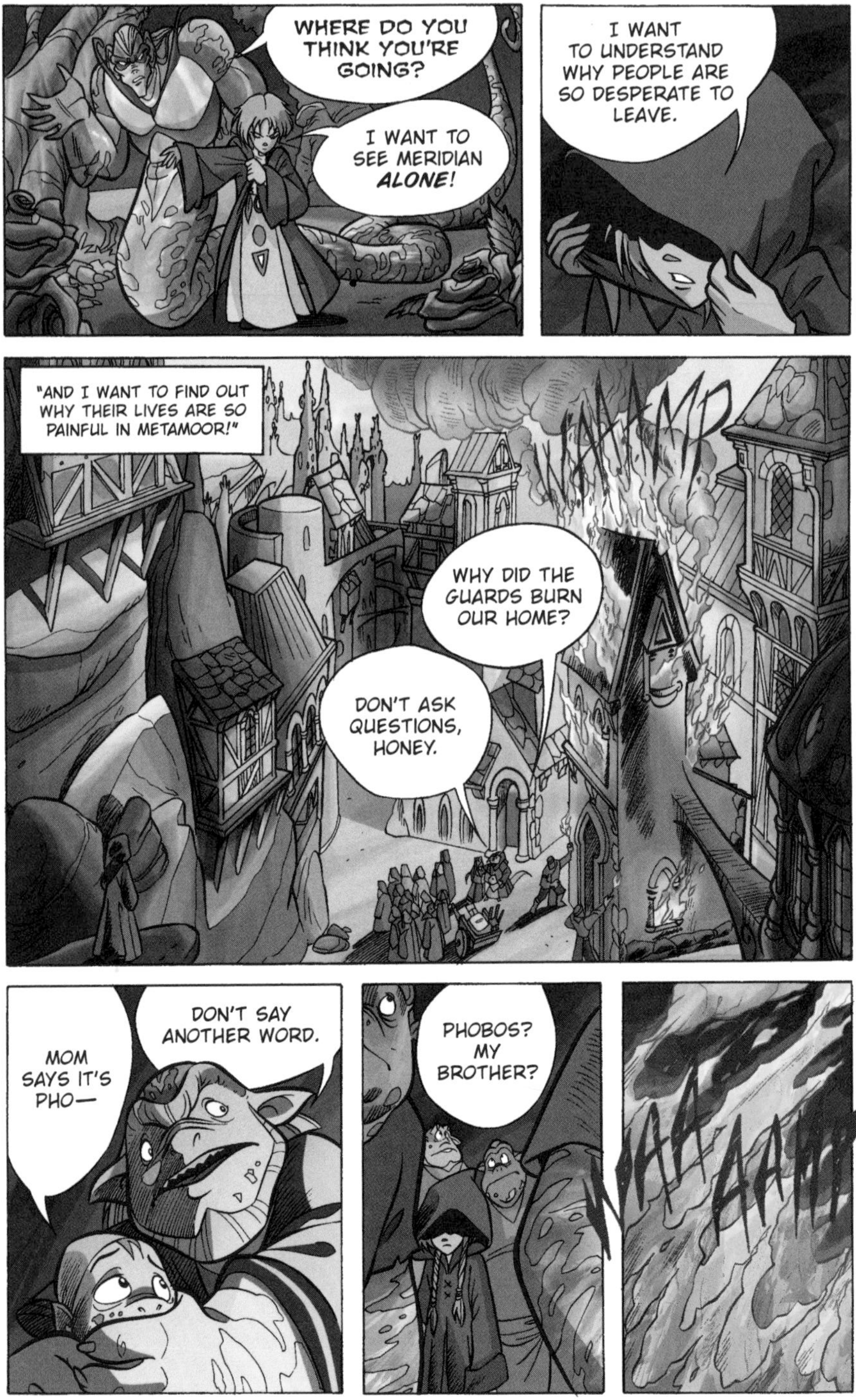
WHERE DO YOU THINK YOU'RE GOING?
I WANT TO SEE MERIDIAN *ALONE*!
I WANT TO UNDERSTAND WHY PEOPLE ARE SO DESPERATE TO LEAVE.
"AND I WANT TO FIND OUT WHY THEIR LIVES ARE SO PAINFUL IN METAMOOR!"
WHY DID THE GUARDS BURN OUR HOME?
DON'T ASK QUESTIONS, HONEY.
MOM SAYS IT'S PHO—
DON'T SAY ANOTHER WORD.
PHOBOS? MY BROTHER?

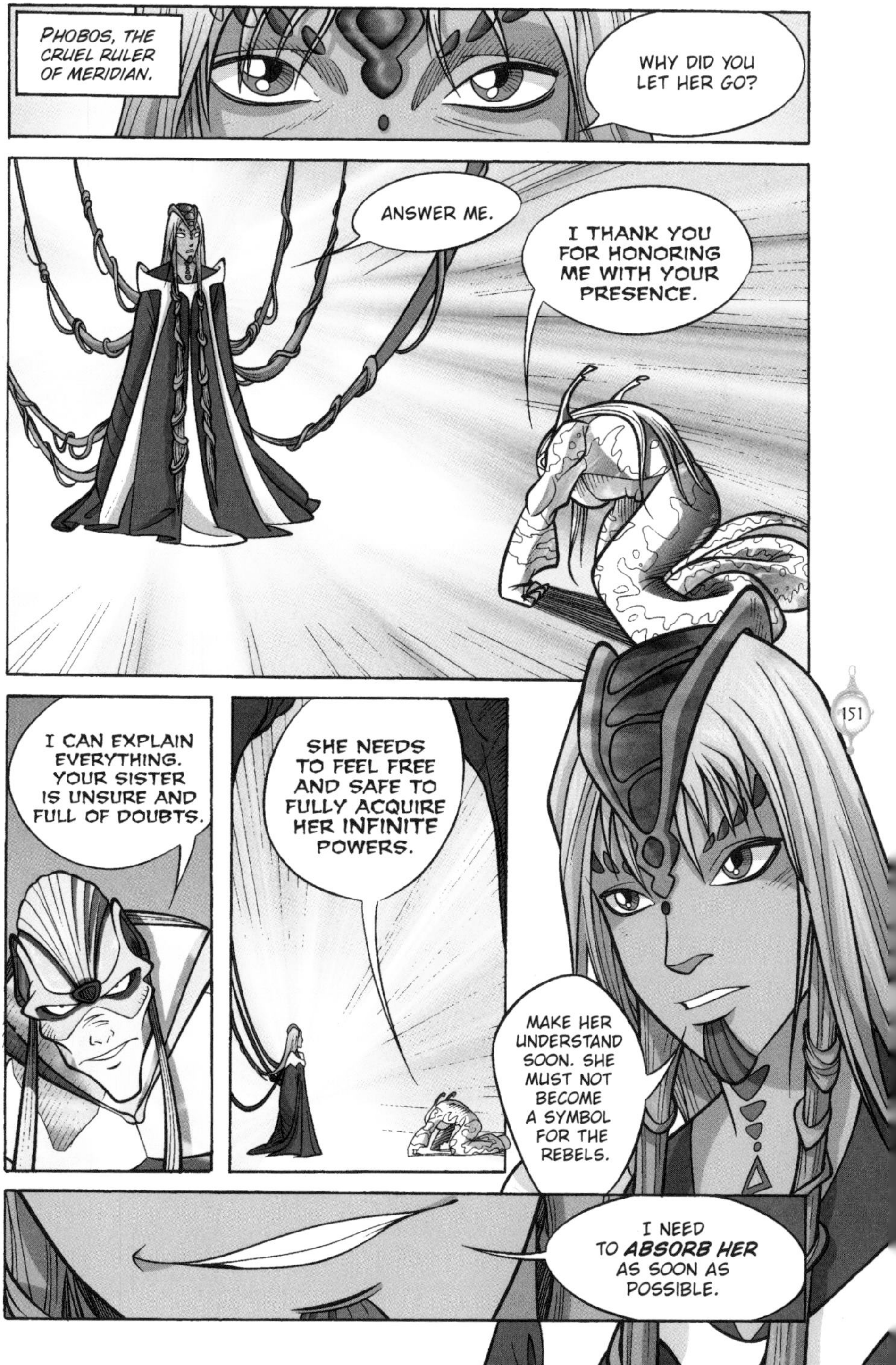
PHOBOS, THE CRUEL RULER OF MERIDIAN.
WHY DID YOU LET HER GO?
ANSWER ME.
I THANK YOU FOR HONORING ME WITH YOUR PRESENCE.
I CAN EXPLAIN EVERYTHING. YOUR SISTER IS UNSURE AND FULL OF DOUBTS.
SHE NEEDS TO FEEL FREE AND SAFE TO FULLY ACQUIRE HER INFINITE POWERS.
MAKE HER UNDERSTAND SOON. SHE MUST NOT BECOME A SYMBOL FOR THE REBELS.
I NEED TO ***ABSORB HER*** AS SOON AS POSSIBLE.

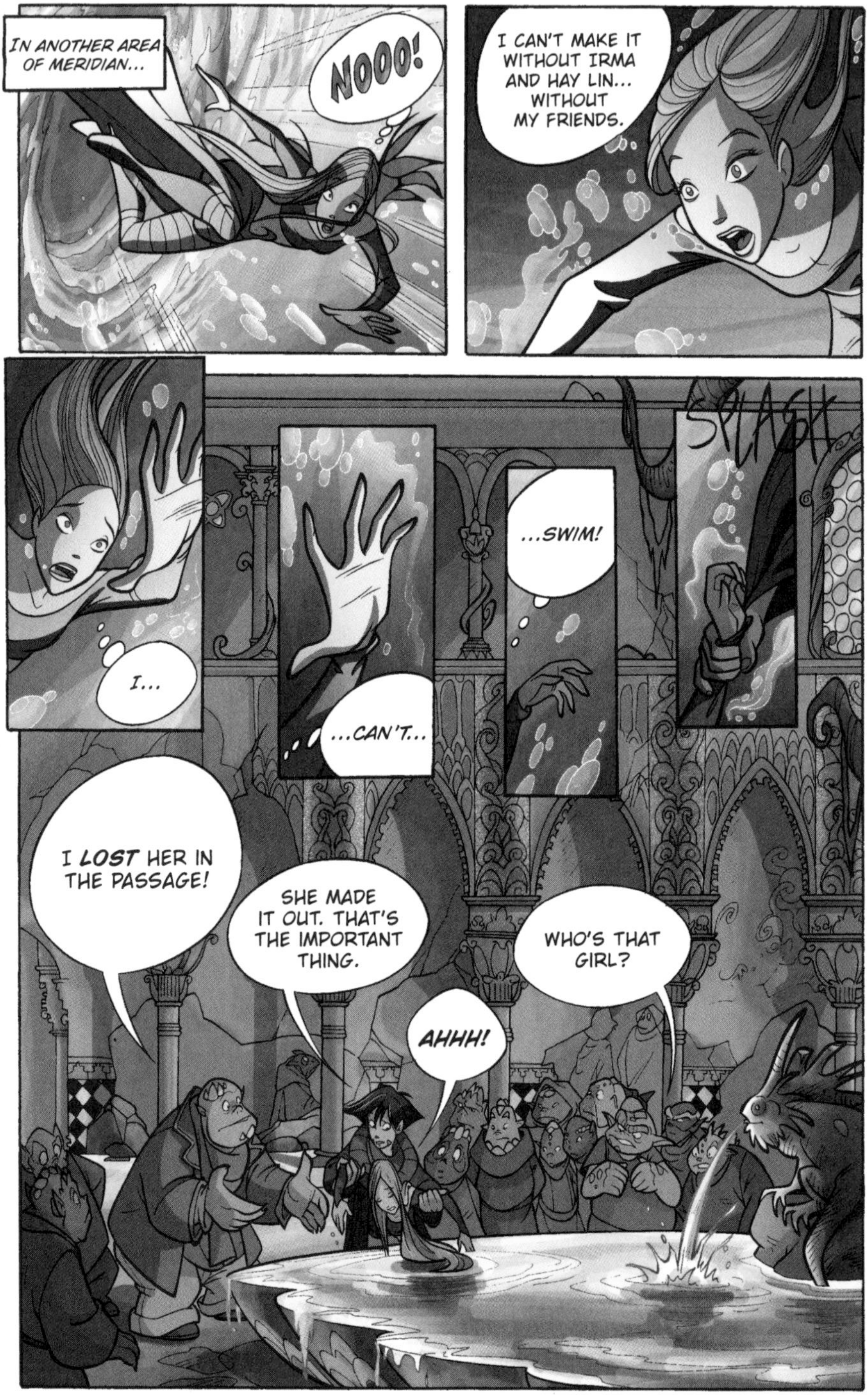
IN ANOTHER AREA OF MERIDIAN...
NOOO!
I CAN'T MAKE IT WITHOUT IRMA AND HAY LIN... WITHOUT MY FRIENDS.
I...
...CAN'T...
...SWIM!
SPLASH
I LOST HER IN THE PASSAGE!
SHE MADE IT OUT. THAT'S THE IMPORTANT THING.
AHHH!
WHO'S THAT GIRL?

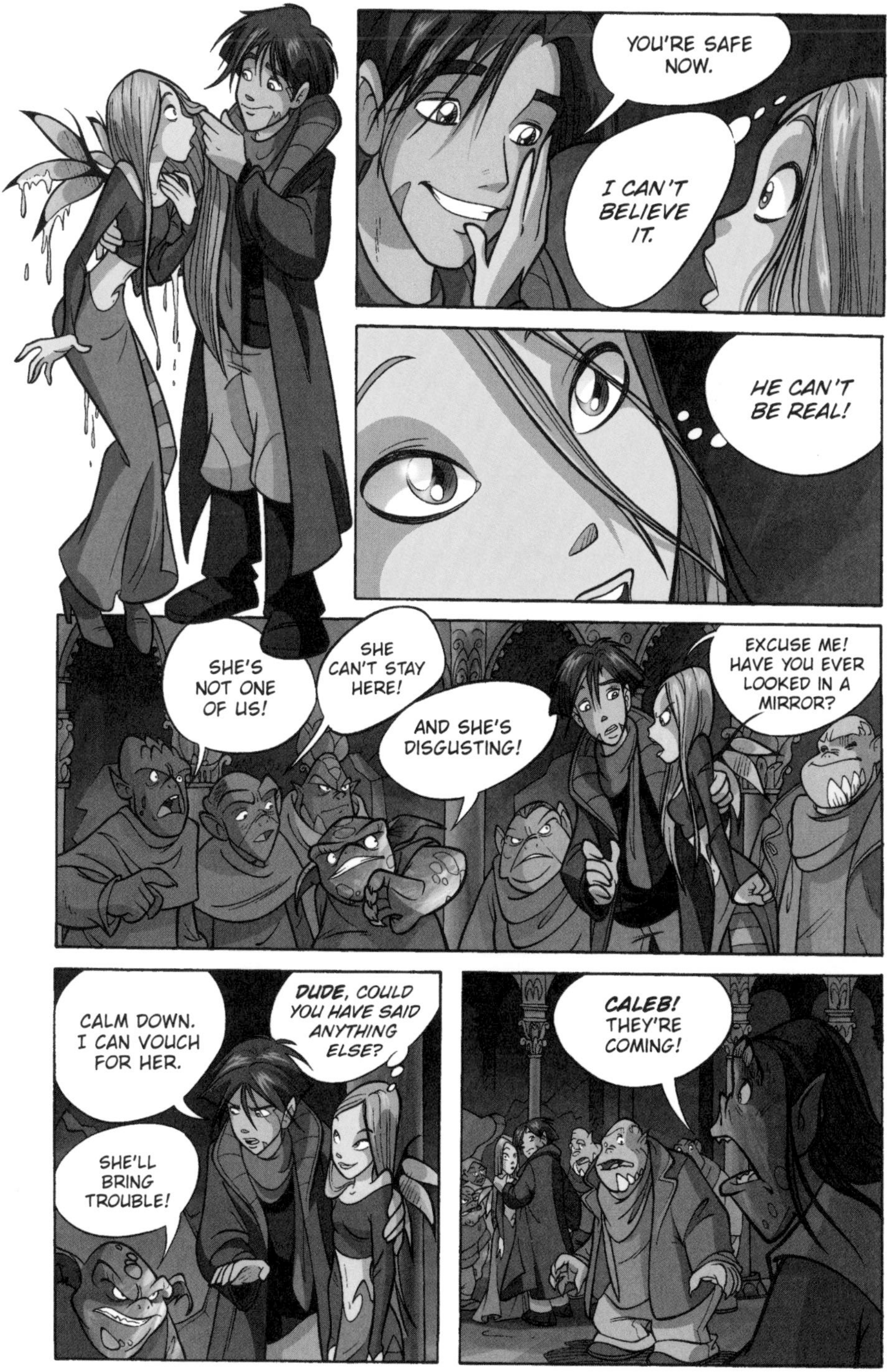
YOU'RE SAFE NOW.
I CAN'T BELIEVE IT.
HE CAN'T BE REAL!
SHE'S NOT ONE OF US!
SHE CAN'T STAY HERE!
AND SHE'S DISGUSTING!
EXCUSE ME! HAVE YOU EVER LOOKED IN A MIRROR?
CALM DOWN. I CAN VOUCH FOR HER.
DUDE, COULD YOU HAVE SAID ANYTHING ELSE?
SHE'LL BRING TROUBLE!
CALEB! THEY'RE COMING!

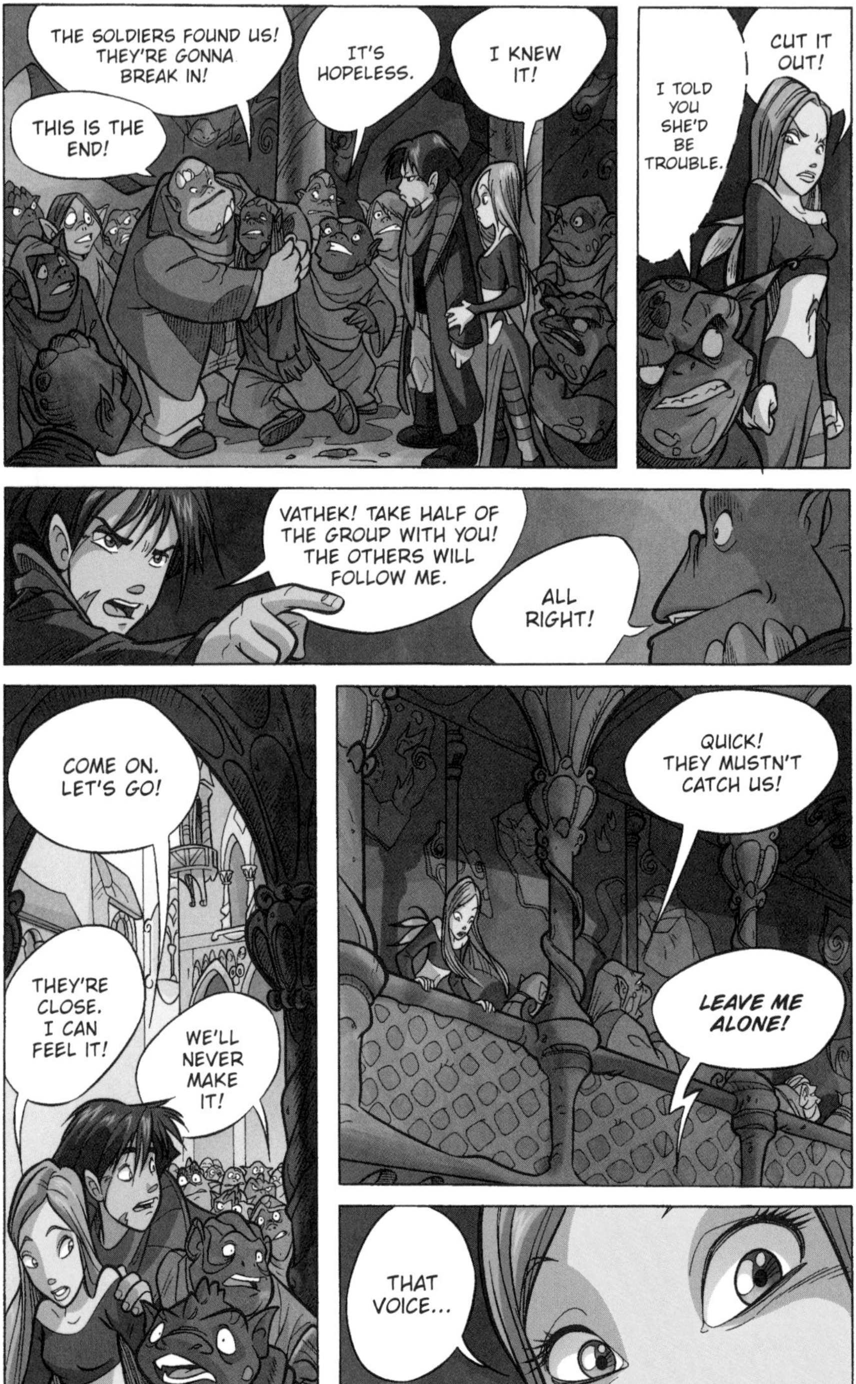
THE SOLDIERS FOUND US! THEY'RE GONNA BREAK IN!
THIS IS THE END!
IT'S HOPELESS.
I KNEW IT!
I TOLD YOU SHE'D BE TROUBLE.
CUT IT OUT!
VATHEK! TAKE HALF OF THE GROUP WITH YOU! THE OTHERS WILL FOLLOW ME.
ALL RIGHT!
COME ON. LET'S GO!
THEY'RE CLOSE. I CAN FEEL IT!
WE'LL NEVER MAKE IT!
QUICK! THEY MUSTN'T CATCH US!
LEAVE ME ALONE!
THAT VOICE...

154

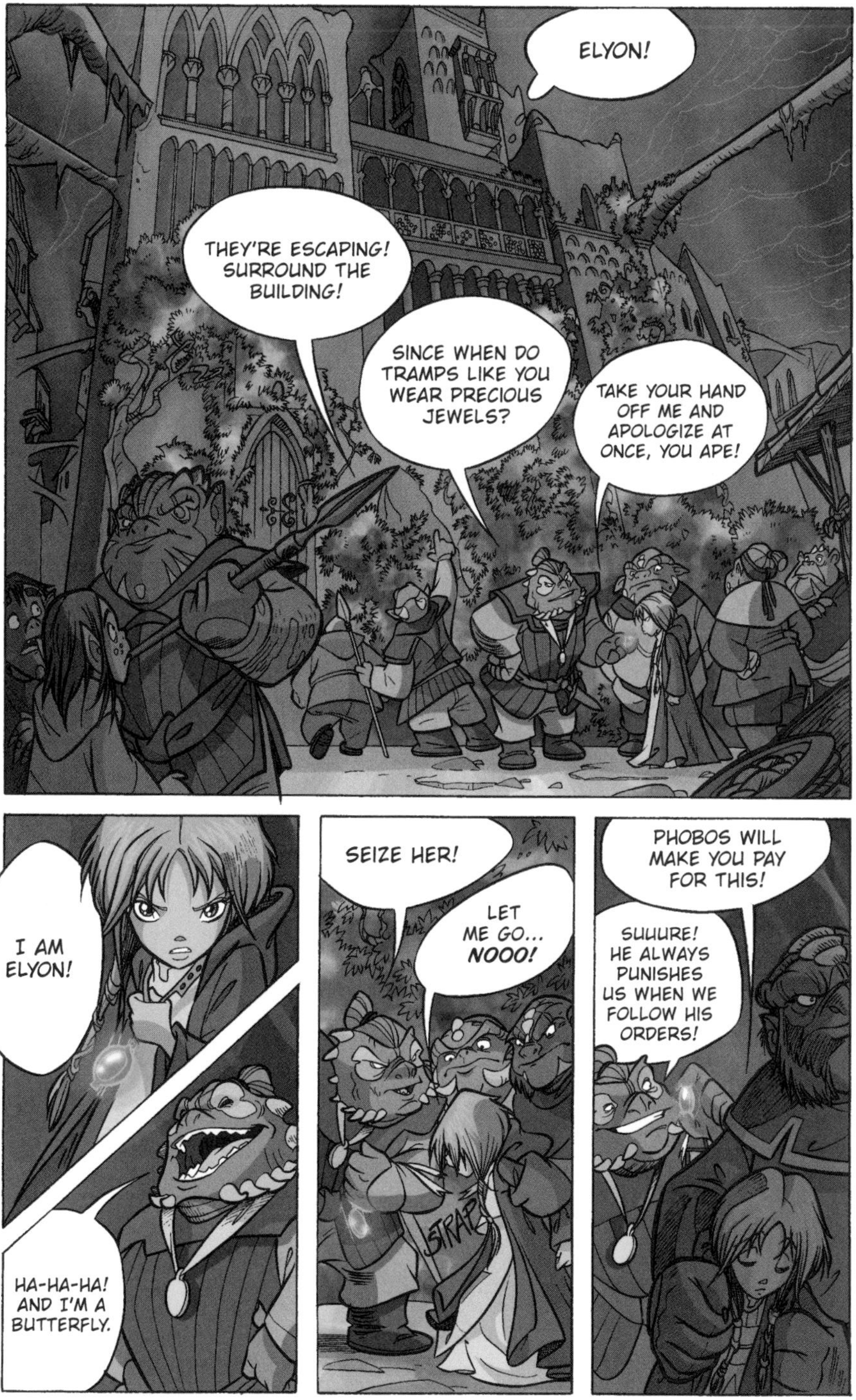
ELYON!
THEY'RE ESCAPING! SURROUND THE BUILDING!
SINCE WHEN DO TRAMPS LIKE YOU WEAR PRECIOUS JEWELS?
TAKE YOUR HAND OFF ME AND APOLOGIZE AT ONCE, YOU APE!
I AM ELYON!
HA-HA-HA! AND I'M A BUTTERFLY.
SEIZE HER!
LET ME GO... NOOO!
STRAP
PHOBOS WILL MAKE YOU PAY FOR THIS!
SUUURE! HE ALWAYS PUNISHES US WHEN WE FOLLOW HIS ORDERS!

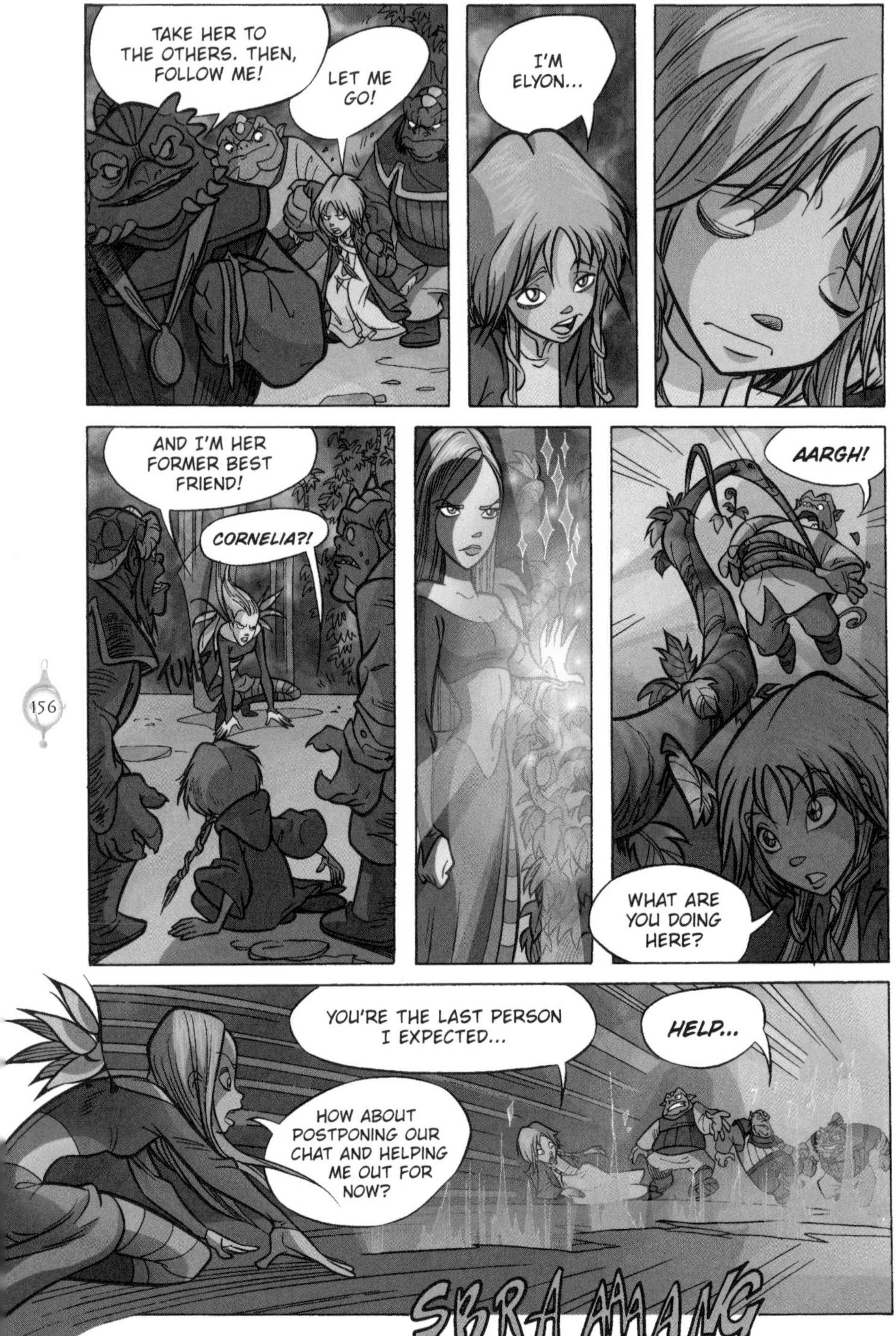
TAKE HER TO THE OTHERS. THEN, FOLLOW ME!
LET ME GO!
I'M ELYON...
AND I'M HER FORMER BEST FRIEND!
CORNELIA?!
TUMP
AARGH!
WHAT ARE YOU DOING HERE?
YOU'RE THE LAST PERSON I EXPECTED...
HELP...
HOW ABOUT POSTPONING OUR CHAT AND HELPING ME OUT FOR NOW?
SBRAAAAANG

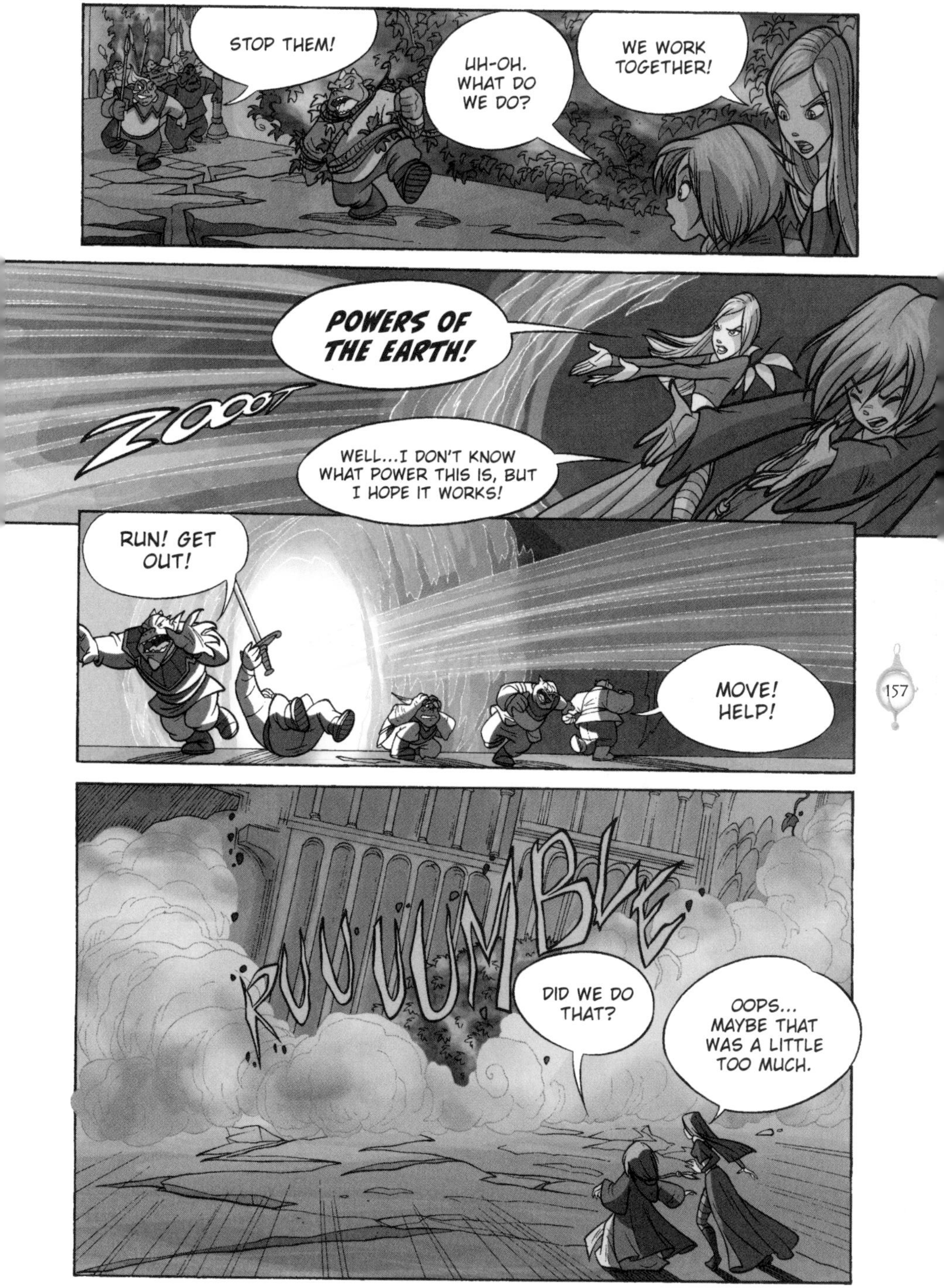
STOP THEM!
UH-OH. WHAT DO WE DO?
WE WORK TOGETHER!
POWERS OF THE EARTH!
ZOOOT
WELL...I DON'T KNOW WHAT POWER THIS IS, BUT I HOPE IT WORKS!
RUN! GET OUT!
MOVE! HELP!
RUUUUMBLE
DID WE DO THAT?
OOPS... MAYBE THAT WAS A LITTLE TOO MUCH.

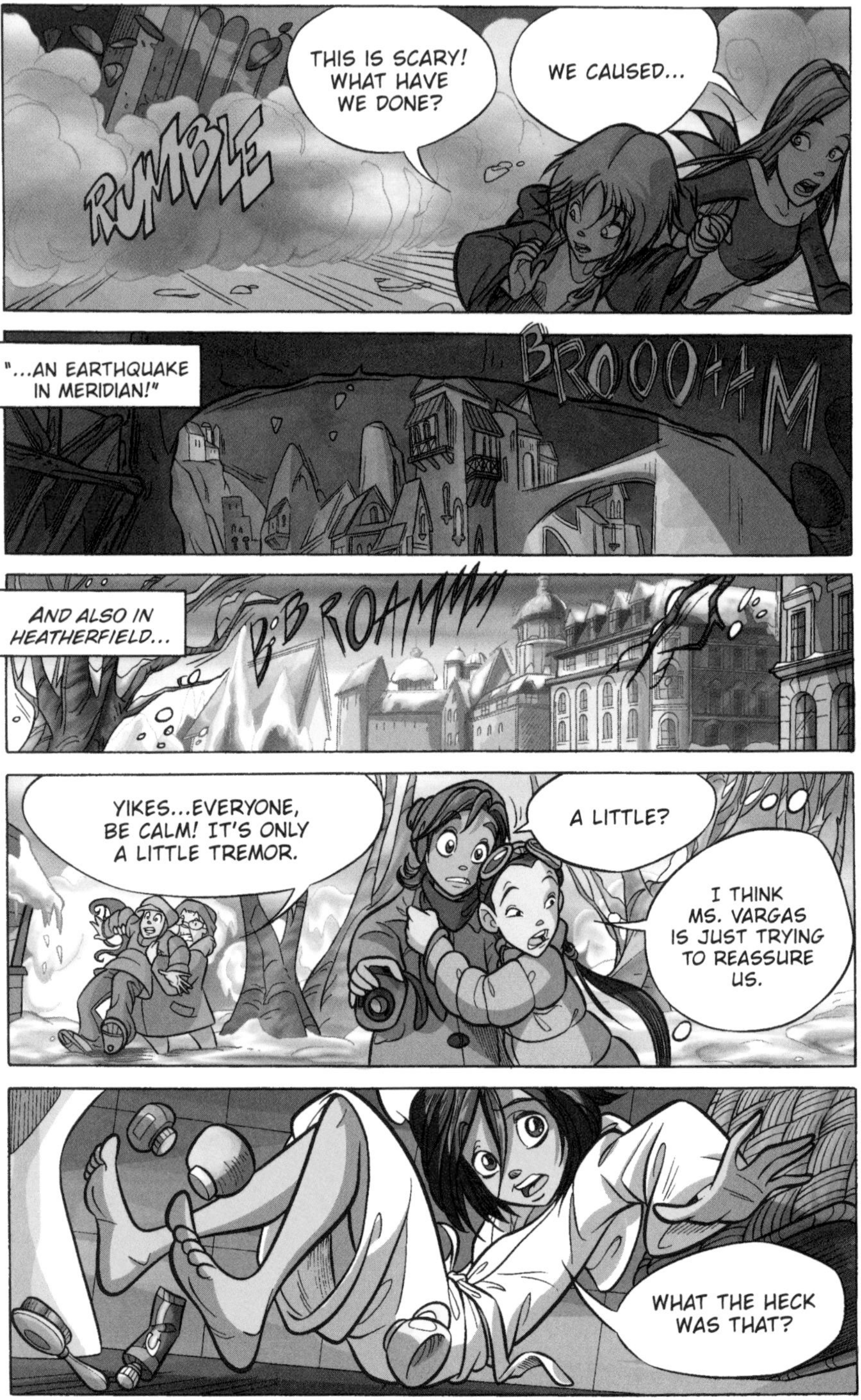
RUMBLE
THIS IS SCARY! WHAT HAVE WE DONE?
WE CAUSED...
"...AN EARTHQUAKE IN MERIDIAN!"
BROOOHHM
AND ALSO IN HEATHERFIELD...
B-B ROAMMM
YIKES...EVERYONE, BE CALM! IT'S ONLY A LITTLE TREMOR.
A LITTLE?
I THINK MS. VARGAS IS JUST TRYING TO REASSURE US.
WHAT THE HECK WAS THAT?

"A promise can be born out of a tear."

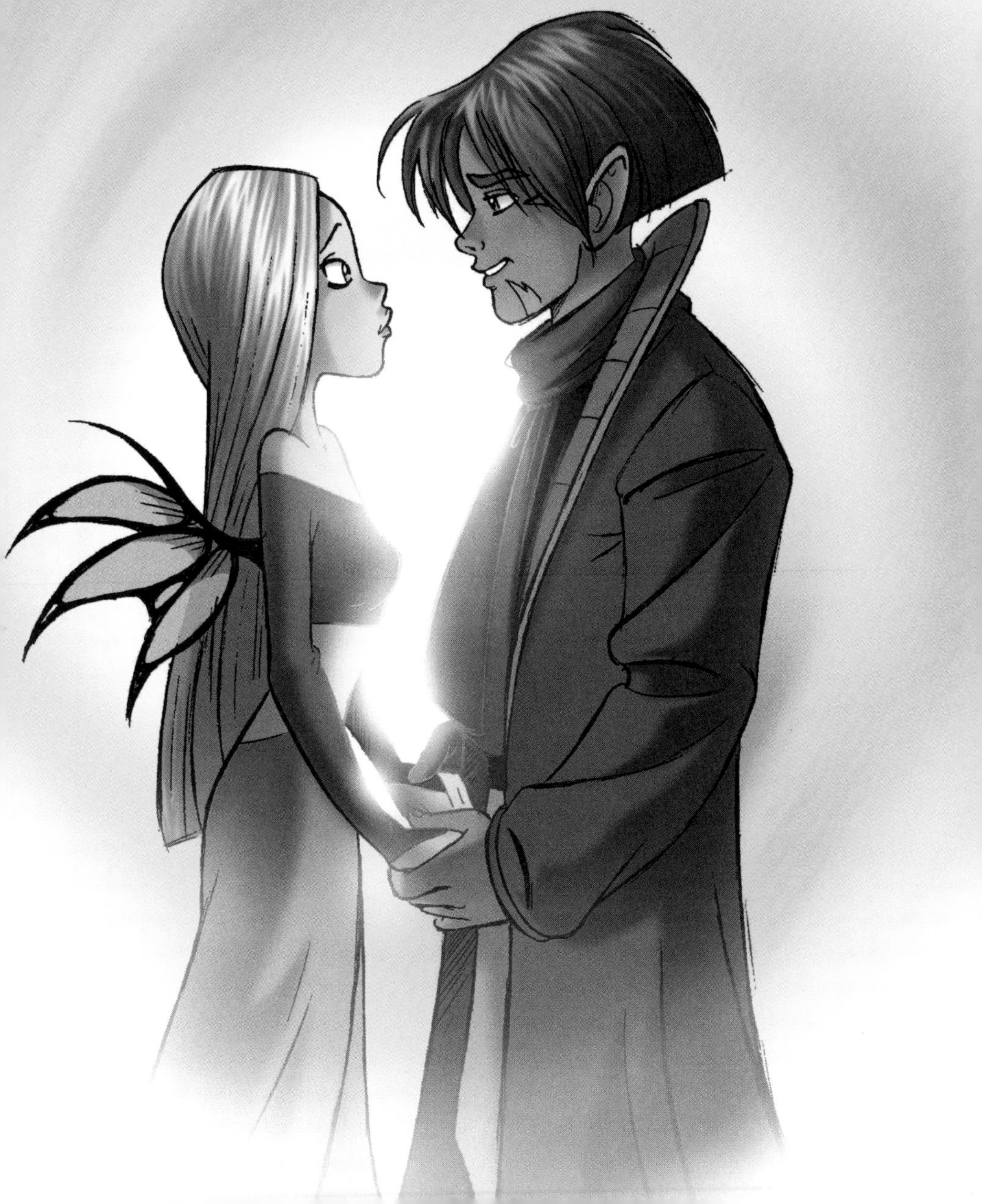

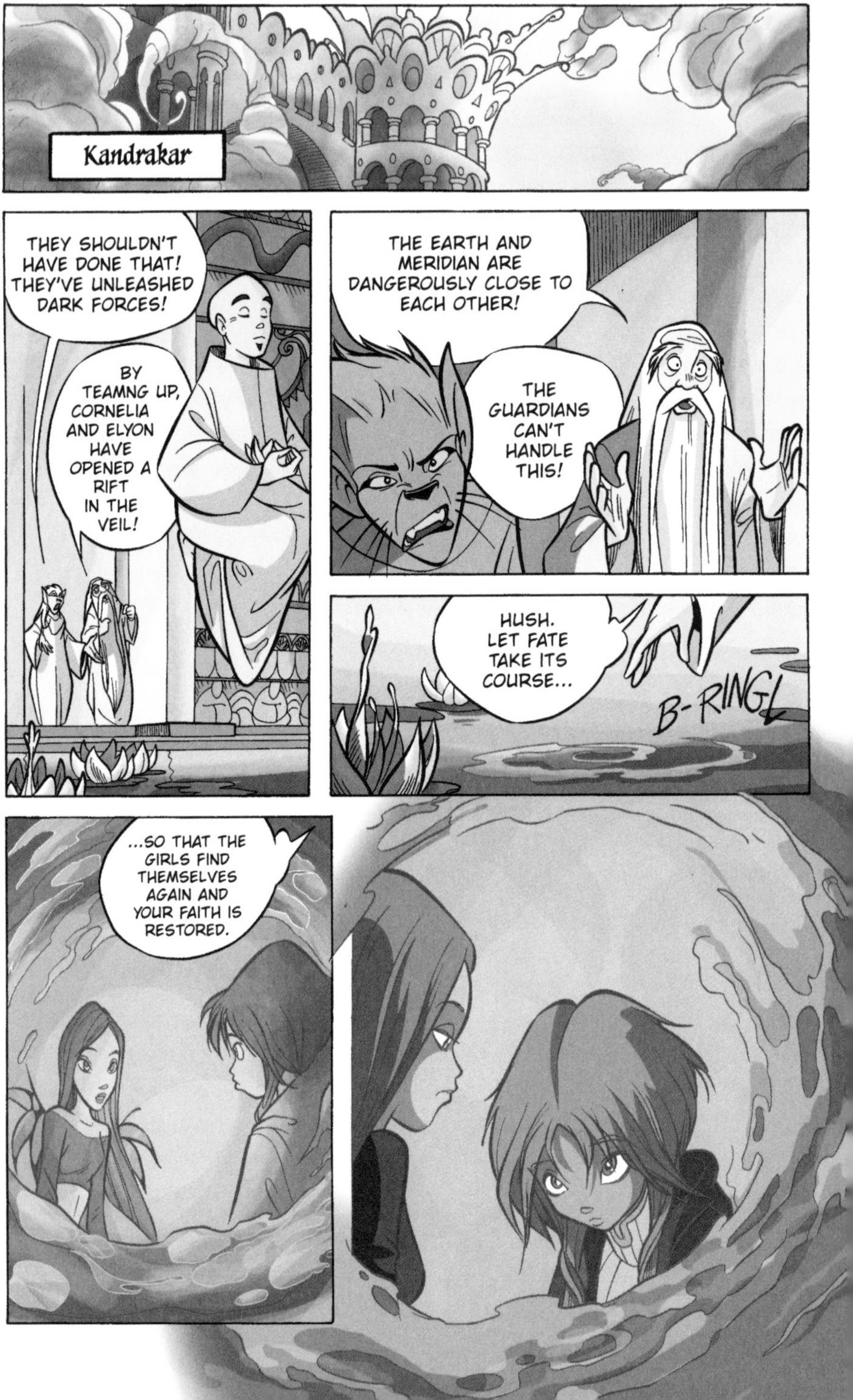

Kandrakar
THEY SHOULDN'T HAVE DONE THAT! THEY'VE UNLEASHED DARK FORCES!
BY TEAMNG UP, CORNELIA AND ELYON HAVE OPENED A RIFT IN THE VEIL!
THE EARTH AND MERIDIAN ARE DANGEROUSLY CLOSE TO EACH OTHER!
THE GUARDIANS CAN'T HANDLE THIS!
HUSH. LET FATE TAKE ITS COURSE...
B-RING!
...SO THAT THE GIRLS FIND THEMSELVES AGAIN AND YOUR FAITH IS RESTORED.

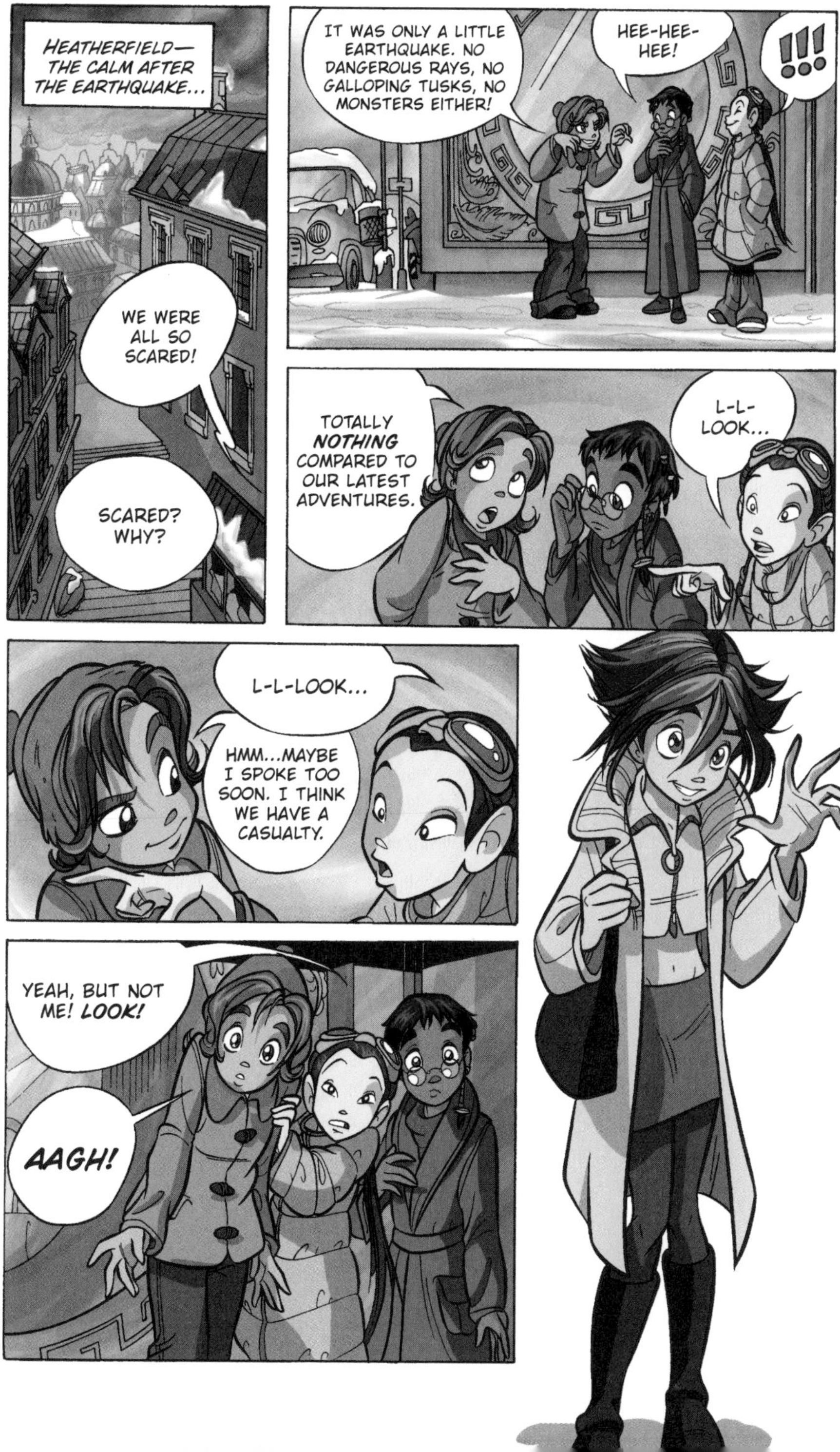
HEATHERFIELD—THE CALM AFTER THE EARTHQUAKE...
WE WERE ALL SO SCARED!
SCARED? WHY?
IT WAS ONLY A LITTLE EARTHQUAKE. NO DANGEROUS RAYS, NO GALLOPING TUSKS, NO MONSTERS EITHER!
HEE-HEE-HEE!
!!!
TOTALLY NOTHING COMPARED TO OUR LATEST ADVENTURES.
L-L-LOOK...
L-L-LOOK...
HMM...MAYBE I SPOKE TOO SOON. I THINK WE HAVE A CASUALTY.
YEAH, BUT NOT ME! LOOK!
AAGH!

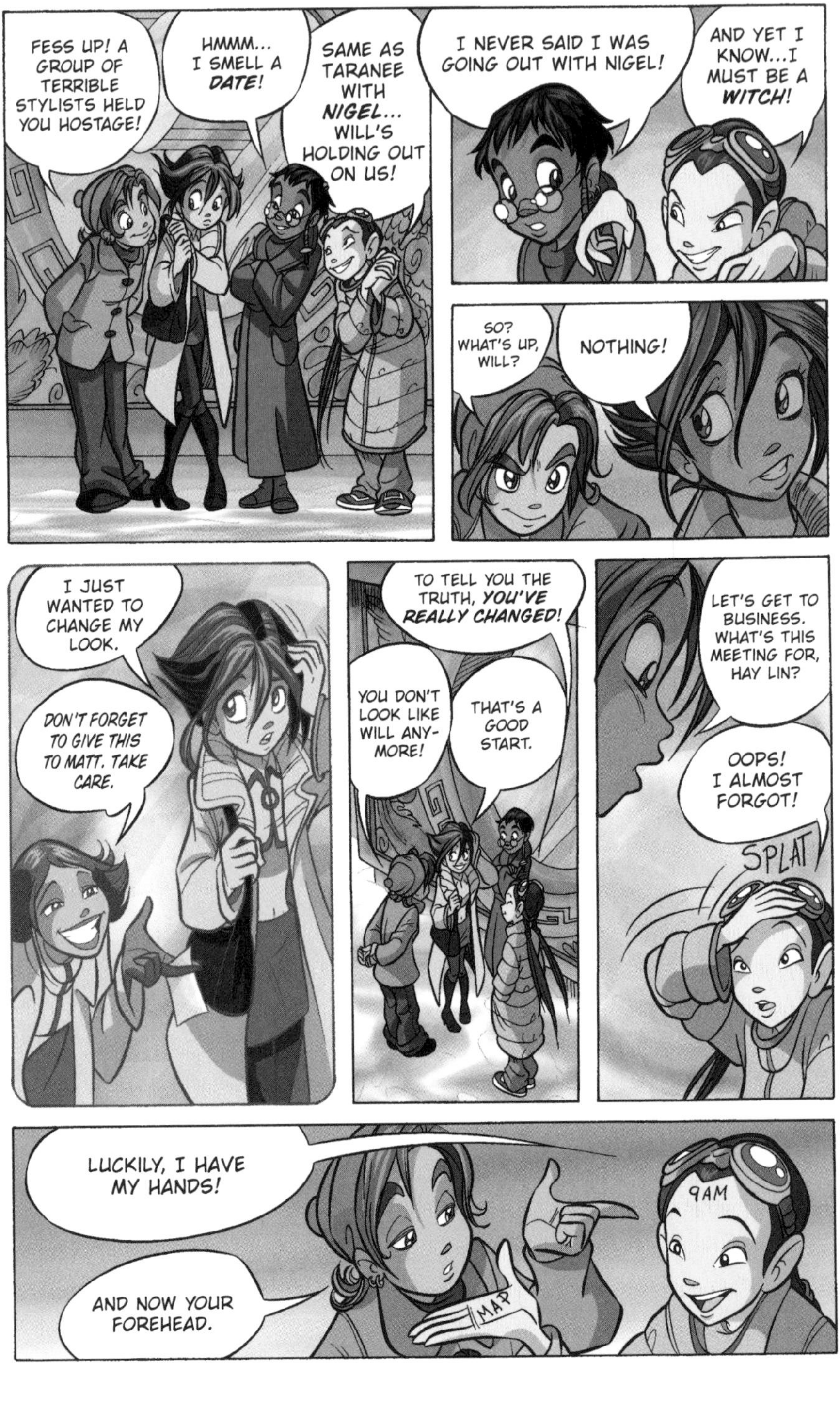
FESS UP! A GROUP OF TERRIBLE STYLISTS HELD YOU HOSTAGE!
HMMM... I SMELL A *DATE*!
SAME AS TARANEE WITH *NIGEL*... WILL'S HOLDING OUT ON US!
I NEVER SAID I WAS GOING OUT WITH NIGEL!
AND YET I KNOW...I MUST BE A *WITCH*!
SO? WHAT'S UP, WILL?
NOTHING!
I JUST WANTED TO CHANGE MY LOOK.
DON'T FORGET TO GIVE THIS TO MATT. TAKE CARE.
TO TELL YOU THE TRUTH, *YOU'VE REALLY CHANGED*!
YOU DON'T LOOK LIKE WILL ANY-MORE!
THAT'S A GOOD START.
LET'S GET TO BUSINESS. WHAT'S THIS MEETING FOR, HAY LIN?
OOPS! I ALMOST FORGOT!
SPLAT
LUCKILY, I HAVE MY HANDS!
AND NOW YOUR FOREHEAD.
9AM
MAP

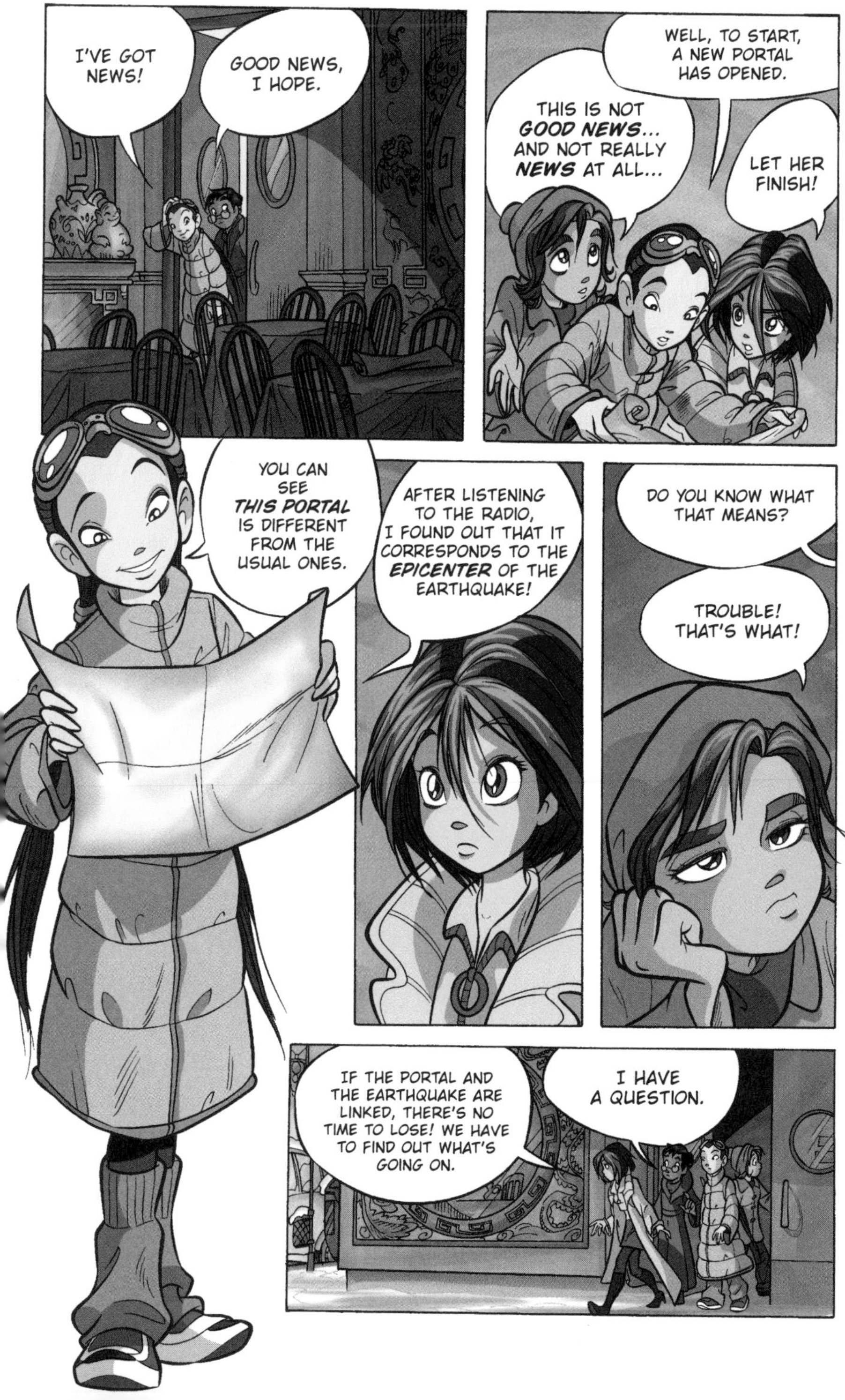
I'VE GOT NEWS!
GOOD NEWS, I HOPE.
WELL, TO START, A NEW PORTAL HAS OPENED.
THIS IS NOT GOOD NEWS... AND NOT REALLY NEWS AT ALL...
LET HER FINISH!
YOU CAN SEE THIS PORTAL IS DIFFERENT FROM THE USUAL ONES.
AFTER LISTENING TO THE RADIO, I FOUND OUT THAT IT CORRESPONDS TO THE EPICENTER OF THE EARTHQUAKE!
DO YOU KNOW WHAT THAT MEANS?
TROUBLE! THAT'S WHAT!
IF THE PORTAL AND THE EARTHQUAKE ARE LINKED, THERE'S NO TIME TO LOSE! WE HAVE TO FIND OUT WHAT'S GOING ON.
I HAVE A QUESTION.

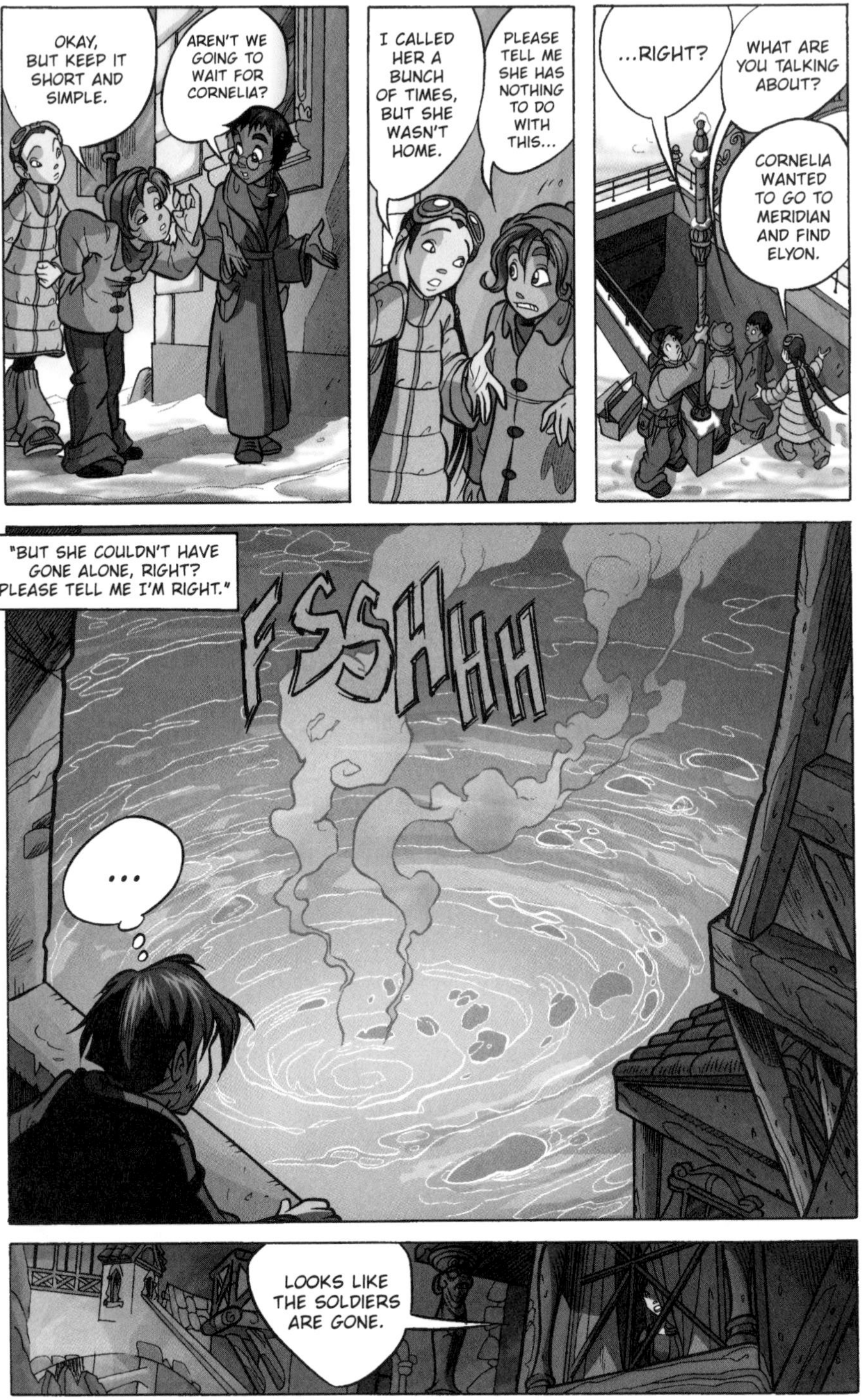
OKAY, BUT KEEP IT SHORT AND SIMPLE.
AREN'T WE GOING TO WAIT FOR CORNELIA?
I CALLED HER A BUNCH OF TIMES, BUT SHE WASN'T HOME.
PLEASE TELL ME SHE HAS NOTHING TO DO WITH THIS...
...RIGHT?
WHAT ARE YOU TALKING ABOUT?
CORNELIA WANTED TO GO TO MERIDIAN AND FIND ELYON.
"BUT SHE COULDN'T HAVE GONE ALONE, RIGHT? PLEASE TELL ME I'M RIGHT."
FSSHHH
...
LOOKS LIKE THE SOLDIERS ARE GONE.

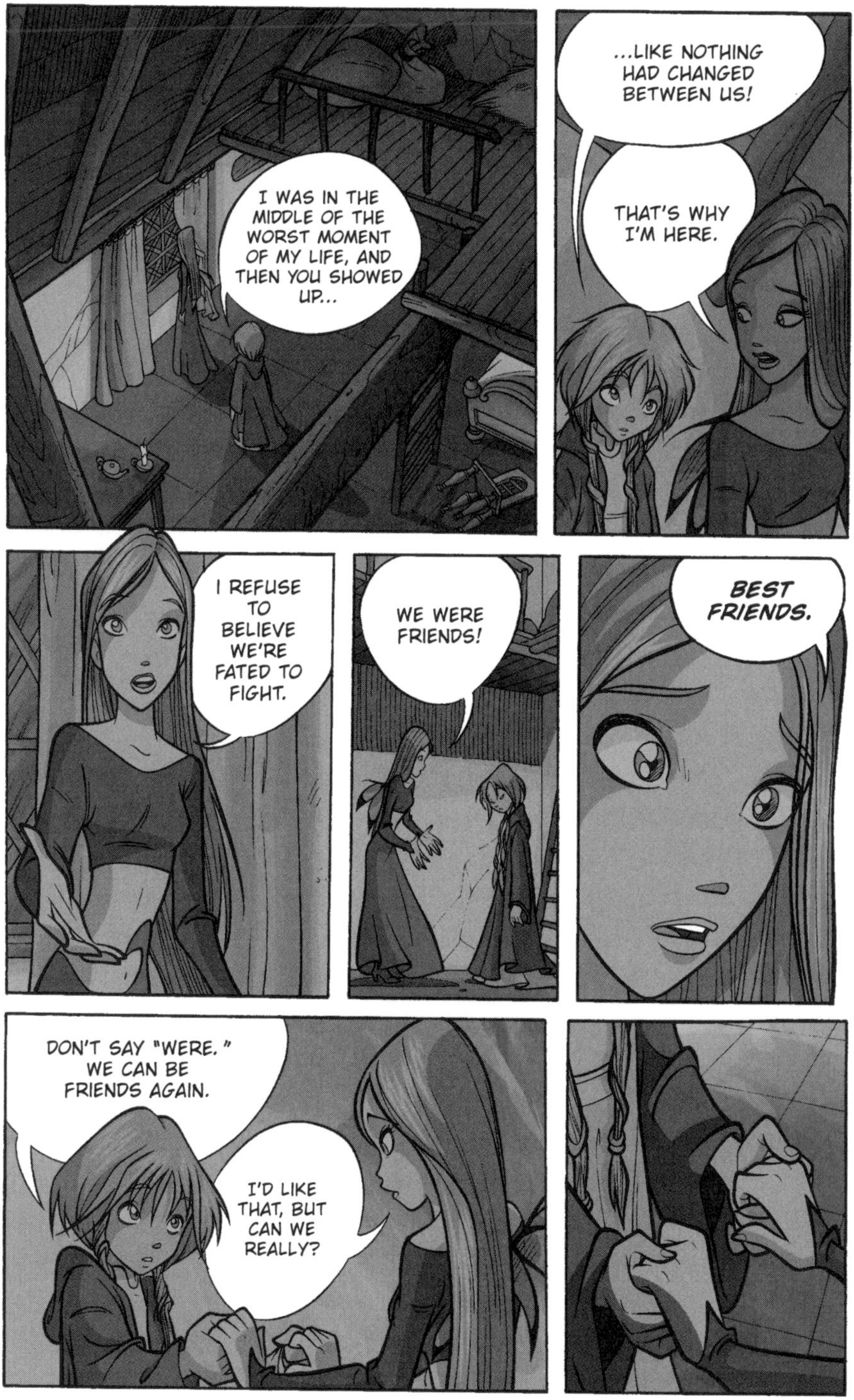
I WAS IN THE MIDDLE OF THE WORST MOMENT OF MY LIFE, AND THEN YOU SHOWED UP...
...LIKE NOTHING HAD CHANGED BETWEEN US!
THAT'S WHY I'M HERE.
I REFUSE TO BELIEVE WE'RE FATED TO FIGHT.
WE WERE FRIENDS!
BEST FRIENDS.
DON'T SAY "WERE." WE CAN BE FRIENDS AGAIN.
I'D LIKE THAT, BUT CAN WE REALLY?

I WAS WRONG! I DID HORRIBLE THINGS TO ALL OF YOU!

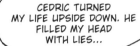

CEDRIC TURNED MY LIFE UPSIDE DOWN. HE FILLED MY HEAD WITH LIES...

...AND I BELIEVED HIM!

AND NOW?

I DON'T KNOW. I DON'T EVEN KNOW WHO I AM ANYMORE!

IN HEATHERFIELD, I HAVE NOTHING.

HERE I'M THE FUTURE RULER OF A WORLD THAT DOESN'T WANT ME.

WE'LL FIX THIS, ELLIE! I DON'T KNOW HOW, BUT WE'LL DEFINITELY FIX IT... TOGETHER.

MERIDIAN SEEKS ONLY YOUR *LIGHT*, YOUR HIGHNESS.

WHAT?

AND THE REBELLION IS READY TO FOLLOW YOU!

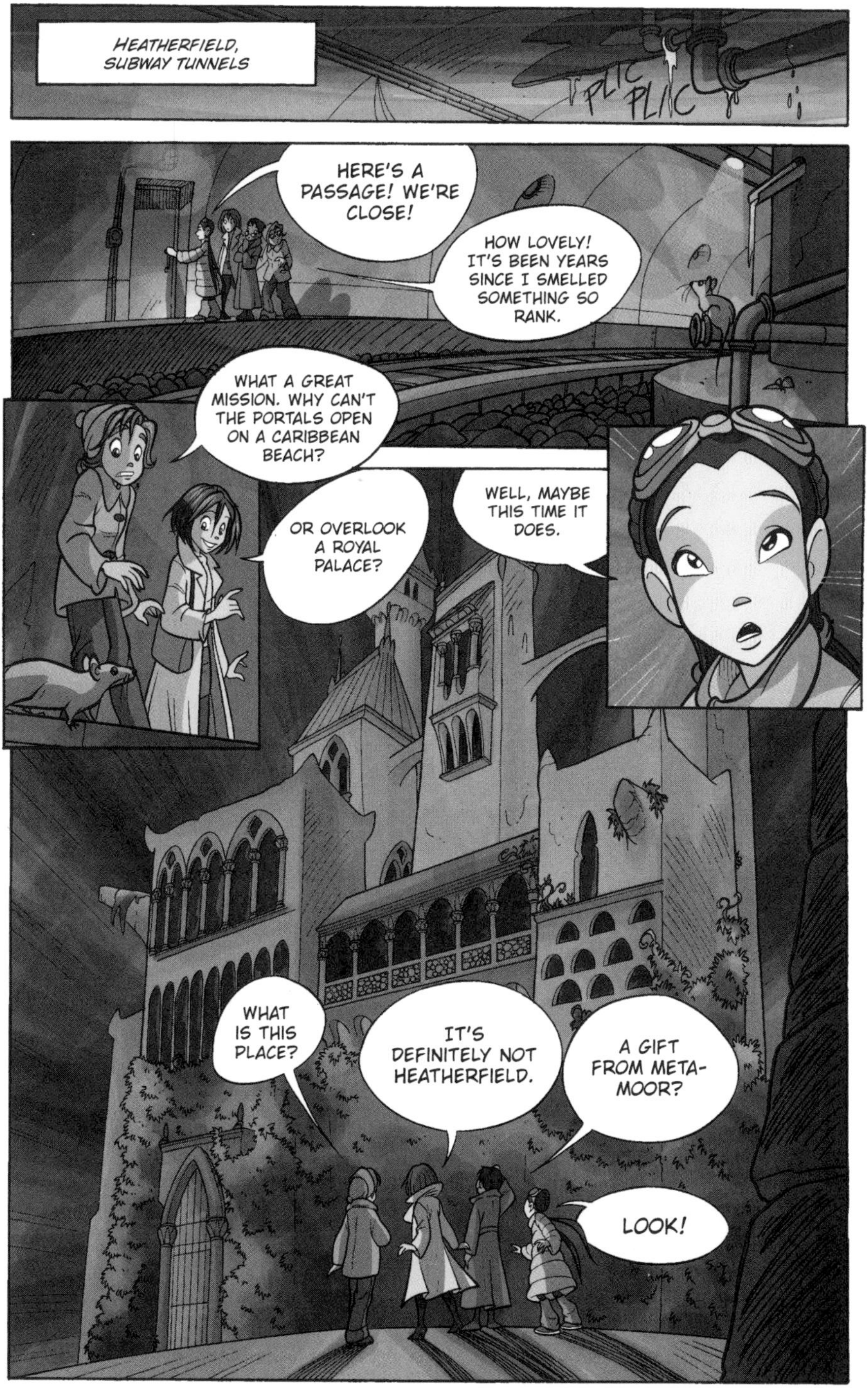
HEATHERFIELD, SUBWAY TUNNELS
PLIC PLIC
HERE'S A PASSAGE! WE'RE CLOSE!
HOW LOVELY! IT'S BEEN YEARS SINCE I SMELLED SOMETHING SO RANK.
WHAT A GREAT MISSION. WHY CAN'T THE PORTALS OPEN ON A CARIBBEAN BEACH?
OR OVERLOOK A ROYAL PALACE?
WELL, MAYBE THIS TIME IT DOES.
WHAT IS THIS PLACE?
IT'S DEFINITELY NOT HEATHERFIELD.
A GIFT FROM META-MOOR?
LOOK!

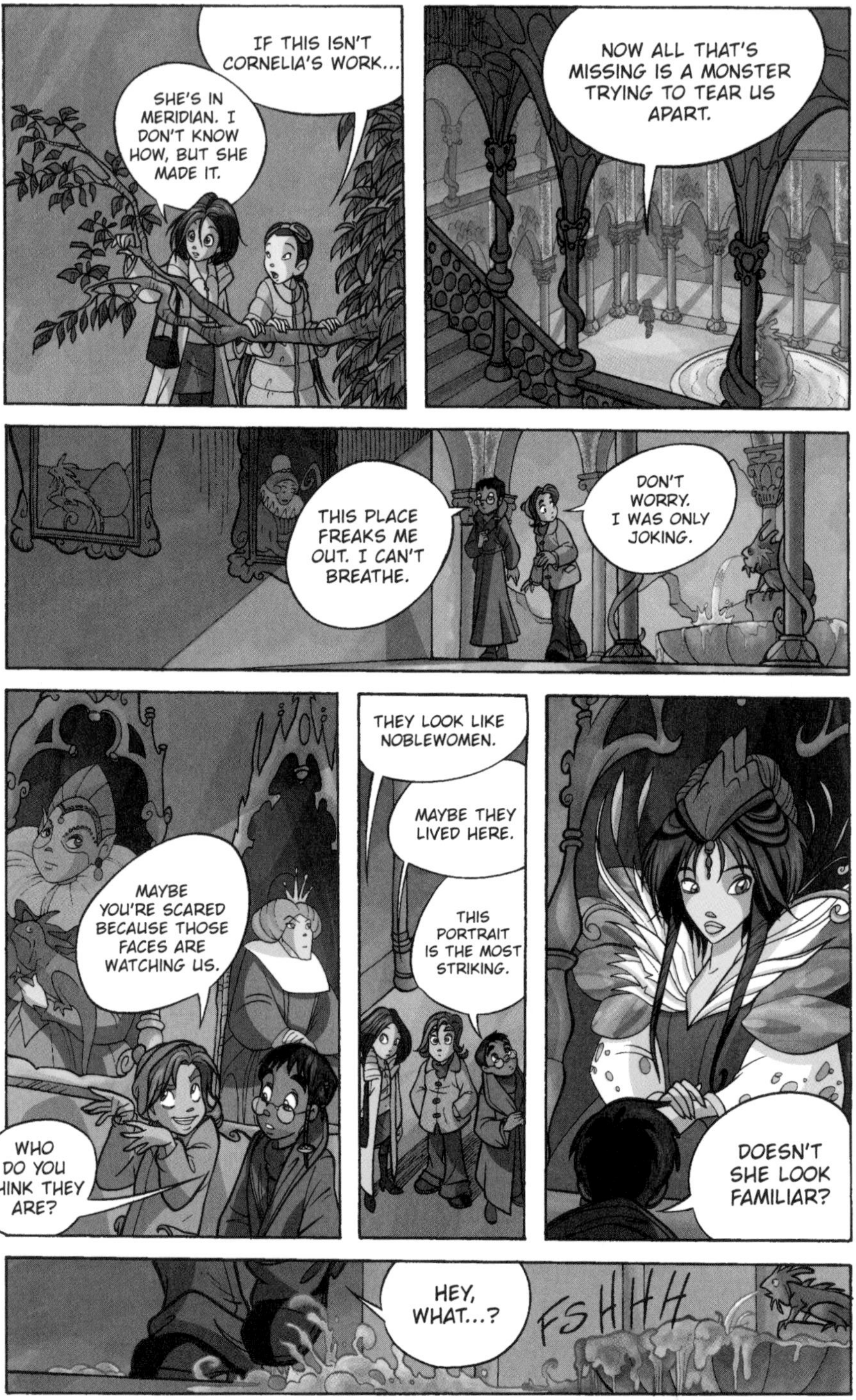
IF THIS ISN'T CORNELIA'S WORK...
SHE'S IN MERIDIAN. I DON'T KNOW HOW, BUT SHE MADE IT.
NOW ALL THAT'S MISSING IS A MONSTER TRYING TO TEAR US APART.
THIS PLACE FREAKS ME OUT. I CAN'T BREATHE.
DON'T WORRY. I WAS ONLY JOKING.
MAYBE YOU'RE SCARED BECAUSE THOSE FACES ARE WATCHING US.
WHO DO YOU THINK THEY ARE?
THEY LOOK LIKE NOBLEWOMEN.
MAYBE THEY LIVED HERE.
THIS PORTRAIT IS THE MOST STRIKING.
DOESN'T SHE LOOK FAMILIAR?
HEY, WHAT...?
FSHHHH

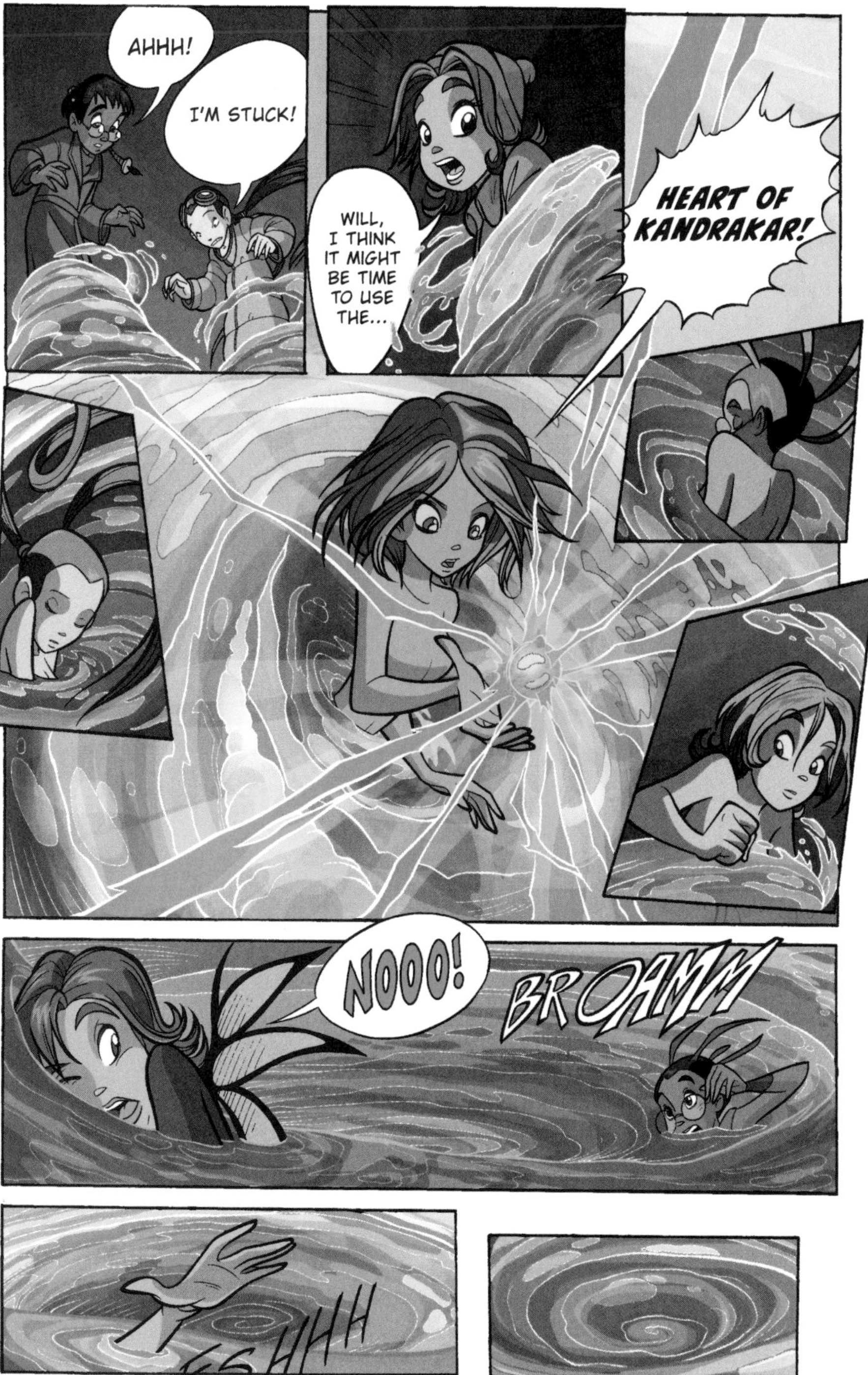

AHHH!
I'M STUCK!
WILL, I THINK IT MIGHT BE TIME TO USE THE...
HEART OF KANDRAKAR!
NOOO!
BROAMM
FSHHH

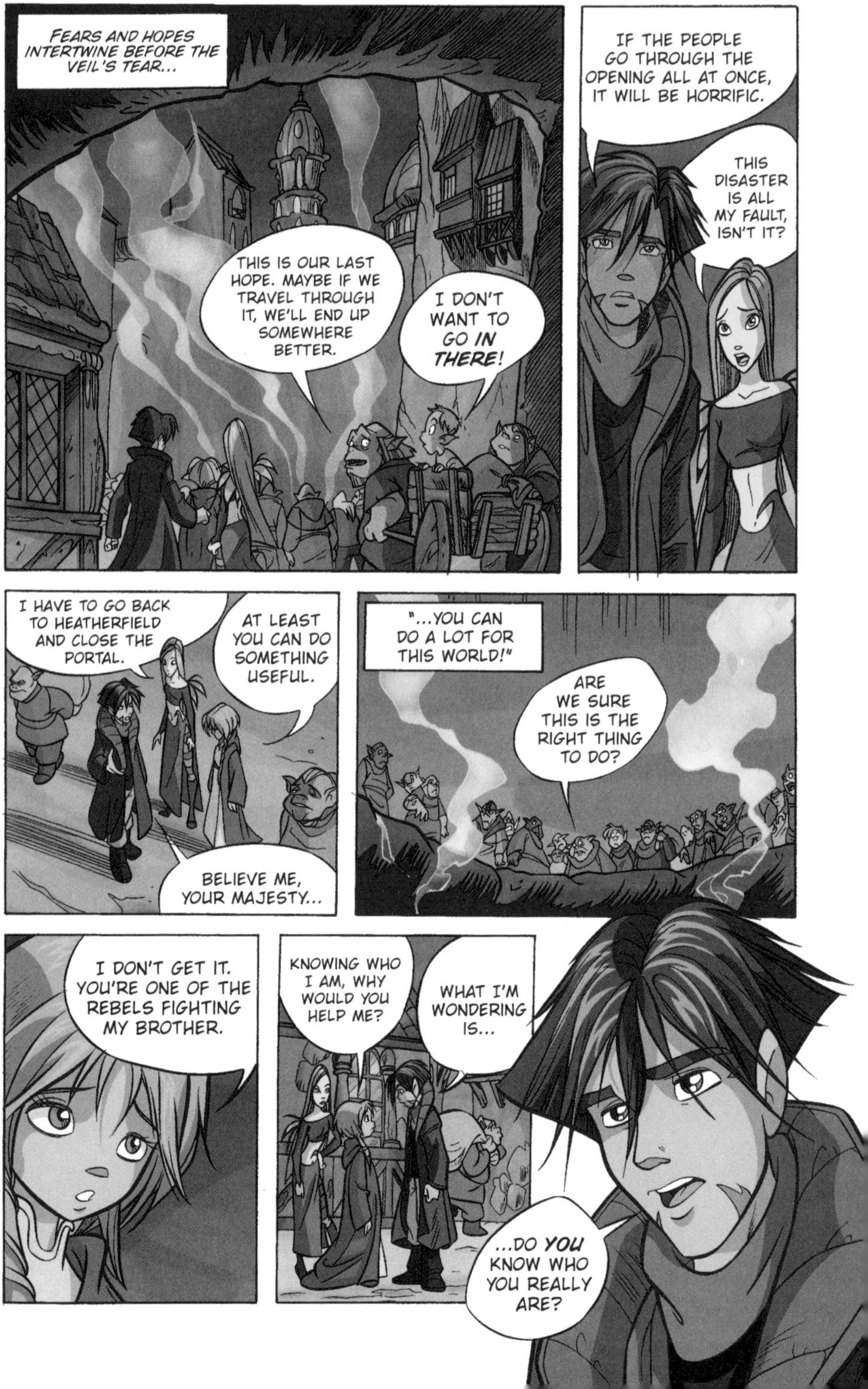
FEARS AND HOPES INTERTWINE BEFORE THE VEIL'S TEAR...
THIS IS OUR LAST HOPE. MAYBE IF WE TRAVEL THROUGH IT, WE'LL END UP SOMEWHERE BETTER.
I DON'T WANT TO GO *IN THERE*!
IF THE PEOPLE GO THROUGH THE OPENING ALL AT ONCE, IT WILL BE HORRIFIC.
THIS DISASTER IS ALL MY FAULT, ISN'T IT?
I HAVE TO GO BACK TO HEATHERFIELD AND CLOSE THE PORTAL.
AT LEAST YOU CAN DO SOMETHING USEFUL.
BELIEVE ME, YOUR MAJESTY...
"...YOU CAN DO A LOT FOR THIS WORLD!"
ARE WE SURE THIS IS THE RIGHT THING TO DO?
I DON'T GET IT. YOU'RE ONE OF THE REBELS FIGHTING MY BROTHER.
KNOWING WHO I AM, WHY WOULD YOU HELP ME?
WHAT I'M WONDERING IS...
...DO *YOU* KNOW WHO YOU REALLY ARE?

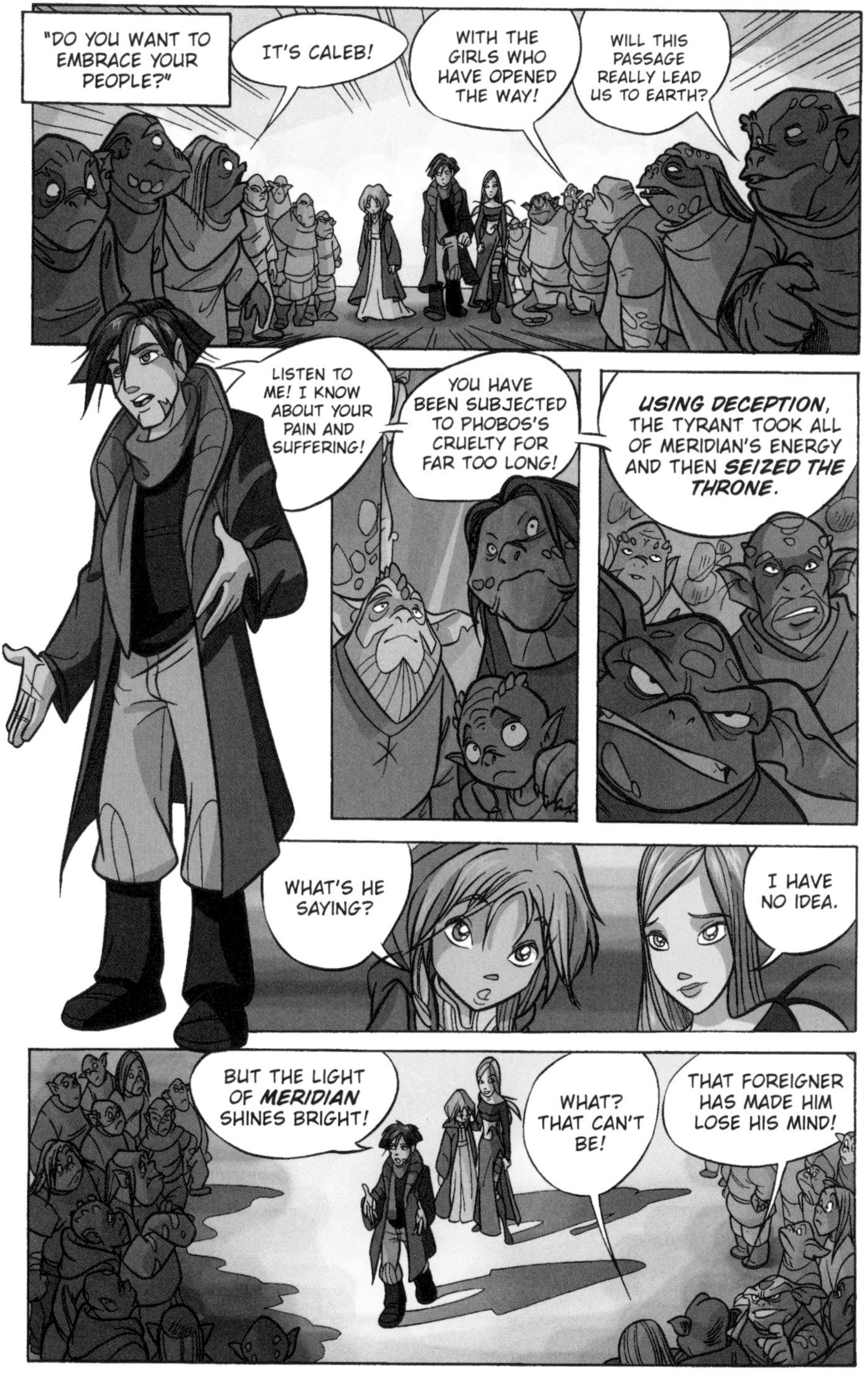
"DO YOU WANT TO EMBRACE YOUR PEOPLE?"
IT'S CALEB!
WITH THE GIRLS WHO HAVE OPENED THE WAY!
WILL THIS PASSAGE REALLY LEAD US TO EARTH?
LISTEN TO ME! I KNOW ABOUT YOUR PAIN AND SUFFERING!
YOU HAVE BEEN SUBJECTED TO PHOBOS'S CRUELTY FOR FAR TOO LONG!
USING DECEPTION, THE TYRANT TOOK ALL OF MERIDIAN'S ENERGY AND THEN *SEIZED THE THRONE*.
WHAT'S HE SAYING?
I HAVE NO IDEA.
BUT THE LIGHT OF *MERIDIAN* SHINES BRIGHT!
WHAT? THAT CAN'T BE!
THAT FOREIGNER HAS MADE HIM LOSE HIS MIND!

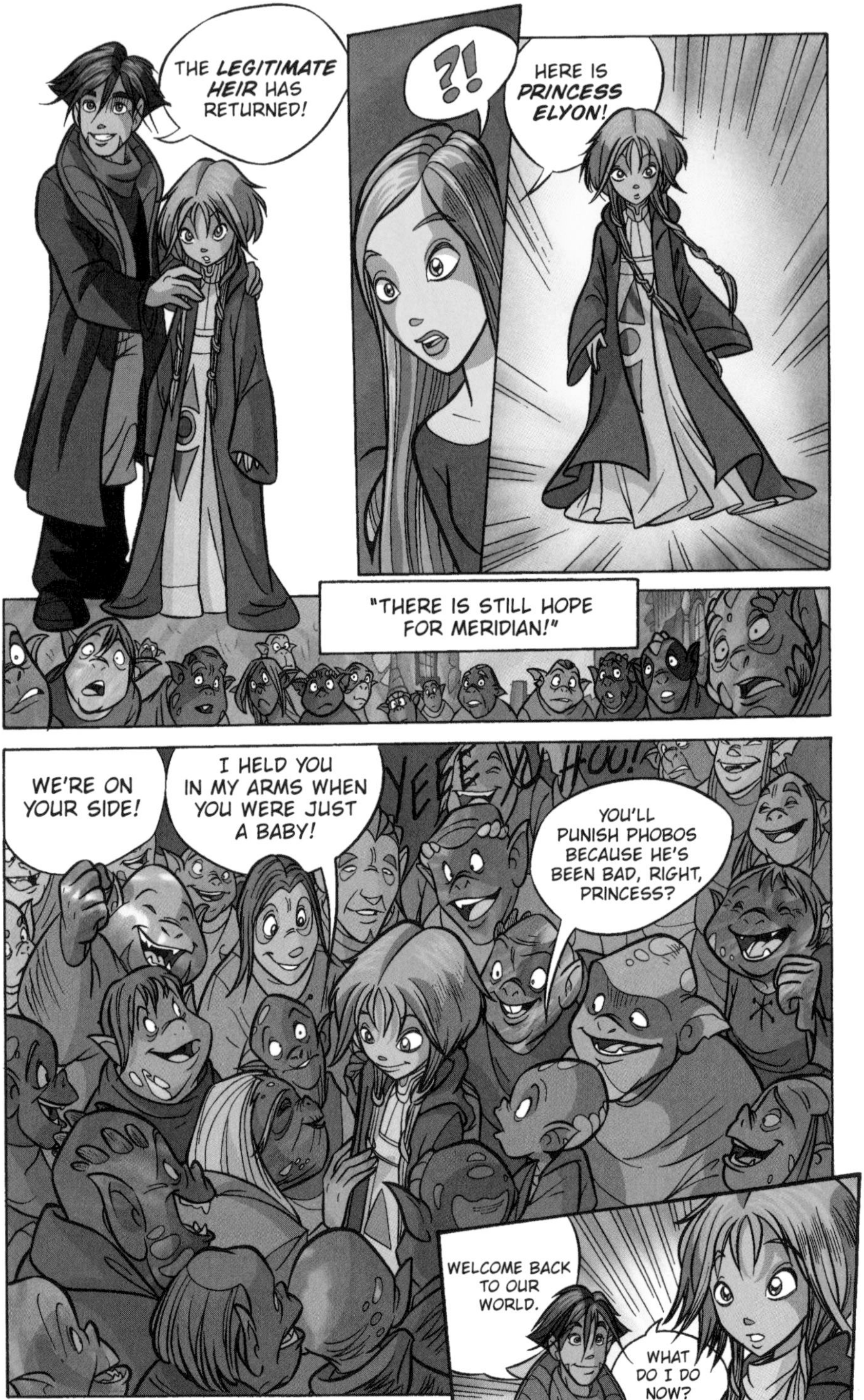
THE LEGITIMATE HEIR HAS RETURNED!
?!
HERE IS PRINCESS ELYON!
"THERE IS STILL HOPE FOR MERIDIAN!"
WE'RE ON YOUR SIDE!
I HELD YOU IN MY ARMS WHEN YOU WERE JUST A BABY!
YOU'LL PUNISH PHOBOS BECAUSE HE'S BEEN BAD, RIGHT, PRINCESS?
WELCOME BACK TO OUR WORLD.
WHAT DO I DO NOW?

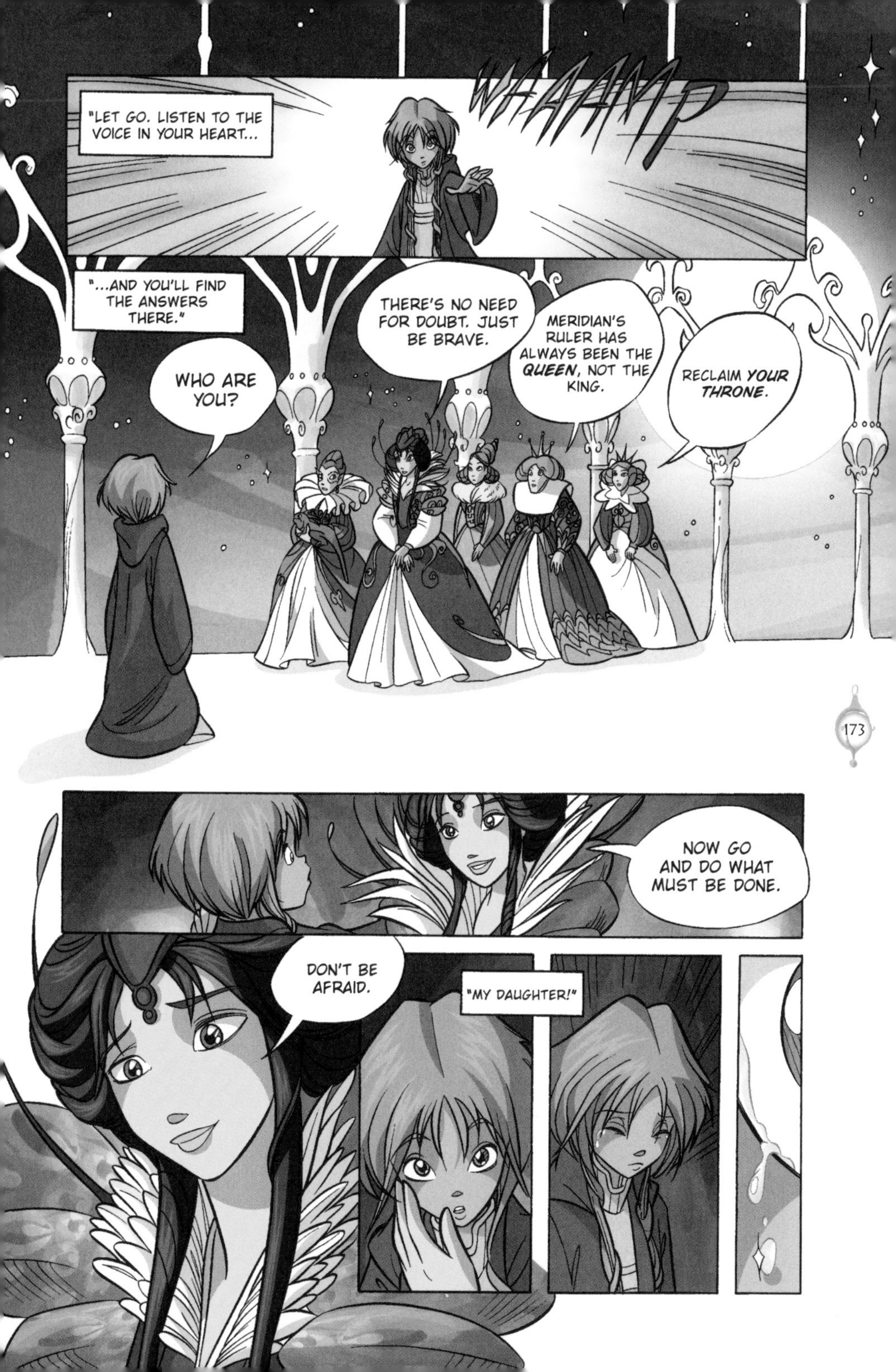
"LET GO. LISTEN TO THE VOICE IN YOUR HEART...
WHAAAMP
"...AND YOU'LL FIND THE ANSWERS THERE."
WHO ARE YOU?
THERE'S NO NEED FOR DOUBT. JUST BE BRAVE.
MERIDIAN'S RULER HAS ALWAYS BEEN THE QUEEN, NOT THE KING.
RECLAIM YOUR THRONE.
NOW GO AND DO WHAT MUST BE DONE.
DON'T BE AFRAID.
"MY DAUGHTER!"

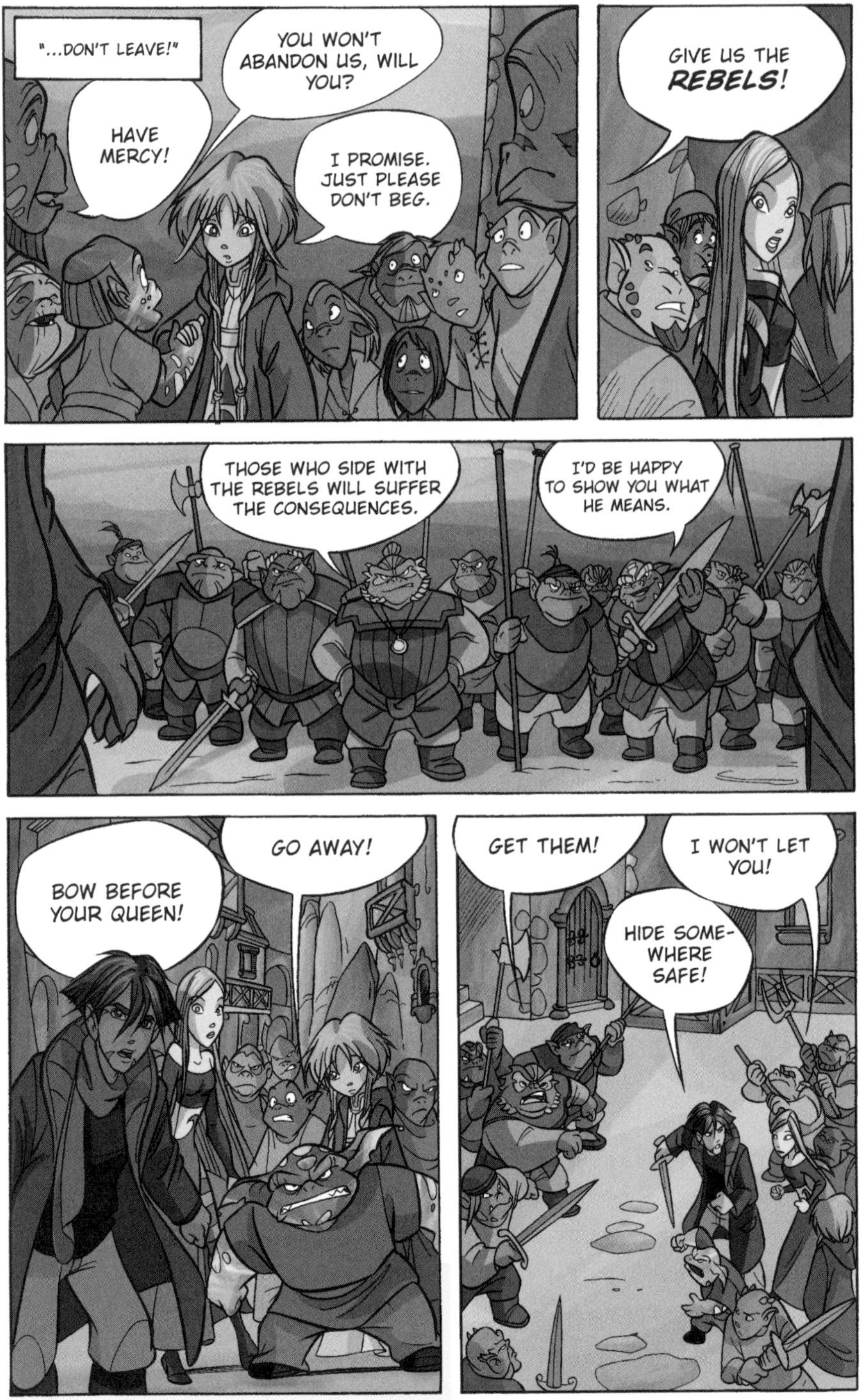
"...DON'T LEAVE!"
HAVE MERCY!
YOU WON'T ABANDON US, WILL YOU?
I PROMISE. JUST PLEASE DON'T BEG.
GIVE US THE ***REBELS!***
THOSE WHO SIDE WITH THE REBELS WILL SUFFER THE CONSEQUENCES.
I'D BE HAPPY TO SHOW YOU WHAT HE MEANS.
BOW BEFORE YOUR QUEEN!
GO AWAY!
GET THEM!
I WON'T LET YOU!
HIDE SOME-WHERE SAFE!

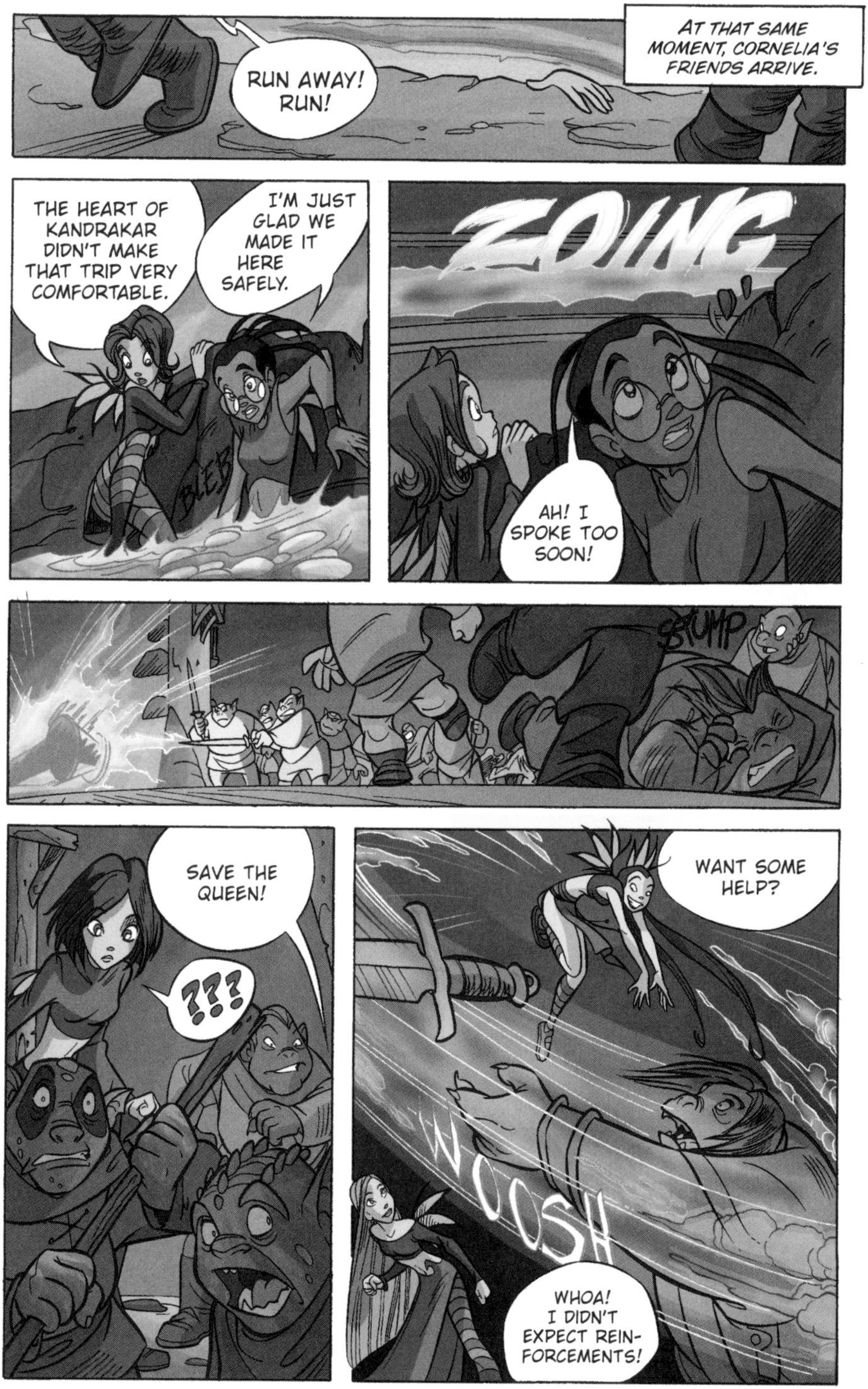

AT THAT SAME MOMENT, CORNELIA'S FRIENDS ARRIVE.
RUN AWAY! RUN!
THE HEART OF KANDRAKAR DIDN'T MAKE THAT TRIP VERY COMFORTABLE.
I'M JUST GLAD WE MADE IT HERE SAFELY.
BLEB
ZOING
AH! I SPOKE TOO SOON!
SAVE THE QUEEN!
???
WANT SOME HELP?
WOOSH
WHOA! I DIDN'T EXPECT REIN-FORCEMENTS!

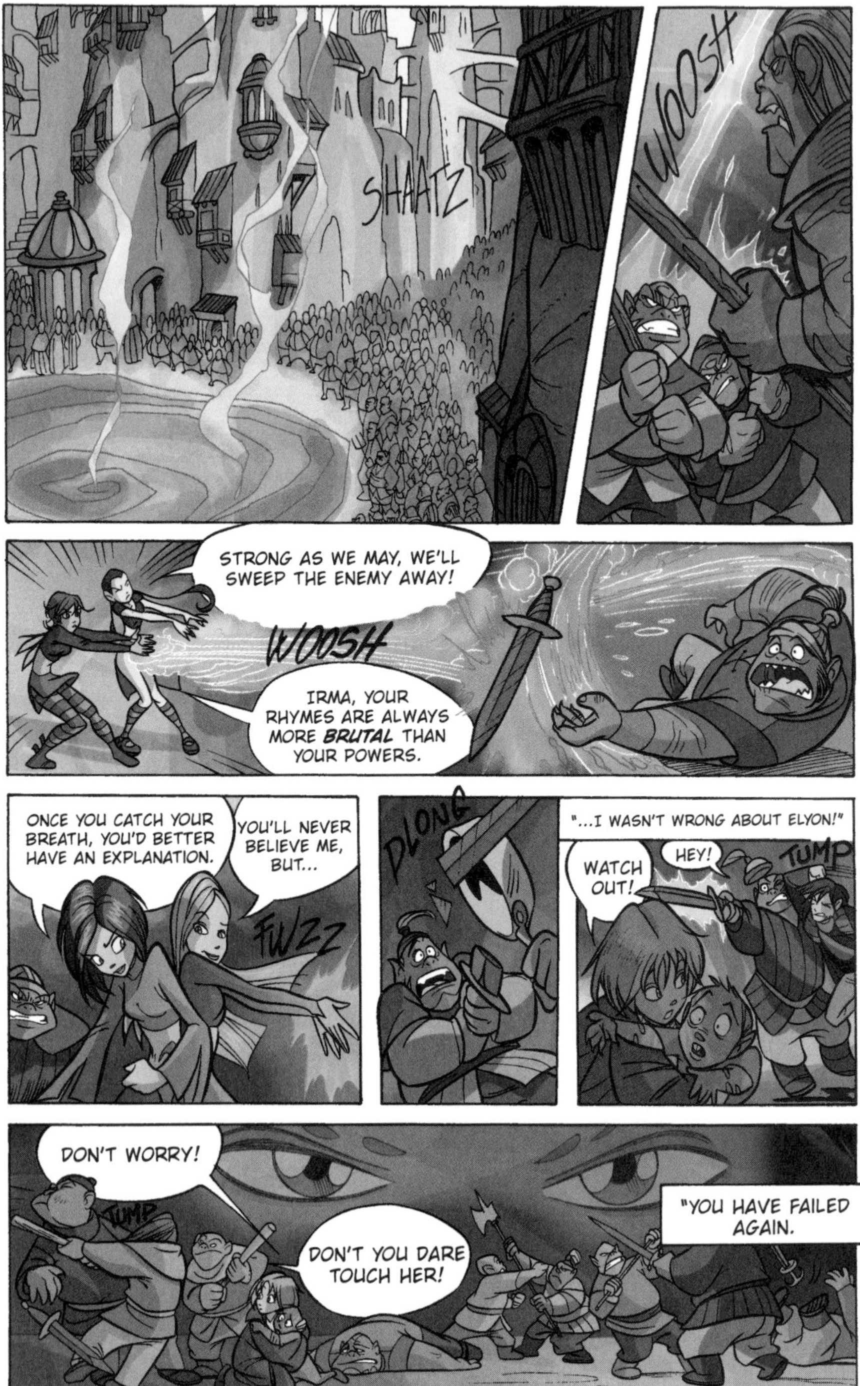
SHAATZ
WOOSH
STRONG AS WE MAY, WE'LL SWEEP THE ENEMY AWAY!
WOOSH
IRMA, YOUR RHYMES ARE ALWAYS MORE **BRUTAL** THAN YOUR POWERS.
ONCE YOU CATCH YOUR BREATH, YOU'D BETTER HAVE AN EXPLANATION.
YOU'LL NEVER BELIEVE ME, BUT...
FWZZ
DLONG
"...I WASN'T WRONG ABOUT ELYON!"
WATCH OUT!
HEY!
TUMP
DON'T WORRY!
TUMP
DON'T YOU DARE TOUCH HER!
"YOU HAVE FAILED AGAIN.

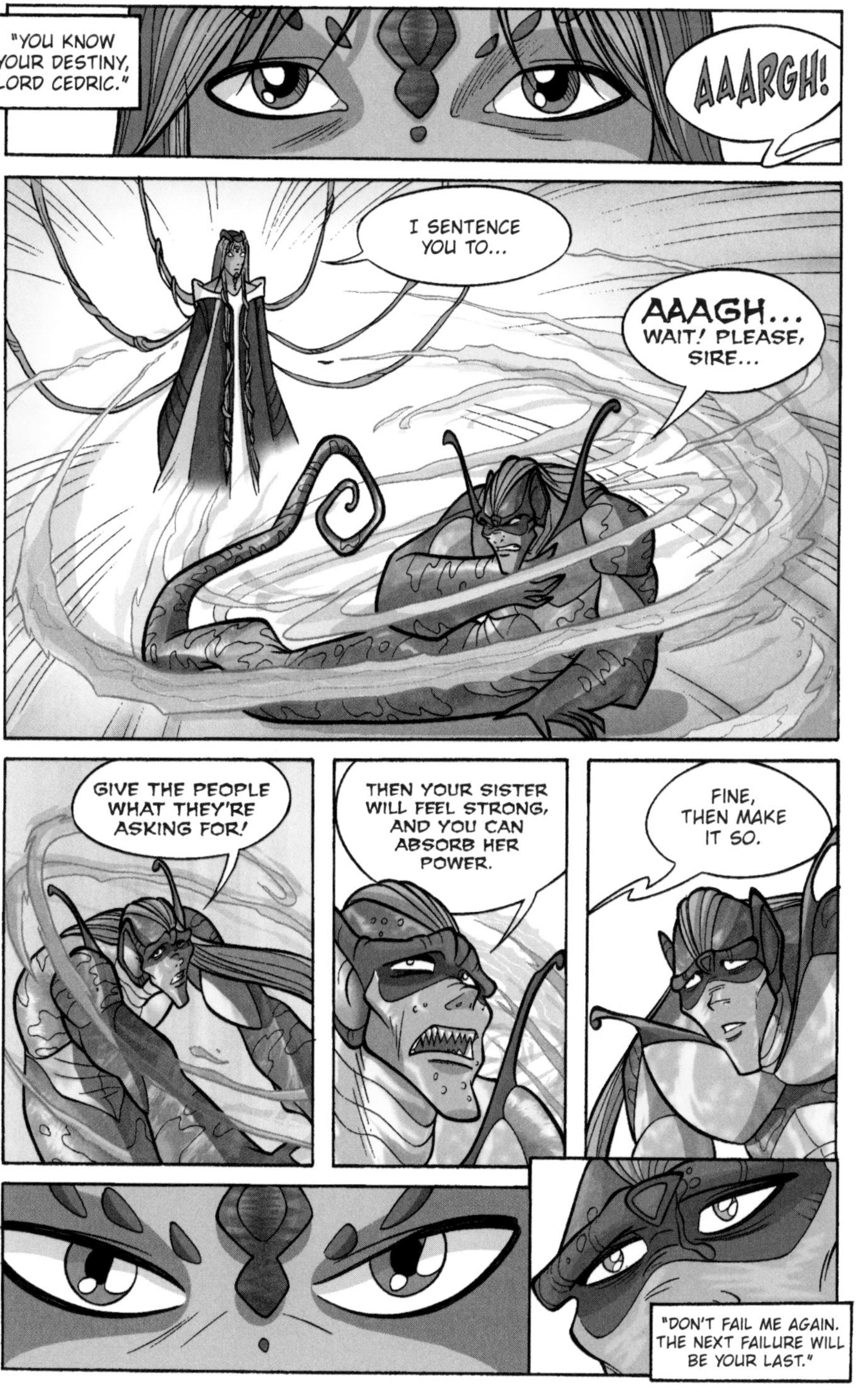
"YOU KNOW YOUR DESTINY, LORD CEDRIC."
AAARGH!
I SENTENCE YOU TO...
AAAGH... WAIT! PLEASE, SIRE...
GIVE THE PEOPLE WHAT THEY'RE ASKING FOR!
THEN YOUR SISTER WILL FEEL STRONG, AND YOU CAN ABSORB HER POWER.
FINE, THEN MAKE IT SO.
"DON'T FAIL ME AGAIN. THE NEXT FAILURE WILL BE YOUR LAST."

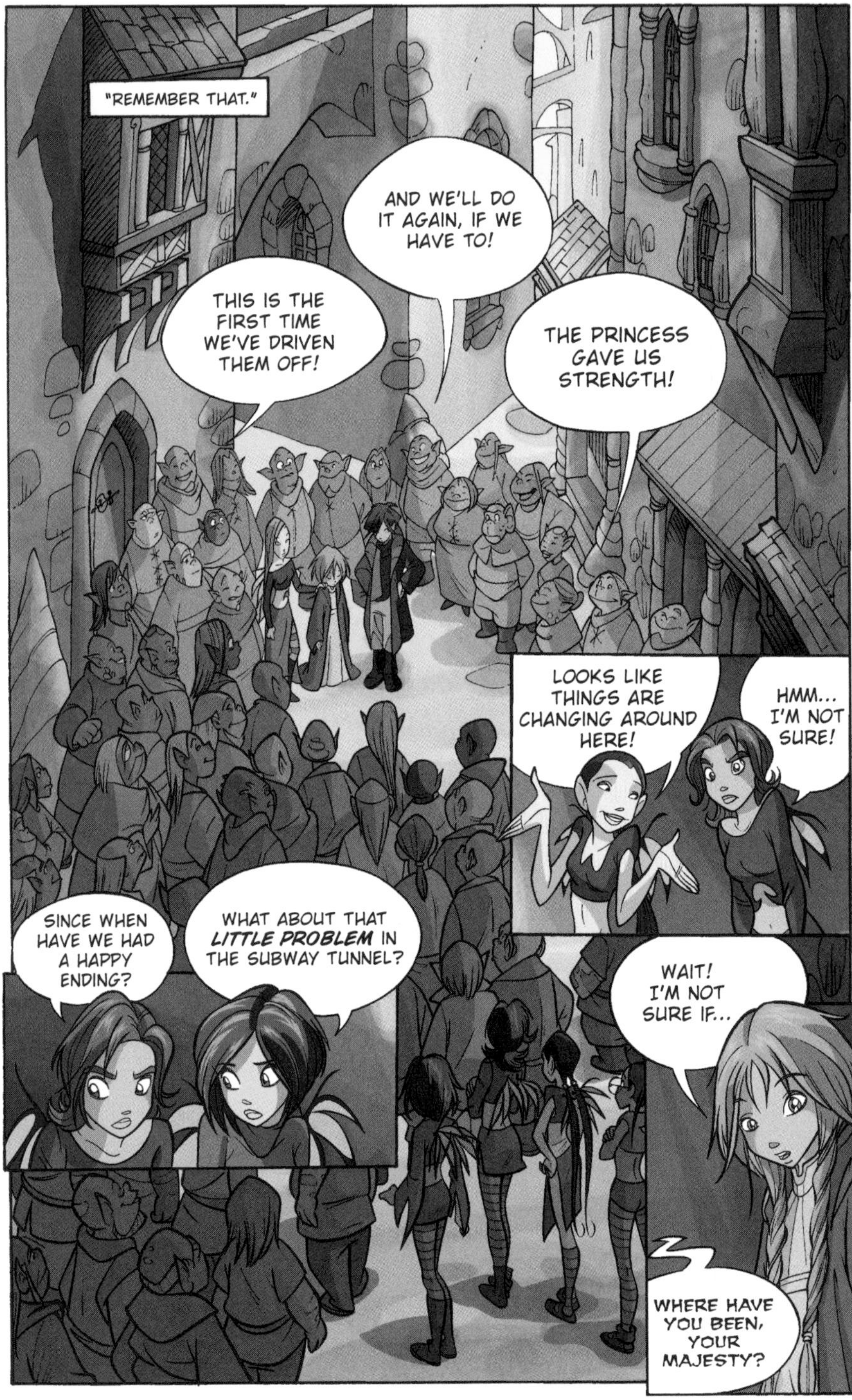
"REMEMBER THAT."
AND WE'LL DO IT AGAIN, IF WE HAVE TO!
THIS IS THE FIRST TIME WE'VE DRIVEN THEM OFF!
THE PRINCESS GAVE US STRENGTH!
LOOKS LIKE THINGS ARE CHANGING AROUND HERE!
HMM... I'M NOT SURE!
SINCE WHEN HAVE WE HAD A HAPPY ENDING?
WHAT ABOUT THAT *LITTLE PROBLEM* IN THE SUBWAY TUNNEL?
WAIT! I'M NOT SURE IF...
WHERE HAVE YOU BEEN, YOUR MAJESTY?

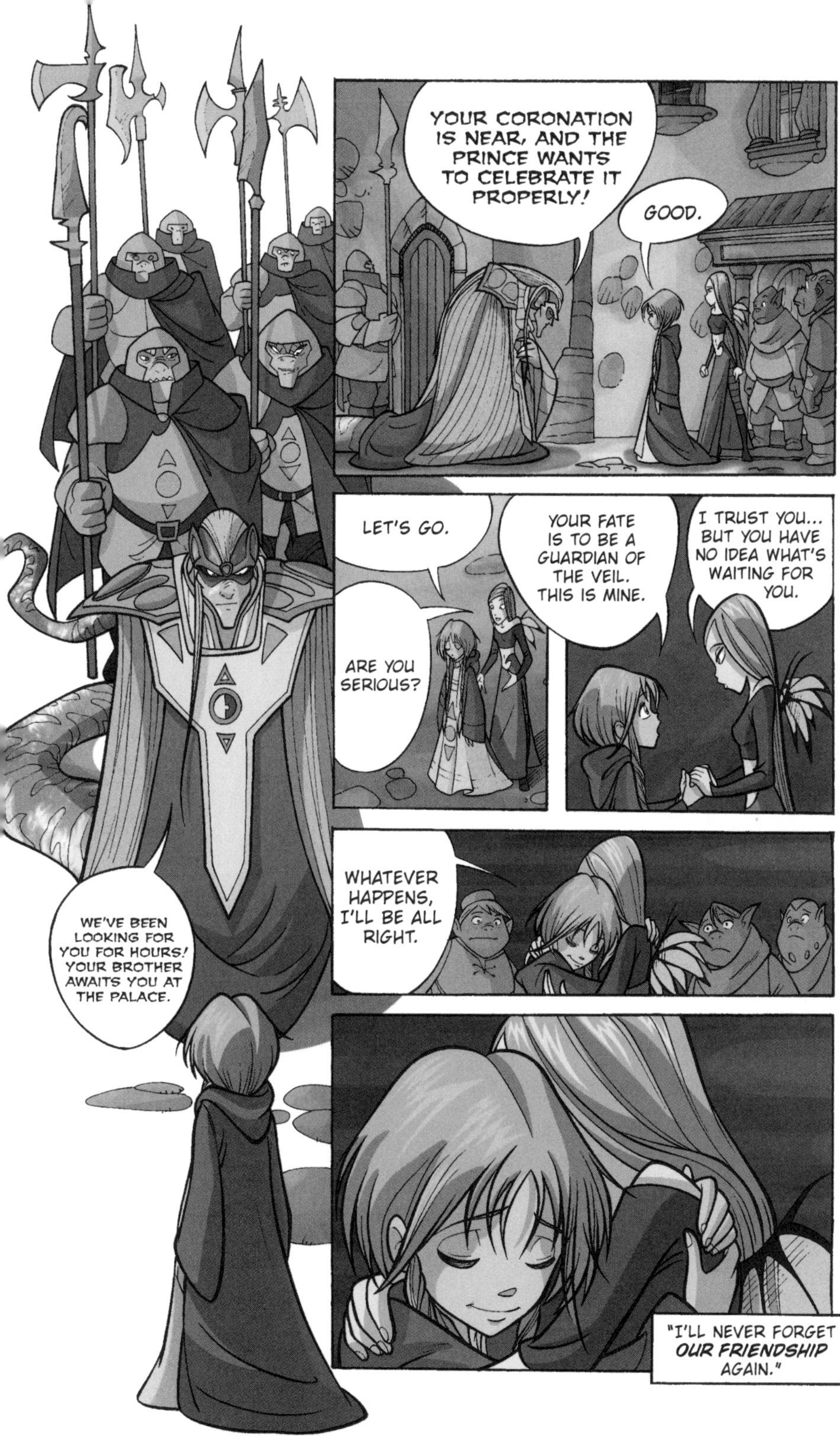

YOUR CORONATION IS NEAR, AND THE PRINCE WANTS TO CELEBRATE IT PROPERLY!
GOOD.
WE'VE BEEN LOOKING FOR YOU FOR HOURS! YOUR BROTHER AWAITS YOU AT THE PALACE.
LET'S GO.
ARE YOU SERIOUS?
YOUR FATE IS TO BE A GUARDIAN OF THE VEIL. THIS IS MINE.
I TRUST YOU... BUT YOU HAVE NO IDEA WHAT'S WAITING FOR YOU.
WHATEVER HAPPENS, I'LL BE ALL RIGHT.
"I'LL NEVER FORGET *OUR FRIENDSHIP* AGAIN."

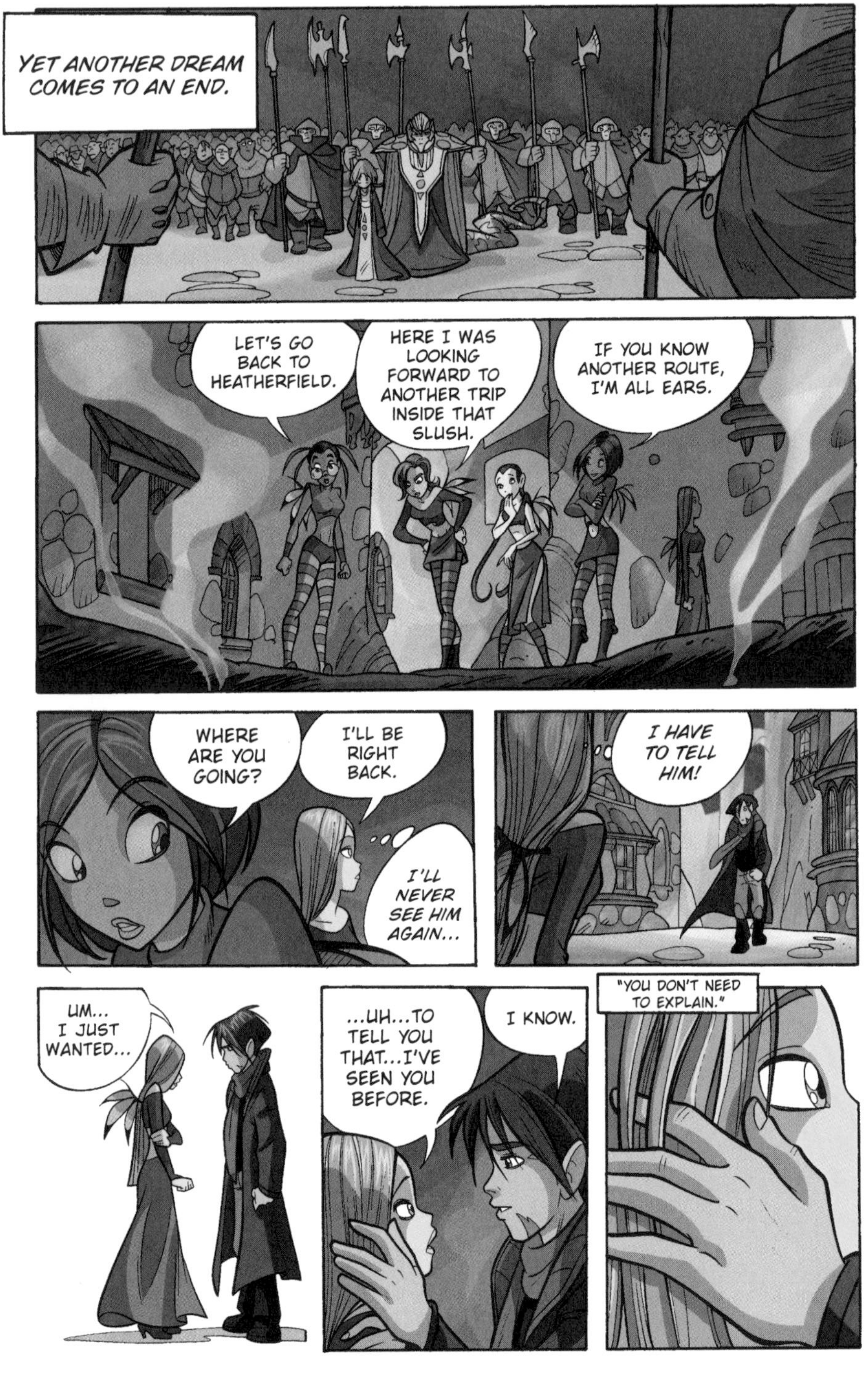
YET ANOTHER DREAM COMES TO AN END.
LET'S GO BACK TO HEATHERFIELD.
HERE I WAS LOOKING FORWARD TO ANOTHER TRIP INSIDE THAT SLUSH.
IF YOU KNOW ANOTHER ROUTE, I'M ALL EARS.
WHERE ARE YOU GOING?
I'LL BE RIGHT BACK.
I'LL NEVER SEE HIM AGAIN...
I HAVE TO TELL HIM!
UM... I JUST WANTED...
...UH...TO TELL YOU THAT...I'VE SEEN YOU BEFORE.
I KNOW.
"YOU DON'T NEED TO EXPLAIN."

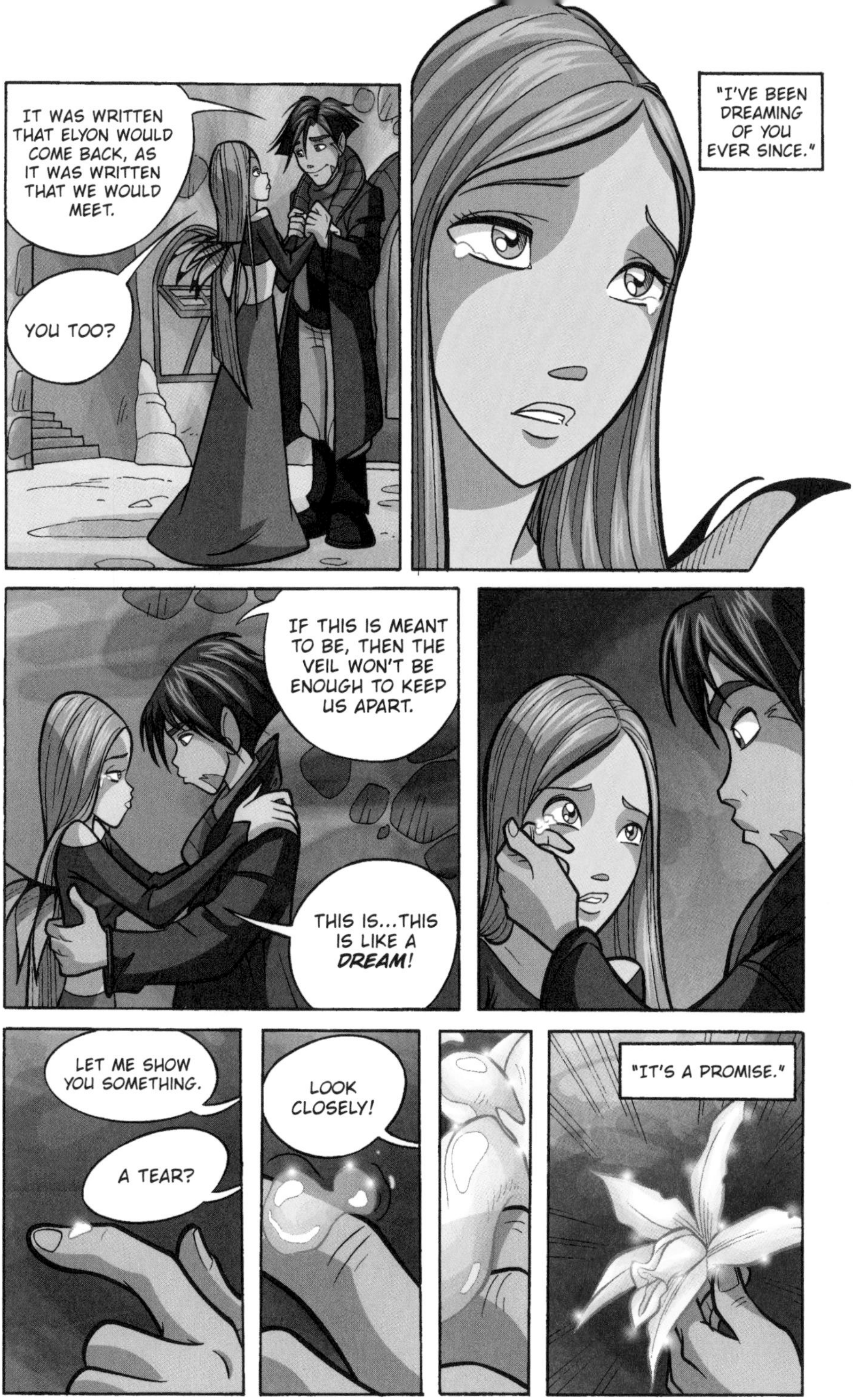
IT WAS WRITTEN THAT ELYON WOULD COME BACK, AS IT WAS WRITTEN THAT WE WOULD MEET.
YOU TOO?
"I'VE BEEN DREAMING OF YOU EVER SINCE."
IF THIS IS MEANT TO BE, THEN THE VEIL WON'T BE ENOUGH TO KEEP US APART.
THIS IS...THIS IS LIKE A *DREAM*!
LET ME SHOW YOU SOMETHING.
A TEAR?
LOOK CLOSELY!
"IT'S A PROMISE."

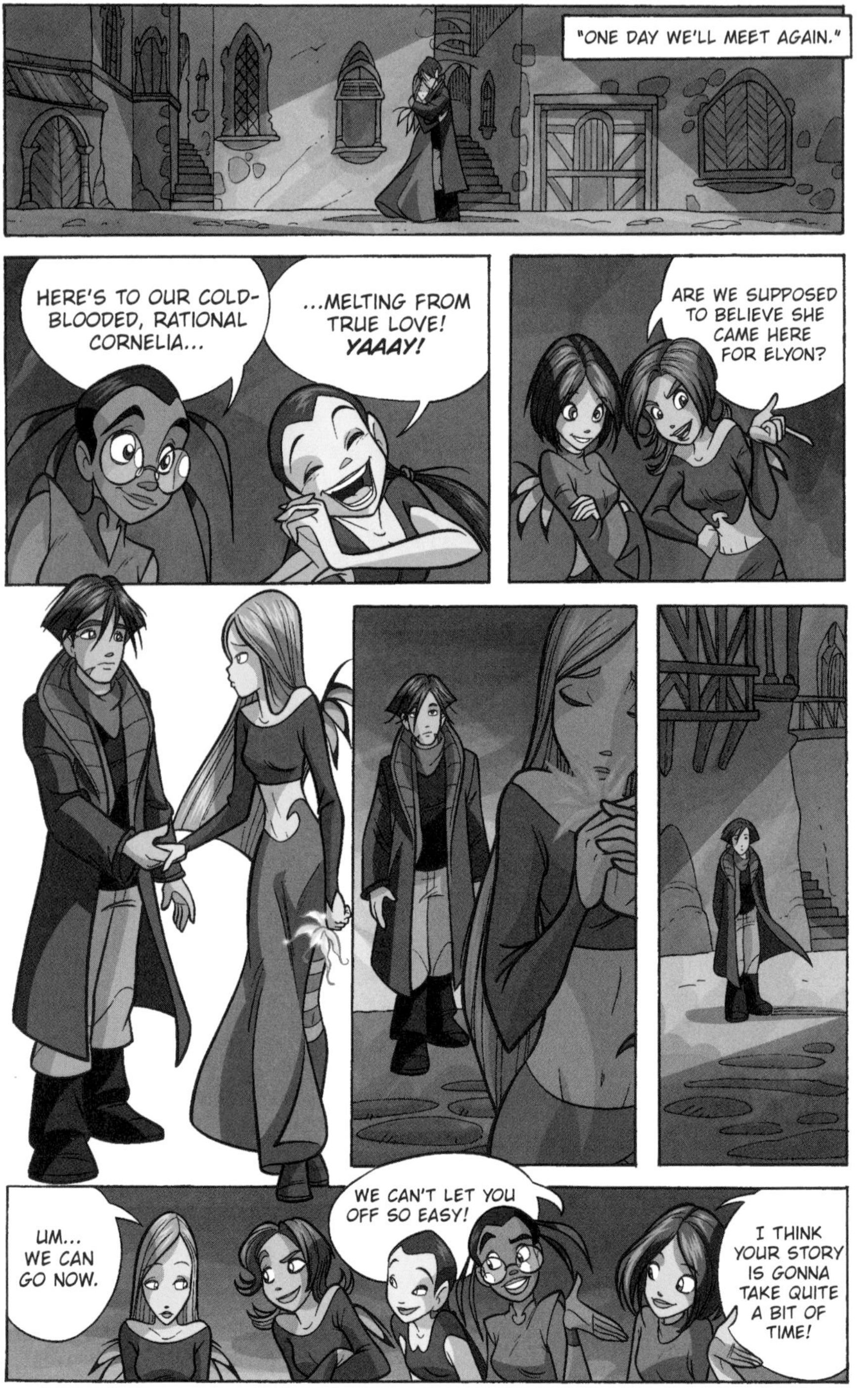
"ONE DAY WE'LL MEET AGAIN."
HERE'S TO OUR COLD-BLOODED, RATIONAL CORNELIA...
...MELTING FROM TRUE LOVE! *YAAAY!*
ARE WE SUPPOSED TO BELIEVE SHE CAME HERE FOR ELYON?
UM... WE CAN GO NOW.
WE CAN'T LET YOU OFF SO EASY!
I THINK YOUR STORY IS GONNA TAKE QUITE A BIT OF TIME!

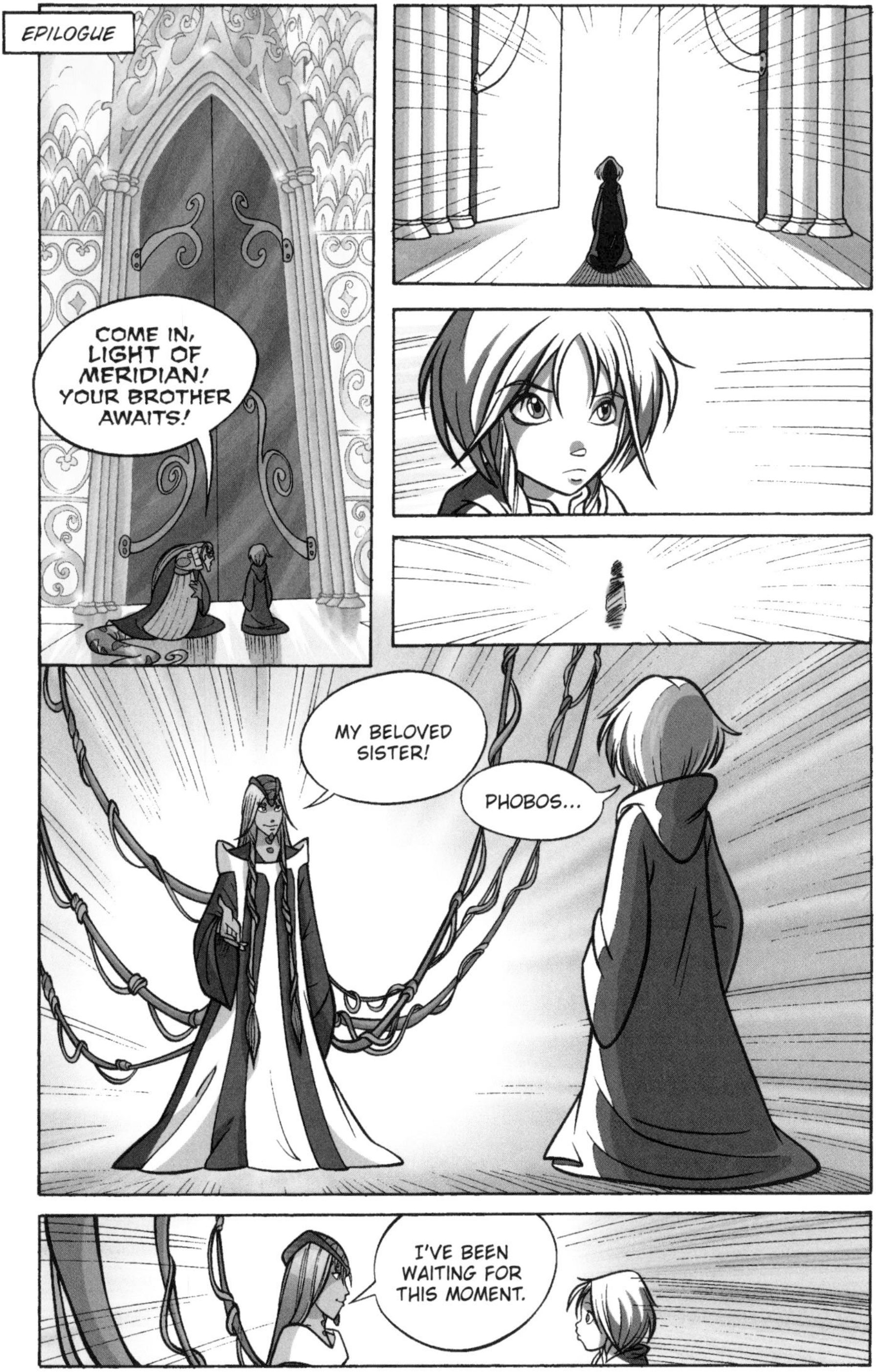
EPILOGUE
COME IN, LIGHT OF MERIDIAN! YOUR BROTHER AWAITS!
MY BELOVED SISTER!
PHOBOS...
I'VE BEEN WAITING FOR THIS MOMENT.

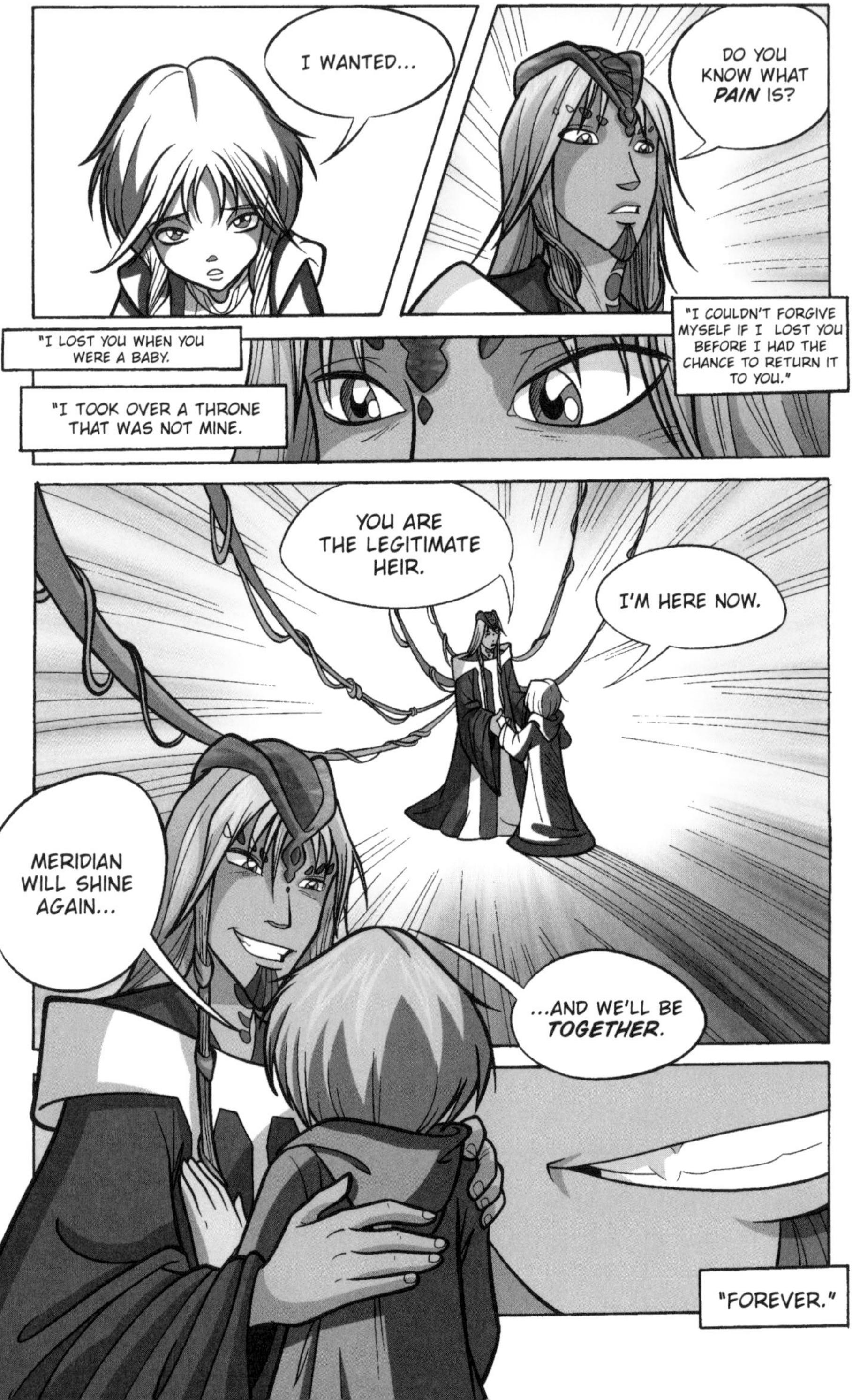
I WANTED...
DO YOU KNOW WHAT *PAIN* IS?
"I LOST YOU WHEN YOU WERE A BABY.
"I TOOK OVER A THRONE THAT WAS NOT MINE.
"I COULDN'T FORGIVE MYSELF IF I LOST YOU BEFORE I HAD THE CHANCE TO RETURN IT TO YOU."
YOU ARE THE LEGITIMATE HEIR.
I'M HERE NOW.
MERIDIAN WILL SHINE AGAIN...
...AND WE'LL BE *TOGETHER.*
"FOREVER."

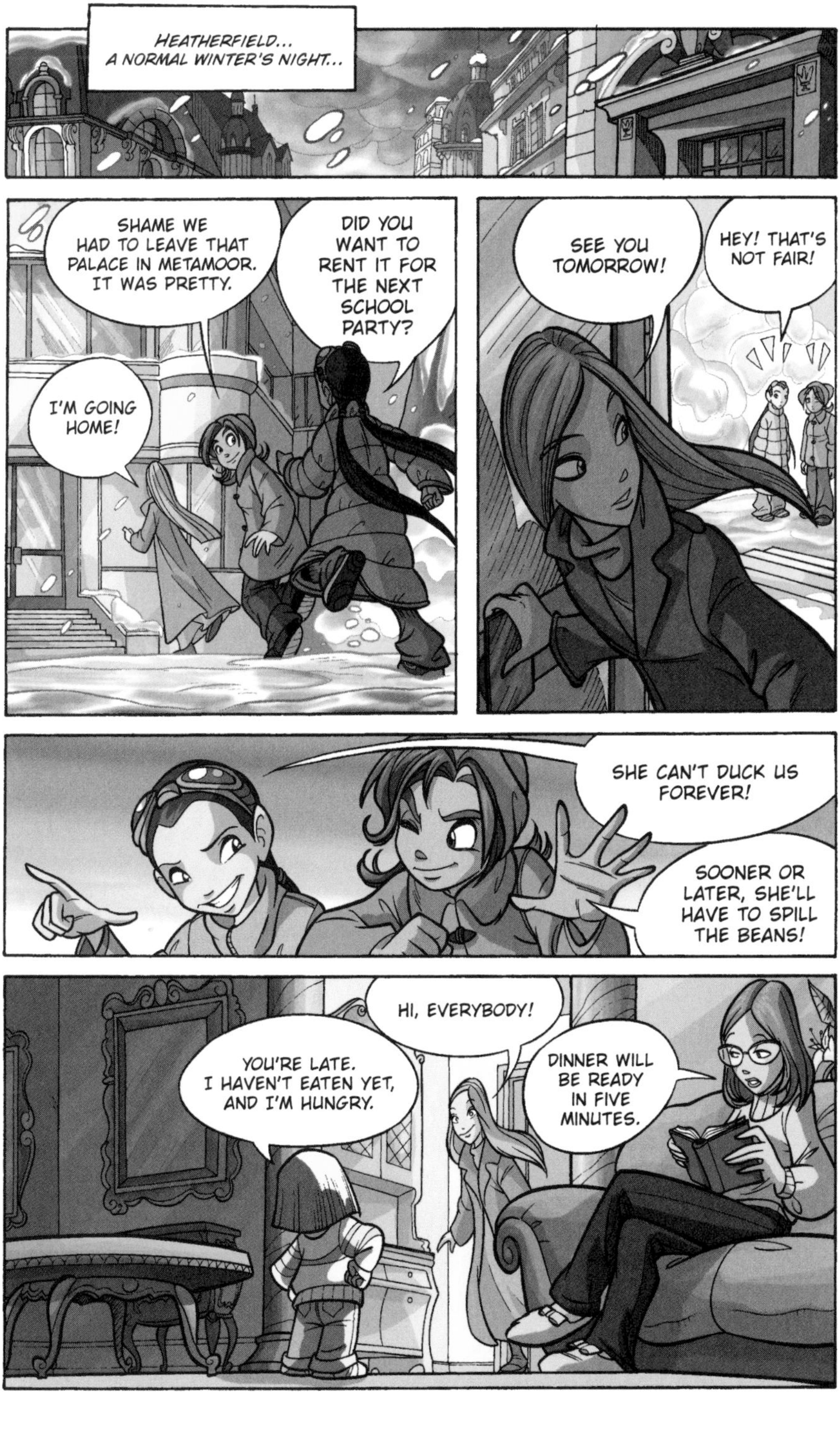
HEATHERFIELD... A NORMAL WINTER'S NIGHT...
SHAME WE HAD TO LEAVE THAT PALACE IN METAMOOR. IT WAS PRETTY.
DID YOU WANT TO RENT IT FOR THE NEXT SCHOOL PARTY?
I'M GOING HOME!
SEE YOU TOMORROW!
HEY! THAT'S NOT FAIR!
SHE CAN'T DUCK US FOREVER!
SOONER OR LATER, SHE'LL HAVE TO SPILL THE BEANS!
HI, EVERYBODY!
YOU'RE LATE. I HAVEN'T EATEN YET, AND I'M HUNGRY.
DINNER WILL BE READY IN FIVE MINUTES.

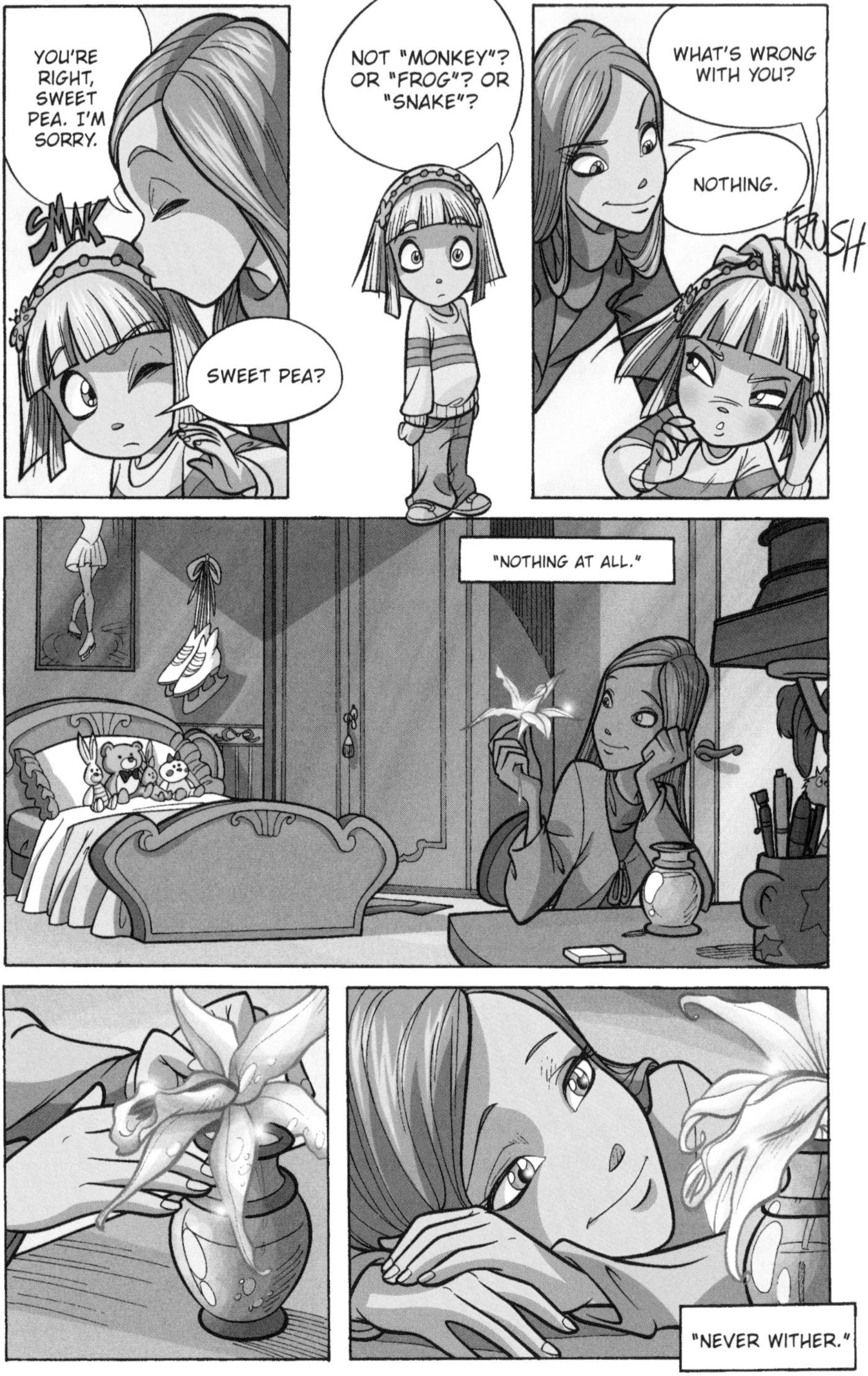

YOU'RE RIGHT, SWEET PEA. I'M SORRY.
SMAK
SWEET PEA?
NOT "MONKEY"? OR "FROG"? OR "SNAKE"?
WHAT'S WRONG WITH YOU?
NOTHING.
FRUSH
"NOTHING AT ALL."
"NEVER WITHER."

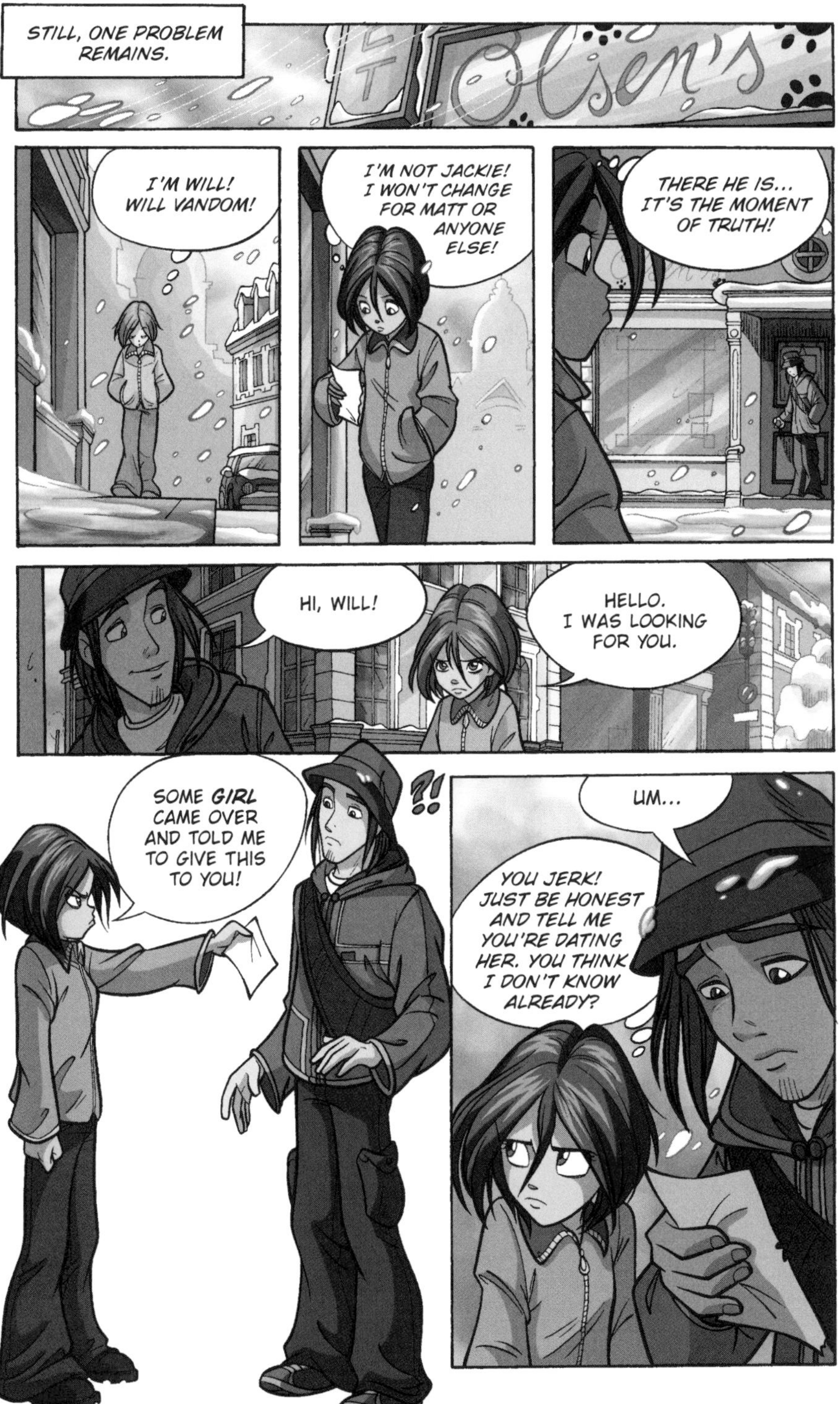
STILL, ONE PROBLEM REMAINS.
Olsen's
I'M WILL! WILL VANDOM!
I'M NOT JACKIE! I WON'T CHANGE FOR MATT OR ANYONE ELSE!
THERE HE IS... IT'S THE MOMENT OF TRUTH!
HI, WILL!
HELLO. I WAS LOOKING FOR YOU.
SOME **GIRL** CAME OVER AND TOLD ME TO GIVE THIS TO YOU!
?!
UM...
YOU JERK! JUST BE HONEST AND TELL ME YOU'RE DATING HER. YOU THINK I DON'T KNOW ALREADY?

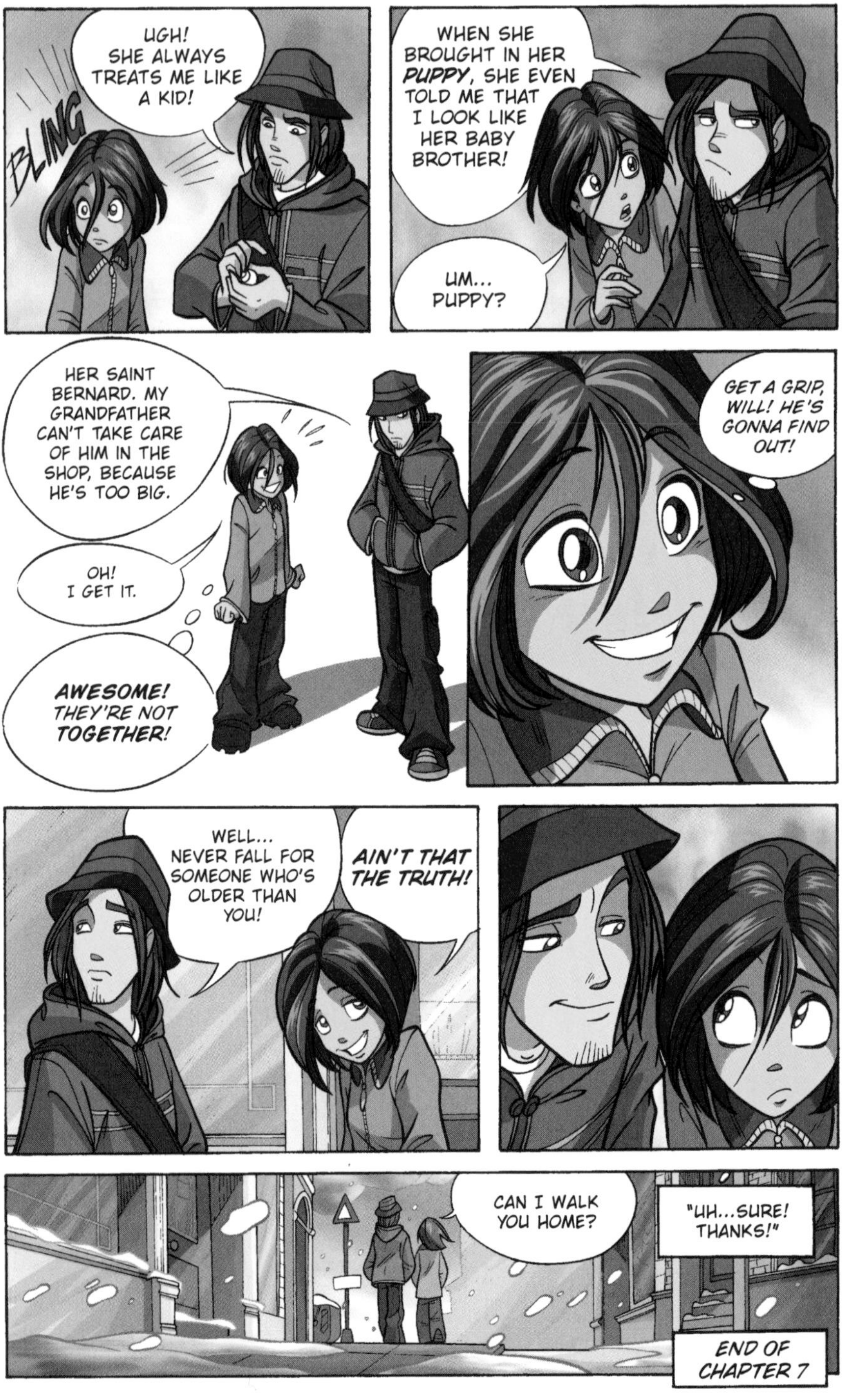
BLING
UGH! SHE ALWAYS TREATS ME LIKE A KID!
WHEN SHE BROUGHT IN HER *PUPPY*, SHE EVEN TOLD ME THAT I LOOK LIKE HER BABY BROTHER!
UM... PUPPY?
HER SAINT BERNARD. MY GRANDFATHER CAN'T TAKE CARE OF HIM IN THE SHOP, BECAUSE HE'S TOO BIG.
OH! I GET IT.
AWESOME! THEY'RE NOT TOGETHER!
GET A GRIP, WILL! HE'S GONNA FIND OUT!
WELL... NEVER FALL FOR SOMEONE WHO'S OLDER THAN YOU!
AIN'T THAT THE TRUTH!
CAN I WALK YOU HOME?
"UH...SURE! THANKS!"
END OF CHAPTER 7

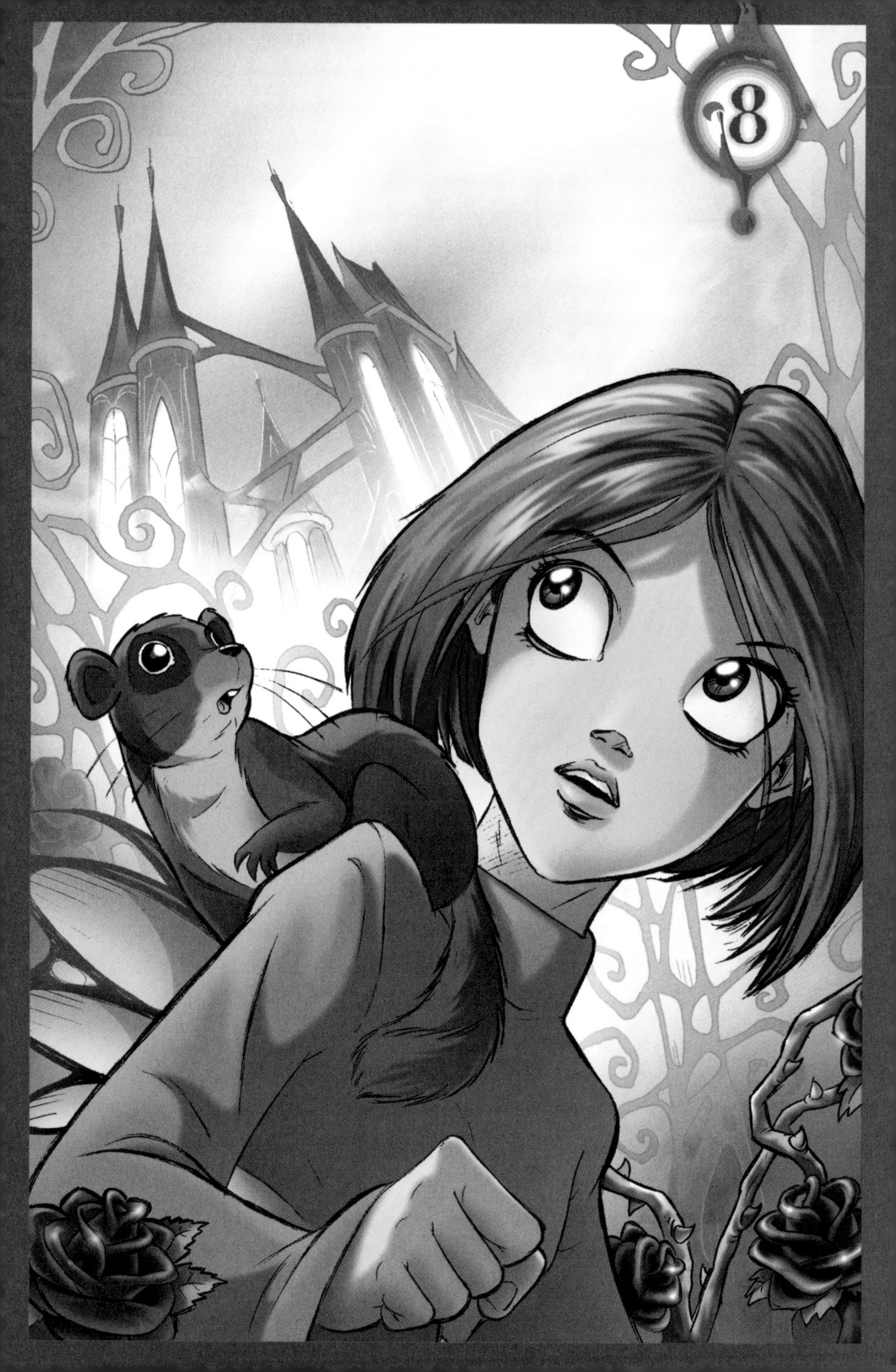
8

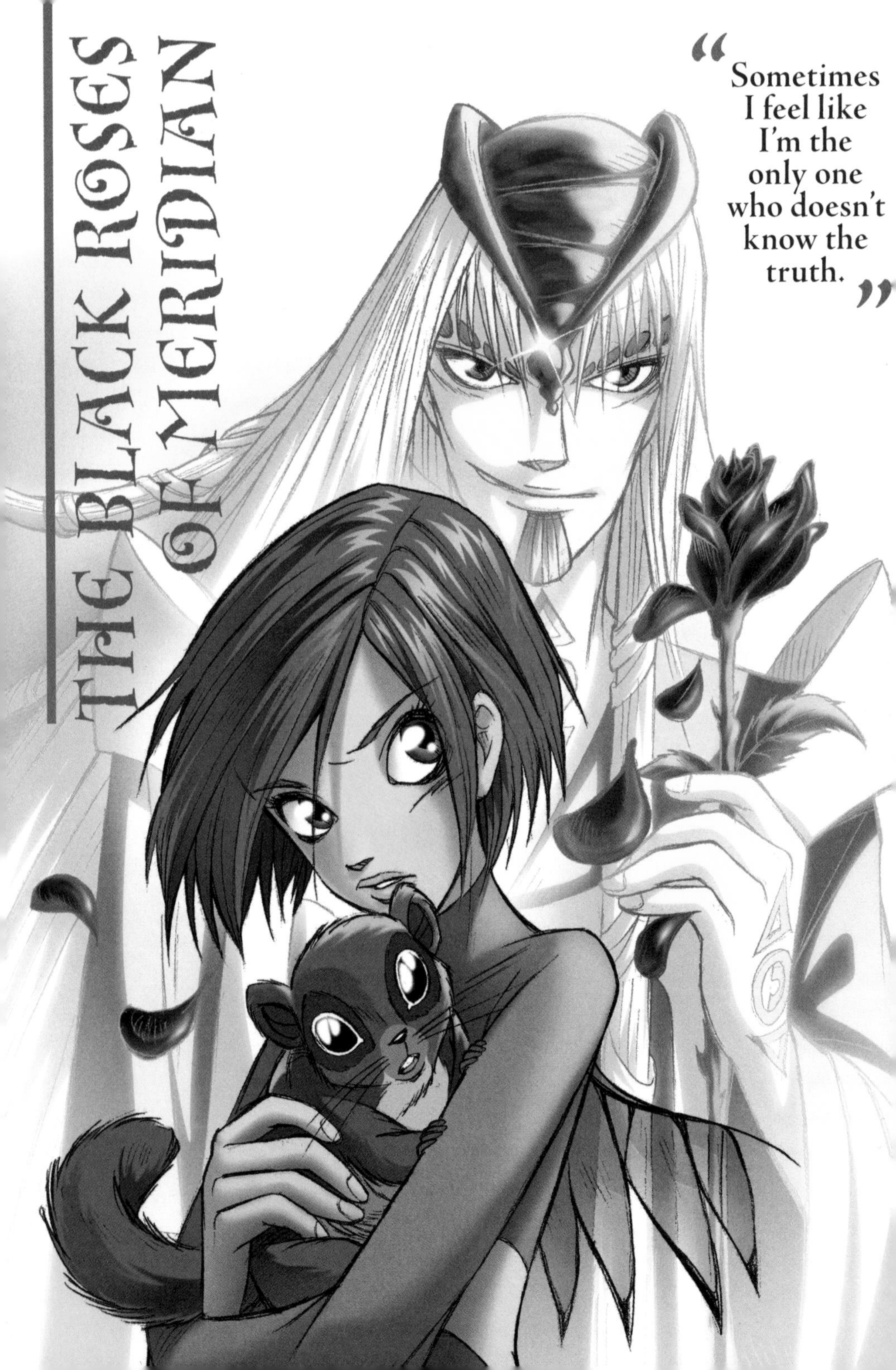
THE BLACK ROSES
OF MERIDIAN
"Sometimes I feel like I'm the only one who doesn't know the truth."

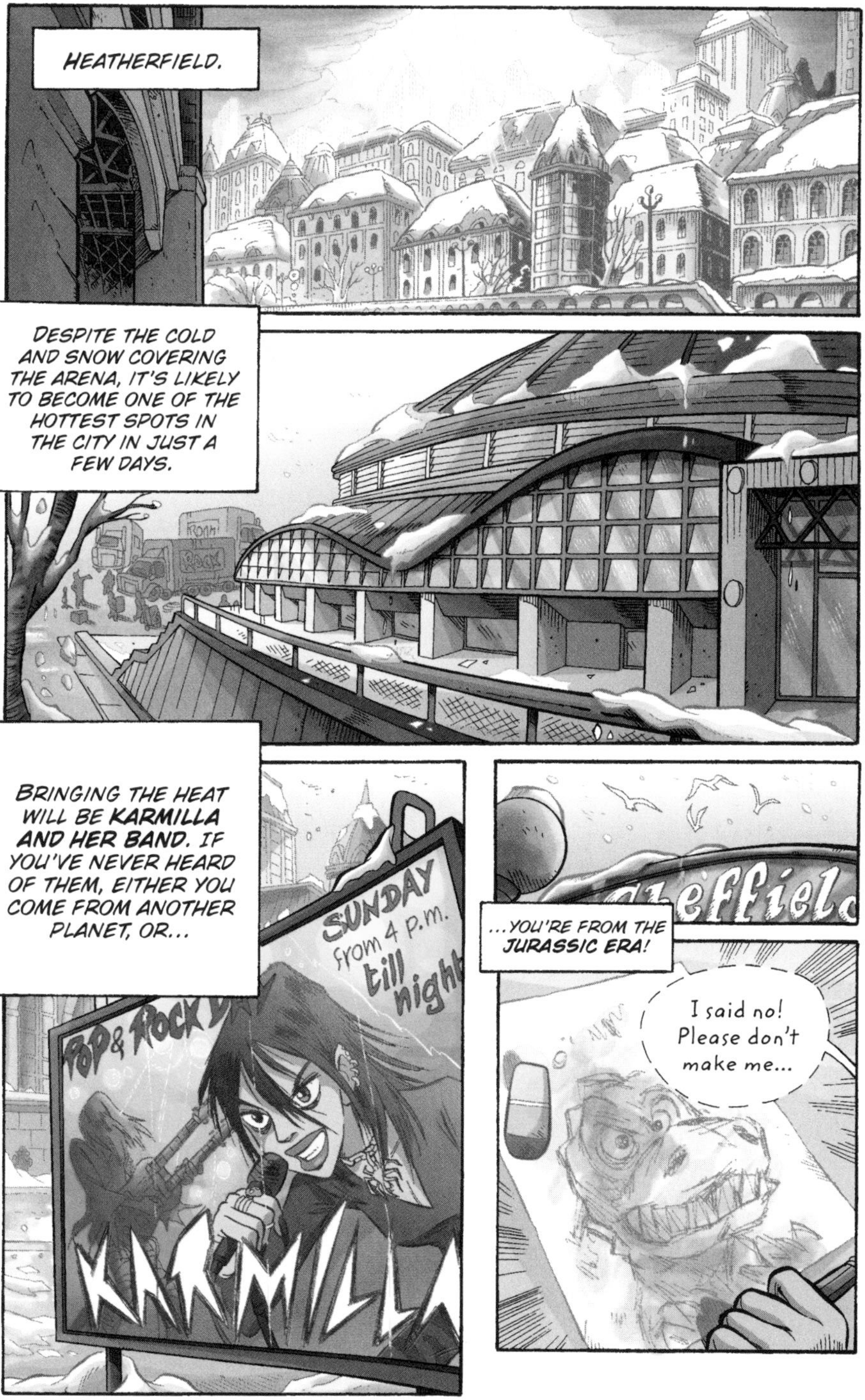
HEATHERFIELD.
DESPITE THE COLD AND SNOW COVERING THE ARENA, IT'S LIKELY TO BECOME ONE OF THE HOTTEST SPOTS IN THE CITY IN JUST A FEW DAYS.
BRINGING THE HEAT WILL BE **KARMILLA AND HER BAND**. IF YOU'VE NEVER HEARD OF THEM, EITHER YOU COME FROM ANOTHER PLANET, OR...
SUNDAY from 4 p.m. till night
POP & ROCK
KARMILLA
...YOU'RE FROM THE **JURASSIC ERA!**
I said no! Please don't make me...

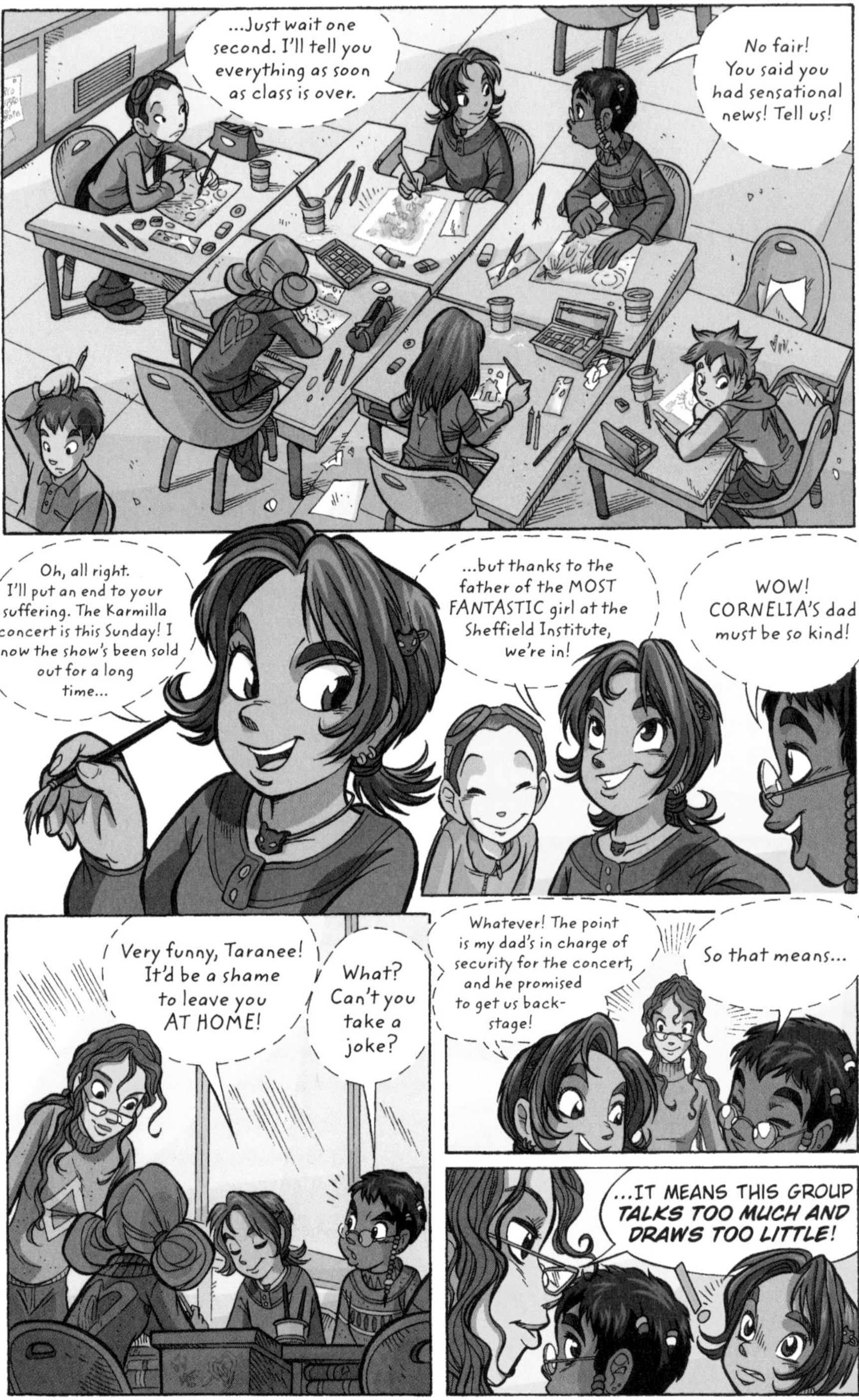
...Just wait one second. I'll tell you everything as soon as class is over.
No fair! You said you had sensational news! Tell us!
Oh, all right. I'll put an end to your suffering. The Karmilla concert is this Sunday! I know the show's been sold out for a long time...
...but thanks to the father of the MOST FANTASTIC girl at the Sheffield Institute, we're in!
WOW! CORNELIA'S dad must be so kind!
Very funny, Taranee! It'd be a shame to leave you AT HOME!
What? Can't you take a joke?
Whatever! The point is my dad's in charge of security for the concert, and he promised to get us back-stage!
So that means...
...IT MEANS THIS GROUP *TALKS TOO MUCH AND DRAWS TOO LITTLE!*

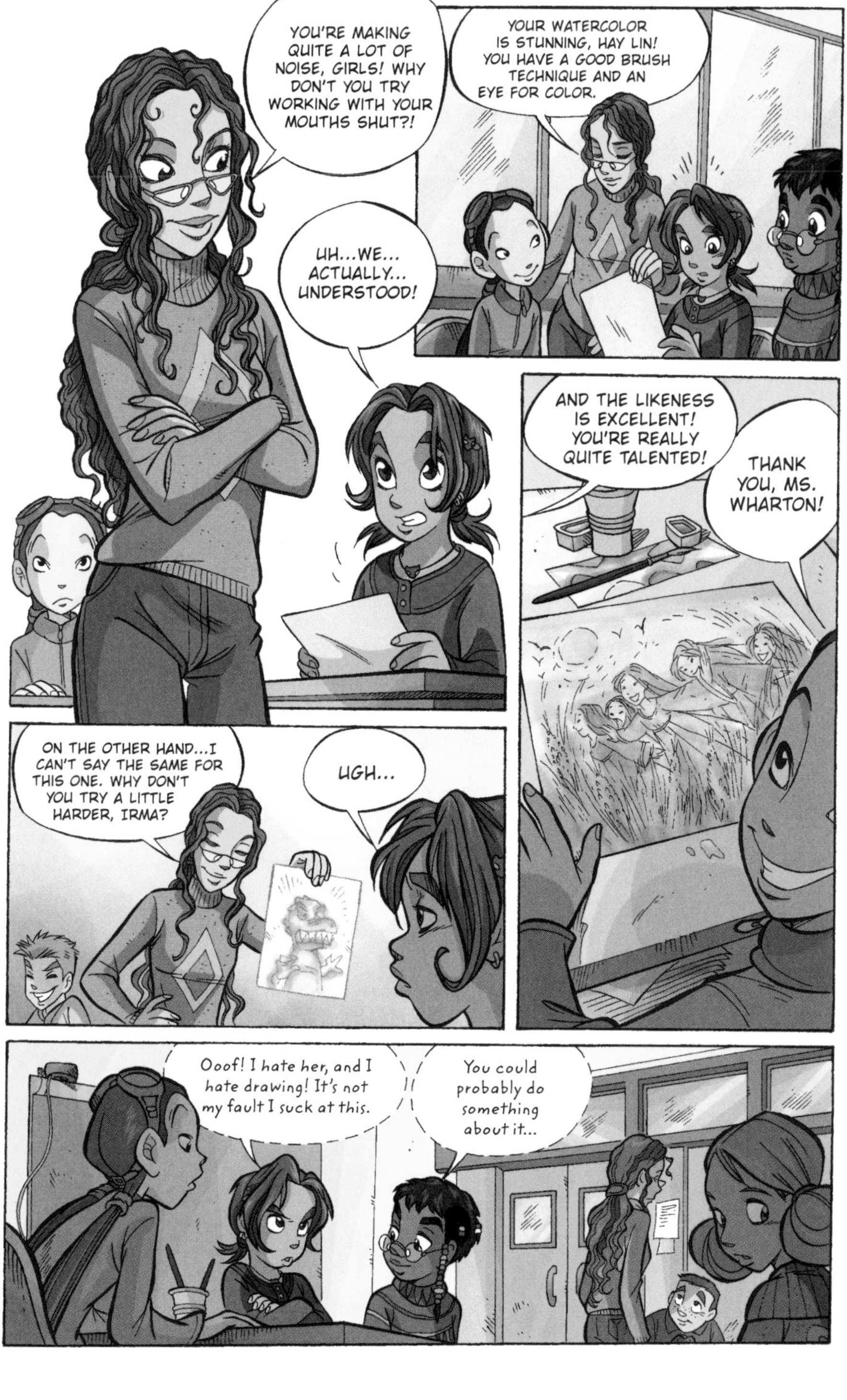
YOU'RE MAKING QUITE A LOT OF NOISE, GIRLS! WHY DON'T YOU TRY WORKING WITH YOUR MOUTHS SHUT?!
UH...WE... ACTUALLY... UNDERSTOOD!
YOUR WATERCOLOR IS STUNNING, HAY LIN! YOU HAVE A GOOD BRUSH TECHNIQUE AND AN EYE FOR COLOR.
AND THE LIKENESS IS EXCELLENT! YOU'RE REALLY QUITE TALENTED!
THANK YOU, MS. WHARTON!
ON THE OTHER HAND...I CAN'T SAY THE SAME FOR THIS ONE. WHY DON'T YOU TRY A LITTLE HARDER, IRMA?
UGH...
Ooof! I hate her, and I hate drawing! It's not my fault I suck at this.
You could probably do something about it...

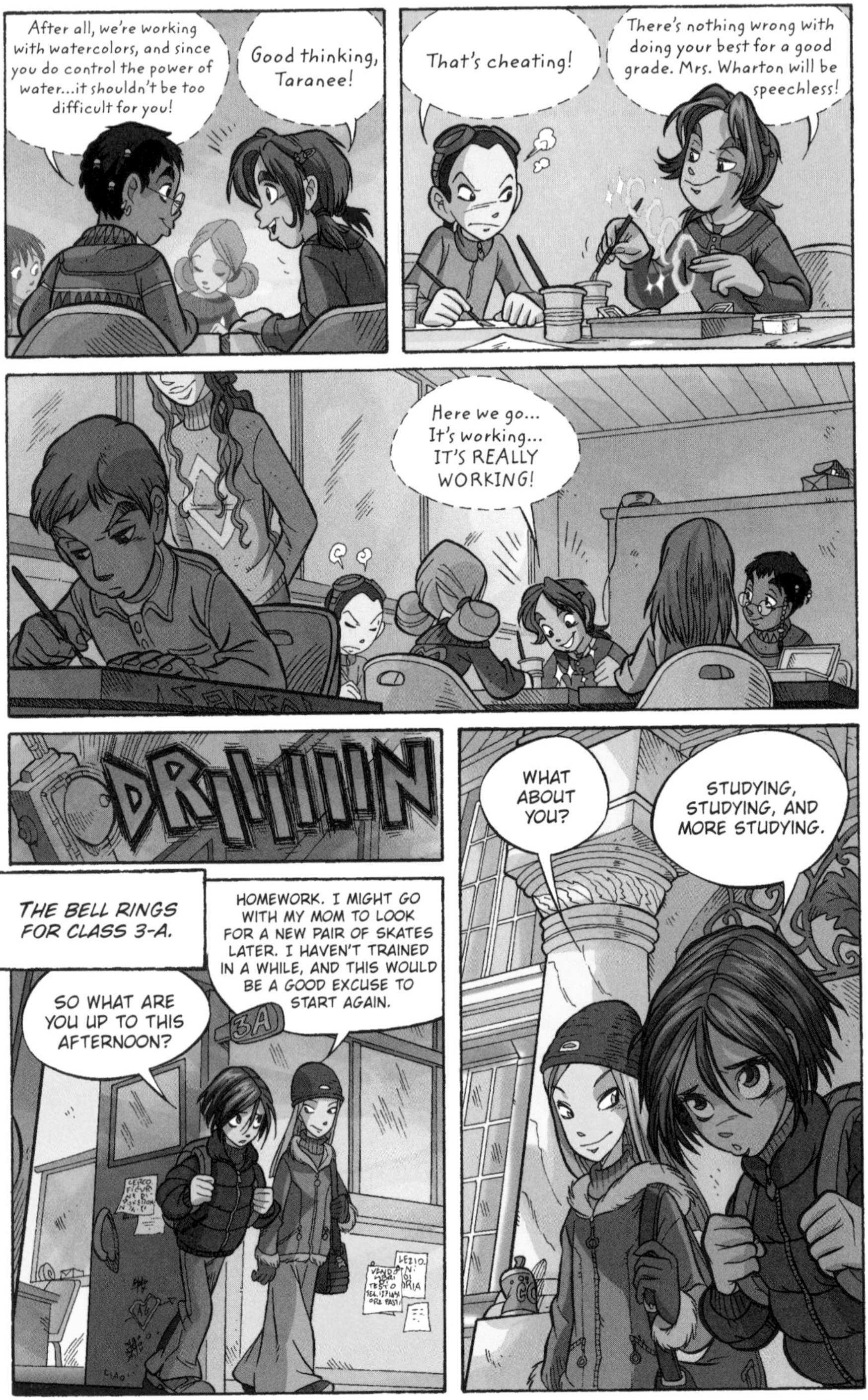
After all, we're working with watercolors, and since you do control the power of water...it shouldn't be too difficult for you!
Good thinking, Taranee!
That's cheating!
There's nothing wrong with doing your best for a good grade. Mrs. Wharton will be speechless!
Here we go... It's working... IT'S REALLY WORKING!
DRIIIIIN
THE BELL RINGS FOR CLASS 3-A.
SO WHAT ARE YOU UP TO THIS AFTERNOON?
HOMEWORK. I MIGHT GO WITH MY MOM TO LOOK FOR A NEW PAIR OF SKATES LATER. I HAVEN'T TRAINED IN A WHILE, AND THIS WOULD BE A GOOD EXCUSE TO START AGAIN.
3A
WHAT ABOUT YOU?
STUDYING, STUDYING, AND MORE STUDYING.

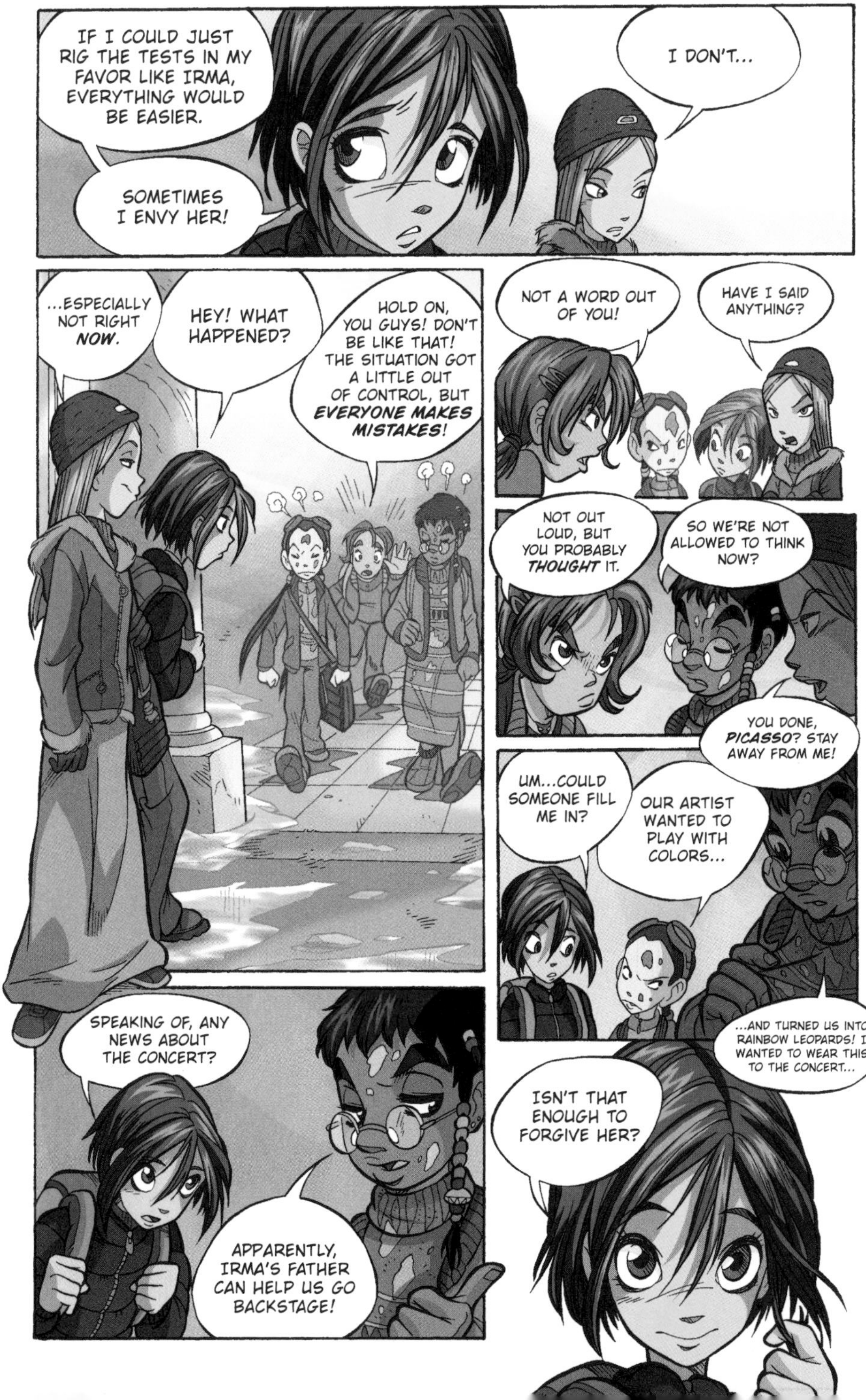
IF I COULD JUST RIG THE TESTS IN MY FAVOR LIKE IRMA, EVERYTHING WOULD BE EASIER.
SOMETIMES I ENVY HER!
I DON'T...
...ESPECIALLY NOT RIGHT NOW.
HEY! WHAT HAPPENED?
HOLD ON, YOU GUYS! DON'T BE LIKE THAT! THE SITUATION GOT A LITTLE OUT OF CONTROL, BUT EVERYONE MAKES MISTAKES!
NOT A WORD OUT OF YOU!
HAVE I SAID ANYTHING?
NOT OUT LOUD, BUT YOU PROBABLY THOUGHT IT.
SO WE'RE NOT ALLOWED TO THINK NOW?
YOU DONE, PICASSO? STAY AWAY FROM ME!
UM...COULD SOMEONE FILL ME IN?
OUR ARTIST WANTED TO PLAY WITH COLORS...
...AND TURNED US INTO RAINBOW LEOPARDS! I WANTED TO WEAR THIS TO THE CONCERT...
SPEAKING OF, ANY NEWS ABOUT THE CONCERT?
APPARENTLY, IRMA'S FATHER CAN HELP US GO BACKSTAGE!
ISN'T THAT ENOUGH TO FORGIVE HER?

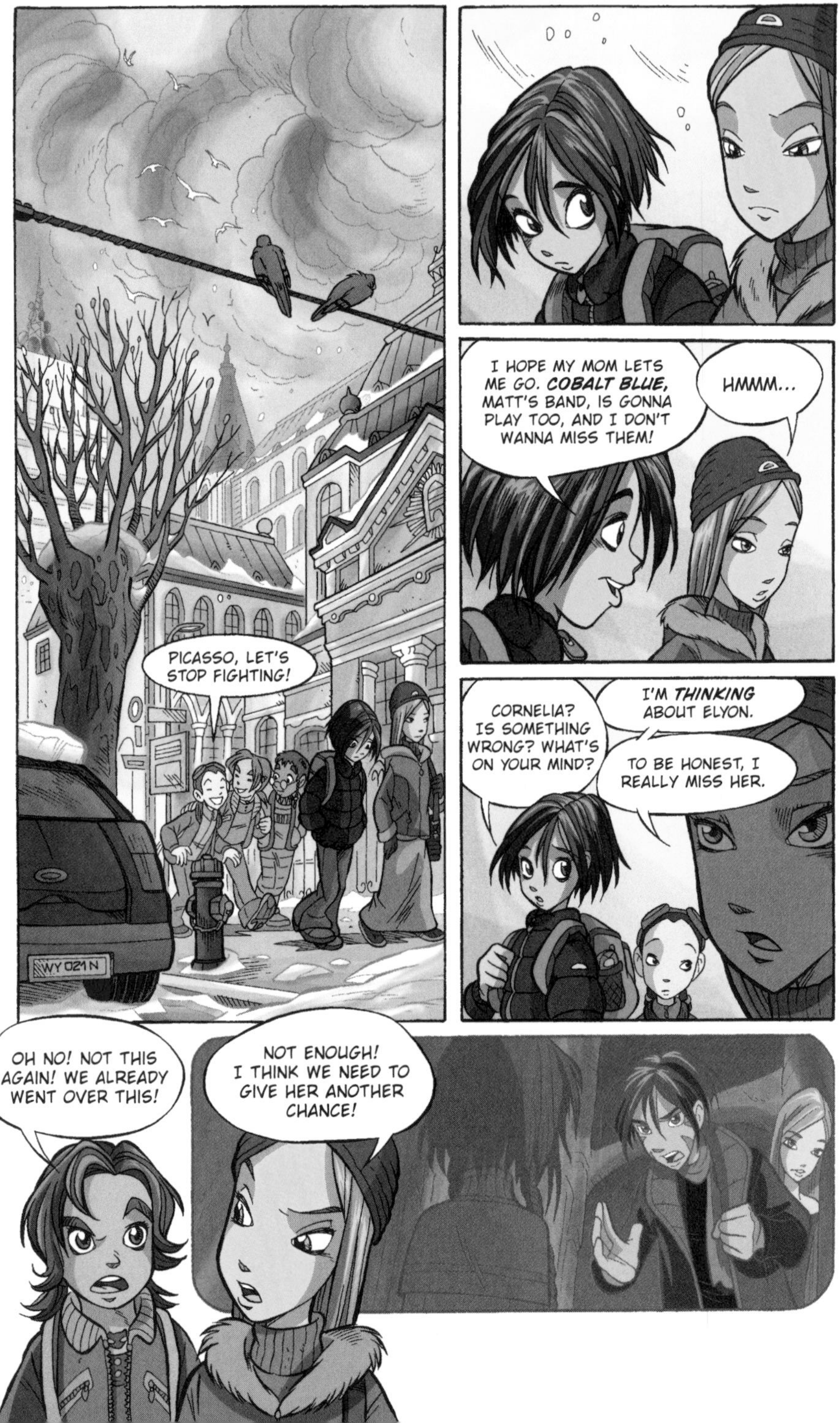
PICASSO, LET'S STOP FIGHTING!
I HOPE MY MOM LETS ME GO. COBALT BLUE, MATT'S BAND, IS GONNA PLAY TOO, AND I DON'T WANNA MISS THEM!
HMMM...
CORNELIA? IS SOMETHING WRONG? WHAT'S ON YOUR MIND?
I'M THINKING ABOUT ELYON.
TO BE HONEST, I REALLY MISS HER.
OH NO! NOT THIS AGAIN! WE ALREADY WENT OVER THIS!
NOT ENOUGH! I THINK WE NEED TO GIVE HER ANOTHER CHANCE!

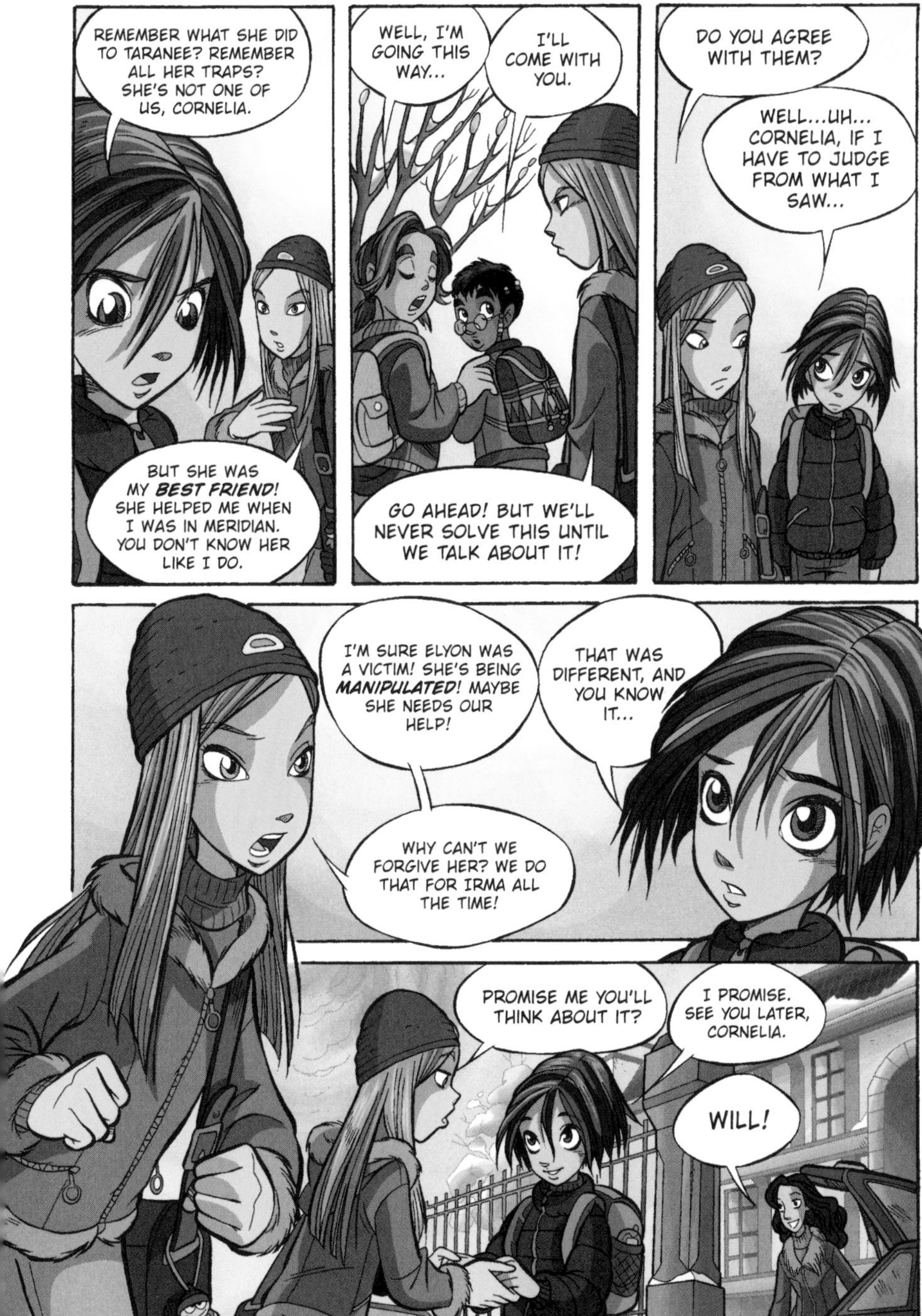
REMEMBER WHAT SHE DID TO TARANEE? REMEMBER ALL HER TRAPS? SHE'S NOT ONE OF US, CORNELIA.
BUT SHE WAS MY **BEST FRIEND**! SHE HELPED ME WHEN I WAS IN MERIDIAN. YOU DON'T KNOW HER LIKE I DO.
WELL, I'M GOING THIS WAY...
I'LL COME WITH YOU.
GO AHEAD! BUT WE'LL NEVER SOLVE THIS UNTIL WE TALK ABOUT IT!
DO YOU AGREE WITH THEM?
WELL...UH... CORNELIA, IF I HAVE TO JUDGE FROM WHAT I SAW...
I'M SURE ELYON WAS A VICTIM! SHE'S BEING **MANIPULATED**! MAYBE SHE NEEDS OUR HELP!
WHY CAN'T WE FORGIVE HER? WE DO THAT FOR IRMA ALL THE TIME!
THAT WAS DIFFERENT, AND YOU KNOW IT...
PROMISE ME YOU'LL THINK ABOUT IT?
I PROMISE. SEE YOU LATER, CORNELIA.
WILL!

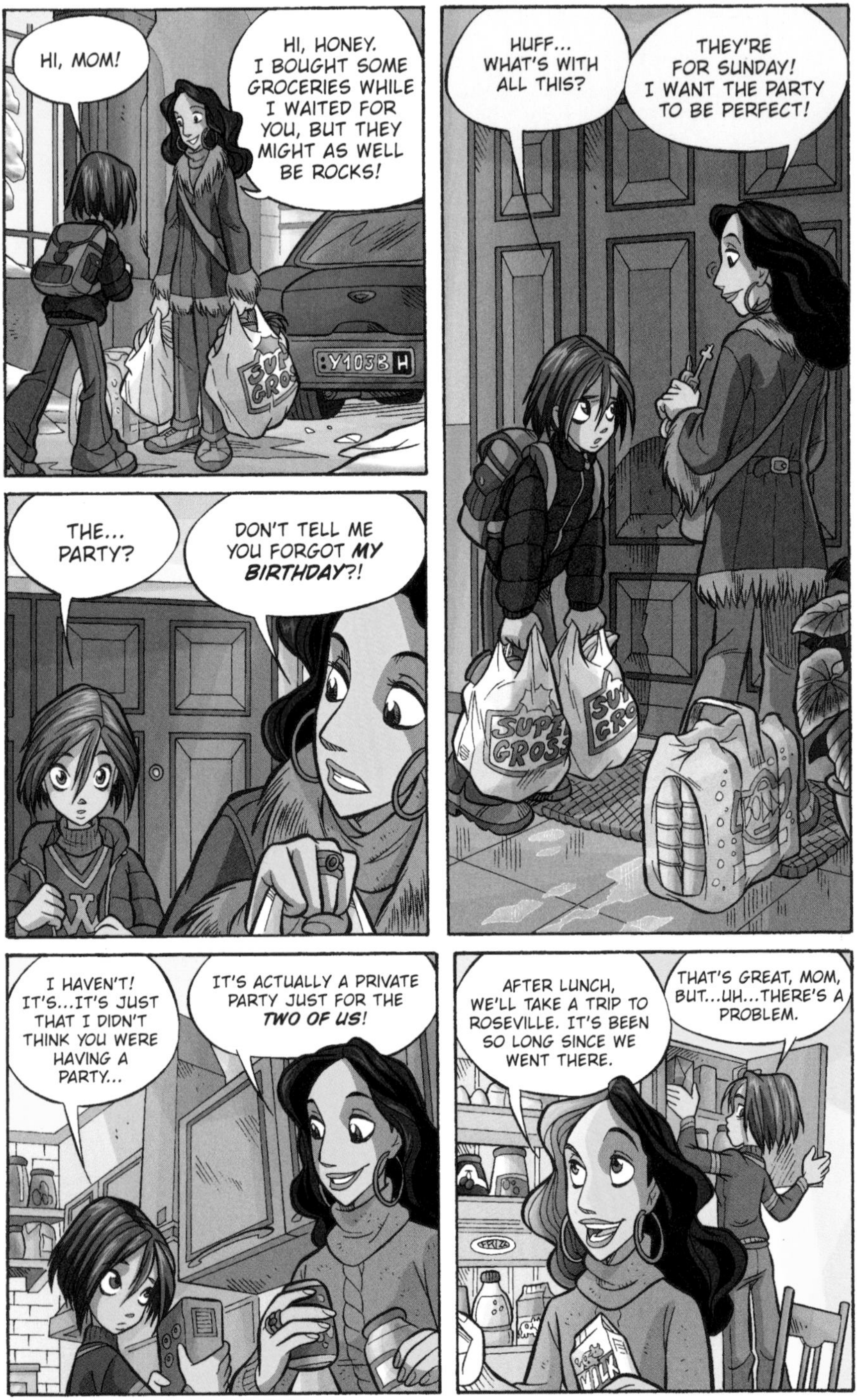
HI, MOM!
HI, HONEY. I BOUGHT SOME GROCERIES WHILE I WAITED FOR YOU, BUT THEY MIGHT AS WELL BE ROCKS!
HUFF... WHAT'S WITH ALL THIS?
THEY'RE FOR SUNDAY! I WANT THE PARTY TO BE PERFECT!
THE... PARTY?
DON'T TELL ME YOU FORGOT *MY BIRTHDAY*?!
I HAVEN'T! IT'S...IT'S JUST THAT I DIDN'T THINK YOU WERE HAVING A PARTY...
IT'S ACTUALLY A PRIVATE PARTY JUST FOR THE *TWO OF US*!
AFTER LUNCH, WE'LL TAKE A TRIP TO ROSEVILLE. IT'S BEEN SO LONG SINCE WE WENT THERE.
THAT'S GREAT, MOM, BUT...UH...THERE'S A PROBLEM.

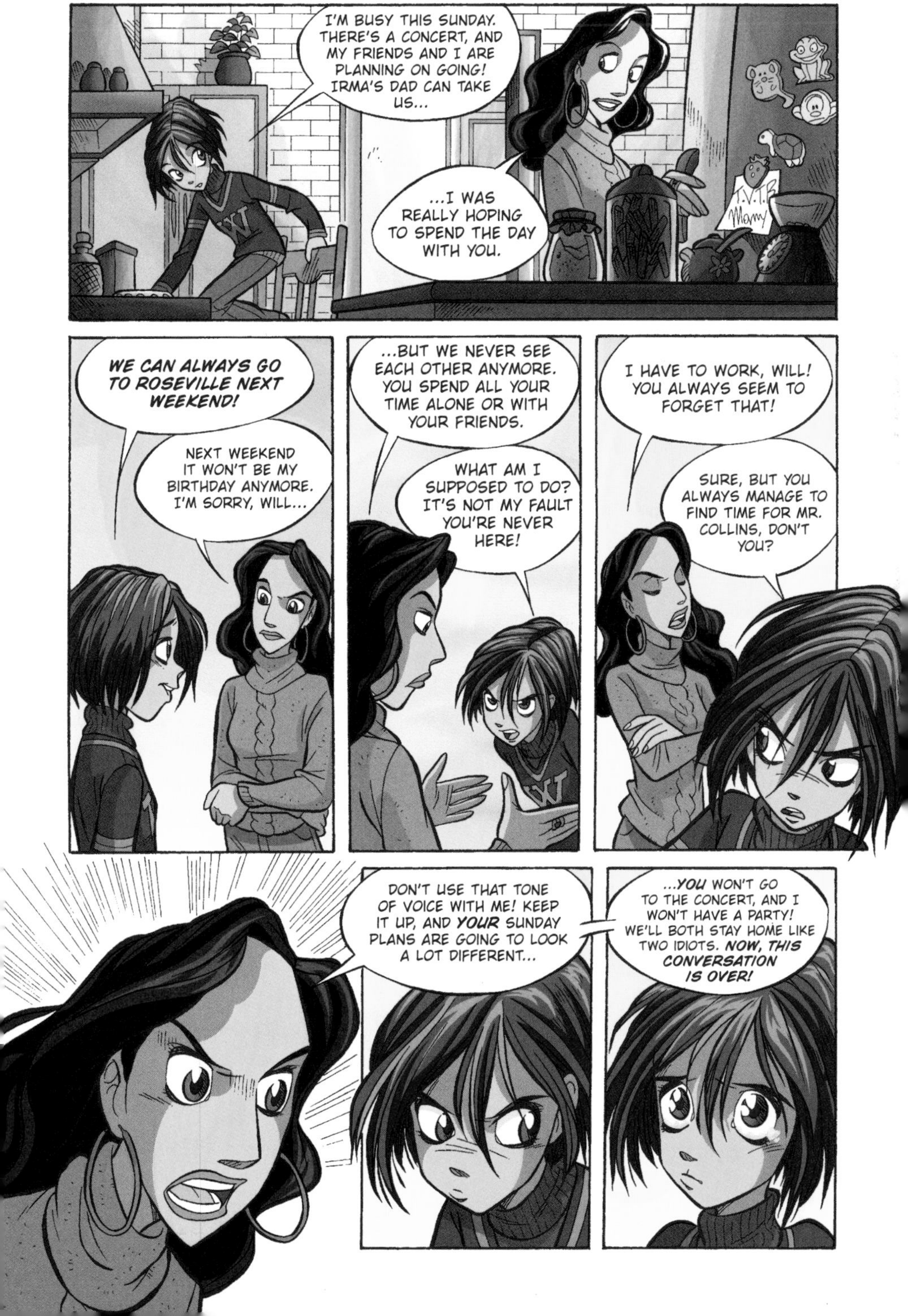
I'M BUSY THIS SUNDAY. THERE'S A CONCERT, AND MY FRIENDS AND I ARE PLANNING ON GOING! IRMA'S DAD CAN TAKE US...
...I WAS REALLY HOPING TO SPEND THE DAY WITH YOU.
T.V.T.B. Mommy
WE CAN ALWAYS GO TO ROSEVILLE NEXT WEEKEND!
NEXT WEEKEND IT WON'T BE MY BIRTHDAY ANYMORE. I'M SORRY, WILL...
...BUT WE NEVER SEE EACH OTHER ANYMORE. YOU SPEND ALL YOUR TIME ALONE OR WITH YOUR FRIENDS.
WHAT AM I SUPPOSED TO DO? IT'S NOT MY FAULT YOU'RE NEVER HERE!
I HAVE TO WORK, WILL! YOU ALWAYS SEEM TO FORGET THAT!
SURE, BUT YOU ALWAYS MANAGE TO FIND TIME FOR MR. COLLINS, DON'T YOU?
DON'T USE THAT TONE OF VOICE WITH ME! KEEP IT UP, AND YOUR SUNDAY PLANS ARE GOING TO LOOK A LOT DIFFERENT...
...YOU WON'T GO TO THE CONCERT, AND I WON'T HAVE A PARTY! WE'LL BOTH STAY HOME LIKE TWO IDIOTS. NOW, THIS CONVERSATION IS OVER!

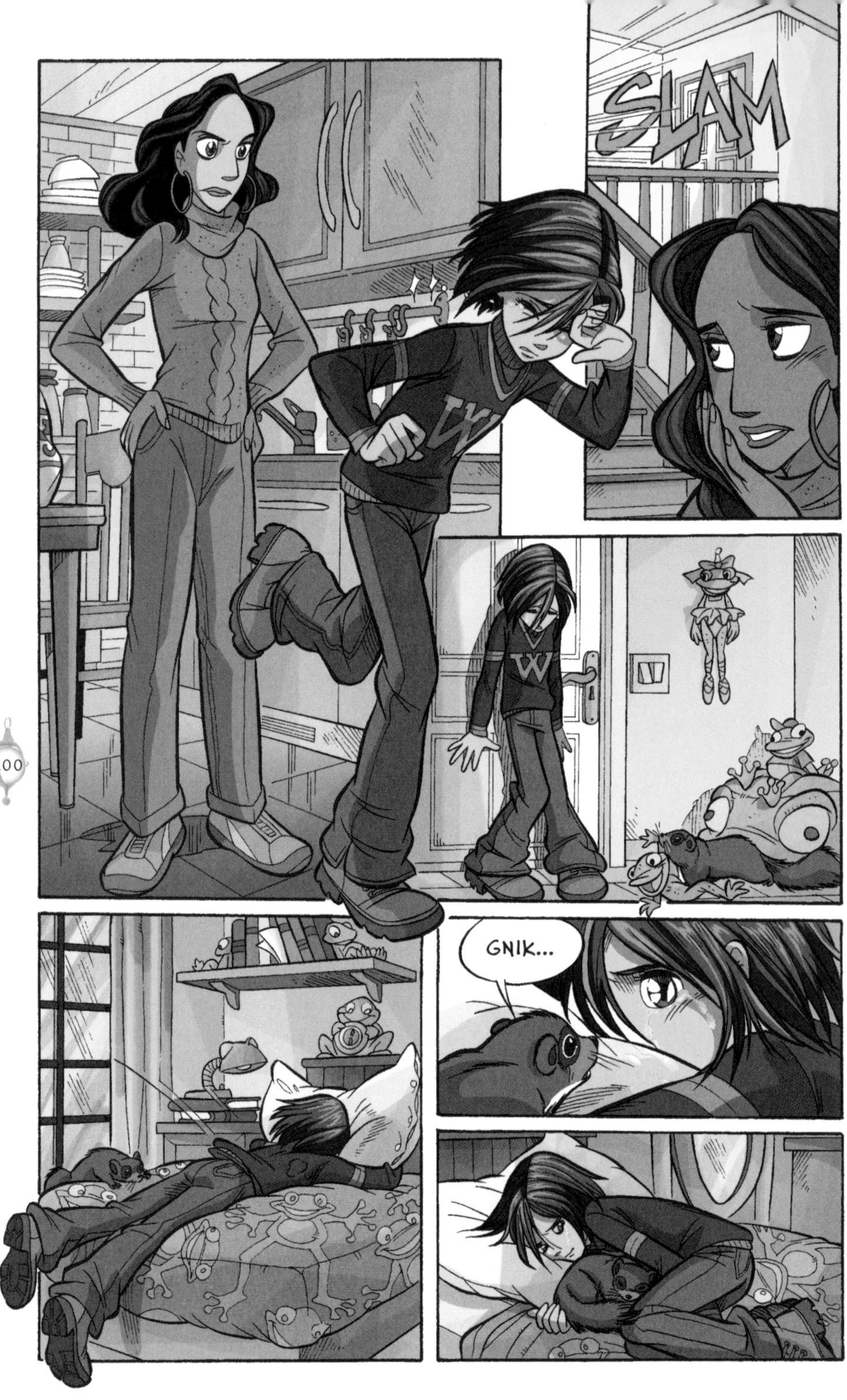
SLAM
GNIK...

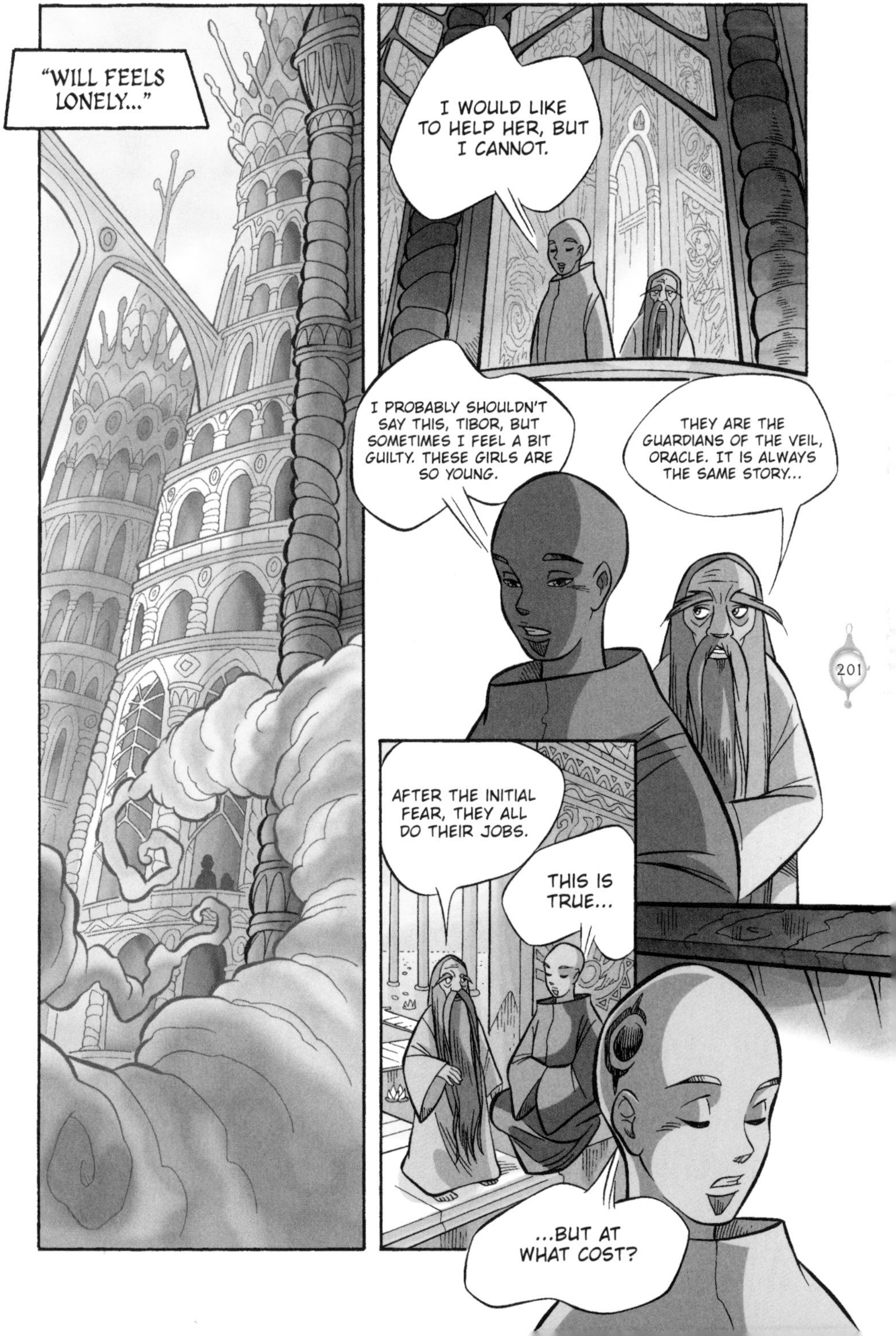
"WILL FEELS LONELY..."
I WOULD LIKE TO HELP HER, BUT I CANNOT.
I PROBABLY SHOULDN'T SAY THIS, TIBOR, BUT SOMETIMES I FEEL A BIT GUILTY. THESE GIRLS ARE SO YOUNG.
THEY ARE THE GUARDIANS OF THE VEIL, ORACLE. IT IS ALWAYS THE SAME STORY...
AFTER THE INITIAL FEAR, THEY ALL DO THEIR JOBS.
THIS IS TRUE...
...BUT AT WHAT COST?

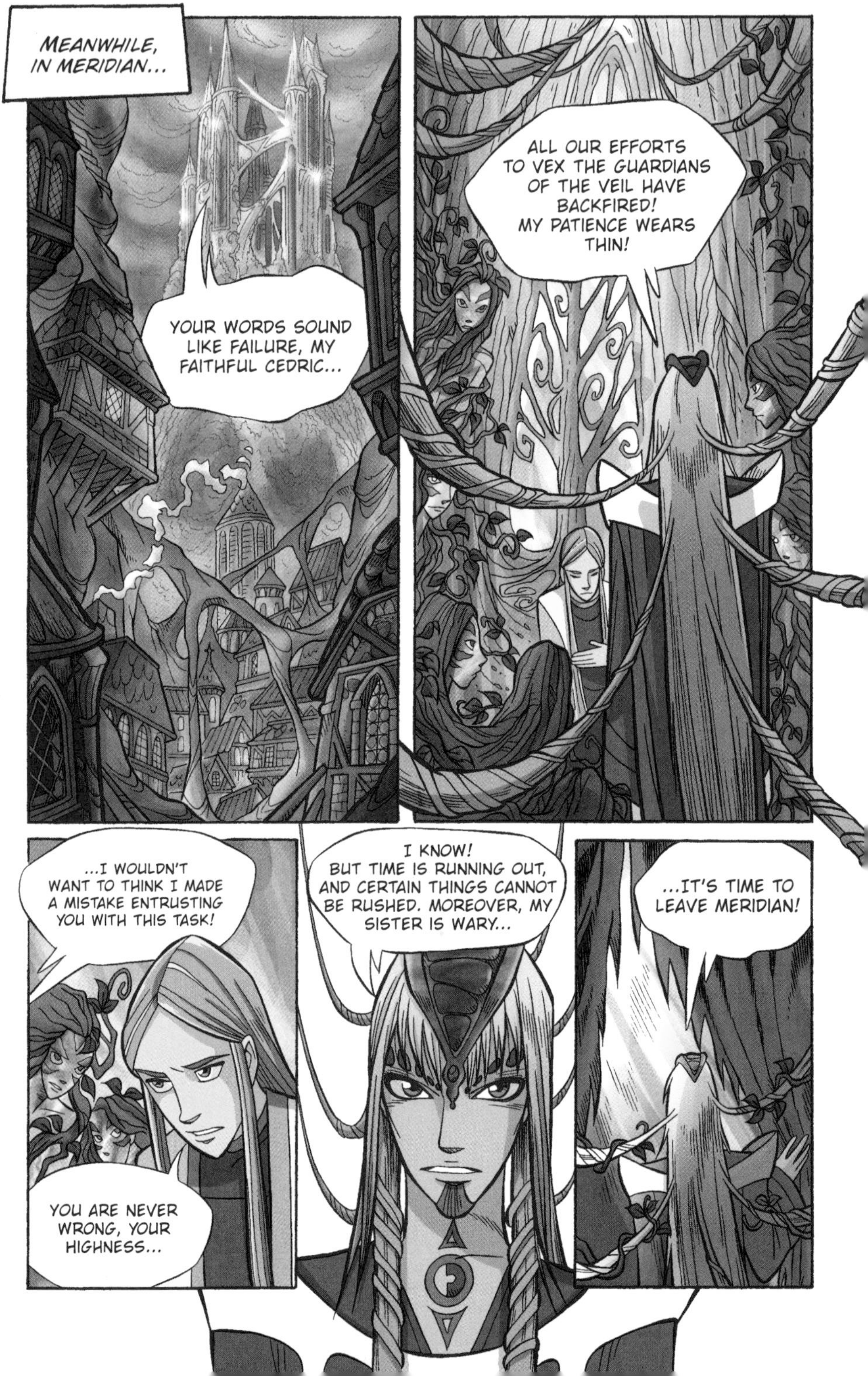
MEANWHILE, IN MERIDIAN...
YOUR WORDS SOUND LIKE FAILURE, MY FAITHFUL CEDRIC...
ALL OUR EFFORTS TO VEX THE GUARDIANS OF THE VEIL HAVE BACKFIRED! MY PATIENCE WEARS THIN!
...I WOULDN'T WANT TO THINK I MADE A MISTAKE ENTRUSTING YOU WITH THIS TASK!
YOU ARE NEVER WRONG, YOUR HIGHNESS...
I KNOW! BUT TIME IS RUNNING OUT, AND CERTAIN THINGS CANNOT BE RUSHED. MOREOVER, MY SISTER IS WARY...
...IT'S TIME TO LEAVE MERIDIAN!

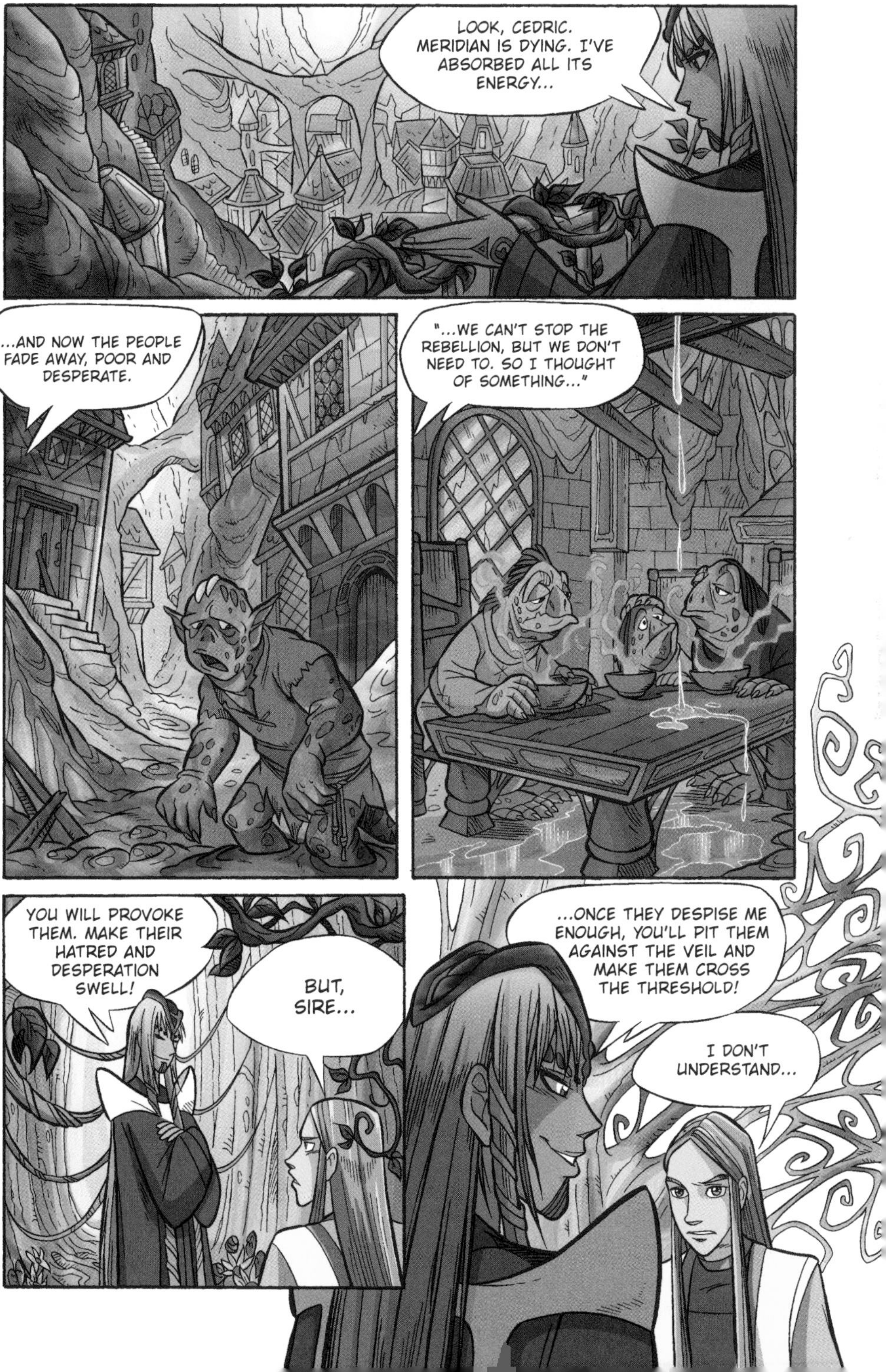
LOOK, CEDRIC. MERIDIAN IS DYING. I'VE ABSORBED ALL ITS ENERGY...
"...AND NOW THE PEOPLE FADE AWAY, POOR AND DESPERATE.
"...WE CAN'T STOP THE REBELLION, BUT WE DON'T NEED TO. SO I THOUGHT OF SOMETHING..."
YOU WILL PROVOKE THEM. MAKE THEIR HATRED AND DESPERATION SWELL!
BUT, SIRE...
...ONCE THEY DESPISE ME ENOUGH, YOU'LL PIT THEM AGAINST THE VEIL AND MAKE THEM CROSS THE THRESHOLD!
I DON'T UNDERSTAND...

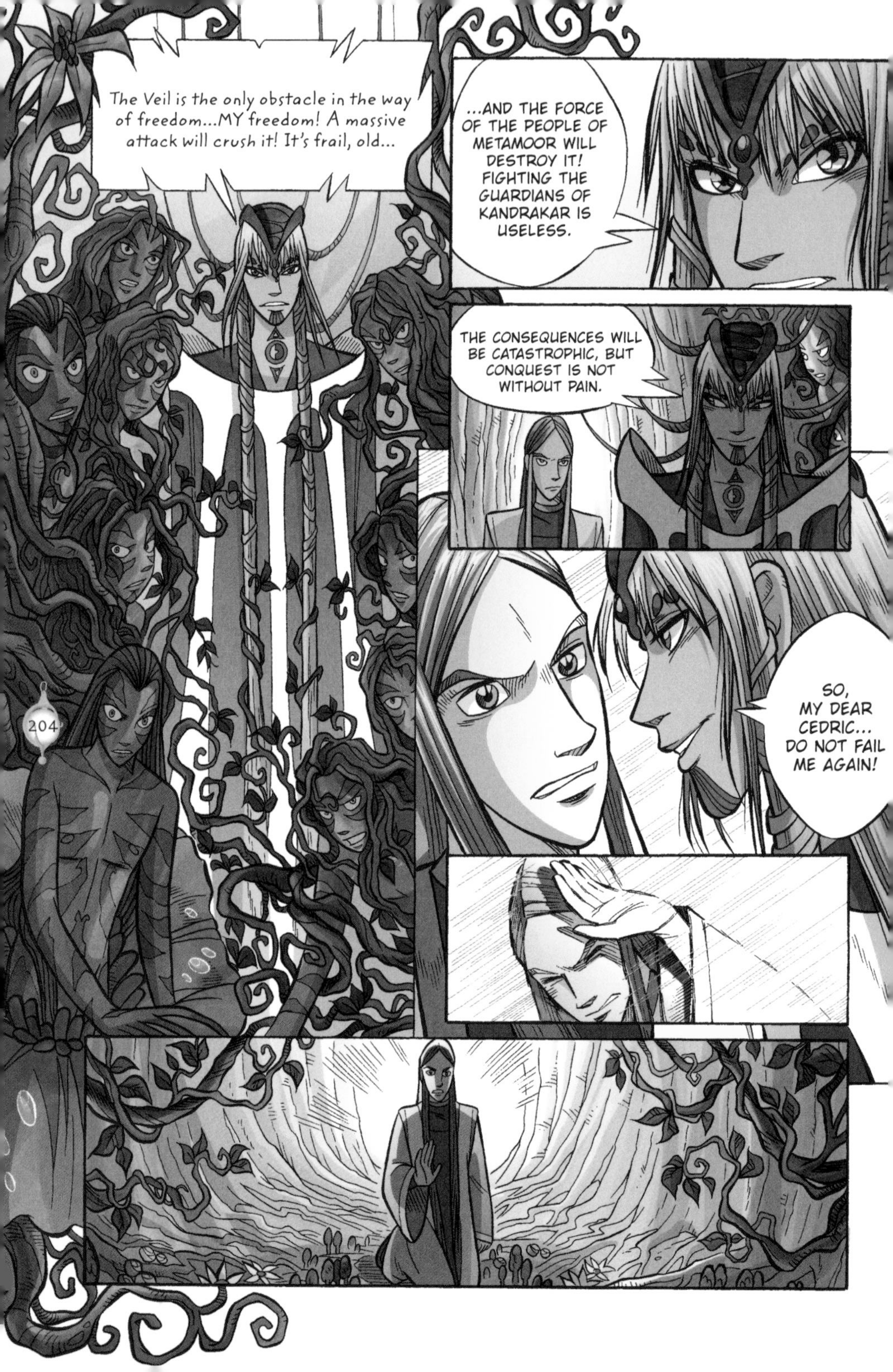
The Veil is the only obstacle in the way of freedom...MY freedom! A massive attack will crush it! It's frail, old...
...AND THE FORCE OF THE PEOPLE OF METAMOOR WILL DESTROY IT! FIGHTING THE GUARDIANS OF KANDRAKAR IS USELESS.
THE CONSEQUENCES WILL BE CATASTROPHIC, BUT CONQUEST IS NOT WITHOUT PAIN.
SO, MY DEAR CEDRIC... DO NOT FAIL ME AGAIN!

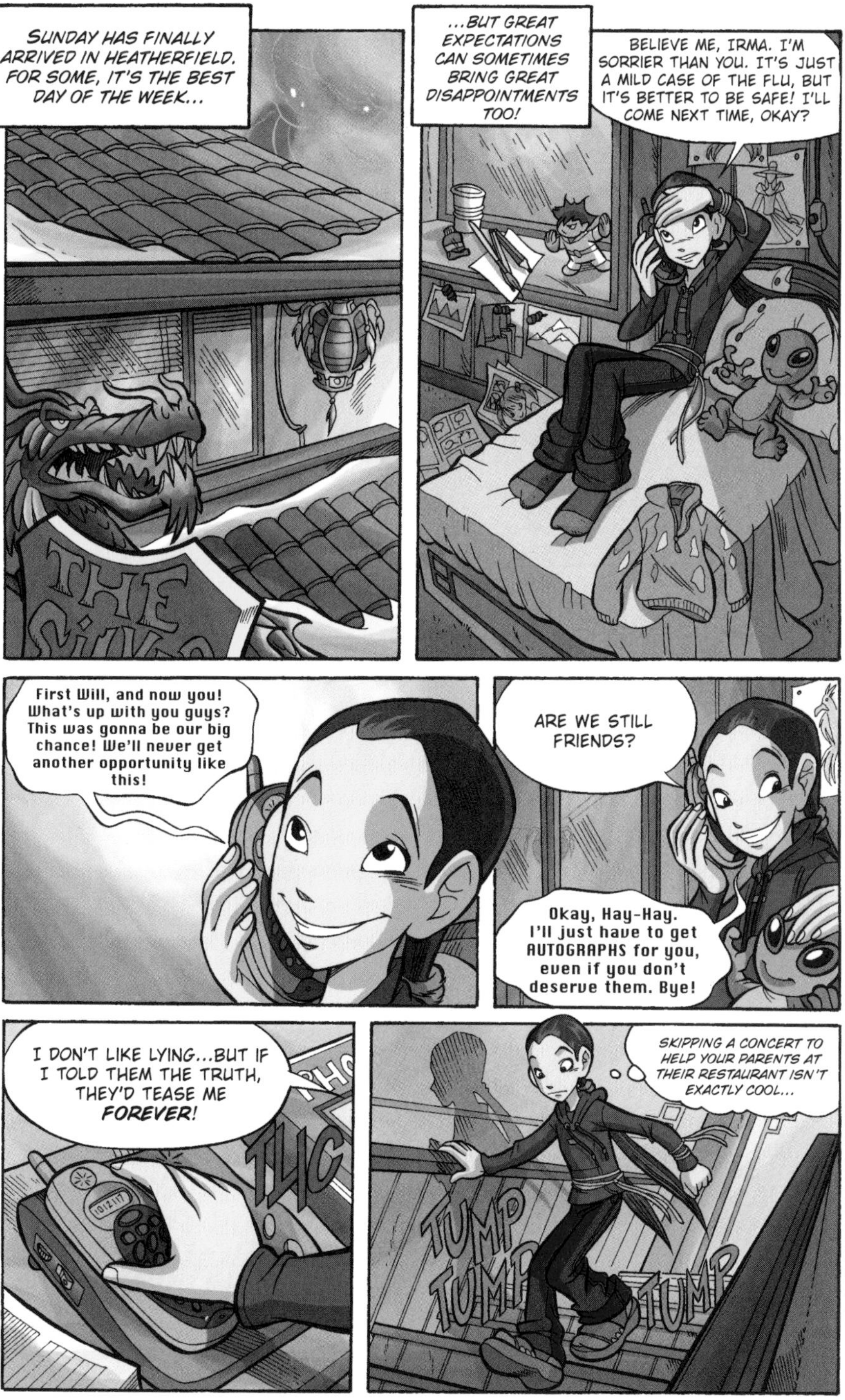
SUNDAY HAS FINALLY ARRIVED IN HEATHERFIELD. FOR SOME, IT'S THE BEST DAY OF THE WEEK...
...BUT GREAT EXPECTATIONS CAN SOMETIMES BRING GREAT DISAPPOINTMENTS TOO!
BELIEVE ME, IRMA. I'M SORRIER THAN YOU. IT'S JUST A MILD CASE OF THE FLU, BUT IT'S BETTER TO BE SAFE! I'LL COME NEXT TIME, OKAY?
First Will, and now you! What's up with you guys? This was gonna be our big chance! We'll never get another opportunity like this!
ARE WE STILL FRIENDS?
Okay, Hay-Hay. I'll just have to get AUTOGRAPHS for you, even if you don't deserve them. Bye!
I DON'T LIKE LYING...BUT IF I TOLD THEM THE TRUTH, THEY'D TEASE ME FOREVER!
TLIC
SKIPPING A CONCERT TO HELP YOUR PARENTS AT THEIR RESTAURANT ISN'T EXACTLY COOL...
TUMP
TUMP
TUMP

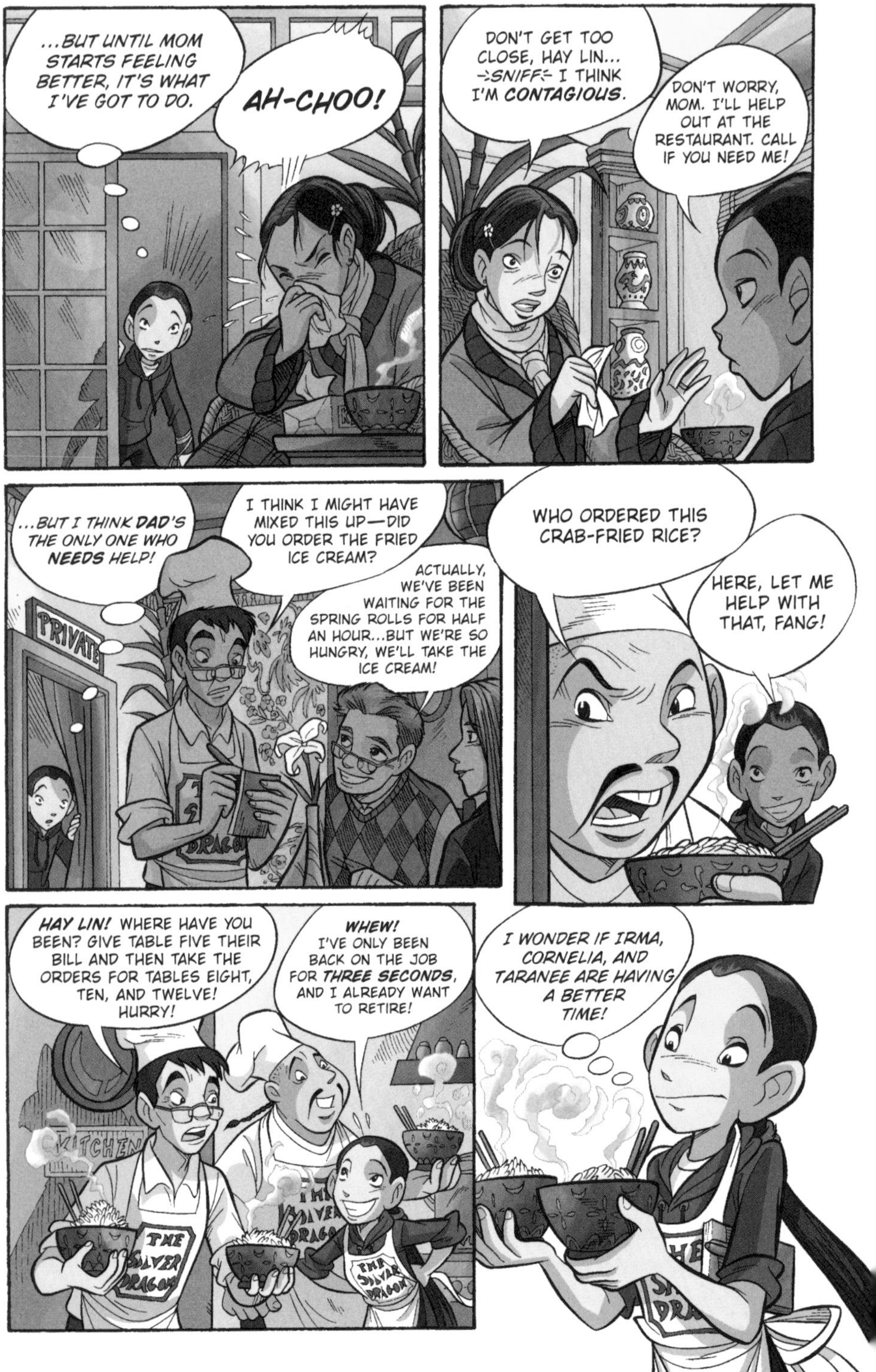
...BUT UNTIL MOM STARTS FEELING BETTER, IT'S WHAT I'VE GOT TO DO.
AH-CHOO!
DON'T GET TOO CLOSE, HAY LIN... ⇝SNIFF⇜ I THINK I'M CONTAGIOUS.
DON'T WORRY, MOM. I'LL HELP OUT AT THE RESTAURANT. CALL IF YOU NEED ME!
...BUT I THINK DAD'S THE ONLY ONE WHO NEEDS HELP!
PRIVATE
I THINK I MIGHT HAVE MIXED THIS UP—DID YOU ORDER THE FRIED ICE CREAM?
ACTUALLY, WE'VE BEEN WAITING FOR THE SPRING ROLLS FOR HALF AN HOUR...BUT WE'RE SO HUNGRY, WE'LL TAKE THE ICE CREAM!
WHO ORDERED THIS CRAB-FRIED RICE?
HERE, LET ME HELP WITH THAT, FANG!
HAY LIN! WHERE HAVE YOU BEEN? GIVE TABLE FIVE THEIR BILL AND THEN TAKE THE ORDERS FOR TABLES EIGHT, TEN, AND TWELVE! HURRY!
WHEW! I'VE ONLY BEEN BACK ON THE JOB FOR THREE SECONDS, AND I ALREADY WANT TO RETIRE!
I WONDER IF IRMA, CORNELIA, AND TARANEE ARE HAVING A BETTER TIME!
KITCHEN
THE SILVER DRAGON
THE SILVER DRAGON

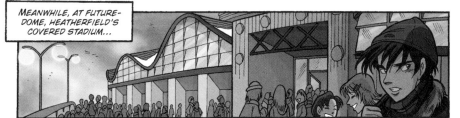

MEANWHILE, AT FUTURE-DOME, HEATHERFIELD'S COVERED STADIUM...

THIS WAY, GIRLS! OKAY...STAY PUT AND TRY NOT TO CAUSE ANY TROUBLE!

WE CAN'T THANK YOU ENOUGH, MR. LAIR!

WELL THEN, JUST ENJOY THE SHOW!

WE WILL!

OVER THERE! LOOK!

DANNY! DANNY! DAAAAAANNY!

207

WHAT'S WITH ALL THE *SHOUTING*? I DON'T SEE THAT *TORTILLA* ON STAGE YET...

EARTH TO DAD! *THAT'S DANNY DOLL, KARMILLA'S BASSIST!*

AND IF HE'S HERE, KARMILLA MUST BE NEARBY!

IS EVERYTHING ALL RIGHT, SIR? DO YOU WANT ME TO *ARREST THESE KIDS*?

NO NEED FOR THAT, SPUD—THIS IS MY DAUGHTER, AND THESE ARE HER FRIENDS...

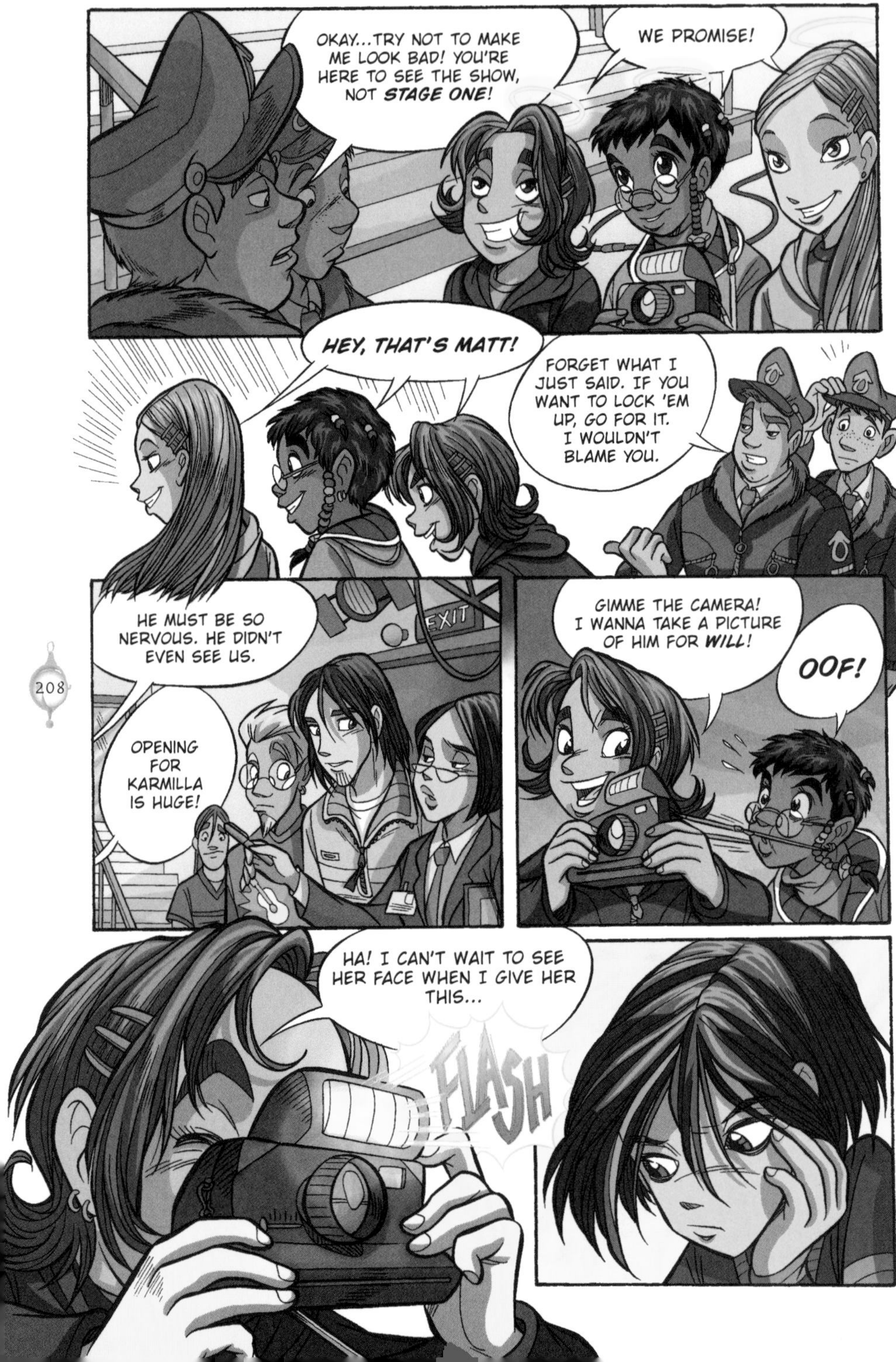
OKAY...TRY NOT TO MAKE ME LOOK BAD! YOU'RE HERE TO SEE THE SHOW, NOT STAGE ONE!
WE PROMISE!
HEY, THAT'S MATT!
FORGET WHAT I JUST SAID. IF YOU WANT TO LOCK 'EM UP, GO FOR IT. I WOULDN'T BLAME YOU.
HE MUST BE SO NERVOUS. HE DIDN'T EVEN SEE US.
EXIT
OPENING FOR KARMILLA IS HUGE!
GIMME THE CAMERA! I WANNA TAKE A PICTURE OF HIM FOR WILL!
OOF!
HA! I CAN'T WAIT TO SEE HER FACE WHEN I GIVE HER THIS...
FLASH

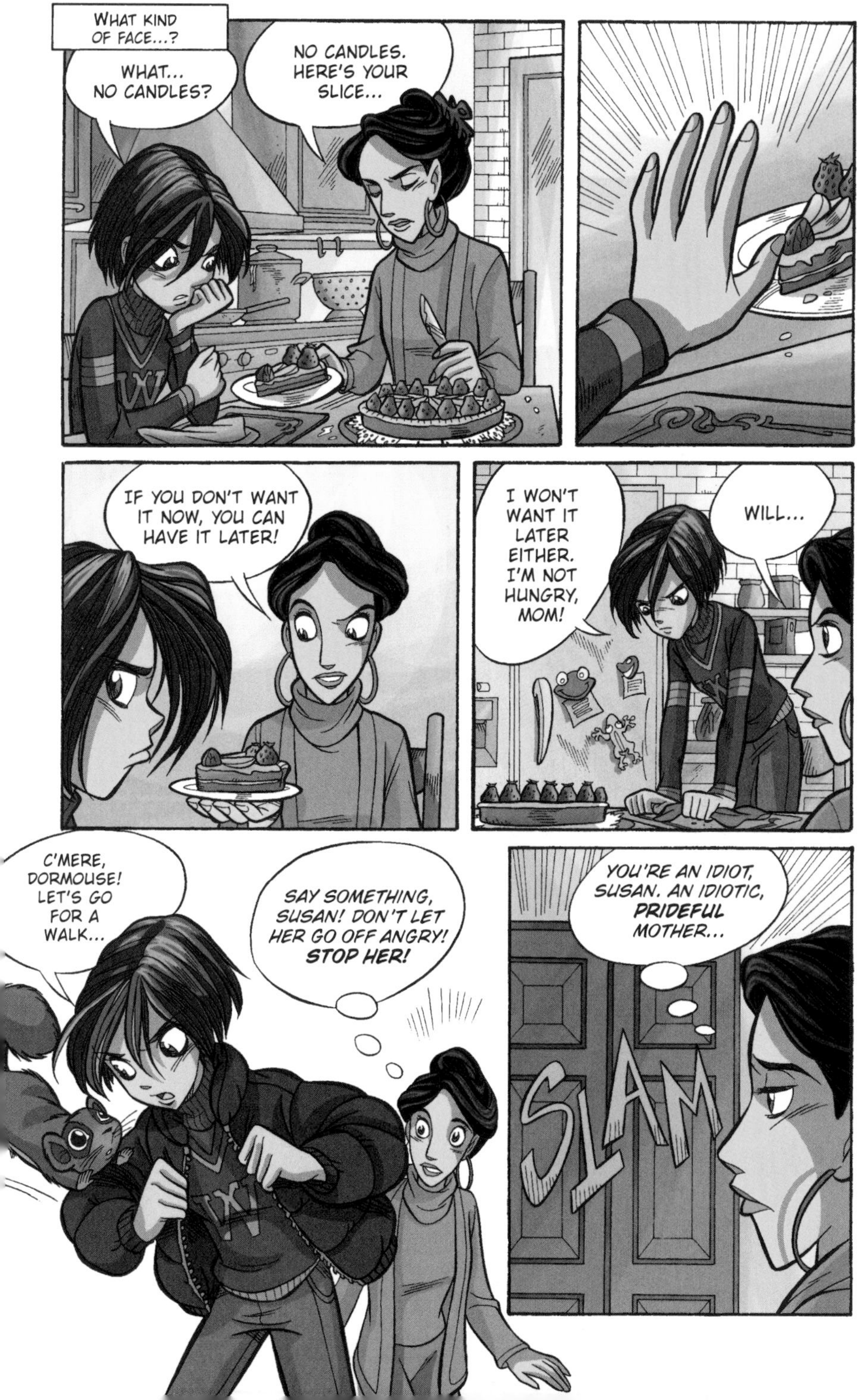

WHAT KIND OF FACE...?
WHAT... NO CANDLES?
NO CANDLES. HERE'S YOUR SLICE...
IF YOU DON'T WANT IT NOW, YOU CAN HAVE IT LATER!
I WON'T WANT IT LATER EITHER. I'M NOT HUNGRY, MOM!
WILL...
C'MERE, DORMOUSE! LET'S GO FOR A WALK...
SAY SOMETHING, SUSAN! DON'T LET HER GO OFF ANGRY! **STOP HER!**
SLAM
YOU'RE AN IDIOT, SUSAN. AN IDIOTIC, **PRIDEFUL** MOTHER...

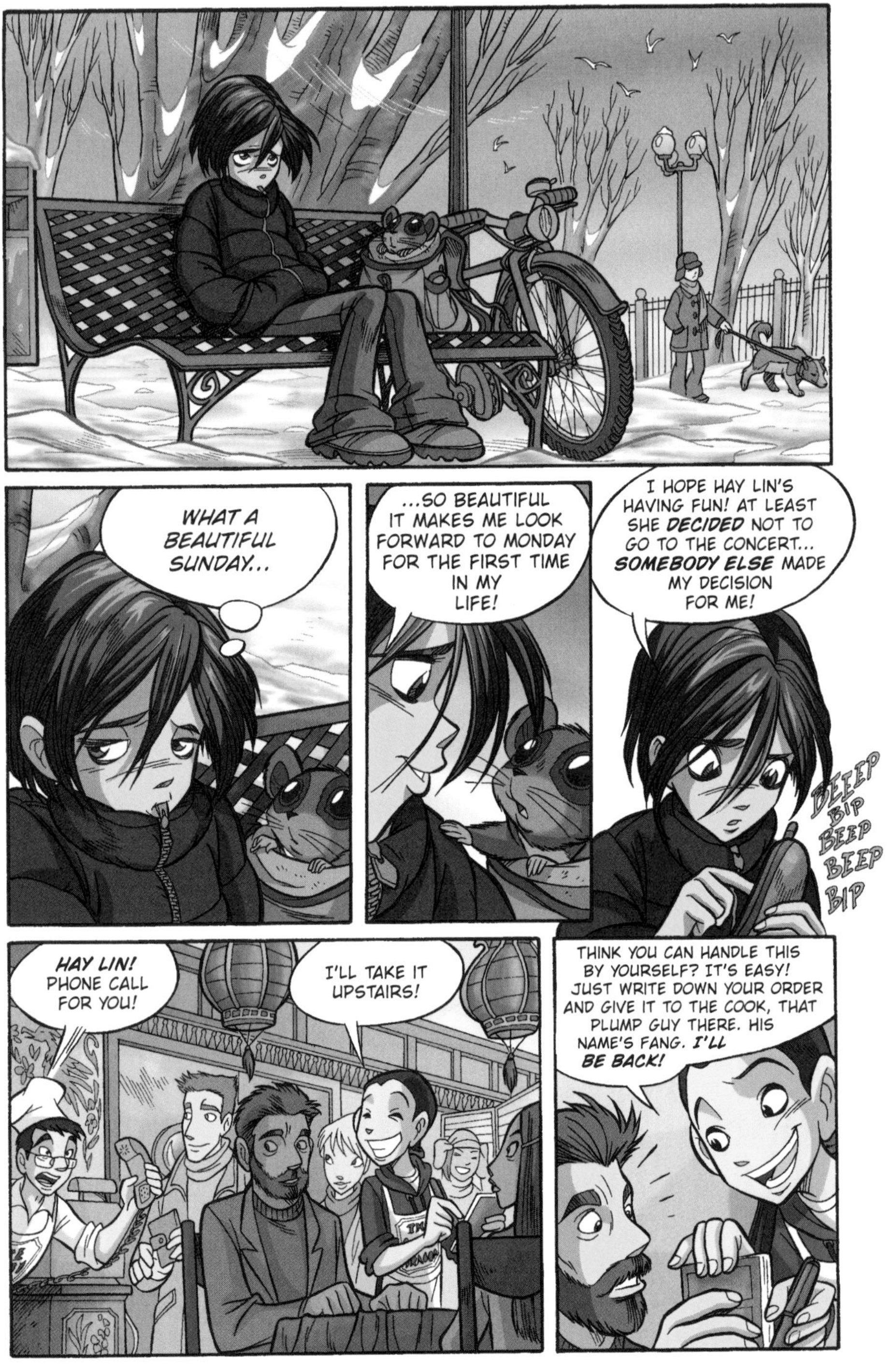
WHAT A BEAUTIFUL SUNDAY...
...SO BEAUTIFUL IT MAKES ME LOOK FORWARD TO MONDAY FOR THE FIRST TIME IN MY LIFE!
I HOPE HAY LIN'S HAVING FUN! AT LEAST SHE *DECIDED* NOT TO GO TO THE CONCERT... *SOMEBODY ELSE* MADE MY DECISION FOR ME!
BEEEP BIP BEEP BEEP BIP
HAY LIN! PHONE CALL FOR YOU!
I'LL TAKE IT UPSTAIRS!
THINK YOU CAN HANDLE THIS BY YOURSELF? IT'S EASY! JUST WRITE DOWN YOUR ORDER AND GIVE IT TO THE COOK, THAT PLUMP GUY THERE. HIS NAME'S FANG. *I'LL BE BACK!*

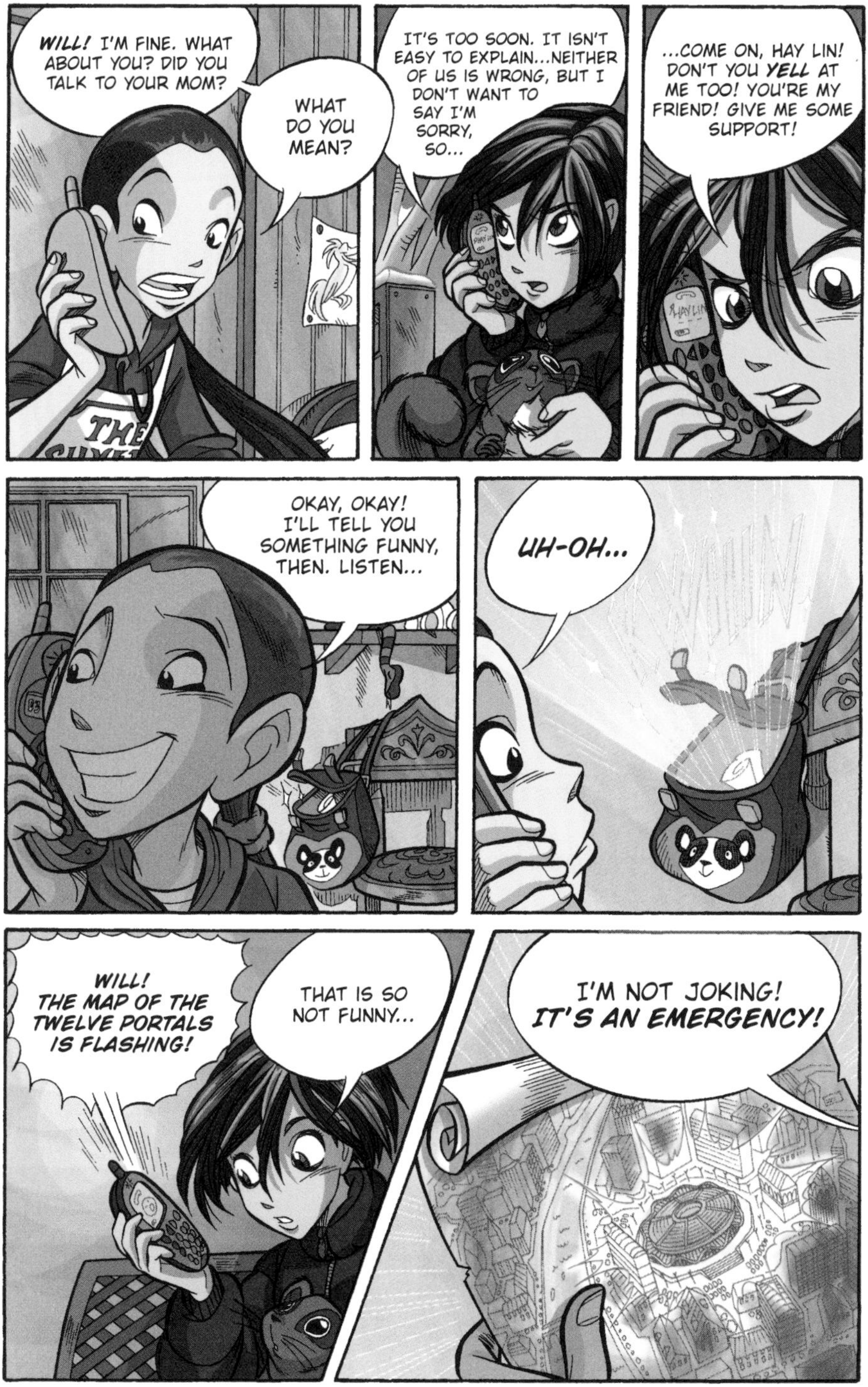
WILL! I'M FINE. WHAT ABOUT YOU? DID YOU TALK TO YOUR MOM?
WHAT DO YOU MEAN?
IT'S TOO SOON. IT ISN'T EASY TO EXPLAIN...NEITHER OF US IS WRONG, BUT I DON'T WANT TO SAY I'M SORRY, SO...
...COME ON, HAY LIN! DON'T YOU YELL AT ME TOO! YOU'RE MY FRIEND! GIVE ME SOME SUPPORT!
OKAY, OKAY! I'LL TELL YOU SOMETHING FUNNY, THEN. LISTEN...
UH-OH...
WILL! THE MAP OF THE TWELVE PORTALS IS FLASHING!
THAT IS SO NOT FUNNY...
I'M NOT JOKING! IT'S AN EMERGENCY!

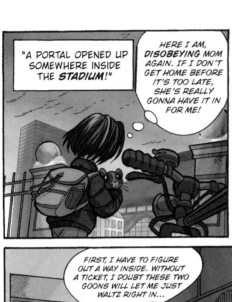

"A PORTAL OPENED UP SOMEWHERE INSIDE THE **STADIUM!**"

HERE I AM, **DISOBEYING** MOM AGAIN. IF I DON'T GET HOME BEFORE IT'S TOO LATE, SHE'S REALLY GONNA HAVE IT IN FOR ME!

HAY LIN WILL BE THERE SOON, AND THE OTHERS ARE ALREADY INSIDE. RIGHT NOW, I HAVE TO MAKE DO ON MY OWN!

FIRST, I HAVE TO FIGURE OUT A WAY INSIDE. WITHOUT A TICKET, I DOUBT THESE TWO GOONS WILL LET ME JUST WALTZ RIGHT IN...

...BUT MAYBE THE HEART OF KANDRAKAR CAN HELP! CLOSE YOUR EYES, DORMOUSE! WE'RE GONNA HIDE!

Don't make that face, dormouse! It's still me.

EERK!

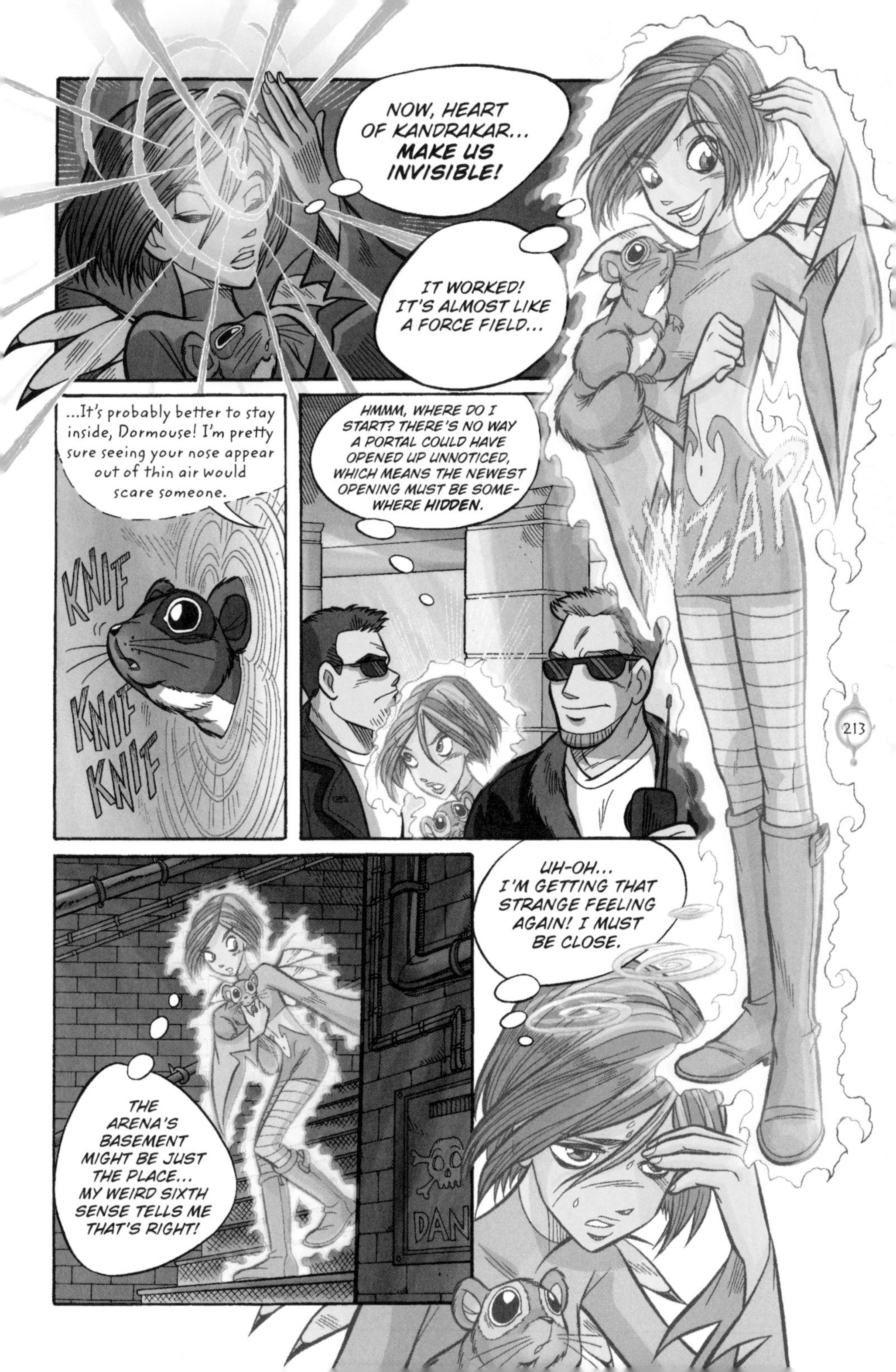
NOW, HEART OF KANDRAKAR... MAKE US INVISIBLE!
IT WORKED! IT'S ALMOST LIKE A FORCE FIELD...
...It's probably better to stay inside, Dormouse! I'm pretty sure seeing your nose appear out of thin air would scare someone.
KNIF KNIF KNIF KNIF
HMMM, WHERE DO I START? THERE'S NO WAY A PORTAL COULD HAVE OPENED UP UNNOTICED, WHICH MEANS THE NEWEST OPENING MUST BE SOMEWHERE HIDDEN.
WZAP
UH-OH... I'M GETTING THAT STRANGE FEELING AGAIN! I MUST BE CLOSE.
THE ARENA'S BASEMENT MIGHT BE JUST THE PLACE... MY WEIRD SIXTH SENSE TELLS ME THAT'S RIGHT!
DAN

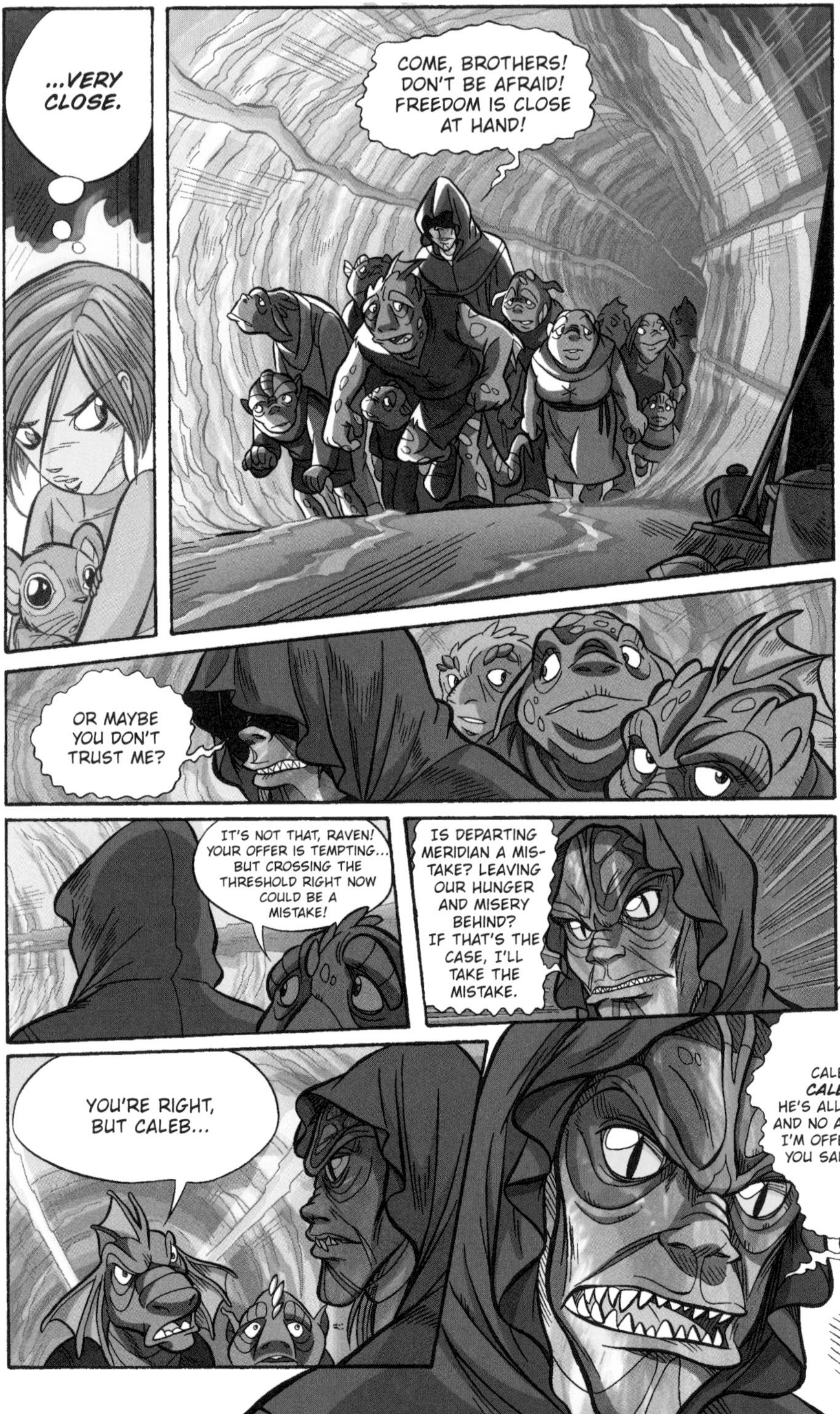
...VERY CLOSE.
COME, BROTHERS! DON'T BE AFRAID! FREEDOM IS CLOSE AT HAND!
OR MAYBE YOU DON'T TRUST ME?
IT'S NOT THAT, RAVEN! YOUR OFFER IS TEMPTING... BUT CROSSING THE THRESHOLD RIGHT NOW COULD BE A MISTAKE!
IS DEPARTING MERIDIAN A MISTAKE? LEAVING OUR HUNGER AND MISERY BEHIND? IF THAT'S THE CASE, I'LL TAKE THE MISTAKE.
YOU'RE RIGHT, BUT CALEB...
CALEB! CALEB! HE'S ALL TALK AND NO ACTION... I'M OFFERING YOU SALVATION!

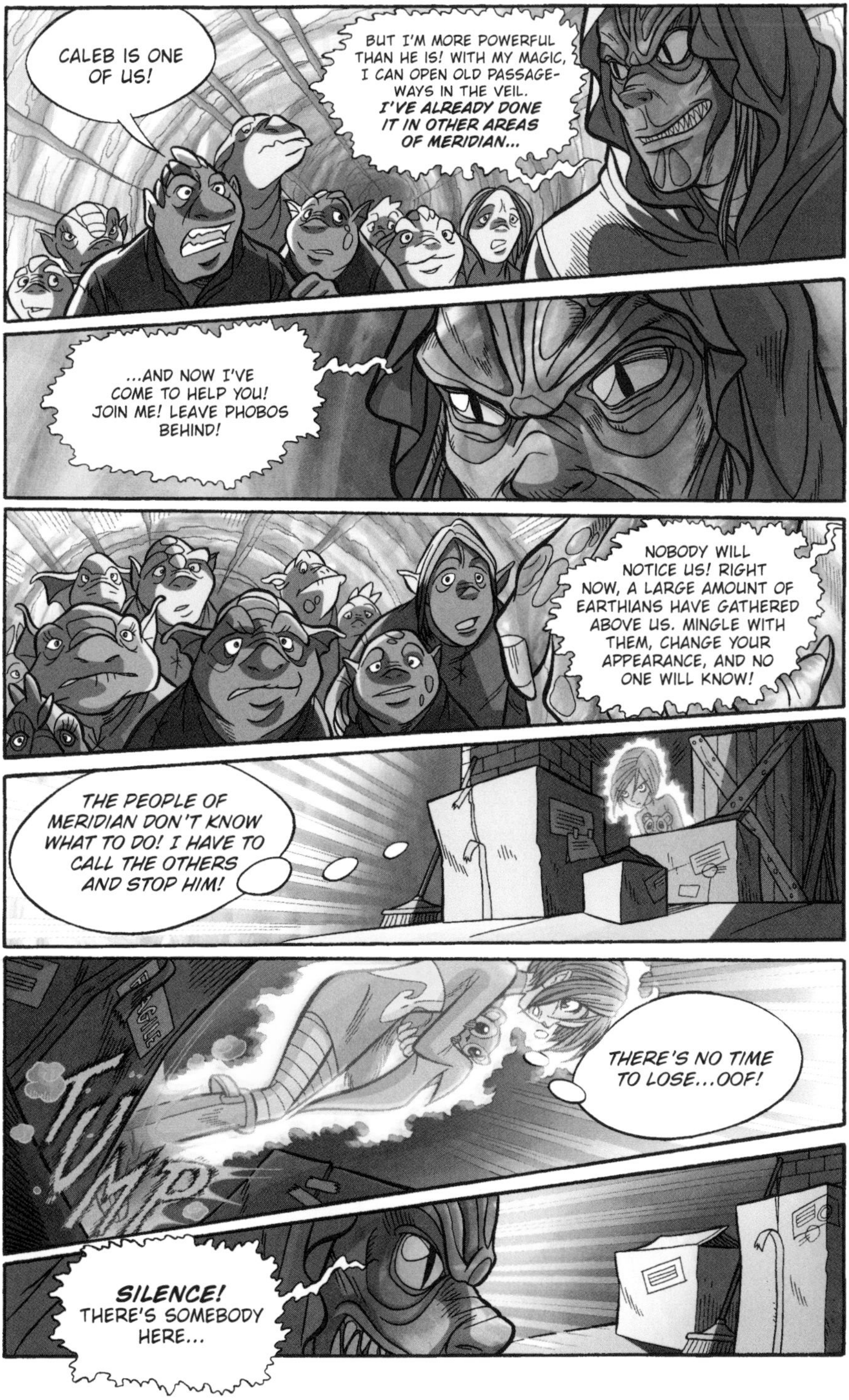
CALEB IS ONE OF US!
BUT I'M MORE POWERFUL THAN HE IS! WITH MY MAGIC, I CAN OPEN OLD PASSAGEWAYS IN THE VEIL. I'VE ALREADY DONE IT IN OTHER AREAS OF MERIDIAN...
...AND NOW I'VE COME TO HELP YOU! JOIN ME! LEAVE PHOBOS BEHIND!
NOBODY WILL NOTICE US! RIGHT NOW, A LARGE AMOUNT OF EARTHIANS HAVE GATHERED ABOVE US. MINGLE WITH THEM, CHANGE YOUR APPEARANCE, AND NO ONE WILL KNOW!
THE PEOPLE OF MERIDIAN DON'T KNOW WHAT TO DO! I HAVE TO CALL THE OTHERS AND STOP HIM!
THERE'S NO TIME TO LOSE...OOF!
TUMP!
SILENCE! THERE'S SOMEBODY HERE...

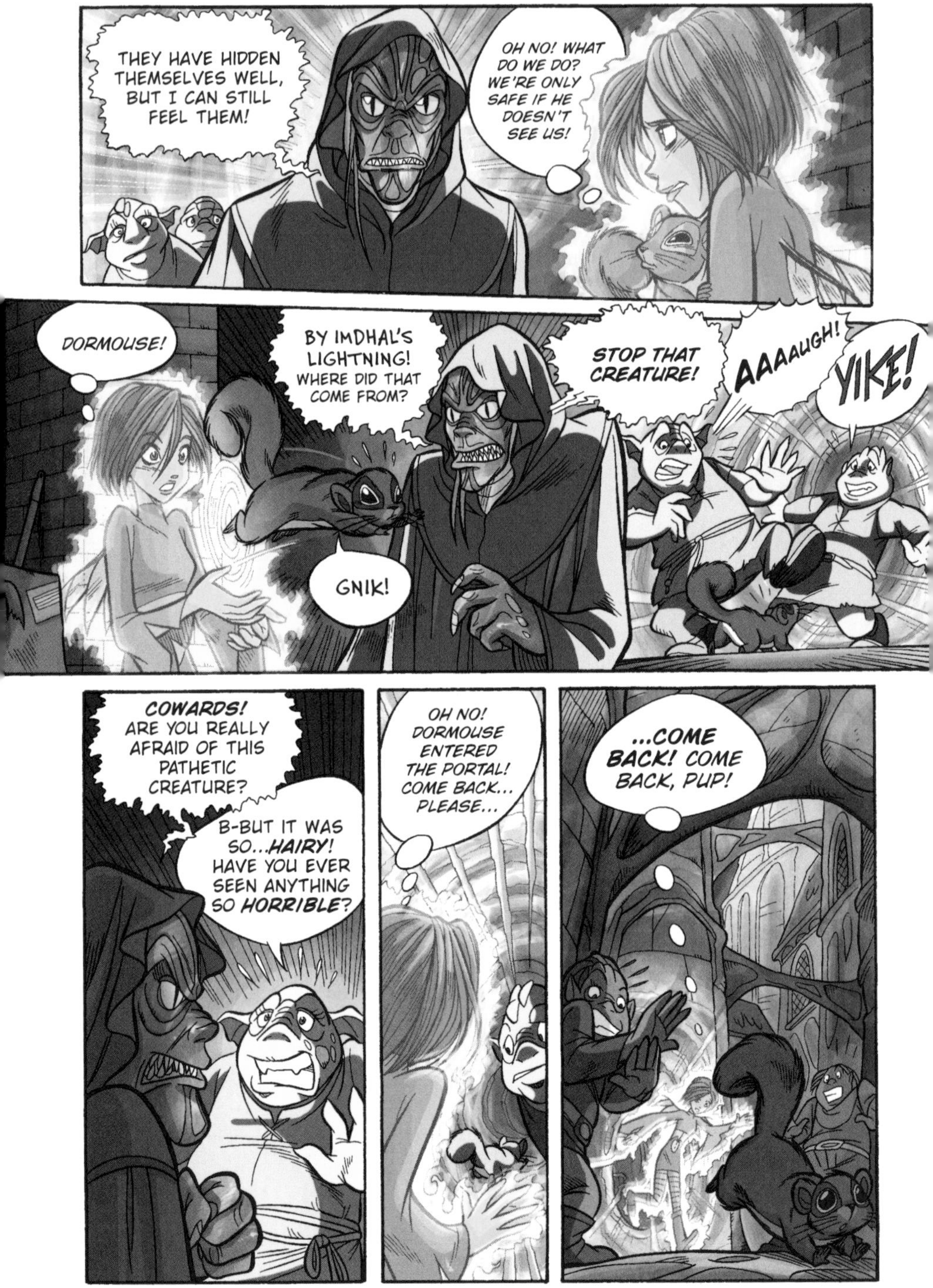
THEY HAVE HIDDEN THEMSELVES WELL, BUT I CAN STILL FEEL THEM!
OH NO! WHAT DO WE DO? WE'RE ONLY SAFE IF HE DOESN'T SEE US!
DORMOUSE!
BY IMDHAL'S LIGHTNING! WHERE DID THAT COME FROM?
GNIK!
STOP THAT CREATURE!
AAAAUGH!
YIKE!
COWARDS! ARE YOU REALLY AFRAID OF THIS PATHETIC CREATURE?
B-BUT IT WAS SO...HAIRY! HAVE YOU EVER SEEN ANYTHING SO HORRIBLE?
OH NO! DORMOUSE ENTERED THE PORTAL! COME BACK... PLEASE...
...COME BACK! COME BACK, PUP!

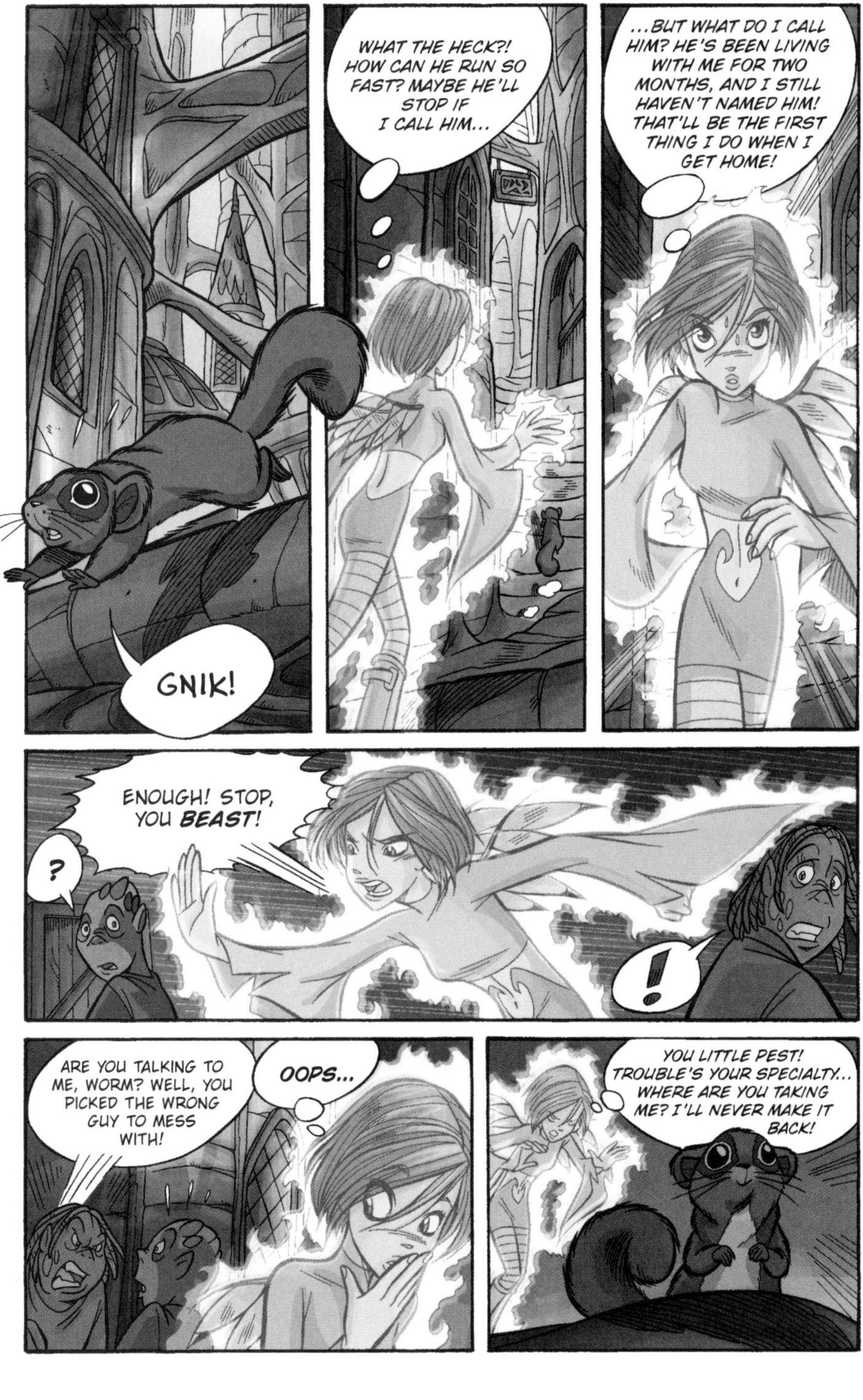
GNIK!
WHAT THE HECK?! HOW CAN HE RUN SO FAST? MAYBE HE'LL STOP IF I CALL HIM...
...BUT WHAT DO I CALL HIM? HE'S BEEN LIVING WITH ME FOR TWO MONTHS, AND I STILL HAVEN'T NAMED HIM! THAT'LL BE THE FIRST THING I DO WHEN I GET HOME!
ENOUGH! STOP, YOU BEAST!
?
!
ARE YOU TALKING TO ME, WORM? WELL, YOU PICKED THE WRONG GUY TO MESS WITH!
OOPS...
YOU LITTLE PEST! TROUBLE'S YOUR SPECIALTY... WHERE ARE YOU TAKING ME? I'LL NEVER MAKE IT BACK!

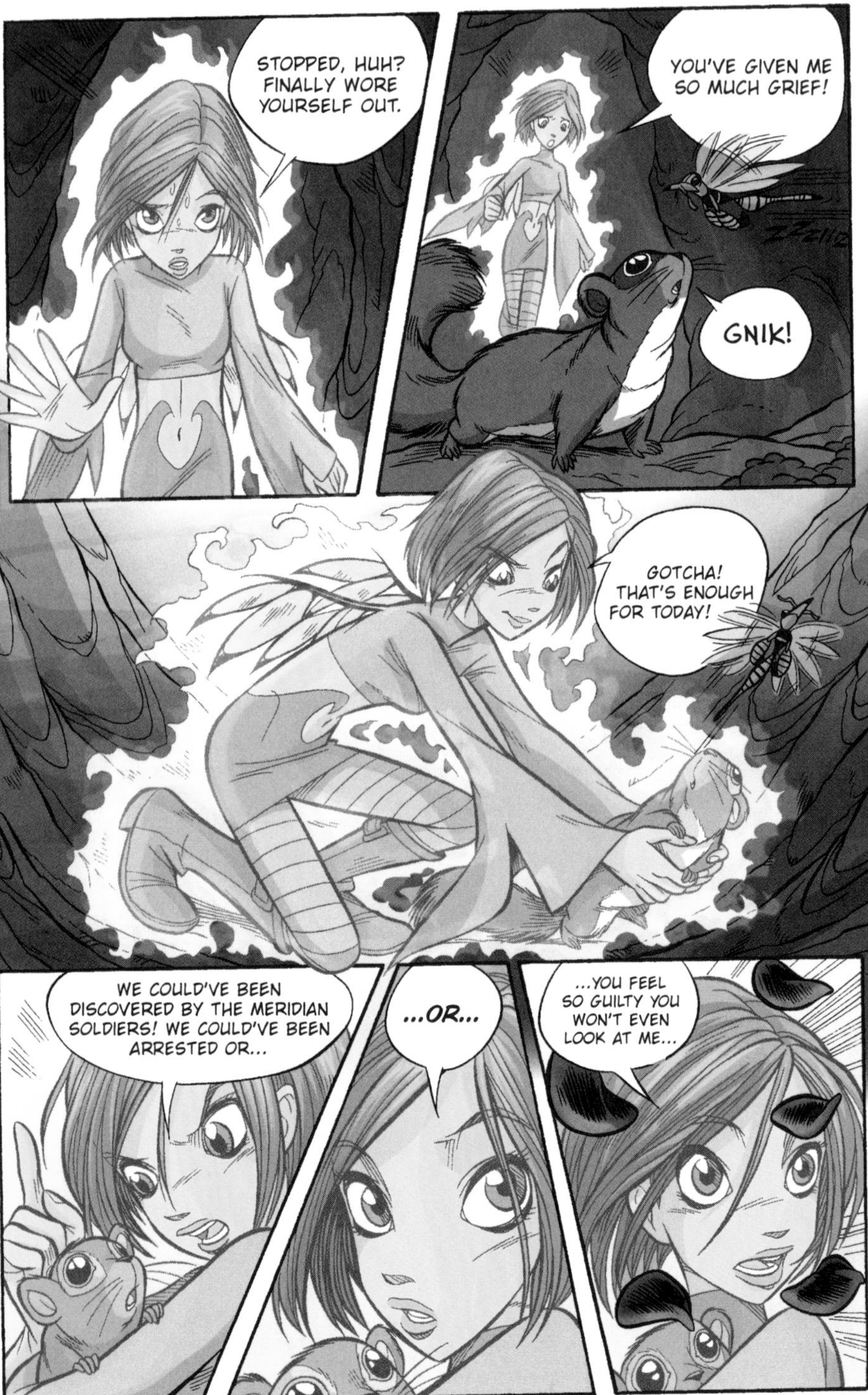
STOPPED, HUH? FINALLY WORE YOURSELF OUT.
YOU'VE GIVEN ME SO MUCH GRIEF!
ZZZIIIZ
GNIK!
GOTCHA! THAT'S ENOUGH FOR TODAY!
WE COULD'VE BEEN DISCOVERED BY THE MERIDIAN SOLDIERS! WE COULD'VE BEEN ARRESTED OR...
...OR...
...YOU FEEL SO GUILTY YOU WON'T EVEN LOOK AT ME...

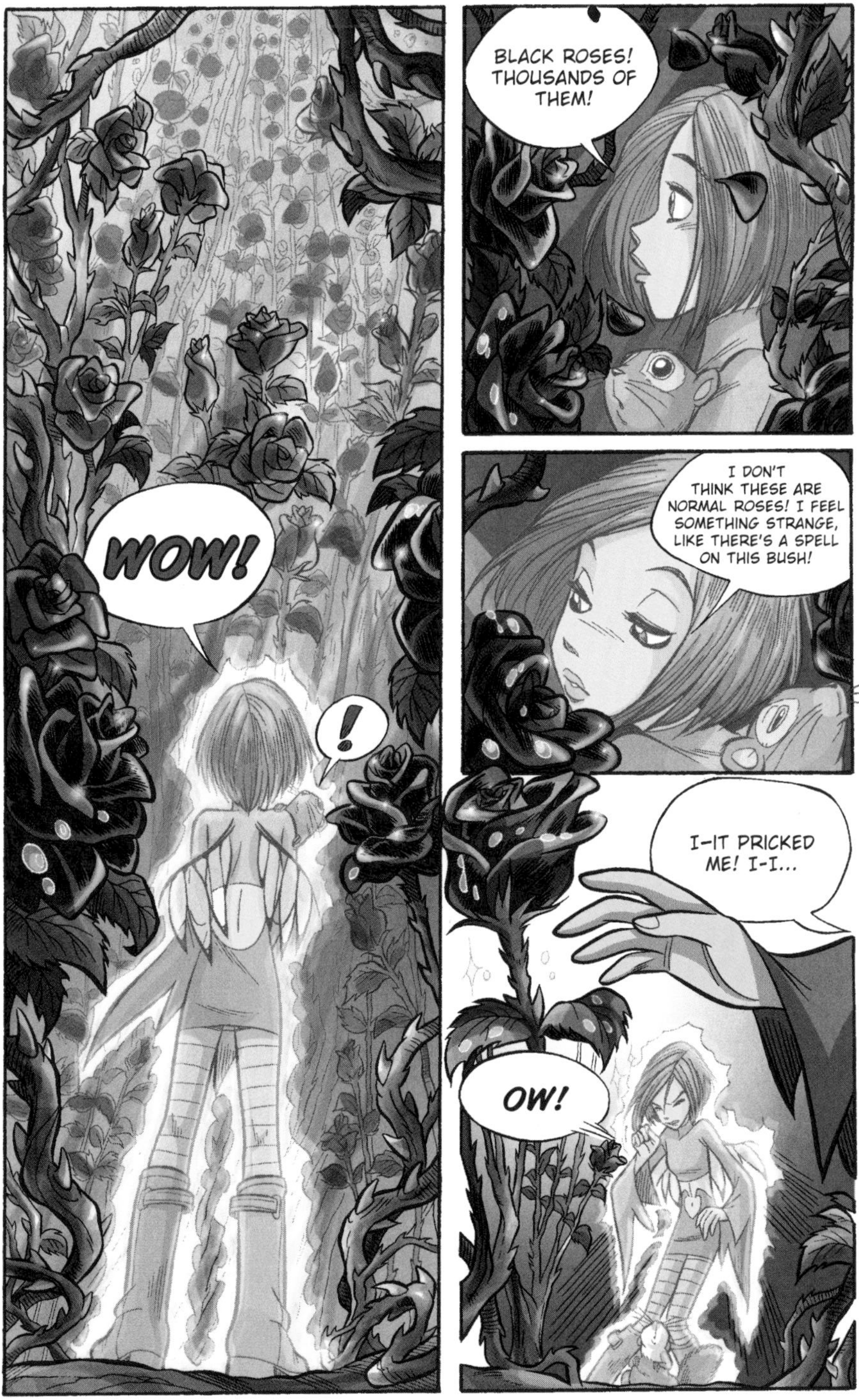
WOW!
!
BLACK ROSES! THOUSANDS OF THEM!
I DON'T THINK THESE ARE NORMAL ROSES! I FEEL SOMETHING STRANGE, LIKE THERE'S A SPELL ON THIS BUSH!
I-IT PRICKED ME! I-I...
OW!

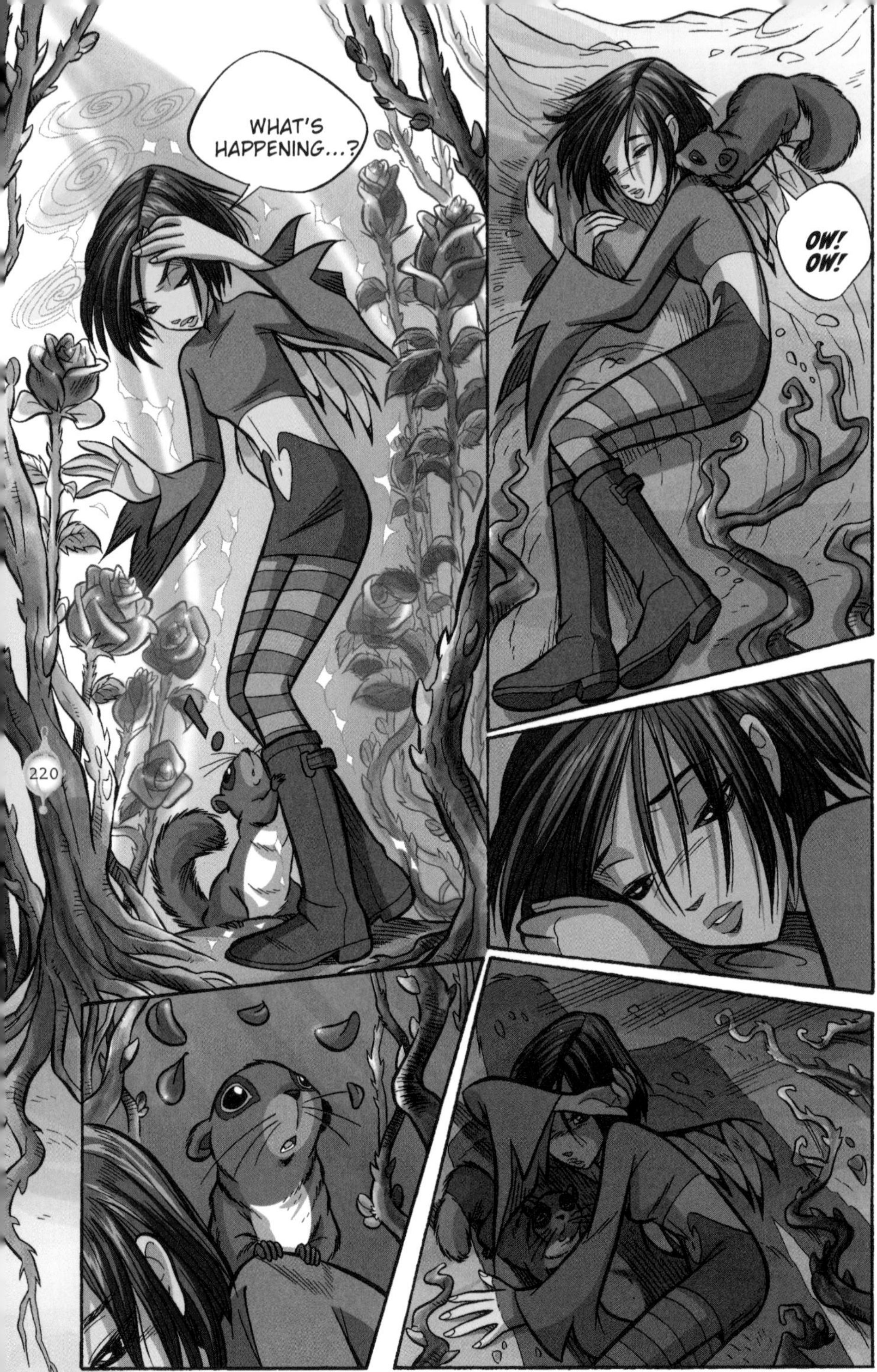
WHAT'S HAPPENING...?
OW! OW!

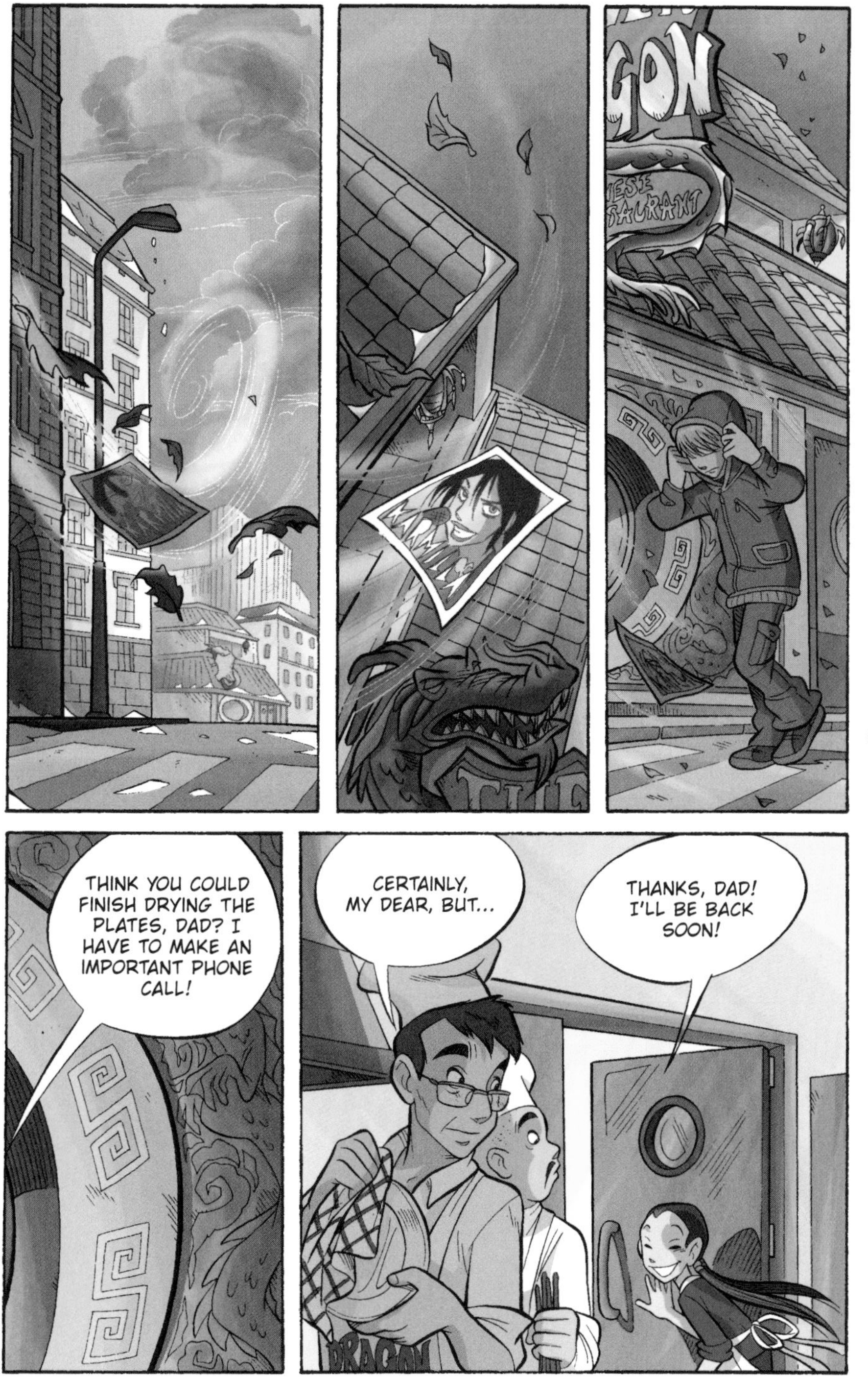
GON
THINK YOU COULD FINISH DRYING THE PLATES, DAD? I HAVE TO MAKE AN IMPORTANT PHONE CALL!
CERTAINLY, MY DEAR, BUT...
THANKS, DAD! I'LL BE BACK SOON!

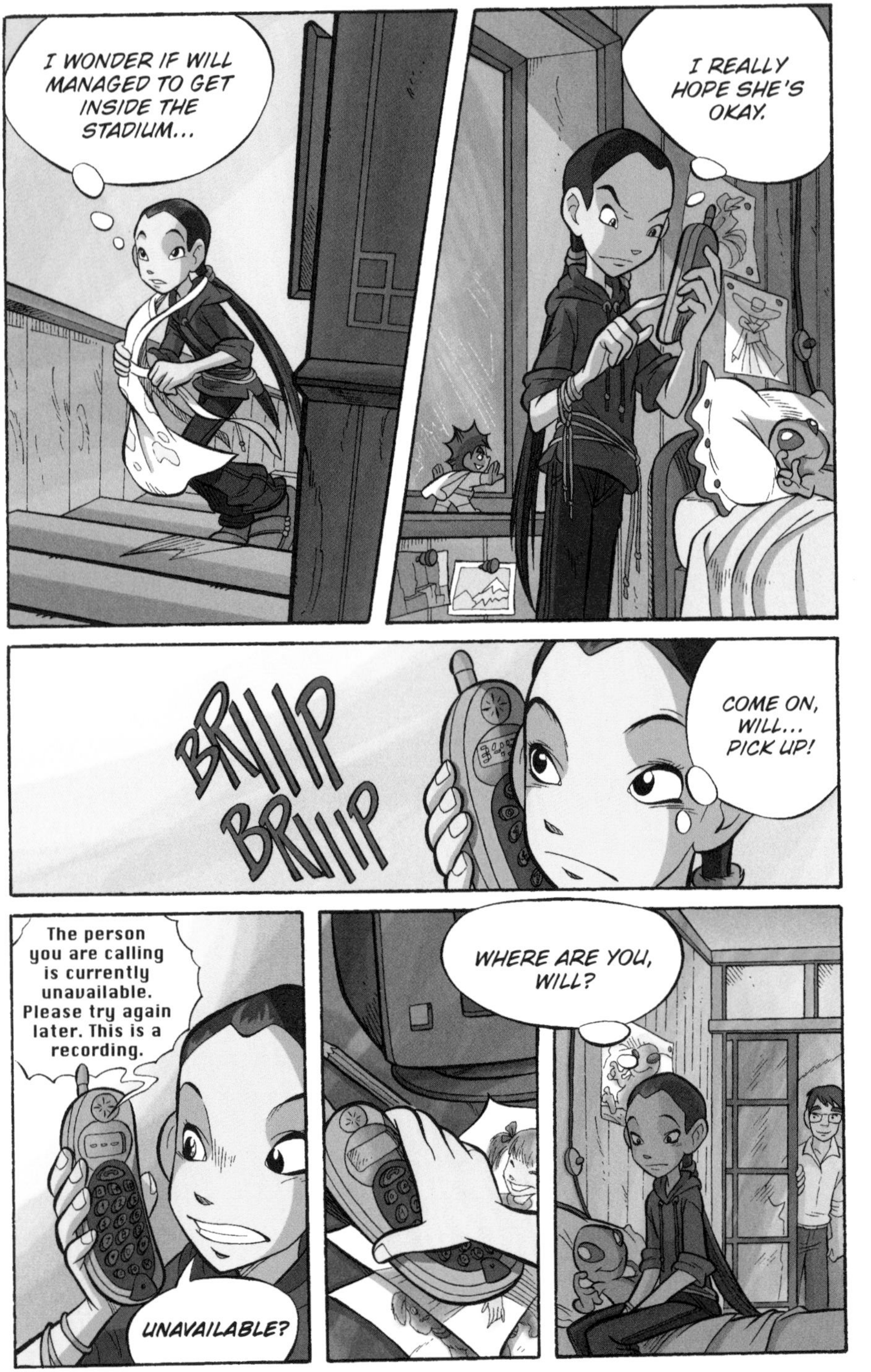
I WONDER IF WILL MANAGED TO GET INSIDE THE STADIUM...
I REALLY HOPE SHE'S OKAY.
BRIIIP BRIIIP
COME ON, WILL... PICK UP!
The person you are calling is currently unavailable. Please try again later. This is a recording.
UNAVAILABLE?
WHERE ARE YOU, WILL?

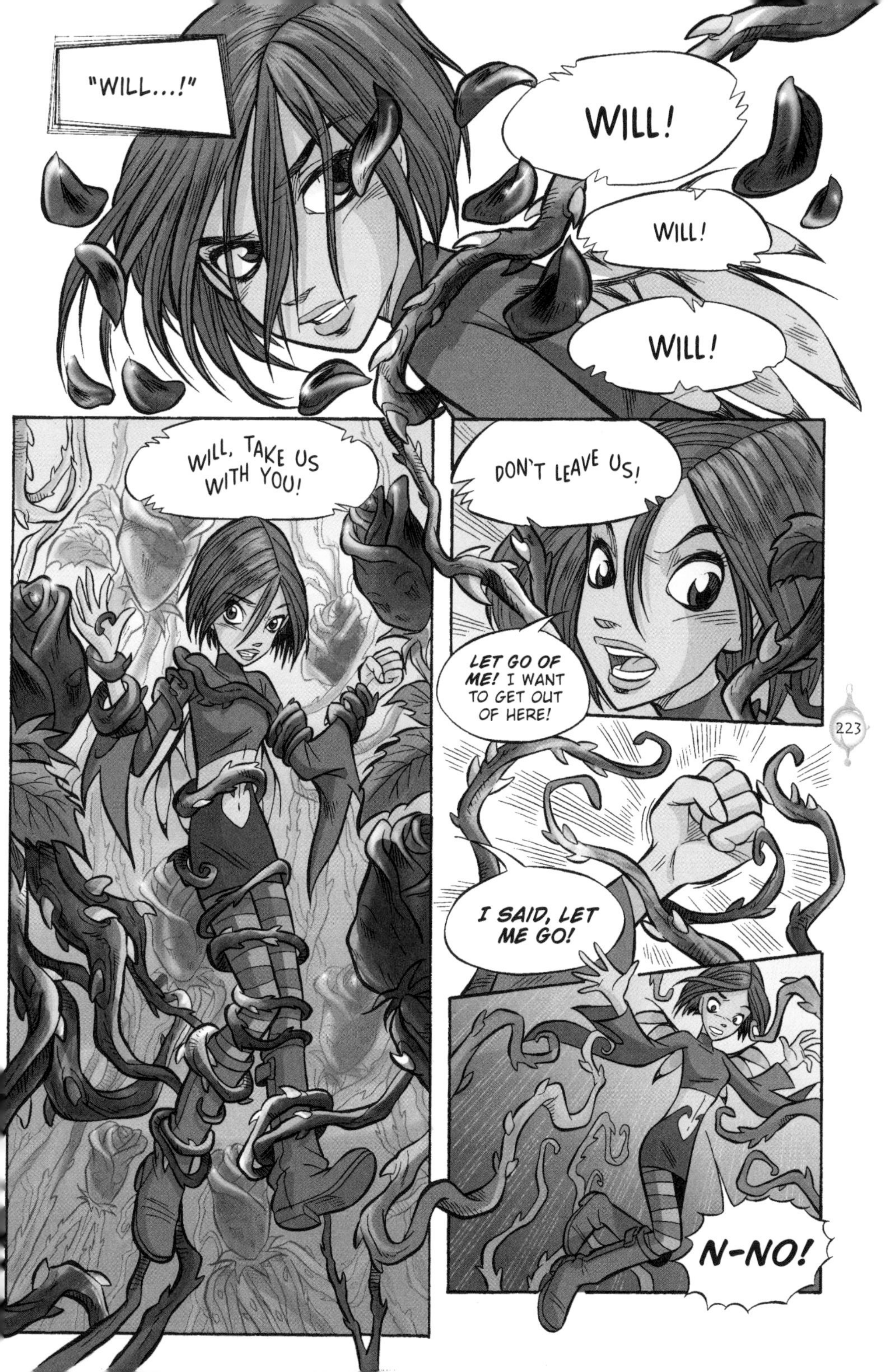
"WILL...!"
WILL!
WILL!
WILL!
WILL, TAKE US WITH YOU!
DON'T LEAVE US!
LET GO OF ME! I WANT TO GET OUT OF HERE!
I SAID, LET ME GO!
N-NO!

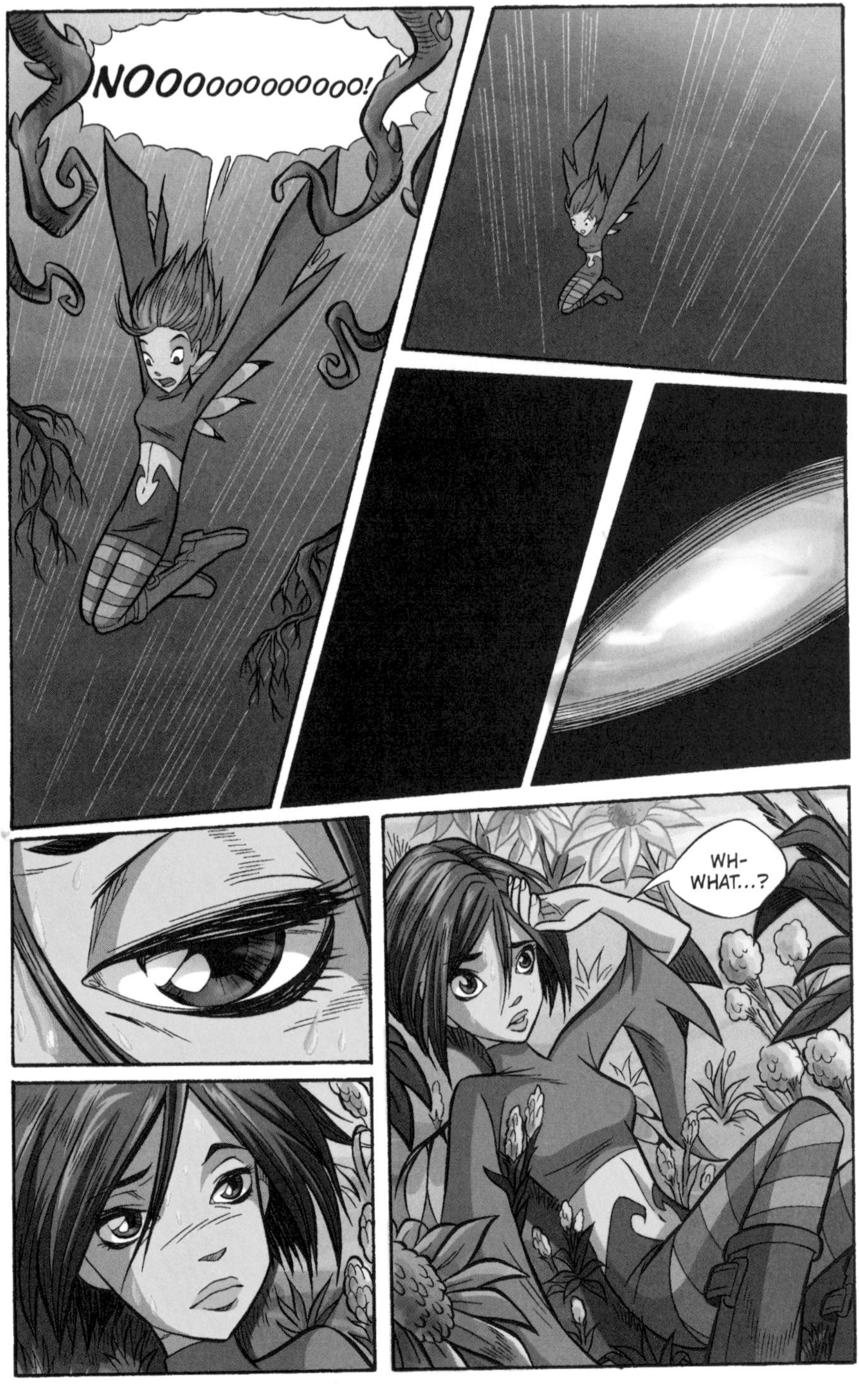
NOOOoooooooooo!
WH-
WHAT...?

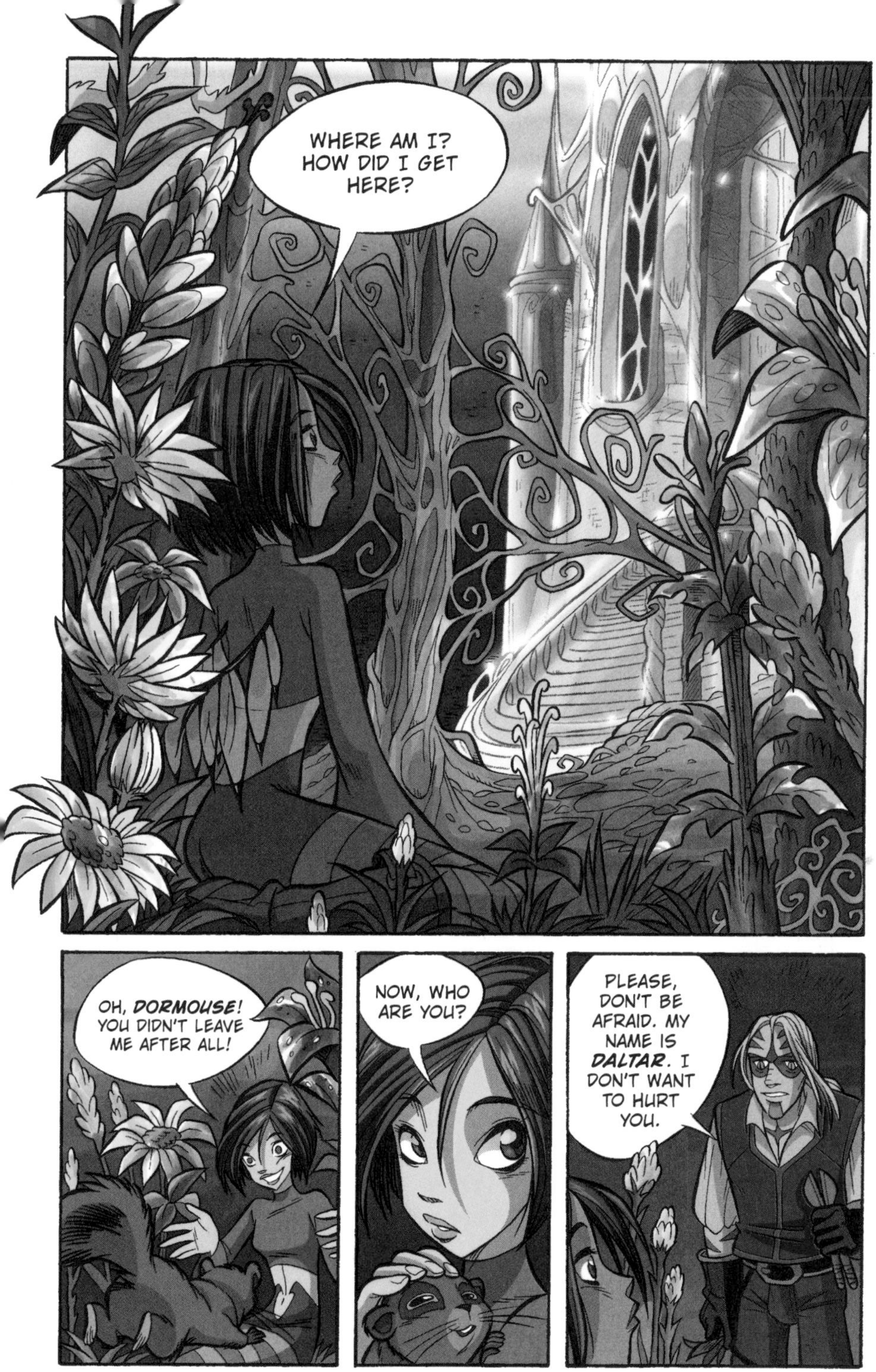
WHERE AM I? HOW DID I GET HERE?
OH, **DORMOUSE**! YOU DIDN'T LEAVE ME AFTER ALL!
NOW, WHO ARE YOU?
PLEASE, DON'T BE AFRAID. MY NAME IS **DALTAR**. I DON'T WANT TO HURT YOU.

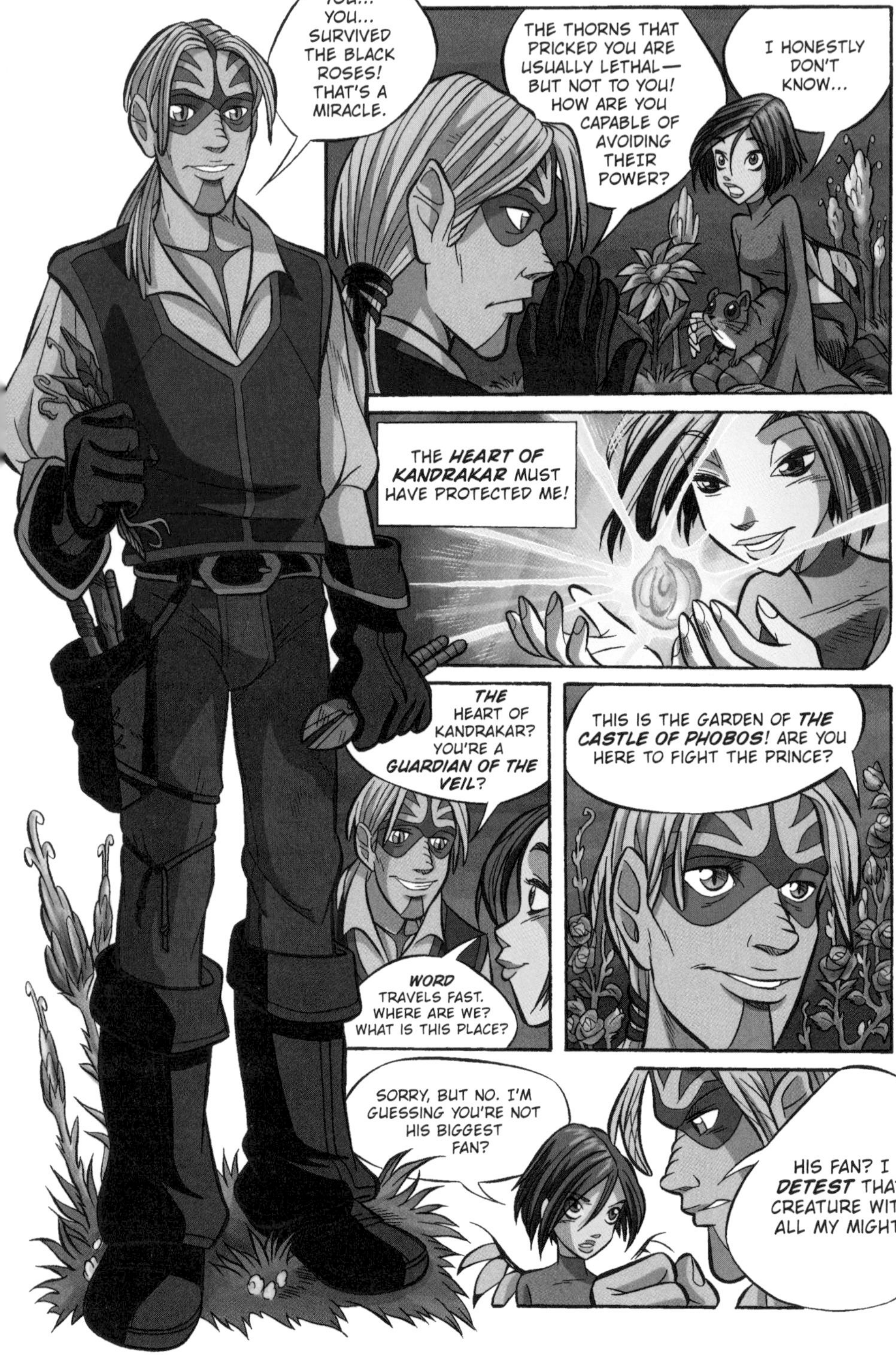
YOU... YOU... SURVIVED THE BLACK ROSES! THAT'S A MIRACLE.
THE THORNS THAT PRICKED YOU ARE USUALLY LETHAL— BUT NOT TO YOU! HOW ARE YOU CAPABLE OF AVOIDING THEIR POWER?
I HONESTLY DON'T KNOW...
THE HEART OF KANDRAKAR MUST HAVE PROTECTED ME!
THE HEART OF KANDRAKAR? YOU'RE A GUARDIAN OF THE VEIL?
WORD TRAVELS FAST. WHERE ARE WE? WHAT IS THIS PLACE?
THIS IS THE GARDEN OF THE CASTLE OF PHOBOS! ARE YOU HERE TO FIGHT THE PRINCE?
SORRY, BUT NO. I'M GUESSING YOU'RE NOT HIS BIGGEST FAN?
HIS FAN? I DETEST THAT CREATURE WITH ALL MY MIGHT!

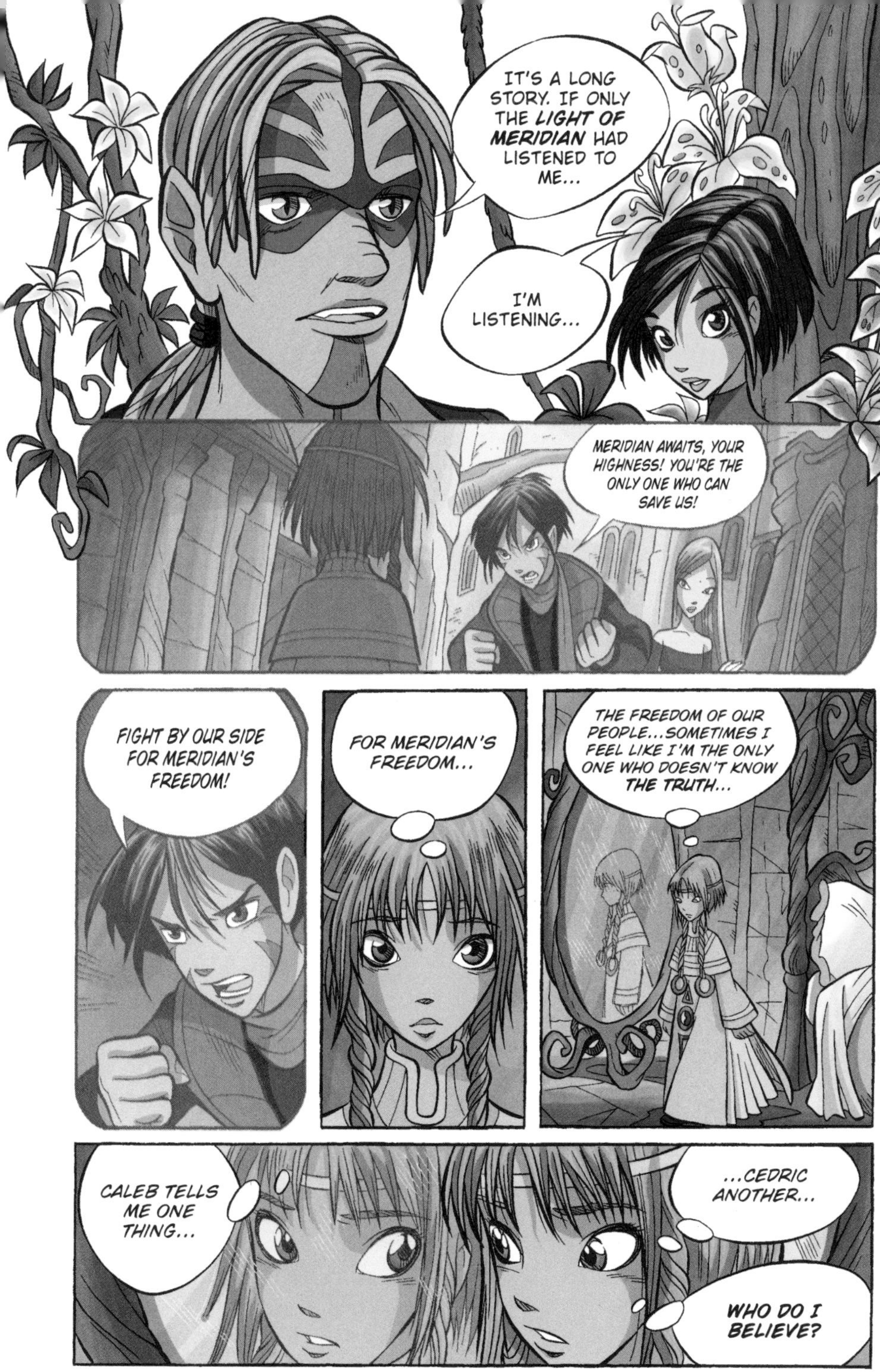
IT'S A LONG STORY. IF ONLY THE LIGHT OF MERIDIAN HAD LISTENED TO ME...
I'M LISTENING...
MERIDIAN AWAITS, YOUR HIGHNESS! YOU'RE THE ONLY ONE WHO CAN SAVE US!
FIGHT BY OUR SIDE FOR MERIDIAN'S FREEDOM!
FOR MERIDIAN'S FREEDOM...
THE FREEDOM OF OUR PEOPLE...SOMETIMES I FEEL LIKE I'M THE ONLY ONE WHO DOESN'T KNOW THE TRUTH...
CALEB TELLS ME ONE THING...
...CEDRIC ANOTHER...
WHO DO I BELIEVE?

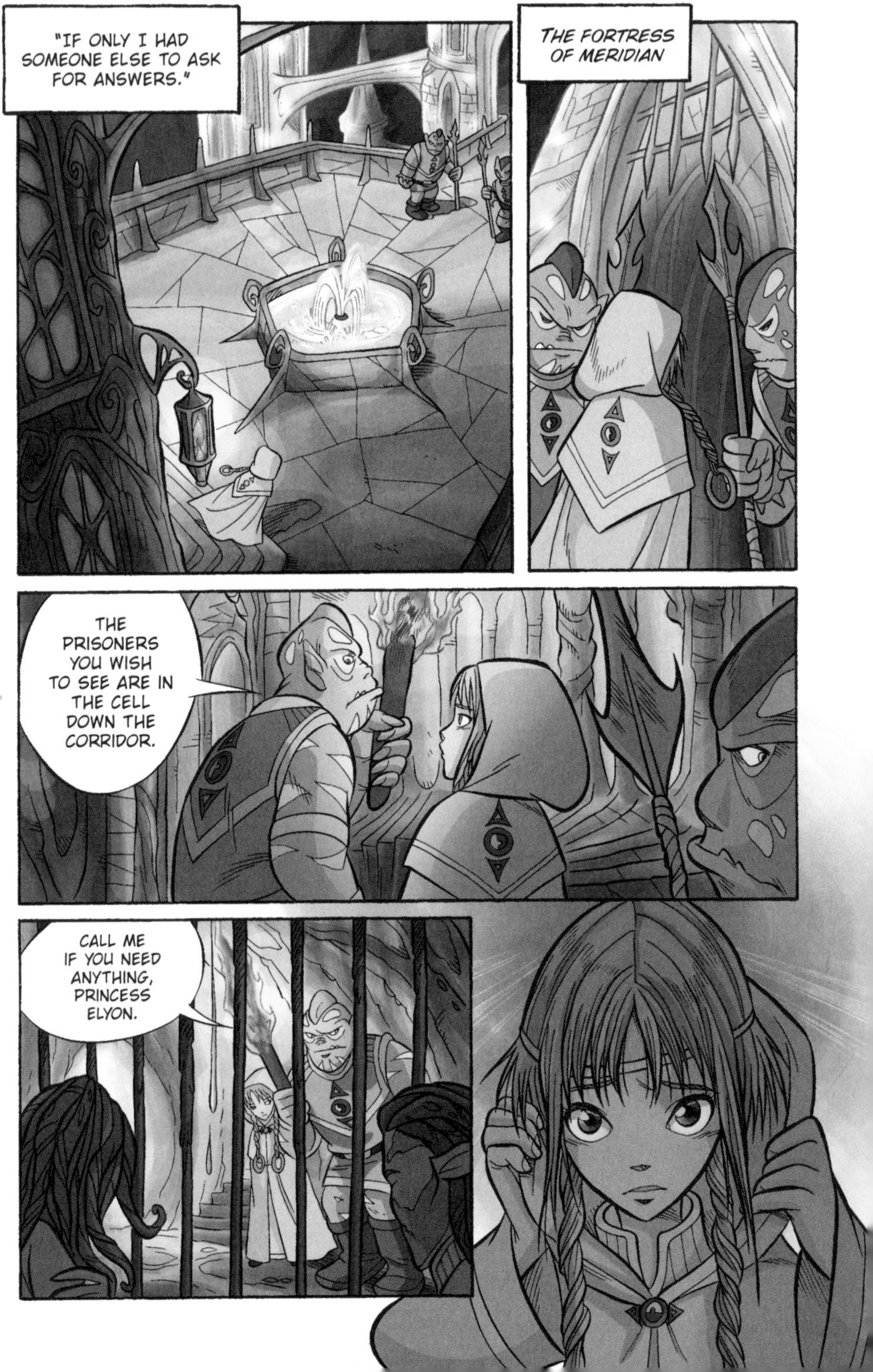

"IF ONLY I HAD SOMEONE ELSE TO ASK FOR ANSWERS."
THE FORTRESS OF MERIDIAN
THE PRISONERS YOU WISH TO SEE ARE IN THE CELL DOWN THE CORRIDOR.
CALL ME IF YOU NEED ANYTHING, PRINCESS ELYON.

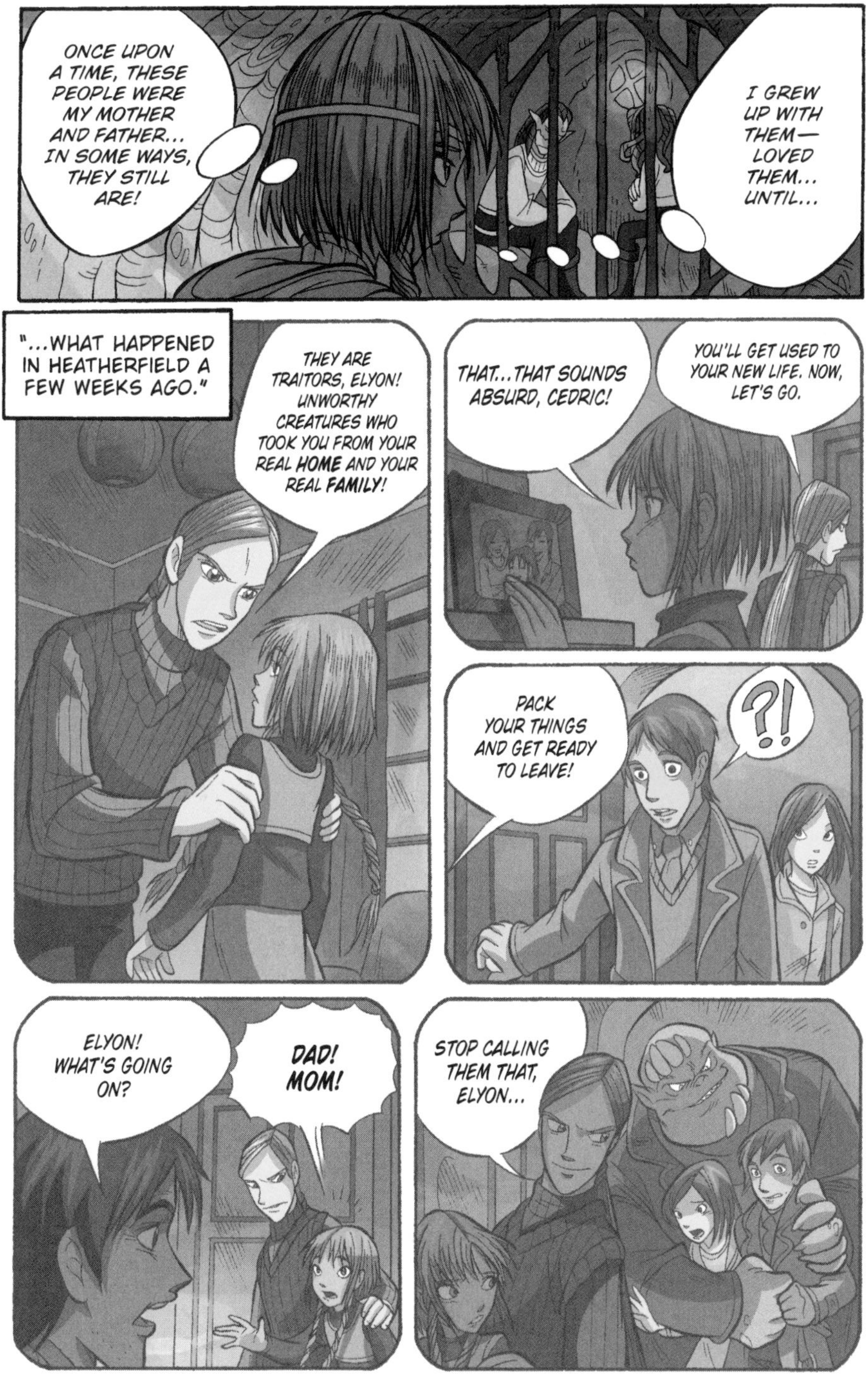
ONCE UPON A TIME, THESE PEOPLE WERE MY MOTHER AND FATHER... IN SOME WAYS, THEY STILL ARE!
I GREW UP WITH THEM— LOVED THEM... UNTIL...
"...WHAT HAPPENED IN HEATHERFIELD A FEW WEEKS AGO."
THEY ARE TRAITORS, ELYON! UNWORTHY CREATURES WHO TOOK YOU FROM YOUR REAL **HOME** AND YOUR REAL **FAMILY**!
THAT...THAT SOUNDS ABSURD, CEDRIC!
YOU'LL GET USED TO YOUR NEW LIFE. NOW, LET'S GO.
PACK YOUR THINGS AND GET READY TO LEAVE!
?!
ELYON! WHAT'S GOING ON?
DAD! MOM!
STOP CALLING THEM THAT, ELYON...

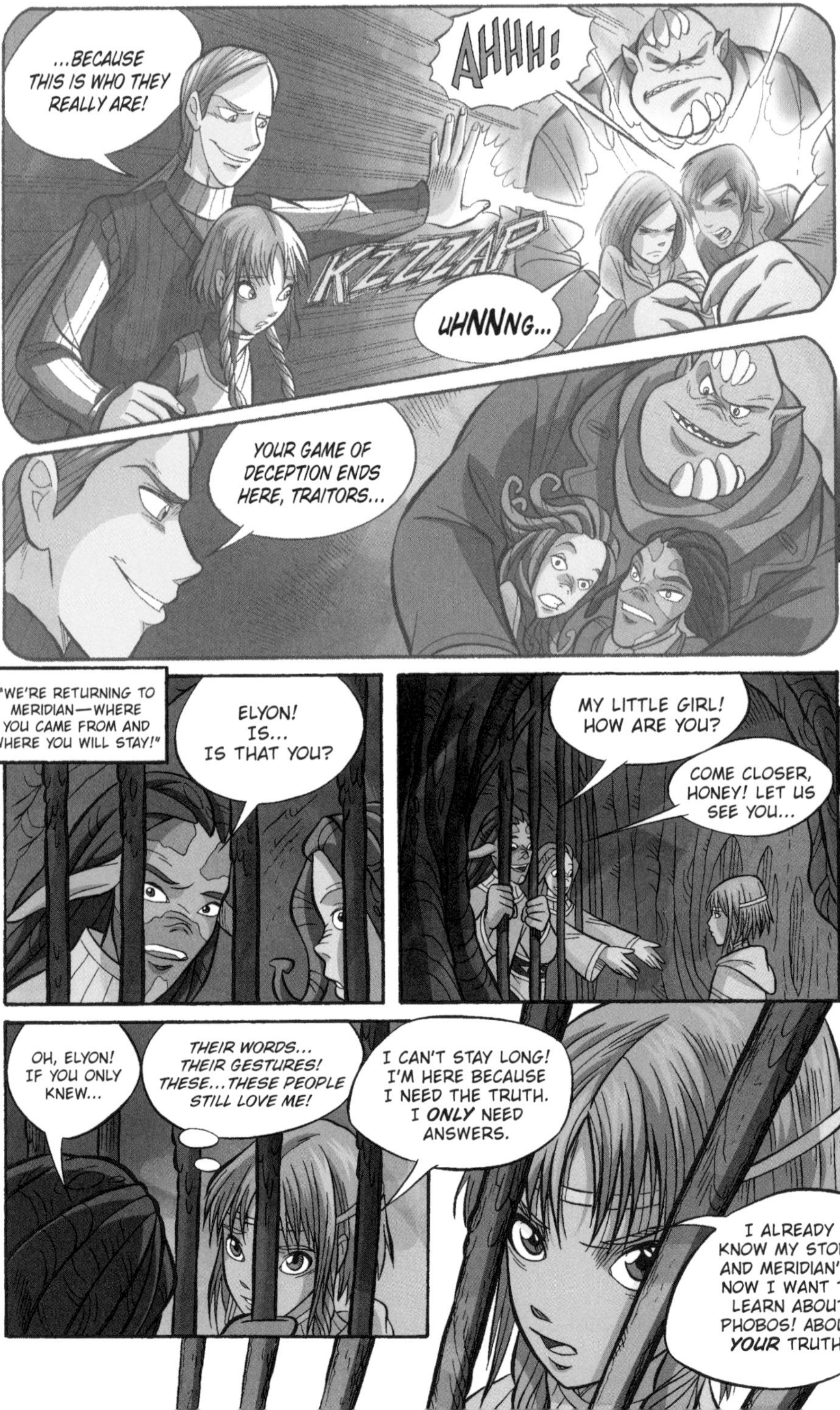
...BECAUSE THIS IS WHO THEY REALLY ARE!
AHHH!
KZZZAP
UHNNNG...
YOUR GAME OF DECEPTION ENDS HERE, TRAITORS...
"WE'RE RETURNING TO MERIDIAN—WHERE YOU CAME FROM AND WHERE YOU WILL STAY!"
ELYON! IS... IS THAT YOU?
MY LITTLE GIRL! HOW ARE YOU?
COME CLOSER, HONEY! LET US SEE YOU...
OH, ELYON! IF YOU ONLY KNEW...
THEIR WORDS... THEIR GESTURES! THESE...THESE PEOPLE STILL LOVE ME!
I CAN'T STAY LONG! I'M HERE BECAUSE I NEED THE TRUTH. I ONLY NEED ANSWERS.
I ALREADY KNOW MY STORY AND MERIDIAN'S! NOW I WANT TO LEARN ABOUT PHOBOS! ABOUT YOUR TRUTH.

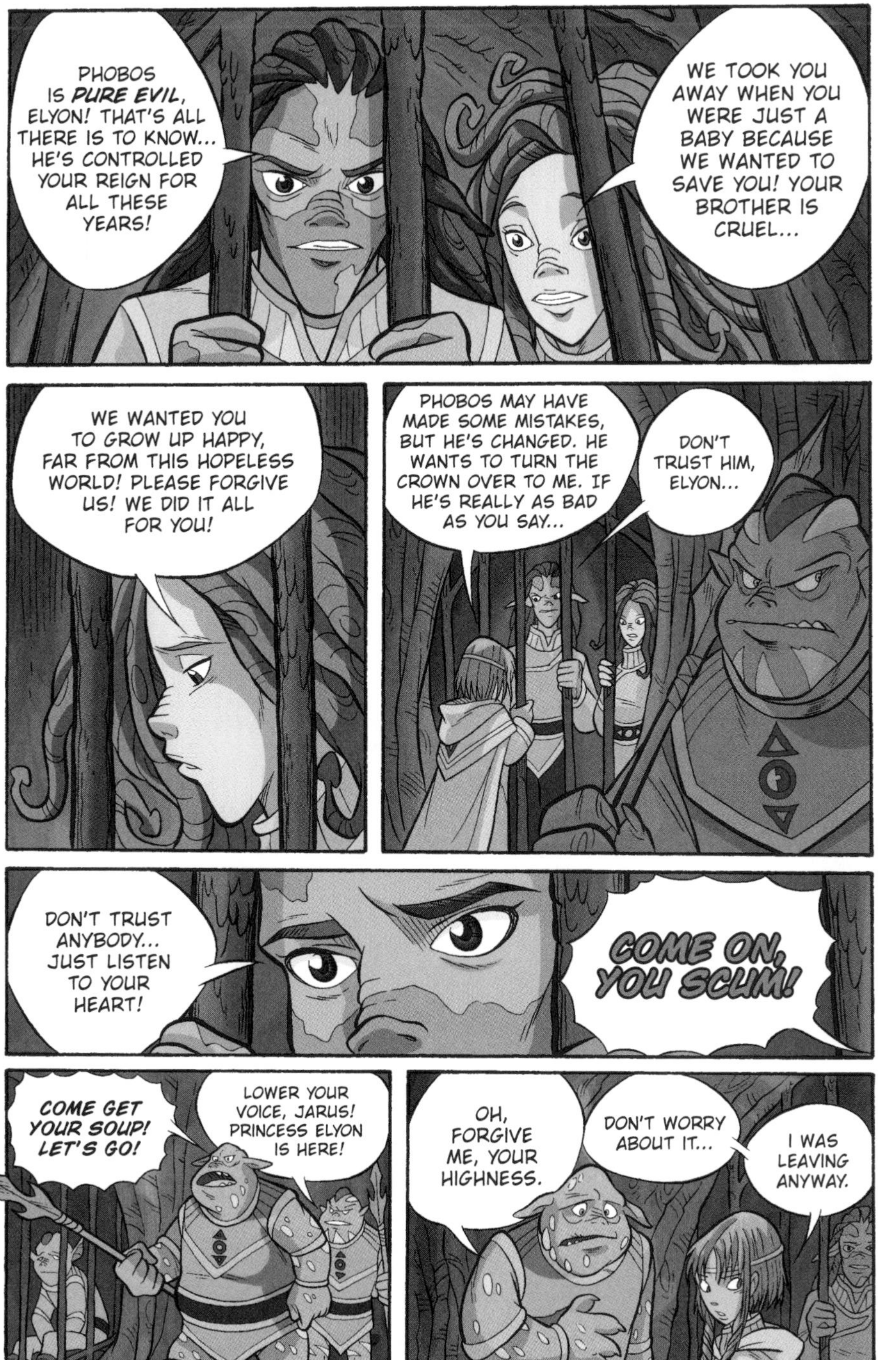
PHOBOS IS PURE EVIL, ELYON! THAT'S ALL THERE IS TO KNOW... HE'S CONTROLLED YOUR REIGN FOR ALL THESE YEARS!
WE TOOK YOU AWAY WHEN YOU WERE JUST A BABY BECAUSE WE WANTED TO SAVE YOU! YOUR BROTHER IS CRUEL...
WE WANTED YOU TO GROW UP HAPPY, FAR FROM THIS HOPELESS WORLD! PLEASE FORGIVE US! WE DID IT ALL FOR YOU!
PHOBOS MAY HAVE MADE SOME MISTAKES, BUT HE'S CHANGED. HE WANTS TO TURN THE CROWN OVER TO ME. IF HE'S REALLY AS BAD AS YOU SAY...
DON'T TRUST HIM, ELYON...
DON'T TRUST ANYBODY... JUST LISTEN TO YOUR HEART!
COME ON, YOU SCUM!
COME GET YOUR SOUP! LET'S GO!
LOWER YOUR VOICE, JARUS! PRINCESS ELYON IS HERE!
OH, FORGIVE ME, YOUR HIGHNESS.
DON'T WORRY ABOUT IT...
I WAS LEAVING ANYWAY.

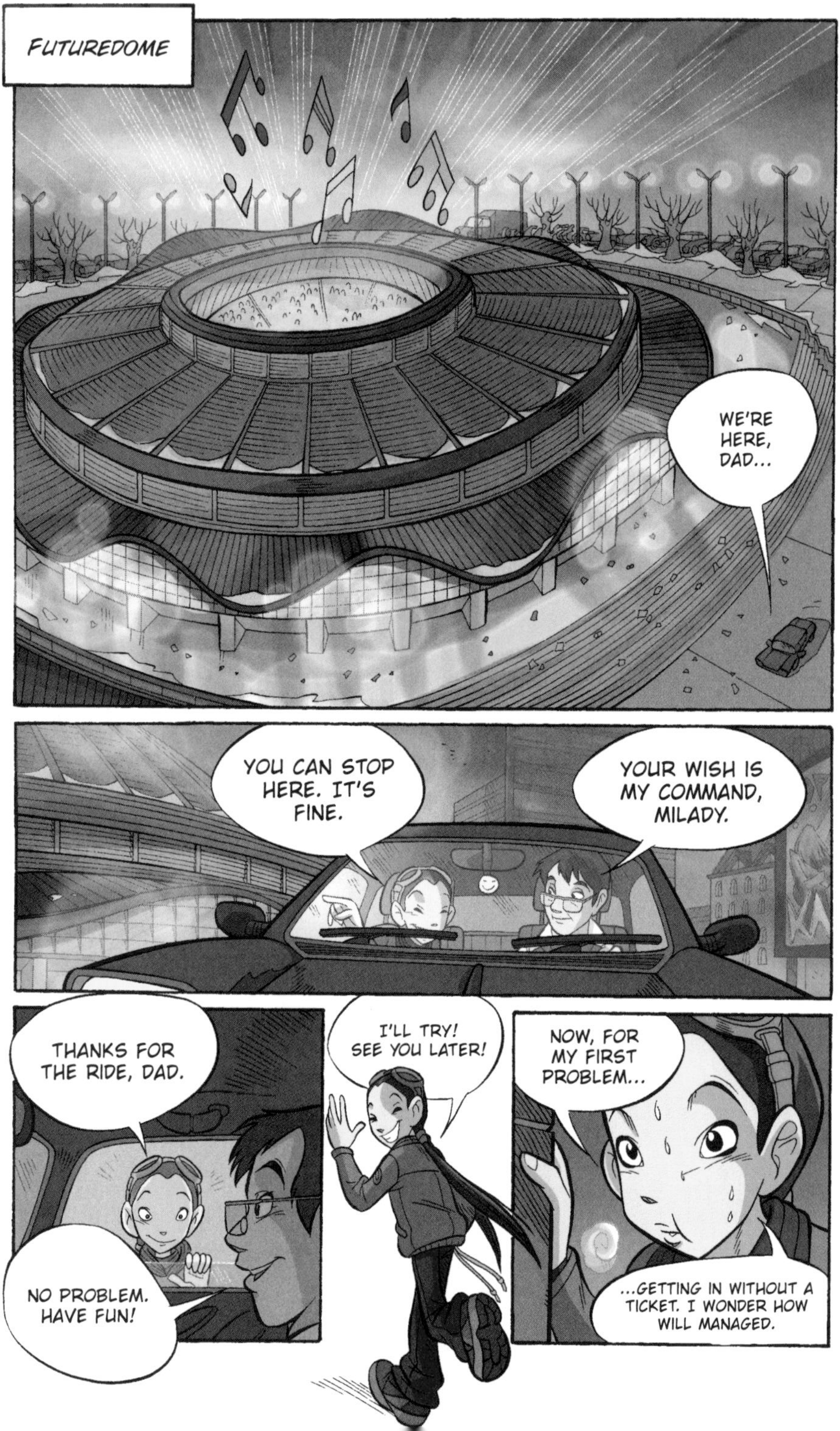
FUTUREDOME
WE'RE HERE, DAD...
YOU CAN STOP HERE. IT'S FINE.
YOUR WISH IS MY COMMAND, MILADY.
THANKS FOR THE RIDE, DAD.
NO PROBLEM. HAVE FUN!
I'LL TRY! SEE YOU LATER!
NOW, FOR MY FIRST PROBLEM...
...GETTING IN WITHOUT A TICKET. I WONDER HOW WILL MANAGED.

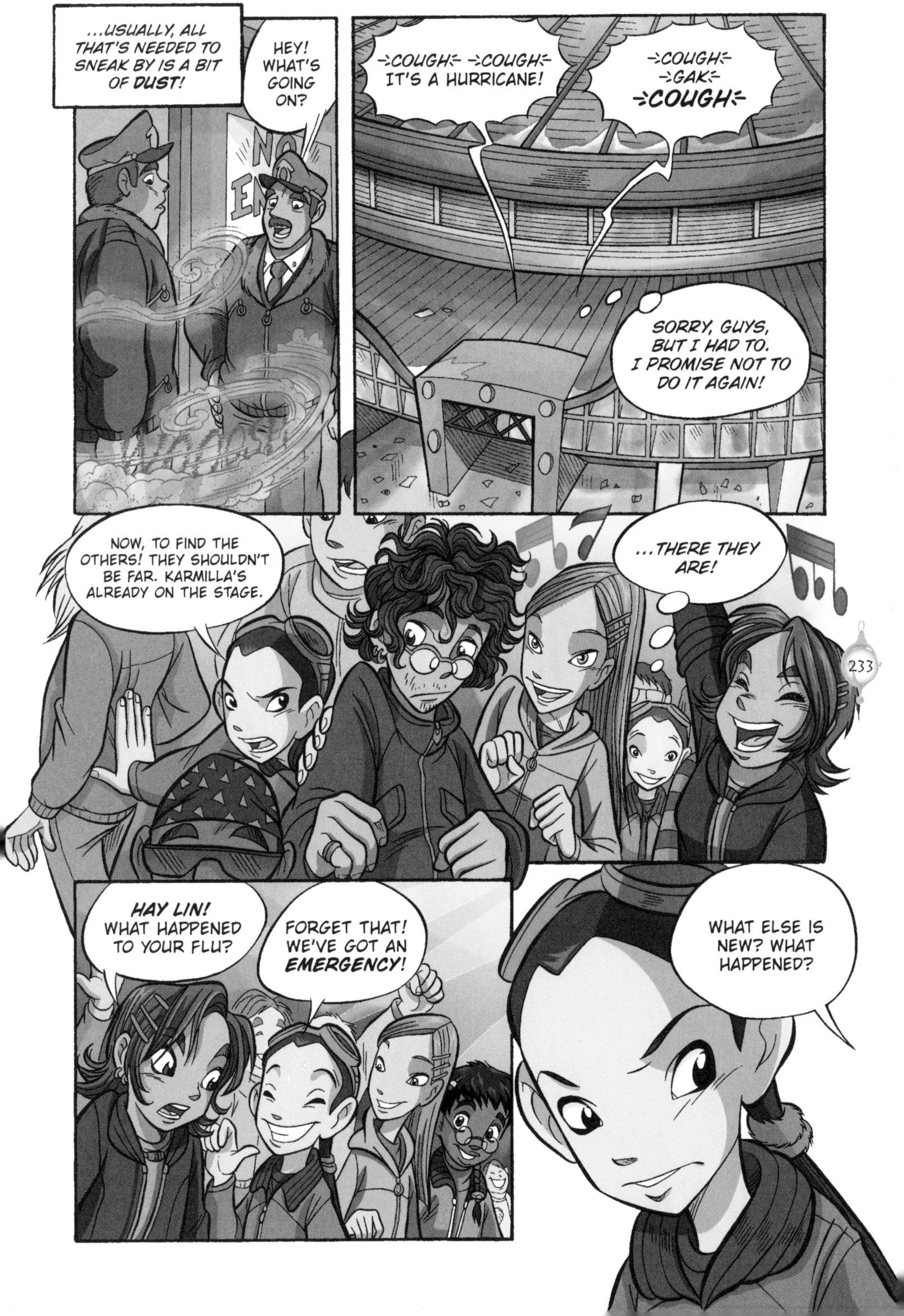

...USUALLY, ALL THAT'S NEEDED TO SNEAK BY IS A BIT OF DUST!
HEY! WHAT'S GOING ON?
-COUGH- -COUGH- IT'S A HURRICANE!
-COUGH- -GAK- -COUGH-
SORRY, GUYS, BUT I HAD TO. I PROMISE NOT TO DO IT AGAIN!
NOW, TO FIND THE OTHERS! THEY SHOULDN'T BE FAR. KARMILLA'S ALREADY ON THE STAGE.
...THERE THEY ARE!
HAY LIN! WHAT HAPPENED TO YOUR FLU?
FORGET THAT! WE'VE GOT AN EMERGENCY!
WHAT ELSE IS NEW? WHAT HAPPENED?

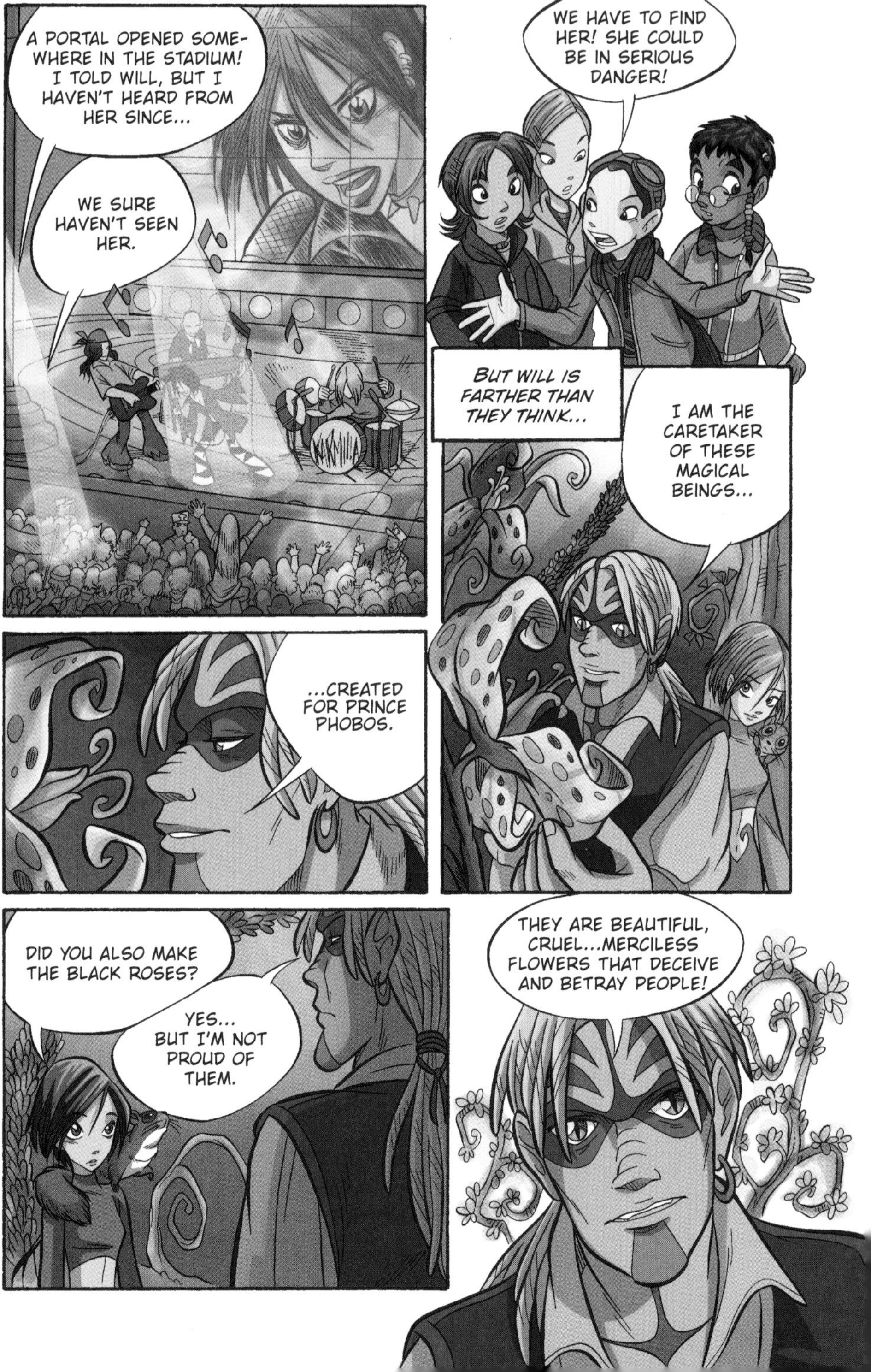
A PORTAL OPENED SOMEWHERE IN THE STADIUM! I TOLD WILL, BUT I HAVEN'T HEARD FROM HER SINCE...
WE SURE HAVEN'T SEEN HER.
WE HAVE TO FIND HER! SHE COULD BE IN SERIOUS DANGER!
BUT WILL IS FARTHER THAN THEY THINK...
I AM THE CARETAKER OF THESE MAGICAL BEINGS...
...CREATED FOR PRINCE PHOBOS.
DID YOU ALSO MAKE THE BLACK ROSES?
YES... BUT I'M NOT PROUD OF THEM.
THEY ARE BEAUTIFUL, CRUEL...MERCILESS FLOWERS THAT DECEIVE AND BETRAY PEOPLE!

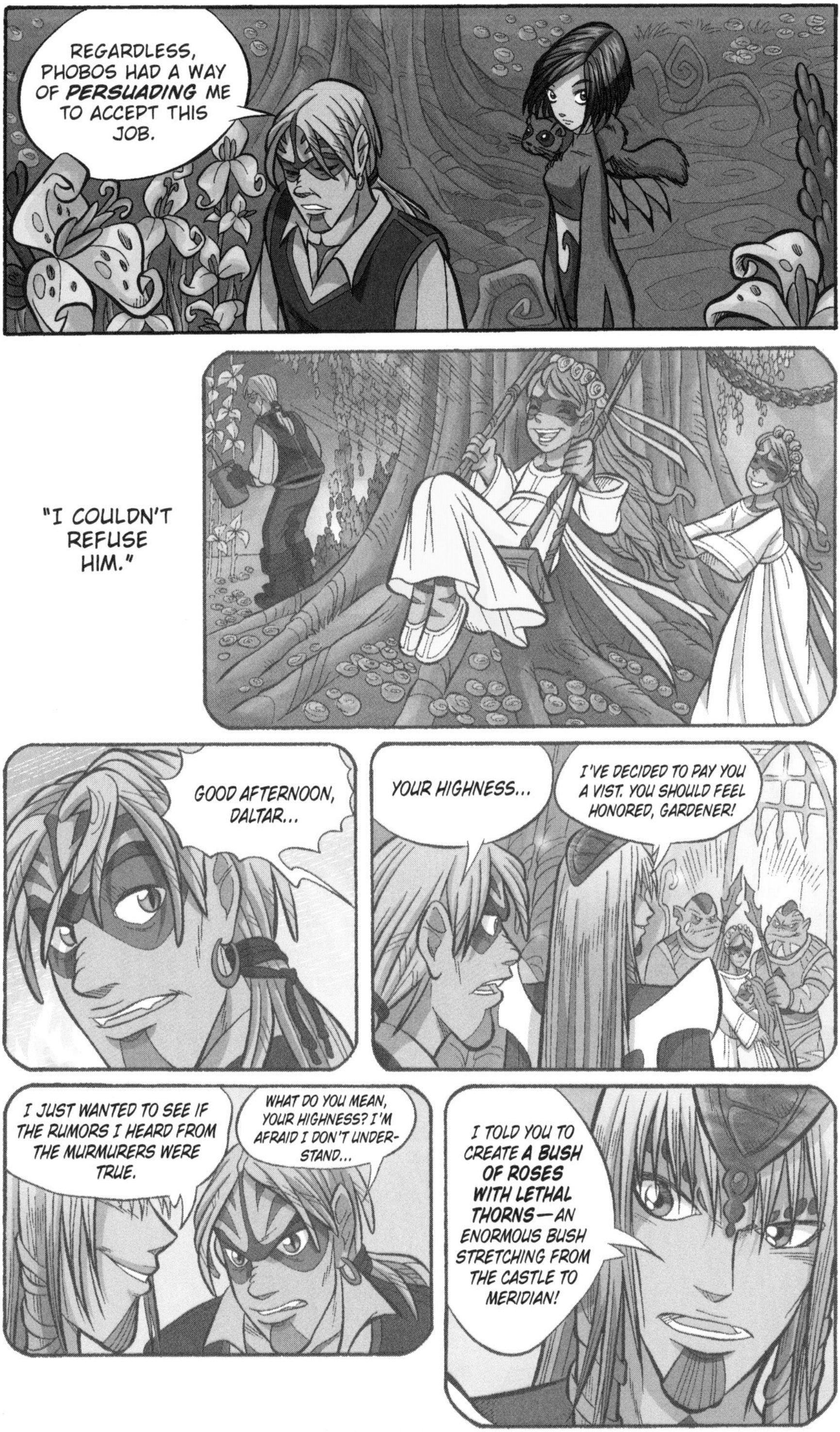
REGARDLESS, PHOBOS HAD A WAY OF **PERSUADING** ME TO ACCEPT THIS JOB.
"I COULDN'T REFUSE HIM."
GOOD AFTERNOON, DALTAR...
YOUR HIGHNESS...
I'VE DECIDED TO PAY YOU A VIST. YOU SHOULD FEEL HONORED, GARDENER!
I JUST WANTED TO SEE IF THE RUMORS I HEARD FROM THE MURMURERS WERE TRUE.
WHAT DO YOU MEAN, YOUR HIGHNESS? I'M AFRAID I DON'T UNDER-STAND...
I TOLD YOU TO CREATE **A BUSH OF ROSES WITH LETHAL THORNS**—AN ENORMOUS BUSH STRETCHING FROM THE CASTLE TO MERIDIAN!

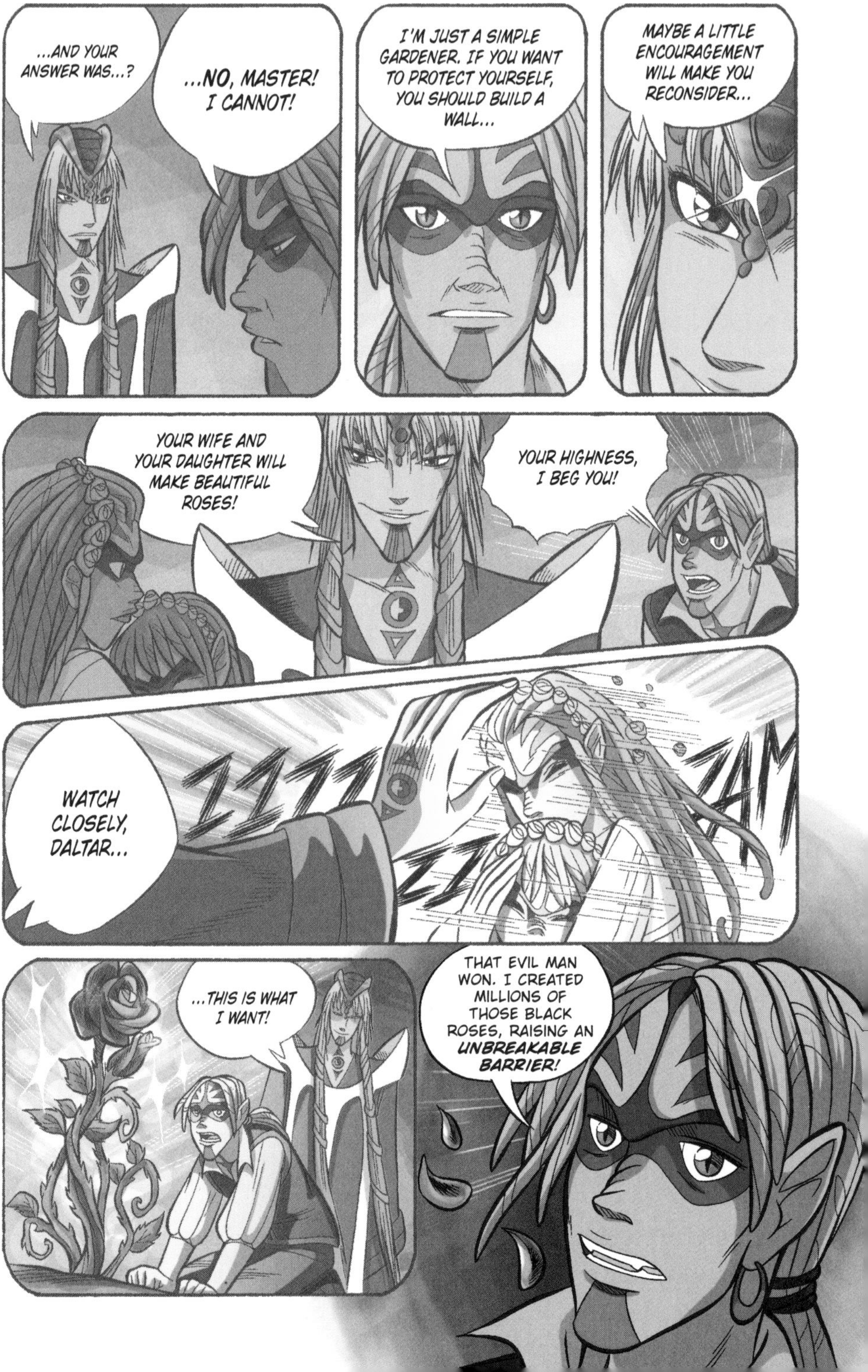
...AND YOUR ANSWER WAS...?
...NO, MASTER! I CANNOT!
I'M JUST A SIMPLE GARDENER. IF YOU WANT TO PROTECT YOURSELF, YOU SHOULD BUILD A WALL...
MAYBE A LITTLE ENCOURAGEMENT WILL MAKE YOU RECONSIDER...
YOUR WIFE AND YOUR DAUGHTER WILL MAKE BEAUTIFUL ROSES!
YOUR HIGHNESS, I BEG YOU!
WATCH CLOSELY, DALTAR...
ZZZZZ
ZZZ
ZAM
...THIS IS WHAT I WANT!
THAT EVIL MAN WON. I CREATED MILLIONS OF THOSE BLACK ROSES, RAISING AN *UNBREAKABLE BARRIER!*

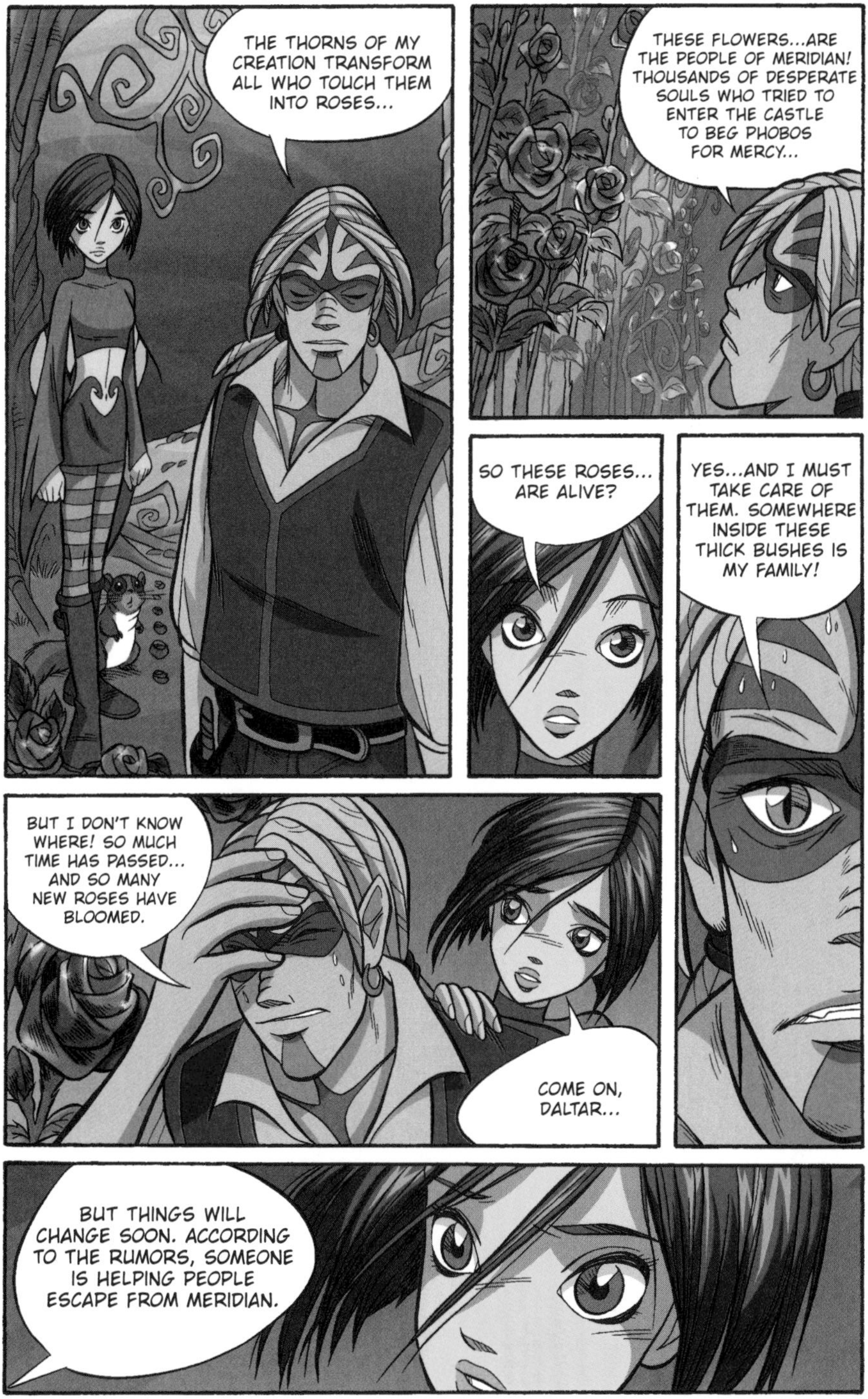
THE THORNS OF MY CREATION TRANSFORM ALL WHO TOUCH THEM INTO ROSES...
THESE FLOWERS...ARE THE PEOPLE OF MERIDIAN! THOUSANDS OF DESPERATE SOULS WHO TRIED TO ENTER THE CASTLE TO BEG PHOBOS FOR MERCY...
SO THESE ROSES... ARE ALIVE?
YES...AND I MUST TAKE CARE OF THEM. SOMEWHERE INSIDE THESE THICK BUSHES IS MY FAMILY!
BUT I DON'T KNOW WHERE! SO MUCH TIME HAS PASSED... AND SO MANY NEW ROSES HAVE BLOOMED.
COME ON, DALTAR...
BUT THINGS WILL CHANGE SOON. ACCORDING TO THE RUMORS, SOMEONE IS HELPING PEOPLE ESCAPE FROM MERIDIAN.

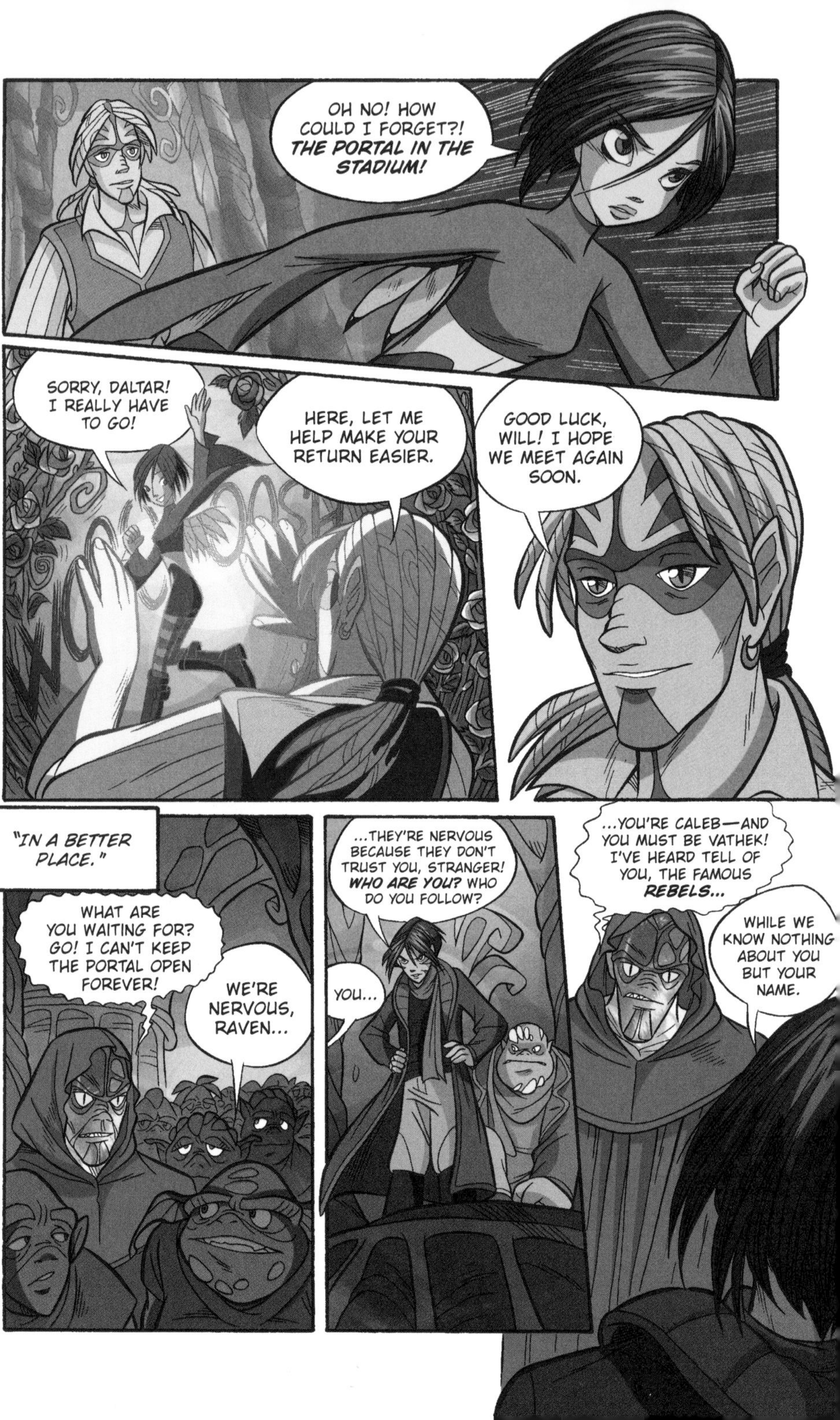
OH NO! HOW COULD I FORGET?! THE PORTAL IN THE STADIUM!
SORRY, DALTAR! I REALLY HAVE TO GO!
HERE, LET ME HELP MAKE YOUR RETURN EASIER.
GOOD LUCK, WILL! I HOPE WE MEET AGAIN SOON.
"IN A BETTER PLACE."
WHAT ARE YOU WAITING FOR? GO! I CAN'T KEEP THE PORTAL OPEN FOREVER!
WE'RE NERVOUS, RAVEN...
...THEY'RE NERVOUS BECAUSE THEY DON'T TRUST YOU, STRANGER! WHO ARE YOU? WHO DO YOU FOLLOW?
YOU...
...YOU'RE CALEB—AND YOU MUST BE VATHEK! I'VE HEARD TELL OF YOU, THE FAMOUS REBELS...
WHILE WE KNOW NOTHING ABOUT YOU BUT YOUR NAME.

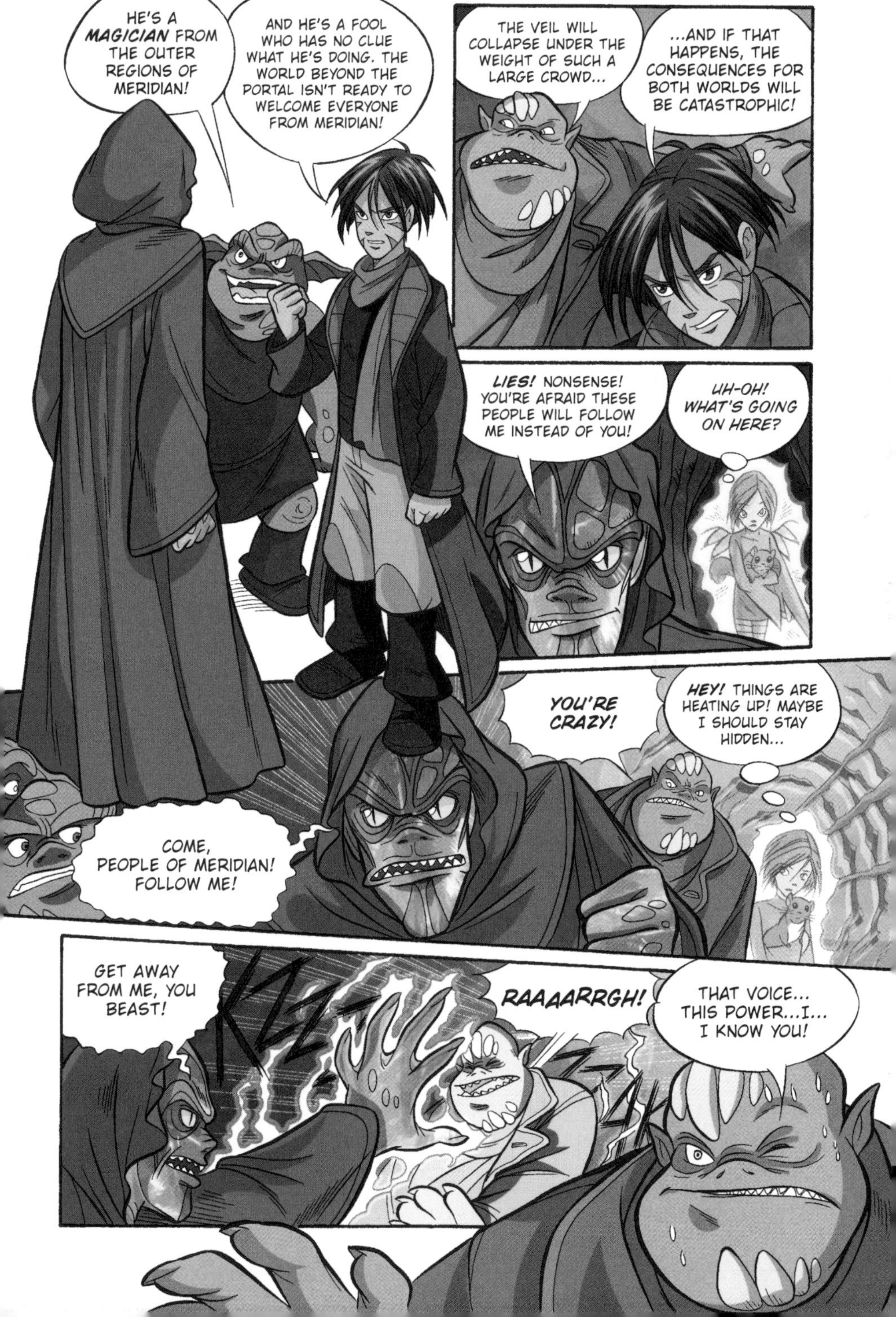
HE'S A MAGICIAN FROM THE OUTER REGIONS OF MERIDIAN!
AND HE'S A FOOL WHO HAS NO CLUE WHAT HE'S DOING. THE WORLD BEYOND THE PORTAL ISN'T READY TO WELCOME EVERYONE FROM MERIDIAN!
THE VEIL WILL COLLAPSE UNDER THE WEIGHT OF SUCH A LARGE CROWD...
...AND IF THAT HAPPENS, THE CONSEQUENCES FOR BOTH WORLDS WILL BE CATASTROPHIC!
LIES! NONSENSE! YOU'RE AFRAID THESE PEOPLE WILL FOLLOW ME INSTEAD OF YOU!
UH-OH! WHAT'S GOING ON HERE?
YOU'RE CRAZY!
HEY! THINGS ARE HEATING UP! MAYBE I SHOULD STAY HIDDEN...
COME, PEOPLE OF MERIDIAN! FOLLOW ME!
GET AWAY FROM ME, YOU BEAST!
RAAAARRGH!
THAT VOICE... THIS POWER...I... I KNOW YOU!

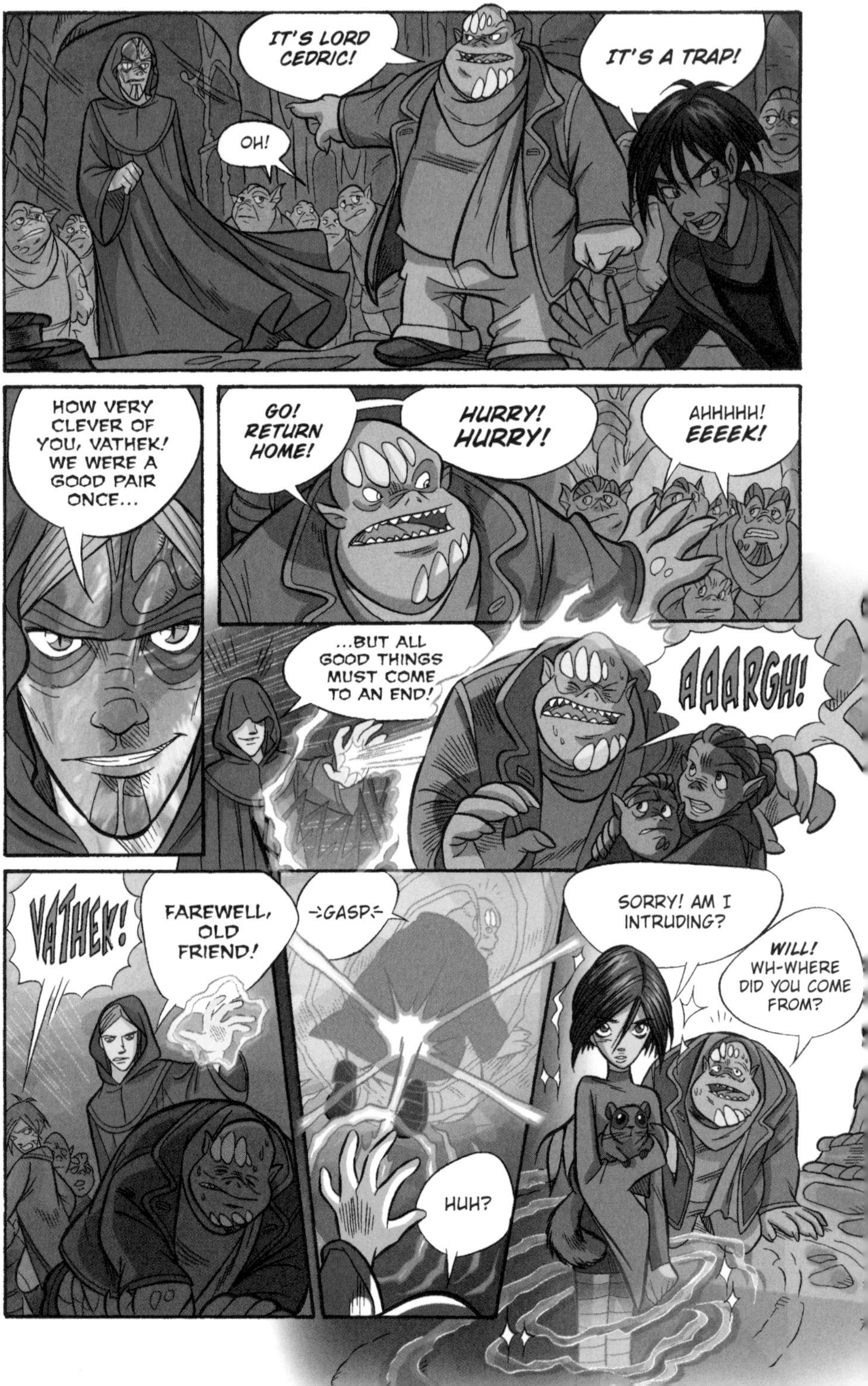
IT'S LORD CEDRIC!
OH!
IT'S A TRAP!
HOW VERY CLEVER OF YOU, VATHEK! WE WERE A GOOD PAIR ONCE...
GO! RETURN HOME!
HURRY! HURRY!
AHHHHH! EEEEK!
...BUT ALL GOOD THINGS MUST COME TO AN END!
AAARGH!
VATHEK!
FAREWELL, OLD FRIEND!
GASP
HUH?
SORRY! AM I INTRUDING?
WILL! WH-WHERE DID YOU COME FROM?

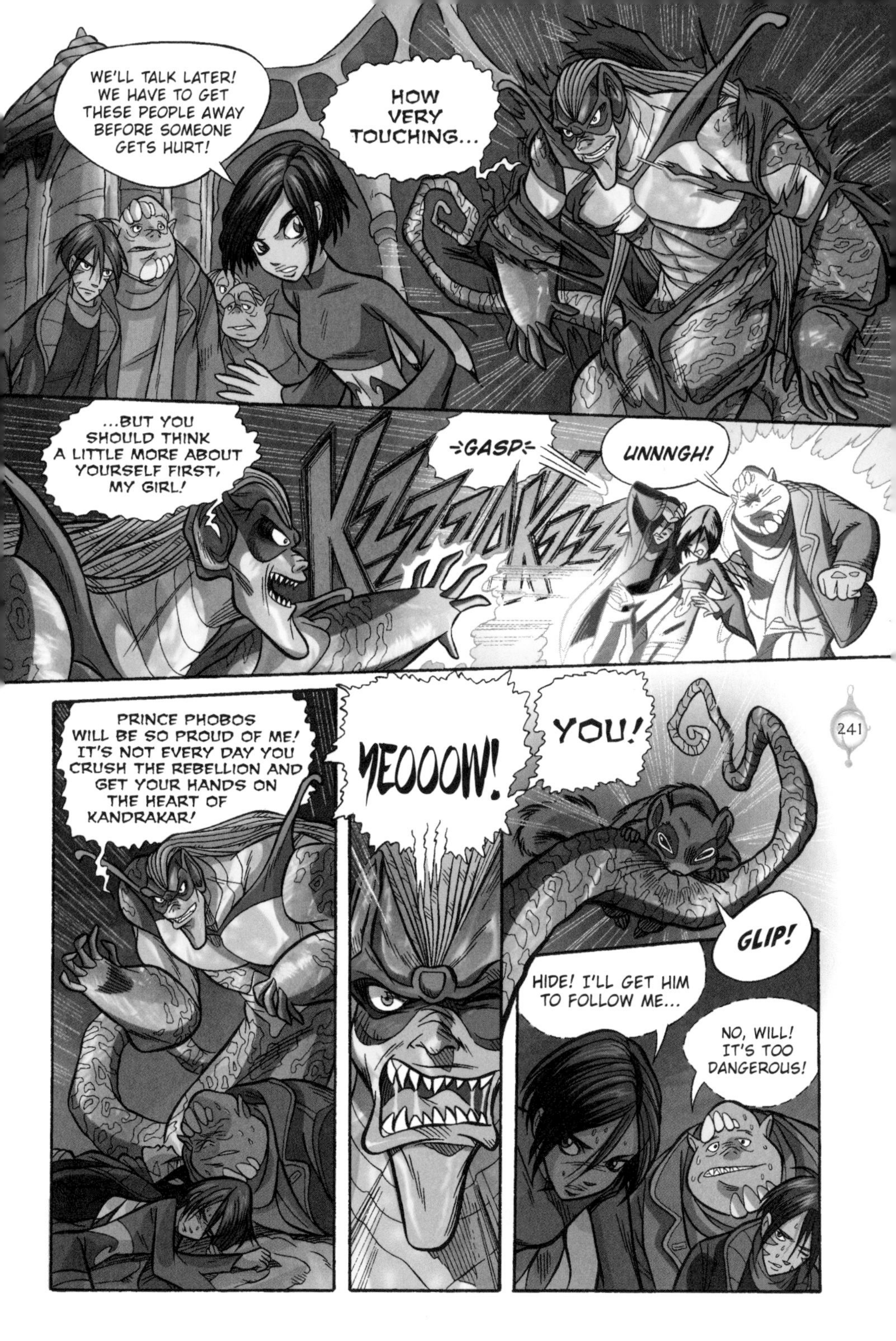
WE'LL TALK LATER! WE HAVE TO GET THESE PEOPLE AWAY BEFORE SOMEONE GETS HURT!
HOW VERY TOUCHING...
...BUT YOU SHOULD THINK A LITTLE MORE ABOUT YOURSELF FIRST, MY GIRL!
GASP
UNNNGH!
PRINCE PHOBOS WILL BE SO PROUD OF ME! IT'S NOT EVERY DAY YOU CRUSH THE REBELLION AND GET YOUR HANDS ON THE HEART OF KANDRAKAR!
YEOOOW!
YOU!
GLIP!
HIDE! I'LL GET HIM TO FOLLOW ME...
NO, WILL! IT'S TOO DANGEROUS!

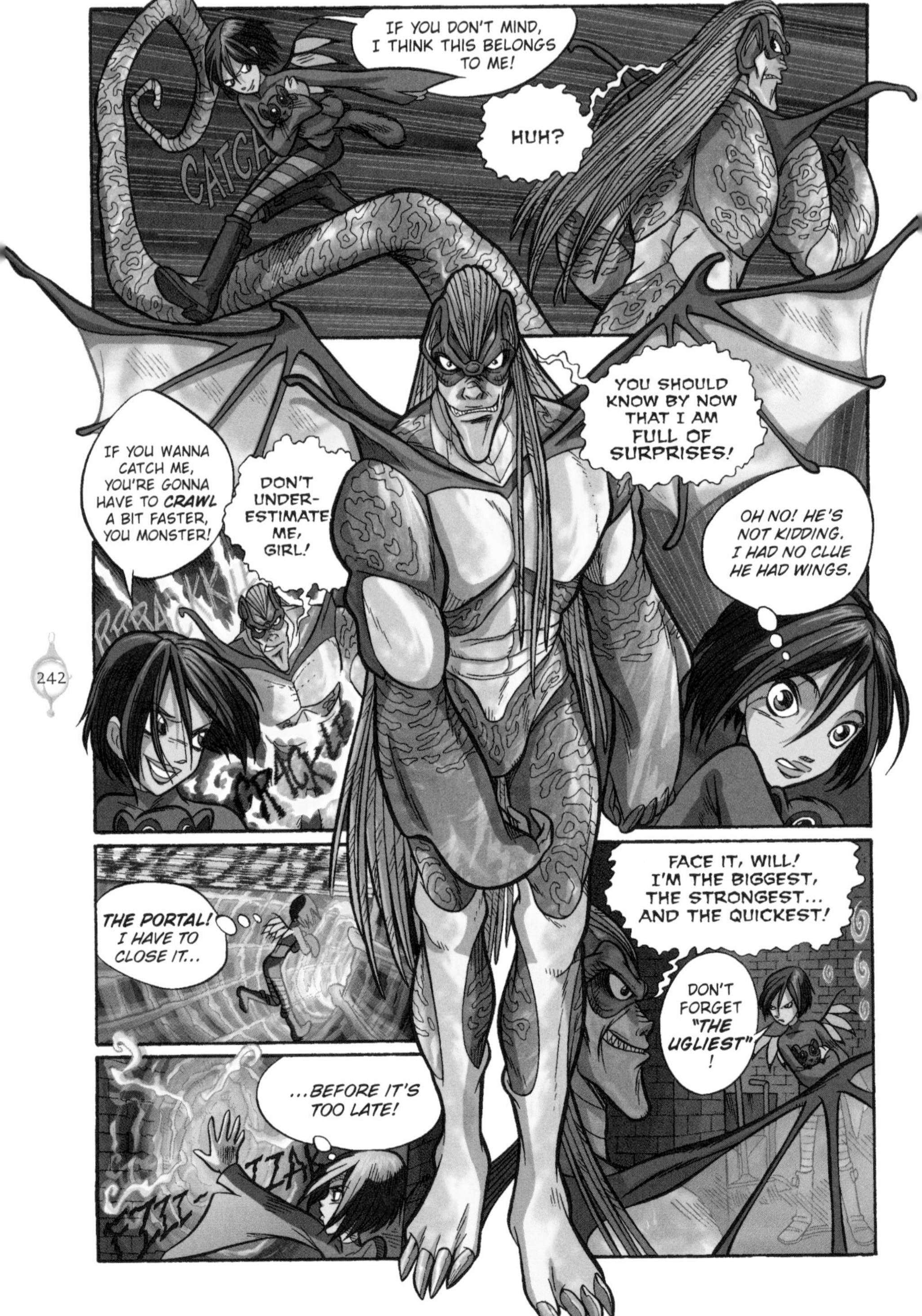

IF YOU DON'T MIND, I THINK THIS BELONGS TO ME!
CATCH
HUH?
YOU SHOULD KNOW BY NOW THAT I AM **FULL OF SURPRISES!**
IF YOU WANNA CATCH ME, YOU'RE GONNA HAVE TO ***CRAWL*** A BIT FASTER, YOU MONSTER!
DON'T UNDER-ESTIMATE ME, GIRL!
OH NO! HE'S NOT KIDDING. I HAD NO CLUE HE HAD WINGS.
CRACKLE
THE PORTAL! *I HAVE TO CLOSE IT...*
FACE IT, WILL! I'M THE BIGGEST, THE STRONGEST... AND THE QUICKEST!
DON'T FORGET ***"THE UGLIEST"*** !
...BEFORE IT'S TOO LATE!

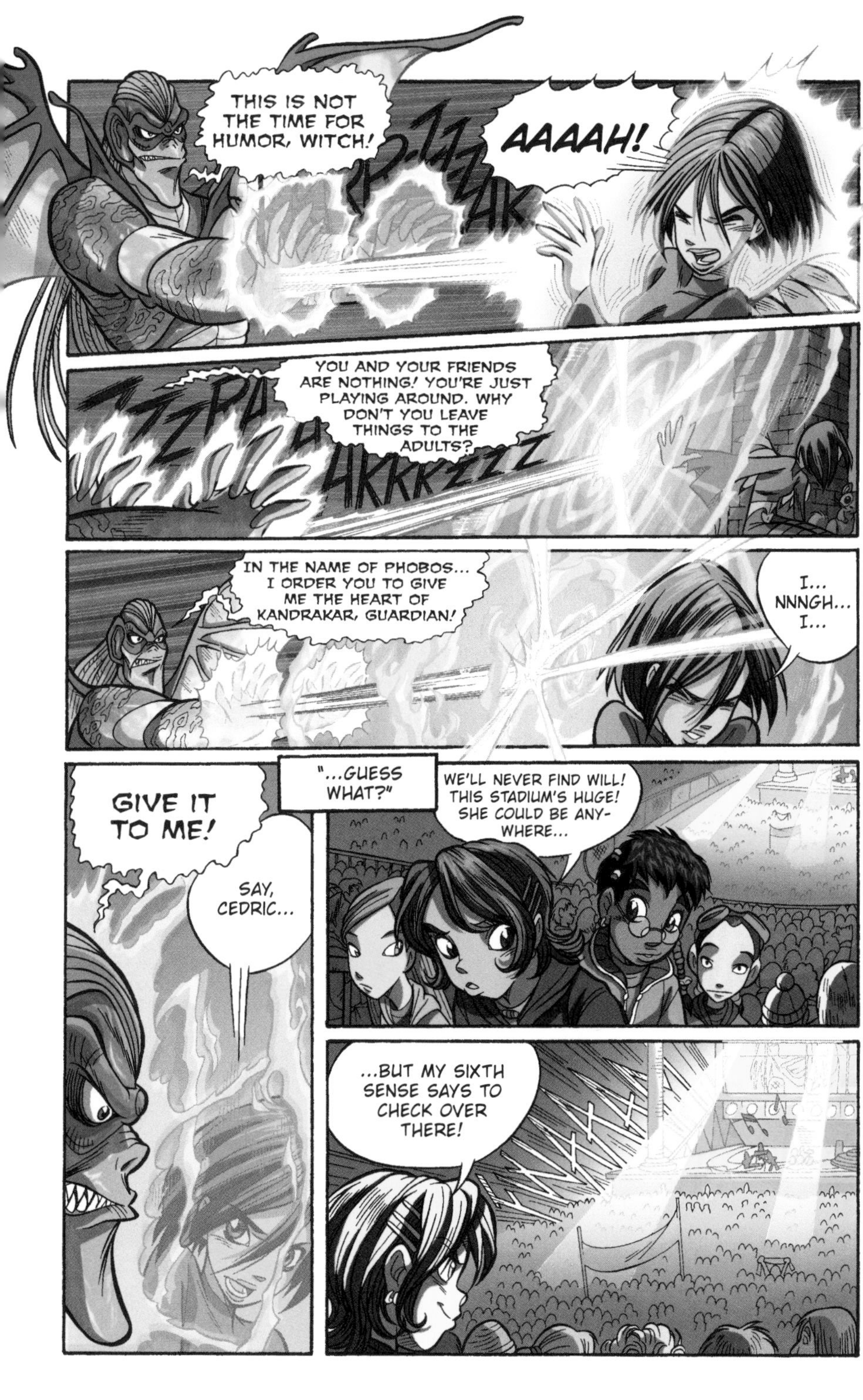
THIS IS NOT THE TIME FOR HUMOR, WITCH!
ZZZAP-TZZZAK
AAAAH!
YOU AND YOUR FRIENDS ARE NOTHING! YOU'RE JUST PLAYING AROUND. WHY DON'T YOU LEAVE THINGS TO THE ADULTS?
ZZZPAAKKKZZZZ
IN THE NAME OF PHOBOS... I ORDER YOU TO GIVE ME THE HEART OF KANDRAKAR, GUARDIAN!
I... NNNGH... I...
GIVE IT TO ME!
SAY, CEDRIC...
"...GUESS WHAT?"
WE'LL NEVER FIND WILL! THIS STADIUM'S HUGE! SHE COULD BE ANY-WHERE...
...BUT MY SIXTH SENSE SAYS TO CHECK OVER THERE!

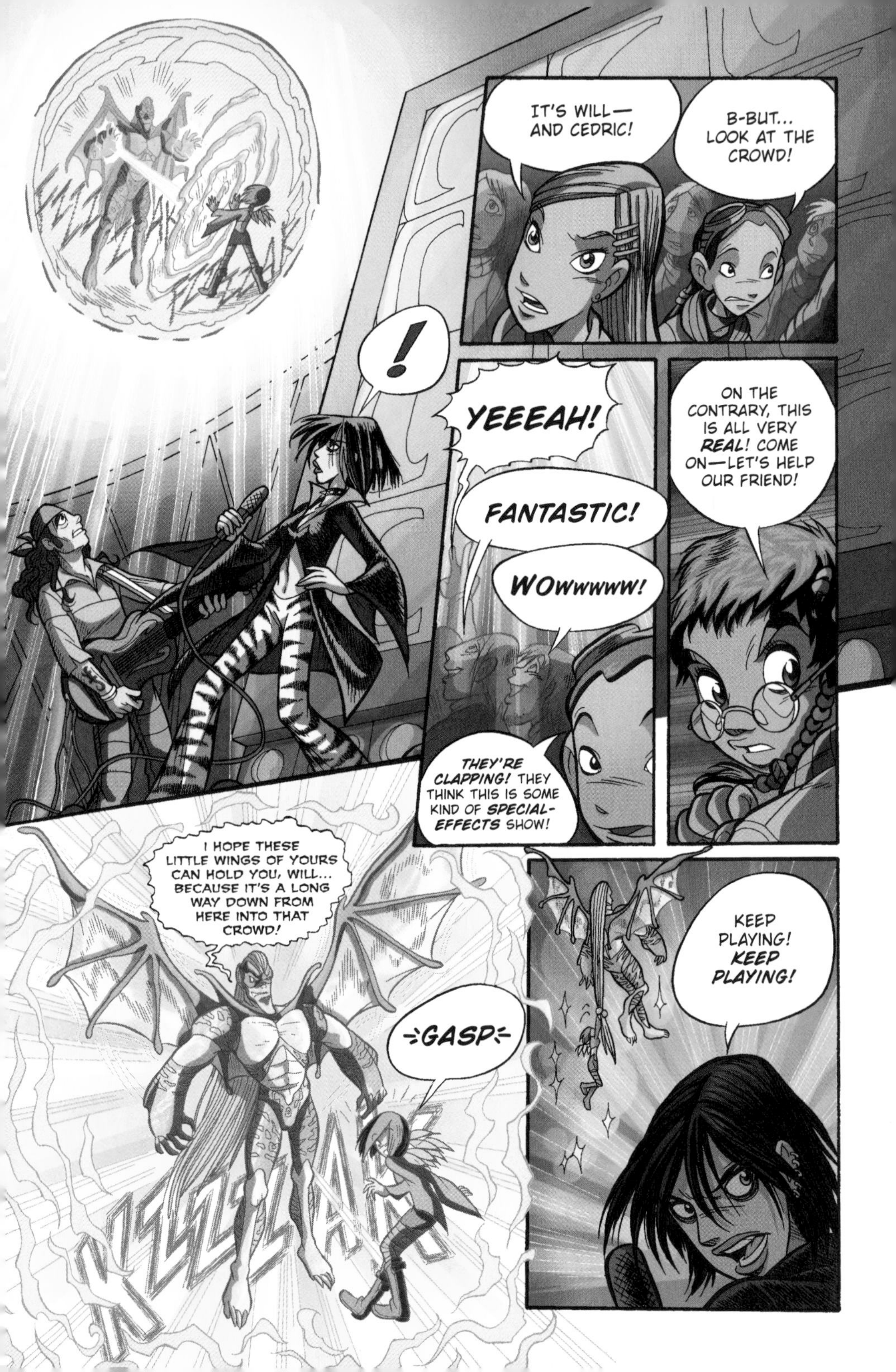

FZZZZAK
FZZZAK
IT'S WILL— AND CEDRIC!
B-BUT... LOOK AT THE CROWD!
!
YEEEAH!
FANTASTIC!
WOwwwww!
THEY'RE CLAPPING! THEY THINK THIS IS SOME KIND OF SPECIAL-EFFECTS SHOW!
ON THE CONTRARY, THIS IS ALL VERY REAL! COME ON—LET'S HELP OUR FRIEND!
I HOPE THESE LITTLE WINGS OF YOURS CAN HOLD YOU, WILL... BECAUSE IT'S A LONG WAY DOWN FROM HERE INTO THAT CROWD!
GASP
KEEP PLAYING! KEEP PLAYING!

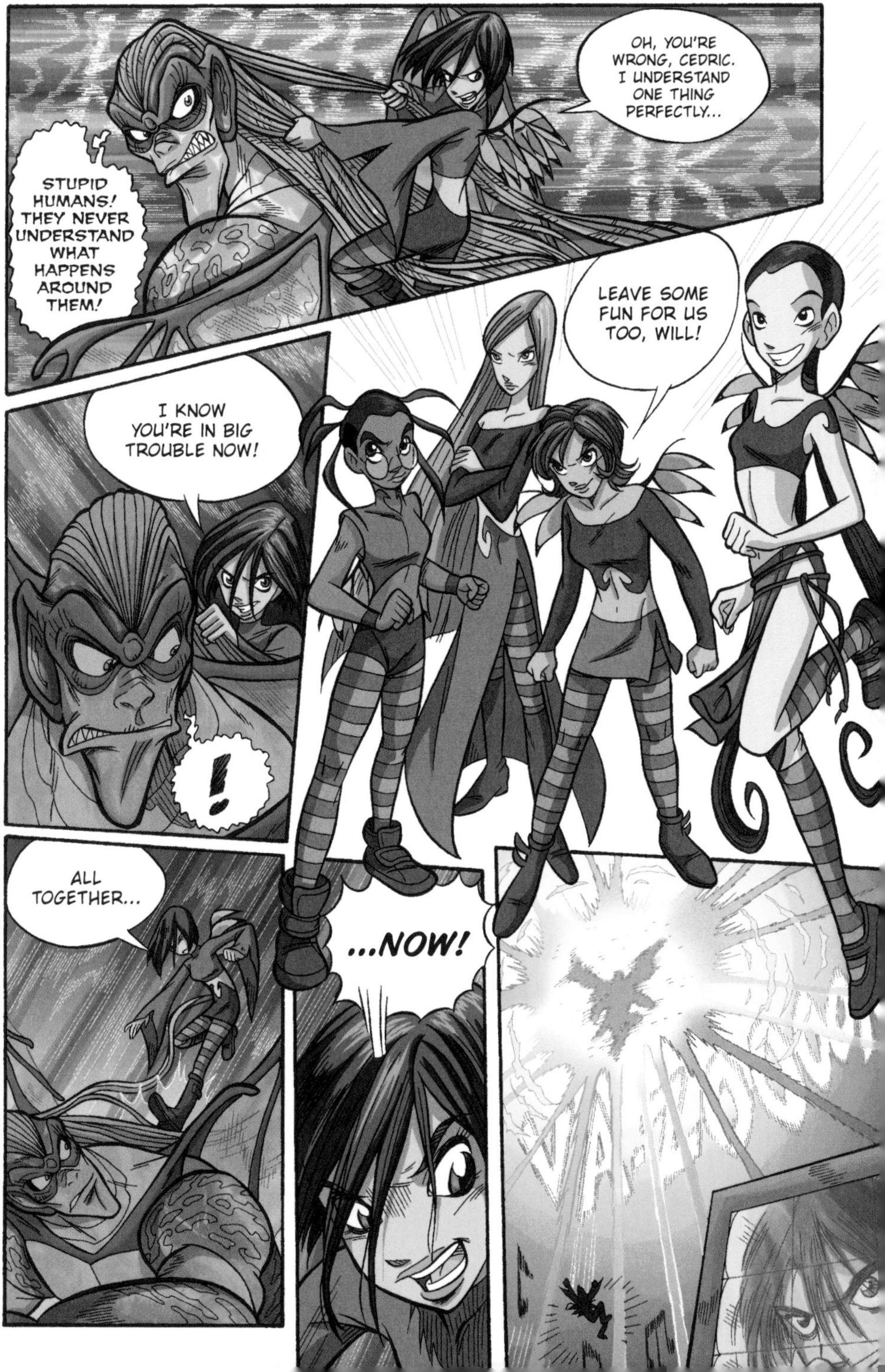
STUPID HUMANS! THEY NEVER UNDERSTAND WHAT HAPPENS AROUND THEM!
OH, YOU'RE WRONG, CEDRIC. I UNDERSTAND ONE THING PERFECTLY...
I KNOW YOU'RE IN BIG TROUBLE NOW!
LEAVE SOME FUN FOR US TOO, WILL!
ALL TOGETHER...
...NOW!

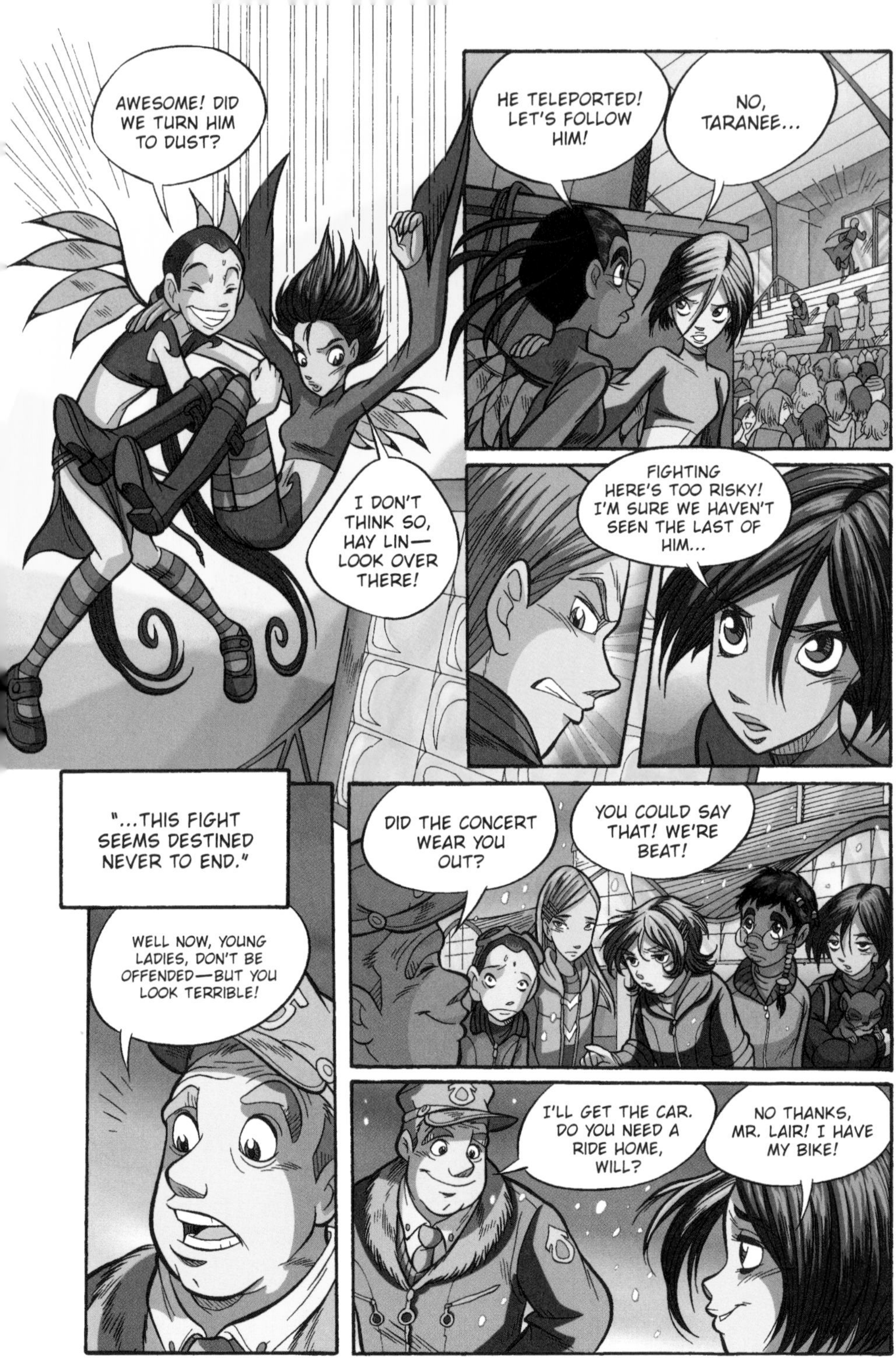
AWESOME! DID WE TURN HIM TO DUST?
I DON'T THINK SO, HAY LIN—LOOK OVER THERE!
HE TELEPORTED! LET'S FOLLOW HIM!
NO, TARANEE...
FIGHTING HERE'S TOO RISKY! I'M SURE WE HAVEN'T SEEN THE LAST OF HIM...
"...THIS FIGHT SEEMS DESTINED NEVER TO END."
WELL NOW, YOUNG LADIES, DON'T BE OFFENDED—BUT YOU LOOK TERRIBLE!
DID THE CONCERT WEAR YOU OUT?
YOU COULD SAY THAT! WE'RE BEAT!
I'LL GET THE CAR. DO YOU NEED A RIDE HOME, WILL?
NO THANKS, MR. LAIR! I HAVE MY BIKE!

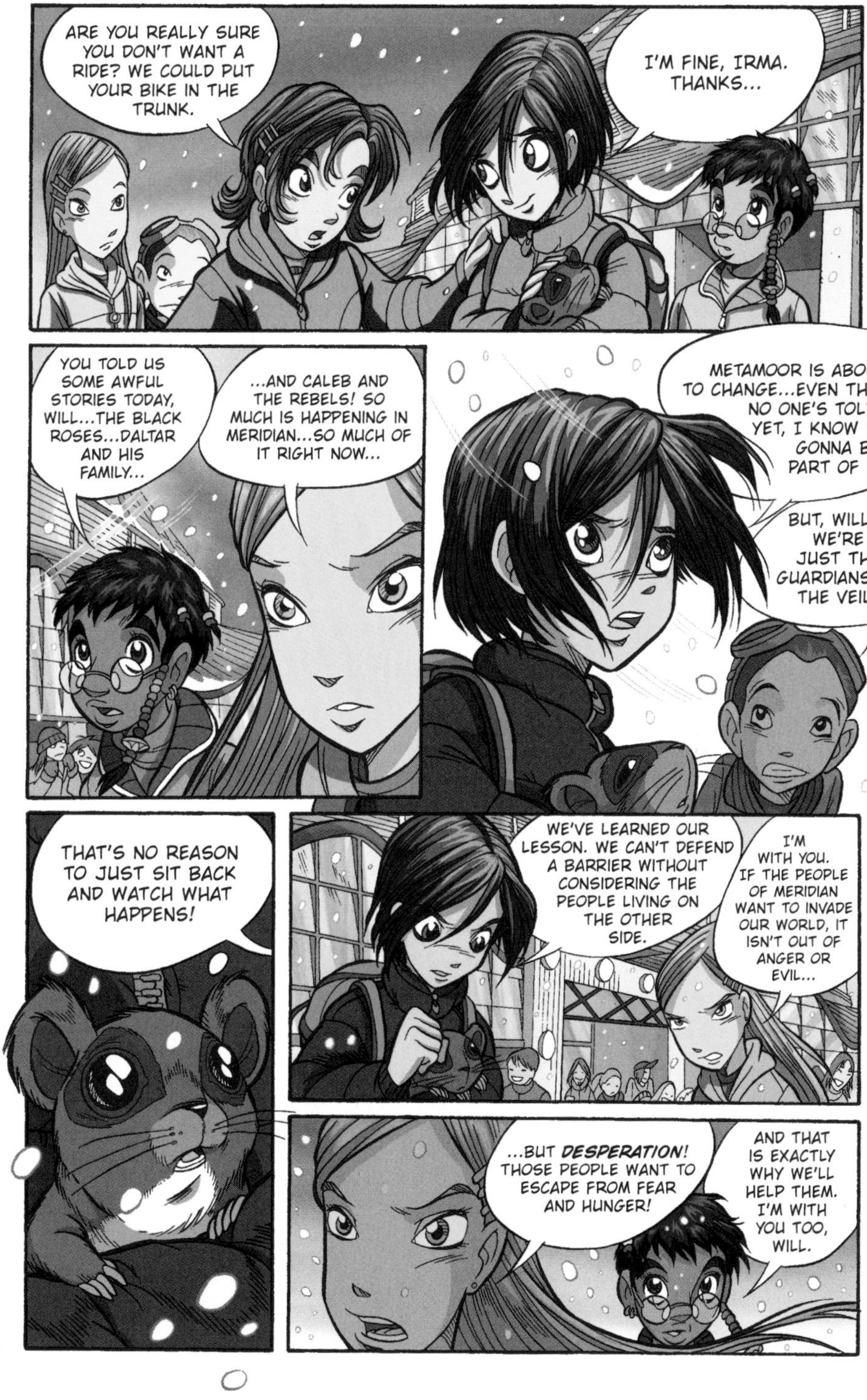

ARE YOU REALLY SURE YOU DON'T WANT A RIDE? WE COULD PUT YOUR BIKE IN THE TRUNK.
I'M FINE, IRMA. THANKS...
YOU TOLD US SOME AWFUL STORIES TODAY, WILL...THE BLACK ROSES...DALTAR AND HIS FAMILY...
...AND CALEB AND THE REBELS! SO MUCH IS HAPPENING IN MERIDIAN...SO MUCH OF IT RIGHT NOW...
METAMOOR IS ABOUT TO CHANGE...EVEN THOUGH NO ONE'S TOLD US YET, I KNOW WE'RE GONNA BE PART OF IT!
BUT, WILL... WE'RE JUST THE GUARDIANS OF THE VEIL!
THAT'S NO REASON TO JUST SIT BACK AND WATCH WHAT HAPPENS!
WE'VE LEARNED OUR LESSON. WE CAN'T DEFEND A BARRIER WITHOUT CONSIDERING THE PEOPLE LIVING ON THE OTHER SIDE.
I'M WITH YOU. IF THE PEOPLE OF MERIDIAN WANT TO INVADE OUR WORLD, IT ISN'T OUT OF ANGER OR EVIL...
...BUT *DESPERATION*! THOSE PEOPLE WANT TO ESCAPE FROM FEAR AND HUNGER!
AND THAT IS EXACTLY WHY WE'LL HELP THEM. I'M WITH YOU TOO, WILL.

HEY! I DON'T WANT TO BE THE ODD GIRL OUT! I'M IN TOO!
GET OVER HERE, LITTLE BIRDIE.
NOBODY WILL COME BETWEEN US!
"NOBODY!"
TLACK
HELLO.
HI.
AHEM I'M A LITTLE LATE.
I NOTICED. QUITE A LONG WALK YOU HAD.

248

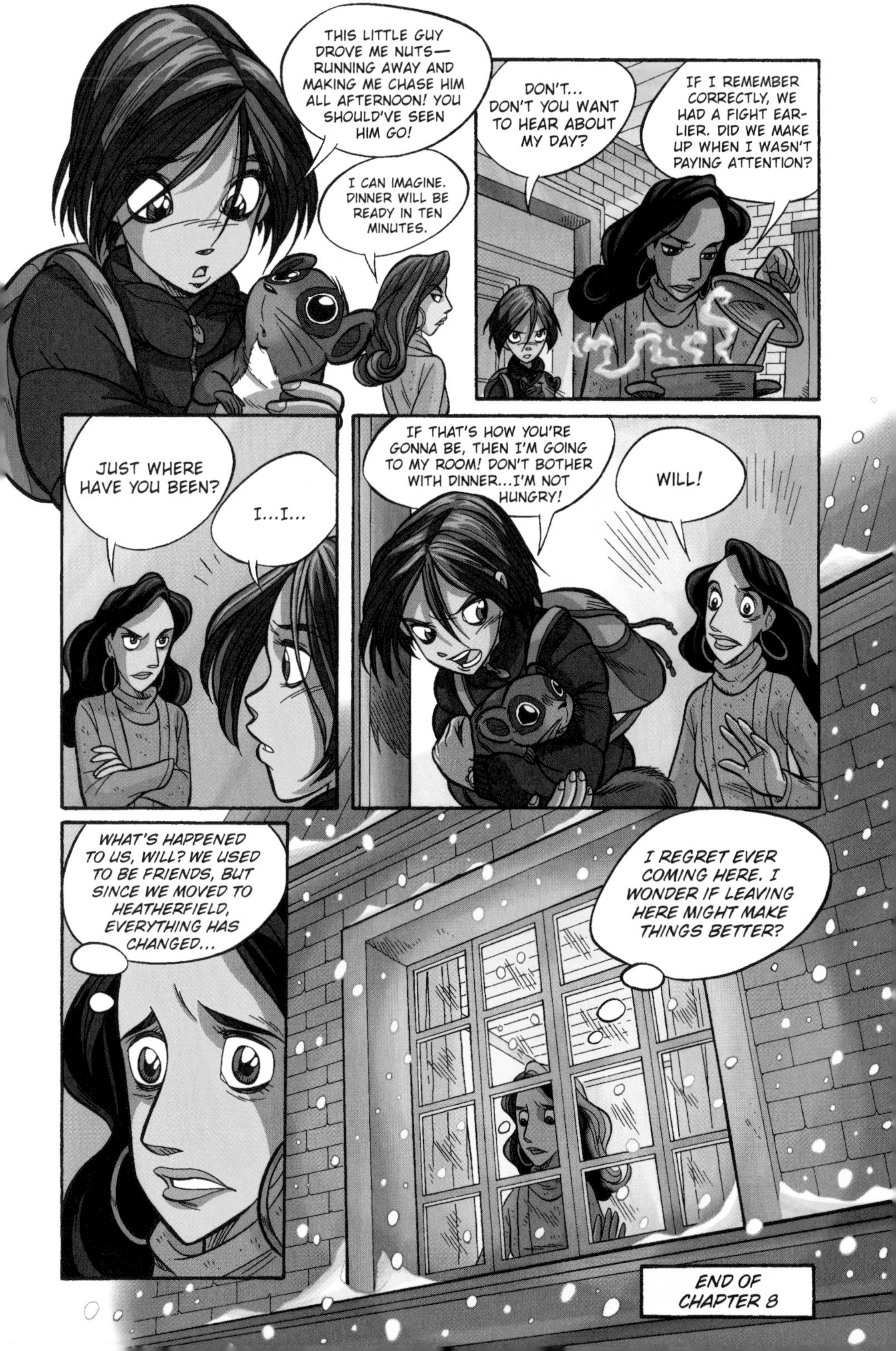
THIS LITTLE GUY DROVE ME NUTS— RUNNING AWAY AND MAKING ME CHASE HIM ALL AFTERNOON! YOU SHOULD'VE SEEN HIM GO!
I CAN IMAGINE. DINNER WILL BE READY IN TEN MINUTES.
DON'T... DON'T YOU WANT TO HEAR ABOUT MY DAY?
IF I REMEMBER CORRECTLY, WE HAD A FIGHT EARLIER. DID WE MAKE UP WHEN I WASN'T PAYING ATTENTION?
JUST WHERE HAVE YOU BEEN?
I...I...
IF THAT'S HOW YOU'RE GONNA BE, THEN I'M GOING TO MY ROOM! DON'T BOTHER WITH DINNER...I'M NOT HUNGRY!
WILL!
WHAT'S HAPPENED TO US, WILL? WE USED TO BE FRIENDS, BUT SINCE WE MOVED TO HEATHERFIELD, EVERYTHING HAS CHANGED...
I REGRET EVER COMING HERE. I WONDER IF LEAVING HERE MIGHT MAKE THINGS BETTER?
END OF CHAPTER 8

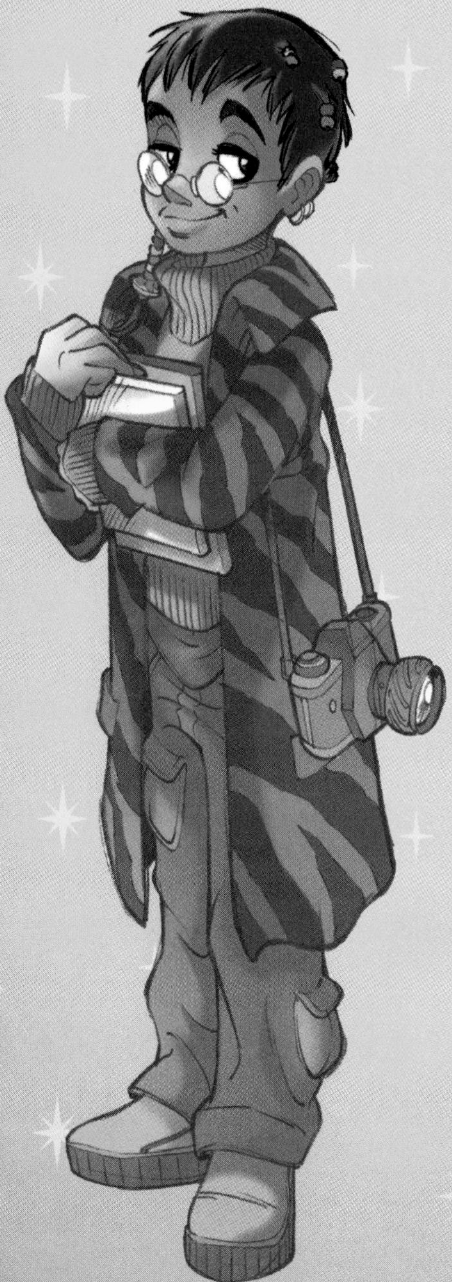

ASTONISHED BY...

Taranee

13 years old

Born March 23, Aries

The most reflective and quiet of the group but is a little bit distracted

Her favorite subject is math.

She's in Class 2B at Sheffield Institute with Irma and Hay Lin. Like Will, she's new to Heatherfield.

She loves classical music and basketball. She's passionate about photography and likes to take pictures of insects even though she gets the jitters around these "flying monsters."

Her mom is a judge, and her dad is a psychologist. She has an older brother who's very cute and loves surfing.

In witch form

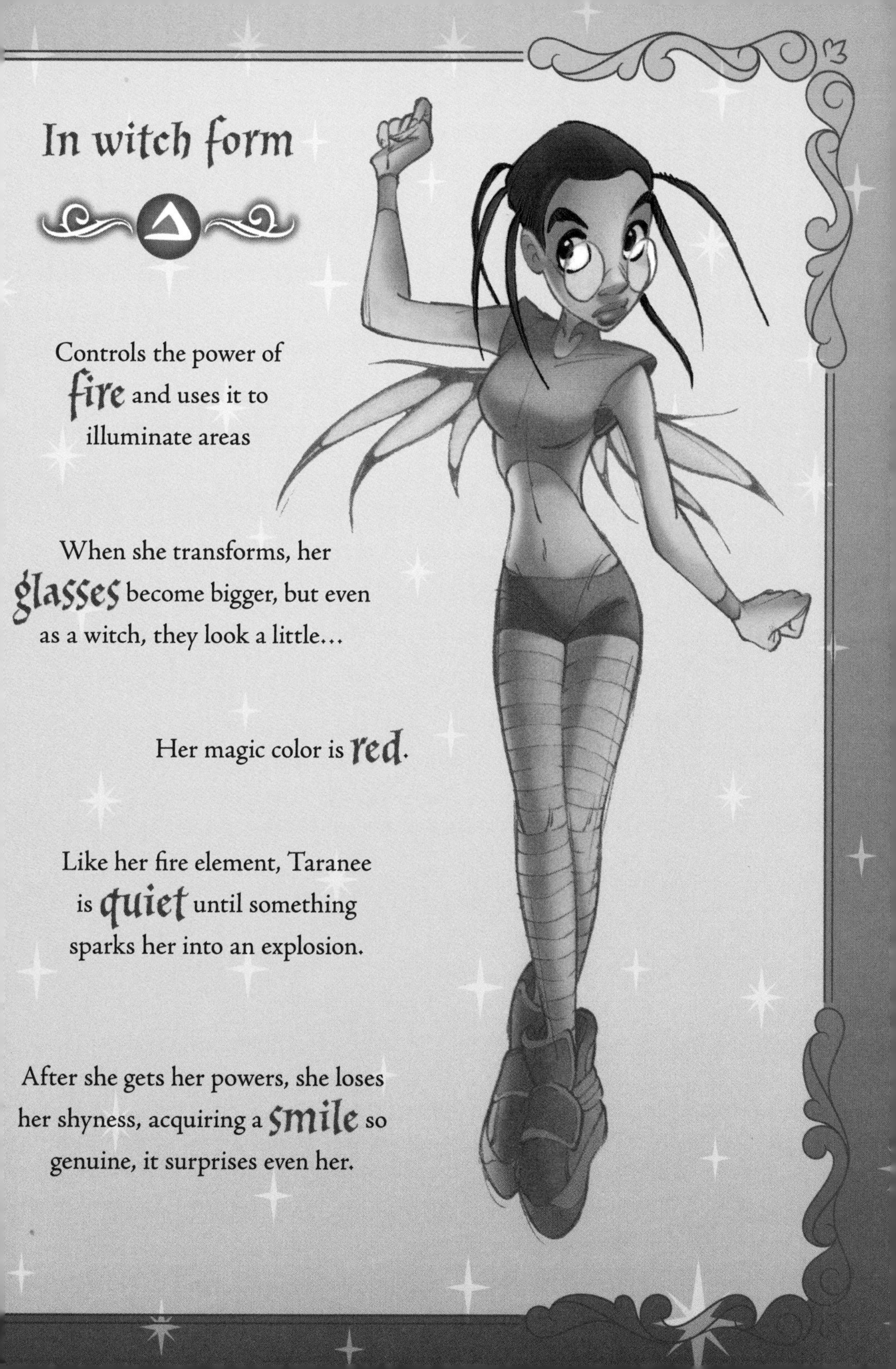

Controls the power of **fire** and uses it to illuminate areas

When she transforms, her **glasses** become bigger, but even as a witch, they look a little…

Her magic color is **red**.

Like her fire element, Taranee is **quiet** until something sparks her into an explosion.

After she gets her powers, she loses her shyness, acquiring a **smile** so genuine, it surprises even her.

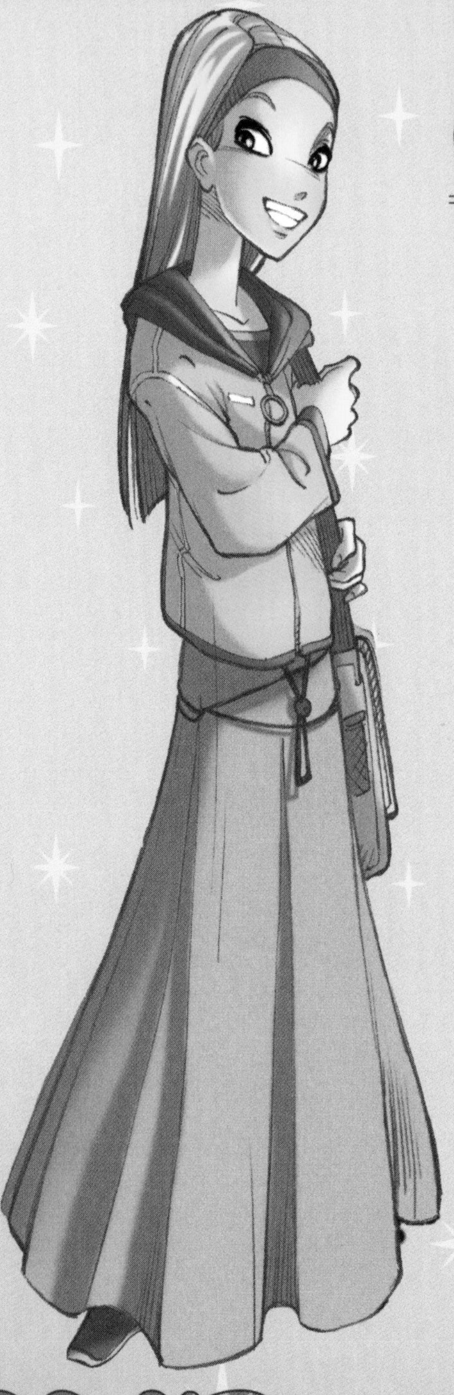

ASTONISHED BY...

Cornelia

She's in Class 3A at **Sheffield Institute** with Will.

Her **calm** and **rational** behavior is challenged by Irma's sense of humor.

Lives with her parents and her **little sister, Lilian**, in a beautiful apartment in one of Heatherfield's most elegant neighborhoods

She loves **ice skating** and has already won many awards in competitions.

She **can't swim** and is afraid of water, but that doesn't mean she won't overcome that difficulty one day.

Controls the power of **earth**, with which she can open gaps in walls and move objects with her mind

Even though her best friend, Elyon, is now her **worst enemy**, she hopes to be friends again.

Her transformation reinforces her **elegant appearance**, making her look the trendiest of the group. She's attentive to fashion.

ASTONISHED BY…

Hay Lin

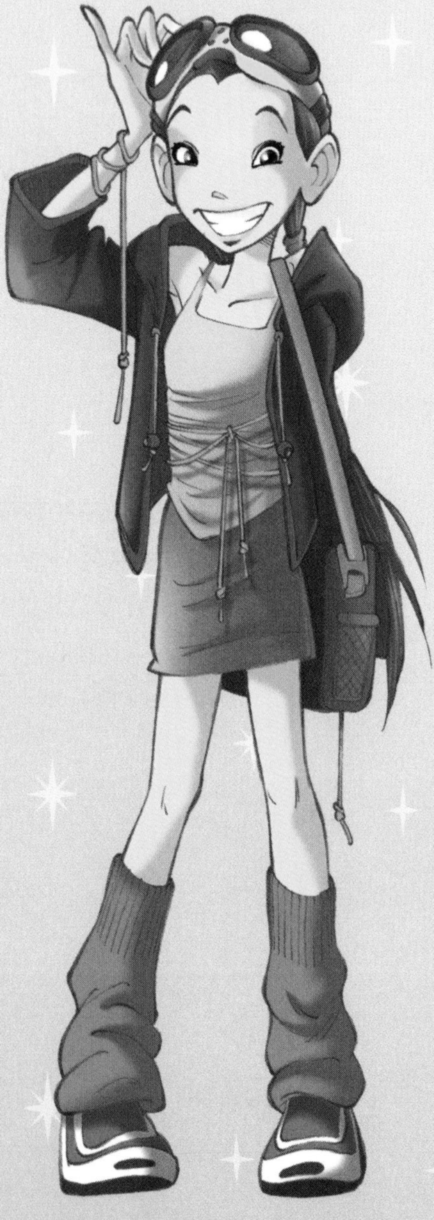

Only just turned 13, on June 4 as a Gemini

Is in class with Irma and Taranee. Her favorite class is art.

Sweet and frequently daydreaming, Hay Lin is the most distracted of the group. She even writes notes to herself on her hands.

She lives with her parents in an apartment above the Chinese restaurant that her family runs.

A science fiction enthusiast, she hopes to meet a scaly, bony alien one day. When she sees something she likes, she says stuff like, "Out of this World!"

She loves glasses, especially big, oddly shaped ones. She also redesigns her clothes with laces, which she uses as distinctive accessories for a distinctive look.

In witch form

Controls the power of **air** to fly. She dominates air currents.

She is entrusted with the map of the **twelve portals**, which indicates all the places to cross to Metamoor.

The map was originally in the hands of her grandmother, the elderly Yan Lin. For the first millennium, she was also a **Guardian of Kandrakar.**

Part I. The Twelve Portals • Volume 2

Series Created by Elisabetta Gnone
Comic Art Direction: Alessandro Barbucci, Barbara Canepa

W.I.T.C.H.: The Graphic Novel, Part I: The Twelve Portals
© Disney Enterprises, Inc.

English translation © 2017 by Disney Enterprises, Inc.

JY
1290 Avenue of the Americas
New York, NY 10104

Visit us at yenpress.com
facebook.com/yenpress
twitter.com/yenpress
yenpress.tumblr.com
instagram.com/yenpress

First JY Edition: October 2017

JY is an imprint of Yen Press, LLC.
The JY name and logo are trademarks of Yen Press, LLC.

The publisher is not responsible for websites (or their content) that are not owned by the publisher.

Library of Congress Control Number: 2017950917

ISBNs:
978-0-316-47696-6 (paperback)
978-0-316-41505-7 (ebook)

10 9 8 7 6 5 4 3 2 1

LSC-C

Printed in the United States of America

Cover Art by Alessandro Barbucci
Colors by Barbara Canepa and Mara Damiani

Translation Assistance by Eva Martina Allione
Lettering by Katie Blakeslee

THE LAST TEAR

Concept and Script by Francesco Artibani
Layout by Alessandro Barbucci
Pencils by Donald Soffritti
Inks by Marina Baggio and Roberta Zanotta
Color and Light Direction by Barbara Canepa
Title Page Art by Alessandro Barbucci
with Colors by Barbara Canepa and Mara Damiani

ILLUSIONS AND LIES

Concept and Script by Bruno Enna
Pencils by Paolo Campinoti
Inks by Marina Baggio and Roberta Zanotta
Color and Light Direction by Barbara Canepa
Title Page Art by Gianluca Panniello
with Colors by Andrea Cagol

ONE DAY YOU'LL MEET HIM

Concept by Francesco Artibani and Paola Mulazzi
Script by Paola Mulazzi
Layout by Stefano Turconi
Pencils by Manuela Razzi
Inks by Marina Baggio and Roberta Zanotta
Color and Light Direction by Barbara Canepa
Title Page Art by Gianluca Panniello
with Colors by Andrea Cagol

THE BLACK ROSES OF MERIDIAN

Concept by Francesco Artibani and Giovanna Bo
Script by Giovanna Bo
Pencils and Inks by Alessia Martusciello
Color Direction by Francesco Legramandi
Title Page Art by Alessia Martusciello
with Colors by Andrea Cagol